The LAST SUITOR

Volume One of
The Raspero Chronicles

A. J. McMAHON

JoJo
PUBLISHING

The Last Suitor: Volume One of the Raspero Chronicles
A.J. McMahon
Published by Classic Author and Publishing Services Pty Ltd.
Imprint of JoJo Publishing.
First published 2015

'Yarra's Edge'
2203/80 Lorimer Street
Docklands VIC 3008
Australia

Email: admin@classic-jojo.com or visit www.classic-jojo.com

JoJo Publishing

Editor: Julie Athanasiou
Designer / typesetter: Working Type Studio (www.workingtype.com.au)
Printed in China by Ink Asia.

National Library of Australia Cataloguing-in-Publication entry
Creator: McMahon, A. J., author.
Title: The last suitor / A J McMahon ; Julie Athanasiou, editor.
ISBN: 9780994275424 (paperback)
Subjects: Fantasy fiction.
Other Creators/Contributors: Athanasiou, Julie, editor.
Dewey Number: A823.4

The Last Suitor: Volume One of the Raspero Chronicles
A.J. McMahon
Published by Classic Author and Publishing Services Pty Ltd.
Imprint of JoJo Publishing.
First published 2015

'Yarra's Edge'
2203/80 Lorimer Street
Docklands VIC 3008
Australia

Email: admin@classic-jojo.com or visit www.classic-jojo.com

Copyright © A.J. McMahon

JoJo Publishing

Editor: Julie Athanasiou
Designer / typesetter: Working Type Studio (www.workingtype.com.au)
Printed in China by Ink Asia.

National Library of Australia Cataloguing-in-Publication entry
Creator: McMahon, A. J., author.
Title: The last suitor / A J McMahon ; Julie Athanasiou, editor.
ISBN: 9780994275424 (paperback)
Subjects: Fantasy fiction.
Other Creators/Contributors: Athanasiou, Julie, editor.
Dewey Number: A823.4

CONTENTS

ONE

The Corruption of Mr Benjamin Clark
by Mr Nicholas Raspero

3:20 PM, Monday 2 May 1544 A. F. (After the Fall)

Nicholas Raspero disembarked from the public flying carriage in Talbert Street with a bag slung over his left shoulder and his right hand resting on the hilt of his wand. It was the day after his twenty-second birthday and so he was still young enough to look eagerly about him as he set off through the bustling streets of New Landern.

Nicholas was of medium height, black-haired and grey-eyed, with an air of composed self-assurance which seemed to stem from the hand he rested on the hilt of his wand. He avoided being handsome by a deft sideways step that made his nose slightly too long and his mouth slightly too wide. His square chin, high cheek bones and strong eyebrows were features which struggled manfully to attain pleasing proportions, but as the Leaning Tower of Hambron keeps its distance from the perfectly vertical, so his face kept handsomeness at arm's length. However, in his favour it had to be said that he walked with an easy grace. His shoulders were set square, his step was light and vigorous, his posture was erect and his good health shone like the sun. His clothes were of good quality but not new and his boots of good leather but cracked and worn, comfortable but getting old. No-one looked twice at him as he walked through the streets of New Landern, the great Metropolis of Anglashia, but Nicholas himself looked more than twice at everything around him. There were the flying carriages passing by overhead, so numerous that they had to be allocated lanes. There were the houses which reached four or even five storeys high on occasion. Above all else there were the people, shouting, jostling each other, laughing and complaining. Everyone seemed to be up to something.

Nicholas found his way to Norell Street in Dejaville and knocked on the door of his uncle's house. It was opened by a maid who looked at Nicholas without saying a word. Nicholas announced himself and she let him in, still without saying a word.

Counsellor Lanford Clark, Mrs Clark, the three children they had had together and Nicholas's cousin Mr Benjamin Clark were waiting for him in the living room. They all greeted each other and Nicholas found them all very formal and stiff. Mrs Clark especially seemed to hide her joy at having Nicholas come to stay with them.

Nicholas was shown to his room by Ben where he put down the bag he had carried over his shoulder, which contained all his earthly possessions, including his only change of robes, and emptied it onto the bed, after which he threw various items here and there around the room and then he was done. This for Nicholas was unpacking. Ben watched this in silence.

'What are your plans for today, Mr Raspero?' asked Ben.

'Could you show me around a bit?'

'Naturally, I would be delighted,' Ben said, sounding anything but delighted.

So they set off through the streets of New Landern.

First of all, Nicholas wanted to see the Bridge of Nerian, where young Adrastos Haddon had been betrayed and trapped, hopelessly surrounded by the Heloise Regiment, but fighting them nonetheless. He had fought the good fight to the very end.

'So what's all this Mr Raspero business about anyway, Ben?' Nicholas asked as they walked along on their way to the Bridge of Nerian. 'You always used to call me Nicholas or Nicky when we were children.'

'We have not seen each other since then.'

'Yes, but we're seeing each other now.'

'That is not an argument that sustains your point.'

'We're cousins, Ben. Your mother was my father's sister. That puts us on first name terms, at the very least.'

'No, it does not, Mr Raspero. It is a mere accident of biology and nothing more.'

'It's your stepmother, Mrs Clark, isn't it? She doesn't like me, I can tell.'

'I am sure that her opinion of you will improve over time in accordance with the measure of your conduct.'

'Well, that's nice, isn't it? I look forward to seeing the measure of my conduct. What's the unit of measurement, by the way? Is it line or volume?'

'You may well choose to be facetious, Mr Raspero, but you cannot expect to receive affection merely because you have just arrived.'

Nicholas laughed merrily. 'I suppose not. I mean, just arriving is only to turn up safe and sound, and what's the good of that? You don't think much of that yourself, I take it?'

'Naturally,' Ben said very stiffly, 'we are pleased that you have safely arrived in New Landern, but it is a presumption on your part to expect a greater measure of affection than that which you have received.'

'Yes, you're all heart, I can tell,' Nicholas said, still amused. 'Well, who knows, Ben, one day we might be friends again and then you'll be pleased to see me when I turn up. How about that? Does that sound good?'

'Indeed, nothing would please me more,' Ben agreed, his tone of voice and the expression on his face suggesting that he found it extremely unlikely that he would ever be friends again with his country cousin. 'It does indeed sound very pleasant.'

Nicholas threw back his head and laughed again as merrily as before as they walked along, which Ben found very annoying though he didn't say anything. They arrived at the Bridge of Nerian, and Nicholas, who had read Humfrey's account of Haddon's last stand, excitedly wandered around matching the account he had read with the plaques positioned here and there marking key places of the narrative. Ben swallowed his exasperation as best he could and nodded in response to Nicholas's cheerful comments, a false but polite smile on his face.

Nicholas now wanted to go and see The House of Display and Records of Wands. Hoping that it was closed by now Ben took him there but it was very much open and Nicholas wandered eagerly around looking at the exhibits and reading all the display notices, drawing Ben's attention to certain comments that Nicholas either disagreed with or thought needed further emphasis. Ben continued to do his best to be polite. Wandlore enthusiasts irritated him and it was clear to him by now that Nicholas was a wandlore enthusiast, which doubled his already existing irritation with Nicholas.

The origin of wands was a mystery, and that in itself was a debating point of the day. Wands had emerged around about five or six centuries after the Fall, how or where no-one knew for certain, although there were, of course, various competing theories. Wands were made of a silvery-grey metal called magneterium formed in a long, thin rectangular shape, with the edges and corners of the rectangular shape being rounded; as the metal was soft, it was encased in wood, with an open end to form the hilt of the wand, which pressed into the palm of the wand-wielder. By use of the wand, objects which had magnetised metal in them could be made to move under the influence of the combinations of the wand-wielder's focused thoughts and bodily movements. Furthermore, the wand could be activated in such a way as to produce an image of the surrounding world in the mind of the wand-user by a process called macchato.

Nicholas next wanted to see Lanston Square. This was the scene of public executions where condemned prisoners were taken to be impaled and beheaded. They sat in the Lanston Box, which closed on them. A metal stake went through their heart while a circular whirling blade, like a very large disc, sliced their head off in one smooth motion. Their now headless bodies were dropped through a trap door and into a coffin, while their heads rolled down a chute, to be picked up by the executioner and impaled on a stake standing nearby. The pole with its head on it was guarded all day and night by soldiers. A lamp on the ground lit up the impaled head during the night just to make what had happened perfectly clear, and then the next morning after sunrise the head was taken down and placed in the coffin with the rest of the body; the coffin was then taken away and buried in the spookiest graveyard in the metropolis. Lanston Square was a very popular destination for visitors to New Landern.

As it was by now after nightfall, Nicholas suggested that they should have a bite to eat. They found a nearby restaurant where Ben was subjected face-to-face across their table to a now unfiltered barrage of Nicholas's questions and jokes and reminiscences of times past, which made Ben regret even The House of Display and Records of Wands, which he now realised had at least protected him in some measure from Nicholas's relentless friendliness. Eventually their meal came to an end; Nicholas insisted on paying the twenty-four strada bill, saying that when he ran out of money he expected Ben to support him, even into his old age, and he laughed to show that this was a joke; Ben somehow made himself laugh as well, by remembering how laughter was done.

Nicholas was too fired up by all the promise of the day to go home once they left the restaurant and insisted they wander around for a while, looking at the sights all around, asking Ben question after question about everything he saw, as if he were a small child in a circus. Ben dealt with it all as best as he could, enduring the unending evening by practising a large measure of self-control. Eventually, Ben suggested it was getting late and it was time to go home. That was when Nicholas surprised Ben.

'All right, it's time to go home,' Nicholas said abruptly. 'Now, let's see. Where is home?' He then turned around in a circle, pointing with one hand and then the other to exactly where they had been during the afternoon and evening, with all the connecting streets that they had walked along. In consequence of the map which Nicholas was drawing in the air with his hands, he now outlined a logical schemata concerning their journey home with regard to the particular route they should follow on the way back. Despite his enormous irritation at even having to stand next to his country cousin, Ben was so impressed by Nicholas's performance that he nodded his agreement without properly thinking the matter through, so glad was he in any case to be approaching the end of this ordeal of an evening in Nicholas's company. So they set off for home, with Nicholas now directing them one way or the other with his hands outstretched high in the air at every street junction, laughing cheerfully every now and then for no reason at all that Ben could see, and so their journey continued. But it dawned on Ben after a while that

Nicholas's proposed route would take them through a part of town that Ben would prefer not to travel through this late at night, and it was now that Ben properly thought the matter through, and having done so Ben came to an abrupt halt in the middle of the road.

'Mr Raspero,' Ben said, 'the route which you propose is inadvisable. It must be amended.'

'And why so?' Nicholas asked interestedly.

'There are certain areas of New Landern that are best avoided at this time of night.'

'And why's that?' Nicholas asked, still interested.

Ben sighed as if he was talking to an idiot. 'They are best avoided, Mr Raspero. You are newly arrived in New Landern — trust me.'

'But what are we talking about?' Nicholas insisted on knowing. 'Giant bears? Crocodiles? I mean, what is it we are avoiding?'

Ben took a very deep breath, sighed very loudly, took another very deep breath, and said, 'Mr Raspero, New Landern is home to a wide variety of people, some of whom may as well be bears or crocodiles in human form; be that as it may, the route you have proposed passes directly through a part of New Landern which presents dangers that we will circumvent by adopting an alternate route. There are dark alleys on the route you have proposed that we should not walk through at this time of night.'

'Do you know who you are, Ben?' Nicholas asked.

'We will go that way,' Ben declared, pointing with his left forefinger to his left, 'then past the Quella Monument, right onto Barclay Street and so on. Yes, that is by far the most sensible choice. It is the longer way, but much the safer.'

'Your mother was Lena Raspero, granddaughter of the twenty-fourth Baron of Raspero,' Mr Nicholas Raspero informed Mr Benjamin Clark. 'There is Raspero blood in your veins, Ben, and that Raspero blood goes back to Daniel himself. For six centuries, the Rasperos have broken their enemies and left them in pieces on the ground, and now you are afraid to go into a dark alley! Think for a moment of how low you have fallen!'

'It is not a matter of being afraid,' Ben said sharply, 'it is a matter of not being foolish.'

'I'll give you a choice, Ben,' Nicholas said equally sharply, 'you can come with me or go your way. It's up to you.' And with that he simply turned and set off without a backward glance. Ben hesitated and then followed him. Later in life, looking back on that moment, Ben wondered why he had after all followed Nicholas. He had every reason to go his own way, not least Nicholas's open acknowledgement that he could, but he did not. He went Nicholas's way, and it did not seem to him later that he had, in fact, made a choice at all. His feet, almost of their own accord, had taken the rest of his body with them as they went after his excitable country cousin. Perhaps it was that Nicholas had for the first time spoken sharply to him; perhaps without having realised it, he had fallen under the influence of Nicholas's relentless friendliness, based as it was on something unconditional, a blood relationship that was neither deserved or earned but which simply existed. For whatever reason Ben followed Nicholas, his apprehensions growing with each street they walked along. Nicholas was as annoyingly cheerful as ever, directing their progress by raising his hands in the air at each street junction and pointing the way they would take with a laugh and by saying out loud the name of the street they were about to walk along.

Everything in general was becoming dirtier and less well-kept. Broken windows like missing teeth began to appear in the walls of the houses. There was a bundle of rags on a nearby street-corner that might have been the cloth wrappings of a human being, or might not have been. Passers-by looked at Ben as if it was obvious he did not belong here, but they did not look at Nicholas in the same way, Ben noted with a certain resentment. Nicholas had no fear of being there, and so his presence was ordinary and unremarked, but Ben's fear was as obvious as a large red balloon in the hand of a child.

To Ben's wide-eyed gaze the most innocent sight, such as a dog's head looking out of a window, began to take on an air of malevolent unreality. The streets seemed to take on more than three dimensions in their journey through time as if shifting geometrically around a complicated axis. Weeds grew in holes where lamp-posts had once stood, taken away too long ago for their light to even be remembered now. The world itself was becoming darker than night.

The further they walked on their way, or Nicholas's way to be more accurate, the more Ben's apprehensions grew, but there was no backing out of anything now, and so it came to be that the two cousins turned down Octave Alley as they travelled together side by side through the dark heart of New Landern.

Octave Alley sloped downwards, its cobbled stones wet from a recent shower of rain. The eaves of the neighbouring houses stood over them as dark silhouettes against the nighttime sky. The bright moon, waxing in its second quarter, shone a silvery light over Octave Alley, forming numerous reflections like silver coins scattered here and there by a generous hand. The moonlit brightness of the centre of the alley, like a Milky Way all of its own, under the star-strewn dome of the nighttime sky arching above and the neighbouring inky darkness of the shadows of the houses lining the alley was a silver-splashed darkness which the two travellers passed through at that time.

Two men emerged from the shadows of a doorway to their left to stand in front of them. Ben's heart leaped into his chest and he looked around, panicking and trying to decide how they could make a run for it.

'Please help us, guvnor,' one of them pleaded, in what might have been a poor attempt at pleading or a mocking pretence of pleading, 'Me and me mate, we're out of work see, we thought maybe a gent like you could help us out with a few spare strada, what you say, guv?' He had a large scar on his left cheek that was so deep it twisted his face sideways and upwards.

It was certainly noticeable, despite their apparent pleading, that they did not have their hands outstretched like the beggars they claimed to be; far from it, they held their wands in their hands in combat readiness.

They were like figures in a nightmare to Ben, and just like in a real nightmare he couldn't run, frozen to the spot by his desperate desire to get away.

'What about your other three companions hiding over there?' Nicholas asked with a vague wave of his left hand. 'Do they need money also?'

There was a harsh laugh from the shadows to their right and three figures emerged, their wands in their hands pointing at Nicholas.

'You're a smart one, aren't you?' said the ringleader. 'Now empty your pockets!'

Ben was trembling from head to foot but as he looked across at Nicholas he saw something so astonishing that his fear momentarily left him. Nicholas, his hand resting on the hilt of his wand, was actually smiling! He seemed to see nothing at all threatening in his current circumstances. It was as if he was in a perfectly ordinary, even amusing, situation which required only the most casual of attention, but even Ben, who was not well versed in such things, could see that his stance was the fighting stance of a wandfighter. 'My pockets are already empty,' Nicholas said calmly, 'so how can they be emptied? I fail to see your logic.'

The ringleader was obviously an impatient man who required his commands to be carried out without delay, because on seeing Nicholas fail to comply with his earlier request he shouted, 'Take them down!' and the fight began.

Wandfighters wore bracelets called karns around their wrists and ankles; these karns were made of leather straps lined with magnetised metal; by use of their wands acting on these karns they could move their bodies through the air at astonishing speeds with enormous agility. They also had mobile karns, usually four each, which could be brought out and used against their enemies in a wandfight, as to fasten these karns onto your opponent's body was to be able to move your opponent's body wherever you chose. Furthermore, if a wandfighter could gain direct control of an opponent's karns already fastened to their body the same result obviously followed, but this required breaking the connection between the opponent's wand and their karns, which alone was the subject of many extensive volumes of wandlore.

Ben took out his wand and backed away until his back bumped into the wall at the side of the alley. He tried to adopt a posture of defence, but luckily no-one was paying any attention to him as the gang of robbers were finding Nicholas more than enough to be dealing with. Nicholas was moving so fast, and the robbers were so confused and scattered around the alley that Ben was having trouble seeing everything even from his priviledged position as a spectator standing right next to the action. Nicholas was taking the robbers down one by one, their hands and feet bound by their own mobile karns, their wands flying through the air into Nicholas's left hand. Nicholas then dragged the robbers into the brightly moon-lit centre of the alley and stood over them with his wand outstretched, while in his left hand he held a bundle of five wands. The fight from start to finish had taken about thirty seconds.

Ben cautiously walked over to them, his wand still in his hand.

'Am I to understand that I have been the subject of an attempted robbery?' Nicholas asked the ringleader with his eyebrows raised.

The ringleader said nothing, too angry to speak.

'I only ask,' Nicholas continued, 'because no-one has ever attempted to rob me before. I am therefore obliged in these unprecedented circumstances to proceed by inference. I see no other explanation of these events other than that you have attempted to rob me. But perhaps you will protest that I have misjudged you.'

'Oh, no, we wasn't robbing you,' said the man with the scar who had first spoken to Nicholas, 'not at all, guvnor, def'nly not.'

'Ah, then I have assigned the wrong interpretation to the request that I empty my pockets. Why then was I requested to empty my pockets?'

There was a long silence which was broken by the man with the scar, 'It was just a bit of a laugh, guvnor.'

'I am glad to learn that you have a sense of humour,' said Nicholas, 'because you will need it. You see, I am minded at the moment of the ancient saying which is *Judge not unless you be judged for with what measure you put forth it shall be returned to you again.* I trust I have made myself perfectly clear?'

It was clear from the faces of the robbers that all they had understood from what Nicholas had said was the word *judge* and this word made them a little apprehensive due no doubt to a past acquaintance with magisterial figures. 'It's just a laugh, guvnor,' the scarred man said again, stubbornly repeating the only defence he could think of, 'just a bit of a laugh, we was all going to laugh about it all, we was, yes, guvnor, that's how it was.'

'You have tried to rob me,' Nicholas told them coldly, 'so I am going to rob you in return. You may either refer to your sense of humour, which you claim to be your governing motivation in this matter or you may refer to the poetic nature of this particular administration of justice. It is your choice and I cannot say that I am particularly interested one way or another.'

Nicholas searched the men and removed from them all the money they had on them. Nothing escaped his attention, not even coins sown into the lining of their clothes which he ripped open in order to remove the coins. Ben watched this in complete and utter disbelief. He was so astonished he could not say a single word, nor could he move a single muscle. Nicholas then freed them from their bonds and walked a few steps away, and stopped to watch them as they clambered back to their feet.

The ringleader had said nothing while all this was going on, but now he spoke. 'You'll regret this,' he snarled.

'There is no need for you to be subject to a long delay,' Nicholas said and flipped the ringleader's wand back to him. With another movement of his wand, Nicholas's disc appeared on the ground before him. 'Take out your disc,' Nicholas told him coldly.

The robber took a firm grip of the wand in his hand but did nothing more than watch Nicholas with an expressionless face.

'You have attempted to rob me but now you no doubt feel that I have treated you wrongly,' Nicholas told him in an icy rage, 'because you have been robbed in turn. How do you think the victims of your robberies feel? Do you care? No, you don't. You are the scum of the gutter and you are incapable of having such thoughts precisely because you are scum. You should thank me for the lesson I have taught you. Now you know from experience what you were unable to understand before by the use of your imagination. But now you have caused me much greater offence. You have threatened me, and I do not like to be threatened.' Nicholas's words became like shards of ice. 'Let me put this to you very simply: take out your own disc or be branded a coward. Now, make your choice.'

The robber had been watching Nicholas more than listening to him and what he had seen, namely that Nicholas was getting ready to kill him, was obviously giving him pause for thought. 'All right, we're even, I got no grudge against you,' he said reluctantly, as if saying these words caused him great pain.

This seemed to Ben like a very good time to wrap everything up and leave, but Nicholas did not seem to think so. 'I see you are a coward,' Nicholas told the robber, 'because you refuse to fight.'

'I got no chance against you,' the robber said in reply. 'I know that.'

'Then why threaten me?' Nicholas asked. 'I mean, what is the point? You are not just a coward, you are also a moron, are you not? You threaten a man you will not fight. Perhaps you might care to explain yourself.'

'Like I said, I got no grudge, we're even,' the robber said then. 'I ain't threatening you no more.'

'Ah, I see, you are withdrawing your threat because you can now see that there will be consequences most unfavourable to you. Well, you have the intelligence of a dog at least.' Nicholas brought his disc up from the ground and returned it to the inside pocket of his robe. He then acted so fast that Ben found himself only catching up with what was happening after it had happened: the ringleader's disc shot up out of his robes into the air, his wand was snatched from his hand and thrown against a wooden beam of a nearby house, with his disc following promptly with the precision of a juggling act in order to cut the wand in two. Ben wasn't the only one who had trouble following what had happened, as all five would-be robbers were themselves staring at the disc embedded in the wooden beam with the cut halves of the wand on the ground below, their mouths hanging open.

Nicholas then threw the other wands onto the ground and with that he seemed to feel that the evening's business had been concluded, for he turned and walked away at a leisurely pace down the alley. Ben hurried after him.

10:20 PM, Monday 2 May 1544 A.F.

The five robbers left Octave Alley sadder and poorer, but not wiser, men. 'Jolly will have to hear about this,' the ringleader, whose name was Merton "No Tin" Nolyn, said to them, and that was all that was said as they trudged towards the Burke Tavern.

The Burke Tavern was crowded as they entered and as noisy as it was crowded. Whores, pickpockets, beggars whose missing limbs had been miraculously restored, even gap-toothed children, swarmed around and over each other in a bedlam of noise. The whores would go through a door at the back and go upstairs in the company of one man or another, and then return to the tavern. The air was thick with tobacco smoke rising upwards to disperse through narrow open windows in the walls below the wooden beams criss-crossing high above the heads of the tavern-dwellers below. A one-eyed man was smoking a long pipe while he watched with his one eye a group of men and women playing cards. A well-dressed young man, who obviously had no idea where he was, being no doubt newly arrived in New Landern, was being played up to by a tableful of admiring men and women; he would be in for a rude awakening as to where he was before the sun rose on the next day, if indeed he ever awakened again at all. Men and women were hunched over tables to bring their heads closer together in order to have conversations that would not be overheard; lone figures here and there drank from their tankards while fingering their hidden weapons as if taking a break in between nocturnal and bloody engagements; money was pushed across table-tops as transactions were concluded. The Burke Tavern was the very inn of lustful larceny.

Ignoring all this activity, and ignoring with a surly face all those acquaintances who waved and shouted over to him, No Tin led his men to the side where he knocked on a door. A panel in the door slid back, a face appeared to inspect the arrival, and with a rattle of bolts the door was opened and No Tin and his men went through.

No Tin and his men walked along a corridor toward Jolly's room, their feet dragging a little as they neared an occasion they dreaded. Jolly's door stood open as always. No Tin stopped ten paces from the open door and pulled on a cord hanging down from the ceiling. A far-off tinkling sound was promptly followed by a bell ringing beside No Tin, signalling permission to enter. No Tin and his men moved forward and entered Jolly's room.

Stepping into Jolly's room was like stepping into a red cave. The walls were covered in plush red velvet; the curtains were made of more red velvet; the ceiling was painted red, with golden chandeliers hanging down; the floor was covered in a variety of red carpets, and the large painting on the wall behind Jolly's desk showed a volcano belching red flames and dark clouds into the air.

Mr Frank "Jolly" Jollison looked up as they entered, smiling, and obviously in a good mood. No Tin knew that this good mood would not last given the news he brought. 'So how's pickings?' Jolly asked them, rubbing the tips of his fingers against his thumb to remind them, even if unnecessarily, such was his good mood, that *pickings* meant *money*.

'We was robbed,' No Tin told him, angry and fearful at the same time.

Mr Taggart "Tagalong" Longman happened to be there that night, sitting at the side, and on hearing this, he threw back his head and laughed.

'Think it's funny, do you?' No Tin snarled, giving him a look sharp enough to cut him open.

'Funny?' Tagalong queried. 'My dear man, it is hilarious.'

'Robbed?' Jolly queried in his turn, his eyes narrowing and his face becoming an angry mask. 'You trying to pull a fast one, No Tin? Is that what you're about? Because let me tell you what I'll do to you, you bag of pigeon excrement.' Jolly then detailed a number of physical procedures that he was about to apply to No Tin that were no less unspeakably brutal than they were unimaginably painful.

No Tin knew this was not idle talk and so he hastened to explain. 'We was robbed,' he said again, and the nods and dispirited demeanour of his men backed up his claim.

'Who robbed you?' Jolly asked.

The same question had been on No Tin's mind. 'We dunno, boss,' he said. 'There was these two gents walking down Octave Alley, all peaceful like they were out for a stroll, and then one of them, he didn't do nothing, but the other one, he just took us all down. You never saw nothing like it, nothing.'

The vigorous nods of No Tin's men throughout were like a silent Greek chorus, but then Helmold "Mould" Nowles, the man with the scar, spoke out, 'He just took us all down, then he just cut No Tin's wand just like that!' He clicked his fingers in the air for extra emphasis.

'He was like nothing else, boss,' Gregory "Grog" Caley added, determined that the unbelievable wandfighting ability of their would-be victim would fully justify their failure to bring home the expected ill-gotten gains of that evening. 'It's no-one could take him down, no-one, I'm telling you.'

It took some time for Jolly to get the full story from them, for his men were more at ease with the application of violence than with the ordered presentation of facts, but in time he came to be fully informed as to what had happened.

Jolly sat there for a while, thinking about this. The others in the room knew better than to say anything at a time like this, so they waited in silence.

Jolly had clawed his way up from the bottom of the gutter to be, if not out of the gutter, at least perched on its rim enjoying the good things of life. He was a rich and powerful man who ruled the underworld of New Landern. In his own way, he was as rich and powerful as the grandees of New Landern, who were its rulers, except that his wealth and power were not expressed in exactly the same way. Like the ruling class of New Landern he had plenty of strada in cash, and like them he also owned properties, and like them he had those who served him, and like them he had a position to maintain which was dependent on the integrity of his reputation. But there the similarities ended, for where they paraded around in the sunlight he lived in the shadows; where they were multiple, he was singular, for he did not allow the existence of rivals; where they prided themselves on being known to all, Jolly made no external show of his existence. Most of the ruling class of New Landern, living as they did in their fine houses, had never heard of him. Those who had heard of him were either involved with the processes of law and order or were themselves visitors to his underworld to partake of the pleasures of gambling and prostitution which he controlled.

Jolly knew what he was and where he was and he was satisfied with that. No-one crossed him and it was important that no-one should ever do so. Jolly knew that what had happened tonight to No Tin and his men was more than an inconvenient loss of money. It was a direct threat to Jolly's power. He knew that the story would be all over New Landern in a flash, and people would fall over themselves laughing, just as Tagalong had done, and the joke would be at his expense. Jolly knew that once people started laughing at him, it was the beginning of the end.

The question was: could he stop the story getting out? Jolly knew that if he forbade No Tin and his men from telling anyone what had happened, they would fail to obey his order. There were five of them, with all of the companions which that entailed, plus the loose talk of drunkenness; it would only be a matter of time before his order was disobeyed. He would then be in a position of having been failed to be obeyed which would weaken his authority. Jolly was wise in the matter of ruling men and women. He knew that authority depended as much on what orders were not given as on what orders were.

Jolly came to his decision. 'Be here at six o'clock tomorrow morning,' he told his men coldly. 'Now get out!'

10: 20 PM, Monday 2 May 1544 A. F.

Nicholas was young and naïve, but he was also intelligent enough to know that he was young and naïve. He knew as he and Ben walked away from Octave Alley that he was in a situation that required an alert attention to detail and context rather than a reliance on past preconceptions. He stole a look at Ben as they walked along. Ben's face was set in shock and his posture rigid. Nicholas decided that it might be wisest to say nothing to Ben right now so the two of them walked along in silence.

Nicholas surreptitiously checked his wand now and then to track the movements of the five robbers they had left behind them. Whether or not they were sufficiently intimidated by his wandfighting prowess to now leave him alone or whether they would seek revenge, was an unanswered question. He decided as he walked along that he needed to know more about them, which was why he was checking their movements. Although he could detect wands at a distance, using a secret of wandlore that went back to the first baron Daniel himself, he could not identify them, so the only way for him to know which of the hundreds of thousands of wands flickering in his mind like fireflies in the macchato space of New Landern were the four wands of the five robbers was by tracking them continually.

This was why he had so generously returned the wands of the robbers to them by throwing the wands on the ground.

As they neared Grenville Street Nicholas suddenly stopped and said, 'Oh, no, I forgot.'

'You forgot what?' Ben asked, coming out of his reverie.

'Never mind,' Nicholas said, who couldn't be bothered to try to make something up right then. 'You go on ahead. I won't be long.' With that, he turned and walked away. Ben called after him, but Nicholas ignored him.

He tracked the robbers he had fought in Octave Alley as he walked along, always able to keep out of sight, until they arrived somewhere and their movements were much slower and jerkier, as if they were entering a building of some kind. Nicholas fixed their location and made his way towards it. As he came around the corner, Nicholas realised the men he was following had gone into the large building ahead of him. The building had a sign hanging off a pole jutting into the street which showed a rosy-cheeked man with a rural smile holding a tankard of beer in one hand and a hunk of cheese in the other. Above the apple-cheeked yokel was the lettering "Burke" and below his cheerful and kindly simplicity was the lettering "Tavern".

The Burke Tavern stood by the side of the river and even had berths for boats to unload and load cargo for river shipping (not all of which was legal). The side of the tavern that faced the street was a large stone-walled front with tiny windows that let in little light, but which would allow the discharge of weaponry upon anyone foolish enough to attack the building. Nicholas stood unobtrusively to one side and waved his wand to examine the lair of his newly acquired enemies: he soon realised, from the motionless position and spacing of several wands within the building that there were guards, and from the layering and arrangement of the wand protection of the security system itself, that the command centre was situated at the back on the ground floor by the river. The Burke Tavern was, in fact, exactly what it looked like — a fortress. A normal tavern it was not. Nicholas didn't know what to make of any of this, but he made a careful note of all this so that he would remember it readily in the future and turned away.

Nicholas turned his steps towards home. When he arrived, Ben was nowhere to be found. Nicholas went to his room and sat in a chair, going over what had happened that evening in a spirit of contemplation. Then he remembered that he had acquired money, so he took it out and counted it. It came to two hundred and seventy two strada in total. Given that he had only had sixty three strada to his credit, he now found himself the proud possessor of three hundred and thirty five strada. He put the money away in his pouch and went back to contemplation.

There was a knock on his door and Ben put his head into the room.

'Can I come in?' he asked.

Without speaking, Nicholas waved him in with generous gestures of his hands.

Ben came in and sat on the bed. He looked calmer and more relaxed, but still tense all the same.

'I didn't know you could fight like that,' he said.

'Father and grandfather both taught me from when I was seven,' Nicholas told him. 'Their training was very thorough.'

'You've put me in an awkward position,' Ben said. 'You realise that, don't you?'

'No, I don't,' Nicholas replied shortly. 'What awkward position are you talking about?'

'Do you realise that under the law I am an accessory to robbery?' Ben asked, without anything remaining of his earlier anger but with a certain residual resentment. 'You robbed them! Are you mad? What the hell were you thinking?'

'Justice was done,' Nicholas said forcefully enough to make clear he would not budge from this point of view.

'Justice?' Ben asked incredulously. 'What's that got to do with anything? We are talking about a clear point of law.'

'Never mind the law,' Nicholas said. 'I'm talking about justice.'

'Never mind the law!' Ben repeated in outrage. 'Why not say never mind the authorities as well while you are about it?'

Nicholas shrugged. 'They're not going to complain to the authorities, are they? They did try to rob us, after all.'

'Mr Raspero,' Ben said carefully, 'that is not the point I am making. Whatever they did, you robbed them. You have committed a crime.'

'A crime that won't be reported,' Nicholas pointed out. 'So forget the law and the authorities. What they don't know won't hurt them.'

Ben hesitated then said, very formally, 'I am afraid I have to reconsider the extent of my associations with you, Mr Raspero. The events of this evening have shown to me a certain aspect of your character and conduct which leave me in such an awkward position that I must reduce all contact with you to a bare minimum.'

'Suit yourself,' Nicholas said indifferently and yawned. 'You can start right now by leaving if you like.'

Ben shifted his posture as if about to stand up but then said instead, 'You do understand my position in this matter, don't you?'

'I understand that you're a rabbit who lives in fear,' Nicholas said with a certain contempt. 'Is there anything more I need to know?'

Ben flushed with anger at this. 'I do not rob people, Mr Raspero, but that does not make me a rabbit.'

'You talk of the law but what of justice. Do you deny that they got what they deserved?'

'Yes, I do deny that,' Ben said. 'They deserved to be reported to the authorities, prosecuted and punished appropriately.'

'I prosecuted and punished them on the spot myself. What's the difference?'

'The difference is that you do not have the authority under law to take such an action.'

'What is authority?' Nicholas asked. 'It's just a bunch of people with titles they've given each other who everyone obeys simply out of habit or fear.'

'I think there is rather more to it than that,' Ben said stiffly.

Nicholas shrugged. 'Maybe. But it was men in authority who —' He broke off then and said nothing further.

'Who what?' Ben asked.

'Ben, I want you to give me your word of honour that you will never tell anyone else what I am about to tell you.'

'Will this pledge of confidentiality require me to be an accomplice to another act of criminality?' Ben asked very stiffly.

'No, this all happened six centuries ago. No-one will get prosecuted now. Trust me! Now give me your word.'

'Very well,' Ben said after a pause. 'You have my word.'

'It was men in authority who took Daniel's family and slaughtered them in front of his eyes,' Nicholas said.

'Who was Daniel?' Ben asked.

'Daniel was the first Baron of Raspero, Ben. He is your ancestor. His blood flows in your veins and in mine. That is the only reason I am telling you this. I would tell no-one else, and neither will you.'

'Why was Daniel's family slaughtered in front of his eyes?'

'Because he was found to be vandrizald. Do you know what that means?'

'Vaguely,' Ben replied. 'Demons, or something.'

'It was once believed that the ability to use a wand was only natural to those of noble birth. It was not realised then, as it is now, that it comes from literacy. Those of low birth who could use a wand were thought to be 'vandrizald', that is, of demonic origin, and they were killed as soon as they were detected. Not only that, but their whole families were slaughtered down to a precisely defined degree of blood relationship, in order to stamp out the emergence of demonic influences into humanity.'

Ben groaned. 'If you're saying that people in authority get things wrong, well, shiver my timbers, I never knew. This was all very harsh for Daniel, but let's all move on, shall we?'

'Daniel escaped,' Nicholas continued, as if Ben had never spoken at all, 'and nothing is known of him until an eleven-year-old boy arrived at the camp of General Galen Sarkisian, a mercenary general of the time. Sarkisian took him as one of his followers and Daniel became in due course of time a Vadim, that's like a captain of horse.'

'This is all very interesting,' Ben said impatiently, 'but what does it have to do with anything now?'

'I am talking about our ancestor, Ben. What happened to him is as real as anything that happens to you or me.'

'Real or not, it is irrelevant to anything now.'

'Daniel was taken prisoner at the age of fifteen in some long forgotten battle and thrown into the Silver Mines of Sacramento as a slave. The authorities did this, Ben. Now are you beginning to understand? How would you like to be taken underground at the age of fifteen to spend the rest of your life in darkness, never seeing the sun or the sky, digging up dirt to be taken above ground to the world you had been banished from? When he arrived, Daniel was shown a man with his tongue cut out. Speak out of turn and this will happen to you, the guards told him. Then he was shown a man with his hands cut off. Raise your hands against us, and this will happen to you, the guards told him. Then he was shown a man with his feet cut off. Try to escape, and this will happen to you, the guards told him. Daniel was searched for weapons and money and tools with which to pick locks such as the lock he was chained with. But Daniel had a wand hidden on him and he was not searched for a wand because the thought never crossed anyone's mind to do so. The wand was disguised as part of a wooden strapping around his legs. He took that wand and that very day he overthrew and killed his guards and freed his fellow prisoners, who you can be sure looked on him as a saviour, for he had indeed saved them.'

'Is there a point to any of this?' Ben wanted to know.

'I am coming to the point, Ben. Picture the scene. Daniel and his fellow freed prisoners emerge above ground. They kill and capture the remaining guards and the personnel who process the silver from the ore they dig up. Now bear with me for this is the interesting part. What Daniel did then was completely unexpected, a bolt from the blue, a stroke of genius. What he did then is why Daniel is the greatest of us all, the greatest of the Rasperos, a man whose name is still held in veneration today by those who remember this tale.' Nicholas was almost in a trance by now, but he came back to himself in order to say, 'Which are not many, of course. This story is not in the history books. It is not generally known. It is confidential, which is why I have sworn you to secrecy.'

Ben waited, but Nicholas stubbornly refused to speak. Ben sighed. 'All right, what did Daniel do next?'

'What would you have done, Ben? I will not answer your question until you have answered mine.'

Ben sat and thought for a while. 'Well, I've escaped from a living hell of being buried alive underground as a slave, I've got my freedom, so I make my way from that place without delay and seek a place of refuge where I can avoid recapture.'

'Very good, Ben, that is excellent.' Nicholas was highly pleased with this answer. 'That is indeed an excellent answer. And can it be faulted? No, it cannot be faulted. It is the answer just about anyone would give to the question: what would you have done then? The obvious thing is to run for it, is it not? To escape, to run with your freedom secure in your hands while you can still get away. But this is not what Daniel did, Ben. What Daniel did was this. He climbed up to where he could address all the freed prisoners and he said to them, "I am Daniel of Sacramento and I claim lordship over these lands. Stay here and serve me, and we will continue to dig up silver from the ground, and we will divide it among ourselves, and we will all become rich men." And they followed him, Ben. Near those mines was the riverside town of Raspero, and in due course of time Daniel became the first Baron of Raspero. He brought the King to his knees and had that Barony created just for him. Now do you understand the nature of authority, Ben?'

Ben sighed in exasperation. 'Your tedious tale is supposed to inform me that one authority can be overthrown and replaced by another. Well, who could have guessed? Now I know! Lucky me! For Heaven's sake, none of this means anything. It certainly doesn't mean that you can do anything you please.'

'It certainly does not mean that I can do anything I please,' Nicholas agreed, 'but it does mean that I can make up my own mind about things. Authority is just a resource to be called upon when necessary, and tonight it was not necessary because I had everything under control. I decided because I could decide. What should authority do, anyway, Ben? Should authority tell you what music to like, how to feel when you see the sunlight fall on the waters of the ocean? You talk about authority as if that means you can't make decisions for yourself. Well, I have a different view.'

Ben was suddenly struck by the sense of what Nicholas had said. It was like a shaft of sunlight breaking through clouds. There was a momentary sense of dislocation, of transposition, during which Ben felt the weight of his own life for the first time. He had never realised before that he carried his own life about with him, that it was his life and no-one else's, and now that he thought about it, he could not deny that there was a certain poetic justice about what Nicholas had done in robbing the robbers. And given that they would never report the robbery to the authorities, he had to acknowledge that the matter had been wrapped up.

'Nicholas, I'm starting to think that you're corrupting me,' he said, shaking his head.

'I'm always glad to help,' Nicholas said with an air of satisfaction.

'Well, it's over and done with anyway,' Ben said.

'Probably.'

'What do you mean *probably*?'

'I mean it's not guaranteed, that's all.'

'How can it not be guaranteed?'

'Well, I think we should both keep our eyes open in case we run into those robbers again, who might after all want revenge. Especially you. Me, they might not attack, but if they find you on your own, well, you'll be on your own, that's all.'

'Well, that's great,' Ben complained. 'Now I have to watch my back every minute of the day.'

'Don't you do that already?' Nicholas asked curiously. 'I mean, I do. I thought everyone did.'

Ben said nothing for a while but just looked at him before saying, 'No, Nicholas, it's just you and those like you. The rest of us don't worry about suddenly being unexpectedly attacked.'

'I've been trained to be ready to be unexpectedly attacked since I was seven,' Nicholas said, shrugging slightly. 'That's where we're different, I suppose.'

Ben got off the bed and moved to the door. He opened the door, and just before he stepped through it he turned to Nicholas and said, 'When I have time I will list our differences, and I assure you, there will be more than one item on the list.' With that he stepped through the door and closed it behind him.

Nicholas smiled to himself. He remembered now that Ben always liked to have the last word.

TWO

....

The Proposal of Lord Percival Breckenridge to Lady Isabel Grangeshield

3:20 PM, Monday 2 May 1544 A. F.

Isabel Grangeshield sat contentedly in her magnificent garden, her fan held lightly in her hands as she contemplated the world at large. The sky was as blue as blue could be, with fluffy white clouds moving across it like clots of cream sliding down the sides of a bowl. Behind her, Grangeshield House rose up into the air like a ship surging through the blue sky overhead, the Grangeshield banner with its two red lions waving in the gentle breeze.

Isabel was looking her best, which was to say formidable. Her dark brown hair had been carefully coiled into a spiral pattern held together by green and white gemstones which had been carefully chosen to augment the dark green dress she was wearing. This dress was cut low to display the cleavage of Isabel's large breasts, then pulled in tight at the waist in order to balloon into cascading skirts which only ended their fall in order to display the demure tips of two shoes peeking forward where they were positioned on the ground. Isabel's large warm brown eyes were framed by darkened eyelashes, her full lips painted a deep red, her rounded cheeks gently rouged to emphasise the sweetness of her face, her bare neck and shoulders gleaming in the sunlight as she sat straight-backed in her chair on this day on which her latest suitor would propose to her.

Beside her sat Lord Percival Albert James Algernon Breckenridge, Count of Anthored, Keeper of The Sixth Key, Knight Exalted of the

Council of Rondreth, and the fifth richest man in Anglashia. He cut a striking figure, with a magnificent moustache and carefully combed reddish hair, blue eyes and the proportions of his nose, mouth and brow all combining to form the regular and pleasing features of his handsome face. His clothes were a glorious fusion of blue and yellow, his ancestral colours, from the gleam of his highly polished shoes to the faded sheen of the carefully folded scarf around his neck.

Isabel and Percival were seated in the ornately carved Grotto of Peace on red velvet cushions at right angles to each other. Discreetly out of earshot at some distance away to Isabel's left sat Lord and Lady Easton in chairs placed within the hexagonal Pavilion of the Sun. With them were Lady Breckenridge, the mother of Percival, and Percival's bored younger brother, the seventeen year-old William. The tableau was not set by accident, for there was a design to it, and the centerpiece of the design were the two figures of Isabel and Percival.

Isabel sat composedly, her hands in her lap holding her fan, which she twirled now and then. Percival himself was anything but composed, fidgeting in his chair continually, straightening in his chair and then slouching down, his legs crossed, the heel of his right foot occasionally tapping at his left calf.

They had exchanged pleasantries, enquired after each other's health and also after the health of various relatives and friends. They then both expressed concern about the international situation, which was bad, as usual. Percival had then spoken at length about harmony, mutual understanding and the merging of destinies. He appeared to have memorised certain quotes because his eyes would slightly glaze over at times as he brought forth segments of highly polished prose containing the wit and wisdom of the ages. Isabel nodded as if attentive to everything he said, the picture of an appreciative audience. In point of fact, she was hardly listening to a word he was saying, but she was enjoying herself nonetheless.

She always enjoyed being proposed to no matter who the suitor in question was. They were all one to her because she had absolutely no intention of accepting any of their proposals. She was twenty two years old and frequently badgered about getting married by her guardians, Lord and Lady Easton, but she was not getting married for several reasons. One was that she enjoyed her independence, another that she enjoyed being chased after by every eligible bachelor in New Landern, and another was that she had never yet met a man who she wanted to marry.

She knew that the Eastons had particular hopes for this match. Percival was twenty-eight, good-looking with a very handsome moustache, from one of the noblest families in the land and incredibly rich. They felt that this match had everything going for it, including the undeniable fact that it was definitely time for Isabel to get married. While never complaining about their own roles as chaperones, it could not be denied that this was also part of their reasoning. They would then have their own time back to themselves rather than being obliged to be Isabel's guardians, but to their credit this was a secondary consideration for them.

Percival had fallen silent for some time while Isabel had patiently waited.

'Isabel,' Percival said, 'well, here we are.'

Isabel saw that he was getting his nerve together to make his proposal. She always enjoyed this part. Her suitors varied in their degrees of anguish, and they each took their varying times about working themselves up to the moment of truth, but when the time came she took a certain interest in watching them go about what they had to do. The sight of the pain, her suitors were going through gave her a warm and pleasurable feeling. She said nothing, her eyes demurely downcast, twirling her fan in her hands.

'So here we are, are we not, Isabel?'

'Yes, we are here, Percival,' Isabel said calmly.

'So,' Percival continued, 'we are here, are we not?'

Isabel looked down at the fan in her hands, peeking up at Percival now and then.

'Yes, we are here,' Percival said, 'and here we are.'

Isabel unfolded her fan and studied the elephant drawn on its opened expanse. The elephant had its trunk upraised as if trumpeting. Isabel wondered what kind of noise an elephant made when it was trumpeting. Was it like a trumpet? Was that why the word *trumpeting* was used? What kind of word was *trumpeting* anyway?

'Isabel,' Percival said, 'there comes a time when a man must decide on questions of the utmost seriousness. This is a momentous occasion, a time of solemnity, a collision of destinies.' He paused to take a deep breath.

Isabel thought that the phrase *a collision of destinies* wasn't bad. She hadn't heard that one before. She thought that *a momentous occasion* was an over-used phrase, though, so Percival lost marks there.

'There comes a time in the life of a man, Isabel,' Percival continued, obviously reaching into his memory for a rehearsed set of words, 'when the pleasures and comforts of the day are not enough, when his soul thirsts for something of which he knows not, when beyond what he sees and understands he hears the call of the unknown seeking an answering call to a question he dares not ask.'

Isabel was very pleased with all this. It was excellent. Percival was doing very well. At this rate, she would give him very high marks for his performance.

'You understand me all too well, I fear, my sweetest Isabel,' Percival said, looking at her closely. 'Do you not, my sweetest Isabel?'

Isabel noticed that he had called her *my sweetest Isabel* twice in the same breath. She could tell he was not far away from his proposal by now.

'I am all at a loss to understand you, Percival,' she said hesitantly, folding up her fan. 'You speak of such high and lofty things that my head spins merely to dare to comprehend matters of such deep import. Oh, you must help me to understand these matters of which you speak. On my own I cannot.'

Percival stroked his magnificent moustache while he pondered her reply. This wasn't the answer he had hoped for. He had hoped that she would have gotten the drift by now, thus helping him over the last hurdle of actually proposing. It was still going to be uphill for a while longer, Percival realised. But the blood of kings, adulterous archbishops and countless counts flowed in his veins, and he manfully squared up to the challenge. 'It falls to my duty to do that which I gladly take up with a shout of joy,' he said.

Isabel wondered if Percival had got that right. Hadn't he misquoted Courtlyn? It didn't sound right, somehow. 'Your eloquence is beyond compare, Percival,' Isabel said in a tone of the deepest admiration. 'How do you express your thoughts with such a fluid and elegant turn of phrase?'

'Ah,' Percival said meaningfully, 'my words fly on wings sent from the deepest least wayward impulses of my heart.'

Well, he got that quote right, Isabel thought, recognising the line from Dacian's epic poem of the love between the mermaid and the doorkeeper of the great castle by the sea.

'So that is why,' Isabel commented. 'But still I cannot understand what it is that you wish me to understand.'

Percival swallowed back the annoyance which had momentarily arisen on hearing her words. How many times, he thought, did he have to use such phrases as *impulses of my heart* before his beloved comprehended the import of his discourse? 'What it is that you must understand,' he said, 'is that however we fly on the wings of our mind, it is the earth that pulls us downward.'

Lorene, Isabel noted, another quote which Percival had actually got right. 'You must think very badly of me,' Isabel said, 'but still I do not understand.'

'Isabel, dearest, my dearest sweetest Isabel, sweet, sweet Isabel, I wish you to be mine, I want to travel hand in hand with you along the great journey of life, together, your hand in mine, I am yours for all of eternity, dearest Isabel, will you grant me that which is in your keeping and all that I desire?'

Isabel realised she couldn't play dumb for much longer. She thought that the sentence *I want to travel hand in hand with you along the great journey of life* was actually not too bad. She memorised it in order to tell her friends later. She wondered if Percival had thought it up by himself or if he'd had help.

'Goodness!' Isabel gasped, raising her hand to her mouth, 'can it be so? But what are you saying, Percival? Surely I mistake what you say!'

'No, beloved Isabel,' Percival assured her, 'I wish you to marry me and be mine for ever.'

So he had finally got to it, Isabel observed. He had used the word *marry* which as far as she was concerned was the actual proposal itself. She noted that he hadn't actually gotten onto his knee and proffered a ring, which brought his marks down as far as she was concerned, because she always liked that touch; she liked to see a man on his knees before her. Still, she reflected, he hadn't done too badly. Even his nervousness had been an artistic enhancement of the overall presentation, even if unintentional. She liked to see a man tremble at the thought of asking her to marry him, because, after all, she expected no less.

Now came Isabel's favourite part, namely her refusal of the proposal. A well-made proposal deserved a gracious refusal; a proposal less deserving of her favour called forth a much blunter response. Percival, she decided, had earned a gracious refusal.

'This is all so sudden and unexpected!' Isabel gasped, unfolding her fan and raising it in front of her face. 'I am caught by surprise. I do not know what to say.'

'Say yes, sweetest Isabel,' Percival urged her.

Isabel said immediately, 'Oh, but you give me no time! Surely I may have time to think.'

'You may have all the time in the world, sweetest Isabel,' Percival told her, 'for what are the minutes you take now, compared with all the years to come?'

Isabel noted that he had given her only *minutes*, which she thought mean of him; also, she couldn't help but note that he had equated *minutes* with *all the time in the world*, which hardly seemed logical. She also couldn't help but feel that the phrase *the years to come* had the slightly depressing connotation of a prison sentence to it, at least to her ears.

'But how can I say yes when I do not love you?' she said. 'Surely it is on the foundations of love that marriage is built?'

Percival took this in his stride. He was prepared for this one. 'Love will grow in time, sweet Isabel. We will grow to love each other as the plant grows towards the sun.'

Isabel approved of that line. It wasn't too bad. 'But in darkness the plant shrivels and dies,' she said. 'And what then?'

Percival was thrown by this. He had no idea what to say. He wasn't prepared for this response. Isabel gazed wide-eyed at him while he thought this one over. 'The plant is just a metaphor,' he said eventually, obviously wishing he had chosen another metaphor. 'Never mind plants. We will come to love each other anyway.'

'Percival, you have granted me the greatest honour I could ever have wished for,' Isabel said admiringly, in tones of the deepest sympathy she could reach for as she warmed up for the kill. 'You have asked for my hand in marriage and by doing so you have gained my deepest attention and most ardent goodwill. Yet, I must refuse your proposal for I cannot see that we are to be together in the way that you seek. I must say no, Percival, no to the proposal which you have made. I refuse your proposal of marriage.'

Isabel looked at Percival, who looked back at her.

Percival opened his mouth to say something, then closed it again; he thought for a while, then opened his mouth as if to speak, then seemed to think better of it and closed his mouth again. Isabel watched all this with a certain disinterest. For her, the drama was all over, and it was time to wrap this all up and move on.

'So, you are saying no?' Percival queried eventually.

'Exactly!' Isabel said, careful not to say it too sharply. 'I am refusing your proposal.' In her experience, which was considerable, suitors very often refused to take no for an answer and pestered her to change her mind, and that was when she could turn nasty. But at this stage, a firm hand was usually all that was needed.

'Well, naturally I am disappointed,' Percival said. 'I had hoped you would accept my proposal.'

Isabel couldn't help but think that Percival did not exactly look heartbroken. He did not even look particularly disappointed. She wondered if he had ever really wanted to marry her at all. Perhaps this course of action had been urged on him by his mother and his financial advisers.

'I have refused your proposal,' Isabel told him gently, 'and that is the end of the matter. I know you are such a complete gentleman that you will not press your suit further.'

'Yes, quite,' Percival agreed, but he did not yet look ready to give up. 'I understand, of course, proposal, refusal, yet I cannot help but wonder if in the fullness of time there might come to be a change which, though gradual and imperceptible in the onset of its influence, might yet bring about such a shift as to render all my hopes fulfilled beyond all measure by that which is only a delay of our mutual happiness.'

Isabel's hands had tightened on her fan during this speech. If Percival had been a more observant man, he might have recognised that as a danger sign, but Percival saw nothing. 'I will not receive a second proposal from you, Percival,' Isabel said gently, 'so it is futile to hope I will change my mind. My mind is perfectly made up. There is nothing more to be said.' She spoke so plainly as to be quite deliberately blunt.

'Yes, quite,' Percival said without moving. 'That is just so. But if the ardour of my suit is to be tested by obstacles which must be surmounted, yet I assure you I am not daunted by any tests I may be obliged to undergo, no matter how plainly I am told these obstacles are impassable.'

Isabel took the tip of her fan in the palm of her left hand, which she held upright with the other end of the fan in her right hand as if it was a dagger. 'I am starting to question whether you are a gentleman, Lord Breckenridge,' she told him coldly.

This stung Lord Percival Breckenridge like a wasp up his nostril. He straightened up in his chair and said, 'I beg your pardon?'

'Your suit is not welcome,' Isabel told him with an edge of fierceness to her voice. 'If you are a gentleman, then accept my refusal with decorum. If you persist in pressing your suit, I shall have no choice but to draw the only appropriate conclusion which can be drawn from the persistence of your unwelcome attentions.'

Percival looked as if she had just hit him several times, which in a sense she had. He was sitting rigidly upright now, his silver-topped walking cane motionless in his right hand. He looked quite pale. 'Of course I will no longer press my attentions upon you if they are unwelcome,' he said.

'I only sought to make you an offer of marriage because of your wholly admirable qualities. I did not expect to be insulted in return.'

'I do not insult you, Percival,' Isabel told him gently, 'but I refuse your proposal and I ask you as the complete gentleman which you undoubtedly are to accept my refusal of your proposal without further argument.'

Percival nodded several times without speaking. 'Yes, quite,' he said, but still to Isabel's growing exasperation he made no move to get going. 'I understand that you have refused this proposal. It is just that I wonder if you might accept another proposal at some future date.'

'No, I will not,' Isabel told him with a careful blend of three-parts severity with seven-parts gentleness. 'I ask you not to be so discourteous as to trouble me again about a matter which is already settled beyond question.'

'Yes, quite,' Percival said, still not accepting defeat. 'Yet I cannot help but hope even now, in the depths of despair, in the darkness of my disappointment, that a light may shine forth to guide me to our shared happiness.'

Isabel then lost her temper. She stood up, walked some steps away, turned to face Percival, and shouted at the top of her voice, 'Your attentions are unwelcome, Lord Breckenridge!'

This public spectacle had the effect that she knew it would. The Eastons, Lady Breckenridge and Percival's younger brother William, no longer looking bored, but his eyes alight with mischief and joy, all jumped up from their chairs and came running over to join them.

'But what is the matter, Isabel?' Lady Dacia Easton asked with concern.

'Lord Breckenridge has proposed marriage. I have refused his proposal. Yet, he persists in continuing to press his suit. I am simply fed up with his behaviour. What kind of man is he to behave like this?'

Percival stood up because everyone else was standing around him, leaving him feeling dwarfed and said, 'Ah, yes, I was merely suggesting that I might make a second proposal at some later date.'

'That sounds very sensible,' Lord Bentley Easton said approvingly. 'Naturally the first proposal is very often refused. It shows nothing but a becoming modesty on the part of the maiden, and it is only to be expected that a second proposal will be proffered.'

'Look at Lord and Lady Preece,' Lady Easton said, backing up her husband. 'She turned him down six times!'

'I am glad to find I am not alone in this matter,' Percival said with some relief, 'for Isabel has suggested I am not a gentleman for continuing to press my suit.'

'Isabel!' Lady Easton gasped, shocked. 'You said no such thing!'

'I certainly said no such thing, Aunt Dacia,' Isabel replied. 'Lord Breckenridge misrepresents me. I said that if he continued to pester me with his unwelcome attentions I would be forced to conclude that he was not a gentleman.'

'If you were to reach such a conclusion, Lady Grangeshield,' Percival said icily, 'I would be obliged to demand satisfaction. Would there be someone to act on your behalf if so?'

'I am sure there is no need for such an action on your part, Percival,' Lord Easton said hastily, trying to hose everything down before the fire spread.

'There is most certainly not!' Lady Breckenridge agreed forcefully, giving Isabel a less than friendly look.

'In the event that you demand satisfaction, I would make enquiries as to who might act on my behalf,' Isabel told him with equal iciness, knowing full well that half of New Landern would jump forward to defend her. 'You will no doubt scorn to refer to First Combat but will refer to a higher grade.'

'Percival will do no such thing!' Lady Breckenridge shouted on the instant.

'First Combat would be the appropriate form of satisfaction for such an offence as this, which in any case has not even been given yet, and will not be,' Lord Easton said firmly, giving Isabel a hard look. He did not often put his foot down, but he was doing so now.

'May I enquire of Lord Breckenridge,' Isabel said coldly, looking directly at Lady Breckenridge as he said this, 'why he cannot comprehend that I have refused his proposal today and I do not wish him to trouble me again with another? I do not want to marry Lord Breckenridge. Not today, not tomorrow, not ever. How much more plainly do I need to speak?'

'Let us agree that there is nothing more to be said about this matter today,' Lord Easton said hastily while Lady Breckenridge was pondering her response.

'It is very becoming of you to be so modest,' Lady Easton said, muddying the waters at a time when Isabel was trying to make everything crystal clear. 'You are fighting like a tigress to defend your modesty, and what could be more commendable?'

Lord Easton was infuriated by his wife's blunder but even as he was opening his mouth to speak Percival made his own blunder.

'Ah, I thought so,' he said, nodding with an air of self-satisfaction, 'your modesty is to be commended, Isabel, and I will return to propose again.'

'You are not a gentleman, Lord Breckenridge,' Isabel said very clearly and forcefully.

Silence gripped the group then. Lady Easton turned to look at her husband only to see him glaring at her with such cold fury she immediately turned away again, wondering why he was so angry with her. She hadn't said anything.

Percival went pale and couldn't speak. He looked at Isabel to see her glaring at him with a hard, fixed look on her face that was so rigid it made her face appear like a mask.

'I must demand satisfaction, Lady Grangeshield,' Percival said eventually. 'Is there anyone who will act on your behalf?'

'Name the time and place of the duel and your opponent will be there,' Isabel told him, furious to the tips of her fingers. 'What form of satisfaction do you require?'

'First Combat,' Percival said. 'Tomorrow at six o'clock at Mildgyd.'

'Very well,' Isabel said. 'I would like to take this opportunity to make something quite plain to you, Lord Breckenridge. If you ever propose to me again, I will tell you again quite plainly that you are not a gentleman and you will find yourself fighting another duel. That duel will not be First Combat, which you will already have referred to once. Is that clear? Now get out! You are not welcome here and you are never welcome to ever set foot here again!' With that Isabel turned and stalked furiously away back to the house.

The Eastons tried to make their farewells as courteously as they could, but the Breckenridges were not to be mollified in any way, no matter how much soothing oil Lord Easton tried to pour on these troubled waters. William had a barely concealed and delighted grin; he had enjoyed the show and now he had a duel to look forward to the very next day. *Life did not get any better than this*, William thought.

Isabel stormed up to the Red Drawing Room and threw herself down in her favourite chair. *What an impossible man!* she thought furiously to himself; it seemed he was so conceited he could not believe she did not want him as her husband. Well, he would grasp that concept fully when he faced his opponent in the duel tomorrow.

She turned her mind then to selecting someone to act on her behalf. She was glad that in her temper she had not pushed the issue further to be a matter of second or final combat. First combat was one thing, second or final combat another. It would be much easier for her to find someone to act on her behalf in a lesser duel. As the Eastons entered the room, she held up her hand palm out to keep them at bay. They sat nearby with expressions of resignation on their faces.

Isabel made her choice, went to her study to write a letter to the lucky man and dispatched it immediately by private messenger. Lewis Hexton was so excited as to come around immediately, and his repeated expressions of delight at being her champion made it plain he was wondering whether to propose to her again. Isabel neither encouraged nor dispelled his illusions, deciding she would not tell him that she would not receive his suit a second time until after the duel was over.

6:00 PM, Tuesday 3 May 1544 A. F.

The duel of First Combat was fought as promised at Mildgyd, in front of a large audience. The duelists faced off against each other, each with four mobile karns floating around them and their fight began. To be brought down onto the ground was to lose the round and there were three rounds in First Combat. There was only one round in Second Combat because that required the breaking of at least one limb. There was also only one round in Final Combat because that required a magnetised disc being used to kill the opponent.

The two men circled each other, wands in hand, slashing ineffectually with various combinations, the one nearly toppling the other and then nearly being toppled in turn. At one point Lord Breckenridge was brought down by physical contact, which was a foul; three fouls would mean the loss of the round. After some twenty minutes or so Lord Breckenridge managed to bring down his opponent with a stray mobile karn that grabbed an ankle and tugged him off-balance so that he fell down. His supporters cheered and Lord Breckenridge, his hair tousled and breathing heavily, nodded briefly in acknowledgement of this support. Then the duel resumed and Hexton in a reckless frenzy attacked so wildly that as much by chance or at least brute force, he brought Breckenridge down. It was now the third round and both men were wary now, for the next victory was decisive. They slashed and grappled each other hesitantly, trying out all the combinations they knew, striking and blocking and parrying all they could. They were both breathing heavily now, their hair matted with sweat. The duel had been going on for fifty minutes or so. Then Breckenridge threw everything he had into a sudden rush that went on without stop while his opponent blocked and parried until overcome by an overwhelming flurry of combinations he lost his footing and fell, leaving Breckenridge standing with his wand upraised in triumph. The cheers of his supporters were deafening.

Isabel was satisfied with the outcome. Her champion had been defeated, which meant she could treat him with disdain for failing to give her victory. There was no need to trouble herself further with his attentions; she could tell him to get lost in the politest but most unmistakable of ways. Breckenridge had by now grasped the concept that he was a rejected suitor, which damaged his pride, but his victory in the duel would go a long way to healing the wound to his pride. He could now walk around New Landern with a victorious swagger and in time he would be merely yet another of her rejected suitors, who were now growing in numbers to the point that there were even jokes being told in New Landern that Isabel's rejected suitors should form a club whose membership criterion would be precisely this status.

Breckenridge and Hexton were now shaking hands and exchanging words. They were smiling at each other and discussing key points of the fight they had just had. What they were saying could not be heard as they were too far away, but it was obvious that neither could praise the honourable bravery of his opponent enough. They knew each other to talk to in passing, of course, but they had never been especially close up until now. They would very likely get drunk together tonight and remain fast friends for life from the looks of how happy they were with each other's company.

All in all, Isabel reflected, everything had ended well.

THREE

The Rescue of Mr Taggart Longman
by Mr Nicholas Raspero

Madeleine's father had died when she was eleven years old, but not before installing in her a sense of self-reliance by so often being away from home. The man in her life had always been away, and now he had departed for good, and the impression this left on her went deep into her soft and malleable feelings. Where the impression of her father should have been, there was only the impression of an absence. Her mother had thereafter managed to take care of them both by sacrificing her pride to the desire evoked in men by her beauty. By the time Madeleine was fifteen she had passed through the hands of no fewer than five "stepfathers", and the unprotected girl had passed through the hands of two of these "stepfathers" in a quite literal sense. Tragedy struck and the beautiful fifteen-year old was left an orphan when her mother died after a lingering illness.

There had been eyes watching Madeleine for quite some time already, eyes that saw her beauty as a commodity, and the mouths that had directed Madame Marlene to befriend the young girl during her mother's last days now directed Madame Marlene to adopt the girl unofficially and take her to her own home, a home which already had a number of women in residence. There she was apprenticed to the line of work which Madame Marlene had chosen for her, given the working name Hailee, and there she was tutored by Madame Marlene in the ways of the world.

'You must be in the world but not of it,' Madame Marlene told the trusting Madeleine. 'That is the only way to be sure that the world does not eat you. Never give a man your heart, or the world will eat you, bite by bite, not all at once but in the end you will be gone. Give men what they can see while never giving your heart and you will be safe.'

Whatever softness remained in Madeleine's feelings did not remain long; like clay baked hard by the fire, the repeated reception of the hot desire of a multitude of men coupled with the clear instructions of Madame Marlene that the world was her enemy hardened the young girl's heart until it could truthfully be said that she was in the world but not of it.

By the time she was seventeen, Madeleine had graduated from her apprenticeship and Jolly himself, the ruler of the underworld of New Landern, took a hand in her future. He installed her in a private apartment as his mistress. She had two servants, Abbey and Hugo, and a life of luxury.

Madeleine turned her attention on Jolly's orders to learning how to behave like a lady. She was instructed by tutors in how to speak and behave with decorum, in the importance of never behaving spontaneously, on the necessity of always keeping her smile in its proper place. She was educated in the literary classics, in the visual arts, in the maxims of philosophy and in all that was necessary to cultivate the appropriate appearance of gentility. She was not expected to understand any of this; she was only expected to reproduce the experience of having encountered it. What she did understand she kept to herself.

She was taught how to polish her natural beauty like a carefully cut jewel by hair-stylists, manicurists, make-up assistants, clothes advisors and fashion designers until she had achieved such a state of calculated attractiveness as for her beauty to appear as a spontaneous flourishing of this moment alone and none other.

The personal demands which Jolly made on her as his mistress were easily met and Madeleine settled into her new life like a weary traveller sinking into a hot bath. She had not realised how accustomed she had become to her life of luxury until one day Jolly threatened to take it all away from her.

8:30 PM, Tuesday 12 July 1539 A. F.

Jolly and Madeleine were sitting in the living room of Madeleine's luxurious apartment; Jolly drinking whiskey with his feet stretched out on a footstool.

Madeleine was looking radiant in a light blue dress which was tied around her slender neck leaving her bare shoulders gleaming; her blue eyes glittered like sapphires; her blonde hair was artfully bound by jewel-encrusted hair-pins in waves that framed her head like a helmet; her delicate lips and nose and high cheekbones had an aesthetic precision that was like mathematics turned into poetry. Her blue dress was tied snugly around her narrow waist, her long legs crossed demurely at her shapely ankles. She was like a sculptor's ideal of beauty.

She held a fan in her hands, and sat as straight-backed as any tutor could desire, her arms and legs collected together with such decorum as to form a living picture of how a young lady should sit.

'Show me what you can do, girl,' Jolly ordered her.

Madeleine looked down at her fan modestly, opened it and said gently, 'But I am at a loss to understand you, Mr Jollison. You must surely think poorly of me for such a failure on my part.'

'Not bad,' Jolly said approvingly. 'Keep going.'

'It is kind of you to show such interest in me,' Madeleine continued. 'I can only thank you for such kindness.'

'What else?'

'A lady can say no more, Mr Jollison.' Madeleine looked up at Jolly demurely and raised her fan to cover up the lower part of her face so that only her eyes showed.

Jolly nodded and considered the picture formed by Madeleine for a while. 'It's time for you to go back to Madame Marlene,' he told her. 'I'm done with you.'

Madeleine lowered her fan and looked down at it. 'Have I displeased you, Mr Jollison?' she asked softly.

'I'm bored with you, Madeleine,' Jolly told her. 'I've had you enough times; what else you got to give me?'

The thought of returning to Madame Marlene filled Madeleine with a dismay tinged with panic. She had become accustomed to both a light workload and a life of luxury. There was neither at Madame Marlene's establishment. 'Jolly, I'm real sorry if I —'

'I spent all that money on teaching you to be a lady and you talk like that!' Jolly roared in a fury.

Madeleine collected herself immediately. 'Naturally, Mr Jollison, I am only too regretful that I have disappointed you to plead my case any further. However, I am only too willing to provide you with any further services which you might be inclined to request from me. You have only to ask, like the kind benefactor that you have always been to me, and I will immediately seek to oblige you without any hesitation on my part.'

Having thrown a scare into her, Jolly could now allow himself to be merciful. 'Well, now, that's more like it,' he told her approvingly. 'Now you mention it, there's another service you can provide for me. You interested?'

'Very,' Madeleine said as composedly as she could, still in a state of shock at the thought of becoming one of Madame Marlene's girls again.

'I'm a man of many interests,' Jolly told her. 'You get me?'

'Naturally, I —'

'Drop the act,' Jolly said impatiently. 'I want you to listen to me. You're going to carry on doing what you've been doing for me. Just one client at a time. Got that?'

'Yes,' Madeleine said cautiously, not daring to say too much unless she said the wrong thing.

'They will be wealthy men, big-shots in society. You don't fool around with anyone I don't tell you to go with. You don't get to have your own personal sweetheart. You understand?'

'Yes, Jolly,' Madeleine said as cautiously as before.

'You tell me everything about these men. Who they see, what their weaknesses are, how they live, anything you can tell me about them, you tell me. You talk to them, you get to know them, you tell me all about them. You getting the picture, girl?'

'Yes, Jolly.'

'You get to keep this apartment, you get to keep Abbey and Hugo but remember they work for me, so do you, don't you forget that. You step out of line and you go back to Madame Marlene's. Got that?'

'Yes, Jolly.'

'Now here's the tricky part, girl. How you gonna do this, hey? Got any ideas?'

'No, Jolly.'

'See, this is why I run the show,' Jolly observed. 'I got the brains. That's just how it is. All right, girl, you're going to become an actress.'

'An actress?'

'That's right. It's all sorted. Ansel Horado is taking you into his company, the Kerrick Company. You're going to see him tomorrow. You keep him at arm's distance, you got that? You don't fool around with a man unless I tell you to fool around with him. You got that?'

'Yes, Jolly.'

'This is costing me money, girl. You're an investment for me, and I'll get that money back plus extra. A lot extra. Otherwise, you'll pay off the money on your back at Madame Marlene's. You know how much money you cost me, girl?'

'No, Jolly.'

'More than seventeen thousand strada, girl. You wanna pay me back that money from your clients at Madame Marlene's, or you gonna do it right?'

'I'll do it right, Jolly.'

'You know what a stage name is, girl?'

'Yes, Jolly.'

'You're gonna take the stage name of "Angela Ashton". After your mother died you were in service for two years as a lady's companion with Mrs Erica Farrar, Mrs Erica Farrar, got that? So you saw that play you were at last week, remember that play I took you to, when I told you to wear that veil, so now you wanna be an actress. That's how you're gonna meet all these big-shots. But you keep a distance from them, you play the lady, got it? Any of them look like they wanna get real friendly, you tell me and I'll let you know which one to choose. You understand everything I'm telling you?'

'Yes, Jolly.'

'What you've been don't exist no more. I'll take care of that. Don't worry, anyone who thinks he remembers Hailee from Madame Marlene will learn different, trust me. Now what am I missing, girl?'

'I don't know, Jolly.'

Jolly threw back his head and laughed. 'You're only forgetting what this is all about for you, girl. How you gonna get paid? Well, what d'ya think?'

'I'm a lady,' Madeleine said cautiously, 'so … so what do I do, Jolly?'

Jolly nodded approvingly to see her turning to him for guidance. 'They give you gifts, girl. Clothes, jewellery, whatever. That's before you give them anything of yours, get me? I'll let you play that yourself. Then you let them have you and they keep on giving you gifts, because they like you so much, see, and you keep on letting them have you and they keep on giving you gifts, that's how it works, girl. It's just a different kind of money, that's all. But those gifts are worth money. You don't steal anything, girl, you get me? If there's ten thousand strada in notes lying on the table, you don't even look at it. You're a lady. But if they give you gifts worth ten thousand strada, well, that's yours, girl. You come to me, I'll see you get a fair price, or you sell them yourself, it's your choice girl, but you make your own money, get it? I don't even take a cut, that's how generous I'm being, I don't even take a cut because you tell me everything you can about these men. That's the deal, girl. You gonna take it or what?'

'I'll take it, Jolly,' Madeleine had said without hesitation, and the deal was done.

11:50 AM, Thursday 5 May 1544 A.F.

Five years had passed and the twenty-two year old Angela Ashton was now on to her fourth client, and there was already a heated competition amongst some of the wealthiest and most dissolute gentlemen of society as to who would be her fifth. The workload was light, the money was good and Angela was pleased with how everything had turned out.

She was not happy. If there were times in her life when she had known happiness, she did not remember them now, but she was not unhappy.

Life was easy and pleasurable and that was the main thing. She never sold a gift until she had moved on to the next client, but with Jolly's expert help she had converted her gifts into a grand total of ninety-five thousand strada in cold hard cash, and the gifts from her current client, Lord Foxley, were piling up nicely. With further advice from Jolly, she had carefully invested the money she had made and her fortune was growing. It was even possible, Jolly had suggested, that she might end up marrying a man with a title and becoming a grand lady, but for now Angela was content with what she had.

She enjoyed being an actress. She had taken to playing roles on stage as easily as if she had always done it. Her success as an actress was the foundation of the success of her other role, the role she played off-stage, which was her real line of work. Acting on stage was fun, but acting off-stage was work.

She enjoyed the feeling of hundreds of hungry eyes feeding on her beauty wherever she went. She liked the power her beauty gave her over the men who sought her attentions. She went through the motions of giving her clients what they wanted, but they never noticed that she was acting even then. She fooled them into believing she received more than passing pleasure from them and so they believed they were worth more to her than the gifts they gave her. They were so wealthy that a necklace worth five thousand strada could be paid for from their pocket change, and Angela was always so delighted with such a girlish delight to receive gifts that they showered her with them just to make her happy and tell them how wonderful they were. She gave her clients what they were so eager to obtain with a personal indifference shrouded by her pretended passion. Their business with her was a material process and nothing more. Angela would later in life remember little of her clients, but every single one of their gifts. Their gifts were her pay and she was a girl who took her pay very seriously.

Now Jolly had brought her to a room in an inn overlooking a square, telling her little of what was going on. She stood by him, wearing a veil as he had instructed her, and having come here by the devious route he had insisted on. Hugo was waiting for her downstairs. Jolly himself had a scarf wrapped around the lower part of his face. They were looking out of the open window, not hiding the fact they were hiding their faces because that could be for any one of a number of reasons.

'There's more than one way to fight,' Jolly said as if thinking aloud.

Angela knew him well enough to know he wanted to be asked to say more. 'What's that mean, Jolly?' she asked.

'There's wandfighting,' Jolly gestured down into the square. Tagalong was standing by a water pump, looking around as he waited. Leopold "Leggit" Gardiner and his five men were walking up and down nearby as they waited in their turn. 'We're gonna see that right now. Then there's what you can do, girl, and that's a kind of fighting that's a lot more dangerous than wandfighting. I'm gonna see if he's as good as they say. Then we'll see.'

'If who's as good as they say, Jolly?' Angela asked, not really that interested but knowing she was there for a reason. Her mind was more taken up with what the value of the emerald-encrusted bracelet Lord Foxley had given her the night before would turn out to be when she sold it. She could almost feel the value of jewellery in her stomach, and she knew that this bracelet was valuable — very valuable — but just how much was it worth in strada?

'Mr Nicholas Raspero, that's who,' Jolly said briefly. 'If Leggit takes him down, you stay out of the picture. If he takes Leggit down, well, we'll come to that at the right time.'

That was when Angela first heard the name of Nicholas Raspero, the wandfighter who had arrived in New Landern three days ago. 'Who's Mr Nicholas Raspero, Jolly?' she asked.

'That's what I want to know,' Jolly said. He said nothing more and she knew him well enough to say nothing more herself.

A boy came running into the square waving. Tagalong and Leggit and his men sprung into action. Some of the spectators worked for Jolly, some were genuine passersby, but all were about to become an audience.

Tagalong started waving his wand and shouting at Leggit. Leggit and his men were gathered threateningly around him, wands out, shouting at Tagalong. Leggit and his men took Tagalong's wand and forced him to his knees. People were starting to look over at them, stopping what they were doing, drawing away to form a space that was like an impromptu stage. The audience had gone quiet. It occurred to Angela then that this was very like a play, and she examined the performances of the main players with a critical eye. *They weren't doing badly for beginners*, she thought.

A man walked into the square, his hand on the hilt of his wand, and stopped on seeing all the commotion.

'That's Raspero, boss,' Pacey "Pay" Yorath said quietly from where he was standing before the neighbouring window.

Angela considered the new arrival. The first thing she thought was that Jolly would not choose him to be one of her clients. He obviously had no money. His robe was shabby and his boots were old and he wore no ornaments. He looked like he didn't even have a watch in his pocket. He was not a man she would normally look at twice, but seeing that Jolly was focused on Raspero to the exclusion of all else she looked again at the newly-arrived stranger standing on the other side of the market-square.

Jolly had guessed that the stranger who had robbed his men must have arrived in New Landern only recently as a wandfighter who was that talented would have drawn attention to himself before now. He had used his contacts at the Post Office to identify every recently registered male recipient of mail in New Landern. He started with the most recent and those who lived in the general direction of where the would-be victims of robbery had been heading. He sent his five men separately to view all the gentlemen whose names had come to light. This strategy had proved immediately successful, and by the end of the first day of his search Jolly knew the name of his man: Mr Nicholas Raspero.

The day after that Ben had been given by an acquaintance at the law courts two free luncheon vouchers at the Hortense Inn for 12 PM on Thursday 5 May but being unable to use them he had given them both to Nicholas, who for his part had wandered along to the Hortense Inn at the time specified. He had arrived at the square where the Hortense Inn was located to find a gentleman being attacked by an armed gang.

'What's going on?' Nicholas asked.

'Get lost, you mongrel!' Leggit snarled at him. 'This ain't none of your business!'

'As the author of a public spectacle, you have forfeited the right to the privacy you claim,' Nicholas told him. 'This is as much my business as I choose it to be. So, what's going on?' Nicholas had an amused look on his face, as if attracting the attention of street thugs had its entertaining side.

'Shut your face!' Leggit snarled at him.

'I am afraid I must persist in my enquiries despite the eloquence with which you attempt to persuade me to do quite otherwise,' Nicholas said, looking as amused as ever. 'So, I repeat, what's going on?'

'I've had it with you,' Leggit shouted angrily. Jolly's instructions had been clear: take Raspero down and bring him bound and gagged to Jolly and he got five hundred strada in cash as a bonus to his pay on the spot, his men got one hundred each. They were among the best wandfighters in Jolly's employ. If they couldn't take Raspero down, then Jolly wanted to know about it. If they did take him down, well, Jolly's eyes glinted at the prospect of having a long and very private talk with the man who had robbed his men, which meant that he had robbed Jolly. No-one crossed Jolly. No-one! If Raspero had handed his men over to the constabulary, fair enough, it was done, but to rob his men was a direct affront to Jolly.

Leggit and his men let go of Tagalong, who as agreed stood up groaning and stretching so that he came between Leggit and Raspero, blocking Raspero's line of sight; Leggit's men attacked Raspero instantly, Leggit coming for Raspero around the side of Tagalong. Except Nicholas was no longer where he had been standing. He was rolling to his left, sweeping the furthest man to his left off his feet and sending him flying into the next man along. As Nicholas rolled to his feet he already had that man's wand in his hand. Leggit's wand followed soon after as Nicholas soared over him, landing and crouching and spinning on his feet in one smooth motion that sent the now wandless Leggit flying into one of his men turning towards Raspero. One after the other Nicholas took them down, taking their wands and binding and tying them with their own mobile karns. His movements seemed effortless, and blended into each other in one continuous sequence of motions that were almost like a dance. Forty seconds after the fight began, Nicholas was standing over Leggit and his men, bound on the ground, their wands in his hand.

'He's as good as they say,' Pay commented, looking over at Jolly.

Jolly turned away from the window. 'Angela, you come see me nine o'clock tomorrow morning.'

'Yes, Jolly,' Angela said obediently, her thoughts already turning back to the emerald bracelet. She would guess as much as seven thousand strada, but that was only a guess.

FOUR

....

The Introduction of Mr Nicholas Raspero
to Lady Isabel Grangeshield

12:00 PM, Thursday 5 May 1544 A.F.

Nicholas surveyed the battlefield as his grandfather had taught him
to do in order to check whether everything was now as indeed over as
it appeared to be — all six wands of his beaten and bound opponents
clasped in his left hand, his right hand still bearing his wand in combat
readiness. Everyone present in the square was staring at him with their
mouths hanging open; Nicholas ignored them with a patrician disdain
as the way they all stared at him and stared and stared and stared showed
them to all be creatures clinging to a lower rung of creation.

Leggit and his men awaited events, not fearful of consequences as they
were under Jolly's protection, their only complaint being the loss of the
bonuses they would have gained had they defeated Nicholas.

Tagalong held himself at the ready, his mind turning around itself
like a complicated machine, waiting his moment to speak, following the
progress of Nicholas's thoughts as they were reflected on his face.

When he saw that Nicholas was thinking about wrapping everything
up so he could move on, Tagalong said to him, 'I cannot thank you
enough, sir, for the assistance which you have rendered me today. May I
have the honour of knowing your name?'

'Introductions are by third party,' Nicholas told him curtly and turned
away.

Tagalong was nothing if not inventive. 'Sir, I demand satisfaction!'

Nicholas turned back with a look of surprise. 'What is the offence?'

'You have refused to tell me your name in a situation which overrides the bonds of courtesy. I am Mr Taggart Longman, and I demand satisfaction for this offence.'

Nicholas sighed in exasperation. 'I am Mr Nicholas Raspero and I accept your challenge. What form of duel do you choose?'

'First Combat.'

'When and where?'

'Here and now.'

'Hang on!' Leggit said angrily. 'What about us?' Leggit's point seemed to be that as he and his men were bound hand and foot and lying on the ground, their predicament took priority over all else, including this duel.

'What about you?' asked Nicholas indifferently.

'You gonna untie us or what?' Leggit wanted to know.

'Do you plan to resume hostilities upon regaining your freedom?' Nicholas asked.

Leggit frowned. He didn't understand what the word *resume* meant.

Seeing his difficulty, Tagalong stepped in. 'I am sure that if you assure this gentleman that our quarrel is over, he will release you from your bonds and peace and goodwill shall prevail over all. All you have to do is to say you are satisfied with everything.'

As far as Leggit was concerned it was time to move on. He had tried and failed to take down Nicholas; there was nothing more to be said about anything. 'All right, I got no problems with nothing,' he growled.

Nicholas waved his wand to untie their karn-bonds and flipped their wands back through the air to hang in front of Leggit and his men. They did not notice, being very unintelligent, that he sent each individual wand correctly back to its owner, but Tagalong did. Leggit and his men clambered to their feet, folding up and tucking away their karns, and pocketing their wands; Nicholas watched them do this, wand in hand, and although his wand was pointing downwards it was understood by all those present from the expression on Nicholas's face that if they were to fight again Nicholas would not let them off so lightly a second time. Leggit and his men turned away, giving Nicholas unfriendly looks before departing the scene.

Nicholas and Tagalong had their duel. Nicholas took Tagalong down three times in succession like the ticks of a clock. Once Tagalong said that he had received satisfaction, he followed this by saying, 'Now that we have been introduced, allow me to thank you for your assistance today, Mr Raspero.'

Nicholas laughed, realising then the trick Tagalong had played. 'It was nothing, Mr Longman.'

'Surely you will allow me to thank you in a manner far more substantial than merely spoken gratitude. Please allow me to take you out for lunch, my good Mr Raspero.'

Nicholas considered this invitation while he appraised the figure of Tagalong standing before him. Tagalong was a tall, slender man with curly brown hair, a freckled face, dark violet eyes and long thin fingers; a spirit of animation possessed him, as if winds gusted about within the hollows of his body making him hum like a tree on a windy cliff. Nicholas sensed at first sight, for he was a good judge of character, that Tagalong was dodgy and untrustworthy but nonetheless he saw no reason why he should not serve as a luncheon companion.

'As it happens, Mr Longman, I have two luncheon vouchers for the Hortense Inn,' Nicholas said, waving vaguely over his shoulder at the Hortense Inn, 'so perhaps you might join me for lunch.'

Tagalong raised his mobile eyebrows in surprise as if he was learning of these luncheon vouchers for the first time, and said, 'But I will now be doubly in your debt, Mr Raspero, both for saving me from those who would do me harm and in feeding me. Very well, Mr Raspero, I accept your kind invitation but on one very strict condition: you must allow me to repay in triplicate your doubled kindness when such a singular occasion shall arise.' Tagalong paused and then exclaimed, 'No!' while holding both hands up in the air palms out as if to stop a runaway horse in its tracks, even though Nicholas had not moved a muscle, 'you cannot deny me in all propriety and duty such a demand as this, which indeed is not even a demand as it does no more than merely express an inevitable consequence.'

'All right,' Nicholas said briefly, his face expressionless, 'fine, you do all that then. Let's go.' With that he turned away and set forth for the Hortense Inn, followed by Tagalong.

The Hortense Inn was owned secretly by Jolly, and the staff had been instructed to give Tagalong and whatever companion he turned up with the best service they could. So it was that Nicholas found himself fawned over by professionals in the fawning business. It was a new experience for him. Most people took one look at his clothes and entirely failed to fawn. The staff at this restaurant seemed to think that they would remember the day they met him for the rest of their lives.

'So what was that all about?' Nicholas asked Tagalong, without much real interest.

'I have alas incurred a debt which I cannot repay at present,' Tagalong told him truthfully, and then continued less truthfully, 'Those men were after repayment of that debt on behalf of a man called Fitzroy, to whom I owe the money.'

'Well, good luck with all that,' Nicholas told him. 'If I'd known that was what it was about, I wouldn't have helped you.'

'You must understand,' Tagalong told him, 'I incurred this debt because of my Aunt Mamie's substantial medical expenses.'

'Even so,' Nicholas said, not looking as if he believed one word of this story, 'you can't incur a debt and not repay it.'

'That is quite so, Mr Raspero. I will repay this debt. I am just slightly late about it, that's all.'

'Whatever,' Nicholas shrugged indifferently.

Throughout the lunch Tagalong was witty, charming, clever, funny and talkative, and Nicholas could not help but enjoy himself. He was too young not to be flattered by the attentions Tagalong was paying him, especially as Tagalong was an expert name-dropper who gave the impression of knowing everyone in town, an impression that was too shrouded by good humour and amusing anecdotes to be clearly discernible as largely a matter of implication. Nicholas laughed along with Tagalong, enjoyed the superb meal, drank two or three glasses of a very tasty wine which went to his head as he was not used to drinking and found the world to be a merry place. By the end of lunch, Nicholas was ready for anything.

'Are you going to the engagement party of Mr Carver and Lady Lachance tonight?' Tagalong asked him as they sat enjoying their coffee and delicious chocolate rolls topped with coconut.

'No.'

'And why not?' Tagalong asked him with a mock sternness which made Nicholas laugh.

'The lack of an invitation is my only excuse,' Nicholas said wittily so that Tagalong roared with laughter which made Nicholas himself laugh proudly at his triumph.

'That is easily remedied,' Tagalong told him. 'I have myself been invited and I am allowed to take a companion with me. Surely you would do me the honour of accompanying me?'

Nicholas was ready for anything, and this sounded good. 'Certainly, Mr Longman, I'm happy to accept. What's this party again?'

So Tagalong told him all about the engagement of Mr Hedley Carver and Lady Sofiya Lachance, with allusion to some mildly scandalous gossip which made them both laugh cheerfully. Nicholas realised that he was on his way to a party where the grandest people in New Landern would be gathered together, about twelve hundred of them or so, in the Regana Palace. It sounded good to him and he was excited at the prospect of being at such a party.

Tagalong had drunk much less than he had pretended to, and his merriness was largely feigned, but Nicholas didn't notice. Tagalong's mind was turning over, thinking everything through, improvising as he went along. His instructions from Jolly were to find out just how good Raspero was with a wand. That meant more than wandfighting; that meant other kinds of wand use. Tagalong's intention was to see if Raspero could break them in to the Regana Palace. Given that the Royal family would turn up, the security there would be as tight as security could be. If Raspero could get them in, he could do anything. Tagalong understood that Jolly did not yet know whether Raspero would be an asset or a liability: if Raspero signed up for Jolly, a man of his calibre could be very useful indeed to Jolly; if Raspero refused to work for Jolly, well, Tagalong knew that Jolly would not be pleased.

Tagalong's job was to find out just how much of an asset or an enemy Raspero would be.

Tagalong realised he had to stay close to Raspero all day long. So as they left the restaurant at around two o'clock, he suggested that they go to Kenina Park. He asked Nicholas if he could do the Three and Nicholas said *yes* quite calmly. The Three was an exercise in the use of the wand requiring talent far beyond the ordinary and those wandfighters who could do the Three constituted an elite. Tagalong believed him but he wanted to see it for himself. His luck was out, however, the Table was closed for the day because of a mourning period for the recently deceased Keeper of the Rolls. Filing it away as a matter to be returned to later, Tagalong suggested they go visit some nearby friends of his. Using code words that told them he was on important business for Jolly, his "friends" received them with such cheer and goodwill, and a glass or two of wine along with earthy tasting cakes, that Nicholas found himself laughing merrily at very little at all. He could not remember when he had last had such a good time or been in such excellent company.

In the midst of his merriment, a warning suddenly came to his mind, some advice given to him by his grandfather, *never drink too much in the company of people you don't know.* So it was that Nicholas woke up to himself and refused all offers of more drink. He declared that he would take a walk. Tagalong thought this was an excellent idea, so leaving Tagalong's "friends" behind them, they strolled down to the river. It was now about five-thirty, Nicholas thought, judging from where the sun was in the sky. As if asking himself the same question, Tagalong looked at his watch and declared that it was twenty past five. They would need to make their way to the party soon, Tagalong suggested. So they started to make their way across town.

Now came the time that Tagalong had been gearing himself up for ever since Nicholas had accepted his invitation to the party. He used the time spent walking to the party to reinforce the impression that attending a party such as this was a regular occurrence for him. Nicholas was sobering up, but he was still too much under the influence of everything he had drunk, and perhaps also eaten, such as those earthy tasting cakes, to be aware that the words Tagalong were speaking were forming nets through his mind that dragged his beliefs where Tagalong wanted them to go. By the time they were halfway to the Regana Palace, Nicholas had no doubt whatsoever that his newfound acquaintance had been handed his invitation to this party personally by a close friend of the fiancé Lady Lachance. Furthermore that Tagalong's attendance at the party was crucial for this close friend to speak to Tagalong about a matter of personal concern to them both. Tagalong made it clear that a gentleman could not speak of matters that were personal and private, but given his affection for Nicholas, he could at least hint that his personal happiness was at stake, and he was sure that Nicholas would understand what he was saying without the necessity of saying anything more. Nicholas's critical faculties were too dulled by drink, let alone those cakes, for him to doubt anything Tagalong was saying. By the time they had reached the Regana Palace, Nicholas understood that Tagalong had to attend this party as a now or never moment in his life concerning his future happiness. It was round about six-thirty and the warm evening was still golden with sunlight.

Tagalong paused and reached into his robe. He hunted about inside his robe, a growing look of consternation spreading across his face. He was looking desperately through all his pockets, turning them inside out, frantically going through pockets he had already gone through. Tagalong groaned and sank to the ground with his head in his shaking hands. It was a performance Angela Ashton would have approved of, and Nicholas was completely taken in.

'What's the matter?' Nicholas asked.

'My party invitation, it's gone,' Tagalong said, his voice muffled. He stood up, a wild look in his eyes. 'It's gone! Leggit took it. I remember now. He made me empty my pockets. Then you came along and I forgot about it because of our duel. Oh God! What am I going to do?'

'Where's Leggit now?'

'He could be anywhere. I'm never going to find him now.'

'Leggit can't come here using your invitation, can he?'

Tagalong shook his head again. 'No, it's by invitation with a spoken code word to go along with it. But what am I going to do?'

'Tell the doorkeeper your name, he'll check the list and let you in.'

Tagalong shook his head yet again. 'This party doesn't work that way. You show your invitation and speak your code word and only then do you go in. You have to have your invitation.'

'Try your code word.'

'No, the code word has to match the invitation. Otherwise, someone could just steal your invitation and make up a code word and try their luck.'

'Bad luck,' Nicholas said sympathetically. He was disappointed himself that he wasn't going to attend this party, but he accepted that this was now his fate without complaint. That was just how life worked out sometimes. What could you do?

'It's more than bad luck, Mr Raspero,' Tagalong said with a desperate look on his face. 'It is a crushing blow of fate, that's what it is.' Tagalong looked towards the Regana Palace. 'Once I'm in I'll be fine. Lady Lachance herself could vouch for me, she knows that this lady and I have an understanding. But no-one could get in. There's no way past that security. No-one could get through. No-one at all.'

Nicholas was young enough to take this as a challenge. He took out his wand and contemplated the Regana Palace thoughtfully, making movements through the air with his wand. 'I could get us in,' he said calmly.

Seeing that his bait had been taken, Tagalong made sure the fish bit harder on it. 'There's no-one who could get past that security, Mr Raspero. No-one at all. I appreciate your offer but to tell the truth I can't deny that I am a little bit upset by your behaviour. To make a false claim such as this when this is all so important to me is, well, it's cruel, Mr Raspero. I must say, well, I won't, you helped me today but you're making boasts that you can't fulfill if you will excuse me speaking so frankly. I am only speaking this frankly because this is all so important to me. I would ask you out of consideration for my feelings, not to make any more boasts of this nature.'

Nicholas turned and looked at him. 'I'll get us in, but on two conditions. The first is that you ask me no questions, the second is that you tell no-one about what I have done. I require you to give me your word that you accept these conditions.'

'I accept these conditions, Mr Raspero,' Tagalong agreed promptly. 'You have my word.' He'd stopped paying attention to any sense of honour years ago, so he had no hesitation in falsely swearing.

'Let's go,' Nicholas said. 'Stick close to me and do what I say.'

It was getting on toward seven o'clock, and still light, although the light was starting to fade. Nicholas led Tagalong down a side street to the palace. There was a side door that was so heavy with wand protection it had only two Force Nine guards standing before it, and even they were merely excessive given the wand protection involved. This entrance was reserved for the Royal Family itself, so no-one else was using it. The Royal Family had already arrived, at which time there had been close to a whole company standing around. The Force Nine guards were the elite, so despite knowing that their roles were merely decorative, they stood alert and at attention. Once out of their sight Nicholas waved Tagalong to a stop.

Knowing that Jolly would want a full report on everything that happened, Tagalong tried to pay close attention to what Nicholas was up to, but the following sequence of events happened so fast that only the outcome found a clear place in Tagalong's memory. Nicholas was waving his wand through the air with an absorbed look on his face, clearly making a series of calculations, then Tagalong found himself being thrown through the air closely behind the figure of Nicholas, who was moving through the air equally fast. The two Force Nine guards were also moving through the air, but upside down and into the neighbouring shrubbery; before they had hit the ground Nicholas and Tagalong were at the side door they had been guarding. Nicholas had the door open and was through it, pulling Tagalong after him and closing the door behind him, all without setting off the alarm, before the two guards had even finished rolling back to their feet.

The highly trained guards, their wands held in combat readiness, angrily looked around them for the source of their downfall. It seemed to have been some kind of prank, but there was no-one to be seen anywhere around. They were too well-trained to leave their post to go looking around so they resumed their guard duty, still angry, but also uncertain. After some time, they both agreed to let the matter go and not report it, given that whatever it had all been about, the security of the palace had not been compromised.

Nicholas and Tagalong were in a hallway with doors to the sides. The hallway led to an open door beyond which could be seen a marble-floored reception area. Nicholas opened the door to his right and led Tagalong in.

An awe-struck Tagalong understood just what Nicholas had done. That side door had been densely woven with a wand protection that Nicholas had simply cut through in an instant, and without setting off an alarm; what Nicholas had just done simply couldn't be done. 'How did you do that?' he whispered, for once expressing an unpremeditated thought.

Nicholas gave him a hard look. 'You gave me your word, no questions.'

He looked so fierce that Tagalong woke up to himself. 'My apologies, Mr Raspero. It is just —'

'Whatever,' Nicholas said with a dismissive gesture of his left hand. He led the way across the room they were in to a door at the side. The door was closed and Nicholas gestured to Tagalong to wait.

Tagalong watched Nicholas. He was using his wand to search the space beyond the door. Nicholas opened the door enough to put his wand through. Tagalong guessed that he was practising macchato. Nicholas waved his wand, there was a yell which shifted in tone as if the person who was yelling was rapidly moving through the air. Nicholas stepped through the door, gesturing for Tagalong to follow him. Above them was a spiral staircase, and Nicholas was up above Tagalong's head in a moment, and Tagalong suddenly found himself plucked upwards and set down beside Nicholas. Gesturing to Tagalong to crouch down, Nicholas led the way up the staircase. The top of the stairs was cordoned off with a red cord and Nicholas briskly stepped over this cord and Tagalong followed. They were just in time, for as they started walking along the wide corridor they had climbed up to via the stairs, a party of laughing merrymakers came their way, paying them no attention. They made their way along the corridor and down another flight of stairs. Merrymakers were all around them now, laughing and carrying on and talking and having pretend battles. The party was gathering momentum and soon it would be in full swing. They were now guests at the engagement party of Mr Hedley Carver and Lady Sofiya Lachance, in appearance at least, and given the nature of these circumstances, appearances were all that were needed.

7:00 PM, Thursday 5 May 1544 A.F.

Isabel was with 'The Gang' at the engagement party of Mr Hedley Carver and Lady Sofiya Lachance. They had discussed the matter of Breckenridge's proposal with varying degrees of agreement and disagreement with Isabel's refusal of this proposal.

'Really, you are being impossible, Izzy,' Miss Uliana Newman said briskly. 'If you are going to turn down a suitor of the calibre of Brecky, who on earth are you ever going to accept?'

'He's really not bad looking,' said Miss Penelope "Penny" Earlson reflectively with a far-away look in her eyes. 'And he's very rich.'

'So's Izzy,' Miss Kora Pryor pointed out. 'She doesn't need to marry for money.'

'She does need to marry, though,' Uliana observed. 'Or is it your intention to never marry, Izzy?'

'I will marry in my own time,' Isabel declared. 'Arabella didn't marry until she was twenty-five, and look at how many suitors she had.'

'You are not going to wait that long until you marry, surely?' Mr Berg Irving asked.

'Izzy's point was that she could wait, not how long she would wait,' Miss Sophie Nicholson told him.

'But what is it that you are waiting for?' Uliana wanted to know. 'True love?'

Everyone laughed at the way she said this except Penny. 'Of course she is,' Penny said, looking at Isabel for support, 'aren't you, Izzy?'

'Certainly not!' Isabel snapped scornfully. 'Any man who will do will be perfectly satisfactory as a husband. I am waiting for when the time is right, that is all.'

'The time is never right, Izzy, only the man is,' Sophie said with an air of wisdom. 'The time will only be right when the right man comes along.'

'First you say the time is never right then you say it is only right when such-and-such has happened,' Isabel rebuked her. 'Am I to abandon logic in order to be married?'

'Logic has nothing to do with it,' Penny decreed. 'Of course you should abandon logic.'

'Or better still, ignore it from the beginning,' Uliana suggested, 'and look only to love.' The Gang knew Uliana well enough to see that she was in one of her contrary moods, saying the opposite of what she believed.

'Albert was telling me about the Guardians of the Hidden Flame,' Miss Samantha Clemens told them. Albert was her piano teacher. 'They believe that only love which is hidden in the depths of the heart is true love. If you declare your feelings then your love is immediately degraded into mere sentiment just as the snow turns to sludge. Your love only remains true if it remains secret and the highest expression of your hidden love is to die from your longing for the beloved who can never be attained.'

'Do these Guardians of the Hidden Flame tend to die off in noticeable numbers themselves?' Uliana asked sardonically. Her pragmatic soul was offended by this kind of talk. 'Or do they fail to follow through?'

Even Penny, always the champion of eternal romance, appeared unconvinced by the philosophy of the Guardians of the Hidden Flame. 'Where is love if lovers are not united?' she objected. 'What is the point of that?'

'Brecky's feelings were sludge from the beginning,' Isabel observed, 'even before he declared them.' It would be a while before she tired of making anti-Brecky comments whenever possible. 'The only love that man has is for himself.'

'There is no love but self-love,' Kora declared grandly. She had taken up reading one of the more pessimistic philosophers lately in order to impress a young man she had recently met. 'Our motivations in life are two-fold: fear, which is the avoidance of pain, and pleasure, which is to exercise our self-love by the pretence of caring for others.' Kora paused there as if for further reflection, but, in fact, she was only wondering if she had got it right so far.

'You forget a third motivation, Kora,' Uliana added, who never passed up a chance to be witty, 'and that is to acquire the wisdom of a philosopher.'

The Gang chuckled.

'Yes, the philosophers always overlook themselves, do they not?' Berg agreed. 'It is that they are modest, I think.'

The Gang chuckled again.

'Oh goodness, are we discussing philosophy?' Sophie complained. 'At a party?'

'What can we be thinking?' Uliana agreed. 'Let us live!' She said this so loudly that everyone jumped and then giggled with the shock of having been so startled.

There seemed to be little more to say. Shortly after this, The Gang set out into the depths of the party to seek excitement, diversion, amusement, witty comments and even, perhaps, true love.

7:00 PM, Thursday 5 May 1544 A.F

Tagalong had now found out all that he needed to tell Jolly. Nicholas was something else, and that was what Jolly had wanted to know. He realised that he had to ditch Nicholas at the first possible opportunity. Even someone as naïve as Nicholas would wonder why Tagalong knew so few people when he had given the impression that he knew practically everybody who was here. But how could he part company with Nicholas right here and now?

'My friends call me Tagalong,' Tagalong said.

'How nice for you,' Nicholas said drily. 'I will call you Mr Longman.'

Tagalong decided this wasn't enough for a quarrel. His ever restless and inventive mind devised a new strategy on the spot.

'Rule Number One: never arrive at a party on time,' Tagalong then told Nicholas with an air of the superiority particular to "one of those who know". Tagalong dove straight for a nearby table and acquired drinks for them both. Nicholas had barely sipped his drink before Tagalong had guzzled his down and was off for another.

He brought another drink for Nicholas, holding one in each hand, but when Nicholas shook his head Tagalong shrugged, downed one drink in three swallows and put down the empty glass. He leaned towards Nicholas and said, 'Rule Number Two: get drunk as fast as possible.'

'I'm learning so much from you today,' Nicholas said with grateful admiration.

'Don't mention it,' Tagalong replied graciously. He might as well have genuinely not noticed Nicholas's sarcasm.

'Who can you introduce me to?' Nicholas asked, the thought crossing his mind that his only acquaintance at this party might be incapacitated before long, just as Tagalong had intended him to think.

Tagalong looked about, humming as if making a selection, but shaking his head as he said, 'Deadly bores, come on, we can do better than this lot.' He led Nicholas off, and before long Tagalong spotted someone that he did know. He introduced Nicholas to Mr Boris Galan before having to discreetly leave to answer a call of nature; in this way he disappeared from Nicholas's side, with every intention of avoiding Nicholas for the remainder of the evening. As he walked around he fought the temptation to engage in petty theft. He could have loaded up his pockets easily with valuable items that would equally easily net him several thousand strada, but he knew that Jolly would disapprove so he kept his light-fingered hands in his pockets.

'Nice party,' Nicholas said.

'Yes,' Mr Galan said coldly. A friend of Tagalong's was not a friend of Boris's, so Mr Galan had accepted the introduction with a cold politeness born of being a gentleman.

'Everyone's having fun,' Nicholas added.

'Yes,' Mr Galan said coldly, looking around as if about to leave.

'It's always a happy occasion when two people decide to get married, wouldn't you say?'

'Yes, will you excuse me?' Mr Galan left swiftly without looking back.

Nicholas walked around on his own, enjoying all the sights and sounds and merriment. He decided he had drunk more than enough that day so he drank nothing but fruit juice. He also made sure to eat plenty of the food in abundant supply on so many tables all over the palace. His sobriety was returning as the food soaked up the remaining alcohol in his system. It was an interesting experience being alone and knowing nobody on such a grand occasion. The palace was enormous and full of people. No-one paid him any attention at all. He might as well have been invisible.

He came across Mr Galan again talking to two men and went up to them, deciding to pretend not to notice that Mr Galan was cold-shouldering him. He greeted Mr Galan by name and looked at Mr Galan's companions immediately afterwards. Mr Galan hesitated, but then decided not to take the hint. Seeing this, Nicholas asked, 'Would you be so kind as to introduce me to your friends, Mr Galan?'

Mr Galan looked for a moment as if he was about to refuse but one of the men, seeing this, headed him off by saying, 'Yes, Boris, would you be so kind as to introduce us?'

Mr Galan reluctantly introduced Nicholas to Mr Haldor Zarek and Mr Alain Eddison. This time Nicholas's attempts to make conversation were received by something like a response, and so Nicholas chatted cheerfully to Mr Zarek while Mr Galan and Mr Eddison silently slipped away. There were merrymakers around them still, coming and going, and while talking to Mr Zarek and looking across upon hearing a blast of laughter to one side, Nicholas saw Isabel for the first time. She was dressed in a strapless scarlet gown streaked with lapis lazuli blue, her hair piled high on her head and held together by a variety of glittering gemstone fastenings. Her large breasts jutted forward, their cleavage encased in a scarlet lacery finery. Her face was round and full like the moon, her eyes large and brown, her eyebrows arched, her lips red and lustrous, and her skin pale as snow. Nicholas felt his stomach dissolve away into nothingness as he gazed upon her. Vaguely he was aware that he was making a spectacle of himself. Vaguely he was aware of someone to one side speaking to the girl; she looked over at him, looked back at her friend; they whispered together; the girl looked at him again, raised her fan to her face so only her eyes showed. He guessed she was giggling. Then with a sudden movement she had turned and was off like a startled deer racing through the forest, her friend chasing after her, both looking back at Nicholas and visibly laughing.

Nicholas looked about to see if anyone had noticed that he had just made a fool of himself, only to find Mr Zarek looking at him with an air of amusement.

'Who was that girl?' he asked. 'The one in the red and blue gown?'

Mr Zarek looked at him with what might have been the kind of sympathy that follows amusement. 'That was Lady Isabel Grangeshield.'

'Lady Isabel Grangeshield,' Nicholas repeated.

Mr Zarek then looked at him with what might have been the kind of sympathy which precedes compassion. 'Not only is she the most beautiful woman in New Landern, but she is also in possession of a fortune of fifteen million strada.'

'She must be popular,' Nicholas commented.

'Indeed,' Mr Zarek replied.

'Can you introduce me to her?' Nicholas asked.

'Unfortunately I do not have the honour of the lady's acquaintance.'

'Then what good are you then?' Nicholas asked pleasantly.

'It is without doubt a lamentable failing on my part, a failing which I can only bear as a burden in silence. I can only beg your pardon for that which I lack.' There was a malicious undertone to Mr Zarek's feigned apology as if he well understood that he was describing Nicholas's condition, not his own.

Nicholas turned away. 'Does this party have any other sight to compare with the vision of loveliness which I have just seen?'

'I find that the bottom of a recently emptied glass can be a vessel of visions, but whether lovely or not can never be foretold, even by the brewers of such concoctions as may only then have been imbibed.'

'You think I should get drunk because I can never have Lady Isabel Grangeshield on my arm?' Nicholas asked.

'I cannot say for sure, but I suspect it might not be the first time that such a development has occurred in the grand metropolis of New Landern. The causes of drunkenness in New Landern may be varied in nature, but a sufficiently insightful contemplative gaze might well identify the unattainable loveliness of Lady Isabel Grangeshield as one cause among those many varied causes of the drunkenness which the citizens of New Landern indulged in daily. More I cannot say. Not even the citizens of New Landern know everything that goes on here.'

'I prefer to face misfortune sober,' Nicholas said in reply. He turned and walked away from Mr Zarek without another word, feeling only that he had to be in motion and that walking would do him good.

The emptiness in his stomach had changed to an ache of loss. What he did not have had been taken away from him and he could feel the weight of this loss in the pit of his stomach, but he walked away from the place of his defeat thinking only of how to try to keep his face looking normal, as if in that way he might preserve what he still possessed.

8:30 PM, Thursday 5 May 1544 A.F

Isabel was standing looking over at Uliana and Berg, wondering whether to go and join them. As she was standing there, Mary Philips came up to her and whispered into her ear, 'Izzy, look! Look! Look over there.'

Isabel looked in the direction Mary had indicated and immediately saw what her attention was being drawn to — a shabbily dressed man standing by the side of the room. He was a young man, her own age or so, staring right at her. He wasn't moving a muscle, and looked directly at her, obviously not giving a thought to the way he was behaving.

'You have an admirer, Izzy!' Mary whispered into her ear. 'Handsome and rich!'

The girls giggled as one. This young man was not at all handsome; in fact, he was very ordinary looking. And judging from the state of his clothes, he had only come to this party as the poor relation of one of the guests. Mary was being very witty, Isabel thought.

The girls looked again at the stranger. He was still standing there, his gaze fixed on Isabel as if he was entirely unaware of anything else but Isabel.

'Izzy, run for it!' Mary cried out and the girls ran for it, laughing merrily as they fled. Isabel looked behind her as she ran and saw that the stranger was still watching her as she departed the scene, turning around to follow her with his eyes.

9:30 PM, Thursday 5 May 1544 A.F

Nicholas felt more than ever that he was in the party but not of it. A growing sense of loneliness spread through him. It was only a matter of time before he left, he decided. It had been interesting for a while to be at a party where he knew no-one to talk to but the interest had faded by now. He liked new experiences, and this had been a new experience, but he was done with it now and he did not care to repeat it. The party was as loud as ever; everyone except for Nicholas was having fun. He went into a room where some men were sitting around a table, looking the worst for wear. He spotted Tagalong amongst them and walked over, deciding to chat briefly before leaving. He stood by the table where Tagalong could see him. Tagalong's companions were talking, naturally enough, of wandlore, from which Nicholas assumed (correctly) that they had finished talking about women.

'This man Raspero,' Tagalong said, pointing to Nicholas with a wavering hand, clearly the worse for drink, 'is a damn good wandfighter. He took down six of Fitzroy's men like that,' Tagalong continued, clicking his fingers, 'and he can do the Three.'

Everyone looked at Nicholas with interest.

Nicholas said nothing.

'Is that true? Can you do the Three?' someone asked.

'Yes,' Nicholas said as if confirming his name.

There was silence, and then someone said, 'And would you care to substantiate such a claim by a demonstration?'

'There's a table right here in Regana Palace,' someone else added.

'I am not a performing circus animal,' Nicholas declared. 'No, I am not going to do the Three just to satisfy your curiosity.'

'Well, of course we believe you,' someone else said sarcastically. 'All you have to do is make this claim and we know it's true.'

Nicholas looked hard at him. 'If any of you accuse me of lying, I will demand satisfaction.'

'Back off, all of you!' Tagalong ordered, waving his hands in the air. 'He took down six of Jolly's men like that!' He clicked his fingers in the air again. Nicholas wondered who Jolly was, when earlier it had been Fitzroy.

'Perhaps we should provide an inducement of some kind,' someone suggested. 'Naturally we cannot expect you to perform such a feat for nothing. What prize would you deserve to receive for such a demonstration?'

Nicholas already knew without needing to think what prize he sought. Matters which reach from one side of your life to the other do not require thought. 'If there is one among you who is acquainted with Lady Isabel Grangeshield, I will do the Three in return for an introduction to Lady Isabel Grangeshield.'

'I know Lady Grangeshield,' someone else present said.

Nicholas looked at Tagalong. 'Can you introduce me to this gentleman?'

Tagalong could not conceal his delight that he could, having just received his own introduction ten minutes earlier. 'Mr Boylent, may I present Mr Nicholas Raspero. Mr Raspero, may I present Mr Timothy Boylent.'

'Mr Boylent, do you agree to introduce me to Lady Isabel Grangeshield if I do the Three?' Nicholas asked.

Timothy shrugged. 'Yes,' he said casually. 'Not a problem.'

'All right,' Nicholas said. 'Let's go.' He was glad now that he had drunk nothing since the afternoon. He would need a clear head for this. Luckily the loneliness he had experienced earlier seemed to have resulted in a complete restoration of his sobriety.

They all trooped off to the rear of the palace, where there was a large wood-panelled room, hung with paintings and decorative swords. The table stood in the place of honour in the centre. Other people standing about came along to watch the show. Mr Odell Ralston tapped his wand on the button and the table whirred into action. Rings began to rotate around each other.

Nicholas went to one end of the table, took out his wand, lifted a disc from the three stacked in a red velvet-lined hollow, and waited. Mr Ralston tapped his wand on the hourglass and sand began trickling through the funnel.

Nicholas crouched, studying the rings. His task was to send the disc flying through the middle of the rings when they were lined up with each other sufficient to provide an opening for the disc to pass through. The difficulty was that the incessantly revolving, rotating and oscillating rings never seemed to provide such an opening.

Nicholas was a statue, not moving a muscle. Then he struck; the disc flew through the rings and sank into the wooden headboard, on the far side of the table. Nicholas took another disc; the sand continued to trickle; another disc went through the rings; he took the third disc; the silence in the room was palpable now; some of those present had never even seen the Three performed. Nicholas waited again, intensely intent; the third disc flew through the rings. Nicholas raised himself up and looked at the hourglass. It had been timed for ten minutes, and nearly a third of the sand still remained.

'That's it, then,' he said calmly, 'it's done. Now to claim my prize.'

Nicholas's guide took him through the house as together they went in search of Lady Isabel Grangeshield. After ten minutes or so they found her. She was again with her companion of before and by chance they looked across at the door just as Nicholas and Timothy entered. They immediately looked towards each other, leaning their heads together and giggling.

Nicholas and Timothy walked right up to them and Timothy said, 'Lady Grangeshield, I present Mr Nicholas Raspero. Miss Philips, I present Mr Nicholas Raspero.'

Then he turned to Nicholas. 'Mr Raspero, I present Lady Isabel Grangeshield. I also present Miss Mary Philips.'

The ladies had not looked at either of them even once throughout this introduction, leaning against each other with their foreheads touching and giggling helplessly. Then, as if by a secret agreement, they both broke away and ran for the door, bursting into shrieks of laughter as if the funniest thing in the world had just happened and it was all too much for them.

Nicholas was utterly content as he watched them go. He felt that everything had turned out perfectly. 'Thank you, Mr Boylent,' he said in all sincerity. 'You have kept your side of the bargain.'

'You are welcome, Mr Raspero,' Timothy said. 'It was really no trouble at all. A mere trifle.'

Which for Timothy, of course, it had been, but for Nicholas it had been one of the great moments of his young life.

10:15 PM, Thursday 5 May 1544 A.F

Isabel was in the Dacian Salon with Mary Philips, who had some additional comments to make on the very choice gossip she had imparted earlier concerning her brother George. The girls were huddling together and giggling over what she had to say when they saw the shabby stranger of before enter the room in the company of Timothy Boylent and approach them. Isabel was feeling very merry. The glasses of wine she had drunk had gone to her head, and she felt floaty and cheerful and giggly.

Mary immediately realised what was happening. 'Izzy, it's your rich and handsome suitor! Look, he's going to be introduced to you.'

The girls were laughing so much that Isabel didn't hear a word Timothy was saying. They waited out of habitual politeness for the introduction to be completed, helpless with laughter. 'Run for it before he proposes!' Mary suggested with her sharp, clever wit into Isabel's ear and the girls ran for it, laughing fit to burst. It was really too funny, this nobody stranger in his shabby clothes wanting to be introduced to Isabel. It was hilarious!

11:00 PM, Thursday 5 May 1544 A.F

Nicholas was again wandering around on his own, enjoying the party. He felt more content now; for one moment, during his introduction to Isabel he had belonged there; at that moment he had been of the party, not just in it. The fact that Isabel had ignored him did not matter. It was not relevant to the fact that he had been introduced. Somehow that had a significance that he could not define, yet felt so deeply that a warmth spread from that significance throughout his mind and body.

He came across Mr Zarek chatting to two ladies and stopped to say hello, and so it was that he was introduced to Miss Amanda Dahl and Miss Eileen Radcliff.

At around midnight, Nicholas left the party. No-one questioned him on the way out, as obviously the defences were maintained against the traffic coming the other way. He was just another figure leaving the party, and by no means the only one; a stream of mostly older people, with reluctant youngsters pulled along behind them, were also leaving.

Nicholas gave no further thought to Lady Isabel Grangeshield in the days that followed. His first sight of Isabel had wrenched him off balance yet Timothy's introduction to her had restored that balance; it had all been perfectly imaginary, yet perfectly real. He felt no interest in trying to understand what had happened. There was either nothing to understand or it would do him no good to understand it. He was content with everything as it had happened and he moved on with his life without a backward glance.

2:00 AM, Friday 6 May 1544 A.F

The evening had been merry, merry, merry. There were many hilarious things that happened that evening; everyone seemed to sparkle with intelligence and good humour. It was the best party Isabel had attended for a while. The conversation was witty and free flowing, the spirits of all the guests cheerful and merry, the food and drink plentiful. The bride-to-be Sofiya looked a little tense, it was true, but then she was now engaged after all; the bridegroom-to-be Hedley was a little forced in his good humour, but then, he also was now engaged. Not everyone could be expected to be happy about being engaged to be married. If anything, the lack of complete enthusiasm on the part of Hedley and Sofiya added a frisson of amusement to the entire evening; the laughter of the guests was sharpened by the dullness of the centrepiece of the evening as a knife is sharpened on dull stone.

Isabel returned home in the early hours of the following morning in her flying carriage, sleepy in the midst of the surrounding sobriety of her chaperones, her body relaxed in the shuddering aftermath of so much laughter. By then she had completely forgotten about her introduction to the shabbily dressed stranger. The incongruity of the presence of the stranger in the midst of all the surrounding wealthy merriness of the evening meant that his presence had not fitted into her perceptions and so he had slipped out of her memory as an item of the evening not in accordance with anything else. The particular memory of his introduction was swallowed up and digested by the more general memory of the merriness of the evening.

It was as if it had never happened at all.

FIVE

....

The Threat Made by Mr Frank Jollison to the Family of Mr Nicholas Raspero

10:00 AM, Friday 6 May 1544 A.F.

Jolly, Tagalong and Angela were sitting in Jolly's private quarters. Tagalong had just recounted the story of his day with Nicholas Raspero, leaving nothing out except the part about Tagalong giving his word of honour that he never tell the story he was telling.

Jolly heard him out in silence, then sat back and went deep into thought. Angela put aside all speculation concerning Lord Foxley's next gift, and paid close attention to what was going on. She knew when Jolly meant business, and he looked as serious as she ever saw him.

There was something about Jolly that immediately inspired trust in the unwary. The gleaming white hair combed back in gentle waves over his noble brow added such an air of distinction to his kindly face that it was made immediately clear that here was a man who would do the right thing. It was true that his lips were lizard thin and his eyes snake-black, but you had to look closely to see these things.

There was a strangeness to Jolly's presence that to those used to his company had come to seem like the inevitability of his rule. His voice had an almost hypnotic quality to it, and the compelling nature of his voice coupled with the commanding look in his eyes made obedience to his orders seem almost a matter of course, as if to hear Jolly was to obey him. It was rumoured that Jolly knew secrets of the world that gave him power over human minds.

Jolly came out of his reverie and looked at Angela. 'Remember what I told you about there being more ways of fighting than wandfighting?'

'No, Jolly,' Angela replied, knowing that this was what he wanted to hear.

'Raspero can't be taken down with a wand. But he's got a weakness for women. A man who'll do the Three just to get an introduction to a beautiful woman, even if it is Lady Isabel Grangeshield, is a man who I want you to get to know. You're a beautiful woman, Angela. You will take down Raspero for me.'

'You mean he's my next client?' Angela asked, not very pleased to learn that a man with no money would be her next client.

'No,' Jolly shook his head, 'you just get to know him, that's all. You do what has to be done. You just make sure that when the time comes, you'll be ready to do what I say.' Jolly turned to Tagalong. 'Now here's where you come in. Angela is going to need rescuing from the attentions of men who would misuse her, and Raspero is going to rescue her. You're going to make sure Raspero is where he has to be to do the rescuing.'

'We've done rescuing already, boss,' Tagalong pointed out. 'We're playing the same trick twice.'

'I'll put Pay in charge of this one,' Jolly continued, as if Tagalong had not spoken at all. 'And you, Angela, once Raspero has rescued you, will be the grateful damsel in distress who worships your saviour. You do what you have to do, but you get Raspero eating out of your hand. You're grateful to him as your hero, the man who saved you from villainy and that makes him responsible for your happiness. Whatever it takes, you do it.'

'Yes, Jolly,' Angela said obediently.

Jolly waved them away with his hands and sank back into his thoughts. Whatever his thoughts were, they were too deep for him to notice them leave his quarters.

2:30 PM, Saturday 7 May 1544 A.F.

Nicholas was walking along Giffard Street the next day when he heard his name called. He turned around to see Tagalong hurrying over to him, a broad smile on his face.

'Mr Raspero! I can never thank you enough for what you have done for me.' Tagalong looked around, and then said in a low voice, 'I spoke to the lady whom I mentioned, and she was so gracious as to inform me that soon she will be mine! And it is all thanks to you, Mr Raspero! I owe you far more than my life.'

Nicholas wasn't quite sure what to make of Tagalong. 'Think nothing of it, Mr Longman.' He turned and continued walking along the street. Tagalong fell into step beside him.

'You are modest and talented, a gentleman after my own heart,' Tagalong cried out. 'But I know where you are going. I was going to go there myself so I would be delighted to accompany you if I might be so bold as to suggest such a pleasing outcome.'

'I'm not going anywhere, I'm just wandering around,' Nicholas replied, perfectly truthfully.

Tagalong looked at him in surprise. 'But surely you are going to see the duel at three o'clock at Mildgyd?'

Nicholas shook his head. 'I haven't heard of it. Anyway, I'm not interested.'

'Not interested in witnessing a duel? My dear Mr Raspero, do you not realise that this is where you can meet people who will appreciate your unique gifts? The story that you have done the Three at the Regana Palace the other day is already spreading amongst wandfighters throughout New Landern. There you will meet people who will adore you, there you will meet people who will wish you to do the Three at Kenina Park and have your name on the List. There you will be a very popular man.' These were guesses in the dark from Tagalong, who was probing Nicholas for his weaknesses, but they were good guesses. Nicholas was starting to feel that he did not know enough people in New Landern. He had been there for five whole days and had hardly met anybody! It was a feeling that had started to grow in him recently, and as he had not given Isabel another moment's thought, he did not connect this sense of loneliness with having seen her.

'It would be good to meet more people,' Nicholas conceded. 'Perhaps you're right.'

'Mr Raspero,' Tagalong proclaimed, 'when you have come to know me better you will realise I am always right. I have only ever been wrong on one occasion.'

Nicholas realised he was expected to ask about this one occasion, so he asked, 'And what was that?'

'You will laugh at me. I will not say,' Tagalong declared, looking away defiantly.

Nicholas went through the motions, not caring less. 'No, I insist on knowing,' he said dully.

'Very well,' Tagalong said, 'I will surrender to your insistent questioning. I once mistook a glass of Yountry wine for a glass of Rehunda wine. Now you know!'

Nicholas didn't even bother to pretend to laugh. This kind of talk had been funnier yesterday for some reason.

'You are very gloomy today, Mr Raspero.'

Nicholas was losing patience. 'I'm fine, Mr Longman.'

'Ah.' Tagalong nodded and fell silent. He knew a quicker way to Mildgyd than the road they were walking along so they turned right down a side alley. A boy crossed the alley below them. They were coming down to a square when a woman's shrill scream, suddenly cut off short, reached their ears.

Nicholas broke into a run on the instant, his wand out. He flipped himself through the air to go around the corner above head height, turning in mid-air to see what was before him. He hit the ground and rolled and jumped through the air. Tagalong jogged along behind without putting too much effort into it. By the time Tagalong reached the corner Nicholas was way out in front. Tagalong did not bother trying to catch him up. There was a carriage standing in the square, its door wide open. Nicholas flipped himself through the open gate of a neighbouring stableyard. The door to the stables was half open, and beyond it was the sound of muffled screaming, struggling and shouting. Tagalong followed him and was just in time to see Nicholas ignore the door and flip himself onto the roof in one movement, landing softly without a sound, after which the wandfighter promptly disappeared over the ridge of the roof. Tagalong ran to the door.

The tableau was set. Angela was struggling in the arms of two men, her dress half torn off, managing to get out a muffled scream now and then. There were seven men in the stables, laughing and making comments. Tagalong ran in, his wand drawn.

'Let her go!' he shouted, knowing that Nicholas would be there any moment now. He wanted Nicholas to see how Tagalong was bravely doing the right thing. 'Let her go now!'

Pay was looking behind Tagalong, wondering where Nicholas was. Tagalong struck at Pay just as Nicholas came in through the back window. Pay shouted in anger and flattened Tagalong with one blow as Nicholas came falling down through the air and landed on the ground behind his enemies. Tagalong looked up from the ground to see Nicholas taking them down one by one. The fight didn't take long. Tagalong got to his feet, holding his hand to his face. His lip was bleeding from the blow he had received. *Beautiful*, he thought. If this didn't make him look like an innocent victim, nothing would. He spread the blood as much out as he could while appearing to gently massage his face, to make the bleeding seem worse than it was.

Nicholas stood over his bound enemies, holding their wands in his left hand, his wand still in combat readiness. He looked over at Tagalong briefly, then at Angela lying on the ground, pulling her torn dress around her in an attempt to preserve her modesty. Nicholas turned and walked away. He then stopped and turned around to look at the scene before him, his face expressionless.

Tagalong prayed that Nicholas wasn't thinking too hard about all the rescuing he had been doing lately. 'Is it you, Miss Ashton?' Tagalong cried out.

'You know her?' Nicholas asked.

'I have never met this lady before,' Tagalong replied, 'but all of New Landern knows her. This is Miss Angela Ashton, the famous actress. Miss Ashton, your deliverer is Mr Nicholas Raspero.' Tagalong performed this introduction hastily, to try to gloss over the fact that he had just declared himself to be not in a position to make such an introduction.

'I can only thank you for your swift and brave intervention, Mr Raspero,'

Miss Ashton said, speaking directly to Nicholas in a sweet, slightly husky voice; it was one of her stage voices that drove men wild. 'I cannot thank you enough. I am in your debt, Mr Raspero. You will surely not be so harsh as to rebuke me for speaking to you so directly in this fashion, although I know it is surely to stretch the bounds of courtesy.'

Nicholas nodded, not really listening to her. 'So these men get handed over to the law now, Mr Longman?'

'They most certainly do,' Tagalong said firmly. 'They deserve to be punished to the full extent of the law for what they have tried to do.'

'Yet surely I will be allowed to depart without further delay,' Miss Ashton pleaded to Nicholas.

'Of course you may, Miss Ashton,' Tagalong said gallantly. 'I have no doubt you wish to leave this place immediately.'

Angela gave a muffled cry as she saw the huddled figure of Hugo by the side. She jumped to her feet and rushed over to his side, her dress falling open in her distress to reveal a delicately sculpted shoulder. Nicholas could not help but notice, though he looked away promptly.

Angela was distraught at the sight of the barely conscious figure of Hugo. Hugo was barely conscious because it had been decided that for him to play at being completely unconscious was too hard. He could moan and move about a bit, which was an easier role to play than being stone cold still. Tagalong asked Nicholas to watch over their enemies and helped Hugo outside to the carriage. He returned with a rug which Angela wrapped around herself.

Tagalong took charge. 'Mr Raspero, I wonder if you would be so kind as to escort Miss Ashton back to her home. I will remain here and see to it that these men are taken into custody.'

Nicholas thought about this for a moment. 'Can you handle them on your own?' he asked eventually.

Tagalong pretended to be offended. 'Given that they are bound hand and foot, Mr Raspero, then the answer is surely yes.'

Nicholas nodded. 'All right then.' He turned to Angela. 'Shall I escort you home, Miss Ashton?'

'If you would be so kind,' Angela said huskily, 'I can only beg of you to take me away from here to a place of safety.' Angela had been wondering how to play this game and she had settled on playing a role based on the waif Serena from *The Gallant Company*, who turned to the strong arms of her protector Sebastian, where she found both safety and love. It was a role she had played to wide acclaim, and she felt she could use this character as a starting point from which to approach Nicholas. She chose decorous clothes accordingly, as the more revealing garments she would later wear would come as a revelation of her beauty, although the torn condition of her decorous clothes helped make everything ambiguous.

'All right, let's go then,' Nicholas said, waving towards the door. 'After you, Miss Ashton.'

Once he had seated her in the flying carriage, Nicholas was only too happy to fly the carriage himself while Hugo huddled in the back seat, woozy and moaning softly. The flying carriage was a Wolstone, a gift to Angela from her first client, the only gift from him she had not sold.

Once Nicholas had arrived at her address, he found himself obliged to help Hugo up the stairs to Miss Ashton's apartment. Once in Miss Ashton's apartment, he was asked by her to wait while she changed, so he waited.

Angela took her time changing, thinking things over. She was not at all happy about having Nicholas in her apartment. She never brought clients here, and avoided any attempts on their part to see where she lived. As they were not interested enough in who she really was to pursue the matter, it was not too difficult to avoid having them here. It was easy enough to distract them with flirtation and bared shoulders if the subject ever arose. Jolly had insisted, however, that she bring Nicholas here, and so she had obeyed.

Nicholas for his part was wondering why there were six wands next door when Miss Ashton had told him she was alone. He was also wondering why the wand that had been where he had left Hugo had moved through space to join the six other wands already present, if Hugo was really so incapacitated as he had seemed.

Nicholas was naïve but he was not stupid and he was starting out on a train of thought that would have alarmed Tagalong had he been able to witness it. He was wondering how Tagalong had just happened to guide him past a place where a lady needed rescuing, given that Tagalong had himself needed rescuing just the day before. He was also wondering, now that he was in a suspicious mood, if Tagalong had ever really been invited to the party they had attended the night before, given that, now that Nicholas came to think of it, he had not seemed to be in the thick of things that night. Nicholas was, in short, wondering what was going on.

Angela came back into the room, in a light green dress (price: five hundred strada) that reached all the way up to her chin and down to her wrists, not too figure hugging. Her hair was artfully done up.

'Please sit down, Mr Raspero,' she said breathily. 'Can I fix you a drink?'

'No, thanks, I'm fine,' Nicholas said, trying to decide whether to leave, or stay and uncover what all this was about.

'But surely you will not leave, Mr Raspero,' Angela pleaded. 'Please stay. I can't bear to be left alone right now.'

'Yes, I'll stay a while,' Nicholas agreed.

'Then please join me in having a drink. I detest drinking alone and without your company I cannot drink.'

'All right, I'll have a glass of red wine,' Nicholas said, his suspicions increasing by the minute but deciding to play along. 'Thank you.'

Angela took two dark red crystal goblets (three hundred strada each) from a shelf, careful to put the one that had a green powder out of sight in the bottom on the right so she could offer that goblet to Nicholas. She poured them each a goblet of wine from the same bottle (Yehunda wine, seventy-five strada a bottle). Nicholas had been raised on stories of his ancestor Etienne, the devious genius whose cunning was legendary, so he was not too impressed by witnessing that the wine she was pouring for him and for her came from the same bottle. Etienne's trick had been to have a button in the neck of the bottle which, when pressed, switched the flow of wine from one compartment to another within the bottle.

Angela brought the goblet over to Nicholas and handed it to him. By then he was standing by the side of the room. He took the goblet and said, gesturing across the room, 'That's a nice painting.'

Angela turned to walk gracefully over to the painting (twelve hundred and fifty strada). Nicholas held the goblet by his side, out of sight of anyone secretly observing him, and tipped the wine into a waste-paper basket that was a hollowed out tree-trunk (eighty strada). He then stood there impassively, pretending to drink from the now empty goblet as she looked back at him.

'It is an original Nadine,' she told him. 'He is such a splendid painter, don't you think?' The painting was an investment that was intended to make Angela a profit.

'Yes,' Nicholas said shortly, pretending to take another sip from the goblet.

'Please sit down, Mr Raspero,' Angela suggested.

'Thank you.' Nicholas sat in a chair facing the door behind which were the six wands keeping him and Angela silent company. He pretended to drink again from the goblet.

'I cannot thank you enough for what you have done for me,' Angela told him sweetly, changing the use of her voice, as her breathy voice did not seem to be affecting Nicholas. She focused on achieving a musical tone.

'That's all right,' Nicholas said. He pretended to drink deeply from the goblet until he had drained it, then set the goblet down on the table. He sat back in the chair, ignoring the footstool nearby.

'Could I pour you some more wine?' Angela asked him.

'No thanks, I'll be leaving shortly,' Nicholas replied, and pretended to yawn. He sat back trying to look a bit sleepy, blinking his eyes.

'Please make yourself comfortable, Mr Raspero,' Angela said in her most soothing voice. 'Close your eyes and rest if you wish. You have been through such a trying ordeal fighting those evil men.'

Nicholas realised his guess had been right. The wine had been drugged, and now she was trying to put him under with her soothing voice and advice about having a rest. He closed his eyes with his hand on his wand and practised macchato. He could see her look at him and then heard her say softly, 'Mr Raspero?' He made no response. She pulled out her wand and tapped on the door opposite Nicholas.

Several men entered the room, their wands out. 'Bind him,' one of them said, and by macchato Nicholas could see which of them it was. As the karns came flying through the air Nicholas moved. He drew his feet up and sent himself over the chair in a backward somersault.

Nicholas waved his wand to pluck the karns out of the air, gathering them in his left hand while his opponents paused, wands outstretched. Then Nicholas flipped himself forward into a somersault which ended in his feet planted in the chest of one of his opponents who went back into the wall with a shout of anger, knocking a vase (five hundred strada) off the table to smash on the floor. Nicholas used his momentum to drop down to the ground and roll to his right. In two movements he had two men down on the ground amidst a shattered table (two hundred strada). He gathered their wands into his left hand, having bound them hand and foot with their own karns, while they were still falling through the air. The man who had been giving the orders stood to one side taking no part in the fighting while his remaining men, who were four in number, including an energetic and much-recovered Hugo, crouched facing him bringing out more karns and attacking him with a variety of combinations. Nicholas soon disarmed them and bound them hand and foot, but not without the destruction of a crystalline sculpture (three hundred strada), a glass tray (two hundred strada) and a ceramic globe of the world (six hundred strada).

Angela looked at the broken Greig vase on the floor; that vase cost five hundred strada. The table it had been on was shattered: two hundred strada. The sculpture, the tray, the globe … she was busy adding up the cost of all this destruction when she found herself bound hand and foot and thrown into a chair. This did not stop her calculations: eighteen hundred strada worth of damage!

Nicholas looked around at his prisoners, who looked back at him without saying a word. Then Nicholas returned to his chair and sat down. This time he pulled over the footstool and stretched out. He looked at the man who had been giving the orders earlier, the man who must be in charge of this lot.

'So what's going on?' Nicholas asked him.

'Introductions are by third party,' the man told him and turned to Angela. 'Angela, my dear, perhaps you will introduce us.'

'Jolly, this is Mr Nicholas Raspero,' Angela said, still angered by the damage to her property. 'Mr Raspero, this is Mr Frank Jollison.'

'So what's this all about, Mr Jollison?' Nicholas asked.

'I would strongly advise you to end this foolishness and untie me, Mr Raspero. I will not talk to you while I am treated in this fashion.'

'So you're a gentleman?' Nicholas asked Jolly, who said nothing in return. 'I can demand satisfaction from you, then?'

'I have already said that I will not speak to you while I am tied up, Mr Raspero. If you wish to speak to me, then untie me.'

'No, I'll make your bonds tighter while you reconsider your position,' Nicholas said. He pointed his wand and tightened the cords until they cut off the circulation to Jolly's hands and feet. Jolly writhed in fury, then began to breathe heavily.

'Mr Raspero, you will loosen these bonds. Do you understand?'

'I thought you weren't talking to me until you were untied,' Nicholas said.

'Mr Raspero, you will untie me or you will make an enemy of me. You do not want me as your enemy, believe me. Untie me, now!'

Nicholas raised his left hand in order to carefully inspect his fingernails. Jolly was breathing heavily, his face twisted in fury, but then he groaned, then said, 'Very well, Mr Raspero, perhaps you might loosen my bonds. I have indeed reconsidered my position.' No-one present had ever seen Jolly back down before.

Nicholas loosened Jolly's bonds and waited. Jolly groaned and strove to move his fingers. It took him several minutes, but in time his fingers were moving normally again. Jolly seemed relieved at this, as if he had worried that his circulation would never return to normal.

'So I can demand satisfaction from you then?' Nicholas asked.

'I do not accept challenges, Mr Raspero,' Jolly replied.

'Then you are not a gentleman,' Nicholas told him, 'are you?'

'I am a gentleman who does not accept challenges,' Jolly said.

Jolly was so used to being an absolute monarch that the indignity of his current position was taking time to sink in. He felt no fear, but rather an anger that was directed now to regaining his liberty so that he could destroy Nicholas. The thought that he might be in danger from Nicholas never crossed his mind. An absolute monarch was never in danger from anyone. As far as he was concerned, this situation was temporary, very temporary, and he would have his revenge.

'So what's this all about, Mr Jollison?' Nicholas asked him.

Jolly looked at him, and then decided he didn't want his circulation cut off again. 'You are a man of rare gifts, Mr Raspero. I wished to learn whether you would be interested in an offer of employment.'

'Do you always tie people up before offering them a job?' Nicholas asked.

As it happened, Jolly did not always adopt such an approach to a job interview, but neither was this exactly the first time that he had. Jolly dodged the question. 'I sought to restrain you to make clear that you have offended me. Once that had been made clear to you, I naturally would have released you without any harm coming to your person. I only sought to make a debating point, Mr Raspero.'

'How have I offended you?' Nicholas asked, feeling that they were coming at last to what this was all about.

'You have incurred a debt that I wish you to repay,' Jolly said.

'What debt? And incurred how?'

'The sum of five hundred and eighty strada, incurred by robbing five of my men in Octave Alley quite recently.' Jolly nodded at the men who were with him, who had all been on Octave Alley that night.

'How come their money is yours?' Nicholas asked, trying to figure out who this man was.

'Because they are my men,' Jolly said.

'Well, firstly, it was two hundred and seventy two strada I took from them, and secondly, I don't accept that I am obliged to repay you the money, whatever the sum.'

No Tin and his men were shaking their heads and objecting to this statement by Nicholas, but Jolly ignored them. Jolly had already guessed that his men had faked the figures, so he was not too surprised to hear Nicholas say this. He decided to be generous for the time being. Vengeance came to those who waited. 'Very well, Mr Raspero. I will accept your own account of the matter. The sum for you to repay me is that of two hundred and seventy two strada.'

Nicholas pointed his wand at the fireplace and banged the fire-starter to light the fire which was set there, given the unseasonable coldness of the weather lately. The paper burned merrily and the kindling started to crackle. 'I take great offence at you attempting to drug me and bind me,' Nicholas told Jolly. 'Very great offence. I think you should be punished for what you have tried to do, and I think you should be punished very severely.'

'You would find that I would be your worst enemy if you were to carry out such a threat, Mr Raspero.'

Nicholas then stood up and went over to Jolly. He searched him and took away everything he had found on Jolly. Nicholas sorted through what he had taken. Jolly furiously said nothing.

There was a wad of bank notes, totaling twelve hundred strada. In the silence of those watching what he was doing, Nicholas threw the bank notes onto the fire.

The attention of all eight of Nicholas's prisoners were fixed on those burning bank notes as if it was the most remarkable sight they had ever seen. They were unable to tear themselves away from the spectacle.

'Perhaps you now wish to say, Mr Jollison, that I owe you an additional twelve hundred strada,' Nicholas said. 'Yes or no?'

'That was a very foolish thing to do, Mr Raspero,' Jolly said, his voice trembling with anger. He could not remember when he had last been so angry.

'Do you live at the Burke Tavern?' Nicholas asked.

'No, I do not. But why should you say that?' Jolly asked, watching the last of his bank notes turning to ash.

'Just a guess,' said Nicholas. 'So this is about money. Have I understood you correctly?'

'It is about a debt you have incurred, Mr Raspero,' Jolly said, still furious at having seen those bank notes burn. 'A debt is not only about money. It involves the integrity of the debtor. Do you claim that a debt should not be repaid?'

Nicholas looked at Jolly in silence, still trying to figure out the situation he found himself in as a result purely of the decisions taken by his would-be captor. Who was he, anyway, exactly? 'So Mr Longman works for you,' Nicholas said. 'I have already guessed that.'

'Who is Mr Longman?' Jolly asked.

'I am surprised that you should go to so much trouble over two hundred and seventy two strada. I am starting to think that this is a matter of principle for you, Mr Jollison.'

'I am glad to see that you are starting to think clearly, Mr Raspero. The preservation of my property is indeed a matter of principle for me.'

'Is it now?' Nicholas said thoughtfully. 'I'm starting to understand you better, Mr Jollison.'

Jolly saw this as a chance to build rapport between himself and his captor. 'I understand you, Mr Raspero, I understand you well. But you do not yet understand me, Mr Raspero. I am a man of many interests. A man of your talents can be of some use to me, you must realise this yourself, Mr Raspero, and I can only hope that you will come to realise the benefits you may acquire through an association with a man of my varied interests. I guarantee you, Mr Raspero, that I can make you a millionaire in less than a year if you agree to co-operate with me on only two or three ventures. I can begin by providing you with the sum of one hundred thousand strada as an advance. Furthermore, just to make plain the sincerity of my intentions, I will forgive you the debt you have incurred and we will say no more about it. Now you understand me, I think, Mr Raspero.'

'So it's back to the job offer now, is it?' Nicholas asked.

'Indeed it is, Mr Raspero,' Jolly agreed, searching Nicholas's face for any kind of clues as to whether he was making progress.

'And how long do you plan to let me live to enjoy the benefits that such a large amount of money would bring me?' Nicholas asked Jolly.

'The benefits of our mutual association will preclude any such intentions on my part,' Jolly said, and at that moment it might even have been true. The chance of having a man like Nicholas working for him was indeed so tantalising that Jolly might have brought himself to put this matter to one side for twenty years or so before taking his revenge.

'Mr Jollison, let me make something perfectly clear right now. After today, I have no desire to ever look upon your stupid face ever again, nor to be subject to the stink of the gutter which you emanate from every pore of your mind and body. If we are to make an agreement, it will be on the basis that I never have to put up with the stinking unpleasantness of your presence ever again. Keep your money. I don't want it. I trust that you understand me?'

Jolly nodded slowly, giving no indication as to whether he had been offended by what Nicholas had just said. 'It is a matter of personal regret to me, Mr Raspero, that we have failed to establish that mutual rapport which I always hoped to establish. But naturally I accept your condition without argument.'

'So, we are enemies now, are we not, Mr Jollison?'

'Mr Raspero, I have only sought the return of what I consider to be rightfully mine. I understand, however, that you see things differently. I have decided accordingly, to let bygones be bygones, and forgive you this debt. There is no need for any further unpleasantness between us. This matter need go no further.'

'But how do we come to an agreement and walk away from this confrontation without concern as to future consequences?'

'You need have nothing further to fear from me, Mr Raspero. You have demonstrated yourself to be such a formidable opponent that there is no need for you to doubt that I have learned my lesson. As I have forgiven you the debt, the bone of contention between us has been removed. I am perfectly prepared to forgive you for what you have done to me today on the understanding that there will be peace between us.'

'If you were a gentleman, I could accept your word of honour that you would be bound by any agreement we make, and in that way we could make an agreement. But you are not a gentleman, and I see no reason to believe you will be bound by any agreement we make once you are no longer bound by those leather cords.'

'That is simply not so, Mr Raspero,' Jolly declared. 'I am bound by my word, and there is no question about it, none at all. You may ask anyone who knows me.' He looked across at his employees. 'Go on, tell Mr Raspero that this is so.'

They all obediently told Mr Raspero that this was so. Jolly was always bound by his word, they insisted. Nicholas did not look too impressed by their testimony.

Nicholas considered this for a while, then shook his head. 'You are a poisonous snake, Jolly. You will coil yourself in a hidden place and strike back at me when you can. It is only a matter of opportunity and patience.'

'You gravely misunderstand me, Mr Raspero,' Jolly said.

'No,' Nicholas said, shaking his head again, 'I don't think I do.'

'You most certainly do, Mr Raspero,' Jolly insisted. 'I have no desire whatsoever to prolong our enmity.'

'Neither do I,' Nicholas said, 'which is why I want to deal with you today.'

'You are no murderer, Mr Raspero,' Jolly said.

'I will not murder you,' Nicholas agreed, 'although if you were a gentleman I would demand a duel of final combat. But then, if you were a gentleman I could accept your word of honour and we could come to an agreement. But we are now going in circles.'

Jolly was relieved to hear that Nicholas was not going to murder him. He had suspected that Nicholas could not do so, by his own code of honour as a gentleman, given that the only offence Nicholas had suffered was merely the threat of being tied up. Jolly brought this into his calculations, starting to feel more confident now. 'May I ask you what you intend to do, Mr Raspero?' Jolly asked calmly.

Nicholas thought for a while in silence and then said, 'What would you suggest, Mr Jollison?'

'I would suggest that you untie me without delay, Mr Raspero,' Jolly said promptly.

Nicholas leaned back lazily in his chair, stretching his feet out on the footstool, and yawned slightly. 'Any other thoughts, Mr Jollison?'

It was then that Jolly made his strategic blunder. He had decided that Nicholas was an insignificant opponent who just happened to have a high degree of skill with a wand. So therefore all he had to do was apply enough pressure and Nicholas would come into line. Jolly was not used to anything except having his own way and so his current circumstances had thrown askew his normally exact judgement. Jolly was also in a temper from having been insulted by Nicholas after having been injured by the same. So it was that Jolly stepped into the abyss.

'My understanding is that you are a recent arrival to New Landern, Mr Raspero,' Jolly said affably. His geniality sent a shiver down the spines of all those of his party present, who knew him well. 'You may not have heard of the unfortunate fate of the Beaman family, who were all murdered not so long ago in their beds late at night, the parents and all three young children. The culprits were never found and are no doubt still at large. It would be a matter of grave concern to me if the Clark family, the parents and their three children and your cousin Mr Benjamin Clark, were also to be murdered late at night in their beds. I am prepared, as a gesture of friendship, to see to it that the Clark family are given such protection that such a fate could not possibly befall them. However, I would require an undertaking on your part that you would accept some form of employment from me, given such terms and conditions as are acceptable to us both. By these means, we may make peace between us while also gaining some benefit from our mutual acquaintance or even friendship.'

'Give me a moment,' Nicholas said. 'Let me think about this.' He plunged deep into thought while his prisoners watched him, occasionally looking amongst themselves, except for Jolly, whose eyes never left Nicholas's face. He was like a snake watching its prey with its gleamingly blank black eye intent on the presence of that prey to the exclusion of all else. Seeing the look on his face, Angela shivered slightly. She knew that look, and she could not help but feel that Nicholas was too soft to prevail over Jolly. His refusal to murder Jolly was not an encouraging sign. He talked well and was talented, but Jolly's stomach was made of granite, and Jolly thought nothing of murder.

Nicholas came to a decision. He stood up and went next door without another word. He came back with a couple of blankets he had taken from a cupboard and started tearing them into strips. Three hundred strada each those blankets cost me, Angela thought in outrage. Six hundred strada! Twenty-four hundred strada!

Nicholas checked their bonds and used the strips of the blanket to tie them all very securely to the chairs where they were sitting and gagged them while he was about it. When he was satisfied with his work he stood back and said, 'I will leave you now for a while. I will return.' Then he left, closing and locking the door behind him as he left.

Jolly wondered what he was up to now. It was most likely that Nicholas had gone to fetch the law. That would be an outcome favourable to Jolly. Even if he was taken into custody, it would only be a matter of time before he regained his freedom. He might even be in a position to demand that Nicholas be questioned by the authorities, and once Nicholas was in their hands, Jolly could very easily arrange for an accident to happen to him. He was a man of influence with connections he could use. He knew a lot of the dirty secrets of those in power, and they would do as he asked to avoid exposure; the accidental death of a nobody like Nicholas Raspero would not be very much for him to ask, or rather, demand of them. There was only one doubt which troubled Jolly, however, about whether or not this preferred outcome would take place, and that was that Nicholas had not turned to the law when he had been subject to attempted robbery in Octave Alley. Like Angela, however, he had decided that Nicholas was talented but soft. He was not too worried about his current predicament, believing it was only a matter of time before he regained his freedom, and thus his chance for revenge, and he would now have revenge, of that there was no doubt whatsoever. Nothing less than the death of Nicholas Raspero would suffice now, and if possible, that death would be the most painful he could devise if Nicholas fell into his hands. But if necessary, a quick death by assassination would have to do. These were the thoughts of Jolly as he waited for Nicholas to return.

SIX

....

The Downfall of Mr Frank Jollison as Brought About by Mr Nicholas Raspero

5:30 PM, Saturday 7 May 1544 A.F.

Nicholas took Angela's carriage and went towards the Burke Tavern. His only decision had been to scout the Burke Tavern, find out if that was indeed where Jolly lived, and see what he could find out. Then he would decide what to do. One idea that occurred to him as he flew along in Angela's carriage was to sit Jolly down in the middle of the street in the worst area of town with piles of Jolly's money around him and leave him to the tender mercies of those who lived in the worst area of town, but that was only a thought.

He parked near the Burke Tavern and made his way to it. He stepped inside and looked around him. There were not too many people around at this time but seeing Tagalong sitting nearby, Nicholas beckoned him over.

'Mr Raspero, we meet again,' Tagalong said. Seeing that Nicholas was very deliberately not looking at him but gazing across the room, Tagalong turned to follow Nicholas's gaze. Nicholas was looking at where the men who had attacked Angela were sitting, enjoying a drink and a smoke; they were looking over at Nicholas with mocking smiles. 'They were granted bail immediately, Mr Raspero and they —'

'Come with me, Mr Longman,' Nicholas said brusquely and set off for the side, where he had already identified the wand protection as being at its heaviest. He went through an alcove, his approach observed by others present in the Burke Tavern but not challenged. If Jolly had a visitor it wasn't their business. Nicholas came to a door and scanned for wands behind it. There was one wand in the space beyond. He opened the door without delay and stepped through, beckoning for Tagalong to follow. As Tagalong followed Nicholas closed the door, took Tagalong's wand and bound and gagged him so swiftly Tagalong had no time to make a sound. He left Tagalong on the floor while he made his way to where the wand was and stepped through a door. He was in a kitchen, and the man sitting with his feet up on the table looked at him with his mouth open in surprise. This was not a promising start to their fight for Jolly's man, given also that he was clutching a huge tankard of beer in his hand. He had not even moved before Nicholas had taken his wand and it was not long before Nicholas had the man, now dripping with beer, tied up and gagged.

Following where the wand protection was heaviest, Nicholas made his way along the corridor and stepped through a curtained doorway into what must be, judging from the luxury, Jolly's private quarters. He returned and helped Tagalong to come with him by the simple expedient of throwing him down the corridor and then through the door into Jolly's private quarters. The gagged Tagalong protested at his treatment but his protests were muffled. Nicholas bound Tagalong to a chair.

Nicholas looked around for where the wand protection was thickest and found the safe behind the painting of the volcano. It was a Basing safe; it had no handles, presenting only a smooth charcoal-grey shiny surface to the observer. It was the most expensive safe on the market, its selling price justified by its widely believed claim that it was next to impossible to break into. Nicholas had it open in less than ten seconds. It was a very large safe, full of money in bank notes, documents, notebooks, jewellery, and various other items. The safe was divided into two compartments, with the notebooks neatly lined up on the top shelf. Nicholas cleared Jolly's desk by sweeping everything off it onto the floor in one wave of his wand, gathered the notebooks with another wave of his wand, and went and sat down at Jolly's desk to look through them. He knew all too little of what Jolly was about and he needed to know more.

Nicholas opened the first notebook that came to hand and started to leaf through it. There were names followed by various comments: highly personal comments, more names of servants with additional comments, references to points of access in various houses, a listing of information of a technical nature such as encoding ciphers and bribes given and received or refused. Nicholas did not bother to read all of it; he picked up the next notebook and leafed through it. He was getting the general idea. He ungagged Tagalong and started to read out these names, asking who they were. Tagalong was very obliging and had no hesitation in telling Nicholas more than he needed to know. Nicholas gained the understanding he sought of what the notebooks were about: they were detailed accounts of some of the wealthiest and most powerful grandees of New Landern which could be used for a variety of purposes such as blackmail, breaking and entering and all sorts of other mayhem. There was also one small notebook, barely the size of the palm of a hand, which was divided into two parts, one headlined *Friends*, one headlined *Enemies*. Nicholas pocketed this notebook while sitting behind the desk in such a way that the watching Tagalong couldn't see what he was doing.

Nicholas pointed his wand at the fireplace, where the fire was already set, as it had been in Angela's apartment, given the unseasonably cold weather today, and set it alight. He waited for it to catch, adding more wood. When the fire had started to burn properly, Nicholas added the notebooks one by one.

'May I enquire as to why you are burning these notebooks, Mr Raspero?' Tagalong asked, his voice shaking a little. He could guess what their contents were and he was privately appalled at the wanton destruction of items of such incredible value. They were not a different kind of money, they were a different kind of printing press with which to make money. Tagalong was shocked, shocked beyond measure at the barbaric destruction which he was obliged to witness of those unbelievably valuable notebooks. He felt that the crouching figure by the fire was like a force of destruction beyond reason on the other side of a line which represented sanity, and when Tagalong considered all the crimes which he could have committed with those notebooks, he could have wept for the world he had lost. As Nicholas had ignored his question he repeated himself a little plaintively, 'May I enquire as to why you are burning those notebooks, Mr Raspero?'

'You wouldn't understand,' Nicholas said.

'I assure you I have an excellent comprehension of many matters pertinent and germane to the subject under discussion,' Tagalong assured him readily.

'Be quiet or I'll gag you again,' Nicholas told him.

Tagalong said nothing further.

Once all the notebooks were merrily burning, Nicholas returned to the safe. He emptied its contents and took them to the desk. There were wads of strada banknotes, worth perhaps nine hundred and seventy thousand or so, a variety of documents, jewellery, a broken child's toy which Nicholas assumed had some personal significance for Jolly, and letters. Nicholas started looking through the documents. He was not able to understand the meaning of any of the terms he encountered in these documents so he enlisted Tagalong's help again. Certified Assets Restricted Funds, Consolidated Financial Trading of the Baskets of Listed Depository Receipts, Asset Backed Securities of Bond Issuer Indentures, Short-Term Securities Tendering of Financial Residuals, Direct Registration Securities of Collateralised Commodities Spread, and many other such terms which Nicholas found incomprehensible.

Tagalong also found them incomprehensible but without hesitation he set forth to pretend that he did understand these terms. It was not just that lying was second nature to Tagalong, if not even perhaps his first nature; it was also that Tagalong had always found it useful to pretend to know things he didn't and he was not going to change his ways now. As it happened, he had once spent an entire dinner under a false name in the company of financial traders and his retentive memory now came up with some of what he had heard on that long-ago occasion. 'Ah, yes,' he said with an outwardly complete assurance of knowing such things as well as he knew his own name, 'Certified Assets Restricted Funds are cross-sectional share holdings of a designated turn-around system as determined by the debt-service coverage ratio of convertible bonds.

Consolidated Financial Trading of the Baskets of Listed Depository Receipts forms the bond equivalent covenant of the adjusted preset value of Certificates of Amortised Revolving Debt. And so on, as one might suppose, Mr Raspero.'

Tagalong had said all this nonsense with such an air of confidence that Nicholas was completely taken in by his performance. A thought struck Nicholas then and he gave Tagalong a look but said nothing further at the time. He shuffled through the documents until he came to the Total Assets Valuation as of 1 May 1544 A.F. He looked up at Tagalong with a speculative look in his eye and read out this term with the accompanying figure of 19,325,547 strada.

Tagalong, all of a sudden, felt seasick. He knew of the enormity of the wealth of the wealthy but to hear this cold hard figure was staggering.

Nicholas looked briefly at the letters, ascertaining that they were personal in nature and therefore either incriminating to others or of sentimental value to Jolly, who was already a dead man as far as Nicholas was concerned, and threw them into the fire. He walked over to Tagalong and said nothing for a moment, while he gave Tagalong a long look and then said, 'Mr Longman, you talk too much. It's time you listened. Now, in the kitchen,' Nicholas pointed in the direction where the kitchen was, 'there is a man who is bound and gagged. You may either join him in the kitchen where you will remain excluded from the subsequent events of tonight or you may remain in this room where important developments will be taking place. Which do you choose?'

'Naturally, Mr Raspero, I would be only too honoured to continue to enjoy the benefits of your esteemed and —'

'There are three conditions which apply,' Nicholas interrupted. 'Firstly, you talk too much. Just say what is necessary. Got that?'

'I will curb my natural loquacity given the —'

'Secondly, you will not pretend to be less intelligent than you are. Got that?'

'I assure you, my dear Mr —'

'Thirdly, you will choose between a continued loyalty to Jolly, or a participation in a scheme of things that is not in Jolly's favour.'

Tagalong said nothing for once after hearing this, but his eyes shifted to all the money on the table. He took a deep breath and exhaled loudly.

'Now we begin,' Nicholas said. 'I demand satisfaction from you for the deception which you have practised on me. Do you accept my challenge?'

'Mr Raspero, I can only beg pardon for —'

'Do you want to go to the kitchen?' Nicholas said furiously. 'Any failure to answer any of my questions and you will spend the rest of the night having no idea of what is happening. Now, answer me: do you accept my challenge, yes or no?'

'No, Mr Raspero. I ask you to —'

'You are not a gentleman, are you, Mr Longman?'

'I am indeed a gentleman, sir. I have fallen on hard times, Mr Raspero, lamentably so, but —'

Nicholas gagged him. Tagalong made muffled protests for a while. Nicholas waited, organising his thoughts. Tagalong fell silent after a while so Nicholas resumed speaking, 'I will explain to you what I am about. You will then demonstrate an ability to participate in my scheme, in which case you might well profit from tonight's developments, or you will fail to demonstrate any intelligence, in which case I will remove you to the kitchen and you will play no further role. I will remove your gag now. If you still have the sense you were born with, you will not babble and you will confine your comments to only those which you judge I will find of interest. Now, let us see whether you do indeed have any intelligence.' Nicholas ungagged Tagalong.

'I shall endeavour to fulfill all your expectations, Mr Raspero,' Tagalong said and carefully stopped there.

'Jolly has many men working for him, does he not?'

'Yes, Mr Raspero.'

'How many?'

'That is difficult to say. Anything from one to ten thousand, depending on how you count them. This is because —'

'I get it. Bribed officials and the like now and then.'

'Yes, Mr —'

'If a flying carriage were to fall on Jolly tonight, who would take over running all this?'

'There is no clear successor to Jolly, Mr Raspero. He is not a man who tolerates rivals or successors.'

'If I were to sit Jolly here in this room, tied to a chair, bound and helpless, and bring his top lieutenants into this room, and leave them all here together with all this money before them, would they free Jolly and continue to serve him, or would they make another choice?'

Tagalong paused. He looked at all the money on the table. More than twenty million strada! 'There is a lot of money on that table, Mr Raspero. But Jolly commands a lot of loyalty. It is not an easy question to answer.'

'What would you decide to do yourself, Mr Longman?'

Tagalong thought about this. He thought about himself, he thought about his situation, and he thought of what answer Nicholas wanted to hear. 'I would choose to turn against Jolly, Mr Raspero,' he said, thankful that Jolly was not there to hear him, 'but only if his downfall was guaranteed. Jolly is not a man to lightly cross.'

'Let us reason from first principles, Mr Longman,' Nicholas said. 'Jolly's time has come and gone. This is simply the way things are at this time. Therefore, someone has to take over from Jolly. But who should it be? Who would you nominate as a candidate, Mr Longman?'

'Naturally, Mr Raspero, it is clear to me beyond rhyme or reason that you stand aligned to the vertical, such that to you alone amongst —'

'Try again, bozo,' Nicholas interrupted. 'Think harder. Jolly's successor has to be at least something like him. I am nothing like him. Give me a name.'

'May I ask how long I may have to deliberate on such an important matter, Mr Raspero?' Tagalong asked with his very best manners.

Nicholas sighed at the difficulty he was having in getting Tagalong to see his own interests. 'What if you took over from Jolly, Mr Longman?' Nicholas asked.

Tagalong laughed. 'Alas, Mr Raspero, I fear that such a development, despite being unheralded, although even if heralded by a comet emblazoned with the letters of my name, would nonetheless —'

'If Jolly's lieutenants fight amongst themselves, and none of them see you as being a rival, your chances of taking over are very good. All you have to do is be the last man standing.'

Tagalong's visible amusement showed how little persuaded he was by this argument. He was an educated man but not educated enough. Nor had he properly grasped the strategy Nicholas had outlined. Although in the coming weeks and months he reflected often on what Nicholas had said.

Nicholas appeared to have given up on this idea, but, in fact, he knew that he had already planted the idea in Tagalong's mind and now it was time to implement his strategy in such a way that Tagalong would not himself realise what was going on. Tagalong might well be an expert in how to deceive people but Nicholas knew how to get things done. 'If you were to select those of Jolly's men who might go against him in return for getting their hands on all his wealth, what names would you come up with?'

Tagalong thought about this. 'Pay, Fitzroy, No Tin, Kassie, Pastime — perhaps. But with no clear successor, they might well fight amongst themselves. Jolly might play them against each other. Do not underestimate Jolly, Mr Raspero.'

'Suppose that I supervised their discussion, thus requiring them to discuss the matter as reasonable men?'

Tagalong licked his lips. He would either be dead tonight, or rich and free from his servitude to Jolly. The stakes were as high as they could be. 'You are a man who might well succeed in such a task, Mr Raspero. Naturally, I hope that as I am to participate —'

'Where would these men be who you mentioned?'

'Pay and Kassie are in the Tavern at this very moment,' Tagalong said. 'No Tin was last with Jolly. The others could be anywhere, maybe not even in New Landern for all I know. Jolly is a man with international interests.'

Nicholas walked to and fro thinking things over. Tagalong waited, unable to keep from looking discreetly at all the money on the table. A love-struck teenager could not have been so secretly attentive. Nicholas looked about him until his attention was caught by a tapestry on the wall. The tapestry showed a man being tortured in a cellar by ten monsters — the detail of the tapestry was lurid and red and stomach-churning — Jolly liked to observe the reactions of people on seeing this tapestry for the first time, for their reactions gave him one of the several measures of their character that he sought to know. Nicholas took down this tapestry with a wave of his wand and settled it over the table to hide Jolly's treasure from sight. He gagged Tagalong again and carefully inspected his bonds. He took down a nearby cloak and ripped it into strips with which he tied the chair Tagalong was tied to so that Tagalong was unable to move this chair an inch. Then he left the room. He re-wrote the wand protection on the door leading into Jolly's quarters so that now only he would be able to open it again and left the tavern. He took the flying carriage back to Angela's apartment. He knew by now exactly what he was going to do to Jolly.

8:00 PM, Saturday 7 May 1544 A.F.

Nicholas's prisoners were exactly where he had left them, although judging from their slight disarray they had made determined efforts to free themselves. Angela was making insistent noises through her gag; Nicholas ungagged her to learn that she was very eager to answer a loud call of nature. Nicholas untied her but at the same time fastened a wand to the back of her lower skirts. He then brought her to her feet and led her away to the bathroom where he left her alone. He then monitored the location of the wand in the bathroom — after being stationary for a while as Angela went about her business, it then moved in such a way as to take it beyond the physical space of the bathroom in a diagonally sloping trajectory. Nicholas, waiting outside the bathroom by a window, opened this window and jumped outside, landing gently on the ground and leaning back against the wall. Angela emerged cautiously from a secret opening in the wall, the very bricks moving aside to form an exit from which her head and shoulders emerged, followed by the rest of her as she tumbled onto the ground. She rose to her feet and brushed herself off and then caught sight of Nicholas and froze in shock, her mouth and eyes wide open. With a wave of his wand Nicholas had the bricks back in place; with another wave of his wand he flipped Angela up and through the open window; with another wave of his wand he flipped himself back up through the open window, which he then closed. Turning Angela around he took back the wand he had attached to her and shepherded her back to the living room where his other prisoners awaited.

Nicholas tied and gagged Angela again; Hugo was making insistent noises through his gag so Nicholas ungagged him only to learn that Hugo was very keen to answer his own call of nature; Nicholas gagged him again and ignored his request, but it gave him an idea which he was later to put to use. He untied Jolly and his five men from their chairs but left them bound. Applying his wand combinations to the karns by which they were tied, he took them to Angela's carriage in a succession of stages by throwing them along the ground, down the stairs and out into the garden to where the carriage was parked. He returned to Angela's living room, checked that Angela and Hugo were tied securely to their chairs then left, locking Angela's front door with a combination that would not be easily unlocked and then flew Angela's carriage back to the Burke Tavern.

Like a bucket with a hole slowly losing water, Jolly's temper was ebbing away as a sense of his predicament began to sink in. It was clear to him that Nicholas had not gone to the authorities; it was clear to him that Nicholas had some idea of what he was about given his purposeful behaviour, and it was clear to him that Nicholas had no intention of making peace with Jolly given the way he was throwing Jolly around like a sack of potatoes. Furthermore, the physical restraints which Jolly had laboured under all this time had by now become real; that is to say, Jolly could no longer ignore the all-too-obvious fact that he was a prisoner. Jolly no longer felt like a king but all too much like a subject of speculation.

Nicholas landed Angela's carriage between the river and Jolly's quarters in the Burke Tavern, entered Jolly's quarters by a side door, checked that Tagalong was still in place and that all was as it should be, then brought Jolly in and tied him to a chair with a deft wand combination. There was only Tagalong and Jolly there to see what he was doing as Nicholas took a jug of water and carefully poured it about Jolly's lower person to make it appear as if Jolly had wet himself (this was the idea which Hugo had inadvertently given him earlier). Jolly protested this treatment through his gag while Tagalong watched everything that was going on with a frightened look of erratic calculation in his sideways looking eyes. Nicholas brought the other five men into Jolly's room and sat them down on the floor along the wall, still tied up. In the meantime Jolly had seen the wide open door of his empty safe; by now his temper had completely drained away and for the first time he began to feel faintly fearful. He tried to attract Nicholas's attention as Nicholas closed the side door but without success; Nicholas ignored him. It was to Tagalong that Nicholas now turned his attention.

8:45 PM, Saturday 7 May 1544 A.F.

'Now is the time for you to make your choice, Mr Longman,' he told Tagalong after having removed his gag. 'You may decide to continue to be loyal to Jolly, in which case I will remove you to the kitchen, where you will play no further role in this matter, and you will certainly receive no profit, no matter what the outcome, or you may choose to consider yourself to be no longer subject to the command of Jolly, in which case you may remain here and profit accordingly. Now make your choice, Mr Longman: are you still loyal to Jolly, or are you not?'

Tagalong looked anything but talkative at that moment. All too aware of Jolly's eyes burning into his face, he licked his dry and cracked lips and said, 'I would hope for an outcome that may suit us all, Mr Raspero.'

'You are to be commended for your loyalty to Jolly even at the very end,' Nicholas told him. 'I will now take you to the kitchen, where you will remain until you learn what the outcome has been from whoever comes to free you from your bonds.'

'No!' Tagalong said as Nicholas began to untie the strips of cloth that held his chair in place, 'I will stay, Mr Raspero, in the hope that —'

Nicholas gagged him then and continued with his task. Tagalong's protests, while muffled, were insistent and desperate. Nicholas paused, looked at him and said, 'I will ungag you and you will have one last chance. If you understand me blink your eyes.'

Tagalong blinked his eyes furiously.

'You will say that you are no longer loyal to Jolly, or you will go to the kitchen. Now: make your choice.' Nicholas ungagged him.

'I am no longer loyal to Jolly,' Tagalong said loudly, clearly and defiantly.

'Then there is no longer a need to restrain you,' Nicholas said and unbound Tagalong, who regained his freedom as if he didn't know whether to make a run for it or not. Jolly made muffled noises through his gag, but Nicholas ignored him. 'We have already discussed how this shall continue,' Nicholas said to Tagalong, whose eyes flickered toward Jolly, 'and now you shall act accordingly. You will go out into the tavern and find three or four men who might well be capable of being successors to Jolly. You will bring them in here so that we can all discuss the matter further.' Nicholas returned Tagalong's wand to him. 'Now go!' He pointed his wand out the doorway and opened the door when Tagalong reached it, then closed it behind him.

Jolly was making insistent noises through his gag but Nicholas continued to ignore him. He tracked the progress of Tagalong's wand, and tracked the return of Tagalong with three wands accompanying him. Nicholas flipped himself up to stand with his feet on the transom above the door frame; as the transom was a wooden strip only a few inches wide Nicholas turned sideways to line up along the wall. Tagalong entered below his feet, followed by three men who moved out through the room looking at Jolly, then back at Tagalong. What followed was not so much of a fight as a slightly confused melee: Nicholas dropped down behind them, all three of their wands sailing through the air into his left hand. Their own cords jumped out of their pockets and wrapped themselves around their wrists and ankles even while they found themselves sitting down heavily, their backs against the wall, still trying to catch up with what was going on. Tagalong had remained motionless with his hands raised slightly and spread out above waist level to signify his non-fighting capacity. Nicholas moved out into the centre of the room and contemplated his latest captives.

'Who are these men, Mr Longman?'

'This is Pay, Kassie, Pastime,' Tagalong replied, gesturing towards each man in turn. 'No Tin here might do as well,' he suggested, pointing to one of the five men who had been with Jolly at Angela's apartment.

Nicholas dragged each of the four men who had been named to their feet one by one. He untied them but kept their wands. They kept looking across at Jolly with an air of disbelief; it was not yet a case of seeing is believing for the sight of their dreaded chief, bound and gagged, was clearly a sight that they could not believe.

'Pay attention, everyone,' Nicholas declared loudly like the master of proceedings at a circus. 'This is going to be interesting.' He then drew back the tapestry which lay over Jolly's treasure on the table, exposing to their lustful gaze the intimacies of Jolly's personal and very private riches.

These men did not avert their eyes from the sight; quite the contrary. Pay and No Tin even licked their lips. They feasted their eyes on the strada bank notes, greedily looked at the documents and jewellery and other items, then back at the strada bank notes. Those bank notes they understood and the jewellery as well. Nicholas watched them watching these goodies, while Tagalong warily watched Nicholas from the side. Jolly was making frantic noises through his gag, but no-one was paying attention.

Nicholas placed the tapestry back over the treasure, hiding it from their sight. They came back to themselves in that crowded room, looking around as if wakening from a dream. Now Nicholas made his next move, hoping that he had gauged it right. He ungagged Jolly. If Jolly pleaded with Nicholas now, Jolly was finished.

'Mr Raspero,' Jolly said as calmly as his panic would allow, 'we have surely continued as far as is necessary with this foolishness. I truly understand the gravity of the offence I have caused you. I entirely withdraw the threat I have made, which indeed I did not make, not even inadvertently. This is a misunderstanding, which has grieved you and I can only apologise for what I have done, because it was not done, not even by mistake. Whatever recompense you require, it shall be rendered to you without delay.'

'You sound as if you're begging me for mercy,' Nicholas said contemptuously.

All eyes in the room were now on Jolly. 'Certainly not, Mr Raspero,' Jolly said, but his composure was visibly impaired as his eyes flickered towards his men who were watching him impassively. The fact that he had apparently wet himself had not escaped their attention. 'I only trust to your inherent good sense, that I withdraw this mistaken threat, your awareness that I will make full restoration of all that has caused you offence, that I understand without reservation that indeed you have cause to feel unjustly treated, indeed you —'

Nicholas gagged him then, and turned to the other men in the room and considered them. They were a bunch who would look at home in a dark alley, he thought. They were evil men who were governed only by fear, and what fear did they have of Jolly now? He could leave Jolly in their hands without a backward glance. Jolly was making ever more frantic noises through his gag but again no-one was paying attention to him. 'It is time for a successor to arise in the place of Jolly,' he told them. 'Or perhaps the enterprise which Jolly runs may be divided up between you, so that all four of you can continue in the place of Jolly. Now is the time to decide how you shall continue your lives as criminals of the New Landern demi-monde.'

Nicholas lifted the tapestry again and began to look through the documents. 'Only two men in this room understand the meaning of these documents. One of them is Jolly, still begging for mercy over here,' Nicholas gestured contemptuously to Jolly, so their eyes swivelled to regard Jolly, still making noises through his gag, 'the other is Mr Longman, standing over here.' With another gesture, Nicholas drew their attention to Tagalong. All eyes swivelled to Tagalong, who nodded with an immediate air of assurance in confirmation of Nicholas's verdict. 'But what are these documents? Ah, that is an interesting question, much more interesting than you realise. You lack education, you lack knowledge, and you are ignorant thugs, are you not? So let us examine what we have here. Here is a Short-Term Securities Tendering of Financial Residuals document which is worth three million, four hundred and twenty five thousand strada.' Nicholas held the document up in front of their disbelieving eyes. 'Yes, you heard me correctly. I am holding three million, four hundred and twenty five thousand strada in my hands right here.' Still more disbelief. 'You are so stupid that you don't even know how stupid you are, do you?'

The four men looked back at Nicholas without expression. Nicholas noted, however, that they did not look hostile. They were fascinated, in their own thuggish way, by what he was saying, even if they did not fully understand it. Nor could men as low as this be insulted by a man holding the wand and offering them more money than they had dreamed possible.

'There is a total of 20 million strada here, one million in cash, 19 million in these documents. If you want to have access to all of this money, then you will require the services of Mr Longman here,' Nicholas told them. Tagalong nodded with the same air of assurance as before. 'He may well choose not to explain these things to you, because he will wish to strike a deal with you concerning his own role in subsequent developments.'

'That is so,' Tagalong eagerly said, 'I must reserve —'

'Shut it!' Nicholas told him harshly, adopting the vernacular of his current circumstances. Tagalong shut it. 'We now turn to the last closing stage of this drama.' Nicholas threw the document back on the table. 'You will all look at me.' They all looked at him. 'I do not expect to be bothered by any of you ever again. If I am, I will see to it that those who serve you are given the same choice concerning your fate as I have given you concerning the fate of Jolly. Furthermore, not one of you will trouble Miss Ashton again. I will take it as a personal offence if anyone troubles her for any reason whatsoever. Stay away from her. That is all. You will decide who is to be the successor of Jolly, or whether or not you will divide up his business between you.' Nicholas drew back the tapestry again and threw it to one side and said, 'This fortune belongs to the successor, or successors, of Jolly here.' With a gesture he drew their attention back to Jolly, who looked at Nicholas and made muffled noises through his gag, clearly wishing to speak at that very moment. Their attention did not linger long on Jolly, however, for it swiftly returned to the fabulous fortune sitting on the table. Nicholas untied the men still sitting on the floor, and then returned all their wands to them at the same time. He was standing by the side door by this time, and as they took hold of their wands, he turned and walked off through the doorway, closing the door behind him. He tracked their wands, but as he had expected, no-one came after him. No-one was going to leave all that money behind with the others. Besides, by now they all had a very healthy respect for Nicholas's wandfighting ability. For whatever reason, Nicholas was not pursued as he returned to Angela's flying carriage.

10:10 PM, Saturday 7 May 1544 A.F.

As he flew the Wolstone back to Angela's apartment, he reflected that Jolly's chances were not good. If he had miscalculated, and Jolly was freed, he would have to deal with whatever situation he encountered as it arose, but Jolly was not likely to live to see the sun rise on another day.

Angela and Hugo were still tied up in place. Hugo made desperate noises through his gag, more eager than ever to go to the bathroom. Nicholas untied them and let Hugo go with a wave of his hand. As far as he was concerned hostilities were over.

Nicholas sat down himself and pulled up a footstool. He considered Angela for a moment, while she considered him in her turn. It was very likely the reaction to everything that had happened, but for a moment Angela seemed to him like a wounded bird that needed to be sheltered and nursed back to health. She was an undeniable beauty, and he was struck by the fact that had she been a painting he would have contemplated that painting for a long while. He felt protective of her for no reason at all that he could identify, given that she had done her best that very day to bring him down, and yet he did not pause to reflect on the undeniable fact that he had already taken steps to protect her without having given any thought at the time as to what he was doing. Everything had happened so fast; he had done what he had done in the time and place of a world revolving rapidly under his feet.

'What is the nature of your relationship with Jolly, Miss Ashton?'

Angela looked down at the fan in her hands and said, 'He has been a kind benefactor to me. After my mother died when I was fifteen, I entered service as a lady's companion with Mrs Farrar. When I chose to go on the stage, Jolly was kind enough to help me to do so.'

'Kind is not the right word, Miss Ashton. There is no kindness in a man like Jolly. He had another motivation to help you, did he not?'

'Where is Jolly now, Mr Raspero?'

'Most likely in the afterlife.'

Angela looked up at him on hearing this. 'Did you kill him, Mr Raspero?'

'No, but I left him in the hands of men who will. Jolly is probably dead by now. If not, it is only a matter of time.'

'I do not understand you, Mr Raspero.'

'I left him tied up surrounded by piles of his money in the company of his men. They can free him, or kill him and take all that money for themselves. You can guess the odds, Miss Ashton.'

'They would not kill him, Mr Raspero.'

'It was a lot of money, Miss Ashton.'

'How much money, Mr Raspero?'

'Twenty million strada.'

'Twenty million strada?' Miss Ashton gasped.

'One million in cash, the remaining money in a variety of financial documents.'

'What kind of financial documents, Mr Raspero?' Angela asked. She was finding this conversation fascinating. Her eyes glowed and she sat upright with her fan held loosely in her hands.

'Oh,' Nicholas said, trying to remember, 'Convertible Adjustable Preferred Stock, that kind of thing.'

'Was it by par value or by cash flow?' Angela asked eagerly.

'Probably,' Nicholas said with a vague wave of his hand. 'But that's not the point. The point is that Jolly will be succeeded by one or more successors, who will now run the show. Jolly will no longer be around.'

Angela could not conceive of a world in which Jolly was not running the show. 'I trust you will excuse me if I express skepticism, Mr Raspero. Jolly is not a man who is easily cast aside as readily as you seem to think.'

'He was begging me for mercy before I left. Trust me, Jolly is finished.'

'I cannot doubt your veracity, Mr Raspero, but neither can I believe what you say.'

'I left him bound and gagged, Miss Ashton. Tell me, how is Jolly to give orders when he is gagged? And if he cannot give orders, how is he to be obeyed by those who have twenty million strada in front of them as theirs for the taking? If you understand what I am saying to you, then you understand the gravity of Jolly's predicament, and you understand why he was begging me for mercy before I gagged him and left.'

'I cannot conceive of a man like Jolly begging for mercy.'

'Then you do not understand that he was pond scum, Miss Ashton. Nor do you understand that he is in the hands of men who are also pond scum, which Jolly himself understood only too well. They only obeyed him out of fear. They have no reason to obey him now. Jolly will not live through this night. I have no doubt whatsoever concerning this point.'

'Perhaps you are right, Mr Raspero,' Angela said, still unable to believe a word of it. For her to be told that Jolly would be overthrown was like being told that the sun would not rise tomorrow.

'I have one more matter to discuss with you, Miss Ashton, before I leave you.'

'And what is that, Mr Raspero?'

'You have my sympathy, Miss Ashton. I wish you to know that I go my way bearing you no ill feelings.'

'That is very kind of you, Mr Raspero.'

'Perhaps. But I have taken certain steps to express this sympathy.'

'Certain steps, Mr Raspero?'

'I made plain to the thugs who will succeed Jolly that you are not to be harmed in any way. I made it clear to them that if any harm were to come to you, I would make them suffer for it. It therefore follows, that they will leave you alone.'

'But why have you done this for me, Mr Raspero?'

Had Nicholas answered truthfully at that moment, he would have said that he didn't know. As it was, he dodged the question by saying, 'You have been obliged by Jolly to obtain secrets concerning Zavanna, Nieves,

Hudson and Foxley, have you not? This was the kindness of Jolly to which you referred earlier. Well, you will no longer be obliged to perform such a service again. You may make your own way in life, Miss Ashton, without recourse to any other will but your own.'

Angela said nothing, but looked down at her fan. She could not take all of this in at once. A world without Jolly? Making her own choices? Never again being threatened with having to go back to Madame Marlene's?

'I leave you now, Miss Ashton,' Nicholas said, getting to his feet. 'One day I hope to see you on the stage.' With that he left, after writing his name and address on a piece of paper and leaving it on her coffee table.

He set off on foot into the cool dark night. Judging by the stars, he thought it must be not long before midnight. He thought of Angela as he walked along. She was a puzzle, he thought. She spoke so well, she had such grace and refinement and beauty, yet it seemed that she had been the mistress of wealthy men in order for Jolly to gain inside information on these men.

He wondered why she had done what Jolly had told her to do. She had played the whore for him. There must have been a reason. Perhaps it was a noble reason, perhaps not. Perhaps she had done this for herself, perhaps not. He had no way of knowing, and he reflected that he probably never would know.

He would make a point of seeing her on stage when he could, he told himself. That would be interesting. Besides, he had never seen a play. He thought of make-believe as he walked off into the night, the stars like bright white candles made of sparkling frost glittering brightly above him.

SEVEN

....

The Vote of the Club of Appreciation for the Most Beautiful Woman in New Landern

11:30 PM, Saturday 7 May 1544 A.F.

Mr Berg Irving was enjoying being in the spotlight so he took his time, withdrawing a folded sheet of paper from his robes and unfolding it with great care. He was reporting to The Gang on the vote of the Club of Appreciation that had just taken place earlier that evening.

The Club of Appreciation had been formed thirty-one years ago during an all-night drinking session between nineteen of the more dissolute gentlemen of New Landern society. Membership was by invitation only. There were currently one hundred and eighty-seven members of the Club of Appreciation, who met once a year to perform the solemn and sacred duty of selecting *the most beautiful woman in New Landern*. The meeting was top-secret and the results known only to the members of the Club of Appreciation, so it followed that the whole of New Landern knew those results within hours. The results were awaited with a mixture of interest, apprehension, amusement, scorn and lustful anticipation, so it can be fairly said that the results were eagerly awaited.

The entrants had only to have set foot in New Landern during the year in question to be candidates for selection and to be at least eighteen years old. The foreign minister of Yelyntrade's wife had been a past winner, for example, even though she had only been in New Landern for one week, but she had been a woman in New Landern and seven months later the hands of many of the members of the Club of Appreciation still shook as they voted for her.

The members of the Club of Appreciation began their meeting by following the sacred rituals as established and honoured by their heritage. They walked around the room, their elbows stuck out and waggling, cackling like geese. They then crawled about the room on their hands and knees barking like dogs. Finally, they stood on their right leg, raised their left leg to one side and mooed like a cow. The members of the Club of Appreciation performed these rituals with greatly varying degrees of enthusiasm.

Then came the business of voting. Names were called out by those present and recorded by the Scribe of Scribes sitting at a desk wearing a hat with a bunch of daffodils stuck to it. Once all the names had been recorded, everyone gathered themselves on one side of the large ballroom their meetings took place in on that one evening of the year. The Scribe of Scribes called out the names one by one; as each name was called out, those who wished to vote for the woman in question walked out into the middle of the ballroom and stood with their hands raised in the air. The Scribe of Scribes counted the votes, called out the total number of votes for everyone to hear and check for themselves, then wrote the number down while two Inspectors of the Count wearing masks peered over his shoulder to verify that he wasn't cheating. The Scribe of Scribes then loudly proclaimed the name and the vote, and the devotees of the beauty in question lowered their hands and walked across to the other side of the ballroom. This process was repeated until all the names had been assigned the value of their vote. The penalty for not voting was immediate expulsion, so everyone always voted. The Inspectors then one after the other from left to right held up their hand and called out the name of their choice, which was noted by the Scribe of Scribes. The Scribe of Scribes had a casting vote in the event of a tie but otherwise did not vote.

The Scribe of Scribes, monitored by the Inspectors of the Count, drew up a List of Ten that was written backwards, with the tenth last name at the top, and the winner at the bottom. He then read out the names and the votes in this sequence, while everyone busily copied down what he was saying.

The name of the winner was then written down onto the Roll of Honour with the date of the year next to it by the Scribe of Scribes, still closely monitored by the Inspectors of the Count to check that even at the very last minute he wasn't cheating, and then the evening was done. The members of the Club of Appreciation went their various ways: some for a drink and a gentle game of billiards, others returned home, while others went and partied with prostitutes. The excitement was over for another year.

This was the event on which Berg, as a member of the Club of Appreciation, had now to make his report to The Gang. He read out the ten names, starting with the tenth beauty of New Landern for that year (*Miss Odilia Fabel*). The third-last name was *Lady Arabella Montlait*, four times a past winner, and still a strong competitor despite her advanced age of twenty seven; the second-last name was *Lady Isabel Grangeshield*, which made everyone look at Isabel with a sympathy she affected not to notice, because of course if she was the second-last name that meant that she had not won, and then with a dramatic pause, during which time everyone's mind was racing trying to figure out who the winner could possibly be, Berg read out the name of the most beautiful woman in New Landern of 1544: *Miss Angela Ashton*. The unexpected result made everyone gasp and then declare that they had known it all along.

'I knew it!' declared Sophie, who had never mentioned this before. 'She was kept out of sight by Hudson, Nieves and Zavanna but Foxley has taken her everywhere with him and she has been widely seen in his company over the past year. Yes, it is that exposure to the public eye which has brought her this success, I think.'

'I said to Arnold just the other day, do you think it might be Miss Ashton this year and he said quite possibly,' Kora added. (Arnold was her sweetheart.) She also had never mentioned this before.

Samantha revealed for the first time her own foresight in this matter, 'Miss Ashton was so widely observed at the Mudfield Stakes that I thought then she might win this year, and I even asked Lane if he would vote for her and he said he might.' (Lane was her brother.)

'The fickleness of men!' Uliana proclaimed as if she had never before suspected such a thing. 'How could they? Isabel, it seems your time has already come and gone.'

Isabel had won the title of *the most beautiful woman in New Landern* for the past three years in a row, and had been a runner-up (to Arabella Montlait) in her first year of competition. Uliana was feeling spiteful — with her square, almost mannish face, a snub nose and a wide mouth with thick lips, she had never made it onto the List of Ten and never would.

'Who is Miss Ashton?' Isabel asked, as if she had forgotten.

Berg looked at her smiling, not fooled for a moment. 'She is an actress who steps out onto the stage of the Emperor Theatre.'

'Ah, an actress!' Isabel observed disdainfully. 'Yes, no doubt she can instruct the Club of Appreciation to cackle like geese better than they do already, if indeed they do need instruction in this matter. I am sure they are already perfect geese.'

'Oooh, it's very hard, Izzy,' Penny consoled her. 'But everyone's talking about Miss Ashton these days. All the men go to the theatre just to ogle her.'

'Men are simple creatures, are they not, Berg?' Uliana asked Berg.

'I assure you I voted for you, Isabel,' Berg said.

'And who else did?' Isabel asked as if she really had very little interest in this matter but was only being polite.

Berg cast his mind back and started mentioning names.

'You have not mentioned Brecky,' Isabel pointed out after he had finished.

'Brecky voted for Miss Ashton,' Berg told her, as if apologetic to be the one to bring her such bad news but looking at her sideways as if eager to see how she took it.

Isabel slapped the table. 'The lowness of that man! He proposes to me and then does not even vote for me.'

'Izzy, you cast him aside like a dirty hat,' Penelope pointed out. 'He's hardly going to vote for you now.'

'That is not the point,' Isabel said firmly. 'Clearly his proposal did not come from the deepest least wayward impulses of his heart as he claimed. He was a charlatan and a fraud and I trust that no-one now will challenge the correctness of my decision when I told him that he was not a gentleman. A charlatan and a fraud cannot be a gentleman,' Isabel continued, warming to her theme. 'A gentleman will do what is right no matter what his personal feelings may be on the matter. Lord Breckenridge has failed to surmount the wound to his pride and voted against me out of a petty vindictiveness and spite that show the lowness of his character, the meanness of his mind and the shallowness of his morals. There is nothing to be said in his defence.'

'Miss Ashton won by twenty eight votes,' Sophie pointed out. 'If she had been less Brecky's vote, which had gone to you, the margin would still be twenty-six votes.'

'Which are not yet the number of your rejected suitors,' Uliana pointed out in her turn. 'You have been beaten fair and square, Isabel. You may well wish to take your own advice about surmounting the wound to your pride.'

'There is no wound to my pride,' Isabel declared. 'But I must confess a curiosity about this Miss Ashton. I propose that we attend a performance at the Emperor Theatre to see this Miss Ashton on the stage.'

'Oh, she's such a wonderful actress,' Penny enthused. 'They are performing *The Lady in Peril* at the moment. It is an interesting and curious play but everyone goes there just to see Miss Ashton.'

'And so shall we,' Isabel proclaimed. So Isabel made arrangements to take out a box but when the time came only Penny and Sophie could come with her, as the others were all unable to make it on the evening in question, and so it was that Isabel set out on Friday, 20 May 1544 A.F. to attend a performance of *The Lady in Peril* starring Miss Angela Ashton at the Emperor Theatre.

EIGHT

....

A Question is Asked of Mr Taggart Longman by Miss Angela Ashton

11 AM, Monday 9 May 1544 A.F.

The death of a king does not pass unnoticed, and the crowds of thousands upon thousands who had brought New Landern to an unexpected standstill for Jolly's funeral had passed by underneath Angela's flying carriage as she went to the Emperor Theatre to attend rehearsals for *The Kingdom of Happiness*, which was the play that would follow her current play *The Lady in Peril*. The respectable half of New Landern had been baffled by the mass attendance of the other half for the funeral of this previously unknown person, and they had turned to *The New Landern Recorder* the next day to find out what was going on, where they had read that the funeral had been for "Mr Frank Jollison, the noted philanthropist". Angela, who no longer had a sense of humour, had read this description impassively; Nicholas had read this nonsense and rolled his eyes and shook his head, wondering to himself, "How do they invent this stuff?" and had then finally laughed out loud, drawing Ben down on his neck, who wanted to know, "What was so funny?" Nicholas had to dissemble on the spot, although Ben had not looked convinced by his performance.

So Jolly was dead; Angela looked down on the crowds thronging the streets of New Landern and knew this straight away without needing to be told in so many words. Rehearsals that afternoon were cancelled; people stood around in the theatre talking in hushed voices, and Angela was not unaware that certain looks were being directed at her, though no-one would say anything directly. The next day was covered with a veneer of normality, as if everyone Angela met were acting from the memory of being themselves, but the next day people were more themselves, and the day after that Jolly was entirely forgotten and life was back to normal.

Angela had maintained her composure throughout and continued as if nothing had happened, despite the fact that the world was simply not the same as it had been formerly. Jolly had been taken from this world in a moment of inattention on his part concerning the nature of his adversary, and it had given Angela reason to pause for reflection. Something like this was enough to turn a girl into a philosopher! Angela had not gone that far, but she was at least reflecting.

Angela did not the least mourn Jolly, nor was she glad that he was gone; or at least, not yet. She had understood the world with Jolly in it; being without Jolly was to be suddenly faced with uncertainty. Angela had one question, and one question only, in her mind at that moment in time: who was Nicholas Raspero?

2 PM, Thursday 12 May 1544 A.F.

Beneath her veneer of calm Angela was apprehensive. As Jolly's investment, she had been protected; now as a woman who lived alone and who was lusted after by half the men in New Landern she was protected only by a passing comment of a gentleman who did not even have a place in the demi-monde. Much of her apprehension was due to knowing nothing of what was going on; so she sent a note to Tagalong care of the head barman at the Burke Tavern (the said head barman being an unofficial one-man postal office of the demi-monde) telling Tagalong to attend her in Kenina Park at 2 PM the next day. She waited for him there at the appointed time and when he turned up she beckoned him into the carriage and then directed the driver to go up in the air and "do the circuit", this being a circular voyage around New Landern which flying carriages took for a number of reasons, not all of them reasons that could be discussed openly in polite society. The reason which Angela had in mind, namely that of private discussion with a captive conversationalist who could not depart the scene, was however as common a reason as any that could be openly discussed in polite society.

'So what's happening, Tagalong?' Angela asked when they were too high up for Tagalong to jump out of the carriage anymore.

'Well, Jolly's dead, as you must know,' Tagalong said, like a chess player opening with one grudging move of a pawn, 'though you didn't attend his funeral, did you?'

'No-one told me anything about a funeral,' Angela responded.

Tagalong looked at her in surprise. 'You didn't get my letter?' He shook his head. 'Someone slipped up. Well, what's there to say about that?'

'Who killed Jolly?' Angela asked, ignoring Tagalong's lies.

Tagalong threw his hands into the air. 'Well, that's the mystery, isn't it? That's what everyone wants to know. Some people say it was Raspero.' 'It is very brave of you, Tagalong,' Angela said, looking out of the window, 'to refer to Mr Raspero merely as Raspero. I will be sure to tell Nicholas that when we next meet.'

Angela was watching Tagalong in a concealed mirror by her side, and so his shadowy look of shock and fear on hearing what she had said did not escape her attention even though she appeared to be looking elsewhere. 'You have misheard me, Miss Ashton. I most certainly said, "Mr Raspero", you simply did not hear the Mister part of my phrase. I do hope you are not losing your hearing. That would be most regrettable for the leading actress of New Landern.'

'No, Tagalong,' Angela said, 'it is you who misheard me. I did not ask, *will you tell me whatever lie first comes to mind?* I asked you, *who killed Jolly?* Answer me, or I will complain to Nicholas, that is Mr Raspero to you, about your disrespect both to him and to me.'

There was a silence, while Tagalong's eyes shifted about the carriage like a rat in a maze considering which corridor looked least likely to have a snake in it. 'Well, all right, Miss Ashton, well, as it happened, well, Pay, Kassie, Pastime and No Tin all threw their discs into Jolly's throat at the same time. Now you know.'

'Did Jolly fight back?'

'No, not exactly, no, he didn't exactly fight back as it happened. He was sort of tied up in a chair at the time so fighting back was not, as one might say, an active option.'

'Was he still gagged?'

Tagalong looked at her warily. He had not said anything about a gag. 'Yes, very slightly gagged, very slightly, in the sense of being gagged I would have to say yes, he was in a manner of speaking actively restrained in his speaking facilities.'

'So who got all that money?'

Tagalong looked warier than ever. 'What money are we talking about, Miss Ashton?'

'The twenty million strada that came out of Jolly's safe.'

'Ah, that money!' Tagalong said with a vigorous nod of his head, as if he had been thinking Angela must have meant some other sum of money, 'Yes, well, that has been apportioned according to merit, station, degree, character, opprobrium, and, one might even add,' Tagalong added with a slightly hysterical laugh, 'the camaraderie of the momentary instability of the once dispossessed upon whose fortunes all has changed.'

'Who got what, Tagalong?'

Tagalong sighed. 'Pay, Kassie, Pastime and No Tin got twenty percent each —'

'That's four million.'

'Indeed,' Tagalong looked at Angela as if impressed by the swift deployment of her numerical abilities, 'I must say —'

'And the remaining twenty percent?'

'Your humble self,' Tagalong said with a slight bow, 'got ten per cent, and the remaining ten per cent went to the remaining warriors of the demi-monde present in the room at the time, but their rewards did not end there, for in return for supporting the successors of Jolly they have gained increased prestige, power, authority and the share of the good life.'

'So who's running the show now?'

Tagalong sighed again. 'This is a matter fraught with implication, innuendo, rivalry, dissent, duplicity, and even a certain —'

'So they're all at each other's throats, is that it?'

'In a nutshell, Miss Ashton, such a characterisation does not entirely fail to serve as a temporary fleeting ephemeral description of the current circumstances, but I would not place too much reliance on such a primarily visual —'

'That's your nutshell? And where's a squirrel going to hide that?'

Tagalong paused, as if wondering if this was a joke that he should laugh at, then said, 'They are not yet all at war with each other, Miss Ashton, if this is what you are asking about.'

'I want the ownership papers of 3/67 Cranston Avenue made over to me,' Angela said abruptly. 'I don't care who does it, or how it's done, just so long as it's legal and above board. Jolly owned that apartment, so as far as I'm concerned, it's mine now.'

'Well, naturally,' Tagalong said, 'I am sure that an appropriate —'

'I got nothing of that twenty million!' Angela screeched. 'Nothing! You make that apartment over to me or I will go to Mr Nicholas Raspero and complain of my treatment at your hands. I will say that you, Tagalong, compromised my virtue in no uncertain manner, and that Pay, Kassie, Pastime and No Tin have all done likewise, and I will seek justice for my mistreatment at your hands, my grave mistreatment which no lady of honour should countenance. I got nothing of that twenty million, *nothing*, but I will get the apartment I live in. It's mine, you hear me? There is one question you want to ask yourself, Mr Tagalong Longman: are you going to give me what I want, or are you going to find Mr Nicholas Raspero walking towards you down the street tomorrow? Because otherwise, Mr Tagalong Longman, you can save yourself time and trouble and just jump out of this flying carriage now!'

'Let us not be hasty!' Tagalong said placatingly, looking as if he had too many thoughts assaulting his mind all at once to know which way to turn, 'Naturally, I —'

'Naturally, you say, "yes", right now! Let's hear you, Tagalong! Yes, Miss Ashton, the apartment is yours.'

Tagalong sighed. 'As it happens, the apartment in which you currently reside, which has the market value of two hundred and thirty thousand strada, is part of the property valuations which comprise part of the aforementioned twenty million strada and as such —'

'Yes, Miss Ashton, the apartment is yours! Or else!'

Tagalong sighed again. 'Yes, Miss Ashton, the apartment is yours. I will see to it myself.'

'Yes, you will,' Angela said fiercely, 'or else I will complain to Nicholas — Mr Raspero to you — about my treatment, and believe me, the content and manner of my complaint will bring about results that you will find deeply misfortunate. You see, Tagalong, you and the others have a lot to lose now, don't you? You've gone from being Jolly's slaves to running the empire yourself. You're a lot higher now, but that just means that you have a lot further to fall, doesn't it? Take a look out of the window at the ground below if you don't understand me. That's a long way to fall, isn't it? Now Nicholas might not actually kill you if I complain about my mistreatment at your hands, but he might remove a certain portion of your anatomy as a punishment that fits the crime, so to speak, if I make a certain kind of complaint about you and the same goes for Pay, Kassie, Pastime and No Tin, and you can tell them so. Do you understand me?'

Tagalong winced and shifted about in his seat. He clearly understood her all too well. 'I assure you —'

'Your assurances mean nothing, Tagalong, they are as worthless as you are. You have three days, until two o'clock on Sunday, to deliver the ownership papers to 3 of 67 Cranston Avenue made over to me. If I have not received those papers by then, I will go to Nicholas in a flood of tears over my mistreatment at your hands. Is that clear?'

Tagalong nodded. 'That is very clear, Miss Ashton. It will be done as you insist.' Angela's repeated references to Mr Nicholas Raspero by his first name had not escaped his attention, nor had he failed to draw the logical inference to be made from her apparent assurance of his intimate acquaintance.

There was a silence for a while as they flew along, with Angela looking out of the window and Tagalong looking at the drinks cabinet. Angela gave in after a while. 'Help yourself, Tagalong,' she said with a gesture to the drinks cabinet.

Tagalong didn't need telling twice. He poured a stiff whiskey, downed it in one, then poured himself an even larger second glass and sat back to enjoy the ride. Angela was an experienced enough courtesan to wait for when the alcohol had dissolved tension before asking the question that was foremost on her mind, the question that troubled her night and day. When Tagalong leaned back in his chair and stretched his feet forward with a gentle sigh, Angela asked, 'Why do you think, Tagalong, that Nicholas — Mr Raspero — didn't take any of Jolly's money?'

'What did *he* say to you about it?' Tagalong prevaricated.

Angela sighed. 'What do *you* think about it, Tagalong?'

Tagalong shrugged. 'How would I know? Mr Raspero is not like you or me, Miss Ashton. I have no idea. Some kind of principle, probably.'

Angela considered this in silence for a while. Tagalong poured himself a third whiskey, his movements as he poured the golden liquid as careful as if he were slightly inebriated.

'Principle,' Angela said scornfully, 'what's the good of that, Tagalong?'

'It's as good as it can be,' Tagalong said with a smile, leaning back in his chair and ready now to be witty. 'And there you have it, if you ever do.' He laughed and sipped more of his third whiskey.

Angela considered him for a moment. She had never understood Tagalong. 'So what's your story, Tagalong? You were a gentleman once, right? You were a man of principle, weren't you?'

Tagalong shrugged, but he was drunk enough by now to say more than he would have normally. 'Yes, I was once a gentleman, and I once nearly lost everything and I had only ten thousand strada so I went to the gaming house of The One Wheel. I lost all that and I got a line of credit and then I lost that. I was fifty thousand strada down, Miss Ashton, and I had really lost everything. So I made a deal with the devil, Miss Ashton, his name was Jolly, and I saved what I could. And there you have it.'

'What did you save?' Angela asked softly, knowing from pillow talk exactly how to extract this confession.

'My sister and my nieces, her two daughters, who to this day live their lives in modest gentility free from the clutches of such as Jolly, or his successors thereof. Yes, and when my nieces grow up, let them live decent lives as best they can. It is a cliché, is it not: the bad man, to wit me, who has sacrificed himself so that others may live free, but there you are, so be it, laugh all you will, this is the truth.'

'Jolly would not have done what you have done,' Angela observed.

'No.' Tagalong sipped his whiskey and said no more.

'Jolly was a man of principle, Tagalong. His principle was that he was the king and no-one crossed him, not even over a single strada.'

'Someone crossed him,' Tagalong laughed, and drained his whiskey glass and set it down as if determined not to have another. 'But I'll tell you something even more unbelievable than Raspero, yes, Raspero-Raspero-Raspero, complain all you like, turning his back on that money, because this is unbelievable, or more unbelievable, if what is unbelievable can ever be more than it already is, Raspero took Jolly's notebooks, with all the juicy details in them, not just about Foxley and your other paramours, but many other equally important New Landern grandees, yes indeed, Raspero took these notebooks and burned them in the fire before my utterly disbelieving eyes. You want to talk about principle? What kind of principle is that? How totally mad is someone who does that?'

'I didn't know that,' Angela admitted, smiling at Tagalong's outrage.

'I wish I didn't know it,' Tagalong complained, interlinking his fingers as if to keep them away from the whiskey bottle, and closing his eyes as if to hide from his memories, 'but can knowledge be unknown? I saw it myself with my own eyes and I cannot now unremember it. I wish I could.'

The driver signalled that they had completed the circuit so Angela instructed him to set them down in Kenina Park. She let Tagalong go with a reminder about the apartment ownership papers being delivered to her (or else!), then set off for the Emperor Theatre for the afternoon's rehearsals. She had a lot to think about, but she was no nearer to the answer she sought, which was how to manage her life in a post-Jolly world.

It was well after two o'clock in the morning when she managed to extricate herself from a sleeping Lord Foxley's embrace and make her way back to her own apartment. There she took up the piece of paper with Nicholas's name and address on it, and contemplated it for the fortieth time. It was then that she came to a decision.

She simply had to speak to Nicholas in person. That was clear enough. So she took up pen and paper and wrote to Nicholas. She invited him to attend a performance of *The Lady in Peril*, and then to visit her afterwards in her dressing room. She asked him to let her know by return of post if he could be so kind as to honour her invitation by an acceptance which could only ensure her happiness.

While waiting for his reply, Angela made arrangements to provide Nicholas with a free ticket for a performance of *The Lady in Peril* for the last night of the season, the most eagerly sought after performance, because she thought that he deserved no less. She wanted a box seat, she wanted a front row seat, she wanted a stall seat, but in the end she could only get Nicholas a seat in "the gods", the cheapest and highest seats at the very tippety top of the theatre, and when Nicholas wrote back to say how delighted he would be to come, she sent him the ticket she had obtained, with a reminder that he was to visit her afterwards in her dressing room, and so it was done.

The paths through time and space of the lives of Nicholas and Isabel, twisting and turning their separate ways through the New Landern continuum, were now lined up and moving along to a second point of intersection: Friday 20 May 1544 A.F. at the Emperor Theatre in New Landern.

NINE

....

The Visit of Lady Isabel Grangeshield to the Emperor Theatre

7:15 PM, Friday 20 May 1544 A.F.

Nicholas stepped into the theatre and stood to one side for a while looking around as people poured past him. He had never been in a theatre before. He was struck first of all by the luxury of red: the curtains were red, the seats were red, the carpeting was red, and the walls and ceiling were ornately painted a mixture of glittering white and red. He stood to one side taking it all in, and then Isabel leaped into his view.

She was sitting in one of the box seats, talking to a companion next to her. At the sight of her Nicholas felt unaccountably nervous, so he ended his inspection of the theatre and began to look for his seat. He was in "the gods", which Ben had told him was right at the very top. They were the poorest seats in the theatre, Ben had told him further, envious that he had not himself got a free ticket, and they were not for people who suffered from vertigo. Nicholas made his way up the stairs, a deferential space around him as he moved amongst the denizens of "the gods", the only theatre-goers poor enough to know who he was, and found his seat and sat down.

He attracted a fair amount of open-mouthed attention from his fellow patrons, which he ignored with a lofty disdain. The story of how he had taken down Jolly had oscillated through New Landern in its rotating voyage changing form as it went along until the form in which it was now most commonly told was as follows: Jolly had abducted Miss Ashton, the most beautiful woman in New Landern and held her prisoner in his stronghold, intending to have his evil way with her. Nicholas Raspero had stormed this stronghold single-handed, taking down hundreds of Jolly's men without killing a single one of them, capturing them as easily as if they had been children; he had freed Angela and taken Jolly prisoner. Jolly had a room full of treasure, with jewellery and strada coins and bank notes piled up to the ceiling, an Aladdin's cave of treasure beyond counting, treasure beyond imagining. Nicholas had tied Jolly up and thrown him into this treasure room, leaving Jolly there and carrying Angela away with him in his arms; all the demi-monde knew that the four successors of Jolly had thrown their discs into his neck at the same time and taken his treasure for themselves.

Nicholas had not replaced Jolly as king of the New Landern demi-monde but he had in a sense become its patron saint. Despite being poor he had turned his back on a fortune and no-one could understand this; it was as inexplicable as the action of a deity. It was fear of Nicholas the wandfighter that led the most violent and dangerous criminals in New Landern to step courteously out of his way as he came walking along but it was something like the honour due to a saint that meant that Nicholas was no longer charged for anything by the poor of New Landern. If he got a drink the barmaid refused to take his money with a disapproving shake of the head; if he bought freshly-baked fish with fire-baked potatoes, drizzled in lemon juice and seasoned with salt and pepper, the street vendor of his meal would wave away the strada Nicholas offered in payment with a furious gesture of his hands as if Nicholas had deeply insulted him by offering to pay for his meal.

Nicholas obviously couldn't know this but some of the streets of New Landern he wandered along would in the decades to come have pubs named "Sir Nicholas" in his honour, their most common sign being that of a man tied up next to a pile of money. The story of what he had done to Jolly would continue to be told and, in time, it would perhaps even become a fairytale.

The play Nicholas was watching tonight had once been a fairytale. A woman had been obliged to remain silent for seven years in order to lift a curse on her twelve brothers who had all been turned into ravens, and so even when falsely accused she had maintained silence despite the imminent danger to her life; the audience, as was common in those days, did not take any of this lying down— they shouted out to her to beware the villain, there was at times a deafening bedlam of conflicting and advisory comments being hurled at the stage when it was clear that innocence was being taken advantage of by evil doers— and everyone cheered with delight when the ravens turned back into her brothers and they all lived happily ever after.

Nicholas enjoyed the performance but above all else he was struck by the presence of Angela on stage: her radiant beauty, her imperiled innocence and the occasional evocative costume combined to form a lasting impression on his youthful senses. He was, in short, star-struck. He even felt a little nervous as he made his way backstage to see her as if he were walking a narrow bridge above an abyss. He was guided to Angela's dressing room by a wide-eyed boy who was himself star-struck to be in the company of the nemesis of Jolly, and then Nicholas found himself knocking on Angela's dressing-room door. He entered on hearing Angela call out.

She was sitting in front of a mirror, wiping at her face with a cloth in her hands.

'Mr Raspero!' she said with pleasure, 'how wonderful to see you again.'

'I hear that all the time, but I never tire of it,' Nicholas said with a smile, closing the door behind him. 'You were magnificent, Miss Ashton. Congratulations on your performance!'

Angela looked as if no-one had ever paid her such a compliment before. 'It is so very kind of you to say so, Mr Raspero. I cannot say how much your words of commendation mean to me.'

'You were amazing, Miss Ashton,' Nicholas continued in the same vein. 'I was thrilled, moved, excited and dazzled by your performance.'

'You are much too kind,' Angela protested, still looking as if no-one had ever paid her so much praise. 'I will blush if you continue with such unmerited endorsements of my poor performance, Mr Raspero. I must beg you to stop before I am too much reminded of my own unworthiness to receive such accolades.'

'All right,' Nicholas agreed as if reluctantly, 'but only if I can sit down.'

'Oh, Mr Raspero!' Angela burst out. 'Where are my manners? Please, sit down.' She gestured to the side, where there was a bench fastened to the wall covered in red velvet cushions. Nicholas closed the door and sat down.

'And how have you been, Mr Raspero?'

'Chugging along, thanks. And yourself, Miss Ashton?'

'Everything is going well for me, Mr Raspero. In no small measure due to you.'

'Your success on and off stage is due to your own ability, Miss Ashton.'

Angela said nothing, resuming wiping at her face with the cloth in her hands. Nicholas looked steadily at her in the mirror stealing glances at him. At that moment there came a knock on the door.

'Come in,' Angela called.

The door opened, shielding Nicholas from the view of the person standing in the doorway.

'Ange,' a man's voice said, 'there're some people here who want to see you.' Nicholas thought the voice sounded like Mr Ansel Horado, the actor who had played Bernard the Yeoman in the play. 'Lady Grangeshield, Miss Nicholson, Miss Earlson, may I present Miss Angela Ashton. Miss Ashton, may I present Lady Isabel Grangeshield, Miss Sophie Nicholson, and Miss Penelope Earlson.'

Isabel entered the dressing room sideways, facing Angela all the while, not realising that anyone was sitting behind her. Nicholas could see her bare shoulders above the strapless low-cut dress she was wearing. He heard Isabel say, 'How very interesting to meet you, Miss Ashton.' Her voice was pitched high, but with a musical sound to it that gave it depth.

Isabel was standing so close to Nicholas that he could have reached out and pushed her in the small of the back. Her wide skirts were brushing his knees. Nicholas straightened his back as straight as straight could be in order to pull himself back as far as possible into the wall. Her presence was overwhelming. He could smell her perfume, he could see every curl in her carefully coiled hair, her right arm hung by her side holding her fan pointing downward; he could see the curves of her biceps and forearm. Nicholas tried to relax so that he could breathe more easily.

'It is very kind of you to say so, Lady Grangeshield,' Nicholas heard Angela reply. He noticed that her voice sounded different, and then he realised that she had pitched it to sound like Isabel's.

'Your performance was astounding,' he heard another woman's voice say from near the door. 'I cried when that cruel man left you all alone in the forest. I cried, I assure you.'

'You are much too kind, Miss Earlson,' Angela said. 'I am overwhelmed by such praise.' Nicholas noticed that she was still using Isabel's voice.

Isabel moved her arm behind her back, waving her fan about restlessly. Nicholas moved his head aside to avoid being poked in the nose. Her hand was so close he could see her fingertips pressing lightly into her palms forming slightly whitened indentations.

'I have never seen the role of Ursula so well performed,' another woman's voice said. 'I could not but believe that all this was really happening. I was on the edge of my seat when you were at the mercy of that terrible man.'

'But then Denver came and saved you!' Penny said. 'Hurrah!'

'Thank you, Miss Nicholson. You are all so very kind,' Angela said, modulating her voice now so that it was slightly deeper than Isabel's. 'I cannot thank you enough for saying such laudatory remarks about my performance. It is only such praise as yours that gives me the courage to step out onto the stage.'

Nicholas was fascinated by how Isabel's bare neck rose above her bare shoulders, her pale skin gleaming in the lamplight of the dressing room, her dark brown hair coiled around her head in a spiral pattern held in place by white and green gemstone hairpins. He was breathing as silently as he could through a wide open mouth, his head turned sideways to avoid breathing onto Isabel's hand.

'We have resisted the insistence of all your admirers that we come and witness your performance for ourselves, and how much we have lost in not coming to see you before now!' Isabel said.

'But you are here now, and surely that is what counts, Lady Grangeshield.'

'And we shall surely be here again, Miss Ashton,' Isabel continued. 'What will your next play be?'

'*The Kingdom of Happiness*, Lady Grangeshield, I believe.'

'Ooh,' Penny squeaked, 'that is my very favourite play of all!'

'That is such a wonderful play,' Sophie said. 'Isn't it, Izzy?'

'I have never seen it,' Isabel said. 'But I am indeed fortunate to have something to look forward to in the future.'

'How can you never have seen *The Kingdom of Happiness*, Izzy?' Penny burst out in astonishment.

'Circumstances,' Isabel said briefly as if all the complexities of her explanation would be irrelevant. 'And when does *The Kingdom of Happiness* open, Miss Ashton?'

'The fifth of August, Lady Grangeshield,' Miss Ashton said.

'I am pleased to hear that it is to happen so soon,' Isabel declared. 'I do not have long to wait.'

'And I so much look forward to seeing you if you are so kind as to visit me again. It was so wonderful for you to have visited me tonight,' Miss Ashton said.

Nicholas was reminded of how Lady Starfeld had brushed him off, but her visitors simply ignored Angela's hint that they leave now. 'But how did you come to take to the stage, Miss Ashton?' Sophie asked.

'I was a lady's companion after the death of my mother, Miss Nicholson, and Mr Ansel Horado was so kind as to allow me to enter the Kerrick Company some five years ago.'

'That is so brave!' Penny exclaimed. 'How very brave of you, Miss Ashton!'

'No, Miss Earlson, I have never had any reason to fear. Everyone has been so kind to me. Surely to be brave means to have a reason to fear. But you know this, of course. I am taking up so much of your time only to tell you what you already know.'

Another hint for them to leave, Nicholas noticed, but Angela's visitors appeared to completely miss it.

'But your greatest triumphs are surely off the stage, Miss Ashton,' Isabel suggested in a neutral tone. She took her fan out of Nicholas's sight, and from her posture he guessed that she was holding it in both hands as a schoolteacher holds a cane. He noticed that her back had straightened. It was as if she were preparing for battle.

'It is kind of you to see me as having triumphs, Lady Grangeshield,' Angela said with unruffled calm.

'You are so thin, Miss Ashton,' Isabel continued with friendly concern. 'Do you manage to eat enough?'

'I eat wonderfully well, thank you, Lady Grangeshield.'

'If you do ever need to eat, Miss Ashton, I will instruct my servants to prepare you some food. They will make a spacious place available for you in the servants' quarters where you may eat in comfort. You have only to ask, Miss Ashton, and I will see that it is done.'

'There is no need to take so much trouble, Lady Grangeshield. But I can only thank you for expressing such a warm and generous impulse.'

'But you are so thin,' Isabel persisted. 'And you hardly have breasts. You are flat-chested, Miss Ashton. I am sure that it must be the result of poor nutrition.'

'Your concern for my welfare moves me deeply, Lady Grangeshield. But I assure you that I eat very well, and your concern is misplaced.'

Nicholas couldn't tell even the least irritation in Angela's voice. It was as if she simply hadn't noticed Isabel's deliberate provocations.

'Do you have a medical condition, Miss Ashton?' Isabel asked in a tone of the sweetest sympathy. 'Your face is that of a skeleton. The bones all show! I know the best doctors in town. I will foot the bill for your medical expenses, I assure you. You have only to ask for my assistance.'

'I am in perfect health, thank you, Lady Grangeshield.' From the sound of Angela's voice, there seemed to be not the slightest crack in her composure. 'But it is so kind of you to be so concerned about me.'

'I hope you are not too proud to seek help, Miss Ashton,' Isabel said, her concern appearing to have grown. 'Please do not feel so ashamed by your notoriety that you dare not seek assistance.'

'I never hesitate to seek assistance, Lady Grangeshield, I assure you. But I need none.'

'But the lifestyle you lead, Miss Ashton, is surely not conducive to good health. Good health is dependent on a sound mind and body and where does that leave you? Why do you refuse my help, Miss Ashton? I do not understand. I reach out my hand to you and you only bite it.'

'I cannot tell you how welcome your kind intentions are, Lady Grangeshield, but surely you must understand that your concerns are entirely misplaced.'

'But you are as skinny as a rake, Miss Ashton. You obviously do not eat properly, you do not have proper medical attention, and yet you say that my concerns are misplaced! Surely you will surmount your pride and seek my help before it is too late! Or do you insist on throwing my concern for your welfare back in my face as you have done until now?'

'Your concern for my welfare is such a blessing as I have never before received, Lady Grangeshield. But the hour grows late, and surely I am keeping you from the rest of your evening?'

'Not at all,' Isabel said reassuringly, 'you are not keeping me from anything at all but the opportunity to help you! You have refused my offer of nutrition, you have refused my offer of medical assistance; well, all that is left for me to offer you, Miss Ashton, is moral guidance. But perhaps you will refuse that as well?'

'I can only thank you for your kind offers of assistance in all these matters, but the hour grows late and we all must be moving on. I can only thank you for having visited me tonight.'

'Your gratitude is surely feigned, Miss Ashton.'

'The time has come, Lady Grangeshield, for me to bid farewell to you and your companions, but I would like to say that I would be only too happy to see you again.'

'But how can you be happy to see us again when you are so unhappy to see us now?'

'Lady Grangeshield, it is not my fault that the Club of Appreciation voted as they have. You must take up the choice they have made with them, not with me. In the meantime, I must bid you farewell.'

'I do not understand you,' Isabel said coldly, though judging from the shifty slightly-shivering barely-perceptible alteration of her posture, Nicholas guessed that she did, in fact, understand Angela all too well, 'but this is beside the point. You are unhealthy, Miss Ashton, in both a physical and a moral sense. The whole of New Landern knows that you are a whore, Miss Ashton, and it is well known that whores lead dissolute and unhealthy lives. Do you really refuse my moral guidance?'

'I never refuse guidance, Lady Grangeshield, but surely guidance must be sought, not imposed.'

'Yes, you will quote Keane to me, Miss Ashton, but without understanding. You are a monkey, are you not, Miss Ashton, a monkey which chatters in imitation of what it imitates? But what do you say yourself from your own understanding, or perhaps you have none?'

'What I say myself, Lady Grangeshield, is that you must address your grievance to the Club of Appreciation. Surely I do not quote someone else when I say this?'

Nicholas could see the muscles flexing in Isabel's back on hearing this. He guessed that Isabel was being fought to a draw, though he could not follow exactly how the blows were being given and received in the battle he was witnessing. What was the Club of Appreciation, anyway?

'You are a whore, Miss Ashton. A whore! Surely that has nothing to do with the Club of Appreciation, unless you slept with all those who voted for you!'

'I did no such thing, Lady Grangeshield. You must take up the reason for their vote with those who voted. But that has nothing to do with me!'

'I see you do not deny that you are a whore, Miss Ashton. Men buy your body for money, do they not? Is your soul also for sale, Miss Ashton? Or have you already sold it?'

'I must ask you to leave my dressing room, Lady Grangeshield.'

'But surely I have not offended you, Miss Ashton?'

'I have other business to attend to, Lady Grangeshield, and if you will excuse me, I must be moving on.'

'Other business? Would this other business be Lord Foxley, by any chance? The whole of New Landern knows that you are his whore, as you were the whore of Hudson before him, and Nieves before him, and Zavanna before him. Yes, I am sure that Lord Foxley is eagerly awaiting you in order to receive the services you will provide for him in those conditions of privacy and secrecy which I am given to understand are associated with such transactions.'

'Lady Grangeshield, I must ask you once again to leave my dressing room. It is only common courtesy on your part to respect my wishes in this matter.'

'Common courtesy? How dare you presume to lecture me about courtesy? You, a whore who has climbed out of the gutter, presume to lecture me about courtesy? How dare you! You know nothing of such matters as courtesy, Miss Ashton. You are merely an ape who mimics the behaviour that you witness.'

'Whatever my understanding of courtesy, Lady Grangeshield, you are in my dressing room and I am asking you to leave.'

'This is not your dressing room, Miss Ashton. It is the dressing room of the Emperor Theatre, and I assure you, if I spoke to the owners of this establishment, they would see to it that you never set foot in this dressing room again.'

'Then you must speak to them, Lady Grangeshield, for I continue to insist that you leave my dressing room. I grow tired of asking you to leave.'

'Yes, you must not grow tired, Miss Ashton. You must conserve your energies for the attentions of Lord Foxley later tonight. Your work for the day is not yet done, is it, Miss Ashton? You have your work as a whore ahead of you still!' With that Isabel left. Her companions must have gone with her without a word of farewell, for Angela stood up and closed the door after them. She returned to her seat before the mirror and resumed inspecting her face, cloth in hand to remove the remainder of her stage make-up. Nicholas could not see that she was the least bit rattled.

'Are you all right, Miss Ashton?' Nicholas asked her.

'Yes, thank you, Mr Raspero, I am perfectly all right.' Angela sounded as if nothing had happened at all.

'Lady Grangeshield gave you a hard time,' Nicholas said cautiously, not knowing whether to say anything or not.

'Did she? I did not notice.'

'She called you a whore several times. Did you not notice that?'

Angela said nothing in reply. She was tidying up the surface of her dressing room table, neatly stacking everything away. Nicholas could tell she was the tidy sort of person who likes to have everything in its right place.

'Will you excuse me while I change, Mr Raspero?'

Nicholas stood up. 'I'll wait outside.'

'Oh no, Mr Raspero, it is perfectly all right. Please stay where you are. I have a screen to change behind.'

Angela stepped to the other side of the dressing room and pulled a screen across the room, leaving large gaps between the screen and the walls. Nicholas sat down uncertainly, not sure whether or not he should step outside anyway. He could hear Angela moving about behind the screen and the rustle of clothes falling to the floor. He tried not to think about what was happening behind the screen, but it was next to impossible for his mind not to wander. He tried to sit perfectly still as if that would help; it helped, but only a little bit.

Angela took her time changing behind the screen, in no rush to be done with her performance. This was the first step she always took when Jolly had selected a client for her. Not one of them had waited on the other side of the screen; they had all put their heads around and playfully manouevred themselves to her side of the screen. After playing the shocked lady who had no idea what to do while they ogled her, she would firmly recover her composure and keep them at bay by being very strict about driving them away, but the tantalised men dug deep into their pockets to come up with gifts to win her favours, and after playing them along for a while and milking them for all she could, she would allow them to obtain the outcome they sought. After that, it was just a matter of staying ahead of them and breaking off relations with them just before they were about to leave her — that always brought them around with a fresh shower of gifts, and she would allow herself to be enticed back into their arms where she would remain, at least until the whole process was repeated or Jolly told her to change clients.

Angela knew she could not expect gifts from Nicholas. Yet, to keep him as her protector would be worth the occasional extra work. It would in a sense be a gift, even if it was not one she could cash in. The successors of Jolly, who had not dared touch her while Jolly was alive because she was his investment, had nonetheless leered at her and made suggestive remarks, as Jolly was indifferent to this kind of treatment of her; now they did not even look her way except politely. They had too much to lose to make an enemy of Nicholas. She wanted to keep Nicholas as her protector, and her seduction of him was beginning now in order to guarantee that protection. Yet, she finished dressing without Nicholas trying to make his way to her side of the screen. She pulled the screen back to see Nicholas still sitting where he had been.

Angela turned her attention to the strategy of jealousy. 'I must leave soon, Mr Raspero. Lord Foxley is waiting for me.'

'Lucky Lord Foxley.'

'I believe he has a gift for me tonight, Mr Raspero.'

'It can't be a surprise gift, then.'

'It is a hairbrush.'

'Don't you have a hairbrush?' Nicholas asked in surprise.

'This hairbrush has a silver backing with an inset ruby. A very large ruby.'

'Does it indeed? Well, that's nice.'

'And why shouldn't I, Mr Raspero?' Angela asked him calmly. 'Tell me that. Why not?'

'You make your own choices now, Miss Ashton. You are no longer Jolly's spy.'

'Tagalong told me you burned those notebooks.'

'I believe that the sight distressed him greatly.'

Angela giggled as if she had not intended to. 'You should have seen his face!'

'I have had this experience. It is not one I care to repeat.'

'Tagalong's all right. The others are worse.'

'They are all rogues, Miss Ashton.'

'And what are you, Mr Raspero?'

'Whatever I am, I am not a rogue.'

'That is what you are not. What is it that you are?'

Nicholas shrugged. 'I am a gentleman with no money.'

'Why did you not take any of Jolly's money, Mr Raspero?'

'Because I am not like the men who did take his money, Miss Ashton.'

Angela considered this answer for a moment.

'Everybody needs money, Mr Raspero.'

'That's true,' Nicholas agreed.

'But you have no money, Mr Raspero.'

'That's true.'

'Do you not want any money, Mr Raspero?'

'I would be very happy to be rich, Miss Ashton.'

'You could have twenty million strada in your pocket right now, Mr Raspero.'

'No, Miss Ashton, that twenty million strada would have me in its pocket.'

'I do not understand you, Mr Raspero.'

'Do you want to?'

Angela made no reply. She sat on her seat by the mirror, which she had turned around so she could sit on it facing him, and played with her fan. Nicholas sat where he was and watched her in the ever-lengthening silence.

'You have done so much for me, Mr Raspero. How can I ever repay you?'

Nicholas considered the question for a moment. 'Free theatre tickets to your plays should cover everything, I think,' he said.

'But is that all, Mr Raspero? I could not deny you anything you asked for. Anything at all.'

Angela looked so meaningfully at Nicholas then that he looked away. He was aware that she was continuing to look at him, and he was also aware of the nature of the offer she had just made.

'I will let you know if anything comes to mind, Miss Ashton,' he said eventually.

Angela laughed then, catching herself by surprise. It was the second spontaneous moment of laughter she had experienced since Nicholas had sat down in her dressing room, and she wondered if Nicholas was having a bad influence on her. She was quite deliberately never spontaneous, yet here she was, laughing without a moment's planning beforehand, laughing before she even knew herself that she was going to laugh. She knew why she had laughed, however. Nicholas was not saying yes and he was not saying no; he was, in short, treating her as she treated her clients in the early stages of her seduction of them. Now she had to behave as a client would behave and it took her a moment to work out the correct response on her part.

'I will still be here if anything does come to mind, Mr Raspero,' she said.

'Yes, well, there we are,' Nicholas said awkwardly, not knowing what else to say, and for the third time that evening Angela Ashton laughed, and this time she threw her head back and laughed merrily for the first time in eleven years.

TEN

....

The Instruction of the Withheld Herakrim
by Lord Adair Zinia

7:00 PM, Saturday 21 May 1544 A.F.

'Always our thoughts return to the Fall and how it can be prevented from happening again,' Lord Adair Zinia proclaimed to the Withheld Herakrim gathered to attend to his words. 'Our ancestors in spirit observed the Fall and kept their heads as only they knew how. And so here we are today in our double world, in which the true knowledge of the past is known only to us while the outer world lives by the images which we supply to them. As the saying goes, we are not born for ourselves alone.'

The men and women assembled together in that room to hear him speak listened attentively to every word he said, only too well aware of the privilege granted them to be present here today. The man speaking to them was a great power in the land and one day his successor would come from the audience seated before him now.

The Herakrim technically no longer existed and so those who followed that now legendary path of ancient times called themselves in secret the Withheld Herakrim. They were of a lineage which had preserved the knowledge of the past which all others had forgotten, and thus was the basis of their power.

'How do we prevent the Fall from happening again?' Zinia asked. 'Do we say that what is natural must be reinforced? But what is natural?'

Lord Zinia was a short, portly man with a short, greying beard, a round, cheerful face and bright green button-like eyes. He seemed somehow ineffectual to the casual eye as if incapable of getting things done, which perhaps came from his habit of speaking at times in an elliptical way; yet this was a masterly act of misdirection, for as everyone present understood, Zinia was as well-informed as he was utterly ruthless.

'Is it natural to be free? What is freedom? Is it the right of an individual to pursue their own good? Or is it the moment of feeling connected to a larger whole? It is said that freedom led to the Fall because it was the freedom to do whatever one wants that led to the Fall. But the freedom to do whatever one wants is not freedom. It is only the freedom to do what you want to do and what you want to do is not chosen by you because what you want to do is who you are by birth. People are never less free than when they are free to do whatever they want. The only escape from this condition is to be in the world but not of it and that is not freedom but death; to be of the world is to want what the world wants you to want and so to be alive means to be unfree. So there must be additional restraints such as the exercise of power and that is where we come in.'

Aranrhod House, the ancestral home of the Zinias, was exactly forty-nine stebas in length from the circumference of the exact centre of New Landern, which was a circle exactly one stebas in diameter. Aranrhod House had been planned and built by the Herakrim as one of the first buildings in New Landern when New Landern had been selected and designed after the Fall. It was here in Aranrhod House where the meetings of the Withheld Herakrim took place. Lord Zinia was speaking in the Room of Remembrance, which was a large circular room with stained glass windows running around the top level and curved oak-wood bookcases lined up around the walls below these stained glass windows. In the centre of the room was an auditorium in the shape of a semi-circle, and here it was that Lord Zinia stood to give his talks while his disciples sat before him on their curved wooden benches.

'We must govern the people in the same way that a doctor acts for the benefit of the patient. This means, among other things, that the people must receive what they need, not what they want. As the people do not know what they need this must be decided for them by those who rule them, and these rulers must be ruled by us. We must always rule by proxy but that is a talk for another day.' Zinia shuffled papers about him on his lectern as if he had lost his place in the talk he was giving, then he resumed.

'We must maintain social stability by the exercise of power but what is power? We think of the exercise of power as a boulder lifted and thrown through the air, but men and women are directed by the thoughts they have and those thoughts are the words in their minds, and in that control of men and women is power. The boulder is lifted and thrown through the air by people who have told themselves to do this and they have told themselves in words. Power is the web of the word, an immaterial web weaker than a spider's cobweb yet stronger than the strongest steel.' Zinia paused here as if to let this sink in, looking about him at the others present, blinking a little absently as if he was losing track of what he was saying, but it was all an act.

'But how do we control words? How do we seize a ghost with our bare hands? Only by beliefs. If you determine what people believe, you can leave it to them to do what you want them to do in a way which seems to them to be free for it seems to be freely chosen. But we do this only to avoid another Fall. Let us remind ourselves: people are never less free than when they are free to do whatever they want. What they want has already been decided by the nature of their appetites and they are as unfree not to seek this as they are as unfree not to walk the path of another Fall. So we must have restraints such as honour — with honour and shame as two sides of the same coin — only through honour can we be aligned to the vertical, for honour is that vertical. People must believe, they must see, they must feel, the vital importance of the sense of honour in their lives. A sense of honour must be like a sense of balance, an empirical condition without which walking upright is impossible or at least extremely unlikely, and this is one of those restraints by which we avoid another Fall.' Zinia paused here to sip from a glass of water by his side then continued.

'There are some who speak of a double Fall as in the Fall that happened before the Fall when the seeds of the later Fall were planted. However, the double Fall is one — when beliefs fall the restraints they have imposed are taken away and from that moment on it is only a matter of time before society falls. The time in between these is merely the time spent in actually falling and what is called the Fall is, in fact, the Impact, and so we have our double world.'

High in the sky far above Lord Zinia and the other citizens of New Landern, fifty or so million tons of water were forming one by one into millions upon millions of water droplets that fell fiercely towards the earth far below, hammering through the air like humming miniature musket-balls on their one-way mission towards cheerful self-destruction. That is the way of rain, to live and die without a thought from beginning to end. The rainfall measured itself out into a myriad separate droplets that smashed into sheets of water that cascaded off the red and black tiled rooftops and ran in dancing rivers down the sides of the streets into the drains, forming pools in the parks and courtyards then and there, and then the lightning began. Great forked tongues of lightning flashed overhead followed by unfolding pounding fists of thunder beating massively on the air overhead as the rain fell madly throughout.

The great metropolis of New Landern, home to the staggering number of two million souls, sprawled out in all its grandeur, was made small and irrelevant beneath the enormous thundering storm which stretched from one end of the sky to the other. The grandees of New Landern and their servants looked out through their windows to watch the show; poets thought of metaphors for lightning; musicians pulled their hair to think of this tune, this melody, this fundamental beat of the rhythm of the rain and the lightning and the time of the happening of this time they felt to think of, and others thought of nothing, nothing at all, only knowing the noise and the light and the hot wet taste of that time that they had in their mouths then.

Isabel looked wide-eyed and open-mouthed through her window, admiring and friendly, pleased with the propriety of the enormous storm, which had everything in the right place; Nicholas stood under the shelter of a marble war monument, his hand on the hilt of his wand, exulting in the drama of the moment; Angela plied her trade with her current client, half-naked by a roaring fire, while pretending to laugh before the background of the thunder; Captain Abner Nevsky was a stone, insensate from an overload of intoxication; Ben paid no attention to the storm, aware of it only as a distraction from the important legal work he was crafting as cleverly as only a lawyer knew how, and the freshly dug earth of Jolly's grave shone fat and wet and dark with pregnant secrets as the rain splashed over the abyss into which he had fallen. Nothing is ever over, the rain said as it fell, but nothing is ever definite, it also said, more softly.

Lord Zinia kept on regardless, fully aware of the storm, fully aware that he had no more weight than a leaf falling from a tree in the face of such an event but also turning over in his mind what he had been saying from the beginning. The power of the storm that raged overhead could not affect the meaning of an equation or a line of poetry. It could rage all it liked, but the human mind would continue. Only logic could destroy logic. A hammer could never make a dent in a word; that was just how things naturally were.

'And now we come to the centre of things,' Lord Zinia said, folding up his papers and putting them away into his pocket to make clear he was coming to the end of his talk, 'the meaning of what we do. We ride the storm to control not the storm but where we land. That is all we do, and that is all we can do.'

ELEVEN

The Hidden Attack of Captain Abner Nevsky on a Lady of Honour

10:20 PM, 21 June 1544 A.F.

The room had been darkened by the drawn curtains. Isabel lay in bed day after day, wounded in pride and body. For more than two weeks now she had not left the room.

Her friends visited, the doctors came and diagnosed *nerves* and prescribed medications which she took without belief or protest.

She felt that her life was over, that her darkened room was the darkness of the grave. Renewed life could not come to her from within; nor could it be granted her from without. There was no hope of recovery from her illness because it was a dagger through her mind whose wound could not close. She had hidden herself away in the dark because the light now hurt her.

She had not seen Nevsky come through the corridor, did not at first understand her danger. He had told her he was Captain Abner Nevsky; she had ignored his presumption. He had called her by name, been familiar with her, laughed at her rebuke, her attempts to turn away and walk past him. There had been men with him, Nevsky had then hauled her into a nearby room; her guardians were there, looking scared, bound, gagged; it was only when Nevsky had thrown her to the ground and lifted her dress that she had understood what was happening.

Her mind then could no longer monitor the movement of time; intervals between moments had become irregular, time itself became scrambled. And along with time went space — the dimensions of the room tilted into geometrically impossible angles.

She had screamed and been gagged; fought and been bound. The further pain of the other men watching and laughing, making obscene gestures; the humiliation, the harsh slap from Nevsky that sent a white light across her vision; trying to scream through her gag; each moment unendurable, her pride mortally wounded; then it had been over and she had wept uncontrollably, lying on the floor, wanting to shut out the world but unable not to be aware of Nevsky standing over her, saying something to her guardians, walking out of the room followed by his men.

Her guardians then, released from their bonds, helping her up from the floor, shock and horror on their faces, rearranging her garments, taking her with them, cajoling her, telling her to put on a brave face, they would go home, and they had gone home.

The nightmare had continued the next day. Nevsky had come calling. Her guardians read the note he had sent in but she refused to look at it. They had said she had to receive him but she refused. She hid in her room while Nevsky was shown in. Nevsky had come with his men, and a lawyer, and a marriage contract drawn up by the lawyer and ready to be signed to seal the forthcoming marriage of Nevsky and Isabel.

Her guardians told her all this after Nevsky had gone. Nevsky's men had signed a contract under oath that Isabel had given herself to Nevsky willingly and now she was bound to marry him. Isabel shuddered and screamed. No, no, no, was all she would say.

Nevsky and his men and the lawyer came back the next day. They were now outraged that they were being kept from seeing Isabel. Her guardians were accused by them of holding Isabel prisoner. Her guardians had also witnessed Isabel's night of pleasure, they said with a knowing grin. They said they would come back the next day and if they were not granted their full rights they would bring in the law.

Isabel threatened to kill herself and it was not an idle threat. Her guardians said that naturally she could not marry Nevsky. Where the matter then stood poised was the question of the law.

If they took Nevsky to a court of law, it was perfectly possible, even probable, that their account of things would be believed. Nevsky would be executed for rape. This Nevsky knew, but Nevsky also knew that it was impossible for them to go to law because everyone would know what had happened and Isabel's reputation would be ruined. Given that it was out of the question for this matter to go to a court of law, Nevsky had nothing to fear.

Nevsky and his men and the lawyer came back with their ultimatum, which was rejected by Isabel's guardians and then the lawyer played his winning card. There was another contract they could sign with regard to the payment of suitable compensation for Nevsky's frustrated expectations. That compensation was the sum of one million strada, payable immediately and in full. The lawyer then pulled out the second contract, a Memorandum of Understanding, which stated that the receipt of one million strada would nullify the marriage contract, which would otherwise have to be signed.

Their nerves run ragged, their backs to the wall, their well-ordered and peaceful lives shattered by this howling storm, Isabel's guardians suggested that she buy Nevsky off. On the edge of a nervous breakdown, shaking in terror, desperate only for this whole ordeal to be over, Isabel agreed. The administrators were called in, the sum of one million strada was made available, Nevsky took the money and the whole nightmare was over; or not quite over. Isabel stayed in her room and refused to come out. The curtains were drawn night and day; the doctors came, her friends came; it was generally understood that she was suffering from *nerves*.

The shadows in her room frightened her; the four posters of her bed seemed threatening in a way she could not define; the lamps in her room stared at her menacingly. Her father, who had been dead these several years, came to the foot of her bed and said, 'What is necessary must be done.' She slept all she could, her mind dulled by medications, hidden under her bedclothes. The looks of sympathy of her guardians stung like acid.

It was the coming of her next monthly cycle that was the beginning of her return to normal life. At least she had not been made pregnant by that monster. Perhaps that had been part of her fear which she had not even identified until that moment. There came a day when she drew back the curtains to let the sunlight in; when she began to have meals in the dining-room again; when she could bear to receive the looks of sympathy her guardians gave her. The appearance of her haughty self began to return if not yet the haughty self as such; she once again began to go out to visit friends, to give and receive social invitations. Slowly her life returned to a semblance of normality. Governed only by the desperate desire that no-one should ever know what had happened, she strove with all her might to behave as if she had only suffered from nerves which had now passed by and she was perfectly all right now. She knew she was ruined and she could no longer hope for a normal life, and that to have the appearance of a normal life was all that was left for her now but she was determined to at least have that. She would appear to be normal; no-one would stare at her; no-one would offer her sympathy or despise her, each of which was as bad as the other, except sympathy was worse.

The external appearance of a normal life returned to her; Isabel went to parties once again, talked with her friends, pretended to giggle over gossip that now meant nothing, pretended to be interested in the latest goings on of society, pretended to pay attention to the normal everyday happenings of her world although these were nothing more to her now than detritus washed up on the beach. Time passed and Isabel began to settle back into her new role as a player pretending to be playing the role of Lady Isabel Grangeshield of Grangeshield House, along with all the other players on the stage of the world. She no longer belonged in her world; she was there now as imposter; she was in her world but she was no longer of it, but she fought to hold on to at least the appearance of continuing to belong. As long as no-one ever knew her secret she was safe. Isabel had hidden herself along with her secret from the world and that now was her life — the half life that was all she could now have.

TWELVE

....

The Duel of First Combat Between Mr Nicholas Raspero and Captain Abner Nevsky

10:20 PM, 21 June 1544 A.F.

Nicholas was leaning against a wall to the side, one hand resting on his wand, a drink which he was barely sipping in his other. He was in the club on the corner next to the Bridge of Nerian that night. People walked to and fro, completely ignoring him, wrapped up in their own wrappings of frenzied gaieties, stimulated by the swirling contents of the dark box-like room with its paintings and curtains and coloured lanterns.

Nicholas had been aware of him for some time but he had tried to shut him out. A large man in a blue jacket had recently entered the room with a shout that drew attention, and was now carrying on at a nearby table, shouting every now and then, making various comments. Nicholas stayed where he was, doing nothing. It was not like Nicholas to have waited for so long in such a situation, but perhaps a presentiment of a future defined held him back. The future in general is undefined, open to any and every possibility. Now a particular future had emerged which cast a shadow over Nicholas leaning against the wall, a definite future with a definite figure, full-bodied and voluptuous, which answered his desire, fulfilled him and brought him forth onto the stage as the man he would be. He was then a glove which a hand would enter and flesh out into living movement, and all he had to do was walk along the arrows painted on the floor; it was as simple as that.

Yet still something, perhaps all his alternate futures joined into one feeling, held him back. He stayed where he was while the blue-jacketed man shouted and carried on as before, disrupting the gathered guests bound by their shared bonds of intended pleasures.

Nicholas was not the only one bothered by the man in the blue jacket. He could see clearly the discomfort all around this blue-jacketed man, could see the attention deliberately deployed elsewhere by those all around who were pretending that nothing was wrong. His shouts grated on everyone's ears, but no-one said anything. Then the blue-jacketed man started making very personal comments about a lady sitting nearby. He made these comments so loudly that she could not but hear, so the gentleman with her stood up and offered her his hand and they left. The man in the blue jacket shouted after them that he knew where they were off to, but they did not look back; they left as if they fled in terror, while pretending to leave normally. And it was then that Nicholas realised what was going on — everyone in the room was terrified of this loud-mouthed figure from a demi-monde opera.

So at last Nicholas made the move that he could perhaps never have avoided given who he was. He had been trained to take anyone down in a wand fight. He was the custodian of wandlore secrets going back for six centuries, which he had inherited purely by virtue of birth and received entirely by virtue of aptitude. He had been born for this fight. He set down his glass on a nearby table and returned to his position leaning against the wall. He looked across at the blue-jacketed man with a strong disapproval of the way that the man was behaving. He had decided this behaviour was inappropriate.

It took a while for the blue-jacketed man to notice, but Nicholas's disapproving gaze was unwavering and it could only take time for events to unfold now that Nicholas was walking along his painted path. Time only had to pass and what was now inevitable would emerge.

The man in the blue jacket looked back at him with a wolfish delight. He even licked his lips and pulled back his upper lip to show even white teeth with long canine-sharp teeth at the sides.

'What you staring at?' he shouted at Nicholas.

'A moron, obviously,' Nicholas replied calmly, loudly enough for the man in the blue jacket to hear him.

A complete silence had fallen over the whole room. Everyone turned around and were staring. A world of longing was in all their stares, and a desire to see blood. They had been too frightened to pay too much attention before; now that fear had turned to an attention to detail that was lustful, an attention that was hot and passionate and sought only its own satisfaction.

The man in the blue jacket took on board Nicholas's reply, and then stood up slowly, the scrape of his chair legs loud in the silence and came towards Nicholas.

'Whad'd you say?' he asked Nicholas. Seen from this close, Nicholas could see that the bright blue eyes of this man were flecked with reddish specks, that his unshaven cheeks had grey points of stubble, a grey that was not apparent in his bushy black hair.

Nicholas had always known he would be in a fight from the moment he had chosen to stare disapprovingly at this man in the blue jacket. 'Do you want me to speak more *loudly* or more … slowly?' he asked his opponent.

His opponent smiled again. He was savouring every moment. Everyone present knew what was happening and where it would lead to and so they stared at the two of them with an almost lascivious hunger. *Fight, fight, fight,* they were thinking as one. It was what they wanted to see happen right before their eyes, so that they could hungrily feed with their minds on the spectacle like piglets suckling on the teats of their great mother.

'Well, you've got a lip on you, don't you,' Nicholas's opponent said with a smile, 'a great big lip that likes to talk. You can talk the talk, my friend, but can you walk the walk?'

'I see you have grasped the concept of an elementary rhyme,' Nicholas observed. 'This must have tasked your intelligence to the limit, mustn't it?'

The man in the blue jacket was now standing so close to Nicholas that Nicholas could have reached out and placed a hand on his blue-jacketed shoulder. 'You're not very bright, are you, boy? Do you know who I am?'

'I know what you are,' Nicholas said, 'and that is enough. But you're so eager to tell me, go ahead. What is your name?'

'My name,' said the man slowly, savouring this fresh and still sprouting development, 'is Captain Abner Nevsky.'

'Well, if I ever have a dog, now I know what to call it,' Nicholas told him.

Nevsky was unfazed by this. He had seen the complete lack of recognition in Nicholas's eyes on hearing his name. 'You've never heard of me before, have you, boy?' he asked.

'No, I have not,' Nicholas replied truthfully. 'But then, I am newly arrived in New Landern.'

'Ah, you are newly arrived in New Landern,' Nevsky repeated, like a wolf making the acquaintance of an exceptionally tasty-looking lamb. 'How very sweet. Well, I am well known here, boy, and if you had been here just another day you would have heard of me. And then you would have minded your manners, boy. You would have minded your manners, boy, trust me. But it's too late now to mind your manners, isn't it, boy? Much, much too late.'

'Surely you have overlooked something, Captain Nevsky. Something so obvious that even a person of your very limited intelligence should have seen it by now.'

'Have I?' Nevsky cried out in pretended surprise. He turned around and stepped away from Nicholas and held his arms out wide as if to embrace all those present in the room, which was very crowded by now. Somehow news had spread like a fire crackling in the shrubs and branches of a drought-stricken tinder-dry forest and people had rushed along to the scene of the combatants, forgetting all else in their haste to see the coming fight, which was already casting its shadow before its arrival. Their wide-open eyes and half-open mouths now surrounded the combatants like low-hanging fruit. 'I've overlooked something, my friends. But what can it be? What can it be?' He bowed his head, scratched the top of his head, then raised his arms wide again and turned back to Nicholas. He was playing to the crowd now was Nevsky, enjoying all the foreplay of banter and humour before the fight which was to come. Yet, this foreplay was part of the fight, part of the drama, intended to reduce an opponent to a nervous wreck before he had even drawn his wand.

Grudgingly Nicholas had to admit he had never seen it better done. Nevsky was in charge, was dictating the course of events, would dictate when they would go out to fight, would even by sheer force of personality, by hypnosis, force his opponent to half-consciously throw the fight in the hope of mercy, in the hope of getting off lightly, and the more vain that hope was the more desperately it would be felt. Nicholas suspected Nevsky had won most of his fights in this way, beaten his opponents before they had even stepped out to fight. 'No, I can't see it,' Nevsky told Nicholas. 'What is it that is so obvious that I do not see it?'

'You don't know *my* name,' Nicholas told him coldly. He pushed away from the wall and faced Nevsky. His look of detachment was gone now. He knew this could go to final combat and there was no thought now in his mind but that of facing Nevsky in the arena of a duel. In his mind now there were only calculations.

The look in his eyes stopped Nevsky cold. He abruptly stopped smiling. Nevsky and Nicholas looked each other straight in the eye, locked together in a shared thought.

'And what is your name?' Nevsky asked him, no longer mocking now.

'My name is Mr Nicholas Raspero,' Nicholas told him.

'Is it now?' Nevsky replied. 'Well, I've never heard of you, Mr Raspero.'

Nicholas noted that despite Nevsky's denial, his eyes had shifted and he suddenly looked wary as if he was no longer quite so eager to fight Nicholas. Nevsky had probably heard of what had happened to Jolly, Nicholas thought. Nevsky had long ago given up on smiling. The cold look in Nicholas's eye told him that this was an opponent who would not be beaten before they drew their wands. This would be settled in combat.

'If you have never heard of me, Captain Nevsky, then why has an ignorant lout such as yourself suddenly acquired manners?'

'I like the way you handle yourself, Mr Raspero,' Nevsky said affably. 'I'm starting to feel like I've found my long lost brother, you and me, Mr Raspero, we can get along just fine, you and me, now let's have a drink together, Mr Raspero.'

'I demand satisfaction for your offensive conduct, Captain Nevsky,' Nicholas said loudly and clearly. 'What do you say?'

'I accept your challenge, Mr Raspero,' Nevsky replied. 'What form of combat?'

'I always start at the beginning, Captain Nevsky,' Nicholas said as calmly as if recounting that morning's walk. 'That means First Combat.' He was, in fact, playing his own tricks on Nevsky's nerves with the implication that the duel could go on to higher stages of combat. Nevsky was now free to worry if he chose to do so and later he might have to worry whether he chose to or not.

'When and where?'

'There is no time like the present, and outside will suit me fine.'

'After you, Mr Raspero,' Nevsky said, stepping back with a wave of his arm towards the door.

Nicholas set off for the door. He kept his hand on his wand to watch Nevsky following behind him, but he doubted Nevsky would launch a sneak attack on him with everyone watching. This animal had to pretend to be human while people were watching. Nevertheless, Nicholas was taking no chances.

They faced off against each other outside. They assumed the position, crouched over their wands. Then Nevsky attacked. Nicholas simply parried, observing what Nevsky could do.

He soon realised why Nevsky was so sure of himself. His combinations used a form that Nicholas doubted even Alexandre had ever seen before. Nicholas could parry it readily enough, but he doubted that anyone who lacked his training could have. After a while Nicholas had seen enough. He had taken Nevsky's measure. He knew what Nevsky could do, but Nevsky had not yet learned what he, Nicholas Raspero, could do. He struck and sent Nevsky flying head over heels, catching Nevsky's wand as it flew past him. There was a gasp from the assembled onlookers and a scattering of applause.

Nevsky found himself lying on his back, wandless, looking up at the stars overhead. He was struck then by a memory of having seen that particular constellation of stars in the sky above as he stood on the deck of the Armoured

Flying Carriage *Hardblast* two years ago now. He had no idea what that constellation of stars was called, but he remembered it clearly — he had looked up during an idle moment and noted it and now he was noting it again.

8:00 PM, Monday 3 March 1542 A.F.

The Armoured Flying Carriage *Hardblast* had set off in the evening carrying the 19th Company under the command of Captain Amery Hartwin, who in civilian life was Lord Whittington. His second-in-command was Lieutenant Quin Warwick, a hard-bitten soldier who had risen through the ranks and would rise no higher; Lieutenant Warwick understood his position and resented it. The third-in-command was Sergeant Nevsky, who even then was a trouble-maker.

It was while flying over the Mountains of Weiden shortly before midnight that Nevsky had looked up and seen that constellation of stars, which had impressed itself onto his memory for no reason that he could think of. Perhaps it was that they were going off to war, albeit a secret war. Captain Hartwin stood on the deck, hands behind his back, a picture of unruffled cool nonchalance. Sergeant Nevsky, tall and burly and bearded (in those days he had a beard) stood nearby.

For no reason that he could think of, Captain Hartwin did not like Nevsky and so he was always unfailingly courteous to Nevsky out of a vague sense of guilt that he was unfair to a man who had done nothing to deserve such dislike. For his part Nevsky, who sensed with an animal's instinct that this courtesy was the opposite of acceptance, wore his role like a stone mask.

They landed in the early hours of the morning and were ambushed as soon as the flying carriage had departed. They fought their way up a ravine where they made a last stand against a cliff. There it was that Captain Hartwin was fatally wounded. In the depths of a cave he wrote a letter, his last act on earth, which he entrusted to Lieutenant Warwick, who for all his faults would have seen to it that the letter was delivered. Nevsky was the only witness to this episode, which meant that later the next day, when Warwick was killed outright Nevsky took hold of this letter. He did this without thinking about what he was doing too much; he acted by instinct. For all that he knew, the letter might be valuable.

'Sealed orders for the commanding officer,' he told the soldiers watching him, 'which is now me.' Nevsky put the letter away in his pocket with an expressionless face and gave his orders; they were to make their way through the foothills of the Maricela Mountains to the town of Kaapo and report to the Anglashian detachment there. Nevsky had led the survivors of the 19th Company by a certain animal cunning through the Maricela Mountains to the safety of Kaapo; there he had been given the rank of Acting Captain in the chaos of the hour and the 19th Company had taken part in the battle of Fedora.

It was the day after this battle that Nevsky, remembering Hartwin's letter, and finding himself alone for a moment, had taken the letter and inspected it. It was addressed to "The 3rd Earl of Whittington" with the instructions "not to be opened by him until his fifteenth birthday" on the reverse of the envelope. Nevsky did not hesitate to do what he should not have done, but then Nevsky was not a gentleman. So it was that Nevsky tore open Hartwin's letter and read what he should not have read — a letter which was an inheritance, the stolen inheritance now in his hands.

Maricela Mountains

3 March 1542 A.F.

My darling son,

Your father is about to die and he considers himself to be a very lucky man. He is so blessed by good fortune as to have time to write this letter to his son and heir the 3rd Earl of Whittington.

All knowledge comes through the senses (and thus you read this letter) but only what we see in the mind's eye is true. So here is something that is true:

A_C\D51deg_B After the Turn the Cut; then of the Six, the Fourth is raised; then the Path is clear.

My time is nearly done. Take your father's love and blessing — life passes on — that is all.

Your loving father, Amery

As the skirmish in the Maricela Mountains should not have happened, being an illegal mission, records were re-written to make it appear that Lord Whittington had died in the battle of Fedora; Nevsky had been returned to his rank of Sergeant but he left the army then and there calling himself "Captain Nevsky", fully aware of the value of the Whittington wandfighting combinations which had fallen into his hands. Nevsky went out into the world at large to make his fortune — and he had indeed made his fortune — but now he found himself stretched out on the ground, looking up at the exact same constellation of stars that had been over his head two years earlier.

It was as if a wheel had turned full circle.

10:45 PM, 21 June 1544 A.F.

Nevsky climbed to his feet slowly, brushing himself down. He had been taken down and his awareness of this took its time filtering through his brain. Nicholas stood there and waited.

'Have you received satisfaction, Mr Raspero?' Nevsky asked, a little awkwardly.

'No, Captain Nevsky, I have not,' Nicholas said, and sent Nevsky's wand flying back to him.

They assumed the position again and this time Nicholas attacked for a little while, testing Nevsky with combinations which Nevsky could easily parry until Nicholas struck again and took Nevsky down for a second time.

The watching crowd took this development in complete silence this time. It was dawning on them all that Nevsky's sun was setting.

'Have you received satisfaction, Mr Raspero?' Nevsky asked again.

'No, Captain Nevsky, I have not,' Nicholas replied and returned Nevsky's wand to him.

This time Nevsky attacked in a flurry of moves, throwing everything he had into it. Nicholas parried almost casually and then struck. He took Nevsky down again for the third, and last, time in their duel of First Combat.

'Have you received satisfaction, Mr Raspero?' Nevsky asked for the third and last time.

Nicholas paused, studying Nevsky. He let the silence draw out while Nevsky was forced to stand there and wait. Then he said calmly, 'Yes, Captain Nevsky, I have received satisfaction.' He sent Nevsky's wand back to him and pocketed his own wand. Nevsky stood there a moment and then slowly put his own wand away. Nicholas walked towards him and stopped a couple of arms lengths away.

'You know, Captain Nevsky,' he said, 'you would be very ill advised to behave with such bad manners in my presence again. You see, I happen to be in a very forgiving mood right now, which is why I will let you walk away from here.' Nicholas said this in a cold fury which made his grey eyes as threatening as a restless cloud-clad sky. 'Your luck is in today. Should you ever cross me in the same way again, however, I would not again be as forgiving. Do you grasp this very simple idea which I am presenting you with?'

Nevsky smiled, but the smile did not reach his eyes. 'Mr Raspero, I see now that we have misunderstood each other. You are a man after my own heart. Mr Raspero, I tell you this from the very bottom of my own heart, I feel like I have met my long-lost brother.' Nevsky's confidence was now restrained by the new-found knowledge that his specially devised wandfighting, which he had thought invincible, had been beaten by movements which he had not been able to even detect. 'A wandfighter like you, well, me and you, can get along just fine. There's been a misunderstanding, Mr Raspero, and it grieves me, it grieves me mightily.' It could not be denied that when Nevsky chose to be charming he could produce an almost involuntary response to his friendliness, as if relief from not having to be afraid of him transmuted into an affectionate appreciation of his animal presence. Nicholas, however, had already made up his mind about Nevsky as being of the scum of the earth, and nothing would change that opinion.

'You are like a dog that licks the boot that kicks it, Nevsky,' Nicholas told him coldly. 'Yes, you will grovel to me now that I have beaten you, just as you tried to lord it over me before.'

'I wouldn't say that I'm groveling to you, Mr Raspero,' Nevsky replied, his smile vanishing.

'I don't think you quite understand me, Nevsky,' Nicholas said very coldly. 'I am saying that you will face me in Final Combat if you misbehave in my presence again. Do you understand this very simple statement? Final Combat means death to the loser, Nevsky, if you don't know.'

'I know what Final Combat means, Mr Raspero,' Nevsky said. 'I have fought two duels in Final Combat.' With what he could summon of his bravado, he stared back at Nicholas as if to say that First Combat was one thing, Final Combat another. 'Have you ever fought Final Combat, Mr Raspero?'

'No,' Nicholas said, 'I have not. Perhaps you might oblige me tonight by being my opponent? What do you say?'

Nevsky said nothing, staring at Nicholas, who waited staring cold-eyed back at Nevsky. The implicit challenge was there, and all Nevsky had to do was help it emerge. They would face each other in Final Combat, then and there. The watching crowd held its breath as one.

'Well, now, Mr Raspero, I never fight without cause. If I have given you cause then say so. I never refuse a challenge. But without cause, Mr Raspero, where then is the reason to fight?'

'Oh, I have cause to issue you a challenge, Nevsky,' Nicholas said. 'The cause is your deliberate refusal to understand what I have said. I have said that if you ever cross me again, I will demand the satisfaction of duel by Final Combat. Either you understand me or you do not. Now which is it, Nevsky?'

Nevsky understood then. Nicholas was going to push this until Nevsky backed down or was faced with a challenge. He also understood, as he looked into Nicholas's cold grey eyes, that Nicholas had no doubt as to the outcome of such a fight, if it happened. Nevsky by then had no doubt as to the outcome either. He had not only lost this fight as badly as he had, but he had indeed heard what had happened to Jolly.

'I understand you, Mr Raspero,' Nevsky replied, backing down.

'Well, then, our business here is concluded,' Nicholas declared. With that he turned and walked away.

It dawned on Nicholas that everyone was staring at him as if he had two heads and a foreign accent. They stared and stared and stared. With that realisation he promptly left the scene and strolled through the late-at-night-largely-deserted streets, looking around him as he went without seeing much of what was around him. Somehow he had a sense that he could not properly grasp as of a future already unrolling beneath his feet, a future that was now shaped and waiting for him. Yet, it was a sense of a presence vanished like that of a dream lost on awakening, its only traces those of an invisible writing that had for one moment been wet and legible. But everything was gone now and Nicholas walked back home, thinking to himself that he was bound to have strange thoughts after having been in a fight with an animal like Nevsky. But still the sense of a future now undetectably present lingered with him, long after he had gone to the bed where he lay awake sleepless, trying to capture this odd feeling of having been captured. It was as if what had happened had been a trap that he had fallen into, and now there was no escape. Finally he fell asleep.

He dreamed that night that he was approaching a great carriage. It was night and the carriage was ablaze with lights. A footman was lowering steps so that he could mount and enter the carriage. The footman was wearing a blue jacket and Nicholas realised all of a sudden that it was Nevsky. Then Nicholas was walking up the steps and lowering his head to step into the carriage. As he stepped into the carriage he found himself in a ballroom. Everyone there seemed to be waiting for him. Then he was dancing with a woman he could not see, her bare arms around him. The dance ended and he stepped back to see her face and just at that moment he woke up from the shock of seeing her face, although he could not now remember what she had looked like.

Soon he fell asleep again, but he remembered the dream when he awoke, and he would remember the dream for the rest of his life.

THIRTEEN

The Gang Set Forth to Find the Mysterious Mr Nicholas Raspero

8:35 PM, Saturday 2 July 1544 A.F.

Isabel was with The Gang at Lady Milburga's Saturday function. A mind-reader had been invited to be the star attraction of the function but none of The Gang were all that interested in Stanislav the Magnificent, a Star brought down to Earth by Providence, because they were huddled together discussing the latest news of the divorce of Lady Fenella. The salacious details of this divorce which had emerged in court could not, of course, be repeated. Yet, their shared knowledge of what those details were left the merest associated reference tinged with a violet hue of unspeakable frissance. A certain well-known chocolate coated biscuit, for example, could not be mentioned without delirious giggles at their own daring in even mentioning it.

Isabel went through the motions of enjoying herself, a pretence that involved smiling when she should, making a comment now and then, and nodding occasionally. Life itself had lost all interest and become nothing but a material process. She thought no-one noticed but, in fact, The Gang had discussed the matter amongst themselves and decided that it was best for Isabel's sake for them to pretend not to notice the state Isabel was in, which they assumed was the remnants of her recent bout of nerves.

A loud voice was all of a sudden nearby, bellowing words into the air of the room. Isabel froze. Her insides turned to ice, her hands started sweating, and she gripped her knees together in her voluminous skirts so tightly the bones pressed against each other through the flesh and linen wrappings. The voice in the air beat on her head like a club while she summoned all her self-control to pretend that nothing was amiss, that she was no more discomfited than the rest of The Gang, who were stealing looks at the cause of all this disturbance.

'Oh ho, what's this?' Isabel looked up to see Nevsky standing before her, looking a little drunk, staring right at her. She felt fear grip her at his presence; she would have chosen to die right then not to have been there. 'Isabel!'

'How dare you call me by my first name!' Isabel said as calmly as she could, furious yet scared, angry yet only wanting to hide somewhere. She looked around the table for help, yet Berg, the only other man present, was studiously staring at the table-top. All the girls looked shocked, but not, Isabel recognised, fearful. Nevsky was only a nuisance to them, not a danger.

'Oh, come on love, don't be like that,' Nevsky shouted so that everyone in the room, who were watching, could hear him. 'Isabel, Isabel, Isabel,' he continued, shaking his head so that his glossy black hair waved back and forth like weeds in a swift flowing river, 'after what we've been to each other, come on girl, give us a smile love, come on, head up, big smile, treat me right and we can go somewhere private, know what I mean?' And then he threw back his head and laughed, his gleaming white teeth opened over Isabel's lowered head like a shark upraised over its victim.

The rest of The Gang (except Berg, whose eyes were fixed on the tabletop as if nailed there) looked at each other and at poor Isabel and didn't say anything. Nevsky was being outrageous and it might be a matter for some head-shaking later, and it really was all a bit too much, and poor Isabel, really, to be picked on like this, but no-one was doing anything about it. The girls knew they had to be careful for if they confronted Nevsky themselves, a male relative might be obliged to issue a challenge on their behalf, and if such a challenge was not forthcoming, they would be marked by that. Out of self-interest, therefore, they said nothing, although later when the time came they would have more than enough to say.

'Captain Nevsky, I find your behaviour objectionable,' Isabel said, trying with all her might to see that her voice did not shake.

'Do you now, do you now?' Nevsky shouted. 'Well, it's a challenge then isn't it?' He looked around the room. 'Anyone up for it? Well?'

The men present in the room averted their gaze from the scene. Berg's eyes were fixed unwaveringly on the tabletop.

'Doesn't look like anyone's going to act on your behalf, Isabel love,' Nevsky told Isabel mockingly. 'What do you say, want to go somewhere private? Just you and me?'

Word had spread quickly about the scene Nevsky was causing with Lady Isabel Grangeshield and Lady Odalys Milburga had wasted no time in coming to her rescue. She approached the table, a formidable large buxom woman, her hair drawn back severely in a bun, with an air of authority as of a nursing matron.

'Are you causing trouble, Captain Nevsky?' she asked briskly.

'Trouble, Lady Milburga?' Nevsky asked, turning towards her and spreading his arms wide to show how innocent he was. 'Trouble, Lady Milburga?' he repeated, as if having difficulty in comprehending such an accusation. 'Not me, not ever, just having a chat with sweet Isabel here.'

'I have already told you not to call me by my first name!' Isabel snapped, her confidence vastly increased by the arrival of Lady Milburga.

'Isabel, Isabel, Isabel,' Nevsky said, turning back to her, Lady Milburga already forgotten, 'we're going to go somewhere private, you and me, and then you'll be singing a different tune, won't you, my love? Oh, a very different tune, you're not going to be so stuck-up and snobby when it's just you and me alone together now, are you, Isabel?'

Somehow her terror at hearing what he said was in no way diminished by knowing that it was impossible. There was no way Nevsky could simply drag her off in full view of those watching. He would hang if he touched her; she knew he couldn't, yet terror grabbed her and churned her stomach into a jagged mass of blackened shards of melded ice as she looked away as defiantly as she could, always gripped by the terror that he might say what had happened then and there, and then and there everyone would know, and still she could see that the rest of The Gang, while prepared to censure Nevsky in the strongest possible terms for his behaviour, were not frightened of his stated intentions to take Isabel off somewhere private where he would be alone with her. The Gang did not, in their innocence, realise the danger Nevsky posed. They were too inexperienced to be frightened. Only Isabel knew that there were such things as monsters.

She knew that Nevsky could not, would not, overpower her, that if she stayed where she was and continued to defy him she would be safe, but her terror was irrational. She was ready to run then, to run anywhere to be out of there, and only the broken remnants of her shattered pride kept her in her seat.

Lady Milburga then came to her rescue.

'Captain Nevsky,' she said loudly, 'your presence at this party is no longer desired. You will leave and you will leave now! Is that understood?'

Her voice had cracked in the air like a shattered glass and it caught Nevsky's attention. He turned his shaggy head towards her slowly, like a large dog that reluctantly looks away from a tasty slab of meat at a compelling command.

Nevsky turned away from the table, took a few steps, stopped and turned to face Lady Milburga. 'Well, now, Lady Milburga,' he said, 'I find that downright unfriendly of you, downright unfriendly.'

Lady Milburga stood there in front of Nevsky and Isabel's heart leaped in her chest to see Lady Milburga standing so bravely in front of the monster, especially as Lady Milburga had taken Isabel's place in front of the monster's maw. As far as Isabel was concerned Lady Milburga could stay there in Isabel's place. After all, this was her party, she was the hostess and she was obliged to see to the wellbeing of the guests. It was only fair that Isabel should be spared. Lady Milburga could, indeed should, confront this monster in Isabel's place, and that was only as it should be.

'I have ordered you to leave my party, Captain Nevsky,' Lady Milburga snapped furiously. 'You are not welcome here. Now get out!'

Nevsky nodded his head slowly, not moving, a large man in his blue jacket and shaggy black hair. 'I'm offended by your behaviour, Lady

Milburga,' he said with an undertone of mockery, fully aware of his own offensive behaviour, 'deeply offended, mortified, mortified, and it's getting so I'm going to demand satisfaction from you, Lady Milburga, yes, that's where this is heading, so who's going to act on your behalf, is there anyone here, is there?'

He looked about the room, which by now was thronged with onlookers, who kept a careful distance from the scene while getting a good eyeful of what was happening. None of the men watching the scene showed any interest whatsoever in stepping forward on Lady Milburga's behalf.

Lady Milburga was unfazed by this apparent lack of support for her position. 'As it happens, Captain Nevsky, I do have a guest who is arriving shortly and who will most certainly be prepared to act on my behalf. If you are still here when he arrives, I will put the matter to him, and I have no doubt that he will accept your challenge.'

'Ah, well, this is more like it, this is more like it, Lady Milburga, because you can't treat Captain Nevsky the way you've treated me, no, no, no, you've told this good man here,' Nevsky thumped himself on the chest, 'to get out, that's what you said, I heard you, so now I ask you, who is this guest of yours, what's his name, do I know him, well, come on, don't be shy, Lady Milburga, tell me who he is.'

'Mr Nicholas Raspero!' Lady Milburga declared loudly.

There was such a long silence from Nevsky that even Isabel looked up at him. Nevsky had not moved, except for having lowered his head slightly, but there was such an alteration in his appearance that Isabel caught her breath. Nevsky's blue jacket somehow seemed to have crumpled, he had shrunk upon himself on the spot, he no longer seemed so large or imposing; nor was he saying anything.

Lady Milburga waited in silence, watching the crumpled Nevsky, and then struck her final blow. 'Captain Nevsky, I have told you to get out! Now get out!' She shouted these last words in a temper.

Nevsky smiled, but Isabel could see that the smile was forced. Nevsky raised his hands high and looked around at all those watching. 'Well, here I am, having some fun, and everyone gets all serious on me! All right, Lady Milburga, you want me to go, I'll go, you just take everything so serious, what's a man to do? Well, let me ask you this, is there any man here who will accept my challenge?' He shouted this last at all those in the room, looking out over them all, watching as they averted their gaze. Lady Milburga said nothing further for fear that her bluff might be called. Had Mr Raspero really been coming, she would have beaten Nevsky over the head all the way to the door. As it was, she waited for him to go of his own accord.

Nevsky chuckled to himself then, his confidence a little returned. 'It's a boring party anyway, Lady Milburga. There'll be some fun somewhere else in town for a man like me. Anyway, I'll be a married man soon, won't I? A bit of fun tonight, then it's off to the ceremony, then it's all about keeping wifey happy, isn't it? But you don't want to make an enemy of a man like me, Lady Milburga. Not when I'm going to be a Member of Council and everything, not when I'll be a Minister of the Crown, not when I'll be sitting next to your hubby in Council. So later we'll let bygones be bygones, won't we, sweetie?'

Lady Milburga said nothing but merely gazed upon Nevsky with contempt. She tried to make her silence seem itself a statement, but the truth of the matter was that the longer this went on the more frayed her bluff became. She was starting to feel much less confident than she looked.

Nevsky looked at her for a long moment, then shrugged and turned for the door. Isabel realised then that this had all been about saving face, that his parting comments had been designed simply to disguise the swiftness of his departure.

As his blue jacket disappeared out of sight, Isabel turned to Lady Milburga and said, 'I cannot thank you enough, Lady Milburga, for coming to my assistance.'

'It was my pleasure, Isabel,' Lady Milburga said, taking a deep breath and visibly relaxing now that Nevsky had gone. 'Besides, it was worth it to see Nevsky run like a rabbit.'

'Is Mr Raspero really coming here tonight?' Penny asked her eagerly.

Lady Milburga looked at the door to make sure that Nevsky had really gone and said in a low voice, 'No, my dear Penelope, but Captain Nevsky didn't know that, did he?'

'It was a bluff!' Sophie declared, seemingly awed by Lady Milburga's achievement. 'How very grand of you, Lady Milburga!'

'You are too kind,' Lady Milburga said with a self-satisfied smile. With that Lady Milburga graciously inclined her head towards Isabel and The Gang and left herself through the same door Nevsky had just gone through, presumably to verify that her unwelcome guest had indeed departed.

There was a momentary silence as Lady Milburga disappeared from view, a silence that was broken by Isabel, who had one question, and one question only, in her mind at that moment in time.

'But who is Mr Nicholas Raspero?' Isabel asked The Gang.

There was a silence while everyone looked at her as if she'd just asked what direction the sky was in. Kora was the first one to realise why she did not know.

'Oh poor Izzy, we keep on forgetting that you had such a bad bout of nerves. You haven't heard. Well,' Kora leaned forward, delighted to be the one to bear such gossip, 'Nevsky fought a duel of First Combat with a young man who gave his name as Mr Nicholas Raspero, and Mr Raspero thrashed Nevsky like a schoolboy. Then Mr Raspero told Nevsky that if they ever fought a duel again it would be Final Combat, and ever since then Nevsky runs like a rabbit at the mere mention of the name of Mr Nicholas Raspero.'

'It is so dramatic and sensational!' Penny burst out. 'The complete unknown revealed in the sight of all!'

'Oh no, I heard that Mr Nicholas Raspero was so far from being unknown to Nevsky that Nevsky tried to back out of their fight as soon as he heard his name but Raspero issued him a challenge anyway,' said Samantha.

'But who is Mr Nicholas Raspero?' Isabel asked again.

'But that's just it,' Kora resumed, 'no-one has ever heard of him. He did the Three at Kenina Park and his name is now on the List but still no-one knows anything about him. He is a complete mystery. It is all too strange for words.'

'There is no mystery,' Uliana said tartly. 'He is simply from outside town, and has a great ability with the wand. I cannot see anything out of the ordinary in that.'

'Ability is itself a mystery,' Berg commented, stretching out his long fingers and flexing them in the air. 'And great ability is a deep mystery.'

'It is merely an inherited talent fostered by education,' Uliana riposted. 'To talk of mystery is mere flipdoodle.'

'You have just now invented the word "flipdoodle", Uliana,' Berg said with mock severity. 'The word itself is not a mystery but your ability to invent it is.'

Seeing the conversation slipping away from its earlier topic, Isabel intervened, 'But I still do not understand. How on earth can no-one know anything about Mr Raspero? Is he a gentleman? If so, he must live somewhere. Someone must know something.'

'He is by all accounts a gentleman,' Uliana replied. 'Beyond that nothing is known. The reasons for this will very likely be found to be trivial once uncovered.'

'You don't know that,' Penny complained.

'Indeed she does not,' Berg, Uliana's future husband, pronounced. 'She merely assumes the world to be less interesting than one would hope if one made different assumptions.'

'I judge by experience, Berg,' Uliana said sharply. 'What do you judge by?'

'Experience, Uliana. Perhaps my experience of the world has been more encouraging than yours.'

'Then please tell us all about it,' Uliana said sweetly. 'I am sure that we are all ears.'

Isabel intervened again. 'But I still do not understand. Has no-one taken steps to find this Mr Raspero?'

Isabel realised then that she was attracting more than one curious look due to her insistence on finding out more about Mr Nicholas Raspero.

One curious look found expression in words, 'You seem to have a particular interest, Lady Grangeshield, in further information concerning this mysterious Mr Nicholas Raspero,' Berg commented with feigned casualness, his eyes shifting like a fox on the prowl. He was always on the lookout for things that were concealed.

Isabel glared at him then. 'I did not notice that you had anything to say when that horrible man Nevsky was here. You kept very quiet then, I believe. Or so I recollect, Berg.'

Her taunt went astray as Berg replied with dignity, 'One does not engage a man like Nevsky in conversation, Isabel. I am surprised that you should even consider it to be a possibility.'

'You sat there and said nothing while that horrible man behaved with the most disgraceful impropriety towards me.'

'Should I have issued him a challenge on your behalf, Isabel?' Berg asked a little mockingly as if to imply that he might have issued a challenge on another's behalf.

'I cannot conceive of a man like you issuing a challenge on anyone's behalf,' Isabel said cuttingly.

This was too much for Uliana who came to Berg's defence. 'You are being very confrontational, Izzy. Berg acted perfectly correctly in refusing even to acknowledge Nevsky's presence. You, on the other hand, spoke to him, thus acknowledging his presence. You are far more at fault than Berg was in this whole deeply regrettable affair.'

'Is that so?' Isabel asked her. 'I had not realised. I thought I was only defending myself against a monstrous imposition. But you no doubt see things very differently, do you?'

'Oh, stop quarreling,' Sophie said impatiently. 'It was bad enough when Nevsky was here. Izzy, you have suffered terribly from the attentions of that dreadful man but he is gone now.'

In one single moment, a thousand thoughts stemming from one anguished feeling washed over Isabel like a waterfall of blood rushing over her brain. She saw clearly how The Gang did not understand how true it was that she had *suffered terribly from the attentions of that dreadful man* and how important it was that they should never know. To them the extreme of suffering was a ruined dress; to her it had once been, but she knew better now. They did not understand anything of what she had been through, and in earlier days she would have been one with them, but neither did they know why she now had to find out who this Nicholas Raspero was. She had not even yet considered her own motivation in making this choice because everything had been happening so fast, yet she had to know in order to properly think about everything. She felt alone now, no longer one of The Gang.

Isabel pushed her chair back and stood up.

'This creature,' she said contemptuously, looking at Berg, 'has plenty to say now but he did not have anything to say earlier. And as for you,' she continued, turning to Uliana, 'if the time ever comes when you have to sit where I have just been sitting, with a deeply offensive man taking familiarities with you, then you will understand why I defended myself as best as I could in the midst of a company of so-called friends who did nothing, *nothing,* to come to my assistance. Lady Milburga is worth more than all of you combined. She came to my assistance, while you stayed silent and said nothing!'

'Izzy,' said Sophie placatingly, 'this was very upsetting for you and we all feel deeply for you. But what could we do? He would only have asked who would act on our behalf and then what would we say? Besides, it was only talk. He would never have dared to have actually done anything. He was unbearable, intolerable, but what could any of us have done?'

'It has come to my attention,' Isabel said, 'that there is a man who could have done something. I have only asked about him, yet it seems that none of you knows anything at all about this man, this Mr Nicholas Raspero. Furthermore,' she continued, looking directly at Berg, 'it seems that simply for inquiring about this man I am subject to an inquisition concerning my inquiry from a man who talks freely now while not daring to say a word before!' She almost spat out these words in Berg's face. 'I will go off and learn about this Mr Nicholas Raspero on my own without your help and I will not trouble you further about this matter. I bid you farewell!'

'No, no, no,' Penny pleaded, 'you mustn't find out all about Mr Nicholas Raspero and not tell us. That would be cruel. Sit down, Izzy. Don't go.'

Isabel allowed herself to be cajoled back into her chair by the protests of all those present. It took some time but the stiff and unbending Lady Isabel Grangeshield eventually resumed her place at the table, giving Berg a look of utter contempt as she did so, a look which Mr Berg Irving took in his stride with a self-satisfied smile. So it was that The Gang turned their collective mind to The Mission: to find the elusive and mysterious Mr Nicholas Raspero and bring him forth to the light of day.

Berg spoke first. 'Shall we offer a prize to the man who can solve this mystery?'

'Did you say "the man", Berg?' Uliana asked sweetly.

'Must you two always quarrel?' Kora complained. 'You are not even married.'

Neither Berg nor Uliana could think of anything to say, but they both blushed.

'Oh, perhaps they have an understanding,' Penny declared, leaning forward with her eyes wide.

'We both understand many things, do we not, Uliana,' Berg replied, looking across the table at her, 'but not, perhaps, each other.'

'Speak for yourself, Berg,' Uliana said, 'I have no difficulty in understanding you at all.'

'How on earth can such a prize be offered?' Isabel asked, redirecting the conversation back to its previously nominated topic. She restrained herself from launching more insults at Berg.

'We could always try the Sheltrades Strategy,' Kora suggested, her face furrowed with suppressed laughter.

'Oh yes!' Penny exclaimed. 'When everyone wrote to Lady Fairbairn, and she had to find out where the baby had come from.'

'That novel is widely known,' Berg said. 'The strategy would be transparent.'

Not as transparent as your cowardice, Isabel thought, who was finding that the very sound of Berg's voice infuriated her, but she again restrained herself. 'But how on earth would that work anyway?' Isabel asked Kora. 'This is not an issue of disputed parentage.'

'This is how it would work,' Kora declared. 'Lady Starfeld is holding a party next Saturday. Have we not all been invited?' Everyone there nodded. 'Well, then, we all write to Lady Starfeld declaring how much we all look forward to seeing Mr Nicholas Raspero at her party, given that he is the "Talk of the Town" and that we have all heard that she has invited him to the party. We try to get as many people as possible to do the same. Lady Starfeld will have no choice but to see to it that Mr Raspero comes to her party or else it will be an enormous embarrassment for her.'

'Brilliant!' Berg said approvingly. 'And if she fails to achieve this goal then the mystery of Mr Raspero will become so pronounced that it will be a matter of general interest to the town at large to resolve it. If this strategy does not succeed of itself, it will pave the way for a future resolution of the mystery.'

'But poor old Lady Starfeld,' Penny observed. She had finely developed feelings for the sufferings of others. 'She will really be put on the spot, won't she? Think of how she'll wail and gnash her teeth and generally suffer. She probably doesn't know who Mr Raspero is any more than we do.'

The Gang thought about the sufferings-to-come of Lady Starfeld and were unimpressed. The general view was that if Lady Starfeld wanted to swan about as New Landern's leading hostess, then she had to do the hard yards. If she was set a challenge and failed to clear the hurdle, she would fall and that would be just too bad! Besides, once The Gang had set to work, the whole of New Landern would believe that Mr Raspero would be attending Lady Starfeld's party and if she failed to meet the whole of New Landern's expectations, she deserved what was coming to her at the hands of a discomfited and disappointed guest list. It would be some time before she could show her face in public if she failed this test. It was not as if The Gang were going to put obstacles in the way of Lady Starfeld achieving this unprecedented success. Penny's objection was over-ruled. Lady Starfeld could suffer all she liked, but she had better come up with the goods or else! Life could be tough sometimes, and that was all there was to it!

They would all write their letters to Lady Starfeld, they decided, and The Mission would be underway.

11:50 PM, Saturday 2 July 1544 A.F.

It was much later, when she was safely back home, that Isabel got the shakes. She rushed off to bed, brushing away the concern of her guardians, locked and double-checked the locks on her bedroom door, checked and double-checked the fastenings of the windows, and then curled up on her bed.

The encounter with Nevsky had thawed something in her that had been frozen since that terrible night in early June when Nevsky had taken her virtue in front of his men. What had been frozen she did not know, what process of thawing she was undergoing she did not know, but what she did know, what was unmistakable, was the fury that consumed her as she shook and sobbed in her bedroom.

She had never known such anger. She had paid one million strada to that animal and for what? As if what he had done had not been bad enough. As if having to pay him a simply enormous sum of money for what he had done was not bad enough. Now he had also tormented her openly in public. He had flayed her fears of exposure with whips of words, and mocked her with their private knowledge hidden in plain sight of the public arena of Lady Milburga's party. He had already destroyed her life; now he stamped on the remaining half-life which was all she had left to her.

Her terror at Nevsky's presence had been above all fuelled by the possibility that he might say what had happened. He might or might not hang for it now, given the money paid to him, which had somehow perhaps legitimised his action. He had five witnesses, after all, who had sworn on oath that she had played the whore. If it now came to light what he had done he might get away with it, might even boast about having had her, might parade her shame before the entire assembled gaze of laughing New Landerners. Death itself could not possibly erase her pain if that were to occur. Death itself would not be nearly enough. Death itself would be merely a rap on the knuckles.

Even if Nevsky hanged and she was spared his strutting braggadoccio, there would still be her unavoidable fate. She would be ruined! She would never again be able to show her face in public. One million strada she had paid this animal, and for what? To be in terror that the silence she had bought would be broken by this drunken lout, this animal!

She realised then that she had always wanted him dead ever since he had assaulted her: dead, dead, dead! Nothing but his death would suffice to satisfy her terrible anger. Isabel's hatred and fear of Nevsky were all one thing, folded together like the one side of a Moebius strip. His effrontery that evening had simply brought her to an understanding which she had always possessed but had hidden even from herself. She had simply not been able to think about what had happened before this point in time. Now she could think, and all she could think of was that Nevsky had to die.

She thought back to what he had said to Lady Milburga, which she had hardly paid attention to at the time, so desperate was she for the terror to be over with. Nevsky had said something about getting married, about being a politician, being in the highest circles of government. She could not believe it. Nevsky was an animal. Surely no-one could have anything to do with him. She shuddered at the thought of Nevsky continuing to move in high society, of being ever present to mock her, to torment her. In time he would simply make a joke of his behaviour that evening with Lady Milburga, when he was a Minister of the Crown, and she would laugh as well. It would be nothing but a quarrel between friends, and didn't everyone know that friends sometimes quarrelled?

Nevsky had to die. He had to die for what he had done.

Breathing steadily to bring her nerves back under control Isabel sat up, then stood up and paced about the room. How could she see to it that Nevsky died for what he had done? It was out of the question for anyone to know what had happened so no-one could kill Nevsky for her knowing what he had done to her. This complicated things.

There were, of course, by repute, such people as assassins. She knew of them only from stage-plays and novels. They were people who would take money to kill other people. She had money. An assassin would do. An assassin would do perfectly well. But how could she go about finding such a person? By the very nature of their work assassins tended to go through the world in an unobtrusive manner. Presumably assassins who drew attention to themselves were the unsuccessful kind of assassins, and she wanted this job to get done. It was an exasperating paradox to find herself needing to find people who could not be found precisely because they were only the right people to be found if they could not be. Discreet inquiries could no doubt be made, but who would make them on her behalf? Furthermore, how could she recruit someone to recruit an assassin without the recruiter knowing what this was all about? There was a danger that any steps she took to destroy Nevsky would expose her own situation and she would end up being destroyed herself.

The name of Nicholas Raspero came back to her then. Raspero was the only man in New Landern Nevsky was frightened of. She and The Gang were already busy tracking him down. The thought occurred to her that perhaps Raspero might kill Nevsky for her. Of course, he could not know what Nevsky had done, which immediately presented a problem. She could not see a way to get Raspero to kill Nevsky without saying why Nevsky deserved death; yet she could not possibly tell Raspero the reason why Nevsky deserved death.

There was always money, of course, the universal solvent. Raspero might not need money. Yet, if he did, he might be persuaded to act on her behalf. But there should be no haggling. Nor should there be anything less than equivalency. If Raspero was offered a million strada to kill Nevsky he might well be tempted. After all, one million strada was an enormous sum of money. *No haggling, a symmetry of payments; there was something poetic about justice done this way,* she thought.

She resolved then to talk to this mysterious Nicholas Raspero. She would play it by ear. She would take one step at a time, but first she had to find Mr Raspero. The Gang's plan was a start. Maybe it would work. If it did, she would invite him here to talk to him. She would write to Lady Starfeld the very next day, as would all The Gang as already agreed, and as it was a Sunday she would send the letter by private messenger. The wheels would then be in motion.

FOURTEEN

The Trials and Tribulations of Lady Marcella Starfeld

11:35 AM, Sunday 3 July 1544 A.F.

Grangeshield House,
New Landern

Sunday 3 July 1544

Dear Lady Starfeld,
I thank you so much for your kind invitation to your party on Saturday
Night coming. Naturally I accept your invitation with pleasure. How
could I not, given the tremendous success with which all your parties
have always been endowed? There are some who say you are lucky,
others that you are tremendously skilled, but there are none, none I say,
who do not stand in awe of your formidable accomplishments as the
leading hostess of New Landern. No one can even hold a candle to you.
You stand alone.

All this is known even to the masses, who hush their voices in awe
when they even dare mention your lofty name. But now the word
is abroad, it is whispered, it is shouted, it is proudly proclaimed
throughout our great Metropolis, that Lady Starfeld, so renowned to
this date as the leading hostess of the aforesaid Metropolis, has reached
high into the lofty heavens and plucked from the highest constellation
the brightest star of our day, that Lady Starfeld has, in short (and
surely the longest praise would not suffice to delineate such a triumph),

acquired the mysterious and elusive Mr Nicholas Raspero as her guest on Saturday Night.

All who know know this: that Mr Nicholas Raspero is the Talk of the Town! And whose guest should he be but the guest of Lady Starfeld! For as long as this world shall roll around the sun, Lady Starfeld, shall your triumph be remembered! To have the Talk of the Town at your Saturday Night party which is already the Talk of the Town, Lady Starfeld, is a double triumph, a two-fold stellar glory, a rising of two suns clothed in splendour, which has left all those blessed to be witnesses to these days in awe, in awe I say of what you have done in the sight of all! No-one will ever dare speak against you again (but naturally I will not again mention those who speak against you, for surely all those who attain to greatness have their envious detractors) for what you have done has shown you are capable of anything! Where all others have failed, you have succeeded! Those who say, those bitter and envious detractors who would drag you down if they dared, who would mock you to your face in public, those detractors who envy you because they have failed to rise to your heights, those detractors, I say, who claim that you have failed to have acquired Mr Nicholas Raspero as your guest on this Saturday Night coming are those who will be overthrown when you unveil your dazzling success in the sight of all. In the sight of all! Words fail me, Lady Starfeld, to fully express my enormous admiration for the magnitude of your achievement.

Roll on Saturday Night, hasten on your way, bring the glorious Truth splendid in your wake, and there I shall be, a guest among all your other guests, humble in my appreciation of your kindness, a devotee at your side, properly grateful to have been invited to your party this Saturday Night coming.

I remain as always your devoted friend,
Lady Isabel Grangeshield.

Isabel read the letter over approvingly. After several drafts it seemed to have turned out just right. She especially liked the phrase *mock you to your face in public* as the very thought would make Lady Starfeld feel faint. She sent the letter immediately by private messenger.

The Gang had not just written their letters, they had talked to anyone who would listen of their inside information that Lady Starfeld had snagged the elusive and mysterious Nicholas Raspero as her guest for this coming Saturday Night. Their plan worked beautifully. The news spread like wildfire. Everyone had heard of the duel between Raspero and Nevsky and hastened to congratulate Lady Starfeld on her enormous triumph. Lady Starfeld, trapped by the praise heaped on her and unable to deny what had raised her so high in the estimation of all, simply smiled while saying nothing in public and had careful fainting spells in private next to a comfortable sofa surrounded by servants with sympathy and smelling salts. The pressure mounted on Lady Starfeld as the week began and Saturday Night coming loomed large like a mountain about to fall on her. Lady Starfeld, after having hysterics, taking to her bed, and complaining of the Unfairness of Life, had mounted a campaign to find this elusive Mr Nicholas Raspero. She even consulted Stanislav the Magnificent, a Star brought down to Earth by Providence, who at some considerable expense, sought for Mr Raspero by his occult arts only to find that dark forces shrouded the elusive gentleman from his sight due to the Dangers which loomed over the unfortunate Lady Starfeld. At further expense he could take steps to protect her from these Dangers, but Lord Starfeld stepped in and said that would not be necessary.

As no-one had any idea who had started this rumour, Lady Starfeld had no idea how to stamp it out. It had become clear to her that the only way out of her present predicament would be to bring Mr Raspero to her party. However, while everyone seemed to have heard of his name with varying degrees of vagueness, and several had met him, no-one knew where he lived or how an invitation could be delivered to him. She found herself between the Scylla and Charybdis of having an unknown guest who might prove troublesome against not having a guest who all her other guests expected to see. Either outcome could spell disaster. Her reputation as New Landern's leading hostess was at stake.

Her husband was of little help. 'It's obvious what has happened,' he told her. 'This is the Sheltrades strategy. You have been put on the spot by a person or persons unknown in order to carry out the task of bringing Mr Raspero to the light of day. It is really quite transparent.'

'But what do I do?' wailed Lady Starfeld.

Lord Starfeld shrugged. 'It doesn't really matter what you do. This is all a storm in a teacup, a kerfuffle and kebabble of no real consequence. Mr Raspero will be there or he will not be. Life will go on.' Up to that point, Lord Starfeld had some claim on her attention. After all, perhaps he was right. But then her beloved husband, the light of her life and guide of her destiny, went and put his foot in it by displaying his utter Ignorance of the Things that Matter by saying, 'After all, it's only a party.'

Only a party! Lady Starfeld could not believe her ears. This most momentous occasion of recent times over which she would so graciously preside was *only a party* according to her husband! She realised then that Lord Starfeld could not be relied upon, that he lacked the proper feelings, that he entirely failed to understand the gravity of her predicament, that, in short, he had no idea at all of what he was talking about.

It was at that moment that Providence, always so kindly to Lady Starfeld, in great matters and small, intervened. Her dissolute son Stanley turned up at Starfeld Manor, coming no doubt from whatever dishevelled bed of disrepute he had somehow managed to drag himself out of, in order to request five hundred strada for urgent expenses he had incurred in a certain matter which he was discreetly reluctant to discuss in any particular detail. All he would say was to imply that somehow his very life was at stake and if his beloved mother failed to save him she would find herself spending a lot more than that on his funeral. Expecting to be haggled down to two hundred strada, he was greatly surprised to find that his loving mother would willingly pay him the whole sum at once, if Stanley could succeed for once in his life at doing something worthwhile and find the address of a certain Mr Nicholas Raspero who Lady Starfeld wished to invite to her party this coming Saturday Night.

Now Stanley had acquired cunning from his dissolute lifestyle and so he did not immediately reveal that he knew how Nicholas Raspero could be found. Stanley, like so many young men of his background and temperament, had a fascination for all things wandfighting. While in conversation with Timothy Boylent, the subject of Nicholas Raspero had arisen due to the fact that Nicholas had just recently done the Three at Kenina Park. Timothy had not spent ten minutes wandering around the Regana Palace with Nicholas for nothing, and so Stanley learned that Nicholas lived with his uncle Counsellor Lanford Clark in Dejaville. That was where Mr Nicholas Raspero could be found.

Stanley, the little rascal, prevaricated while his mother fretted. He complained about expenses, about slipping the necessary monetary inducements into the necessary hands, spun an imaginary tale of the lengthy and complicated processes which he would have to set in motion to find Raspero's address, and by hook and crook managed to push his beloved mother up to nine hundred strada. Then he went forth, found the address of Mr Nicholas Raspero that very day, and went off whistling with nine hundred strada cash in his pocket. Lady Starfeld herself could not have been happier with this outcome, which reassured her yet again of the kindliness of Providence.

8:20 PM, Thursday 7 July 1544 A.F.

Starfeld Manor,
New Landern

Wednesday 6 July

Dear Mr Nicholas Raspero,
I am holding a small reception this coming Saturday Night, a humble gathering for those select refined few of New Landern I consider sufficiently cheerful and noble in word and deed to gather together for the express purpose of raising in common voice a rousing shout of joy in these troubled times (but then the times are always troubled, are they not? — but I speak to no purpose when I instruct one of the leading minds of our age, or indeed any age).

In consideration of this venture upon which I have embarked, I cannot help but wonder if you would be so kind as to attend my party this Saturday Night coming. Your presence shall be a light unto us all, the very words you shall speak a blessing!

There will be no more than seven hundred attendees or so (do not ask me to count, my dear and most esteemed Mr Raspero! I leave those who do not count to count). I am sure you detest crowds — don't we all?

How can I implore you to come? A man of your glorious modesty will certainly not overlook a woman in her hour of need — I cling to this hope for indeed it is my hour of need. What will become of me if you do not come? I tremble at the thought! You must come otherwise I am lost! What I shall do if you cannot come I do not know — I dare not think of it, I dare not!

I know you will not, in your gracious kindness, require me to fall to my knees and beseech you to attend my party this Saturday Night coming. Without you I am lost! Surely you will come! I know you will! Yes, I know somehow you will come! Somehow — do not ask me how I know!

I remain always your affectionate devotee,
Humbled to invite you this Saturday Night coming,
And always affectionately yours,
Lady Marcella Starfeld.

Nicholas started to read this letter again, trying to make sense of it.

'Who's the letter from?' Ben asked him curiously. Nicholas did not often receive letters.

'It's a bit strange,' Nicholas said in reply. 'It's from this Lady Starfeld inviting me to her party.'

'Lady Starfeld!' Ben whistled. 'Wow!'

'You've heard of her?'

'Well, of course I've heard of her. She's one of the tip-top society ladies. People would kill to get invited to one of her parties.'

'She's saying that her life would be some kind of stricken wasteland if I don't go to her party.'

'They always talk like that. It doesn't mean anything.'

'She also says I'm one of the leading minds of the age.'

Ben laughed loudly, a little more loudly than Nicholas thought necessary. 'You never told me that. I certainly would never have guessed it.'

'But why is she inviting me to her party?'

Ben considered this for a moment. 'You know, I have absolutely no idea. What have you been up to lately?'

'Not much.'

'Do you know anyone who knows her?'

'Not as far as I know.'

'Well, that is a puzzle,' said Ben, and yawned. He had been up late the night before over legal papers. 'Are you going to go?'

'Will you come with me?'

'I can't if I'm not invited.'

'I can't go alone,' Nicholas protested. 'What if I don't know anyone there and I have no-one to talk to?'

'Then leave after a discreet interval of time,' Ben said in what Nicholas thought was a very cavalier fashion.

'If her life will be a scene of devastation if I don't attend, then she can't stop you coming with me, can she? I'm practically saving her life by attending so what can she say? You'll be just one more face among the seven hundred or so attendees.'

'Only seven hundred?' Ben whistled again. 'Wow! It must really be a tip-top party!'

'So you're coming then?' Nicholas asked.

'Nicky, you don't understand,' Ben told him, with the wise, world-weary air of the city sophisticate faced with his country cousin. 'If I'm not invited then I'm not on the list. If I'm not on the list, I don't get in. It's like going to heaven or something. You can't just go with someone else.'

'But what about all her talk about my presence being a blessing and all that? She says that without me she is lost!'

'That's just talk. I already told you, it doesn't mean anything.'

'Well, I protest!' Nicholas said, like a religious heretic faced with an arbitrary tyranny. 'I protest! Words have meanings and without those meanings what's the point? Why doesn't she just write to me and say, Nicholas my hunky-chunky friend, come to my party if it's cool, and if not, that's cool too. Then I go or don't go. She makes it sound like a life or death matter!'

'I keep on telling you, it's all talk.' Ben sounded exasperated at the slowness of his country cousin.

'But that's my point! Talk is made up of words. As far as I'm concerned, I can take this letter at face value. It says what it says! Lady Starfeld is desperate for me to come to her party, so if you come with me she can't refuse you entrance. Then we go together.'

'I will be refused entrance,' Ben told him. 'Because ... my ... name ... is ... not ... on ... the ... list.'

'Then I'll refuse to go in and that's that. I got her invitation, turned up and didn't get admitted. Look, she's a complete stranger. Does she really expect me to just go on my own when I probably won't know anyone there? That's unreasonable!'

'Nicky, you go or don't go. Leave me out of this!'

Nicholas looked at Ben with a slow smile. 'Ah, that's just it with you, Ben, isn't it?'

Ben did not want to bite the bait. He knew there was a hidden hook. 'Absolutely,' he agreed. 'That is indeed just it. And quite right too!'

'You just want to stay hiding in your hole, don't you? Little Ben Clark, the legal eagle, no, the legal beagle with a runny nose and flapping ears hiding in a hole!'

'I am not even going to begin counting your mixed metaphors,' Ben said stiffly, but he was trying not to smile all the same.

'Ben, fortune favours the brave! Now, the question you have to ask yourself is: are you feeling brave?'

'Not today, no, as it happens.'

'Let me get this clear,' Nicholas said thoughtfully. 'As a legal person embarking forth on your career, you are going to refuse to attend a party where the tip-top grandees of New Landern are all gathered together in one place at your very fingertips. This is what you are saying? Is it? Well?'

Ben took a deep breath and sighed. 'No, Nicky. I am refusing to waste my time trying to go when I can't.'

'Ah, but on a cost-benefit ratio, what will you lose by trying compared to what you might gain by winning? What would you advise a client of yours in your position to do?'

Ben considered this. The magic word *client* made him think, as Nicholas had known it would. 'I would have to say it would be worth a shot because the gains would be considerable, the loss negligible, and you never know how things might turn out.'

'So there we are!' Nicholas cried out in triumph. 'I'm going and you're coming with me! It's settled!'

Ben buried his face in his hands to signify his own recognition of his defeat. Nicholas leaned back in his chair with a sigh of satisfaction. Outside the watchmen marched past, their heavy tread marking the time of the hour of that night, the Thursday night before that of Saturday Night coming.

7:25 PM, Saturday 9 July 1544 A.F.

The streets were crowded with people going to their varying destinations, talking and loudly laughing, shouldering each other like apprentice pickpockets, which some perhaps were. In the midst of the crowd were two contrasting figures who were both friends and cousins.

Ben had dressed up at his very best, which helped him to look at least moderately prosperous and respectable. Ben was a tall, broad-shouldered man with a fine head of dark curly hair and greyish-green eyes, and he was impressive-looking in his best clothes. Beside him the shorter Nicholas largely failed to impress; he was as shabbily dressed and average-looking as ever.

As they neared the district of Old Nuroy the crowds began to thin out as if its ordinary citizens were falling to the thinning air of the prosperity of such altitudes. Soon they were on their own on the cobble-stoned streets, accompanied only by flying carriages passing by overhead.

'Ben, whatever I do, back me up,' Nicholas ordered.

'That sounds like a recipe for disaster,' Ben commented.

'If we go down in flames,' Nicholas proclaimed, 'then the flames we go down in will be such flames as Lucifer himself would envy.'

'Why am I not encouraged by all this talk of going down in flames?' Ben asked.

'Because you are by nature a pessimist,' Nicholas pointed out. 'You mistrust the universe.'

'I wonder why,' Ben said sarcastically. 'Silly of me, isn't it?'

'Leave everything to me,' Nicholas said, spreading his hands out palms down in a gesture which embodied him then and there as an incarnation of knowledge. Ben shook his head and sighed very audibly.

They were walking alongside a tall wall coming up to large wrought-iron gates which stood wide-open. No-one seemed to be about as they entered and walked along a driveway lined with flowerbeds. The large imposing edifice of Starfeld Manor loomed over them, ominously in Ben's eyes, who was already deeply regretting having agreed to come.

'Nicholas, I really don't think this is such a good idea,' Ben said fearfully, his nerves getting the better of him as the coming confrontation loomed larger and larger in his mind's eye.

'Well, run for it, then,' Nicholas said with contempt. 'And don't forget to tuck your tail between your legs so you can run faster.'

Ben stayed by Nicholas's side, trying to tell himself that the worst that could happen would be that he would simply be turned away.

Large wooden doors stood open, leading into a large marble-floored entrance hall, with wooden paneling on the walls, and paintings of various ancestors of the Starfelds, several of whom looked darkly villainous. Spiked maces lay on neighbouring tables next to sharpened pikes, mementoes of a more direct age.

Ben's stomach had hatched a cloud of butterflies by now. He stole a sideways look at Nicholas, who looked amused, which only served to agitate Ben's nerves still further. He had seen that look on his wandfighting cousin's face before and it was always when trouble was already on the way.

They walked through the entrance hall to the large double doors standing wide open at the end. They could hear the sounds of the party beyond the doors, a distant splashing murmur like the waves of the sea falling on rocks.

Before the door a servant sat at a table, dressed in the livery of the Starfelds. Before him was a scroll of paper, unrolled and held flat against the table-top by silver candlesticks. Even the paper weights here were silver candlesticks, Ben thought, feeling more and more intimidated with each passing moment.

'Sirs, your names, please,' the servant said grandly. He was the doorkeeper and he wanted them to know it.

'I am Mr Nicholas Raspero, and this is my cousin, Mr Benjamin Clark. We are attending Lady Starfeld's party by invitation.'

The doorkeeper took his time checking his list, his movements slow and deliberate. 'You may enter, Mr Raspero,' he said at last, 'but Mr Benjamin Clark may not.' He declared this as if his judgement in these matters were final.

Ben wanted to say, 'Well, that's that, have fun, bye,' and then run for it, but his tongue was glued to the roof of his mouth by his thickened saliva. For a lawyer not to be able to say a word was not good, he reflected a little feverishly.

'My cousin Mr Clark is with me,' Nicholas told the doorkeeper. 'If he does not enter, then neither do I.'

The doorkeeper had a sallow face, pale and greasy, with long, black hair pushed to the sides. He also had a nasty smile, which he now displayed to the newcomers.

'That, of course, is your choice, Mr Raspero,' he said. He said nothing more, as if he had no need to say one more word.

'All right, call Lady Starfeld and ask her to judge in this matter,' Nicholas ordered him.

The doorkeeper said nothing but smiled his nasty smile again.

'You are starting to get on my nerves!' Nicholas shouted at him. 'You are nothing but a jumped-up flunkey. I demand that Lady Starfeld make this decision.'

'What seems to be the problem?' a voice asked from behind. Ben jumped.

Nicholas turned around, unsurprised by this latest development. His hand resting on the hilt of his wand, he had already identified where all the security people were, and he had monitored their approach.

'And you are?' Nicholas asked, studying the man who would now be his opponent. He was a slim man with thinning, blond hair and sunken eyes.

'I am Ryan Marchant,' the newcomer told him, his eyes cold as he appraised Nicholas. 'I am in charge of the security here.'

'This jumped-up flunkey here,' Nicholas said, gesturing behind him with a thumb to the doorkeeper, 'is presuming that he has the right to deny my cousin entry to the party. I insist that Lady Starfeld herself should make this decision.'

'Borchardt the doorkeeper has the authority to deny a person of any standing whatsoever entry to the party if their name is not on the list, which alone identifies those who may enter,' Marchant told him. He said all this with the ease of long practice. He obviously knew it by heart.

'Ah, but Borchardt doesn't realise how desperately keen Lady Starfeld is for me to attend her party,' Nicholas responded. 'She said she will be lost if I do not come. In view of this, surely you must realise that the usual rules do not apply.'

'The usual rules always apply, Mr Raspero,' Marchant said, unmoved by the tale of his employer Lady Starfeld's plight. 'I am afraid I must ask your cousin, Mr Clark, to leave the premises.'

'Well, now,' said Nicholas, moving his feet apart and taking a firmer grip on the hilt of his wand, 'I thought it might come to this. But first of all I have to tell you something very important, so listen carefully. You have three men out of sight on the stairs, two outside the door, and you yourself, which makes six. Six men won't be enough to take me down, Mr Marchant. Trust me.'

Marchant looked at Nicholas, and Nicholas looked straight back at Marchant. Borchardt slipped his hand down under the tabletop.

'Nor will seven,' Nicholas said, not looking away from Marchant. 'Pull that wand on me, Borchardt, and I will break your arm.'

Marchant's eyes flickered past Nicholas to glance at Borchardt, whose hand was now emerging above the tabletop back into plain sight, held open to show that it was empty. 'This unpleasantness is not necessary, Mr Raspero. I ask you once again to step aside, while Mr Clark leaves these premises.'

'You're not listening to me,' Nicholas told him. 'This is really a fight you should walk away from. I tell you again: Lady Starfeld will decide this matter, not this jumped-up flunkey Borchardt.'

Nicholas moved at the same time as Marchant, but much less quickly. Marchant's strength was his speed;. Marchant's wand flew into his hand while Nicholas was still drawing his, yet Marchant's combinations had no effect. Nicholas flipped Marchant head over heels, while taking his wand and rolling to the side. The men from outside were already rushing in, wands drawn; Marchant barrelled into one of them while in three movements Nicholas had taken the wand away from the other two. One by one Nicholas took them all down, then whipping out their own cords he had them bound and trussed and lined up against the wall.

Nicholas looked around him with the air of a conqueror. Borchardt had gone pale and was not daring to move a muscle.

'I told you six men were not enough to take me down,' he told Marchant.

Marchant was furious but spoke with a fiercely clenched calmness. 'There will be consequences, Mr Raspero, I trust you realise this.'

'And will those consequences be in my favour or yours?' Nicholas asked him. 'Your security isn't up to much, is it? Fancy facing the sack, do you?'

Judging from the expression on his face Marchant did not fancy facing the sack. 'I thought your name sounded familiar, Mr Raspero,' he said. 'You are the man who took down Nevsky. Are you not?'

Nicholas ignored this request for information and turned back to Borchardt. 'Lady Starfeld will pronounce judgement on this matter, not you. Now get going!'

Nicholas pointed his wand at Borchardt, flourished it and physically threw the doorkeeper through the open doors onto the floor beyond. Borchardt scrambled to his feet and disappeared.

The later arrivals to Lady Starfeld's party, cautiously and courteously waiting some distance away, were staring at Ben and Nicholas as if they were naked. It was clearly not customary for Lady Starfeld's guests to get into a fight with security immediately upon arrival and Ben felt acutely the exceptional nature of this situation. His nerves had temporarily disappeared, as if he were in a barrel that had already gone over the waterfall. Ben had long ago prudently and discreetly withdrawn to one side before the battle began and had stood throughout leaning against the wall. He had completely ignored Nicholas's wandfight with Marchant and Co., not giving the action a single glance, all the while inspecting his fingernails absent-mindedly as if his thoughts were elsewhere. Now he crossed his arms over his chest and spoke. 'Tell me, Nicky,' he asked casually, 'what is all this bravery about? Is it because you are too scared to go to the party on your own?'

Nicholas laughed merrily. He was in an excellently, merry mood. 'I'll have no lawyer talk from you, Ben my boy.'

'You will need my lawyer talk before long the way you're going,' Ben told him flatly.

'Always the pessimist,' Nicholas observed.

'Always barking mad,' Ben observed right back.

'I will let you have the last word, of course,' Nicholas said cheerfully.

'Yes, you will,' Ben replied.

Nicholas laughed again as merrily as before. Nothing could put a dent in his cheerfulness right then.

Nicholas was not kept waiting long. Borchardt returned with a tall, thin, avuncular man, kindly and welcoming.

'I understand that we have a slight difficulty, Mr Raspero,' he said in a silky voice. 'I am Arvedun, Lady Starfeld's steward. Can I be of some assistance in this matter?'

'Lady Starfeld is desperately keen to have me attend her party, she told me so herself in a letter of invitation,' Nicholas told him. 'My cousin, Mr Benjamin Clark, has come with me. If he doesn't enter, neither do I. If Lady Starfeld is so keen to have me attend she will accept my cousin's presence as well, won't she? And if she is not she should phrase her invitations differently. Now, as to the security people,' Nicholas looked at Marchant and his men, trussed up on the floor, 'well, that's too long a story, I'll skip over that part.'

'I quite understand, sir,' Arvedun said smoothly.

'I will only accept Lady Starfeld's judgement in this matter and no-one else's.'

Now Arvedun knew full well of the desperate plight Lady Starfeld had been placed in by suddenly having to produce Mr Nicholas Raspero as her guest and so he pronounced his verdict without hesitation. 'I am empowered to over-rule Borchardt's decision, Mr Raspero. You are perfectly correct in your estimation of Lady Starfeld's eagerness in having you tonight as her guest. Therefore, if you will allow me to be so bold as to speak in the place of Lady Starfeld, I will grant you and your cousin entry to the party.'

Nicholas considered this. 'What I meant to say before was that I would only allow either your judgement or that of Lady Starfeld to be final in this matter.'

'I quite understood that to be so, sir,' Arvedun said with an almost reverential air.

'So that's settled then,' Nicholas asked slightly suspiciously, as if on the look-out for some kind of trick.

'Indeed it is, sir,' Arvedun agreed.

Nicholas freed Marchant and Co. almost absent-mindedly. Marchant clambered back to his feet a little stiffly, stretching his limbs. Nicholas flicked his wand and the wands of Marchant and his men appeared in the air before them. It did not escape Marchant's attention as he took his wand back that Nicholas sent the correct wand back to each owner even though he had taken those wands from their owners during the hectic hurly-burly of their fight. With that slightly awed recognition of Nicholas's ability much of Marchant's resentment evaporated.

'Lead on, Arvedun,' Nicholas told the steward, waving him forward as imperiously as an emperor. Arvedun courteously bowed without a word and led the way through the open doors, Nicholas and Ben following him a few paces behind.

They went along a long corridor to where more double doors stood wide open. They could see people moving and talking, laughing, drinking and eating, in the room beyond.

Arvedun courteously and with the merest of gestures required them to remain just outside the door while he entered and whispered into the ear of a large florid-faced man standing rigidly at attention to one side of the door.

'Mr Nicholas Raspero and Mr Benjamin Clark!' the announcer called out loudly.

The silence spread through the room like the contents of a falling wave rushing swiftly in its shallow flow over the level sands of a beach. It was in this hushed, almost reverential silence that Nicholas Raspero, the Talk of the Town, entered the reception room of Starfeld Manor.

FIFTEEN

The Meeting Between Mr Nicholas Raspero and Lord Adair Zinia

7:55 PM, Saturday 9 July 1544 A.F.

The Reception Room of Starfeld Manor was a more civilised version of the Great Halls of old: warm and welcoming foreign carpets covered the polished wooden floorboards, and from the high ceiling were lowered large chandeliers which descended through the air to float through the room like islands of light, while staircases departed from the sides of the room to zig-zag out of sight; an enormous painting of the battle of Niedbala and portraits of significant Starfelds and weaponry ornaments hung on the walls. A variety of people dressed differently yet with a glittering alikeness stood about the room, the splendour of their appearance filling even the enormity of the Reception Room with an unearthly glow. All these people had turned as one to gaze upon the newest arrivals to the party, and so it was that Nicholas and Ben entered the room to find themselves the centre of attention in the midst of a hushed silence. Nicholas calmly stood there looking around, the picture of unruffled relaxation, while Ben, whose apprehensiveness had abruptly returned in full force, was a tangled ball of nerves. His rational mind was telling him that the craziness of the night was now over, while the irrational part of his mind was telling him that it had only just begun, and these two parts of his mind were having a shouting match about who was right.

Having scanned the room with a composed mind and attention to detail, Nicholas set off towards a group of people sitting at the side.

Ben followed nervously. Nicholas approached the group and came to a standstill.

Not by chance, The Gang were there, seated and attentive to the approach of Nicholas Raspero. It had come to their attention that Miss Dahl had made the acquaintance of Nicholas Raspero and so they had made sure that she was by their side; nor was it by chance that Miss Dahl had taken up her seat in such a position as to afford a view of the entrance of the guests, for she had after all gained the distinction of having been introduced to Mr Nicholas Raspero at the engagement party of Mr Carver and Lady Lachance at the Regana Palace, and so it was that it was Miss Dahl, and Miss Radcliff sitting next to her that Nicholas Raspero made a bee-line towards, thus bringing him right before The Gang in his very own person!

The Gang feasted their collective gaze on the mysterious Mr Raspero, who was standing before them in the flesh. They saw a man of medium height, black-haired and grey-eyed, composed and deliberate in his movements, with a self-assurance which seemed to stem from the way he stood with his hand on the hilt of his wand. Yet, it could not be denied that he was very ordinary looking and shabbily dressed and were it not for his reputation having preceded him they very likely would not have given him a second look.

'Good evening, Miss Dahl,' Nicholas said.

'Good evening, Mr Raspero,' Miss Dahl replied, delighted to have been singled out in this way. 'How are you?'

'Never better,' Nicholas replied. 'And good evening to you, Miss Radcliff.'

Miss Radcliff said nothing in reply, paralyzed by nerves, especially as everyone turned to look at her, no-one having known that she had met the elusive Mr Raspero. Nicholas turned his attention back to Miss Dahl.

'This is my cousin, Mr Benjamin Clark. Ben, this is Miss Amanda Dahl.'

'Delighted to meet you,' Ben said politely.

'Delighted to meet you, Mr Clark,' Miss Dahl said with equal politeness.

'Ben, this is Miss Eileen Radcliff,' Nicholas continued. 'Miss Radcliff, Mr Benjamin Clark.'

'Delighted to meet you, Miss Radcliff,' Ben said as politely as before but much more truthfully. For the first time, as he considered the Miss Radcliff he had just been introduced to, he started not to regret coming tonight.

'Yes,' Miss Radcliff said. It was a reply which was all her shyness could manage yet Ben took it very differently. His turning brain slipped a cog, perhaps as a delayed reaction to stress, giving rise to the belief that Miss Radcliff was saying *yes* to the implicit prospect of receiving his romantic advances sometime in the future. It was a curious misreading of one of the simpler words in the Anglashian language, but by then Ben was not entirely in his right mind.

'Miss Dahl, I wonder if you might do me a favour?' Nicholas asked.

'But of course, Mr Raspero. I would be delighted,' Miss Dahl replied.

'I have been invited to this party by —' Nicholas turned to Ben. 'Who was it again?' Nicholas asked him.

'Lady Starfeld,' Ben told him in a low voice, embarrassed and not believing for a moment that Nicholas had really forgotten her name.

'Exactly!' Nicholas proclaimed, holding his left hand out in the air, his forefinger protruding as if pointing the way. 'Lady Starfeld. However, as I don't know her at all, I was wondering if you would be so kind as to introduce me to her?'

'But of course, Mr Raspero. It would be my pleasure.' Miss Dahl gracefully arose to her feet, her long tennis-playing legs hidden under her even longer skirts, and gestured for Nicholas and Ben to follow her.

The Gang watched their quarry walk away.

'He doesn't *look* like a terrifying wandfighter,' Penny complained.

'That's exactly what Nevsky thought, apparently,' Berg observed. 'But by the time Mr Raspero was finished with him, Nevsky was shaking like a leaf from head to toe.'

'Leaves don't have heads and toes,' Uliana corrected him. 'I do detest mixed metaphors. They are so slovenly.'

Berg fell silent. He was shattered. This was the worst thing that had happened to him all year.

Uliana's fan fluttered a little in triumph.

Miss Dahl reached Lord and Lady Starfeld with her two charges safely in tow. With a studied and theatrical nonchalance, Miss Dahl introduced Nicholas and Ben to the Starfelds, feeling as if her life was for once being played out on centre stage.

Lady Starfeld was a short, plump woman with bright blue eyes, curly black hair in a gold netting and red-painted lips. She had been a noted beauty in her youth. Lord Starfeld was tall and thin with short-cut grey hair, a deceptively vacant expression that masked a very sharp mind, and long-fingered hands that restlessly pulled on the lapels of his coat. They both looked closely at Nicholas Raspero, who was only here tonight due to a trick played by a person or persons unknown and who had thus become their guest in this elliptical fashion.

'We are so thrilled you are here, Mr Raspero,' said Lady Starfeld.

'Why is that?' asked Nicholas.

Lady Starfeld was momentarily thrown by this question. Looking up into Nicholas's disconcertingly direct grey eyes she realised that Nicholas had asked his question with perfect seriousness. He really wanted to know. Lady Starfeld thought that it was very bad manners to actually show that you wanted to know something. A person of refinement would pretend to know rather than ask such a direct question.

Lady Starfeld only smiled, looked away as if to hint that some mysteries were never spoken of directly, and then said, 'I see you are witty, Mr Raspero.'

'I have my moments, Lady Starfeld,' Nicholas said. 'So you're thrilled that I am here, did you say?' Clearly Nicholas wasn't going to let go of this point.

Lady Starfeld looked at him with the sweetest of smiles, and said in a husky throaty voice that in her younger days had been known to weaken men to the point of dropping their wine-glasses, 'It was so wonderful to have met you.' This eloquent reference to a past event made it abundantly clear to Nicholas that his introduction was over and he should go away now.

As he turned away he found two young ladies standing in front of him, their gaze fixed directly on him. One of them said to Miss Dahl, who had turned away from the Starfelds with Nicholas, 'But surely, Amanda, you are going to introduce us to Mr Raspero.'

Miss Dahl looked as if this was not an idea that would have occurred to her on her own, but put on the spot in this way she could not refuse without seeming ungracious. She had enjoyed her brief shining moment as one of the few known acquaintances of Mr Raspero too much to let it go easily, however. Lady Starfeld, during the days she had spent hunting Nicholas Raspero, had gathered up Miss Dahl as a party guest solely due to her one claim to fame: that she had been introduced to Mr Raspero. She knew she might never come here again and that knowledge had a bitter taste.

'But I would not wish to impose on Mr Raspero,' she said, turning to Nicholas. It was a delaying tactic made in the interests of a forlorn hope.

'Not at all,' Nicholas said magnanimously, 'go ahead and introduce us.'

Miss Dahl, reluctantly and grudgingly, made the necessary introductions to Miss Sophie Nicholson and Miss Penelope Earlson.

'You must come and meet our friends, Mr Raspero. They are dying to meet you,' Sophie said immediately.

'So I am summoned on a mercy mission, am I?' Nicholas asked with a mock-serious turn of his head.

'Yes!' exclaimed Penny, delightedly. 'So you can't say no.'

'Think of all those deaths on your conscience, Mr Raspero,' Sophie implored him.

'Very well, lead on,' Nicholas replied, amused.

They led him across the room to where The Gang all sat in armchairs, watching them approach. Isabel had miscalculated by fretting too much and missed a seat and was standing behind the chair Sophie was sitting in. So it was that in their excitement Sophie and Penny omitted to include Isabel in their introductions of Mr Nicholas Raspero to all those who were seated. Isabel was not at all happy about it, but there was nothing she could do.

'Surely you will sit and join us, Mr Raspero,' Uliana said invitingly. Everyone agreed with her, gesturing to an empty chair which they had strategically placed in their midst for the purpose of getting him to sit in it.

'All right,' Nicholas said noncommittantly as he sat down. Ben had disappeared like a faithless and untrustworthy companion, leaving him all alone. (Ben, however, would have put it differently, complaining that he might as well not be there for all the attention Sophie and Penny had paid him. Indeed, Sophie and Penny had not even noticed that Ben had gone, so eagerly did they observe every detail of Mr Nicholas Raspero's appearance, demeanour and behaviour.)

'Tell us everything about yourself, Mr Raspero,' Penny said excitedly.

'Everything?' Nicholas queried. 'Well, that won't take long. I am from Little Batton in Surrafield, my father Mr Emmett Raspero has an independent income, he married Miss Catherine Bell from Burravilde, her father was a schoolteacher, I have two younger sisters Gemma and Tamina, and I am staying in New Landern with my uncle Counsellor Lanford Clark. So that's it. Now you know everything.'

'You have a strange name, Mr Raspero,' Sophie commented, throwing caution out of the window in her eagerness to learn something out of the ordinary about the mysterious Mr Raspero, whose mysteriousness was rapidly disappearing by the prosaically passing minute of mundane detail.

'My grandfather, Alexandre, was the second son of the twenty-fourth Baron of Raspero in Westrigonia,' Nicholas told them. They gasped silently. This was more like it! The talk of schoolteachers and lawyers had been disappointing. Foreign barons sounded much more promising. 'He settled here in Anglashia and married Miss Lydia Knight, one of three daughters of the Reverend Lennard Knight. They have four children, Anatole, who is the Comptroller-General of the Second Port and who married Miss Iolanda Marmaduke, the daughter of General Peregrine Marmaduke, Pamela, who married Mr Casper Ingram, a horse trainer down in Lower Torse, and —'

'Mr Ingram!' exclaimed Samantha. 'But he has won the Mudfield Stakes four times!'

'Don't mention my name to him,' Nicholas warned her. 'I once commented that I couldn't understand why people still rode horses when the flying carriage had been invented, and he has never forgiven me for it.'

'But what a thing to say!' Samantha said in shock. 'Horses are intelligent, sensitive creatures who carry one beautifully on their backs. Carriages are merely wooden and nothing more.'

'That was what he said,' Nicholas replied. 'Yes, it's all coming back to me now. Whatever he said, exactly, it was the same sentiment.'

'But please carry on, Mr Raspero,' Uliana urged him, uninterested in horses versus carriages.

'Then there was Lena, who married Mr Lanford Clark; she died about fifteen years ago, she was Ben's mother.' Nicholas looked around the room but there continued to be no sight of Ben anywhere. 'And then my father Emmett, the youngest son. So that's everyone. My tale is done, I believe.'

He wasn't getting let off that easily.

'Have you been to visit your relatives in Westrigonia, Mr Raspero?' Penny asked, fired up by all the romantic promise of the day.

'No,' Nicholas said shortly.

'But why ever not, Mr Raspero?' asked Uliana.

'Why should I?' Nicholas told them. 'What do they have to do with me?'

'But they are your relatives, Mr Raspero,' Uliana insisted.

Nicholas shrugged. 'My father went there once long ago, before I was born, he had some interest in seeing them, but the Baron, Alexandre's father, turned him away at the door.'

'But why did that happen?' Uliana asked him.

'When Alexandre married Lydia, he went against his father's wishes, so the Baron sent him a letter with crossed swords drawn on it. In Westrigonian it meant that if Alexandre ever returned to Raspero he would be put to death.'

'Goodness, how awful!' Penny exclaimed, her knuckles pressed against her teeth, thrilled to the core.

'But what were the wishes of the Baron?' Uliana asked.

'Why, to return home and follow the programme the Baron had devised for him, to go into their equivalent of the Civil Service, to enter into an arranged marriage and, in short, be a dutiful son.'

'I see,' Uliana replied, 'but even so, the Baron must be very strict.'

'Well, the Barons of Raspero are the oldest baronial family in Westrigonia so they must be doing something right,' Nicholas said dismissively, as if nothing more now needed to be said.

'The oldest baronial family in Westrigonia!' Penny exclaimed. 'How old? How did the barony begin?'

'Daniel was made the first Baron back in 942. He was a bandit in the forest whose armed band controlled the region of Raspero. The king got so fed up with not getting his taxes that in the end he gave up, made Daniel a Baron, and the royal revenue resumed flowing into the royal treasury.'

'A not uncommon beginning of a noble house,' Berg observed.

'How did Daniel become a bandit?' Penny asked. 'Was he a disinherited nobleman driven from his rightful lands by a tyrannical uncle?'

'No, he was low-born, the son of a master-of-arms and a miller's daughter,' Nicholas told her.

'Perhaps they only pretended he was their son,' Penny suggested, 'because they had been handed a baby from a boat which came over the waves of a windswept lake.'

Nicholas considered this comment and decided to completely ignore it. 'Well,' he said, looking at Sophie and Penny, 'I was told that your friends were dying to meet me, and I believe that they have now been restored to life. So, now it's my turn to ask the questions. Tell me: why was I invited to this party tonight?'

There was a sudden shifty silence during which no-one would directly look Nicholas in the eye. 'But whatever do you mean?' Sophie asked eventually, trying to look the picture of innocence.

'Exactly what I say. Why did Lady Starfeld invite me to her party tonight?' Nicholas asked her.

'I'm sure I do not know,' Sophie replied. Trying to shift Nicholas's inquisitorial gaze away from her she turned to Penny and said, 'Do you know why, Penny?'

Nicholas's inquisitorial gaze shifted to Penny. 'No!' she shrieked and collapsed into a fit of the giggles, her face buried in her forearms with her unfolded fan over the top of her head. Her giggles proved infectious and soon fans were unfolded and faces hidden with only peeping laughing eyes emerging now and then. Berg didn't have a fan, so he steepled his fingers and rested his forehead on them.

For Nicholas their reaction to his question only deepened the mystery of his invitation. But he realised that there was nothing further to be done for now, so with a smile he arose from his chair and said, taking a leaf from Lady Starfeld's book, 'It was so wonderful to have met you.' He then departed in search of Ben.

He spotted Ben in the neighbouring room deep in conversation with an elderly gentleman in a wig. Guessing (correctly) that this was a deadly dull legal conversation, Nicholas continued in search of someone he knew, or failing that, food and drink. He spotted Mr Albert Yancy standing nearby on his own, leaning against the wall with a drink in his hand. Nicholas went up to him and soon they were chatting away.

8:45 PM, Saturday 9 July 1544 A.F.

There were strategically placed eyes watching the figure of Mr Nicholas Raspero and mouths which directed certain actions; Mr Alwyn Hardy, by gaining an introduction to Nicholas by having been introduced by Mr Emmerich Blaze, who had just been introduced by Timothy Boylent, asked Nicholas if he could come with him for a moment. Nicholas trustingly went along. They went through a door to the side and down a corridor and Nicholas's guide turned right into a room.

Nicholas followed to find himself in a large, pleasantly appointed room with comfortable chairs scattered about, and a suit of armour in the corner. There were four men seated in the room. Nicholas's guide introduced Nicholas to them: Lord Adair Zinia, Comptroller Dacre Ingelbert, Commissioner Mark Cable, and Lord Lesley Kristoff, after which Nicholas's guide discreetly withdrew from the room, closing the door behind him.

Nicholas wasn't sure what was going on, but he did realise that he had been expertly culled from the pack of the party by these men, who therefore must be figures of some importance in order to have been able to do this. Ingelbert, Cable and Kristoff were studying him with the unabashed curiosity of five-year-olds while Lord Zinia, having looked at him during their introduction and only nodded briefly, was too busy packing his pipe with tobacco to pay Nicholas any more attention. No-one was saying anything, so Nicholas looked about him for a minute or so, before breaking three rules of proper conduct in quick succession. Firstly, he drew his wand, which he shouldn't have without permission; he then whipped around a chair from the side and placed it to one side facing his newly found companions, and thirdly he pulled up a footstool, pocketed his wand and sat down. Ingelbert stroked his moustache to hide his smile.

He joined them in the silence in which they were sitting. He quite openly studied Lord Zinia with his own unabashed curiosity, having already guessed that Lord Zinia was the most senior figure there, given how he was sitting and how he was ignoring Nicholas.

Lord Zinia lit his pipe with a slow calm deliberation, sending puffs of smoke up into the air, then leaned back slightly in his chair and looked steadily at Nicholas for a moment or two.

'I did not give you permission to sit down, Mr Raspero,' he said.

'Yes, I noticed that.'

'Are you choosing to be deliberately rude, Mr Raspero?'

'Is this why Lady Starfeld invited me to her party? So I could be brought here to stand before you in your chair?'

'I am not a man to be impressed by bravado, Mr Raspero.'

'Well, I'm not a man to be impressed by pomposity, Lord Zinia. So there is at least one difference between us. Perhaps others will emerge.'

Lord Zinia smiled slightly. 'How old are you, Mr Raspero?'

'Twenty-two.'

'Ah, that is a splendid age to be. It is also an age to be young and foolish, is it not?'

'People of an advanced age can also be foolish, Lord Zinia. Would you not agree?'

Lord Zinia smiled more widely until he chuckled. 'You have spirit, Mr

Raspero. You also have talent, by all accounts. My concern, however, is whether you have character.'

'And what is it to you?' Nicholas asked cautiously, still trying to make some kind of sense of who this man was and what this was all about.

'Order does not maintain itself, Mr Raspero,' Lord Zinia said. 'It must be maintained.'

'What kind of order are we talking about, Lord Zinia?'

'The order which you have disrupted by what you have done, Mr Raspero. The question is, what are you about? The consequences of what you have done can be managed, but what about you, Mr Raspero? Can you be managed?'

'Definitely not, Lord Zinia,' Nicholas said firmly. 'If you want to manage something, go and buy yourself a horse. But first of all, why not tell me what it is I have done so that I can at least know why it is that I am telling you to go jump in the lake?'

Lord Zinia lit his pipe again and took his time about it. Nicholas waited patiently, unfazed by this deliberate attempt to wear his nerves down as it was a standard technique of wandfighting strategy. Seeing that his attempt to intimidate Nicholas was going nowhere Lord Zinia spoke. 'Before we proceed any further, Mr Raspero, I require you to give me your word that you will honour the confidential nature of this discussion we are having.'

Nicholas considered this impassively for a moment, then nodded. 'Very well, I give you my word.'

'It has come to our attention, Mr Raspero, that you were instrumental in the downfall of Jolly. We know this, at least. But what we do not know is what you are about, what your intentions are, and what, if any, further plans you have.'

'What's the downfall of Jolly to you?' Nicholas asked very cautiously. 'Jolly was a poisonous snake, the world's a better place without him.'

'The world has become a less ordered place without him,' Lord Zinia said.

'What's that got to do with anything?' Nicholas protested. 'And who was Jolly to you, anyway?'

'Jolly was not a *who* to us, Mr Raspero, he was a *what*. He was useful to us as an instrument. Naturally, we lament his less pleasant activities as much as anyone, but given that even worse outcomes could conceivably follow in his absence, we tolerated his presence.'

'Jolly worked for you?' Nicholas asked in puzzlement.

'No, Mr Raspero, Jolly was very much his own man. He saw himself as the king of the demi-monde, and kings do not see themselves as working for anything other than their own grand destiny. Yet, he was on occasion willing to do certain things beneficial to us in return for the odd favour or two.'

'What kind of odd favour or two?' Nicholas asked.

Lord Zinia shrugged. 'The early release from prison of an associate, permission for a financial transaction that might otherwise be unlawful, the lack of an investigation into a crime, that kind of thing.'

'And what did he do for you in return?'

'He saw to it that political radicals were dealt with swiftly before their turbulence could spread. Political radicals can come from either side of the social divide, Mr Raspero. Due to a variety of circumstances, it is very often the case that political radicals flourish in the dirtier, less well kept corners of our world, and the eyes and ears that see and hear what goes on there do not belong to us, but to the inhabitants of the demi-monde. As soon as some political agitator started to stir to life, Jolly would stamp hard on the beginning of this disturbance. In short, as we are unable to properly monitor and eradicate political radicalism that takes place out of our sight, Jolly did this for us. Our concern is the maintenance of order, Mr Raspero. Political radicals seek to overturn the social order to institute another more to their liking. We seek to maintain this social order.'

'I'm not a political radical, Lord Zinia,' Nicholas said. 'I like our world exactly the way it is.'

'I am glad to hear this, Mr Raspero,' Lord Zinia said approvingly, but Nicholas could tell that Lord Zinia's approval was tempered by the suspicion that this was exactly what a political radical would say anyway in these circumstances. 'But I hope you now understand why it is that I would like to know what it is that you are about.'

Nicholas sighed. 'It is a long story, Lord Zinia, but suffice it to say that your fears are groundless. I have no political agenda. I did not bring about the downfall of Jolly for anything other than personal reasons and the successors of Jolly are just as greedy and stupid as he was, so you can continue to deal with them as you did with Jolly.'

Lord Zinia nodded. 'If you choose not to tell me this story, Mr Raspero, I will of course not argue with you about it. It would be highly discourteous of me to impose on you in such a fashion. But please, do not let me keep you from your much more important business.' Lord Zinia gestured towards the door with the stem of his pipe.

Nicholas sighed again. 'Well, on my first day in New Landern, I was walking down Octave Alley when five men attacked me and tried to rob me. I took them down, and robbed them. I did not do this for their money but to teach them a lesson about what it was like to be robbed. I was newly arrived in New Landern, and knew nothing of what the consequences of this action might be so I followed them discreetly as they went on their way, and noted that they went to a place called the Burke Tavern.

'Now some time later, a woman was attacked near where I was walking past, so I came to her rescue and then she asked me to escort her home. She told me she was alone but I sensed the presence of others in her apartment and was suspicious so I only pretended to drink the wine she offered me which was drugged, so when I was attacked by men who came from the next room I was able to defend myself and I took them down. There were six men, five of them the robbers who I had robbed, and the sixth being Jolly, who I had never seen before. Jolly said that I owed him five hundred and eighty strada, the sum of money taken from his men. I said it had only been two hundred and seventy two strada, but in any case I did not consider myself liable for this debt, whatever the sum.

'Jolly said he would accept the revised figure of two hundred and seventy two strada but that I had to repay this supposed debt. Jolly was starting to annoy me by now, so I searched him, took the sum of twelve hundred strada in bank notes from his pocket and threw it on the fire so he could watch it burn. He was not happy about this and pointed out that I had made an enemy of him but I was no murderer. I agreed that I would not murder him. He then said that the Clark family of my cousin Ben, his stepmother and my uncle and their children, would all be murdered in their beds late at night as happened to the Beaman family some time ago, by implication on Jolly's orders, Jolly being this shiny clean instrument of yours that you were just telling me about, but that this fate of the Clark family could be avoided if I would submit to his authority. I decided that Jolly had just pronounced a sentence of death on himself but I wasn't sure how to go about it. I left them all tied up and went to the Burke Tavern, where I did some breaking and entering and opened up Jolly's safe. He had one million strada in cash and nineteen million in financial documents, which I put on the table. I then went and fetched Jolly and gagged and tied him to a chair, then I sent Mr Tagalong Longman into the public area of the Burke Tavern to bring back some of Jolly's closest followers, and pointed out to them that they could direct their affections towards Jolly or the money. I left them there. By the way, I did not take one strada of Jolly's money. That was my whole participation in this affair. Now you know.'

There was a long silence while Lord Zinia and his companions considered the account of events Nicholas had just given.

'Who was the woman who tried to drug you?' Lord Zinia asked.

'She is not involved in any of this. She is innocent.'

'Miss Ashton is many things, but innocent she is not.'

'Well, how innocent are you, Lord Zinia? You might not even know the meaning of the word *innocent* for all you know.'

'Why did you not take any of Jolly's money, Mr Raspero?'

'If you need me to explain, Lord Zinia, then you wouldn't understand anyway,' Nicholas told him.

Lord Zinia set about lighting his pipe again. He puffed away, sending a gathering cloud of smoke around his head while he plunged deep into thought. Nicholas waited patiently, looking around at his interrogators. Lord Zinia came to a decision. 'I would like to thank you, Mr Raspero, for your courtesy in so kindly telling us what happened. I am reminded yet again of how much happenstance there is in the world. From what I can see, I can only say that I approve of your character and I understand that you did what you had to in circumstances that were not of your making.'

'That is very kind of you, Lord Zinia, and I can only say how pleased I am to have you approve of me.'

Lord Zinia smiled to acknowledge that he had noted the sarcasm and rose to his feet. 'We have all been kept away from the party long enough. Let us return.'

Nicholas walked back along the corridor with them and back into the Reception Room. Lord Zinia turned to Nicholas and patted him on the shoulder saying, 'It was a pleasure to have met you, my young friend, and I look forward to meeting you again, Mr Raspero.'

'It was likewise a pleasure to have met you all,' Nicholas said, 'and I look forward to meeting you all again as well.'

They all went their separate ways.

SIXTEEN

The Pursuit of Mr Nicholas Raspero
by Lady Isabel Grangeshield

8:40 PM, Saturday 9 July 1544 A.F.

Isabel started to manouevre herself away from her current position next to The Gang, whose giggles had subsided and who were now excitedly talking of what they had accomplished. They were on a high, like a military strike force which had succeeded in its mission against all the odds. Isabel was too upset to be angry with them, although she planned to be angry with them at the first available opportunity, especially Sophie and Penny, who had failed to introduce her to Mr Raspero. Yet, she could not afford the luxury of recriminations now. She had to be introduced to Mr Raspero in order to invite him to visit her so she could ask him to kill Nevsky for her, or to be more precise, for one million strada. She set off after Mr Raspero, barely paying attention to Mr Hubert Huppanstall, who followed her as attentively as a pet dog.

The party was by now in full swing. By a mysterious alchemy which somehow only the Lady Starfelds of the world could conjure, the guests were already fired up and animated, finding interesting conversations, attractive people to flirt with, and new revelations of matters that had only been dimly suspected before. Everyone but Isabel had come to life and was having a ball. They were on fire with the unlimited possibilities of the universe with its myriad stars brightly shining in the heavens above.

Isabel's difficulty stemmed precisely from the structured ordered society of the day. You could not simply walk up to a stranger and start talking to them. It simply was not done, any more than one could walk around naked. Introductions were done by third party, and without those third party introductions one simply could not approach another person. The dirty creases of society were replete with all sorts of stratagems for getting around this obstacle: to faint next to the person of interest, thus requiring their immediate personal attentions and subsequent acquaintance, had been done to death and was looked upon with scorn; to always be standing nearby until at some point a mutual acquaintance appeared, had also once been too popular to now be employed by any person of sense. It was the mark of an inferior person to adopt a stratagem that could be seen through, and as always reputation was everything.

Isabel somehow had to find a mutual acquaintance who would introduce her to Mr Raspero. As she circulated among the party guests, always keeping Mr Raspero in sight but at a distance (a neutral stratagem which conveyed no opprobrium even if detected) she found that as Mr Raspero's circle of companions grew as the night went on they came to include mutual acquaintances. Yet, her attempts to manouevre herself to a position adjacent to Mr Raspero whenever a mutual acquaintance was present always came to naught. Mr Huppanstall stayed by her side throughout, and she nodded politely at what he said, barely listening. It was not long before Mr Huppanstall noticed the frequent direction of her gaze and began darting Mr Raspero jealous glances, which Isabel was entirely oblivious to due to being caught up in her self-appointed task.

Ben encountered Miss Eileen Radcliff standing by herself during his wanderings. His earlier delusion returned in full force and without hesitation he walked up to her, said, 'I believe this next dance is mine,' took her hand in his and led her onto the dance-floor. Miss Radcliff obeyed him in a state of confusion, not quite sure what was going on.

Nicholas was enjoying himself. He was meeting one interesting person after another, carefully memorising their names and faces so he would remember them again. Seven hundred people was a lot of people to remember! Nicholas enjoyed meeting people and talking to them, and this party was nothing but meeting people and talking to them. He ignored the dancing tonight, although usually he loved dancing.

Time was passing and Isabel was getting more and more into a state. Whenever she made her way towards Nicholas in the company of a mutual acquaintance, he would be on his way elsewhere and she would find herself obliged to meet and greet with those he had left behind. She would engage in interminable pleasantries, only to tear herself away eventually and go in search of Mr Raspero and then go through the whole thing all over again. None of her approaches hit their target. The party was still in full swing but she knew it was only a matter of time before things started to slow down and when the party ended then so did her chances of being introduced to Mr Raspero.

Mr Zarek saw Isabel looking over at him while he was chatting to Nicholas. He uneasily remembered that he had told Nicholas at the engagement party of Mr Carver and Lady Lachance that he was unacquainted with Lady Isabel Grangeshield. Now that Nicholas was considered the best wandfighter in New Landern, this little white lie hung over his head like a sword. Seeing Isabel starting to walk his way, he made a hurried excuse to Nicholas and made for the nearest door leading out of the room; Isabel swerved like a spiraling falcon to intercept him.

'Who was that man you were talking to?' Isabel enquired.

'What man?' Mr Zarek asked as if he hadn't been talking to anybody.

'That man!' Isabel snapped, gesturing towards her fan towards Nicholas.

'Oh, Raspero or something, I think,' Mr Zarek said vaguely, as if trying to remember.

'Would you be so very kind as to introduce me to him?' Isabel asked him in her sweetest and gentlest manner. She knew she was behaving in such a way as to raise eyebrows but she no longer cared. This farce had gone on for too long.

Mr Zarek did, in fact, raise his eyebrows. 'I am sorry, Lady Grangeshield, but that would be out of the question.'

'And why so?' Isabel asked, no longer sounding at all sweet and gentle.

'I am not at liberty to say,' Mr Zarek told her. 'I am sure you understand.'

'No, Mr Zarek, I entirely fail to understand. Perhaps you might be so kind as to explain?'

'Would you excuse me?' Mr Zarek sidestepped and was gone before Isabel could stop him.

Isabel stood there and fumed. Her quarry stood a mere ten paces away, chatting cheerfully with two admiring wandfighting aficionados, but he might as well have been standing on a distant horizon for all the good that did her.

'So, I am to court you, I believe,' Ben was saying to an astonished Miss Radcliff. 'Naturally, I need to know your address first.'

9:20 PM, Saturday 9 July 1544 A.F.

Mr Huppanstall stuck to Isabel throughout, his hostility towards Raspero growing through the incubating medium of his jealousy. Then the time came when Isabel's patience ran out and she had had enough, both of Mr Huppanstall's never-ending presence and Mr Raspero's never-ending elusiveness. There came a time, perhaps inevitable in the circumstances, when Isabel finally flipped.

This had gone on for far too long. She was used to having things her own way. She was usually the target of this kind of pursuit and to be the one doing the pursuing seemed such an indignity for a personage such as Lady Isabel Grangeshield of Grangeshield House that it verged on being an outrage.

Why on earth would this man not stay still? He kept on charging about the place like a horse. Isabel had not kept count of the approaches she had made (there had been six) but she was fully aware that she was getting fed up — with everything, absolutely everything. Her repeated failures to gain an introduction to a man vastly her social inferior was beginning to tell on her. Her blood was slowly coming to the boil. It was not, for Heaven's sake, as if she sought an audience with a monarch, who alone would be sufficiently above her on the social scale to warrant such an indignity as this. She was suffering for an absolute nobody, a mindless wandfighter, a man birthed from a family of schoolteachers and lawyers and foreigners and bandits in the forest, a man with no social status who, judging from how shabbily he was dressed, had no money either. Once the fuss over his defeat of Nevsky had died away, this jumped-up Talk of the Town would slide back into his nobody obscurity.

A deep and abiding hostility towards the very person of Mr Nicholas Raspero started to grow in her. There was his laugh, for a start. Every now and then he would laugh out loud as merrily as if he had not a care in the world, and whoever happened to be with him at the time would smile or chuckle or laugh out loud themselves, instead of drawing away from this unseemly exuberance with looks of distaste. A gentleman should not laugh out loud in such a manner, unless of course he could be excused for doing so, and nothing in the world would excuse Mr Raspero for doing anything at all in Isabel's view at that time. But then came a time when Isabel, having manouevred herself into a position neighbouring that of Mr Raspero and his companions, heard Mr Raspero say cheerfully, 'There's nothing like New Landern in Little Batton.' This comment was followed by laughter all around and at last Isabel had some idea of what this such said laughter had been about. This such said laughter had been about jokes as feeble, as dim-witted, as thoroughly stupid, as this one! This was what she had been witnessing unknowingly from a distance all this time! How stupid did a stupid man have to be to make such a stupid joke as this stupid joke! *There's nothing like New Landern in Little Batton.* Just how pointless and unfunny could a joke be!

And yet everyone had laughed, as everyone else had laughed at whatever other jokes this imbecile had told that evening, while she had been following him around. And it was this joke-telling imbecile who she was trying to be introduced to in vain, this backward provincial who would not keep still long enough for her to reach him, this obscure nobody who was the objective of all her advances which he did not deserve and yet did not receive anyway because he was never there when she arrived! His mere presence, which was a recurring absence, was starting to annoy Isabel nearly as much as his laughter.

Even more annoying than his laughter was his generally favourable reception by all those who he encountered. People seemed to like him despite his shabby dress and obvious lack of money. But still what annoyed her most of all was the way he kept on moving away just as she made her approach. Her luck was simply rotten and as far as she could see it was all the fault of Mr Raspero for not keeping still at the right time.

The more she brooded over everything, the more her blood came to the boil at being the victim of indignity invisible.

Isabel would have been twice as indignant as she was already had she known that the elusiveness of Nicholas was not simply a matter of bad luck on her part. Nicholas was using macchato to deliberately avoid her. He had been all too aware of Isabel's background presence while chatting to Miss Nicholson and her friends and he was by now all too aware of Isabel's repeated attempts to approach him. It was perhaps strange that he did not stay still long enough for her to reach him given that he wanted nothing more than to be further acquainted with her, but out of instinct he avoided her for no reason that he could have put into words. It was true that his legs turned to jelly at the mere thought of speaking with her; it was true that he felt short of breath when she was near, but it was also true, that in a dimly sensed fashion, he understood that meeting Isabel again would be to cross a threshold that would close all roads behind him.

Just then Mr Huppanstall summoned up all his nerve and said, 'Would you like to dance with me, Lady Grangeshield?'

She wasn't listening and so replied automatically, 'That is quite so but surely you will excuse me,' and moved off, leaving Mr Huppanstall behind aware that she had not even heard what he had said. It was then that Isabel made her seventh approach and seeing her prey turn away yet again and start to move towards a nearby corridor she finally snapped — she turned abruptly away from the welcomes she was about to receive, walked at top speed and overtook Mr Raspero, passing so close by that she brushed his shoulder, and then when she was clear of him she stopped as if remembering something, and then quite deliberately stepped into Mr Raspero's path as she turned around to her left, her manouevre stopping Mr Raspero in his tracks, and then at last Lady Isabel Grangeshield of Grangeshield House found herself face to face with Mr Nicholas Raspero of Nowhere.

They were standing at an arm's length from each other. Nicholas could have reached out and laid his hand on her gleaming bare shoulder.

The beauty he had seen before in the distance was right before him and Nicholas found himself smitten all over again. Her eyes were a deep warm mahogany brown, her black eyebrows arched like dolphins leaping out of the water, the full, red lips pouted slightly, her round and sweetly formed face was framed by a cascading waterfall of long, dark brown hair fastened by a gold netting with bright white and green gemstones. Her bare shoulders rose like cliff walls above the deep cleavage of her large breasts which were enclosed with the bright blue lacery finery of her figure-hugging dress.

Isabel grasped everything in a flash. Too many men had been smitten by her beauty for her not to instantly recognise all the signs, and then, feeling herself standing so near to a man who was all too obviously filled with a hot desire for her, she reacted instinctively by stepping backwards and raising her arm to point the folded fan at Nicholas's chest like a sword to keep him at bay; she was now two arms' lengths away. Nicholas stood still as meekly as if he were under arrest. Then she coolly withdrew her extended arm and took hold of the other end of her fan so as to hold her fan in front of her like a schoolteacher's cane, while she raised her eyebrows imperiously.

'Good evening, Lady Grangeshield,' Nicholas said.

Isabel couldn't believe her ears or her luck. This jumped-up nobody had brazenly addressed her directly by name without having been introduced to her. This descendant of bandits in the forest knew nothing of the laws of civilisation! He was now a socially dead-man walking. Her eyes glinted at the possibility of now drawing blood from this upstart, then crushing him under her boot like a bug, and then forgiving him his trespass only if he very carefully followed the instructions she would then give him about coming to see her tomorrow afternoon.

'Have we been introduced?' she asked very frostily, tapping her fan on her knuckles in sequence as she prepared for battle.

'Yes, we have,' Nicholas replied, his grey eyes looking directly into her brown ones.

Nicholas paused then, savouring the moment. He knew full well that she didn't remember having met him and he was going to let the silence draw out until she admitted it. It wasn't revenge; it was just his mood right then at that moment in time.

Isabel realised Nicholas was looking at her with an amused look in his eyes because he could see she did not remember him being introduced to her. He seemed so confident they had been introduced that she felt that she had to believe him; yet she could not believe him. She could not have forgotten those direct grey eyes or the self-assurance which emanated from him; he had far too much of a presence for her to have forgotten him. Had she met this man before, she would remember him now, of that much she was certain. He was not a man she would forget so completely as to be quite sure in her own mind that she had never met him before. Yet, he seemed to have no doubt that he had been introduced to her. It was an impossible situation for her to be in, and it came on top of an already difficult evening.

She could also see he had no intention of saying anything more but was enjoying seeing her at a loss. The corners of his mouth were even being tugged upward as if he was holding back a grin. The silence dragged on, he was still quite deliberately saying nothing, and Isabel's instincts kicked in when Nicholas lost his inner battle and openly and blatantly grinned cheerfully like a schoolboy. 'Explain yourself!' she ordered him imperiously.

The grey eyes, which she had surely never seen before, which, she *knew* she had never looked into before, looked even more amused at the sight of how bossy she was being. 'I was introduced to you at the engagement party of Mr Hedley Carver and Lady Sofiya Lachance by Mr Timothy Boylent. It was in a room by the stairs with a mermaid painting in it. You were with a Miss Mary Philips at the time.' Nicholas said this so matter-of-factly that Isabel could not disbelieve him; yet neither could she believe that it had happened. Isabel had no idea of what was going on, but remembering the importance of this meeting with Mr Raspero she decided to simply ignore all these anomalies for the time being.

'Ah, yes, I remember,' Isabel said, nodding her head very slightly to confirm that she did, in fact, remember the occasion to which Mr Raspero referred. She knew where the room with the mermaid painting was though, and that helped her to place where the introduction had taken place. 'That was in the Dacian Salon! There, you see! I remember it better than you do.'

'If you say so, Lady Grangeshield,' Nicholas said in a skeptical tone of voice.

'But I do say so,' Isabel said with an edge of anger to her voice. 'Why, do you wish to argue about it?'

'Definitely not,' Nicholas said hastily. He found himself grinning foolishly just because she was looking at him. Not knowing what to say because Isabel was simply gazing at him while saying nothing, Nicholas added, a little weakly, 'I mean I'm not, ah, arguing. About anything.'

Isabel considered Nicholas with a careful eye as to his awkwardness, his foolish grin and his feeble attempts at appearing composed, and felt herself fully in control of the situation. He was obviously smitten with her beauty and she knew full well how to deal with men who were in such a state. He would do anything she told him to do, that was clear; it was just a matter now of explaining to him what he had to do.

Just then Lord and Lady Rolkandet came along and Lord Rolkandet said affably, 'Hello again, Isabel.' The elderly but incurably lecherous Lord Rolkandet was standing to her left, taking a good look at Isabel's cleavage, while the long suffering Lady Rolkandet stood impassively further back. Lord Rolkandet was clearly oblivious to the distress he was causing Isabel by interrupting a scene of vital importance to her.

'Good evening once again,' Isabel said, furious at how rotten her luck was this evening. She said *once again* in such a way as to indicate that *once* had been more than enough, let alone *again*, but Lord Rolkandet was deaf to her implication.

'We were on our way to the Juggling Show,' Lord Rolkandet said. 'Would you care to join us?'

'That is very kind of you,' Isabel replied, trying to think of a polite way to tell Lord Rolkandet to get lost.

At that moment, Nicholas, who had been discreetly edging away, but not discreetly enough to escape Isabel's attention, started to turn away.

'Mr Raspero! Where are you going?' Isabel asked sharply.

'Away,' Nicholas replied.

'It is very rude of you, Mr Raspero, to leave in such an abrupt manner.'

'I assumed you wished to be left alone to talk with your fellow guests,' Nicholas said as calmly as he could under fire from this dazzlingly beautiful woman, his pulse racing and his hands starting to sweat.

'I will make your assumptions for you, Mr Raspero,' Isabel said firmly.

This was such a totally bizarre thing to say that Nicholas was thrown. He had never heard anyone say anything like that before, and the unexpectedness of her comment, coupled with her dazzling beauty, had him as bound and helpless in her hands as she could wish. 'Naturally I will remain here to converse further with you,' he said as formally as he could manage.

'Yes, you will,' Isabel told him forcefully and then turned back to Lord Rolkandet. 'I am not coming to the Juggling Show at present,' she informed him, 'but I shall be along shortly.'

'It's starting any time now,' Lord Rolkandet said, unaware that Isabel was wishing him gone with every ounce of her barely concealed disdain. 'You don't want to miss the beginning.'

'Ah, but I *do* want to miss the beginning,' Isabel said in exasperation. 'But you go along now with Lady Rolkandet and thank you once again for your kindness.' As she hadn't even thanked him once, she thought that saying *once again* would be a clear hint of the superfluity of his presence.

'You want to miss the beginning?' this utterly imbecilic Lord Rolkandet said to her, entirely unaware in his doddering utter imbecility that she had merely been wishing him gone. 'Why is that?'

Isabel's luck that whole evening, as rotten as ever, now took a turn even for the worse. Ben came along and said to Mr Raspero, 'Nicky, these people are giving me hell unless I introduce you.' Ben waved vaguely behind him.

'I can't, Ben,' Nicholas told him, briefly glancing at Isabel. 'I'm on probation. I've already tried to get away once.'

'What do you mean?' Ben asked a little nervously. He was wondering what Nicholas had done now.

'I wish I knew myself,' Nicholas said with a smile, looking again at

Isabel, who was standing listening to this exchange with her head tilted to one side.

'But why should you wish to miss the beginning?' Lord Rolkandet again asked Isabel, still in an obvious state of perplexity.

All of a sudden Isabel had had enough. 'Come with me, Mr Raspero,' she ordered peremptorily and set off at once. Nicholas opened his hands out wide for Ben in a gesture signifying that he didn't know what was going on either, and set off after Isabel.

Isabel stomped through the room, unfolding her fan and holding it in front of her face whenever anyone tried to gain her attention. She marched to a place by the window where no-one was near and turned around to wait for Nicholas to catch up with her. She had not bothered to check that Nicholas was following her. She had had no doubt about that particular matter at all — when men looked at her the way Mr Raspero was doing, they would follow her anywhere.

'Mr Raspero,' she told him, 'I wish you to visit me tomorrow at three o'clock in the afternoon.'

'Certainly, Lady Grangeshield,' Nicholas said as composedly as he could.

'You will not tell anyone of this visit. It must be strictly confidential.'

'My visit has to be kept secret, did you say, Lady Grangeshield?'

'Yes that is correct, Mr Raspero.'

'Why must my visit be kept a secret?' Nicholas asked cautiously.

'Because I wish to discuss a highly confidential matter with you.'

'Ah, I understand,' Nicholas said, relieved and disappointed at the same time. 'Very well, I will come to see you and I won't tell anyone about it.'

'That will be all,' Isabel said in a tone of dismissal.

'Wait a moment,' Nicholas said, holding his hand up to forestall her departure. 'We're overlooking something.' He knew perfectly well what they were overlooking, but he spun out the moment to spend just that much longer in her company. 'Oh yes, I know. I need to know where you live. What is your address?'

Isabel looked at him in some astonishment. 'I live in Grangeshield House,' she told him briefly.

'Where's that?'

Isabel took a deep breath, as if needing to exercise self-control. 'It is on Jennyann Avenue.'

'Where's that?'

'Kasia. Do you know where Kasia is?'

'It's in New Landern,' Nicholas said, grinning widely at his own wit.

'Three o'clock, Mr Raspero,' Isabel told him coldly, entirely unimpressed by his feeble attempt at humour. 'Don't be late!' And with that parting comment she was gone, leaving behind her a hopelessly smitten Nicholas watching her superb and shapely figure moving away out of sight.

Mr Hubert Huppanstall had lurked here and there, spying on Lady Grangeshield's meetings with Raspero from a distance. He felt sick with jealousy, furiously foamingly sick with the greenest cadaverous envy at the sight of Lady Grangeshield talking with Raspero.

A vein was throbbing on his forehead, standing out like a worm wriggling through his skin. His hostility towards Raspero was now hatred. His whole body was slippery with sweat. He followed Raspero following Lady Grangeshield with his hands twitching slightly as if in his mind they had closed around Raspero's neck.

Lady Grangeshield had stopped on the edge of the crowd gathered to watch the Juggling Show, which was well under way by now. Raspero came up beside Lady Grangeshield and stood there. Lady Grangeshield looked over at Raspero standing right next to her and then quite markedly turned and walked away. She walked some twenty paces or so away and found another vantage point to watch the juggling. Yet, Mr Huppanstall noticed with the feverish attention to detail of the jealous mind that she was standing so as to observe Raspero as easily as the evening's entertainment. The idea that she might be doing this simply to keep Raspero at bay never occurred to Mr Huppanstall, who could only interpret her action as that of a woman who was giving her affections to a man, despite the fact that she had walked away from him, and then it was that Mr Huppanstall's feverish jealous mind gave birth to an idea which immediately seized the mind that had conceived it and took over Mr Huppanstall on the spot.

Mr Huppanstall acted immediately on the idea. He walked at top speed towards Raspero at an angle designed to shoulder Raspero aside on impact. He would push Raspero aside while Lady Grangeshield was watching, thus humiliating Raspero in her eyes and elevating Mr Huppanstall as a man of consequence.

Mr Huppanstall had simply not registered the name of his perceived rival for Lady Grangeshield's affections as being the name of the man who was known all over New Landern for having taken down Nevsky. He would have made the connection had his mind not been so clouded, and if he had done so, he might have acted differently but he did not make the connection.

Nicholas had his hand on the hilt of his wand as always, and with his habitual practice of macchato, observed Mr Huppanstall's approaching him from behind like an asteroid on a collision course and simply stepped out of the way and deftly tripped Mr Huppanstall up as he passed by. Had Nicholas been asked why he had done this (but he never was) he would have had a perfectly good explanation. The trajectory of Huppanstall the Asteroid was such that he would barrel into the lady and gentleman standing arm in arm just in front of Nicholas if he continued. So, Nicholas tripped Mr Huppanstall to spare the couple being bowled over, an action which Nicholas considered perfectly justified, everything considered.

Mr Hubert Huppanstall howled as he fell over, which attracted attention from all those standing nearby. Lying on the ground, he could not help but look to see if Lady Grangeshield had seen what had happened. Seeing that she had, Mr Huppanstall's humiliation was such that while still lying on the ground he shouted, 'I demand satisfaction!'

Nicholas looked down at him impassively. 'You are obviously unacquainted with the formalities attendant upon the issuing of a formal challenge,' he told Mr Huppanstall. 'You are obliged to state your name, bozo.'

'I am Mr Hubert Huppanstall,' Mr Huppanstall shouted, while scrambling to his feet. 'I demand satisfaction!'

By now this local distraction had spread through the crowd to become the growing centre of attention of those nearby, displacing the jugglers from the crowd's affections.

'I accept your challenge,' Nicholas said. 'My name is Mr Nicholas Raspero. What form of satisfaction do you require?'

'First Combat,' said Mr Huppanstall.

'When and where?' Nicholas asked disinterestedly, as if bored by the tedium of all this.

'Now outside,' Mr Huppanstall said in his rage. All he could think of right then was how to regain favour in Lady Grangeshield's eyes by redeeming himself with a victory in a duel. He did not consider the possibility of sinking further through defeat because nothing but redemption existed for him right then.

'I accept these terms,' Nicholas said, formally completing the exchange. 'Let's go,' he said, and turned away and set off.

News had spread rapidly and the entire assembled company of guests trooped off after them to watch the duel, leaving the jugglers forlornly behind, but the jugglers looked at each other, shrugged and followed them all outside to watch the duel as well.

Outside in the garden Nicholas and Mr Huppanstall adopted their positions; Nicholas waited only long enough for it to be clear that the duel was under way, then he struck, sending Mr Huppanstall flying and collecting his wand.

Mr Huppanstall stood up and gathered himself together.

'Have you received satisfaction, Mr Huppanstall?' Nicholas asked him.

'No, I haven't, Raspero,' Mr Huppanstall said, foolishly omitting Mr Raspero's title of "Mr" in his feverish anticipation of the next round.

Nicholas returned his wand to him and they fought again; Mr Huppanstall went flying and Nicholas collected his wand a second time.

Once again Mr Huppanstall had not received satisfaction, and once again he omitted to say "Mr Raspero" in his fury.

The third round saw Mr Huppanstall taken down again.

'Have you received satisfaction, Mr Huppanstall?' Nicholas asked.

'Yes, Raspero, I have,' Mr Huppanstall said, aware then that it was over and somehow hoping that his bravery in fighting the duel would gain him favour in Lady Grangeshield's eyes.

Nicholas returned Mr Huppanstall's wand to him. Then he quite deliberately slapped Mr Huppanstall and waited.

Mr Huppanstall glared at him while holding his hand to his face and said, 'What was that for?'

'You continuously address me as Raspero, instead of as "Mr Raspero",' said Mr Raspero. 'I find your behaviour merits a slap.'

And so it was that Mr Hubert Huppanstall awoke to his current predicament as if awakening out of a sleep. All around him people were staring at him, eager to see him issue another challenge, the challenge which he was bound now to make, having just been slapped in public. He could not now ask for First Combat again; all he had left was Second Combat or Final Combat. Final combat meant death; Second Combat meant a broken arm at best and much worse at worst. Now that his mind had cleared Mr Hubert Huppanstall shrank from the circumstances he had awoken to find himself in so late in the evening.

'I do not believe that these grounds require a further duel,' Mr Huppanstall declared.

Nicholas slapped him again.

His hand to his face, Mr Huppanstall was forced to accept the inevitable. 'I demand satisfaction. Second Combat,' he said then.

'I accept your challenge. When and where?'

Mr Huppanstall considered this, tempted to postpone everything, but then he decided to get it all out of the way now. 'Here and now,' he said with a certain resignation.

The two combatants adopted the dueling position; before long there was the sound of a crack, a yelp of pain from Mr Huppanstall and Nicholas had Mr Huppanstall's wand in his hand while Mr Huppanstall writhed on the ground with a broken arm.

'Your attempt to avoid the second duel did not speak in your favour,' Nicholas declared like a judge pronouncing a verdict; with a speed of action that seemed almost instantaneous he pulled Huppanstall's disc out of its pocket and threw it high into the air while flipping Huppanstall's wand against a nearby tree and then cutting it in half with Huppanstall's disc with a casual expertise that excited a gasp of admiration from the watching wandfighting aficionados. So the duel was over, but Nicholas, still fired up and ready to fight on, had not finished yet. Nicholas scanned the crowd until he saw who he was looking for, then walked quite deliberately towards that person.

He came to a standstill not far in front of Lady Starfeld, considered her coldly for a moment, and then said to her, 'This would seem to be a good time for me to leave your party. But before I thank you for your hospitality there is something I would like to ask you first. Why did you invite me to your party?'

Lady Starfeld found this a difficult question to answer. She felt that she could hardly say while everyone was listening that she had been tricked into inviting Mr Raspero. 'Why, whatever do you mean, Mr Raspero?' she asked uneasily.

'I mean that we are complete strangers to each other. So I will ask you again, Lady Starfeld. Why did you invite me to your party?'

'But whatever do you mean, Mr Raspero?' Lady Starfeld asked again, stubbornly clinging to her previous statement. As everyone by now knew, Lord Zinia had patted Nicholas on the shoulder, and this seal of approval could not be disregarded by anyone. Lady Starfeld felt that she was in the grip of unseen forces and only wanted to find somewhere to hide.

Nicholas took a deep breath and let it out in a sigh of exasperation. 'I mean what I say, Lady Starfeld. So answer my question: why did you invite me to your party?'

Lady Starfeld could not think of anything to say. By now her mind had gone completely blank. Her husband stepped in. 'We invited you to our party, Mr Raspero,' he said in a friendly manner, 'because you are the Talk of the Town.'

'Oh yes,' Lady Starfeld agreed fervently, clutching at this explanation which she now remembered after having been reminded of it. 'You are the Talk of the Town, Mr Raspero. That is why we invited you.'

'And why am I the Talk of the Town, Lady Starfeld?' Nicholas asked, raising his eyebrows to show that this was complete news to him.

'Why, I'm sure I do not know,' Lady Starfeld said in her most reasonable tone of voice.

'What do you mean, you do not know?' Nicholas asked, a little sharply.

'I mean what I say, Mr Raspero,' Lady Starfeld said a little apprehensively. 'I mean that I do not know.'

The guests all watched this exchange avidly. What was happening now would be the talk of the town for the next week or more. They all knew a potentially scandalous scene when they saw one.

'How can you not know?' Nicholas asked, exasperated. 'If I am the Talk of the Town, then that talk must be about something. What is that talk about?'

Silence.

Nicholas tried again. 'Lady Starfeld, I am but newly arrived in New Landern but I have heard of a place called Malapense House. It is the madhouse of New Landern. Perhaps this household of yours, Starfeld Manor, is a second Malapense House. It certainly seems to me to be a madhouse. You say I am the Talk of the Town without knowing what this talk is about. But this is utterly absurd. If you continue to refuse to answer my question I will be generous and attribute your failure to stark raving lunacy rather than calculated malevolence. So now: for the last time, why am I the Talk of the Town?'

Then one of the other guests spoke. 'It's because you took down Nevsky, of course. Thrashed him like a schoolboy. Everyone's talking about it. I believe it now that I've seen you in action. You're the best wandfighter I ever saw.'

Nicholas sighed loudly again. 'I am the Talk of the Town because I defeated Nevsky in a duel. I see. This town can't have much to talk about then. Whatever.' Nicholas waved his hand through the air to demonstrate that *whatever* stood for every conceivable comment that could be made. 'I will make my farewells now, Lady Starfeld, with all the necessary pretended politeness attendant upon this tedious obligation. Thank you for your misplaced hospitality. Don't bother inviting me to your next party because I will certainly misread the time and place of the nominated venue and that would be no fun for you. Goodbye.'

With that Nicholas turned on his heel and walked to the garden gate. Ben hurriedly made his politest farewells to Lady Starfeld and hurried after Nicholas. Without breaking step Nicholas whipped out his wand and threw the garden gates open. The expensive security system simply collapsed without a fight and Nicholas and Ben walked out, the gates shutting behind them with another wave of Nicholas's wand.

Lady Starfeld's guests returned to the house, chattering excitedly amongst themselves. Some talked wittily of the latest fashions in straitjackets now that they were returning to the second Malapense House. Isabel went along with them, eyes cast down to the ground, reserved and silent.

Isabel was encouraged by what she had just seen of Mr Raspero's ability with a wand, but the puzzle of their introduction remained so she looked around for Timothy. She spotted him, with a group of wandfighting friends, deep in an animated discussion of the duel they had just witnessed, making movements through the air with their hands to illustrate the points they were making as it seemed that the spoken word alone was insufficient to express the extent of their excitement. Timothy was a happy member of this group until Isabel arrived and dragged him by the arm away from his friends with an imperiousness that ignored his protests and asked him, 'Timmy, did you introduce Mr Nicholas Raspero to me at Sofiya's engagement party?'

'Yes,' Timothy confirmed briefly, looking impatient to be on his way.

'Are you acquainted with Mr Raspero?'

Timothy hesitated; a wary look appeared on his face, which did not escape Isabel's attention. Timothy wasn't sure how Isabel might take the story of his introduction of Nicholas to Isabel being a wandfighting prize. However, he had a strong feeling she would not take it well, so he ducked the question. 'Am I under interrogation, Isabel? If so, why? And what am I being charged with?'

Isabel could see that Timothy was being evasive, and she geared up to find out what he was hiding from her. 'You are being very foolish, Timmy.'

'Are we done, Izzy? Excellent, bye,' and Timothy was off in the instant before Isabel could make a move to stop him.

Isabel watched him disappear around a corner, holding her folded fan like a sword she could not use. It did not make sense that she had been introduced to Nicholas without remembering the occasion, yet Timothy had just confirmed it. But why had Timothy been so evasive as to run for it? What was going on?

Well, it did not matter, Isabel told herself. She had achieved what she had come here to achieve. Nicholas was going to come to Grangeshield House tomorrow, and she would offer him employment as an assassin. Surely a man dressed in rags whose ancestor had been a bandit in the forest could only thank her for this. She would graciously decline to accept his thanks; she would tell him that there was no need for him to be thankful as he was going to be acting in the interests of justice, even if he could not know what those interests were, exactly. He could never know what had happened, no-one at all could ever know what had happened, but a million strada would make up for all that missing knowledge. *He would thank her fervently for her offer of employment as an assassin, given that no doubt he was suited for little else, but perhaps she would after all,* Isabel thought, *graciously accept the poor man's gratitude rather than decline it.* Yes, she would pat him on the head while his tail wagged; that would only be kindness because of how extremely grateful he would be to her for her offer.

After all, a million strada would call forth a lot of gratitude from a man dressed in rags, would it not?

SEVENTEEN

A Request is Made of Mr Nicholas Raspero by Mr Benjamin Clark

12:05 AM, Sunday 10 July 1544 A.F.

The wide and well-kept road was empty at this time of night although flying carriages passed by above them. Stars glittered overhead through gaps in the clouds; the waning moon was like a lantern carried in the steady hand of a giant; the footsteps of Nicholas and Ben made smart sounds on the neatly paved road as they stepped along.

'I suppose none of that was your fault,' Ben commented.

'It certainly wasn't,' Nicholas agreed blandly, taking Ben's words at face value.

'It's funny how everyone else but you manages to go out for the evening without getting into a fight. Strange that it's never your fault, though.'

'It is strange,' Nicholas agreed innocently, still taking Ben's words at face value. 'It makes you wonder what's going on, doesn't it?'

Ben sighed. 'You understand that by insulting Lady Starfeld in the way you did, you will never be invited to a party anywhere in New Landern ever again, at least not in high society. I won't ask why you did it because I already know you'll just tell some story of some lunatic Westrigonian ancestor hundreds of years ago who did something crazy that somehow makes your own crazy behaviour make sense.'

'Ben, this happened the day after Etienne's wedding, as he and his newly wed —'

'I'm not listening!' Ben said, his hands over his ears, 'I'm not listening!'

'As he and his newly wed wife travelled to a nearby town, she said she wanted to make a pilgrimage to Oxtanisienth. Her lover was waiting for them there in an ambush in order to kill Etienne. Etienne, by the way, was the eleventh Baron of Raspero. They both attacked Etienne together, planning to take him by surprise, but Etienne wasn't a man you took by surprise. His shadow was in the shape of a corkscrew, as the Westrigonian saying goes. He took them both down, and then guess what he did, Ben? Can you guess what he did then?'

'No,' Ben said in resignation, having given up not listening. 'Please tell me, Nicholas, what did Etienne do then? Please, please tell me.' Ben was reaching for all the mocking sarcasm he could possibly gather into the fewest possible words.

'He gave his beloved a choice, after having a good laugh. Interesting, isn't it? He actually found it funny and you can imagine how much that annoyed his newly wed wife!' Nicholas paused to laugh merrily himself. 'He told her she could run off with her lover or continue with Etienne on his journey as Etienne's wife. Then he walked off back to their flying carriage. And what did she do? She quickly made arrangements with her lover for him to follow her and Etienne so they could make another attempt together at killing Etienne, then she went off with Etienne on his journey. How about that? Do you see how clever Etienne was being? Well?'

'No, Nicky,' Ben said in exasperation, 'I entirely fail to see how clever Etienne was being. He kept someone who wanted to kill him by his side. Brilliant! Perhaps you might explain.'

'Well,' Nicholas explained, 'if he'd taken her bound hand and foot with him she would only have escaped at the first opportunity she got and he would have lost her and he was starting to fall in love with her by then. But he gave her a choice so she went with him of her own free will. Now that's clever, isn't it? You can't deny that's clever, can you?'

'You said she went with Etienne in order to kill him,' Ben said, reluctantly discussing the story despite not really wanting to.

'Yes,' Nicholas agreed impatiently, 'but she only tried to kill him three times and then she gave up on it and they were very happily married, Ben, they were happily married for forty years and had five children and they loved each other deeply. It was a great love story, Ben, and now you have to see how clever Etienne was being then when he gave her that choice after the second time she tried to kill him.'

'The second time?'

'Well, of course she tried to kill him the first time on their wedding night because she didn't want their marriage consummated. She tried to stab him in the back with a knife she'd hidden in her hair as a hair pin, but Etienne saw the reflection of her attacking him on the polished surface of a bronze water jug and dodged out of the way in time.'

'This was just another day in the town of Raspero, was it? It makes you wonder why our grandfather ever left, doesn't it?'

'It was an arranged, political marriage, Ben, which was a set-up to destroy Etienne, but that's a whole other story; I'm just talking about the set-up of the second time she tried to kill him, with a particular emphasis on the words *set-up*, in case you're not paying enough attention to what I'm saying.'

'I am not only wondering why you are telling me this story, Nicky. I am also wondering why I am listening to it,' Ben said as sternly as a headmaster.

'My story is done, Ben, and you know exactly what question to ask now, don't you?'

'Oh, heaven help me! This is when you come to the totally demented point of all this, isn't it? Well, I am not going to ask what it is,' Ben said with a determined look on his face. 'I ... am ... not ... going ... to ... ask.'

'Exactly!' Nicholas said in triumph. 'With your brilliant legal mind you have observed that the time has come to draw a moral from all of this that is relevant to the events of tonight. You can see the point I'm going to make, can't you? About things being a set-up?'

'No, I can't, Nicky,' Ben said in his continued state of exasperation. 'Trust me on this one. I really, really can't!'

'Let's consider the facts,' Nicholas said, like a lawyer in court. 'Fact number one, Lady Starfeld invites me, a complete stranger, to her party.'

'Yes, because you're the Talk of the Town!'

'Objection over-ruled! Now, when I get there, and this is fact number two, I ask these girls I'm talking to, oh, why was I invited to this party, and they all burst out laughing! I'm telling you, Ben! You weren't there. You should have seen them. They had hysterics. Honestly, I swear! They couldn't stop laughing.'

'Well,' Ben said, 'maybe you just said it in a funny way. Maybe it just seemed odd to them that you should ask such a question. Maybe no-one else before you has ever asked such a question in the whole history of party-going. I mean, I've never heard of anyone arrive at a party and ask their fellow guests why they were invited. It's actually a peculiar thing to do if you ask me.'

'Fact number three,' Nicholas continued, 'or really it's number two if the facts are to be listed in a chronological sequence, is the behaviour of Lady Starfeld. Note that you were admitted to the party with me, despite you saying it was impossible, an error of judgement on your part which I have yet, by the way, to hear you acknowledge. And so Lady Starfeld says how thrilled she is to have me there, you heard her, you were standing right by me, and when I ask why, she brushes me off! I mean, what was that all about?'

'I saw Lady Starfeld being polite, that's all. She didn't expect you to take her seriously.'

'Fact number four, that duel happened because of an entirely pointless provocation by that Huppanstall fellow, it just came out of the blue, I hadn't even spoken to him, I assure you Ben, I did nothing I can think of to bring about that attack he launched on me.'

'Nothing that you can think of,' Ben repeated, with the barest of emphasis on *you*.

'Fact number five, after the duel, when I asked Lady Starfeld why she invited me, she couldn't answer. You were there, you saw it yourself. Then her husband stepped in and said I was the Talk of the Town, and Lady Starfeld said, oh, yes, I'm the Talk of the Town, and when I ask, well, what's the talk about then, they have no idea! Now you can't deny that that's weird!'

'That does seem peculiar on the face of it,' Ben conceded reluctantly, 'but there might be a perfectly reasonable explanation.'

'But there is, there is a perfectly reasonable explanation and I'm coming to it! Fact number, um, what number did I reach?'

'This would be fact number six if these were facts, which they're not. You obviously don't know the meaning of the word *facts*.'

'Fact number six,' Nicholas continued, 'is that someone else said that I'm the Talk of the Town because I beat Nevsky in a duel. Note that it's not Lord and Lady Starfeld who tell me this! Oh no, that would make their game all too clear, wouldn't it? So when we put all this together, what conclusion do we reach, Ben? What is the one and only explanation of everything that makes sense of all this?'

Ben sighed. 'Feel free to tell me, Nicky.'

'They invited me to their party to fight a duel for their guests to watch, as if I'm a performing circus animal! That's what they were all about! It was all a set-up from the beginning! So now you see why I gave Lady Starfeld such a hard time. She knows now that I know what she was about, and I bet she wishes now that she never tried to play a trick like that on me! Doesn't she?'

'I am sure Lady Starfeld regrets inviting you to her party,' Ben said in a neutral tone of voice.

'Too right she does! And it serves her right for pulling a stunt like that!'

Ben sighed and shook his head. 'Nicky, there are several problems with what you are saying, not least being your evasiveness whenever I ask you why all my criminal clients know your name. Would you care to comment?'

'That has nothing to do with me being some kind of Talk of the Town,' Nicholas said.

Ben looked about him, and without appearing to look anywhere in particular he saw that Nicholas's left forefinger was curled up so the fingernail pressed into the ball of his left thumb. With his lawyer's eye for the behaviour of witnesses Ben had long ago noted that when Nicholas was dissembling, being evasive or lying through his teeth, his left forefinger invariably curled up to press against the ball of his left thumb.

'Nicky, for some reason I now have a waiting list of clients faced with a variety of criminal charges who all want to have me as their lawyer. Strangely enough, whenever I interview them for the first time, they all want to know if it's true that I am the cousin of Mr Nicholas Raspero. I have mentioned this to you before, but you always say that you have no idea at all why this should be so, except for mumbling something vague about how maybe you've been in a couple of wand fights. You are happy to tell me stories about things that happened centuries ago, but you duck out of telling me what is happening right now, don't you?'

'Well, it's kind of complicated and probably not relevant to anything,' Nicholas said evasively, 'and anyway it might not be of too much use to you so there we are, I mean, what else is there to say?'

'Nicky, you never told me that you defeated Nevsky in a duel, perhaps because this didn't happen hundreds of years ago. I had to hear about this from other people. Whatever else you're not telling me, fine, just don't make out that I'm some wonderful cousin of yours. You've done something to make you the Talk of the Town, but you won't tell me. Fine. Well, as it's not too much use to me anyway, according to you, that's just fine. And thanks for not telling me by the way. I'm sure you have my best interests at heart, don't you?'

Nicholas sighed. 'Ben, you hit the roof when I do the smallest thing like when I robbed those robbers who attacked us and then complain if I don't tell you anything that might be a little bit slightly more controversial than that. I mean, you carry on as if none of this has anything to do with you, oh no, I mean, you're the innocent party, aren't you, or do I misunderstand your self-righteous complaint?'

'You did something more controversial than rob those robbers?'

'Just a little bit more, it was hardly anything, but see, you're already gasping for breath, aren't you? I kept this from you for your own good and now my consideration is something terrible, isn't it?'

'Oh no, Nicky, what did you do? I mean, really, what did you do? Did you rob someone else?'

'Not exactly.'

'What does *not exactly* mean?'

'See what I mean, you're already hitting the roof and I haven't even said anything yet. You over-react, Ben, and then it's all my fault because you just get hysterical.'

'Nicky, what did you do?'

Nicholas sighed. 'If I explained that one thing led to another and that really things happened as they happened but in a sense I'm innocent because events followed a logic of their own that, in a sense, I was a kind of spectator, would you be prepared to bear all that in mind?'

'Nicky, what did you do?'

'You do understand that the morality of all this might get complicated, Ben? I mean, can I hear you say that in advance?'

'Nicky, what did you do?'

Nicholas sighed again. 'Have you heard of a man called Jolly? Otherwise known as Mr Frank Jollison, the noted philanthropist who died recently?'

Ben took a deep breath and let it out very slowly. 'Yes, Nicky, I have, funnily enough. Not that this has anything to do with my career in criminal law, you understand, such as in hearing my clients tell me in great detail things which I subsequently can't repeat due to legal confidentiality. But yes, Nicky, I have heard of Jolly. But why do you ask?'

'Well, I sort of had a bit of a run in with the man, after which his closest followers killed him. That might be why your clients have heard of me.'

'But you didn't kill him,' Ben said, just to get this straight.

'Ben, I give you my word of honour, I have never killed anyone by my own hand.'

'By your own hand,' Ben repeated, having noted this careful caveat.

'I tied Jolly up in a chair and gagged him, and that was how his successors killed him, so in a sense I paved the way for his death, which was what I meant by the aforementioned moral ambiguity, but given that he could have been freed and lived as a logical possibility, it can't be said that I killed him.'

'And why,' Ben asked carefully, 'did you tie Jolly up in a chair and gag him?'

'Well, do you remember the night when I robbed those robbers and then I left you because I had to go somewhere?'

'Yes, Nicky, I do, as it happens,' Ben said with a subdued sarcasm, as if he could never forget.

'Well, I followed those robbers because the thought crossed my mind that I should know something about them in case they might seek revenge. I followed them to the Burke Tavern, then came home.'

'You didn't tell me this at the time.'

'You didn't ask me where I had gone. I assumed it was because you didn't want to know, given that you didn't ask. But it's all my fault now that I didn't tell you, isn't it?'

'The Burke Tavern, being the home of the late Jolly, criminal kingpin of New Landern,' Ben said. 'So go on, Nicky, with your tale.'

'Well, the robbers who I robbed were led by a man called No Tin, that was the fellow I challenged to take his disc out, and they went and complained about me to Jolly. So Jolly tracked me down and set a trap for me. He got an actress named Angela Ashton to invite me to her apartment and slip me some drugged wine. But I didn't drink the wine, so I was able to defend myself and take them down when they attacked me. So what was I to do then, Ben? You tell me!'

'Did Jolly say what he planned to do with you if he had taken you down?'

'He said I had to repay him the five hundred and eighty strada I had supposedly taken from his men, but when I pointed out that it was actually two hundred and seventy two strada he said he would accept that sum in repayment. He was after getting his money back, according to him.'

'So what did you tell him?'

'Well, my reply was actually more in the line of actions speak louder than words, given that what could you tell someone in such a state of delusion? I searched him, took a roll of bank notes from him that were a total of twelve hundred strada, and threw them on the fire so he and his men could watch them burn.'

'And why did you do this?' Ben sounded faint.

'Why did I do this? Who did this idiot think he was? He tried to drug me and tie me up to recover an illusory debt. I was giving him a wake-up call as to what reality was all about!'

'I personally would think twice about putting you and reality in the same sentence,' Ben said, 'but never mind that. Go on with your tale.'

'Well, we weren't getting anywhere because he said he was a gentleman but he wouldn't accept my challenge and he kept on saying how he wanted to give me a job, he wanted me to work for him, and I said no way could I work for a man like you, so that was how our conversation was going.'

'We are in rare agreement,' Ben said, 'certainly you could not work for a man like Jolly. So then what happened?'

Nicholas hesitated. 'Ben, you have asked me to tell you what happened because you complained that I didn't tell you. All right then, this is what I have been keeping from you. Jolly threatened to have the entire Clark family, that's you and your stepmother and father and siblings, murdered in your beds during the night, just as happened to the Beaman family some time ago, if I didn't submit to his authority.'

Ben stopped still in the middle of the street where he was walking. He looked at Nicholas without saying a word, his face pale and shocked. Nicholas stood where he had stopped and looked right back, also without saying a word. Ben took one deep breath after another. Time passed, and Nicholas waited where he was. Ben started walking again, moving a little jerkily, as if he had forgotten how his limbs were supposed to move, and he said as he walked along, 'Just tell me the story, Nicholas.'

'Well, I decided then and there that Jolly was a dead man. But as I couldn't kill him myself, I had to work out some other way to attain this end. So I went to the Burke Tavern, did some breaking-and-entering, which you no doubt would consider to be against some clear point of law or other. I emptied his safe, which had twenty million strada in it, one million in cash and nineteen million in various financial documents. I put it all on a table, then I took Jolly there, tied and gagged him to a chair, went into the public tavern, invited some of his men into Jolly's private quarters and showed them the money on the table and Jolly in the chair and left them to make up their own minds. Well, they took the money and killed Jolly. That's it. By the way, I did not take one strada of Jolly's money, just so you know. My tale is done.'

Ben said nothing for a while and then said, 'Well, that's why you're the

Talk of the Town. No wonder. But you must understand how I feel about learning that my family was endangered in this manner.'

'Why do you think I didn't tell you before? I didn't want you to worry. Anyway, Jolly's dead now. So it's over.'

'Until you do something crazy to endanger us all again.'

'Ben, don't talk like that,' Nicholas said, a little worried by the expression on Ben's face. 'Jolly brought this on his own head. What would you say instead? That Jolly should just have everything his own way because he was an evil man? Is that what you are saying?'

Ben lowered his head as he walked along, and Nicholas had the good sense not to interrupt his thoughts. Eventually Ben raised his head and said, 'No, Nicky, you did the right thing. I'll tell you something you've taught me, that I've never seen so clearly before you came along, and that is our normal solid lives which we take so much for granted and never think twice about, well, the ground we stand on is always thin ice, it could break at any moment and there's nothing solid about anything. Everything could go at any moment, what we rely on could just simply not be there the very next minute. I should thank you but I won't, I liked my earlier illusion, it was at least comforting. The most I can do is not blame you for showing me the truth.'

'If I'd known you'd take it so well,' Nicholas said cautiously, 'I would have told you before. I just assumed you would be extra critical of the whole business.'

'Oh, believe me, Nicky, I can see why you didn't tell me any of this before. Oh yes, indeed, even for you this is totally insane, and no wonder you preferred to keep quiet about everything. But I would like to ask one thing from you, Nicky, if I may?'

'And what's that?'

'I want you to promise me to avoid yet another mad venture into moral ambiguity, to avoid another crazy stunt like this, in short to try to behave like a normal person, given that your behaviour reflects on relatives, such as myself, who might be murdered late at night in bed otherwise.'

'You talk as if I asked for all this to happen!' Nicholas complained. 'I'm trying to explain to you that everything followed a certain logic.'

'From the time that you robbed those robbers,' Ben pointed out. 'If you hadn't done that, then the later consequences would not have followed.'

'Wait a minute! I thought you agreed that I did the right thing when I robbed those robbers!'

'All right Nicky, let's not argue,' Ben said placatingly. 'My point is this. Will you promise to try to behave like a normal person? Is that really too much to ask?'

'All right Ben,' Nicholas said as if in meek surrender, 'I promise to be a completely normal person from now on. Happy now?'

'Very,' Ben said, with a sideways look of scepticism at his wild country cousin. 'And I will hold you to your promise.'

'Lucky me,' Nicholas said, 'lucky, lucky me.'

'Yes,' Ben agreed, 'lucky you.'

Nicholas said nothing more. He knew Ben liked to have the last word, and besides, he was free now to use their companionable silence as they walked along the late-at-night deserted street, to wonder what Lady Isabel Grangeshield wanted to see him about the next day. It was the first chance he'd had to consider the matter since she had invited him to Grangeshield House, given everything that had happened since. His heart leaped in his chest at the thought of sitting down and talking with her, just the two of them, for hadn't she said that this matter was highly confidential, which implied that they would be alone together, just the two of them, ensconced in confidentiality. Before long he had half-forgotten the promise he had just made to Ben, which he hadn't taken seriously in the first place, given that he did not understand what Ben meant by it anyway. Surely being a normal person was a concept that was subject to a wide variety of interpretations? He had only made such a half-promise to keep Ben quiet in the first place, and the second place was to forget all about it.

Furthermore, in his heart he had already broken the half-promise he had made to Ben, because where Lady Isabel Grangeshield was concerned, Nicholas didn't care about anything except getting to know her better. His promise of being a normal person could go jump in the lake if that got in the way of getting to know her better. There was something about her that affected him in a way he could not explain. It was no longer just her visible beauty now, the beauty he had seen at a distance; it was the way she looked at him when she spoke, the way she held her fan, the way she had walked away from him when he had stood next to her. This was the same as her beauty, but it was her beauty given expression beyond what his eyes could see alone, it was now her mind speaking directly to his. She had spirit and poise and grace, she was critical and bossy, her eyes narrowed when she decided he was being stupid, such as when he hadn't known where she lived; she tilted her chin when she believed things had been decided and there was nothing more to say; yet there was something sweet and gentle about her that took his breath away.

Yes, he would see Lady Isabel Grangeshield tomorrow, and wherever that path took him, he would walk down it as long as she was there with him. He couldn't wait to see her again, and his thoughts of seeing her again enwrapped him in folds that led his thoughts along the weave of his own folded thoughts, until he fell asleep seeing her tapping her fan on her knuckles, beautiful and gentle and imperious, and waiting for him to visit her tomorrow in Grangeshield House.

EIGHTEEN

A Bell is Rung by Mr Nicholas Raspero

The original Grangeshield House had been built by its first Master, Sir Arevik Grangeshield, to go along with his newly acquired title of Knight Exalted of the Realm. Sir Arevik was a man as fierce and hard as the times in which he lived. He had acquired a fortune by means which were only whispered of during the day and only spoken of out loud late at night among friends sitting drinking bravely around a fire. It was said of Sir Arevik that he could kill a man at a distance of one hundred yards with a single look from his baleful, bloodshot eyes, and while this was obviously a wild exaggeration it was nonetheless felt to be a poetic truth because it had been noticed that his enemies did tend to die off in mysterious circumstances.

After having been knighted by a pale and trembling king, Sir Arevik, who by now was all but a solar god, had turned his mighty attention to building a house worthy of housing both his noble knightly person, and the noble persons of his lady wife Marigold and twelve energetic children. The house had to be strong and it had to be knightly. Sir Arevik was a man who knew what he was about.

He had started by considering the inevitability of death and in consequence digging a crypt deep in the earth so that the end of all things would never be more than a step away. The north wall of the crypt was made entirely of natural rock while the remaining walls were made of a mixture of limestone and granite blocks cut to fit so snugly together that the lines could barely be seen. Ventilation shafts and drainage channels were appropriately positioned, while the stone platforms on which the stone sarcophagi of Sir Arevik and his descendants could be stacked were brought into place to stand through the ages that would follow. Over the crypt were laid the foundations of the house itself, while over the foundations which were over the crypt was placed the Great Hall, which was entered into directly from the front doors. The Great Hall had its fireplace to the west, because that was where the sun set, and this said fireplace was a crescent shape fifty feet wide and five feet high with its inset grate being twenty feet wide. The ceiling of oak-trunk roof-beams was fifty feet high above the heads of the innocents below, while to the north stood the dining table, which was thirty feet long and could seat twenty-two people at one comfortable spread-out sitting, and more if they were to sit more closely together as on such special occasions as a royal visit; the dining table stood with easy reach of the kitchens, which were directly behind the neighbouring wall, so food from the kitchens could be carried directly to the table. The walls of the Great Hall were of granite and over the years came to be hung with insignia mementoes of the inexorable onward march of the Grangeshield clan: paintings of the Grangeshields themselves and instances of various weaponry with perhaps a secret or two behind them (e.g., "this was the dagger which killed Lord Stoager late at night") which would never later be told or even remembered. Above the Great Hall, reached by stairs at the sides, was the floor of the servants' quarters, while above that floor were all the various bedrooms, bathrooms and drawing rooms of the Grangeshields themselves.

A man like Sir Arevik was never one to forget the obvious, and so Grangeshield House was designed to be defended against an armed foe marching against it: the walls were thick and the estate on which it stood, while scenic with its ponds and trees and mossy walkways, had open spaces on which horses could charge down an approaching enemy. Sir Arevik knew all about such things, and so the House he built did as well. Furthermore, finally and ultimately, the walls, foundation stone, crypt, battlements and boundary stones, were aligned extensively enough with the solstices and equinoxes and key points of the nodal axis of the sun and moon so as to satisfy the most esoterically-minded of mortals. Everything that was known of the world in which we live had gone into Grangeshield House.

And so matters stood for a while, and obviously enough so they stood, because what more was there to be done? Grangeshield House was complete, and the word *complete* has a meaning. But time will always take its toll, and so it came to be that Grangeshield House came to be changed.

Nothing succeeds like success and the Grangeshield Estate, via the careful networking of shrewd marriage alliances and the acquisition of various trade advantages, had expanded swiftly through the following generations, and the sketches and blueprinted plans of the third Master of Grangeshield House, which had lain around all dusty and ignored until the seventh Master of Grangeshield House chanced upon them, were expanded upon and set into motion until by the time of the birth of the eleventh Master of Grangeshield House, everything from these plans had been completed. At each corner of the original Grangeshield House was built a square tower, with a great library on the ground floor of one tower, a music room in another, a conservatory in another and a ballroom in another; between them were walkways with a variety of reception rooms, piano rooms, studies, medical stores of pharmacies, servants quarters and storage rooms. Above these walkways were guest bedrooms, bathrooms, drawing rooms and private studies and artist studios; above these were various sunroofs and roof gardens, while unchanged in the centre remained the Master Bedroom of the Master and Mistress of Grangeshield House, arising above its surrounds like the carefully protected kernel of a great plant, its windows still looking over the surrounding landscape as they always had, the Master and Mistress of Grangeshield House like captains on the deck of their ship as they had always been since the very beginning. Some things had not changed at all.

This was the house that Nicholas now stood in front of as an invited guest.

3:50 PM, Sunday 10 July 1544 A.F.

Rankled by Isabel's bossiness in saying, 'Don't be late!' Nicholas had made sure he was late. He had wandered around Kasia and up and down Jennyann Avenue looking at the grand houses with their immense gardens and finally come back to Grangeshield House to look at it again, looking up at how it arose high into the air, the size of a small castle. Nicholas understood now why Isabel had been astonished that he had not known where she lived. Anyone who lived in a place like this would expect everyone to know about it.

Nicholas was far from intimidated about being so small in front of such a large place because as a master of wandlore he was aware that force was dependent as much on direction as size. With his wand in his hand he contemplated Grangeshield House in terms of what could only be seen in the mind's eye.

The magnetised metal that formed the hinges and locks of doors and windows were bound together in a network of commands that formed the security system of the house; only the appropriate commands could activate the necessary process to open a door or window. As with all old houses, the various security systems, changes, updates, building extensions, repairs and modifications had combined in at times unpredictable ways to form an almost living being. As Nicholas contemplated Grangeshield House, he came to realise that there was a door at the side which had a doorbell that didn't work. At some time in the past something appeared to have gone wrong with the security system. He saw why attempts to fix it, if any, had failed: while a minor flaw that only affected the bell, attempting to restore the missing function only transferred wand command from elsewhere in the house, resulting in the system going haywire. The entire security system needed to be re-done.

Nicholas rang the dysfunctional bell, using a simple re-routing command to attach a direct connection, which he cancelled afterwards. He did not examine his own motives in doing this. Most likely he was showing off to impress Isabel by making an Entrance. It is true that an impish grin appeared on Nicholas's face when the idea first occurred to him, so it might have been simple mischief. Whatever the reason for his behaviour, he gave a wand command which resulted in the AU135 Bell ringing in the Secondary Servants Ante-Chamber.

Benson was not there at the time. He was in the Long Yellow Room supervising the cleaning of the woodwork of the Cabinet of Curiosities, *supervising* meaning that he was standing around doing nothing while Fey, Cara and Daffar did all the work. He was not the steward of Grangeshield House for nothing. That was where he was when Beth rushed into the room, obviously in a state.

'Benson!' she gasped, short of breath from running even that short distance. She spent a lot of time in the kitchen surrounded by appetising food. 'Benson! You must come! Immediately!'

'What has happened?' Benson asked, straightening up and squaring his shoulders as if preparing to take the weight of a drama onto those very shoulders.

'The AU135 Bell just rang!'

'No it didn't!' Benson declared immediately, as if he had been there himself. 'That bell doesn't work. It hasn't worked since — You're imagining things, Beth.'

'No,' Beth insisted, 'Maura and Cassidy were there, they heard it, you ask them. They're watching the bell right now, Mr B, right now. You ask them! Go on then! Imagining things! I don't imagine things, Mr B!'

It was true that Beth didn't imagine things. Benson considered how very true this was for a moment or two before saying, 'Very well, Beth. I will come. You lot,' he continued, turning to address Fey, Cara and Daffar who had stopped working and were standing listening to all this, cloths and opened jars in their idle hands, 'back to work!'

Benson strode off, followed closely by Beth. Fey, Cara and Daffar promptly dropped to the ground and lazed about, enjoying their unexpected work-break, gossiping and giggling on the floor of the Long Yellow Room.

Benson and Beth arrived in the Secondary Servants Ante-Chamber. Maura and Cassidy had been joined by Gordon and Harvey from the Garden; Shevaun, Hatty, Terrence and Larry from the Kitchens, and Simmy and Rassen from the Second Floor Wardrobe Department. Word had quickly spread about the mysterious goings-on in the Grangeshield House servants' quarters. They were all staring at the AU135 Bell intently. The AU135 bell just stayed where it was fixed on the wall, its bronze casing gleaming defiantly at them as if it refused to give up its secrets no matter how long they interrogated it with their accusing stares, and then at that very moment, as they were all staring at the AU135 Bell, the AU135 Bell rang again! It rang long and it rang loud and it rang to be heard! It was as if it was tired of being disbelieved.

Benson felt a cold shiver go up his spine as if someone had walked over his grave. Beth groaned and managed to stagger to a nearby chair, which she promptly dropped onto like a falling stone. There were head-shakings, comments and uneasy movements from the assembled servants.

'That ain't natural,' Gordon commented, shaking his head like a prophet of doom.

Benson knew his duty and he knew it well. Lady Grangeshield had to be informed immediately. 'I will return shortly,' he informed his fellow servants and departed immediately for the Red Drawing Room.

Nicholas, who had been tracking the movement of wands through Grangeshield House, and had rung the AU135 Bell the second time accordingly, saw a wand moving from the space where he supposed the AU135 Bell to have been ringing, judging from the number of wands clustered around it, to an upstairs room where there were three wands, two close together and one further away. He had already guessed that was where Isabel was waiting for him. Nicholas waited for the right time to ring the bell the third time. He grinned to himself like a boy playing the world's best ever prank.

Benson entered the Red Drawing Room and walked straight up to Lady Grangeshield, breaking normal protocol, which he knew that he could given the extraordinary nature of the news he brought. Guessing that something was up, the Eastons stood up and followed him over to Isabel.

'Lady Grangeshield, the AU135 Bell has rung,' Benson said in a state of agitation.

Isabel, who was dreading the coming interview with Nicholas, and who was both relieved and annoyed that Nicholas was so late, had no idea what Benson was talking about. She had never heard of the AU135 Bell. She had no idea of how the machinery of Grangeshield House worked as she left that for the servants to manage.

'The AU135 Bell has rung, did you say?'

'Yes, your ladyship.'

'And what does that mean?' Isabel asked without any real interest.

'We don't know, your ladyship. We don't know, and that's a fact. What's to be done though, your ladyship?'

'Another time, Benson,' Isabel said. She had no time for domestic matters now. 'I am waiting for a Mr Raspero to arrive, and when he does you are to show him up here immediately.' She had already told this to Benson two or three times already, but she said it again as if that would make it more likely to happen.

'Yes, your ladyship,' Benson replied obediently, but he didn't move from where he was standing. He was trapped between two things he couldn't do: disobey Isabel; or leave without directions from Isabel about what to do about the AU135 Bell.

Lord Easton stepped in. 'What is the purpose of the AU135 Bell, Benson?'

'The purpose, my lord? It's a bell. It rings, except it doesn't.'

'If that bell were to ring for a reason, what reason would that be?'

'That's just what we don't know, my lord. It's a mystery. There's no reason, my lord.' Benson looked at Lord Easton meaningfully and added with an air of grave seriousness, 'That is, no earthly reason, not in this world!'

Lord Easton was unmoved by Benson's implication, but then Lord Easton did not believe in the supernatural. 'The bell has rung in this world, Benson, therefore we shall look for an earthly reason as to why it has rung. If someone were to make this bell ring, what purpose would they have in mind in order for them to do this?'

'How would I know, my lord?' Benson replied, a little aggrieved at being expected to decipher the logic of a ghost. 'It's not for me to say, begging your pardon.'

Luckily Lord Easton was a patient man. He changed his line of questioning. 'By what process does this bell come to ring? What action is taken to bring about this result? What makes the bell ring?'

'But it doesn't ring, my lord. That bell doesn't work. It never rings, my lord.'

Lord Easton's patience was still there, but it was much reduced in volume by now. 'But you have said that it did ring, Benson! Did you not?'

'Yes, my lord, but that's just it. The bell has rung, sir, I was there, I heard it myself, yet it doesn't ring, sir. And what's to be done now?'

Lord Easton's patience was starting to run low. 'Benson!' he said sharply, 'pull yourself together, man! There are bells to summon you to Lady Grangeshield, bells for the doors, bells for dinner, bells for this, bells for that. What kind of bell is this one?'

'It's the doorbell for the Rose Garden door, my lord,' Benson told him.

Lord Easton sighed with relief at having finally got somewhere. 'Then go and see if there is a visitor at the Rose Garden door who is ringing the bell.'

'But there can't be no-one there, my lord,' Benson said, his grammar showing cracks under the strain of all this. 'That bell don't work for a visitor to ring.'

'In which case,' Lord Easton declared, 'having found no visitor at the door ringing the bell, you have eliminated this hypothesis and we shall consider another.'

'This hypothesis, my lord?' Benson queried.

Lord Easton lost his temper. 'Go and answer that door now, Benson! Right now! This very minute! Get going!' Lord Easton went so far as to raise his arm to point at the door through which Benson would be passing on his travels.

Benson looked at Isabel, who had been observing all this with an air of detachment, her thoughts very much elsewhere. 'Do as he says, Benson. Go and answer the door,' Isabel ordered him.

'Yes, your ladyship,' Benson answered promptly and left the room without any further delay.

It was times like this, he reflected as he descended the stairs, when he wished himself back to being a lowly footman again. People sought to rise in this world, he reflected further, only because they had never borne the weight of responsibility. There was no thought in his mind of disobeying Isabel, whom he served (Lord Easton's instructions had been merely advice to Benson) but he felt dread at what he might encounter on opening the Rose Garden door.

The AU135 Bell had not worked since the day Master Terence had died all those years ago. Some time after that, when life in the household was returning to normal, or at least back to a creaking state of normality which was all that the grief of the household could manage, the experts had been summoned to fix that bell. After a week of scratching their heads, they had declared that it was impossible for that bell to work and the Grangeshield House would just have to live without it. As it had been a little used door in any case (a clue, if anyone had stopped to consider it, as to why its doorbell had stopped working) it had been a very minor inconvenience for Grangeshield House to live without this one door, given that there were no less than eight other entrances, which were dedicated to visitors ranging from workmen and tradesmen to the grandees of New Landern.

Seeing a wand leaving the space where he assumed Isabel was waiting Nicholas rang the AU135 Bell a third time, long and loud with the insistency of a child throwing a tantrum. Benson could hear it faintly in the distance and so he wasn't surprised to see Beth running towards him. 'Mr B, it rang again!'

Benson entered the Secondary Servants Ante-Chamber grim-faced. The servants were still all there, plus a few more who had turned up, including Fey, Cara and Daffar who had given up pretending to clean the Cabinet of Curiosities and come to watch the show. 'Cassidy, you're coming with me. We're going to open the Rose Garden door.'

'I'm not coming with you,' Cassidy protested.

'Then pack your bags and get out now!' Without waiting for an answer Benson strode off. Cassidy looked about him for help but the other servants only drew away from him as if he were diseased. Running over to the fireplace, Cassidy grabbed an axe and ran after Benson.

'What if it's a ghost, Benson?'

Benson had been asking himself the same question. He looked approvingly at the axe in Cassidy's hand but said only, 'Less talking, more walking, Mr Cassidy.'

As the AU135 Bell hadn't worked since the day that Master Terence had died, the servants of Grangeshield House had come to believe superstitiously that the failure of the bell to work was somehow connected in a supernatural way with the death of Master Terence. Another point of view which they might have considered was that the breakdown of the bell had something to do with the events at Grangeshield House on the day Master Terence had died, but that was all so long ago now that no-one bothered thinking about it any more. All they knew for certain was that the bell didn't work and the bell didn't work because the ghost of Master Terence forbade it to had become folklore amongst them.

Seeing the Eastons looking out the window, Isabel went to join them wondering what was up. They were watching Benson and Cassidy make their way down the driveway. Isabel wondered why Cassidy was carrying an axe, but without too much interest in the question. She had too much on her mind already.

Benson and Cassidy walked down the driveway, the gravel crunching under their feet, and turned left through the Rose Garden to the door hidden out of sight behind a hedge. The secluded nature of the door had guided the tutor of Master Terence into using it for his clandestine comings and goings, just as his own inexpert attempt to re-wire the commands of the door had resulted in the bell becoming uniquely dysfunctional. Benson and Cassidy approached the door cautiously, their footsteps slowing. Benson waved Cassidy to the side before slowly and with enormous apprehension opening the door only enough to poke his head through.

A man was standing there, obviously waiting for the door to open. Benson looked at him and said, 'Yes, what do you want?'

The stranger raised his eyebrows at the manner of his reception, hesitated, and then said, 'To gain entry, of course. Why else would I have rung the bell?'

'You rang the bell?' Benson queried, just to make sure he had everything right. 'It was you then?'

The stranger took a deep breath, his face carefully impassive; it was not clear whether he was trying to keep his temper or keep from laughing. 'Yes, it was.'

'Why do you wish to gain entry?' Benson asked him suspiciously.

'Because I am visiting Lady Grangeshield.'

Benson looked around. 'Where is your carriage?'

The stranger also looked around and behind him and then replied, 'What carriage?'

'But how did you get here?' Benson asked in the spirit of a man enquiring as to a mermaid's choice of transport, given the deep mysteries into which he seemed to be plunged.

'I believe it is my turn to ask a question, is it not?' the stranger said. 'Tell me: are you a servant of the Grangeshield household, or are you an escaped lunatic from the local madhouse?' He raised his eyebrows to signify he had finished asking his question.

Several things were dawning on Benson all at once. The stranger was shabbily dressed but he spoke with the quiet authority of a natural-born gentleman. However, he had rung the bell or arrived here, it was not Benson's place to question him about it. And it was undeniable that his reception of the stranger had certainly been odd enough to warrant an accusation of lunacy.

Benson pulled himself together, opened the door wide as Cassidy edged to the side so as to still be concealed behind the door, and asked deferentially, 'May I enquire as to your name, sir?'

'Mr Nicholas Raspero,' said Mr Nicholas Raspero.

'Welcome to Grangeshield House, Mr Raspero. Lady Grangeshield is expecting you.' Benson stepped back and courteously bowed, a decorous wave of his hand inviting Nicholas to enter.

Nicholas didn't move from where he was standing.

'Why is there someone waiting behind the door?' Nicholas asked Benson.

Nicholas opened the door wider with a movement of his wand, banging the door repeatedly on the figure of Cassidy to oblige him to step back so the door could swing fully open. This development revealed Cassidy standing there with an axe in his hand.

'Let me re-phrase that question,' Nicholas said calmly. 'Why is there someone waiting behind the door with an axe in his hand?'

'We thought you was a ghost,' said the man with the axe.

'Ah,' said Nicholas calmly, nodding his head as if this kind of mistaken identity happened to him all the time. 'I won't ask why. Call me incurious, but there we are. Nor will I ask why you believe an axe to be an effective weapon to employ against a ghost. What I will ask, however, is when you plan to resume your duties as servants of the House of Grangeshield. Will it be any time soon?'

'Go back, Cassidy, now,' Benson ordered him. As Cassidy stood there, still catching up with the fast-changing pace of events, his mouth hanging slightly open, Benson added sharply, 'Now, man, go!' Benson even shooed him with his hands as if he was a cow that had strayed into the vegetable garden. Cassidy finally got the message and trudged off up the driveway, casting glances behind him as he went.

Nicholas moved then, entering the residence of the Grangeshields since 1247 in the year 1544. He set off up the driveway. 'What's your name?'

'Benson, sir.'

'What position do you hold in this household?'

'I am the steward, sir.'

Nicholas said nothing more after that as they walked up the driveway. Benson held himself back from stealing covert glances at this bell-ringing stranger who could tell as if by magic when people were hiding behind doors. Then Nicholas came to a stop and Benson could not help but follow the direction of his gaze.

They had come clear of the trees that lined the part of the driveway near the door. Grangeshield House lay before them. High up on the second floor, a figure in white stood at the window. As Nicholas and Benson watched, the figure abruptly moved away out of sight. Nicholas moved on as well. Benson followed him, with yet another topic to think about.

Isabel had stayed at the window gazing into space only to return to the present moment to see Cassidy coming back up the driveway followed by Benson and a figure she immediately recognised as Nicholas. She had a sudden attack of nerves. She looked at the time: it was ten past four. She wondered if Nicholas was so late that she could refuse to see him; then turned away from that moment of weakness.

She went back to her chair and sat down and prepared herself for the coming interview.

Nicholas found himself walking up an enormous flight of stone stairs to large double doors made of carven oak wood. As the doors themselves were only opened on special occasions, they entered through an inset door. As he entered into the Reception Hallway he looked straight ahead at the ancient blackened doors of the original Great Hall, some distance ahead of him; on either side were two large marble staircases, with curved bronze handrails, at the base of each handrail were two large bronze statues, one of a lion and the other of a lioness. Benson took Nicholas up the right-hand staircase, and then along a labyrinthine sequence of corridors and open spaces housing a variety of statues and artworks until he came to a halt outside a large pair of oak double doors; Lady Grangeshield had told him to bring Mr Raspero to see her *immediately* so that was what he did.

Benson then entered the Red Drawing Room, leaving the door only partly open so Nicholas could not see inside. Benson returned, opened the door wide and waved for Nicholas to enter.

The Red Drawing Room stretched before Nicholas into the distance like the deck of an ocean going liner. Ornately designed carpets lay over the polished wooden floorboards while golden chandeliers with red tips hung over chairs and armchairs and card tables; there were reading nooks at the side overlooking the garden; there were two fireplaces, several bookcases, paintings aplenty and a profusion of curios and ornaments. Despite its name, the décor of the room was largely a mixture of crimson reds and azure blues.

To his right Nicholas observed a seated lady and a gentleman standing politely to her side; the lady was short and plump with ringed curls of an old-fashioned style falling around a delicately shaped face; the standing gentleman was of average height but slightly stooped, with a long thin face and bright observant eyes. They were looking at Nicholas with no more than polite curiosity. Nicholas realised that they were obviously Isabel's chaperones.

Further down the room sat Isabel in a large armchair with complicated carvings at the sides. Benson was waiting dutifully to one side so Nicholas set off to where Isabel was sitting and came to a halt in front of her.

Isabel had ignored his approach, gazing into the distance as if he were not there. Now she took her watch from the table-top in front of her, opened the watch-face, inspected the time, and declared, 'You are very late, Mr Raspero.'

Nicholas thought this was absurd for several reasons. Firstly, there were five clocks in the room, placed so that any one of them could be seen from any vantage point, as if an earlier Grangeshield had desired a puzzle of geometry laid out to serve a theology of time. Secondly, Isabel would have known what the time was, given that she had just been looking out the window at his approach and she would have been bound to have checked it then, so she did not need to look at her watch now. Thirdly, it was too obviously a calculated move to be plausible. Despite all this he found himself all of a sudden wondering what time it was anyway and sneaked a glance at a nearby clock. (It was quarter-past-four.)

Yet, despite everything his rational mind told him about her behaviour, he admired her action, even as he resented it. He admired her action because he was still smitten by her; she could have done anything and he would have thought it was absolutely wonderful. Even the way her lips moved as she formed words took his breath away. Yet, he resented her action because he felt as far from her as ever, and that resentment was as powerful a motivation in his turbulent chest as his love-struck admiration.

'I rang the bell three times to gain admittance to your house, Lady Grangeshield,' Nicholas said, implying that his lateness was all her fault.

Isabel considered this answer while she considered him quite coolly. 'May I enquire as to your current circumstances, Mr Raspero?' she asked.

Nicholas looked about him. 'My current circumstances are Grangeshield House. You would know more about these circumstances than I would.'

'That was very clever, Mr Raspero,' Isabel said in a tone of voice that made plain it was anything but. 'You know very well what I mean, do you not?'

It was dawning on Nicholas that she intended to keep him standing before her like a supplicant. His admiration of her beauty that urged him to be a doormat for Isabel to walk across if that was what she wanted was at war with his resentment of the unattainability of her beauty that urged him to just sit down without being invited and then get thrown out for his rudeness. He fought off his resentment, but it was a close-run thing.

'My current circumstances, Lady Grangeshield?' he said reflectively, as if thinking about her question. 'Well, I enjoy my life, as it happens. I walk sometimes at dawn along the Freestarte beach, where the cockle pickers are at work in the distance where the sea is shallow, and I wonder what life must be like as a cockle picker. Don't you ever wonder that? No? Well, perhaps you should. They are only silhouettes, those cockle pickers, and so you can't help but wonder what they are really up to. You only see the façade, but what is behind the façade? But what have I seen? I wander through the Straendern market and watch everything that's going on: pickpockets, housewives, servants from households such as yours, and they all seem to be having fun, even when they're miserable, each in their own way, which is good. What's life without having fun? I've been to the Yellastezanis garden, I've done the Three in Kenina Park, and I've met interesting people from all over. I went to Trevarden because I'd never seen the sea and I sat on the cliff and looked at all the dazzling points of sunlight glittering and moving on the surface of the sea but it was all just a feeling I had then. I've seen a play and I've danced at the Plartendrawe bonfire. You ask about my current circumstances, Lady Grangeshield? Well, they're just fine. Everything is just dandy. Thanks for asking.'

Isabel had listened to all this without a change of expression, if indeed she had listened to any of it at all. She was bound up with her own agenda, and she had little interest in anything else other than achieving her own very strictly defined goals. She was vaguely aware of what Nicholas had been saying, in a general sense, but she was focused on more practical matters. But then Nicholas's resentment overcame the slavery his admiration had reduced him to and he made several moves all in a row.

Firstly, he took out his wand; then he turned and grabbed a chair with his wand and shifted it in one movement to be positioned at an angle close (but not too close!) to Isabel's chair; then he whipped up a nearby footstool and positioned it before the chair; then he sat down in the chair with a lusty sigh of relief, stretched out his feet on the footstool, pocketed his wand, interlinked his hands over his stomach and leaned back with his head resting on the headrest of the chair. Isabel watched all this in silence.

Nicholas sat there in the aftermath of this thunderclap feeling relaxed and at peace with himself. He knew he was bound to be thrown out any moment now, but he welcomed that. He looked forward to it.

There was something about the way Isabel's dark brown hair was piled up in a bun on the top of her head that twisted the insides of his stomach. There was a hair-pin in her dark brown hair made of a green gemstone that somehow seemed to point at him even though he had done nothing wrong. She wore diamond earrings that glinted distractingly. There was something about her warm brown eyes that made him need to take a deep breath. Her beauty was a constant sound in his ears. Above all else, what annoyed him more than anything, was the way he had been kept standing in front of her chair like that. She had invited him, for Heaven's sake! It was not as if he had banged on the door demanding entrance. He had come out of courtesy because she had invited him. As far as he was concerned, he was done being polite, and if she didn't like it, she could tell him to leave. He would leave immediately, and gladly, and while he wouldn't exactly slam the door on his way out he would certainly leave without a backward glance. Yes, he was done being polite. As far as he was concerned right then, being polite was overrated.

Isabel for her part was busy counting the ways in which Nicholas had been rude, and she certainly didn't consider politeness to be over-rated. As far as she was concerned, politeness could not possibly be over-rated. There were five counts of rudeness she identified with ease: one, being very late in arriving; two, taking out his wand in her house without her permission; three, moving furniture in her house without her permission; four, sitting down in her house without permission to do so, and five, putting his feet on that footstool.

In all her years (twenty-two) Isabel had never seen that footstool actually being used as an actual footstool, for the simple reason that it was not to be used for that purpose. It had been bound where it was by wand-commands that no-one could countermand (yet Nicholas had done so instantly, she observed) in the event that an uninformed guest had tried to take the footstool by mistake. It was the Footstool of Mangatha, and there Nicholas sat, his feet propped up on it! Isabel resolved not to say one word about the footstool. Not one word!

She further decided to show her far superior courtesy by saying nothing about his behaviour. She reminded herself then what this meeting was all about. She tried to remember what had been going on before Nicholas had distracted her with his wild wand-waving. She had asked him about his current circumstances. In reply, he had babbled something about cockle pickers and how wonderful they were, she remembered. She tried to think of her next move.

'Are your current circumstances all that you would desire, Mr Raspero?' she asked. When he said *no*, then she would lead him on to contemplate how she could help him improve them. She had worked it all out the night before.

'No, definitely not,' Nicholas replied. It was perfectly true, given that his current circumstances were a world away from the dazzlingly beautiful girl sitting right next to him.

'I am sure you would like to improve your current circumstances, would you not?' Isabel continued, ticking off the next item on the list she had made the night before.

'Wouldn't everybody?'

'Well, yes, of course. But what I must now ask you, Mr Raspero, is this: what do you plan to do in order to improve your circumstances?'

'Not a lot,' Nicholas said casually, 'I mean, I think I'll just wait for something to come along.'

He looked such a picture of lazy nonchalance, sitting there lolling back with his feet stretched out on the Footstool of Mangatha, that Isabel's self-control cracked in two.

'Mr Raspero, do you know what your feet are resting on?'

Nicholas glanced down at his feet. 'It's a footstool.'

'It is the Footstool of Mangatha,' Isabel told him with some severity.

'Well, that's interesting,' Nicholas said politely. 'Is it indeed?'

'It is not intended, Mr Raspero, for feet to rest on.'

'What is it intended for then?'

'To be an ornament of some elegance for contemplation, Mr Raspero. Contemplation! It is not supposed to be used to actually put feet on.'

'Is it a footstool or is it not?'

'It is a footstool that is not to be used.'

'What kind of footstool is that?'

'I have just told you,' Isabel said in exasperation. 'It is for contemplation, not use.'

'Well, it works just fine for me,' Nicholas said, as if that settled the matter. 'It's doing its job like no other footstool I've ever seen. Full marks to this footstool, that's what I say.'

'Mr Raspero,' Isabel said forcefully, 'you will remove your feet from that footstool now! Is that clear?'

'Yes,' Nicholas replied, not moving a muscle, 'that is perfectly clear. I am your guest in your house and I am obliged to respect your wishes. And when my feet hit the ground, my body will rise into a vertical position following which my feet will propel my body towards the door and through it and out of here. I will say *goodbye* on my way out, by the way, in case you don't understand what is happening. Now, is that clear?'

Isabel unfolded her fan and studied the markings on it as if that was of relevance to the ultimatum she had just received. She already knew, however, without needing to inspect very closely the markings on her fan that he could not leave until she had spoken to him of the reason she had invited him here in the first place. She folded up her fan again. 'I will say nothing of your rudeness in sitting down without permission, in moving my furniture without my permission, in taking out your wand in my house without permission, in using the Footstool of Mangatha which is not to be used as a footstool, nor of being so late. You may notice the far superior courtesy which I display on this occasion to your own lamentable caveman antics and I can only trust that it will be a lesson to you, an instructive occasion from which you may improve yourself.'

Nicholas noted to his surprise that he was not going to be thrown out after all. 'That is very kind of you, Lady Grangeshield.'

'Have you a position, Mr Raspero?'

'No.'

'Have you an income?'

'No.'

'Have you any money?'

'No.'

'That must be very unfortunate for you, Mr Raspero.'

'Thank you for offering me your sympathy, Lady Grangeshield.'

'I can offer you more than sympathy, Mr Raspero.'

'Like what?' Nicholas asked, raising his eyebrows.

'I understand that you are capable of defeating Captain Nevsky in a wand fight?'

'I've got Nevsky's measure,' Nicholas said cautiously, wondering where Isabel was going with this. 'I can take him down.'

'I wish you to kill Captain Nevsky for me,' Isabel said flatly. Now that the moment of truth had arrived her nerves had disappeared and she felt perfectly calm.

'Now that's something you don't hear every day,' Nicholas said, his face expressionless. 'Is this your own idea?'

'I will pay you well,' Isabel replied.

Nicholas practised one of several methods of self-control that he had been taught. 'So you believe me to be a murderer-for-hire, or an assassin to use a nicer-sounding word. You will pay me to kill Nevsky, is that what you are saying? Have I understood you correctly?'

'You may name your price,' Isabel said.

'Oh, I have a price, do I? That's news to me. What price is that? Do you know?'

Isabel sensed that this was not going well. Nicholas had no expression on his face, his voice was calm, yet his hands were gripping the sides of his chair so tightly that his knuckles were turning white. She played her last card, which she had kept in reserve believing it to be the winning card in her hand.

'I will pay you one million strada to kill Nevsky for me.'

Nicholas took a deep breath, let it out slowly, took another deep breath and then started to speak. He spoke very calmly. 'I think you have entirely mistaken the nature of my identity, Lady Grangeshield. I find as I sit in your drawing room that my nostrils are filled with the stench of the gutter. You have insulted me so deeply that if you were a man the only satisfaction I could demand from you would be that of Final Combat. As it is, perhaps there is someone who will act on your behalf if required. Is there such a person?'

'No, Mr Raspero, I am alone. There is no-one.'

'Well, then, I will leave. There is nothing more for me to say to you and there is certainly nothing more for you to say to me. You have already said far more than enough. Goodbye, Lady Grangeshield.'

With that Nicholas stood up and began walking towards the door. Isabel jumped to her feet and raced after him.

'Please do not go, Mr Raspero. You judge too quickly. You do not know the circumstances.'

Nicholas took a deep breath, stood there a while and thought about this, breathed out heavily and took another deep breath. Despite his anger, he was struck by the magnitude of her offer. A million strada! 'Lady Grangeshield, you will apologise for your conduct. Now!'

'I apologise for my conduct, Mr Raspero,' Isabel said automatically, her eyes fixed on his face.

'I accept your apology,' Nicholas said and took another deep breath. 'But there is no point in telling me anything further. I will not do as you ask of me, so why tell me the reason you ask it of me?'

'I ask you only to hear what I have to say, Mr Raspero. Is that really too much to ask of you?'

'It probably is,' Nicholas declared, still coming down from his bout of fury. 'It probably is too much to ask of me, as it happens. But very well, I will hear you out.'

He returned to his seat, leaned back and put his feet up on the Footstool of Mangatha again. 'You may proceed.'

Isabel took a deep breath and launched herself into what she had to say like a diver falling from a great height into unknown waters.

'A friend of mine was … gravely mistreated by Captain Nevsky.'

Nicholas felt abruptly disconnected from himself, as if his head was floating in the air, because he did not want to know what she had just said, which could not now be unsaid. He had a sudden vision of Isabel in her red and blue gown, resplendent in her magnificent innocence. 'And then what happened?' he asked calmly.

'Nevsky and … his lawyer Balustrade came the next day. There were … witnesses.'

'What witnesses?'

'Five men … who … watched.'

'Then what happened?'

'Nevsky said my friend had to marry him. She refused. Balustrade had a marriage contract. They said she would be sued for breach of promise if she did not marry him.'

'Then what happened?'

'She refused. So they said they would forego the marriage contract if she paid them one million strada in compensation.'

'Then what happened?'

'She paid them the money.'

'Did they leave her alone after that?'

'Yes, but Nevsky … torments her whenever he sees her in public.'

'When did this mistreatment happen?'

'On the fifth of June.'

'So this is what you are telling me,' Nicholas said, his head still floating in the air. 'Nevsky raped you and then blackmailed you for one million strada.'

'I said it happened to my friend.'

'I heard exactly what you said,' Nicholas told her, looking into her wide brown eyes. 'Let me think about this for a moment.'

He turned away, stretched his legs out further and stared off across the room.

A wave of anger surged through Nicholas then. The blood drained from his face as if it was gurgling down a plughole, leaving his widened eyes shining in his white face like grey gemstones embedded in a bank of snow. He felt that the world had become confusingly layered, with different parts of different layers showing through at the same time to form a picture of the world that was not all one thing. The world had become disordered.

The world might have become disordered, but there was one thing that was immediately apparent to him and which could not be denied or avoided. Nevsky had to die. That was simply beyond any kind of dispute. Furthermore, as he was the only man who could defeat Nevsky, he had to be the one to do it. His duty was clear. Everything that remained was merely a matter of detail. There was nothing to be thought about with regard to this decision because this decision made itself, it simply appeared as a complete resolution already formed and to which he could only respond. Nicholas was a man of his time and there was simply no other choice he could make.

Nicholas turned back to look at Isabel. Her eyes were fixed on his face. She looked away, then defiantly, with a stiffening of her face, looked back into his eyes.

'Nevsky must die,' Nicholas told her. 'And clearly I must be the one to do it. Very well, I will kill Nevsky for you.' With that Nicholas stood up. 'I will see myself out, Lady Grangeshield.'

Isabel stayed in her seat to watch him cross the room; then he was gone, and she was left to her thoughts.

NINETEEN

....

The Secret Visit to the House of Captain Abner Nevsky
by Mr Nicholas Raspero

5:10 PM, Sunday 10 July 1544 A.F.

Nicholas made his way by retracing his steps through Grangeshield House, oblivious now to the magnificent nature of his surroundings. A servant seeing him passing by unaccompanied raced off around a corner and by the time Nicholas had reached the driveway Benson was trotting briskly after him.

'Are you leaving, Mr Raspero?' Benson asked, puffing for breath and alarmed at how white-faced Mr Raspero was.

'Play time is over, Benson,' Nicholas told him harshly. 'No stupid questions, got it?'

'Yes, Mr Raspero, indeed,' Benson said, a little shaken and looking over his shoulder and up at the windows of the room where Isabel had received Nicholas. There was nothing there to be seen, and Benson could only worry. 'You have made your farewells to Lady Grangeshield?' Benson insisted on knowing.

Nicholas understood him. 'She's fine. I'm not. Shut up.'

Benson said nothing more, as he had been requested to do.

They walked in silence to the door. Nicholas was in such a temper that he threw open the door and slammed it shut behind him, leaving Benson standing still where he stood.

Nicholas hardly noticed where he was or where he was going. Everything was a blur. Yet, an intention of some kind must have guided him, because he found himself at the Thorburn Bridge, on the outskirts of New Landern, a lonely and deserted place, especially at this time of the early evening.

Without thought, Nicholas knew that this was where he would kill Nevsky. That was decided. But how would he get Nevsky to come here?

He went to the side, sat on a flat stone and thought the matter over. Nevsky would not come if he knew why he had been summoned, so therefore he had to be summoned under a false pretext. But what false pretext? What would bring him here? The question somehow answered itself: if he was promised a way to get revenge on Nicholas Raspero. Fine, that was settled. The precise detail could wait. It would come to him in time.

Just then another thought occurred to Nicholas, a thought which interrupted the sequence of ideas assembling themselves into a plan. The thought then occurred to him out of the blue that if Nevsky was killed then the authorities, bless their little hearts, would set to work to investigate. Secret duels were forbidden and in consequence counted as murder; there would be a criminal investigation, which meant that Nevsky's personal effects would be placed under scrutiny. And what if documents relating to Isabel were uncovered during the course of that search and what had happened to her at Nevsky's hands came to light? Nicholas was troubled by this possibility, and it is to his credit that his thoughts did not even continue to their further implication, namely that the association of Isabel Grangeshield with Nevsky's death might lead to the identification of Nicholas Raspero as his killer, which would lead to him being executed for murder. His only thought was to protect Isabel.

Nicholas set his mind to consider this new perspective that had just opened up. He saw immediately that he would have to burgle Nevsky's place and search it for documents of this nature before proceeding with the actual killing of Nevsky himself. He had never done anything like this before, but he knew that logically the place with the greatest wand-made protections would be the place where what was most treasured by their owner was hidden. If he broke and entered into Nevsky's place, and used his wandlore to identify where Nevsky hid his most valued possessions, he would have solved this particular problem and would then be free to move on to the second problem.

First of all, Nicholas realised, he would have to find out where Nevsky lived. He stood up then and there and set forth to achieve this goal.

Finding where Nevsky lived was not as simple a task as might be supposed, Nicholas reflected as he walked along, heading back home. There was the Post Office, which would list addresses, but how would such an enquiry work? Furthermore, he could not simply go around asking anybody he met where Nevsky lived, because later when Nevsky was found dead they would very likely remember his enquiry. He could not wait to spot Nevsky somewhere and follow him; Nevsky would notice. Since their fight, each man had acquired a keen awareness of the other's presence whenever their paths happened to cross. Nevsky wanted to avoid another duel, Nicholas wanted to avoid getting a bolt through his neck from around the corner. How could he find Nevsky's address?

No answer came to him that night, but Nicholas was patient — to hunt down an idea was like any other kind of hunting. The very next day a possibility suggested itself. There was a street urchin who appeared to idolise Nicholas, no doubt because he was famous as the conqueror of Nevsky and as a man whose name was on the List for having done the Three in Kenina Park. This street urchin seemed to be a leader of those of his kind, resourceful and energetic, always on the lookout for opportunities. Whenever Nicholas passed by he stopped whatever he was doing and gazed in the direction of his hero. Hitherto Nicholas had simply ignored him, but now as he walked along Crest Street that Monday morning, he gave the matter more thought when he noticed the street urchin standing paused in the middle of some motion, gazing at Nicholas passing by with a fixed attention. Nicholas stopped, turned and caught his eye, and then beckoned him over with a wave of his hand. The street urchin came running over. He had pale blue eyes, curly reddish hair and a cheerful freckled face.

'What is your name?' he asked the boy.

'Bailey, sir,' the boy replied.

'Do you know who I am?'

'You are Mr Nicholas Raspero, sir,' Bailey said promptly.

'Do you know where Captain Nevsky lives?'

'Yes, sir,' said Bailey.

'Take me there,' Nicholas ordered him.

On the way Nicholas pulled forth a hooded cloak from underneath his robes. He wrapped it around himself and pulled the hood over his head, tying the drawstring to pull the sides of the hood around his face so that his face was hidden from view. Bailey looked up at him doing this but said nothing.

Bailey stopped. 'That's where Captain Nevsky lives, sir,' he said, pointing to a house across the way.

'Don't point,' Nicholas said sharply and the boy dropped his arm as if it had been slapped down.

Nicholas stopped and considered the house. It was a large mansion, set well back from the road; it had plenty of trees and shrubbery to provide cover for an uninvited intruder, Nicholas noted with satisfaction.

This was a good area, Nicholas realised as he looked around. The people who lived here had money and social standing.

Nicholas stared at Nevsky's house and wondered what his plan of action would be. He could keep a watch on the house until Nevsky left to go somewhere or other, leaving the field clear for Nicholas to burgle the house, but how long would that take? In a wealthy area like this a stranger could not simply stand about as he could in a poorer area. His presence would soon be noted and someone would come along to question him. Nor could he simply walk about for too long, for the same reason. Nor could he identify a place of concealment from which to carry out his surveillance. Furthermore, Nevsky was a rich man now; he would be bound to have servants. Nicholas would have to take them down and tie them up. Nevsky would then know he had been burgled, and if documents had gone missing he would be alerted to the seriousness of the danger he was in by the nature of the missing documents. He would go to ground and it would be impossible for Nicholas to lure him out.

Nicholas had already decided how to draw Nevsky out to the secret duel, but what now? He stood there and thought while Bailey stole glances at his hooded companion.

Bailey had been born premature into an already hostile world, literally kicked out of his mother's womb when his drunken father, doubting the paternity of the child, kicked his pregnant wife in her stomach, thus inducing a premature birth. This was Bailey's start in life. The boy was naturally cheerful and inquisitive, intelligent and energetic. So, perhaps it was to his advantage that his father was thrown into a debtor's prison when he was three and his mother, unable to care for her brood of five, slimmed down the numbers of her dependent children by leaving Bailey on the steps of the Halen Charity Home for Boys. At least there he was fed and clothed adequately for the first time in his life, and he learned to read, write and do sums. But then his luck turned bad again when a recently appointed Supervisor took a liking to the seven-year-old boy and after two years of being at the receiving end of the Supervisor's affections Bailey climbed out of the window one night and left to make his own way in the world.

He slept where he could, stole food, ran errands and earned a few coins here and there, occasionally so desperate with relentless hunger as to receive the attentions of men like his former Supervisor for money to buy food, and even his own wand, his proudest ever possession. He once saw a wealthy child drop a toy onto the street and he swiped it for himself; it was a wind-up duck that walked about quacking. Bailey was so entranced by his toy that when it broke he hid it carefully away as if the broken toy was a treasure.

It wasn't long before he made his way to the periphery of a group of street kids who were connected to Gross of Gross, who was connected to Pay, who was connected to Jolly himself, the absolute monarch of New Landern's demi-monde.

Jolly was too distant to be a hero for Bailey. Bailey had never even seen him, though he had kept his eyes open. After looking up to a number of figures in his life, he found his hero in Captain Abner Nevsky. Nevsky was brash, loud and feared, but more than anything, he was the best wandfighter in New Landern. In the past two years he had won eighteen wand fights, two of them duels of Final Combat. Six duels had been Second Combat, in which he had broken the arms and legs of his opponents, leaving them crippled for life. The other ten had been First Combat duels, which he had won with such ease his opponents had trembled at the thought of ever crossing him again. People crossed the street to avoid him. No matter how offensive his behaviour, no-one ever dared say anything. Bailey idolised Nevsky, and the greatest moment of his young life came when he was twelve and Nevsky called him over, ruffled his hair and gave him a few strada. And then came the calamitous news that Nevsky had fallen to a newcomer called Nicholas Raspero, and Bailey's world was shaken. Even the later news that Nevsky had suddenly become rich due to an inheritance from an uncle in Yerlandergard across the sea had failed to restore Nevsky to heroic status, despite the enormous grandeur which being rich conferred. Nevsky had strutted around as if he was invincible and Bailey had needed to believe in Nevsky's invincibility because of a deep and abiding sense of his own powerlessness. If Nevsky could be invincible, then Bailey could be as well one day, or so thought Bailey, and the fall of Nevsky was a personal tragedy for Bailey.

It had been a top priority for Bailey to see Nevsky's nemesis, and it wasn't long before he caught his first sight of Nicholas Raspero. He took to noting all the differences between Nevsky and Raspero: where Nevsky was loud, Raspero was quiet; where Nevsky was a fountain of money, Raspero was poor; where Nevsky threw himself about, Raspero stood quietly in the background largely unnoticed. But Bailey was an observant boy and he also noted all the similarities between the two: both men always kept their hand resting on the hilts of their wands; both men always stood in the same posture, relaxed and balanced but only a foot movement away from the wandfighting posture; both men were always aware of everything going on around them as a matter of habitual reflection and both men had a certain indefinable air of command about them.

But then came the time when Bailey noted the key difference between them which settled his choice of hero. Where Raspero was, there Nevsky was not. He noticed that if Raspero came walking along, it was only a matter of time before Nevsky left the scene. Nevsky's departure would be disguised as brought about for one apparent reason or another but Bailey was not fooled: Nevsky ran from Raspero, and so it was that Nicholas Raspero became Bailey's hero and Nevsky became yesterday's news.

And now had come the day when Bailey was walking side by side with his hero, who even knew his name now, and Bailey could not have been prouder. This was now the greatest moment of his young life.

'Come with me,' Nicholas instructed Bailey and walked away from Nevsky's house. He directed his steps towards the river and stopped by a tree which he leaned on, looking around him fairly casually.

'Do you know what discretion is, Bailey?'

'No, sir.'

'It means keeping your mouth shut. Think you can do that?'

'Yes, sir.'

'I have a job for you, but I cannot pay you,' Nicholas told him. 'You may have whatever chance throws your way. Do you understand me?'

Bailey hesitated, as if he had questions, but then said only, 'Yes, sir.' He seemed to be in awe of Nicholas, as if he was in the presence of a god.

'Above all else, however, this employment requires the utmost in discretion. That is clear enough, I take it?'

'Yes, sir.'

'You will meet me here at six o'clock this evening. I will instruct you as to what you will then do. You will tell absolutely no-one, no-one at all, about our arrangement. Do you understand me?'

'Yes, sir.'

'Until six o'clock this evening then,' Nicholas said and walked off. He pulled off his hood and cloak as he walked along and stuffed it back under his robe. Bailey's heart beat much faster than usual as he watched his hero walk away.

Nicholas had been taught by his grandfather that sometimes the most careful of plans could go wrong and sometimes the wildest of plans could go right. There was never any telling how life would work out. His ideas had all come to him seemingly of their own accord rather than being deduced by a process of reasoning, and so he acted on them without too much reflection.

He went to Veron Street and spoke to Ben. He casually inquired if Ben had any spare parchment scrolls for him.

'Parchment scrolls?' Ben asked. 'What do you want them for?'

'I'm taking up calligraphy,' Nicholas told him, leaning against the door jamb of Ben's lawyer's office in Veron Street.

Ben glanced down to see Nicholas's left forefinger curled up against his thumb. 'Calligraphy? Why?'

'To improve myself. Is there anything wrong with that?'

Ben shook his head as if giving up on Nicholas. 'Parchment scrolls, let's see,' and a short while later Nicholas was on his way clutching his newest possessions. The only clue left for Ben to ponder was that Nicholas had wanted several different types and sizes of parchment scrolls.

Nicholas returned home and composed a letter with care, the care taken being to ensure that the letter was not only semi-literate but also badly written as if by a hand not used to producing alphabetical symbols. The letter was written on a torn off piece of parchment, which added to the impression given of an uneducated man sending a letter. The letter was addressed to "Kaptin Nevski".

He then readied himself for the evening's work by making himself a black mask. Not being skilled with needle and thread, this took him some time, but as all he cared about was the functional requirement that the mask shield his face from view, while providing him with normal vision he got there in the end. He then took off his robe, checked the various weaponry strapped to his body, tied the mask and parchment scrolls to his body, and put his robe back on again. Then he waited.

He left early to avoid Ben's return, and walked leisurely as if out for a stroll. By six o'clock he arrived at the meeting place.

Bailey was already there, as if he'd made triple sure that he was on time. He looked eager and nervous. Nicholas looked down at the boy and pulled out his letter.

'You will go to Nevsky's house and say that you are delivering a letter to him. You will say that you have been instructed not to hand it over to anyone but Nevsky himself, and that Nevsky himself will be furious if any other hand but his receives this letter. If Nevsky is not there, you will enquire as to when you might return to deliver the letter to him. If Nevsky is there you will deliver the letter only to his hand. If anyone asks who sent the letter you will say you do not know. You will only say that the man looked like a sailor, with a tattoo of an anchor on his arm, his left forearm, and he was short and stocky with short white hair, with an accent of someone from the north. The sailor gave you five strada which you do not have on you because you have already hidden it. The sailor gave you this letter in Strepton Street an hour ago. Make up any further details you care to as long as you remember what they are if you are questioned further. Then you return here and report to me. Do you understand everything I have told you?'

'Yes, sir,' said Bailey, his heart pounding madly in his chest.

'Off you go then,' Nicholas said and handed him the letter.

Bailey ran down the street at top speed and soon he was out of sight. Nicholas sat down on a nearby tree branch and waited.

Bailey arrived at the Nevsky residence and rang the bell by the gate. The gates swung open and he walked briskly up the driveway, holding the letter in his hand very visibly. As he neared the door it swung open and there stood a butler, elegant in his butler-wear silver-haired and deceptively kindly by appearance. This particular butler, Rand, had been in and out of jail most of his life and knew little of being a real butler but he suited Nevsky and that was what counted in the Nevsky residence.

'Wha'dja want?' Rand asked with a yawn.

'I've got a letter for Captain Nevsky,' Bailey told him, holding the letter up as proof of his contention.

'Give it here,' Rand said with little interest, holding out his hand to take the letter.

'No,' Bailey protested, backing away, 'I been told that Nevsky gets this letter, no-one else, and Nevsky's gonna be mad at anyone that even touches this letter, see?'

This gave Rand pause for thought. He knew from personal experience what Nevsky was like when he lost his temper and he had no desire to be on the receiving end of that particular firestorm. Rand came to a decision.

'In,' Rand said, standing aside and jerking his thumb towards the hallway.

Bailey stepped through the door. He was only nervous at being here, because luckily for him he had no idea of the nature of the game in which he played his crucial role. Had he known, he would have been too terrified to speak. As it was, he knew that the secretiveness of Nicholas Raspero meant that something dodgy was going on, but beyond that he had no idea of what this was about.

'C'mon you,' Rand said and set off down the hallway. With a downward gesture of his forefinger he instructed Bailey to wait outside a door he entered. Bailey waited, his hands sweaty as they clutched the letter between them. Rand returned, opened the door, gestured with his thumb as an invitation to enter the room, and then closed the door behind Bailey as he went in.

Nevsky was sitting at the end of the room, with four or five men sitting around in their shirtsleeves. Nevsky's blue jacket was thrown over the back of a nearby couch; he wore a black woollen sweater with the sleeves cut away at the shoulders, his powerful bare arms lying along the sides of his chair. The air was blue with the haze of tobacco smoke, Nevsky himself puffing on an enormous cigar. No-one seemed to be troubling themselves with the use of an ash-tray. The men were laughing at something as Bailey approached Nevsky, nervous at being there but not any more nervous than that, which was as well for the success of Nicholas's plan. Nevsky could sense the approach of danger as an animal can sense a change in the weather.

'Over here, my boy,' Nevsky cried out cheerfully, 'this way, don't be shy, don't be shy, a fine boy like you, I know you, don't I, boy, know you, don't I?'

'I'm Bailey, sir,' Bailey said as calmly as he could.

'Well, of course you are, who else would you be?' Nevsky laughed at his own wit and his companions all laughed out loud as well. 'You're not no-one but Bailey,' Nevsky added to make the joke even clearer, and everyone laughed even harder.

Nevsky's laughter gradually subsided and sharp eyes suddenly looked sideways at Bailey as Nevsky turned his head to tap his cigar ash onto the floor by his chair. Bailey stood there without moving, clutching his letter in both hands.

'Got a letter for me, have you, my boy?' Nevsky asked him.

'Yes, sir,' Bailey replied.

'Give it here,' Nevsky ordered, holding out his hand.

Bailey went up to him obediently and handed over the letter then retreated a few steps.

The letter and envelope were all one thing, folded into a rectangle so the name of the addressee was written on the facing side of the envelope, which was the reverse side of where the message had been written onto the parchment. The torn edge of the parchment had been glued into place. Nevsky inspected the letter briefly then tore it open. It read:

> *Kaptin Nevski, I knou Rasparos seakrit. Mit me 10 oklok tumora nait at Thorburn Bridge. Kum aloan. Itl kost ya tun thowznd stradas koynz oanli.*

Nevsky read this letter over again then looked up at Bailey with an air of menace. 'Who gave you this letter, boy?'

'I don't know, sir,' Bailey said, frightened by the look Nevsky was giving him.

Nevsky could sense his lie. He whipped out his wand and on the instant Bailey was dangling in the air. Nevsky stood up, his eyes level with Bailey's and shouted, 'Who gave you this letter, boy?'

At that moment all Bailey could think of was the story Nicholas had told him. 'I dunno, it was a sailor or someone, he had a tattoo on his arm, an anchor,' Bailey gestured desperately to his left forearm, 'he was like from the north or something, I dunno who it was, I swear, Captain Nevsky, I never saw him before.'

Nevsky considered this answer, glaring red-eyed at Bailey, then flicked his wand: Bailey dropped to the floor, trembling from head to toe. Bailey had given the only answer he could think of, and it had therefore seemed like the truth to Nevsky. And that was the last moment when Nevsky could have taken a different path to this one. Had he treated Bailey more kindly, who knew what different outcome might have manifested itself? But Nevsky could not have behaved differently — it was not in his nature. Even Bailey, observant as he was, had not noticed the real key difference between Nicholas and Nevsky: Nevsky was consumed by fear, while Nicholas had been taught by his grandfather to be frightened of nothing, not even his own death. No-one had ever taught Nevsky anything. Nevsky's fear became the anger which drove his actions. And the letter he had received from Nicholas, reminding him of his fear of Nicholas, which was his fear of his own death, had become the anger he had directed at Bailey.

'Get out, boy,' Nevsky ordered, with a wave of his hand at the door. Bailey did not need telling twice. Rand was not surprised to see how eager Bailey was to be on his way, given that he had heard Nevsky's voice upraised in anger. Rand smirked as he opened the door with a deliberately agonising play-acting slowness as if the door were incredibly heavy, enjoying the sight of Bailey trembling. Bailey dodged sideways through the door as soon as it was just wide enough and ran for it.

Bailey returned to where he had left Nicholas and told him everything that had happened. Nicholas nodded approvingly and said, 'Well done, Bailey. You have done very well indeed.'

'Thank you, sir,' Bailey said, his fear lessening and his pride in what he had done growing. He could tell from the expression on Nicholas's face that Nicholas was pleased with his delivery of the letter, and Nicholas's approval made his pride grow to the very tips of his finger-tips.

'You will meet me at ten o'clock tomorrow evening at the Montague Monument,' Nicholas told him. 'Do you know where that is?'

'Yes, sir,' Bailey told him.

'Once again, Bailey, I must impress upon you the importance of discretion. You remember what discretion is, don't you?'

'Keeping my mouth shut, sir.'

'I have a concern that if you told anyone about what has happened,' Nicholas told him, 'it would be bound to get back to Captain Nevsky and Nevsky would be angry with you. Therefore it is best if you tell no-one at all about any of this, nor about our next meeting. Do you understand what I am saying?'

'Yes, sir,' said Bailey, so proud at that moment he couldn't care less about a thousand Nevskys but would do anything for Nicholas. 'I'll keep my mouth shut, I promise, sir.'

'Good. You go that way,' Nicholas said, pointing down the street. 'Ten o'clock tomorrow at the Montague Monument. If I am late, wait for me.'

'Yes, sir.'

With that Nicholas was off and Bailey looked after him until his hero was out of sight.

Nicholas wandered around until it was dark, then wandered around some more to let it get even later, and then returned to the Nevsky mansion. He didn't have a watch but he guessed it must be getting on toward ten o'clock or so.

The Nevsky mansion was ablaze with lights. To the side were several carriages, drawn off to one side. Nicholas went over the wall in one movement: one moment he was walking along the street, the next he was over the wall, nullifying the wand protection as he went through so he landed on the ground without setting off the alarm bell.

Dogs had been on his mind, but as he crouched in the darkness by the wall he could not detect any canine presences. A flying carriage was coming down and Nicholas watched it land. Three well-dressed people descended to the ground and went towards the door, obviously familiar with visiting the Nevsky mansion. The door was standing open and they just went straight in. Nicholas guessed that wand messages must be sent and received by any new arrivals.

Nicholas pulled out his mask and put it on, then used his wand to go down the side of the garden in three stages. If anyone was looking his way at that particular moment in time, he would have noticed a movement, but Nicholas could only hope that his luck would be in. Chance itself should be on his side, as it was unlikely that Nevsky had sentries. There were no wands outside the house, so there were no sentries hidden outside. Furthermore, the entrance of the new arrivals should have momentarily become the focus of attention, thus making it less likely that anyone would happen to be looking out of the window. Or so Nicholas hoped; he was making everything up as he went along.

Nicholas studied the side of the house. He could see lighted windows but no visible movement. He had already studied the wand protection of the house, but now he carefully checked everything again. There was a window of a darkened room high above him; Nicholas opened the window with his wand from where he was, went up to it in one parabolic movement through the air and landed with his feet on the window sill. He entered the room, closing the window behind him. His entrance had taken no more than three seconds from start to finish. The room was dark but by macchato Nicholas determined that he was in a storeroom full of trunks, packing cases and various oddments. Picking his way carefully through the dark room, dependent entirely on macchato, Nicholas made his way to the door. There were no wands in his immediate vicinity so Nicholas cautiously opened the door and poked his head through.

A corridor went to his left, then ended and turned right. To his right the corridor stretched for some distance, running the whole length of the house from the looks of it. Nicholas pulled his head back in, closed the door softly, and started his search.

Within the house there were few wand protections, just the usual domestic arrangements. But there was one particular cluster of wand protections that caught Nicholas's attention. They were below him to the left in the house — and they were exceptionally strong. Nicholas noted that Nevsky had used his specialised wandfighting combinations to devise these wand protections. Where those wand protections were, Nicholas realised, would be Nevsky's most closely guarded secrets. Anything that could endanger Isabel would be there.

Nicholas now scanned the house for the presence of wands. There were thirty-eight in total, the bulk of them not far from Nevsky's treasure. Nicholas thought about his next move.

He wasn't worried about being detected and therefore caught. He could take down anyone who attacked him. But Nevsky must not know that there had been an intruder, not when he had just been summoned to a secret meeting with someone unknown. It was vital to the success of his meeting tomorrow with Nevsky that he enter and depart undetected.

Realising there was nothing for it but to try his luck, Nicholas left the room and set off down the corridor. There were rising and falling sounds of merriment downstairs. Coming to a staircase, Nicholas slowly made his way downwards, scanning constantly for the movement of wands in the room below. He would not be able to detect anyone moving about without a wand in their pocket, but the chances of that were low; his luck would really be out if that happened.

There was a small window set in the wall of the room for a servant to spy on proceedings in order to maintain an unobtrusive flow of hospitality to guests, and Nicholas peered cautiously through this window now.

The room was large and filled with people. Nevsky stood laughing at something someone had just said. Near him lying on a sofa was Lady Arabella Montlait, who Nicholas had met at Lady Starfeld's party. She was one of society's beauties and Nicholas had thought that she was flirting with him at the time, but had made little of it, given she was married to the Keeper of the Royal Seal who had been standing nearby. Lord Montlait, Nicholas remembered, had been elderly and reserved, while Lady Arabella had been young and vivacious. Nicholas observed she was barely dressed in undergarments that were in some disarray, her thin shift rucked up over bare legs, while she gazed admiringly up at Nevsky who was standing bare-chested and bare-footed wearing baggy trousers. Nicholas couldn't help but take a second look at Lady Arabella before his attention moved on. She was not acclaimed as one of society's beauties for nothing, and the sight of her bare shoulders and her bare legs did not detract from this status. Another one of Lady Starfeld's party guests who Nicholas recognised was Lord Yamila, Minister of the Crown for the Defence of the Realm, thin-faced with a mop-top of black hair. Lord Yamila, Nicholas noted, was sitting with a completely naked woman on his lap — she was large-breasted and sprawled out all over Yamila, who was paying her little attention. Nicholas did not recognise any of the other guests except Nevsky's dogs, five men who he had seen following Nevsky about New Landern just like loyally attentive dogs, hence their nickname.

Well, well, Nicholas reflected. He had heard that Nevsky was planning to enter politics and it seemed that his political career was off to a flying start. But time was passing and he was no closer to his goal. He scanned the room now for where it provided access to Nevsky's treasure, and then he saw it — a door at the far end. It was beyond that door that Nevsky's treasure was located, and between him and it was Nevsksy's party. He understood now that this was deliberate on Nevsky's part — no burglar could get there while Nevsky was partying, and no doubt that was where Nevsky slept at night.

Nicholas refused to allow himself to despair. He would find a way. Where there was a room there would be a window, and where there was a window he would gain access. Or so he hoped. Taking account of the location of his destination, he went back upstairs and moved along until he was above the room where he had guessed that Nevsky's treasure was located.

There were no wands outside. He opened a window and cautiously put his head through and looked down. He saw what had to be a window but there was something odd about it; it had some kind of cage attached to it. It was too dark for him to make out anything more, so he brought out his wand and used macchato. It did not take him long to realise that the cage was full of snakes, and he very much doubted they were harmless ones. The wand protections he could deal with, but the snakes he could not go past without killing them, and remaining undetected was key to his whole plan. He closed the window and paused for thought. He wondered what Nevsky put outside the door to his room when he was out, but put aside the speculation as a distraction.

His grandfather had taught him, *when there is no way to go through, make a way,* and this advice came back to Nicholas now and he had his solution to the problem. He would cut his way through the ceiling and just hope that if he did it cleanly enough he could restore the damage he had done on the way out so that it would not be noticed. It was risky but it was all he could think of and so he acted on his decision. The best bet, he thought, would be the bathroom. Who looked up at the ceiling in a bathroom? In a bedroom you might well look up at the ceiling; you might also look up at the ceiling while lying on your back on a sofa in a living room, but in a bathroom? He went along the corridor and around the corner, looking out of the windows until he saw below him pipes going out through the wall and into the ground. Nevsky would want a bathroom near where he slept, he thought, so he should be able to get to Nevsky's room from here.

The toilet itself, he decided, should be near where the pipes were. He was by now in a room with chairs and a piano and artwork on the walls, so looking down at his feet he took out some tools and set to work. He pressed hard with one swift motion to make clean cuts. Before long he had cut a manhole-sized hole in the floor. Setting aside the floorboards he knelt and peered down. The floorboards were set on a lattice work of sturdy wooden beams crossing each other, and below them was plasterboard. He cut through the plasterboard cleanly in four straight strokes to form a rectangle, making the cuts at an angle inwards so the cut through section rested on its newly acquired bevelled edges, then levered it upwards and laid it aside. The light was dim in the room below but he could see he had guessed correctly: there was a toilet below him. Taking out a thin coil of rope, he tied one end to a beam and lowered himself down.

He looked up: the sides of the cut were clean but a direct look upwards would more than likely uncover their presence. There was nothing he could do about it now. He moved toward the door, wand in hand. Nevsky's treasure was very close to him now; he could read its presence just on the other side of the door he was approaching. He scanned for wands but there was no-one nearby. Slowly he opened the door and looked through.

He used macchato to locate a lamp, clicked its button and the gas-fired flame flared into life. He found himself looking into Nevsky's bedroom. There were a large four-poster bed and a drawn curtain covering the window where the cage of snakes was located. A blue velvet dress, presumably Lady Montlait's, was on the floor; Nicholas threw it at the foot of the door leading to the room where the party was taking place in order to block out the light of the lamp he had just lit. He threw a black under-garment with a satin sheen, no doubt another of Lady Montlait's, over the door handle to cover up the keyhole.

A wave of his wand located where Nevsky's treasure was hidden: behind a painting on the wall. The painting was laced with wand-protections designed to set off an alarm bell so Nicholas rewired the commands before lifting the painting off the wall. Behind the painting was a safe, set into the wall. The safe had no handle, being a Basing safe of the same make as Jolly's. There was another layer of wand protection, even more complicated than before. Nicholas rewired the commands and the black metal door clicked open. By the light of the lamp he could see a jumble of money and documents. The money was in bundles of high-denomination strada; there must have been twenty or thirty thousand strada worth of money there. Nicholas ignored the money for two reasons: firstly, he was no thief; secondly, Nevsky must not look into the safe and see anything missing.

He could still hear the noise of the party going on in the next room with gusts of laughter and shouting currently going on but he could only now trust to luck. The door from the next room where the party was going on led straight into Nevsky's bedroom, where he was at that very moment busy burgling the safe, and if Nevsky chose this moment to come in everything would be blown sky high. There was nothing he could do to stop that happening so he ignored it. He sifted through the contents of the safe. There was four scrolls so he took those, plus a letter in a torn open envelope: he took the letter but left the envelope behind. He took the four scrolls and extracted the blank scrolls he had brought with him. Matching them as best he could, he placed four blank scrolls to one side, took all the scrolls and the letter in his possession and bound them in one bundle and tied them securely under his robe. He then placed the four blank scrolls in the safe, jumbling them up with the money as they had been before. He then closed the safe, replaced the painting, went back to the door, threw Lady Montlait's clothes back onto the floor, turned off the lamp and went back into the bathroom, closing the door behind him.

He waited for his eyes to adjust to the dark again, looking up at the hole cut in the ceiling. The ceiling had been long ago painted an ivory white; the cuts were very sharp and clean so with any luck they would escape anything but a direct look. He used a towel to flap about the toilet to remove any dust that might have fallen. He climbed back up the rope, replaced the cut-off section of ceiling carefully, lowering it into place and giving it a pat or two. Then he replaced the floorboards he had cut through so that they once again rested on their beams, dragged the rug back over them and made his way to the door. Scanning for wands, he made his way back to the window where he had first gained entrance. Fifteen seconds later he was back by the wall taking off his mask and stowing it away. He then pulled out his hooded cloak from under his robe and put it on while he walked away from the Nevsky mansion along Bowden Street, pulling the hood around his face and tying the drawstring to secure it into place.

He went straight back home, not even able to guess at the time. As he passed by the Office of Registration, he looked up at the clock-face: twenty past eleven was the time. Removing his hooded cloak and stowing it away beneath his robe, Nicholas arrived back home at ten to twelve.

'Been out practising calligraphy?' Ben asked as Nicholas went past his room. The door was open and Nicholas could see Ben sitting at a table strewn with papers, a lighted lamp up on a shelf throwing its light down over the table.

'I've decided calligraphy is not for me,' Nicholas told him, standing in the doorway with a smile.

'Give me back my scrolls then,' Ben said.

'I used them up practising already and threw them away,' Nicholas replied, unaware that his left forefinger was curled into the ball of his thumb.

'That's a pity,' Ben said. 'I would have like to have seen your penmanship.'

'Trust me, you're better off being spared the sight of my penmanship.'

Ben wondered whether to ask how Nicholas had managed to avoid getting ink-stained hands but decided to let the matter go. 'If you say so,' he said with a barely detectable emphasis on the word *say*. Nicholas gave no sign of whether he had noticed any such emphasis but merely bid Ben good night and went to his room.

He closed and locked his door to prevent any unexpected intrusion. Ben could think what he wanted if he came along and found the door to Nicholas's room unusually locked. He lit a lamp, drew his curtains and took forth the scrolls and letter and sat down with them. It was late but he was not the least tired. There was still work for him to do that night before going to bed — and then there would be the actual business of killing Nevsky tomorrow.

He read through the Nevsky-Grangeshield Memorandum of Understanding and in the light of a flare of anger he saw again why he had set out to kill Nevsky; he read the Nevsky-Walherich Contract of Marriage by which Captain Abner Nevsky and Miss Piritta Walherich became pledged to be married; he read the letter from Lord Whittington to his son which explained where Nevsky's wandfighting prowess had come from; he inspected the Nevsky-Jollison Memorandum of Understanding, which made it clear that Nevsky and Jolly had bound their fates together, and finally he looked through the Nevsky-Balustrade Contract of Assignation by which Nevsky retained the legal services of Advocate Alpin Balustrade.

By now it must have been about three in the morning, Nicholas guessed, but he had one more task to perform. He quickly wrote a letter to "Captain Nevsky" in which he made up a succession of nonsensical statements with a smile on his face, and then he went to bed to get some sleep as he had a big day ahead of him which would end, all going well, with the death of Nevsky.

TWENTY

The Secret Duel of Final Combat Between Captain Abner Nevsky and Mr Nicholas Raspero

8:00 PM, Tuesday 12 July 1544 A.F.

Nicholas arrived early at the scene of his forthcoming duel with Nevsky. He had specified ten o'clock in his letter so he arrived at eight o'clock. There were a few wands about, so he wandered around here and there while they passed by, then approached Thorburn Bridge once the scene was deserted. He more thoroughly went over the area than he had done before, and realised that while nothing was perfect this place would do as well as any other and better than most. The days when it had been a well-used thoroughfare were long gone; traffic moved in other ways now; yet the remnants of its glory days gave it a spaciousness that its isolation did not warrant. By the bridge was a patch of level ground that would serve as the dueling arena; to the left was a copse of trees around a large rugged rock that would serve as Nicholas's vantage point from which to observe Nevsky's arrival.

Nicholas whipped himself on top of the rock with a wave of his wand and settled down to wait, lying flat so he would be out of sight. He scanned for wands where Nevsky's house was and after a while six wands left there travelling fast, which meant that Nevsky was bringing his dogs with him and they were coming in a flying carriage. Nicholas got down off the rock and crouched down by its side. The last tip of the sun was just going down over the horizon, which meant that it was around about quarter past nine, when Nevsky and his dogs arrived. They landed not far from the rock Nicholas was hiding behind. Nicholas moved back on top of the rock and waited.

There was the sound of movement and some muttered comments. Nicholas guessed that Nevsky and his dogs were having a look around. Nevsky moved off alone to the bridge. Nicholas could see his blue jacket through some shrubbery in the darkening twilight; there was a low murmur of voices from his dogs while they waited. Soon Nevsky was back. 'Get out of sight where you can see me,' he ordered his dogs and then set off back to the bridge. It was still twilight but it was starting to get dark.

Nicholas waited until the sound of Nevsky's movements faded into the distance and then stopped. The board was set — it was now Nicholas who would make the first move.

He had already scanned the wands of Nevsky's dogs and he knew where they were hiding. He took out five bolts, which were heavy cylindrical-shaped pieces of metal ending in a sharpened point, and with a wave of his wand came out flying from on top of the rock. Using both his vision in the fading light and macchato, he hit the dogs hard in their necks with the bolts, taking them down one after the other in a blur of motion that an observer would have been hard pressed to distinguish as separate movements. Nevsky's dogs died as silently as Nicholas had moved. Nicholas gathered back his bolts, blood-soaked now, and wrapped them in a cloth and stowed them away beneath his robe. He checked that his disc was ready, then stood up and stepped out of the copse of trees and walked towards Nevsky, his wand in his hand.

Even in the dim twilight, Nevsky recognised Nicholas despite his mask just from the way he walked. Nevsky's wand came out.

'What's with the mask, Raspero?' he shouted, as if hoping to attract attention, his eyes looking behind Nicholas to where he had left his dogs. Nevsky was not an imaginative or artistic man, but the sight of a masked Raspero with his wand out walking towards him in a lonely spot after dark had a certain nightmarish quality to it that brought him as close as he had ever been to an aesthetic experience. At that moment, Nevsky was a frightened man.

'Captain Nevsky, I demand satisfaction in final combat on behalf of a lady whom you have dishonoured,' Nicholas said as he came closer to Nevsky.

'What you talking about?' Nevsky said as if puzzled, his first instinct being to deny everything. 'I haven't done anything to any lady.'

'Do you accept my challenge or do you not?' Nicholas asked. By now he was twenty feet away from Nevsky so he stopped. They were now at dueling distance and Nicholas could feel in the tips of his fingers how close he was to killing Nevsky. He adopted a wandfighting posture and by an instinctive response Nevsky did the same.

'Like I already told you, Mr Raspero,' Nevsky said, 'I never refuse a challenge. But where there is no cause to fight there can be no challenge. What cause have you?'

'You cannot deny what the lady herself has told me and what the documents signed by you and your *dogs* say in plain legal terms,' Nicholas said, barely paying attention to their conversation, which for him now was merely a matter of form. Nevsky was not walking away from this, no matter what they said to each other. Nicholas's wand was bound now to his disc by command, and he only waited to give another wand command to bring it forth.

'Yeah, well, I'm marrying the girl, ain't I?' Nevsky said coolly, 'so I'm doing right by her. There's no cause for final combat there. It's all squared off. You don't have cause for challenge there, Mr Raspero.'

'It's not your fiancé, Nevsky. It's the one you blackmailed for one million strada.'

This gave Nevsky pause for thought. The pause lengthened into a minute or two while Nevsky thought this one over. Nicholas's attention didn't waver for a moment. He waited, ready to act at an instant's notice. He knew that Nevsky could have his disc out of his pocket and into Nicholas's throat in less than a second. He was not going to be distracted by anything.

'That Grangeshield slut?' Nevsky said, still trying to talk his way out of the duel. 'She begged me for it. Anyway, I wasn't the first. Everyone's had her, Mr Raspero. There's no cause for final combat there.'

'Why has she asked me to act on her behalf if you did not dishonour her?' Nicholas asked, still only half-paying attention to this conversation, which to him was entirely pointless but which for Nevsky represented his only way out of here alive. It seemed to Nicholas to be honourable to allow Nevsky the chance to say what he could before they took out their discs.

After a pause for more thought Nevsky said, 'Maybe it's because I didn't give her any more. She was after me night and day begging for more. I didn't want nothing to do with her.'

'Why did she pay you one million strada not to marry her as stated in the Memorandum of Understanding document, if she wanted more of your affection?'

Nevsky breathed deeply while Nicholas waited for his reply. 'Women, Mr Raspero, women, eh, who can understand them?' Then he said with an abrupt discontinuity, 'We could rule New Landern together, you and me, Mr Raspero, with me in second place, Mr Raspero.'

'We're done talking, Nevsky. Take out your disc.' Nicholas's disc came out and he held it in front of him, just above the ground.

Nevsky's disc remained in his pocket. 'I don't fight secret duels, Mr Raspero. That's illegal. You gotta call me out in public. Then I'll accept your challenge.'

'I do not want this conversation we have just had to take place in the arena at Mildgyd where everyone can hear it,' Nicholas replied, waiting now to give a command to send his disc into Nevsky's throat.

'All right, Mr Raspero,' Nevsky said slowly, sensing now that his options were running out. 'I won't say nothing about any of this. You've got my word of honour on that, I can tell you. My word of honour, Mr Raspero.'

'You have no honour, Nevsky. Now take out your disc, or I'll take it out for you.'

'I'm refusing your challenge, Mr Raspero,' Nevsky said very clearly, insistent on being understood by Nicholas. 'I am refusing your challenge, Mr Raspero,' he said again very clearly.

Nicholas switched his wand command to take control of Nevsky's disc and brought it out and then sent it hard and deep into Nevsky's throat. As Nevsky staggered backward Nicholas sawed the disc swiftly from side to side to sever Nevsky's head completely from his neck. Two seconds after Nicholas had taken command of Nevsky's disc, a headless Nevsky was falling backward to the ground. A fountain of blood gushed in repeated spurts which lessened in volume and intensity, while Nevsky's head rolled to a stop a few feet away.

Nicholas approached Nevsky's headless body and knelt by it. It was nearly the end of twilight and soon it would be too dark to see. He found the letter to "Kaptin Nevski" in Nevsky's inside pocket and replaced it with the letter to "Captain Nevsky" that he had written in the early hours of that morning. A quick search of Nevsky's body turned up nothing further, certainly not ten thousand strada in coins, which Nicholas needed for the next and final stage of his plan.

Nicholas went back to the flying carriage using macchato to make his way in the darkening light. He clicked on a lamp in the carriage and made a quick sweep with his wand. A cabinet in the corner had heavy wand protection so he opened it. Inside was a bag full of twenty, fifty and one hundred denomination strada coins — this must be the ten thousand strada which Nicholas had assumed Nevsky would bring in order to close the deal he had come to make, given how badly he must have wanted "Rasparos seakrit". Nicholas had not even thought of any use for the money at that time but had put it in the letter to make the letter seem more believable to Nevsky, as Nevsky would be suspicious of getting something for nothing. Now he had come to think of a use for the money so he was pleased that it had turned up. Nicholas cut off two squares of cloth from the velvet curtains of the flying carriage and wrapped them around a lamp before leaving with his two bundles in his left hand.

He used macchato in the dark. He had no idea what time it was but he saw Bailey waiting by the side of the Montague Monument. There were no wands about but Bailey's. Bailey heard him coming and looked his way; even by macchato Nicholas could see how eager he looked.

'Come with me Bailey,' Nicholas told him. He led the way to one side and sat down and lit the lamp, turning the flame down low. Bailey sat down next to him.

'I have one more job for you to do for me, Bailey, and it is vital that you do exactly what I say and get everything right. Are you ready to listen very carefully to what I am about to tell you?'

'Yes, sir,' Bailey said eagerly.

'Captain Nevsky has just been killed in a duel of final combat at the Thorburn Bridge,' Nicholas said. Bailey looked quickly up at Nicholas, then looked as quickly away again. 'The man who killed him was tall and well dressed with golden hair that fell down to his shoulders and a pointed, golden beard. He came in a flying carriage from the north with his servant, who was a short stocky man with a tattoo on his left forearm, like a sailor.' Bailey looked quickly up again at Nicholas and looked as quickly away again. 'After he killed Nevsky he flew off towards the north with his servant. Have you got all that?'

'Yes, sir,' said Bailey.

'Repeat it then,' Nicholas demanded.

Bailey repeated all the key points without a single slip. Nicholas was satisfied with his performance.

'Now here's what you are going to do, Bailey. You are going to go around town and talk to people who like to drink. You will tell them that this story is going around town and people who have been witnesses to this event are being bought free drinks so people can hear their story. You will use your own wit and invention to decide which people to approach and how to tell them this story in such a way that they will go off and pretend they have been witnesses to this event themselves in order to get free drinks. Do you understand the task you have been set?'

Bailey hesitated. 'Yes, sir, I think so,' he said uncertainly.

'It might assist your understanding of the matter if I explain to you the consequences which I intend to be brought about as a result of your actions. I want to find tomorrow that the whole of New Landern is talking about how Nevsky was killed in a duel in the way which I have just outlined for you. I want them to believe that this is how things happened because there were witnesses who saw it happen and who have told this story as an account of what they have themselves witnessed. Now do you understand?'

'Yes, sir,' Bailey said in a very uncertain tone of voice, 'I'll do my best, sir.' He looked and sounded reluctant to perform the task Nicholas had just set him; he either felt that such a task was beyond his capabilities or just sounded a little bit nutty.

Nicholas had already decided that he had to draw Bailey in deeper to ensure his silence. Bailey might now swear on his soul to keep silent for all eternity, but would such an oath hold his tongue for longer than a week? Nicholas had therefore turned to the old stand-by of self-interest with which to govern Bailey at this time.

'You will not just do your best, Bailey,' Nicholas told him. 'You will do this right so that it works. Now we come to the question of payment. Do you remember that I said you would receive what chance threw your way? Do you remember I said that?'

'Yes, sir,' Bailey said without too much visible enthusiasm. He knew that Nicholas had no money.

'Let us contemplate what chance has thrown your way,' Nicholas said. He laid down on the ground the two squares of curtain cloth he had cut away so they overlapped slightly and then opened and upended the bag of money over them so the coins all streamed forth into a big gleaming pile of red, gold and silver coins.

Bailey's mouth fell open. He had not known there was so much money in all the world, although now he came to think of it, of course there must be because there were so many people and they all had a little money each.

Nicholas watched him like a hawk, wanting to time his remarks to coincide with Bailey's thought processes. Bailey looked too dazed right now to hear anything Nicholas said, so Nicholas waited. Bailey reached out a hand tentatively, as if to touch the coins to check that they were real, but paused in mid-movement and looked up at Nicholas a little fearfully as if just then remembering that he sat next to a man with bloodstains on the sleeves of his robe.

'Do you know how much money is there, Bailey?' Nicholas asked him.

Bailey shook his head. He couldn't speak.

'Let's count it then, shall we?' Nicholas suggested.

Bailey breathed heavily through his mouth, his gaze fixed on the coins.

Nicholas picked up a silver coin with his wand. 'Do you know what this is worth, Bailey?'

'One hundred strada, sir,' Bailey said in a very faint voice. He had once, only once, seen a hundred strada coin in all the twelve years of his whole life.

'This one?' Nicholas asked, picking up a red coin.

'Fifty strada, sir,' Bailey said, his voice a little firmer now. He was recovering from his first vision of Aladdin's cave, and the world was starting to swim back into focus. Something like sentience seemed to have returned to Bailey.

'This one?' Nicholas asked, picking up a gold coin.

'Twenty strada, sir.'

'Good, let's count them then.' Nicholas sorted them into separate mountains of coins, dividing them into piles on each of the two squares of cloth. The count ended with five thousand strada on one cloth and five thousand strada on the other cloth. Bailey watched the movement of each coin as it went to make up the differing and growing piles of coins with a hungry fascination as if nothing else existed in the whole world but this utterly compelling spectacle. 'Five thousand plus five thousand. That makes ten thousand, does it not, Bailey?'

'Yes, sir,' Bailey agreed. He had done sums involving figures this size at the Halen Charity Home for Boys. He knew the number ten thousand all right. He had met it before, but never in this form.

'We have agreed, have we not, Bailey, that you would have what chance has thrown your way, and chance has thrown this ten thousand strada your way so this money is yours, is it not?'

'Mine, sir?' Bailey looked up at Nicholas, his mouth open, his eyes wide, breathing heavily through his mouth. He was grasping the concept that this money was all his for the first time, so Nicholas waited a moment or two to let the hook set before reeling in his fish.

'Well, I should say, nearly yours, because you haven't earned it all yet, have you?'

'Earned it all yet, sir?' Bailey repeated mechanically.

'Do you remember the task I have set you? That the whole of New Landern must tomorrow be talking about how Nevsky was killed by a well-dressed man with golden hair falling down to his shoulders and a golden beard and a servant who looked like a sailor? Do you remember that, Bailey?'

'Yes, sir,' Bailey said.

'When you have successfully completed this task by getting drunks, poor people and any of those who you think are suitable witnesses to this event to tell anyone who will listen that they saw this duel themselves, then you will have completed this task and all of this money will be yours — the whole ten thousand strada.'

'The whole ten thousand strada?' Bailey repeated mechanically, forgetting to say *sir* in the state he was in.

'You get half now, half tomorrow, if and only if you have successfully completed this task,' Nicholas said, hoping that his repetition of the phrase *successfully completed this task* would have an hypnotic effect on young Bailey.

Nicholas wrapped half the money in one square of cloth and tied it up then he wrapped the other half of the money in the other square of cloth and tied that up. Bailey watched this as if unable to move a muscle. Nicholas then handed over one bundle of five thousand strada to Bailey. Bailey clutched that bag of money to his chest as a mother clutches her infant child rescued from a river.

Nicholas watched him and waited. 'I do have one concern, Bailey,' he said when Bailey gave signs that he was starting to notice the world around him again, 'and that is that the authorities will take this money away from you? Do you know why that will be?'

'Take this money away from me, sir?' Bailey asked.

'It will be because you have failed to perform the task I have set you tonight. You can see why that is so, can you not?'

Bailey obviously couldn't but Nicholas said no more — to frighten Bailey by pointing out that he might possibly be identified as being the deliverer of a letter to Nevsky might either paralyse the boy or make him run for it out of New Landern altogether while he could.

'If you succeed in completing this task, then all will be well: you will keep the money, which you have now and also earn the remaining five thousand strada. You will be the proud possessor of ten thousand strada. You'd like that, wouldn't you, Bailey?'

There was silence for a while, as if Bailey was bewildered by having too many thoughts at once. 'Yes, sir,' he said eventually.

'Then you will successfully complete the task I have set you, will you not, Bailey?'

'Yes, sir,' Bailey said automatically.

Nicholas realised that Bailey had to walk for a while to recover from the shock of suddenly becoming enormously rich under the dread shadow of losing his wealth just as swiftly. 'Then we are done for today,' he told Bailey. 'Walk with me for a while.' He turned off the lamp, gathered it and the bundle of money into his left hand, stood up and moved off a few steps, using macchato to help him in the dark. Bailey stood up, disoriented in the dark. 'This way, Bailey,' Nicholas said as he moved off and Bailey stumbled after the sound of his voice.

The quarter moon was getting low on the horizon, but it shed a little light for them to walk by as their eyes adjusted to the night-time. Nicholas said nothing, deciding he had said all that he could. Bailey also said nothing, carrying his bag of money. But the walking was doing him good, as Nicholas had known it would, and he was coming back to himself looking about him more.

Nicholas stopped abruptly and said, 'Here is where we part company, Bailey. Go and hide your money somewhere safe and then do what I have told you to do. If you succeed, I will meet you at the Montague Monument tomorrow at eight o'clock to give you the remaining five thousand strada. If you fail … well, you will be on your own and good luck to you. But you will not fail, Bailey, you are an exceptionally talented boy. No other boy in New Landern could do this task I have set you, but you can. Off you go.'

With that Nicholas turned and walked away. He used macchato to observe Bailey staring after him for a while, and then, as if recovering the use of the decision-making part of his mind, Bailey turned away himself and hurried away into the darkness. The moon went down over the horizon as the two went their separate ways in the dark of the night.

TWENTY-ONE

The Exchange of a Story for Drinks Between Five Witnesses and the Citizens of New Landern

10:25 PM, Tuesday 12 July 1544 A.F.

Bailey hurried off into the dark, hunched over his bag of money so he was almost bent double, although the bag was not heavy. His feet had wings. He went to a place by the river where he crouched down and looked around him like a fox besieged by hounds before he carefully stowed his wealth away by digging a hole in the earth and placing a rock on top. It was only then that his thoughts turned to the task which he would successfully complete that night. The thought of failing in his task simply did not occur to him. He would do it, he would do it right, and he would earn the remaining five thousand strada, and then ... well, his thoughts turned away from that vista of happiness, guided astray by an ingrained skepticism that he could really be that fortunate. Yet, he had no doubt that he would successfully complete his task. Failure was simply not an option. His quick and alert mind started running over the likeliest people to recruit to his cause even as he was running at top speed towards Dunstan Square. He knew the streets of New Landern and the people who lived in them as only a boy of his background and experience could know them. He was the perfect employee for this particular form of employment — none better.

Even as he was running deeper into New Landern at top speed, Bailey's mind was turning around and around even faster than he was running. The people he would speak to popped up seemingly of their own accord before his mind's eye. Barney first, he decided. He knew where Barney would likely be found.

Barney was begging just down the road from the public lecture hall. (The public lecture that night was on the Ethics of Compassion.) He was begging, as usual, for money to buy drink. Alfred was with him, which gave Bailey pause for a moment; then realising that time was tight, he went ahead anyway.

Bailey sat down next to him and said excitedly, 'Barney, guess what? Nevsky was killed in a duel!'

'Was he now?' Barney said with little real interest. 'Well, isn't that something?'

Alfred was looking over at Bailey and listening as well.

'Finn's in the Boar's Head pub telling everyone about it, cos he saw it hisself. An' guess what, Barney? Everyone's buying him free drinks just to hear his story! Isn't that something?'

Barney's attention was as caught by this as Bailey had intended it to be. 'Free drinks, did you say?'

Alfred's attention was also caught by this phrase. Bailey had an audience of two.

'Finn saw it all happen, just not an hour ago. Nevsky was at the Thorburn Bridge, he fought a duel with a man who had golden hair coming down to his shoulders and a beard, he was real well-dressed like a lord and he killed Nevsky in a duel of final combat. And then he went to his carriage, there was his servant there, he looked like a sailor with a tattoo on his arm of an anchor, and they got into the carriage and flew off towards the north. Isn't that something, Barney? Finn saw it all happen, and everyone's buying him drinks just to hear him tell the story. Isn't that something?'

'Ah, that's something,' Barney agreed a little absently, as if entirely unaware of the personal advantages which could accrue to him for being in possession of this knowledge.

Bailey was going to walk Barney through what Barney was going to do no matter what; Bailey wanted the other half of that money. 'Do you know what Finn did? He walked into the Boar's Head pub and shouted, "I just saw Nevsky killed in a duel. Someone buy me a drink and I'll tell them all about it." And so someone said, "Sure, Finn, and what are you having?" And Finn said, "Nothing but a pint of honey mead," and that's exactly what he got. Then he told his story. And then they all wanted to hear it again, so he got another drink. How about that, Barney, isn't that something?'

'Oh yes, that's something,' Barney agreed, still completely unaware that he could be getting free drinks himself in the same way as Finn.

Eager-eyed and bushy-haired Bailey was going to spell this out for Barney. 'Just think, Barney, if you went into the Lion's Paw pub and shouted out, "I just saw Nevsky killed in a duel, someone buy me a pint of honey mead and I'll tell you all about it," guess what would happen, Barney? You'd get a free drink because they'd all want to hear the story. You just tell them you saw it yourself. Finn won't go against you, he'll back you up, he'll say you were there as well, he's a decent sort, all you have to say is the same story as he's telling, about this man with golden hair down to his shoulders and a beard, real well-dressed like a lord, who killed Nevsky in final combat, then went off in a carriage towards the north with his servant, who looked like a sailor with a tattoo of an anchor on his arm. Everyone's buying Finn drinks because he's telling that story, everyone'd buy you drinks if you told the story just the same. Tell them Finn was there as well. And wouldn't that be something, hey, Barney, wouldn't that be something? But you'd have to do it right now, Barney, because pretty soon everyone in New Landern's gonna know this story and there'll be no more free drinks then.'

Barney sat there while Bailey waited. Barney seemed entirely at sea with the opportunity with which he had just been presented but it was then that Alfred took a hand in proceedings.

'Well, we was there, Barney,' he said turning to Barney with a wink, 'sure, we was, the both of us there, we saw it all. Come on,' he struggled to his feet, slapping Barney on the shoulder, and staggering around in a circle once he had reached the vertical, 'come on Barney, let's go. Free drinks, now isn't that something?' Alfred set off down the road towards the Lion's Paw pub, not in a completely straight line, but looking likely to reach his destination.

Barney started to get up, and before long he was walking after Alfred. Bailey watched them go, with the feeling of a gambler who has thrown the dice onto the table and can now only wait to see the numbers turn up.

There was another roll of the dice for Barney before his evening's work was done, and he went on the run to Rockham Park. As he'd hoped, Finn was there in his usual corner, with Ted and Larry. Barney went up to them and told them all about how Barney and Alfred had witnessed Nevsky being killed in a duel of final combat, and before long Finn and Ted and Larry were off to the Boar's Head pub to tell this story for themselves.

Everything was now in motion and Bailey could only wait. He lurked about on the streets, watching and waiting and before long he noticed a crowd of people marching along from the Boar's Head pub, followed by another crowd marching from the Lion's Paw pub. Other people were caught up in the general excitement, and Bailey tagged along with them.

They marched towards the Thorburn Bridge, followed now by night watchmen on the ground and night watchmen in a flying carriage in the air. There was an excited babble from the crowd as they saw Nevsky's body lying on the ground.

By now all five witnesses to the duel between Nevsky and the golden-haired man who had come from the north had been brought together in the mingled crowds of the two pubs, and these five witnesses had swiftly formed a camaraderie of shared mendacity as they delighted in their new-found fame. They told their story all over again, turning to each other and saying, 'You remember that, don't you?' and they would all nod and laugh excitedly. They demonstrated how Nevsky had stood like this, and his opponent had stood like that and how the discs had flown through the air between the combatants; they re-enacted the savage struggle they had witnessed not so long ago, taking turns to play the roles; they repeated their statements to the night watchmen who came and took down a written account of their eye-witness accounts of the duel between Nevsky and his unknown opponent; they discussed the sailor-servant and the carriage, which had been painted a dark blue. Bailey stood at a distance and watched all this, his fingers crossed in his pockets as he listened, carefully keeping out of sight. The night watchmen searched Nevsky and found the letter on him and read it by the light of a lamp; the crowd demanded to know what the letter said; the night watchmen shook his head and said this was official business; the crowd demanded again, much less politely this time, to know what the letter said, and the night watchman reluctantly read the letter out loud, feeling his dignity to be impaired by their importunity but all too aware of how vastly outnumbered he was by the drunken and belligerent crowd.

Soon the authorities arrived in force and cleared the area. Important-looking officials arrived and stood about talking amongst themselves; the witnesses were called forth again and questioned; by now their mutual story had solidified into a coherent account which withstood official questioning, and their account was taken down as a genuine eye-witness account of the secret duel between Nevsky and this well-dressed man from the north, and so Bailey won his hand of cards with his five aces drawn straight from the top of the deck.

8:00 PM, Wednesday 13 July 1544 A.F.

Bailey was already at the Montague Monument, looking apprehensive, when Nicholas arrived.

'How are you, Bailey?' Nicholas asked him.

'I am well, thank you, sir,' Bailey said, his eyes fixed on the bundle in Nicholas's hand.

'Come with me, Bailey,' Nicholas said and led the way to where they had sat the night before. He lit the lamp and sat down. Bailey sat down opposite him.

'I am very pleased with your work, Bailey,' Nicholas said. 'You have earned the second half of the money. Shall we count it again?'

'Yes, sir,' Bailey said.

Nicholas opened the bundle and meticulously counted all five thousand strada again. Bailey was transfixed by the sight which held him in place like glue.

Nicholas carefully wrapped the bundle and handed it over to Bailey, who grabbed it tightly, breathing heavily through his open mouth.

Nicholas could see that Bailey was fearful of losing his wealth now that he had come into it.

'It is one thing to possess wealth, Bailey,' Nicholas told him, 'it is another thing to keep it. You do not want to have all this money taken away from you, do you?'

'No, sir,' said Bailey.

'I know of only one way in which you can keep this money. Shall I tell it to you?'

There was a long silence. Bailey's eyes flickered up to Nicholas's face and back down. 'Yes, please, sir,' he said eventually.

'You must not spend so much money at once that you attract attention. If you do that, others will come and beat you and rob you. Or the authorities will arrest you and rob you in their own way. You must pretend to have found a good job. Give the matter careful thought. Then you can spend a little money now and then, buy good clothes, shoes, have a good place to live, as if you are earning that money from your employment. Do you understand what I am telling you?'

'Yes, sir,' Bailey said.

'And above all else, Bailey, get an education so you're fit for something in life.'

Nicholas considered the sight of Bailey sitting there, his eyes downcast, and decided he had done all he could. 'We now go our separate ways, Bailey. Remember the importance of discretion.'

With that Nicholas took up the lamp and stood up and led the way. Bailey followed. Nicholas switched off the lamp and walked off without another word.

TWENTY-TWO

The Correspondence Between Mr Nicholas Raspero and Lady Isabel Grangeshield

5:10 PM, Sunday 10 July 1544 A.F.

Isabel couldn't move a muscle for some time after Nicholas had left Grangeshield House. The shock of Mr Nicholas Raspero having learned of what had happened to her was so great that it had eclipsed her fear of Nevsky. Another man knew of what had happened to her. He knew! The simple fact that he knew was unendurable. He knew! Somehow this made everything so much worse that Nevsky's death was no longer the solution it had been. She knew that Nevsky was now a dead man; Nicholas had been so white-faced with anger that she had known just from the sight of him that Nevsky's fate was sealed. The one man in New Landern that Nevsky ran from in terror was now after him with a vengeance. Yet, Mr Nicholas Raspero knew what had happened to her. He knew!

She could not bear the thought of ever being in the same room with Nicholas, of ever even seeing him across the park in the distance. He would look at her and he would know what had happened and there was absolutely nothing she could do about it. Everything had become so much worse than before. He would stare! She felt hot and cold with horror whenever she remembered Nicholas saying he had heard *exactly what she said.*

The rest of that day passed in a blur. She hardly noticed where she was or who she was talking to. She slept badly that night, waking up from nightmares in which Nevsky chased her while Mr Nicholas Raspero watched. The next day she spent as much by herself as possible, avoiding all company; she felt shivery, nauseous; she wanted the world to go away and be somewhere else for a while, but the day after that she began to feel more accustomed to this new state of affairs, as if life had become more difficult than before but she would manage somehow. She resolved to no longer be the victim of her nerves.

10:15 AM, Wednesday 13 July 1544 A.F.

Isabel came down to breakfast determined to try to eat something, having eaten hardly anything for the past couple of days. There was a certain air about Lord and Lady Easton as they looked over at her. They were both hunched over that day's issue of the *New Landern Recorder*.

'Interesting news, Isabel,' Lord Easton told her. 'Very interesting news.'

'And what is that?'

'Captain Nevsky has been killed in a duel.'

Isabel froze. 'Who killed him?'

'That's just it,' Lady Easton exclaimed. 'No-one knows. It was a Lord from the North but no-one knows who he is. He came in a carriage from the north with his servant, fought Nevsky in a duel and killed him, and now he's gone back to the north. It is all a great mystery.'

'Clearly a man like Nevsky must have made many enemies,' Lord Easton commented, not looking at Isabel as he poured himself another cup of coffee. 'We should not be too surprised that he should have been killed by one of these many enemies.'

'May I see the newspaper?' Isabel asked, reaching out her hand.

The article was headlined *Captain Nevsky killed in mysterious circumstances*:

A leading citizen of our fair metropolis ... the article began, stretching the meaning of the adjective "fair" to breaking point,

... lies dead in mysterious circumstances which are at this time the subject of investigation by the authorities. The decapitated body of Captain

Abner Nevsky was found last night at Thorburn Bridge by concerned citizens of New Landern who had been alerted to the slaying of Captain Nevsky by the report of witnesses to what appears to have been an illegal duel of Final Combat.

Isabel liked the phrase *The decapitated body of Captain Abner Nevsky* so much that she read this sentence a second time.

These witnesses to the duel, who are known to their confreres to be poor but honest men, witnessed a tall bearded man with golden hair streaming down to his shoulders, handsome and well-proportioned, with the manners and dress of a great lord, arrive at Thorburn Bridge by a flying carriage which approached from the north. The unknown lord was accompanied by his servant, a short burly man with a tattoo of an anchor on his left forearm who appeared to have once been a sailor. Captain Nevsky, who was already upon the scene awaiting the approach of the unknown lord, spoke briefly with his opponent, exchanging words that the witnesses did not overhear, then stepped back and the two men followed the time-honoured rituals of dueling. The close-fought combat ended with Captain Nevsky falling to the ground with his head flying from his shoulders in an enormous spray of blood. The Lord from the North bowed to his fallen opponent as if to honour his departed spirit, then departed from the scene with his servant in his flying carriage, which flew off in the same direction from which it had approached the dueling grounds, namely the north. A further search of the dueling grounds uncovered the bodies of five men, who were identified by several of those present as close followers of Nevsky who were commonly referred to as 'Nevsky's dogs'. All five had been killed by bolts through the neck. The witnesses were unable to provide any explanation for these deaths, which must therefore have occurred at some time previous to the duel.

A search of the body of Captain Nevsky brought to light the following letter found upon his person:

"To the Captain of Infamy called by his twisted tongue Abner Nevsky, You rogue, I have found you out, tracked you down and now I stand

outside your door. Yes, run if you choose, but I will find you out wherever you hide. I know what you have done; you know who I am if I mention the swinging gate, the horse and the hat by the road, do you not, Nevsky?

I summon you to a secret duel of Final Combat at Thorburn Bridge at nine o'clock tomorrow evening; the offence is known to us both.

I sign myself the Lord of the North."

The authorities continue their investigation into this modern-day mystery of our times, a mystery without parallel or standard of measurement by which it can be appraised, but all our eyes now must turn to uncovering the mystery of this Lord of the North, who will surely be discovered before long.

The newspaper article ended here somewhat abruptly as if the author had been bludgeoned by an imperative deadline into coming to an end no matter what. Isabel laid aside the newspaper article, careful to keep the features of her face composed given that the Eastons were studying her as carefully as she was composing herself, and so the matter rested.

It was not easy for Isabel to appear composed. The Eastons no doubt were studying her reaction to the news that Nevsky had been killed, but Isabel was bewildered by this sudden and unheralded appearance of this Lord of the North. Who on earth was the Lord of the North? Was "the North" some kind of land or realm? How could a man be a lord of a compass direction in any case? What was this Lord of the North's connection with Nevsky? Had Mr Raspero brought the Lord of the North onto the scene, and if so, did this mean that the Lord of the North knew what Nevsky had done to Isabel? Was this simply an enormous coincidence: had this Lord of the North come along to kill Nevsky for reasons of his own and simply beaten Mr Raspero to it? In which case, if she had done nothing, would this have happened anyway? Surely it was too much of a coincidence that Nevsky should just happen to have been killed by another wandfighter just when Mr Raspero had himself set out to kill Nevsky. Yet, surely Mr Raspero had not told this Lord of the North of what had happened to Isabel; surely not! Yet what was all this talk of swinging gates and hats by the road?

Isabel's bewilderment was given no rest all that day. At the garden party of the Rushtons that afternoon, the talk was of nothing else but the Lord of the North. At the evening exhibition of the latest paintings of Miss Apolena Calogera, which Isabel dutifully attended the talk was again of nothing else but the Lord of the North.

Key topics were already emerging, to be debated fiercely by partisans of varying philosophies. Given that Nevsky was far from mourned by anyone, should this Lord of the North be prosecuted for murder if (or more likely when) he was identified, given that deaths in secret duels of final combat were legally classified as murder? Definitely yes, argued some; it was after all a clear point of law. Probably not, argued others, given that it was not yet known why the duel had been fought in the first place. More than probably not, argued yet others, who by the end of the week would be arguing "Definitely not", as clearly this Lord of the North was too noble to have acted for any motives other than noble motives. Who were these legal sticklers to say otherwise? They were nothing but bungling pipsqueaks who should really keep quiet if they knew what was good for them! Tempers were rising as disagreements grew more marked. The cryptic contents of the letter, which some already knew by heart, could be interpreted in a large number of ways and this large number of ways was already being made manifest. Some argued that the letter was obviously in some kind of code; others poured scorn on this notion as the action produced by the letter, namely the duel, was stated clearly in the letter and what kind of code was it anyway to say things uncoded? A code that was not a code hardly needed to be deciphered, did it? Well?

It was said that an artist's impression of the Lord of the North had already been produced using the witnesses to the duel and there was a widespread eagerness to see this drawing. Clearly the Lord of the North himself would soon be identified, given this eyewitness representation of his appearance: someone would soon enough identify him. A great lord, such as this, could not be unknown, after all, and so it was only a matter of time before he was found.

The very latest news was that Nevsky's butler had said that a street urchin had delivered a letter to Nevsky from a short, stocky sailor with a tattoo of an anchor on his arm. A reward of fifty strada was offered by the authorities to this street urchin if he would come forward to tell them what he knew. No fewer than fifteen street urchins came forward to claim the reward, each saying that the other fourteen were lying. Nevsky's butler said that none of them was the street urchin who had delivered the letter so that approach came to nothing. This was yet another layer of mystery; what kind of street urchin failed to claim a reward of fifty strada? It was like a stone refusing to fall through the air!

Isabel said hardly anything to anyone all that day. What made everything worse for her was that all this confusion over the Lord of the North was preventing her from rejoicing over the death of Nevsky. It was no longer now only the catastrophe that Mr Raspero knew of what had happened to her at the hands of Nevsky that clouded her mood of good cheer on hearing of Nevsky's death; it was also all this talk of the Lord of the North, who might or might not know of what Nevsky had done to Isabel, and who had flown off into the north with his sailor servant as if that was that so goodbye to you all! What kind of unmannerly behaviour was that from a supposedly great lord? On the other hand, if he did know what had happened to Isabel, perhaps it was best that he did leave, but what if he were found and arrested? What then? Would he tell the authorities what he knew about Isabel? Surely not! But did he even know? And what was his quarrel with Nevsky anyway? Isabel wanted to rejoice over Nevsky's death but was restrained by all these questions from such said rejoicing; it was like wanting to shout but not being able to take a deep breath of air into your lungs.

Isabel felt so beset by all these perplexities that she wanted to break something, or destroy a country.

11:00 AM, Thursday 14 July 1544 A.F.

Isabel went through her letters for that morning. Some were social letters, some were business letters, but among them was one from a Mr Nicholas Raspero. Isabel left the letter from Mr Raspero to one side to be the last letter she opened. It lay waiting on the desktop, glaring at her with such intensity that she could hardly properly take in what any of the other letters were saying, but the time came when she had no choice but to pick up the letter from Mr Raspero.

She contemplated the handwriting of the addressing of the letter. The handwriting showed her that Mr Raspero was a disciplined man with a strong sense of tradition and an occasional disregarding of convention. Isabel's upper lip curled in disdain on seeing this occasional disregarding of convention. No-one could be excused for disregarding convention, Isabel believed, even if only occasionally.

She picked up her favourite letter opener, with its sharp bronze blade and its silver owl's head, and cut open the letter.

71 Norell Street,
Dejaville,
New Landern

13 July 1544

Dear Lady Grangeshield,
How are you? I trust you are well and in good health.
I am myself in excellent form.
The weather continues fine, which is good although I am sure that the farmers would be pleased if it rained.
I was wondering if it would be possible for me to call upon you at Grangeshield House at 3 o'clock in the afternoon of this Friday 15 July.
Yours sincerely,
Nicholas Raspero

Isabel read this letter over and over again with mounting disbelief. She had never received such a letter in her life. The man who had written this letter was a clown, a man utterly without social sensibilities, a man she could not possibly receive as a guest. To say something as banal to Lady Isabel Grangeshield of Grangeshield House as *the farmers would be pleased if it rained* was beyond a joke; it was either an act of inadvertent stupidity or an act of deliberate insolence, which were each as bad as each other except that stupidity was worse. Isabel wrote her reply in a handwriting which sloped slightly like a faint yawn to demonstrate her crushing superiority over the rural Raspero.

Grangeshield House,
New Landern

14 July 1544

Dear Mr Raspero,

I thank you so much for your very interesting letter, which I received earlier this morning and took the greatest pleasure in reading. I must compliment you, I am compelled in this matter to compliment you, on the elegance of your literary style, the choicest use of phrase which you employ with such disarming effect, and I dare not even refer to the charm and wit of your insightful observations. You even include a weather report!

I feel at a loss in bearing such a heavy burden as to compose an epistolary reply equal to your own. What can I say that can possibly stand comparison with the outstanding literary qualities of your superb letter, a letter which positively flows with all the glittering eloquence at your command? Nevertheless, I must do my best and I do hope you will overlook such deficiencies as are unavoidable in one so less gifted in these matters than yourself. I implore you not to judge me too harshly for so lamentably failing to rise to those heights through which you freely roam to such great effect.

I observe in your letter that you have requested an audience with me this Friday afternoon at three o'clock. Nothing would please me more than to receive you at the time you have suggested and yet, though it is with a heavy heart, I must respectfully yet firmly decline your request at this time. I do hope that you understand that my decision is taken with the utmost regret, and the deepest concern for that very slight disappointment which a man of your tact and sensitivity of feeling must surely experience upon receiving this reply. But I assure you that my adverse reply is due to the most unforeseen of circumstances whose untimely advent cannot be turned aside, even for such a welcome visit from a man such as yourself, whose qualities I cannot praise highly enough and whose intelligence is such that all those who have the great good fortune to experience your company come away singing your praises. You will, of course, with the modesty with which you are so generously endowed, accept such praise with the greatest reluctance, a reluctance which only serves to raise you higher in the estimation of all those fortunate enough to be blessed with your acquaintance.

I can well understand that you must now wonder if another, more opportune time, might serve you in seeking an audience with me. It is with the utmost regret, indeed with the greatest concern for the sensitivity of your feelings, that I must inform you that no such time exists at all. There is no time at which I can grant you an audience. Naturally, I understand that you must experience a certain degree of surprise to learn that I am so busy at present that I cannot receive you at all, and yet this is so. I have assiduously, and with the greatest of care, considered my current appointments, as the business which I must conduct with regard to my estate, while embarrassingly slight and inconsiderable, nevertheless makes many insistent demands on my attention, not to mention those social engagements with others in society who, while vastly superior to my own humble rank, are so gracious as to grant me the pleasure of associations with the very highest in the land, a gracious kindness which I know only too well I do not deserve and yet I accept with such humility as is only proper on my part; as I say, Mr Raspero, I have considered my current circumstances with the greatest care and I find in consequence that I cannot receive you now, or at any time in the future, due to these aforesaid considerations.

I do hope that the disappointment which you must necessarily experience upon receiving this news will be only slight and fleeting when you give proper consideration to the circumstances in which my decision has been made. As you by now well understand from the praise I have heaped upon you in this letter, no-one stands higher in my estimation than yourself. If only I had the time to receive you I would only be too happy to grant you an audience, but alas, this is not possible. It is completely out of the question for you to come here tomorrow or any other day. It is with the deepest regret that I inform you that I cannot receive you at all at any time.

I have surely imposed enough on your time with your perusal of this letter, humble as it is by comparison with your own mighty literary missive. I will impose no more on your time, Mr Raspero, and bid you farewell without further delay.

With warmest regards,
Yours sincerely,
Lady Isabel Grangeshield

Isabel dispatched the letter immediately by private messenger and sat back with a feeling of satisfaction, tempered with a slight apprehension due to the unprecedented nature of her situation. She had insultingly and with enormous sarcasm refused a request to see her from a man who had sawed Nevsky's head off with his own disc. Yet, she could not see any reason for her to fear him. In any case, she would prefer Nicholas to cut off her own head rather than endure the humiliation of meeting him knowing that he knew what had happened to her. Death was preferable to having him look directly at her while she knew that he knew of her shame.

She received his reply on Saturday.

71 Norell Street,
Dejaville,
New Landern
15 July 1544

Dear Lady Grangeshield,
I hope you are well and in good health and enjoying the fine spell of summer weather of the past few days.

I am in good spirits myself.

Thank you for your letter of 14 July. It does not matter in the least *that you cannot receive me. There is no need for me to see you in person. I was only going to tell you that it is done.*

  I wish you well for the future.

  Yours sincerely,

  Nicholas Raspero

Isabel's first feeling on reading this letter was one of relief. Nicholas would not come to see her and he would not argue with her about it. He had accepted her refusal to see him and she had nothing further to do with keeping him at bay. In order to confirm this outcome she read the letter again. There was no doubt about it: he would not make any attempt to come and see her again. She did not have to endure the unendurable ordeal of having him stare at her, while he knew what had happened to her.

It was on the third reading that she was shaken where she was sitting by the implacable indifference of the letter. He simply could not care less. It meant nothing to him that she would not receive him, nothing at all. Such implacable indifference!

Nor would her questions about this whole Lord of the North business now be answered. The implication of the sentence *I was only going to tell you that it is done* was that Mr Raspero himself had killed Nevsky; there was no mention anywhere of the Lord of the North. Isabel felt that her questions now would never be answered — it was like waving goodbye to someone on a boat going down the river — the last question could no longer be asked and answered.

Suddenly Isabel felt that she had to have Nicholas sitting in front of her. Never mind if he despised her, never mind if he held her in such contempt that he would not even write her a proper letter. He could think what he liked. He could look at her in her shame as much as he wanted, but she would not be treated in this way. This was worse than being stared at by a man who knew what had happened to her.

Grangeshield House,
New Landern

16 July 1544

Dear Mr Raspero,
Once again I have been honoured to receive a letter from you. What can I say in praise of this letter? What indeed? You have mastered such a brevity of style, such a conciseness of expression, that all other literary expressions pale by comparison.

I find to my embarrassment that I do have a suitable time in which to grant you an audience after all. By an oversight, which I simply cannot explain (and I know that you will excuse failings in others even though you lack such failings yourself, by the generous breadth of your noble character), as I say, by an inexplicable omission of observation, I have earlier failed to notice a time at which I can receive you, and in consequence of this observation I find that I can grant you an audience at three o'clock in the afternoon of Sunday 17 July.

I hesitate to impose on you at such short notice, for as you are well aware (and what gentleman of social standing is not), it is highly discourteous to make appointments at such short notice. I know that you yourself would never do such a thing. I can only ask you to overlook yet more of my failings on the grounds that although you yourself have none, you have such courtesy and nobility of character that allow you to overlook such failings in others.

I remain yours sincerely,
Lady Isabel Grangeshield

TWENTY-THREE

The Restoration of Lady Isabel Grangeshield of Grangeshield House

3:00 PM, Sunday 17 July 1544 A.F.

Nicholas came on time and rang the Bell That Could Not Be Rung. Benson promptly came to open the door for him.

'Welcome to Grangeshield House, Mr Raspero,' Benson said in his warmest, most friendly voice.

'Everything normal today, Benson?' Nicholas asked, looking at him closely.

'Yes, sir.'

'You haven't brought an axe-wielding ghost-hunter with you today. It's his day off, is it?'

Benson laughed wheezily. 'We are all most mortified about the occasion to which you refer, Mr Raspero.'

'What's life without a bit of fun, Benson?'

'Indeed, sir.'

'Everything would be very dull if we were just serious all the time.'

'That is very true, sir.'

'Lead on, Benson,' Nicholas ordered him.

'Very good, sir.'

Now Benson was not without intelligence and like everyone else in New Landern he had heard that Mr Nicholas Raspero was the only one capable of defeating Captain Nevsky in combat. He had also observed that Nevsky's death had followed soon after Nicholas's meeting with

Isabel, and like a select few in the Grangeshield household he knew what Nevsky had done to Isabel. He had been forty years in the service of the Grangeshields, from when he was a fifteen-year-old foot servant, and he had known Lady Grangeshield from when she had been Miss Isabel and he had walked beside the three-year-old as she first rode a horse, ready to catch her if she fell. Benson would have killed Nevsky himself if he could.

Benson wasn't distracted by this Lord of the North business, as a man who could ring the AU135 Bell and tell that Cassidy was hiding behind the door had powers beyond the ordinary. With a disregard of the spurious details of golden haired Lords from the North and a direct insight into correlation that a logician could only envy, Benson had deduced that Nicholas had killed Nevsky. Nicholas didn't know it, but he had become Benson's hero.

As they came clear of the trees along the driveway, Nicholas looked up at the upstairs bay windows, and there he saw the distant figure of Isabel, looking down at him. He stopped as before to register that he saw her, but she did not move. Benson followed the direction of his gaze, but said nothing.

As instructed, Benson showed Nicholas straight in to see Isabel. She was sitting as before at the end of the room. Sitting to one side were the same two people who had been present on his last visit, who Nicholas guessed from the Nevsky-Grangeshield Memorandum of Understanding to be Lord and Lady Easton, watching Nicholas as he approached Isabel.

'Good day to you, Lady Grangeshield,' Nicholas said politely.

Isabel did not look up at him. 'Good day to you, Mr Raspero,' she replied after a moment. 'I trust you are well.'

Without being asked, Nicholas stepped up to a chair, pulled it around, whipped up the Footstool of Mangatha and sat down, leaning back and stretching out with his feet on the Footstool of Mangatha. Isabel watched all this in silence from the corner of her eye, making no comment.

'I can tell you everything that happened if you like,' Nicholas told her. 'It was a duel of honour, a secret duel. But maybe the details don't matter. The important thing is that Nevsky knew that he was going to die because of what he did to you so your honour has been avenged.'

Isabel had listened to this with her face averted from Nicholas's gaze. 'I know very well that you must despise me,' Isabel said. 'Is this not so, Mr Raspero?'

'No, it is not so, Lady Grangeshield,' Nicholas immediately replied.

'You need not dissemble, Mr Raspero. I will not, indeed I cannot, take offence that you now look down on me as unworthy to be in your company.'

'I do not despise you, Lady Grangeshield, and I do not look down on you.'

'I'm afraid I cannot believe you, Mr Raspero. You are only being kind.'

'It wasn't your fault,' Nicholas said uncomfortably, not happy at being required by his hostess to have this particular conversation. 'You were blameless. I do not despise you because you are innocent of everything.'

'You must have sympathy for me then,' Isabel said. As it happened, Nicholas had a lot of sympathy for Isabel. He was opening his mouth to say so, when his instincts warned him against it. Nicholas closed his mouth without saying anything. He was not a man to question his instincts. Isabel, her eyes still resolutely downcast, saw none of this. She saw only his silence.

'Everybody has their troubles, Lady Grangeshield. You are not the only one with problems.'

The indifference of this statement stung Isabel like a slap in the face. Her fingers whitened as she tightened her grip on her fan in a fit of anger. How could this man not have sympathy for her after all she had suffered? He clearly had no proper feelings. Did he not know how she had suffered? She had suffered! She had suffered! If anyone deserved sympathy, she did, and all he would say was that *everybody has their troubles* as if she were not Lady Isabel Grangeshield of Grangeshield House. This was outrageous!

It occurred to her then that she was in the company of a brutal murderer who flung her furniture about the room! The more she thought about it, the more she realised that because of her fallen state she had come to be in the company of a man even lower than herself, a brutal murderer who lacked proper feelings and did not know how to behave himself as a guest in Grangeshield House.

Isabel had not once looked directly at Nicholas up to this point because she lacked the nerve to do so. But on hearing what he had just said she forced herself to look up and across at him to meet his gaze, whereupon she noticed something astonishing.

The astonishing thing she noticed was that he did not look at her with appalled curiosity, as if she were a freak in a circus. He did not gaze at her with a lascivious avidity derived from speculative thoughts writhing like snakes about a lurid vision of how everything had happened to her. In short, he simply did not stare! There was something entirely normal and everyday about the way he looked at her. His grey eyes were simply observant, as if he saw nothing other than Isabel sitting next to him.

'How wisely you have spoken, Mr Raspero,' she said, still unable to believe that he had said anything quite so stupid. 'Indeed, everybody has their troubles. But do you have no sympathy with any of them?'

'Well, life can be tough and there you have it,' Nicholas matter-of-factly told her.

She was only half-listening to what he was saying. Of far more importance to her was to see his eyes. His grey eyes looked neutral, as if she were a completely normal person who he was talking to. As if she were completely normal! But then she registered the comment he had just made and she was so taken aback at the sheer inanity, the sheer imbecility of this comment that she almost whimpered with a sudden onset of fury, Her fingers whitened further on her fan. Isabel's temper was coming to a quick boil in the face of Nicholas's heartlessness. 'But surely a person deserving of sympathy should receive such sympathy, Mr Raspero?'

Nicholas shrugged. 'Whatever,' he said, with an impatient gesture of his left hand, as if fending off an importunate bee.

His absurdly insolent letters, his use of the Footstool of Mangatha, his lack of sympathy, and now this arrogant *whatever* — all of Nicholas's insults collided in one blazing hot moment as Isabel lost her temper then and there, 'You have no sympathy for me, I see, but then, you are nothing but a brutal murderer, are you not, Mr Raspero? You are never happier than when you are cutting off people's heads. Is this not so, Mr Raspero?'

'No, it is not so,' Nicholas said sharply, stung by her ingratitude. 'I acted on your behalf in a matter of honour and this is all the thanks I get? Thanks a lot!'

'Should I thank you for what you have done, Mr Raspero?'

This set Nicholas back on his heels while he thought about her question. There was a long silence. 'No,' he conceded eventually. 'Justice was done and that is all that counts.'

'First you rebuke me for not being thankful, then you say I need not be thankful. Which is it, Mr Raspero?'

'The not needing to be thankful one,' Nicholas acknowledged. 'I withdraw my earlier complaint, Lady Grangeshield.'

'You are very erratic, Mr Raspero. First it is one thing, then it is the other. How can anyone hope to keep up with you?'

'Yes, well, there we are,' Nicholas said. 'As we are done now with this topic —'

'No, Mr Raspero, we are not *done now with this topic*, as you put it,' Isabel snapped, concealing her delight at the swiftness of her victory. 'Allow me at least to display consistency. You may very well learn something to your advantage by observing such behaviour. You do not despise me; you have no sympathy for me, and yet you complain when I say that your behaviour is that of a barbarian, a wild man of the woods!'

'You may think of me as you wish, Lady Grangeshield, but —'

'Oh, that is very kind and gracious of you,' Isabel said sharply, 'to give me such permission! But I tell you plainly that I will think of you as I please, with or without your permission, Mr Raspero!'

'Fair enough,' Nicholas said as reassuringly as he could. He looked about the room for a moment or two, not really seeing anything, while Isabel glared at him, and then Nicholas gave Isabel a keen eagle-eyed look to show that he understood her after having carefully considered the matter. 'Yes, of course, think of me as you wish, absolutely, yes. So, there we are. Now, with regard to —'

'Do you want to know what I think of you, Mr Raspero?'

Nicholas nearly said *not really*, but caught himself in time. 'Of course I would, Lady Grangeshield. I would be only too pleased.'

Isabel was very angry. She was not going to pull her punches. 'You do not despise me because you have no judgement; you have no sympathy for me because you have no feelings; so there is nothing to be said for you, Mr Raspero, except that you are not a gentleman!'

Nicholas was so shocked by this that for a moment he could not speak. He was the descendant of generations of Barons of Rasperos for over six centuries, the custodian of wand secrets that made him the warrior who had broken Nevsky and the careful student of the wisdom of the ages concerning the beliefs and behaviour of a gentleman, and here was Lady Grangeshield telling him to his face that he was not a gentleman! This was outrageous! This was beyond belief! This was completely unacceptable! Yet he could see that Isabel was angry and upset, with her brown eyes smouldering like the smoking bark of a log in the fire, and given that he knew why she was angry, he felt himself to be that log burning in the fire.

For a moment he wished that he did not have to deal with this situation, that his father or grandfather had to come up with a response to this iniquity, but with the wish came like its shadow the counter-wish, that his father or grandfather were not there to hear the accusation which Isabel had just thrown in his face, because their response would be axiomatic: *Challenge!* Furthermore, and from his unbending grandfather this went without saying, it would mean Final Combat without doubt. Nicholas was struck all of a sudden that he was profoundly thankful that his father or grandfather were not there, and why was that? Because, and the absurdity struck him such that he nearly laughed, he would have to defend Isabel!

Time was ticking in all the Grangeshield House clocks as Nicholas was only too well aware, just as he was only too well aware that he had still not responded to what Isabel had just said.

'That comment is unacceptable, Lady Grangeshield, and I must require you to withdraw it.'

Isabel considered this response for a moment, her face veiled in her passing thoughts, before saying, 'But I do not understand you, Mr Raspero. Is it the truth that you object to, or the unacceptable nature of that truth?' She almost smiled, as if there was almost a difference between these options.

'Do you have any idea, any idea at all, of what my father or grandfather would say if they heard you say such a thing?'

Isabel now openly smiled like a skier leaning forward into the gradient of a slope. 'No, Mr Raspero, now that you ask I have no idea at all what your father or grandfather would say if they heard me say such a thing. Why, what would they say?'

'They would say, Lady Grangeshield, that when your pitiful ancestors were striking together stones to make a fire, the Barons of Raspero sat in their castle looking down on them,' Nicholas replied, improvising on the spot.

'Then it is a great pity,' Isabel replied without hesitation, 'that these very same Barons are not here today to look down upon you, Mr Raspero, to lament the decline of their estate.'

It crossed Nicholas's mind then that a battle of words with Isabel was not one that he would win. But then there still remained the problem of what she had just said.

'Lady Grangeshield, I am a gentleman whether you like it or not, whether you know it or not and whether you say otherwise or not. If you continue to dispute this point I will consider this conversation to be at an end and I will leave this place without delay. Is this clear?'

Nicholas understood that he had retreated from demanding that Isabel withdraw her comment to the greatly weakened position of insisting that she not say it again, and judging from the glint in Isabel's eye this had not escaped her notice either.

Isabel, without hurrying, very calmly unfurled her fan to consider its markings carefully in the most contemplative of moods before saying, 'But I am not the one who is disputing this point, Mr Raspero. I am only too happy to accept that I am mistaken in my estimation of your character. But first I must be persuaded by an appropriate argument. You do not despise me; you have no sympathy for me, and yet you still claim to be a gentleman! Tell me that you despise me, or tell me that you have some sympathy for me, and I will accept that you are a gentleman. But how can I otherwise?'

She looked up at him then, and Nicholas felt trapped in the maze of those warm brown eyes. Neither logic nor emotion were of any use to him then: logic would accept either choice, emotion both at once, and he himself was left with nothing but his own perceptions. He looked away from Isabel to try to see what to do.

Nicholas came to a decision. 'Lady Grangeshield, I will respond to each charge separately. Firstly, I do not despise you because you looked so innocent the night I saw you at the engagement party of Mr Hedley Carver and Lady Sofiya Lachance. I don't care if it's not logical, it's just the way it is. I can't give you a reasoned argument about it because I don't have one. So that's my defence to the first charge. Secondly, I do not —'

'One moment, if you please, Mr Raspero,' Isabel interrupted. 'I require you to explain yourself. What do you mean by your first defence?'

Nicholas hesitated. He really didn't want to get into any of this.

He looked over at Isabel to tell her this but then stopped short. Isabel was wearing a yellow dress that had belonged to her grandmother. A yellow dress that came up to her chin and down to her wrists. A yellow dress which sprouted so many ribbon-like folds of cloth that Isabel herself was rendered shapeless, her head emerging from the dress as if poking up out of a barrel. Her hair was made up into a severe bun, and she wore no jewellery of any kind. She was looking at him, composed and angry, her brown eyes wide-open, sitting straight-backed in her chair, her fan held folded in her hands. For no reason at all that he could think of, the sight of Isabel made Nicholas feel obscurely obliged to answer her question.

He tried to think of a way to avoid letting her know the full truth while answering her question in a technical sense. 'Well, at this party I saw this girl. She was wearing a red and blue gown. I asked someone nearby who the girl was and he said she was Lady Isabel Grangeshield. So what happened to you later, well, it wasn't your fault and I know that because I saw you then, the night I was introduced to you. So I think that wraps it all up.' Nicholas said all this with an air of caution that was all too evident to Isabel, whose anger was lessening as her confidence began to return to her. Nicholas was keen to avoid telling Isabel that he had been smitten with her at the time, and his avoidance of this point was making this point all too clear to Isabel.

Isabel was reminded then that she still did not know how she had come to be introduced to Nicholas. With her own caution fully concealed, she said, 'No, Mr Raspero, it does not *wrap it all up.* You must realise that the account you have given is insufficient. I require you to explain yourself more fully.'

Nicholas dug his heels in to keep from being dragged down this path by saying, 'It's really much too long a story, Lady Grangeshield.'

'If it is true that you do not despise me, Mr Raspero, then you will oblige me in this matter.'

It was true that Nicholas did not despise Isabel, but it did not follow he had to explain himself more fully. Yet, to refuse her request would bring an automatic accusation from Isabel that he did despise her after all. In any case, he was only being asked to say in more detail what he had already said. Seeing no way out, Nicholas began cautiously to tell her of how he had seen her for the first time that night. Unaware that he was blushing bright red in embarrassment, but fully aware of Isabel's eyes fixed on his face throughout, he described the whole scene in all the detail which she demanded of him with her constant interruptions, he had to say, what she had been wearing, how her hair was done, how she had been standing, the markings on the fan she had held before her face. With his vivid memory of seeing her that night he was able to answer all these points perfectly, not realising in his innocence how revealing he was being. Isabel observed all this and secretly gloated. After recounting his failed attempt to gain an introduction to her from Mr Zarek, who had said that he was not acquainted with Isabel, Nicholas ended by saying, 'So that explains everything fully. Good, now we've got that out of the way we can —'

'No, Mr Raspero, this matter is not *out of the way.* You have entirely failed to justify yourself. If you do not despise me, you do not understand anything at all,' Isabel told him with a secretly delighted fierceness. 'You are incapable of making the correct judgements. You should despise me and the fact that you do not shows your lack of character and moral sense.'

'Well, there we are,' Nicholas said, not exactly agreeing with her but making no attempt to defend himself from her attack. This was not the conversation he had come here to have and he was trying to think of a way to steer everything back to discussing the topic of Nevsky's death, but he took too long about it, which gave Isabel plenty of time to extend her growing control over their conversation.

Still cognizant that she needed to be informed of how they had been introduced on the night in question Isabel stated firmly, 'You may continue, Mr Raspero, with your account of the evening we are discussing.'

'Continue? What do you mean?' Nicholas asked apprehensively.

'I require you to explain how you succeeded in gaining an introduction to me,' Isabel explained with a regal air of command.

'I don't think so, Lady Grangeshield,' Nicholas protested, feeling a certain degree of alarm at the prospect of telling this particular story. 'I mean, there's really nothing to tell, I just met someone who could introduce me, that's all.' On this particular issue he was prepared to dig in his heels deep into the ground. She could harangue him all she liked, but this was going too far — it was really not necessary, and he would not do it! His defiance was written all over him and Isabel had no trouble reading it.

Isabel opened her fan, considered its markings, and spoke with her eyes downcast. 'I understand my position in these circumstances, Mr Raspero. You are fully entitled to disregard any request I may make of you. I cannot ask you to show me any respect, for I am deserving of none. I understand that I may not insist and so I do not. I will say no more.'

Nicholas had no idea what to say. Isabel sat there in silence, her eyes still downcast. The silence dragged on. Nicholas felt a heavy feeling in his stomach at the sight of her sitting there looking so humble. It was still as embarrassing as ever to tell her how he had come to be introduced to her but it had somehow become far worse not to tell her.

So, Nicholas began to tell her the story she had asked to hear. He told her that after he had seen her for the first time, he had wandered around the party and come across a group sitting around a table, among whom was Mr Longman. He explained that he had come to the party with Mr Longman, upon which Isabel interrupted and wanted to know how that had happened. Her humility had disappeared instantly as soon as he began to speak. Nicholas told her of how he had met Mr Longman, a tale which caused Isabel to shake her head and say, 'So you are a street-fighter, Mr Raspero, a common man who engages in public brawls, a brutal wandfighter who slugs it out with his opponents in the public eye without regard for decorum or decency.'

'You have clearly not understood a word of what I have just said,' Nicholas said defiantly, 'but I will not say it all again, if that is what you hope. I doubt if you would understand anything no matter how many times I told you the story. No doubt you think I should have just walked by without intervening, which says a lot about you, doesn't it?'

Isabel sighed. 'My only point, Mr Raspero, is that the manner of your intervention was unseemly. A more decorous intervention would have preserved precisely that civilised element which you threw away by leaping down into the gutter with these brutes. But I will say no more — there is little hope you will understand such matters as these, which are too far above you to be explained in terms which you can comprehend.'

Nicholas resumed his story, and soon came to how he had gained an unauthorised entry into the engagement party of Mr Carver and Lady Lachance. This was a tale of misbehaviour that evoked a hissing uptake of breath from a shocked and disapproving Isabel, who lost no time in thoroughly castigating him over the matter.

'But this was breaking and entering, Mr Raspero! This was the behaviour of a common thief, a criminal, a law-breaker! Is that the kind of man you are, Mr Raspero? I am shocked, shocked to hear that you have behaved in this manner. I can only trust that you are deeply ashamed of this now.'

With a very guilty look on his face, Nicholas admitted that it was even worse than that because he later came to understand he had been tricked by Mr Longman, who had never had an invitation in the first place and was not even a gentleman; Isabel kindly said that as Mr Raspero was obviously a person of low intelligence, he could not be blamed for being tricked in this manner; Nicholas observed that everyone made mistakes and wondered if Lady Grangeshield was the one exception to this otherwise universal rule; Isabel graciously acknowledged that she did indeed make mistakes but *never* such ones as those of *criminal behaviour*; Nicholas said no, she didn't, she just kept interrupting all the time; Isabel said that no doubt Mr Raspero preferred to avoid attention being drawn to his behaviour out of a natural modesty that did him credit; Nicholas said one more interruption and he would no longer tell his story.

Isabel snapped her fan shut menacingly with a fierce look on her face but said nothing more. She was, in fact, happier than she had been in a long time. She couldn't remember when she had last had such a good squabble.

Nicholas continued his story, telling of how Mr Longman had set out immediately to get drunk and so Nicholas had soon gone off on his own, seen Isabel, and wandered around for a while, and there was soon nothing for it but to tell Isabel that he had nominated an introduction to her as a prize for doing the Three, which he managed to do by determinedly not looking at her while recounting the event. Nicholas felt a sense of relief as he neared the end of his tale — he needed no prompting to tell the story of their introduction in detail but if he hoped to embarrass Isabel in the slightest his hope was in vain — Isabel was supremely indifferent now to his account of how supremely indifferent she had been to him then.

Not wanting to leave Isabel with the embarrassing impression that he was one of her admirers, Nicholas ended his story by saying almost truthfully, 'After that night I never gave you another moment's thought. Now, as far as —'

'You never gave me another moment's thought?' Isabel enquired, not at all pleased by this comment.

'Not a single thought at all,' Nicholas assured her trying to put as much distance as possible between then and now. 'Now, and here's my point,' he continued, holding up a forefinger to forestall yet another of Isabel's interruptions, 'all this goes to show why I don't despise you now and why I consider you to be innocent of any blame.'

That word *innocent* again, Isabel noticed. She was trying to decide how offended she should be that an introduction to her had been a prize for thuggish wandfighters to contend for in this manner. No wonder Timothy had run for it! Should she be very offended, merely contemptuous or simply disregarding of a matter far beneath her dignity? She filed the matter away to be decided upon later.

'Mr Raspero,' Isabel began, still displeased from hearing that Nicholas had never given her *another moment's thought* after that evening, 'from what you have said it is clear you were smitten with me on the occasion to which you refer. Is this not so?'

Nicholas guiltily looked away, and frowned in puzzlement as he looked into the distance as if he was trying to figure this one out. 'Well, maybe just a little bit,' he conceded, holding his forefinger a fraction of an inch away from his thumb to show just how little.

'I consider it very impertinent of you to have been so smitten with me,' Isabel said reprovingly. 'I trust you are not smitten with me now.'

'Definitely not,' Nicholas lied, careful not to look at her while he said this.

Isabel hid a smile of triumph behind her fan. She was starting to feel her old self again for the first time in an age. 'That is just as well, Mr Raspero, for I would not tolerate any such impertinence from you.'

'Of course not,' Nicholas agreed hastily, 'I was just explaining that I don't despise you, that's all.'

'Very well, Mr Raspero, I accept that you do not despise me.' Isabel conceded this point graciously. 'Yet, whatever you say, I have lost what I should not have lost, have I not? My life is no longer worth living.'

'Ah, well, yes, that brings me to your second charge, that I lack sympathy. I don't pity you, because that would be insulting, and I don't feel sorry for you for the same reason. So you'll get back on your feet. It'll just take time, that's all. So, there we are. That's my second defence. So we're done.'

'*Get back on my feet?*' Isabel repeated in disbelief. 'Just how many stupid things are you capable of saying in one day, Mr Raspero?'

'You may not be impressed with this argument, Lady Grangeshield —'

'Argument? It is not an argument, Mr Raspero. It is a collection of stupid sentences leaning against each other out of weakness.'

'It's what I'm saying for my second defence,' Nicholas insisted stubbornly. 'Think of it what you will.'

'I am ruined, Mr Raspero,' Isabel told him.

'I have avenged your honour, Lady Grangeshield. At least you have received that satisfaction.'

'I am ruined, Mr Raspero,' Isabel repeated, trying to get this simple point across. 'So what good does it do me to have my honour avenged?'

'This was never about what might do you good, Lady Grangeshield,' Nicholas replied.

'Then what was it about?' Isabel asked.

'It was about justice,' Nicholas told her. 'Nevsky had to die, of that there could be no doubt. I acted on your behalf in a matter of honour. Nevsky is dead. It is over.'

'Do you say that justice has been done? But what good does that do me? I am ruined.'

Nicholas hesitated on hearing this *I am ruined* statement yet again, realising that he was not properly responding to her inquiry. He looked away, and then looked back at her. Once again she observed with surprise that he did not stare even though she was repeatedly referring to something she could not even think about. He talked to her as if he made no judgement about her loss of character. Her heart started beating faster and she took a deep breath to keep her hands still as they held her fan.

'I take your point, Lady Grangeshield. But justice was done in any case, wherever it leaves you.'

'What I have lost cannot be recovered,' Isabel told him emphatically. 'Do not pretend that you do not understand.'

'Of course I understand,' Nicholas said uncomfortably, looking away from her. 'I understand perfectly. But in any case, I'm not the right person to talk to you about this.'

'You are the *only* person I can talk to about this,' Isabel retorted immediately.

Nicholas nearly groaned out loud as he contemplated the way in which any hoped-for end to this conversation turned out to be a twist and turn into a new phase of the conversation. Yet, somehow he could not openly refuse her demands. He did not even ask himself why this was so; he simply went along with what she wanted.

'Ah, I see,' Nicholas said. He sat there and thought while Isabel stared at him. 'Well, I'm really no expert in these matters, so I can't tell you much about it, but of course you could always go to a Restorer.'

'A Restorer?'

'Yes,' Nicholas said, looking into her eyes meaningfully without saying anything more.

'What is a Restorer?' Isabel was obliged to ask.

'Well, they're these women, they're called Restorers, it's all very hush-hush, but with a needle and thread and a sac of goat's blood or chicken's blood or something like that they can provide a woman with a similitude of virginity. It won't fool a medical examination but as your reputation is spotless no suitor would demand one. Maybe that might work.'

'But what on earth are you saying, Mr Raspero?' Isabel was vastly intrigued by what she was hearing. Her life had been much too sheltered to have had any idea that this kind of thing went on.

'Well, if you accept a proposal of marriage, you can go to a Restorer and be a virgin on your wedding night.'

'Are you suggesting, Mr Raspero, that I should deceive the bridegroom who has pledged his honour to my virtue in such a way as this?'

'Yes,' said Nicholas, nodding vigorously to confirm that she had caught on straightaway. 'Exactly, deceive him so he doesn't know. Then you're married and in the clear.'

'But, this is preposterous, Mr Raspero. What you are suggesting is simply outrageous. Your claim to be honourable is cast into doubt by talk like this. You are obviously depraved.'

Nicholas tried to come up with more advice. 'Well, then, suppose that you have a suitor that you look favourably on due to his excellent qualities. He is obviously a man of honour, because otherwise you wouldn't look favourably upon him. Well, make him swear on his honour not to tell anyone else what you are about to tell him, and then when he has done that, tell him the truth. If he won't marry you after that then no-one will know because he is sworn to secrecy, but if he's prepared to overlook it, then you can accept his proposal.'

'Mr Raspero,' Isabel said firmly, 'I would despise a man who would be prepared to marry me after learning the truth. I could not possibly accept his proposal if he were still prepared to marry me regardless. How on earth could I marry a man like that?'

'Ah, well, that's awkward,' said Nicholas. 'Then it's back to the Restorers. Nothing is guaranteed, of course, but if you play your hand right you should pull it off.'

'I have never been so shocked in all my life,' Isabel declared. 'Never! You appear to be a man utterly without morals, without decency, utterly incapable of telling right from wrong. It seems that you divide your time between murdering people and advocating immorality, Mr Raspero.'

'Ah, well, there we are,' Nicholas said weakly. 'It was just a thought.'

Isabel was silent long enough for Nicholas to make a grab at trying to regain some measure of control over this conversation. 'Lady Grangeshield, we have been side-tracked from the —'

'Side-tracked?' Isabel snapped, not at all happy to be told that the ruin of her life was only a side-track.

'Not side-tracked,' Nicholas immediately corrected himself, 'that was the wrong word. I mean only that I came here to have one conversation with you only to have another. Which was, of course, the perfectly correct thing to do,' he hastened to say, seeing her lips tighten on hearing this, 'but now that we're done with that conversation we can —'

'We are not *done with that conversation*, as you put it, Mr Raspero,' Isabel interrupted. 'I entirely fail to understand you. How would you feel if a woman were to deceive you in the way in which you propose?'

For a moment Nicholas couldn't think of anything to say; then a moment of happy inspiration struck. 'Your question is a logical fallacy because you presuppose that I know exactly what I don't know — being deceived means that you *don't know* about things.'

'You are evading the issue, Mr Raspero. A moral principle is to be obeyed, is it not?'

A fragment of a conversation with a philosophically-minded person came back to Nicholas's mind just then. 'Should we only obey what we understand?' he asked.

Isabel, who was no more philosophically-minded than Nicholas, said immediately and with authority, 'That is beside the point.'

'Well, yes,' Nicholas agreed hastily, 'of course it is. But perhaps you could remind me of what the point is.'

Isabel sighed. 'I begin to see that you are hopeless, Mr Raspero, utterly, utterly hopeless. You are no good at all.'

'Yes!' Nicholas agreed enthusiastically. 'Absolutely! I told you from the beginning I wasn't the right person to talk to.'

'I begin to see what you are saying, Mr Raspero,' said Isabel thoughtfully. 'You are saying that if I deceive my husband in this way, then I will provide him with an illusion which is all that counts because it is all only an illusion anyway.'

Nicholas thought about this, biting his lower lip in concentration. 'No,' he said eventually, 'I'm not saying that. Look, it is a deception and you will always know that even if he doesn't. But what choice do you have? I mean, are you just going to give up on the rest of your life?'

'Of course I am not going to give up on the rest of my life, Mr Raspero. I shall never marry, that is all.'

'Never marry!' Nicholas was shocked. 'But that is giving up on the rest of your life!'

'Not at all, Mr Raspero. It is conducting my life according to moral principle. I do not expect a man like you to understand a matter such as moral principle. Suffice to say that I am ruined so I cannot marry and that is all there is to it. To conduct my life according to moral principle is not to give up on it but to conduct it in the only way that is honourable.'

'You are going to be a spinster all your life, never get married and have children and a family of your own just because you can't do something wrong?'

'This is not merely to do something wrong, Mr Raspero. We are talking about moral conduct, about the qualities of character which distinguish ladies and gentlemen, about the values which form the foundation of civilisation. You are saying I should just do as I like, are you not, without regard to whether or not what I do is right or wrong.'

Nicholas shook his head. 'I can't say I agree with you, Lady Grangeshield, but it is your choice.' He felt all of a sudden impatient with this whole conversation. All he had been asked to do was kill a man and now he was expected to produce an entire philosophy of life! 'In any case, I do believe we have reached the end of this conversation. It has just banged on and on with no end in sight. We have talked more than enough about a topic of conversation that is of far more interest to you than to me.' Nicholas said all this with a cold decisiveness that shattered Isabel's hold over him with one blow. He was a free man again.

Isabel immediately saw her blunder and without a moment's hesitation she set out to rectify it.

'For all your many faults, Mr Raspero,' Isabel said, fiddling with the latch that held her fan closed, 'you do strike me as an intelligent man. Clearly, I will not attempt to prevaricate when such an attempt would only prove to be in vain as you will only see through it immediately. When I say that I will never marry, I do of course mean this as a declaration of intent rather than as an actual choice that has been made. But surely, Mr Raspero, you will not rebuke me any further than you have already done.'

'Ah, it's a declaration of intent,' Nicholas said, no longer feeling as decisive as before. 'Well, yes, of course it is. That's clear enough.'

Isabel continued in the same vein, her eyes demurely downcast, 'You will surely not deny me the freedom to declare intentions, Mr Raspero. I would never deny you are, after all, a gentleman, which is why I have listened to everything you have had to say without a word of protest. Even when some of the things you have said have been well outside of the normal range of experience which I have been accustomed to from birth by my upbringing.'

Nicholas considered what she had just said. He was dimly aware that he should at least roll his eyes at this complete re-writing of history, which Isabel had carried out. Instead, he couldn't help but see her regal disdain for the truth to be immensely charming, even elegant, especially given the delicacy of the way she tilted her head to one side as if not daring to look up at him. 'Not at all,' Nicholas said reassuringly, 'of course, I would never deny you the freedom to declare intentions, I mean, good for you, it's very commendable really.'

'I hesitate to say anything more lest I provoke you into another display of temper, Mr Raspero. I dare not say another word.'

'I didn't mean that I didn't very much enjoy our conversation, but, well, I don't really know what to say about such things, it's really not my thing. But of course, I'm happy to help you all I can.'

'But you have made plain that I am imposing on you and surely you must understand how distressed that makes me feel. I detest discourtesy and now you tell me I have imposed on you.' Isabel raised her wide-open brown eyes to gaze with a certain hesitant uncertainty into his observant grey eyes, and as their eyes met Nicholas's freedom slipped through his fingers and was gone just like that!

'No, no, no,' Nicholas hastened to assure her, 'not at all! You haven't imposed on me in the least! This is a misunderstanding on your part, or rather I didn't explain myself properly. You have been a most wonderful hostess throughout my visit and I have been treated throughout with impeccable courtesy.' Nicholas could hardly believe even as he was saying this that he was actually saying it, but somehow it seemed very important that she should no longer be distressed, and the truth could go take a holiday.

Isabel began her tirade by saying, 'Well, I am obliged to observe that *you* have not behaved with impeccable courtesy, Mr Raspero.' Isabel now held forth for some time about how freely Nicholas had expressed himself. She referred to expressions such as *banged on and on,* which he had earlier used, without giving the least thought to the offence; she now revised her earlier opinion that he was *an intelligent man* given that *an intelligent man* would not say such *unintelligent* things, and she wondered aloud if anything could be done to improve Nicholas or if such a task was beyond the powers of anyone then living.

Nicholas sat there and took it all without a murmur of protest.

The regular practice of macchato was second nature to Nicholas and so he noticed the entry of Benson and his approach while Isabel was holding forth on Nicholas's deficiencies. Benson stood deferentially some distance away, completely unobserved by Isabel. So when during a lull in Isabel's offensive Nicholas looked over at him, Isabel followed the direction of his gaze.

'Your ladyship,' Benson said, 'Lord and Lady Sabina and Miss Nicholson have arrived.'

'Show them into the Stanton Room,' Isabel ordered, 'and appoint someone to take care of them. Do not bother me again until I call for you.'

'Very good, your ladyship,' Benson said, bowing and leaving.

The arrival of guests had shifted Nicholas's point of view again. He was not himself really a guest as such and he was reminded that he could never have the dazzling Lady Isabel Grangeshield on his arm. His stomach twisted itself into knots as he contemplated how far apart he was from Lady Isabel Grangeshield of Grangeshield House, and with that contemplation came a sense of loss, and with that sense of loss came a sense of himself as an independent person. So as Isabel resumed her barrage of criticism, Nicholas held up his hand to forestall her. 'I get the general idea, Lady Grangeshield,' he told her. 'But let me make something quite plain: your guests are arriving and so I am leaving. You have simply taken over this whole conversation and not let me get a word in edgeways even though I came here quite specifically to discuss a certain subject. But don't let me stop you holding forth on your favourite topic — the faults of Nicholas Raspero.'

Isabel guessed everything in a flash. 'You will be staying for dinner, Mr Raspero,' she informed him. 'So, as you are my guest, you are not leaving.'

'Well, naturally I would be delighted to stay for dinner,' Nicholas said, mollified by his sudden elevation in status. 'But my earlier point remains, does it not? With regard to the conversation we have been having, I really think that Lord and Lady Easton might be much better suited for a variety of reasons to talk to you about your current situation.' Nicholas glanced up the room at Lord and Lady Easton while he said this.

'Oh, do you know Lord and Lady Easton?' Isabel asked.

'No, but I've guessed who they are.'

'And how have you guessed?' Isabel asked.

'Well, that's a much more tricky question than you might suppose,' Nicholas said a little evasively. 'And it might be late in the day to answer it now.'

Isabel contemplated his evasiveness in the way a cat contemplates a mouse. 'But it is not at all late in the day, Mr Raspero,' she objected, looking at a nearby clock. 'It is only five-past-six. Surely, as my guest for dinner tonight, you need have no concern for the time.'

'Well, there's that,' Nicholas said. 'It's just that it's a long story, that's all. But briefly, then, well, the thought crossed my mind as I was planning everything that after I had killed Nevsky the authorities might go through his personal effects and find documents or something of that sort referring to what happened before, and thus you might be exposed by such a development, if you see what I mean.'

Nicholas stopped there, seeing from the expression on Isabel's face that this was not a possibility that had occurred to her. He enjoyed seeing Isabel momentarily at a loss, but then seeing fear appear on her abruptly stricken face he hastily continued to spare her any further distress, 'So the night before I killed Nevsky I burgled his house. I stole the Nevsky-Grangeshield Memorandum of Understanding from his safe. So no-one now can ever know.'

Isabel said nothing, but she was no longer looking fearful.

'As I said, it's a long story —'

'It is a story you will tell me, Mr Raspero, long or not, and you will tell it to me in full,' Isabel declared imperiously.

'Yes, I will, I will tell you everything, I promise,' Nicholas assured her, holding his hands up placatingly, 'because you have a right to know everything. But my point is this: once I had the document, I kept it to show you before it was destroyed so you could see for yourself that it had been destroyed. But then you wrote to me to say that you would not receive me, so I wondered what to do with the document. I still felt that you should see it before it was destroyed, just to put your mind at rest, so I kept it while I tried to decide what to do next. But then you wrote to me inviting me to come here today so I brought the document with me. It's here,' Nicholas said, patting the side of his robe with his hand.

'Give it to me,' Isabel commanded, holding out her hand.

Before he complied with her request, Nicholas held his left hand up palm out and said decisively, 'Once you have inspected the document, and satisfied yourself as to its authenticity, it will be destroyed here and now. Is that understood?'

Isabel said nothing, taken aback by the note of authority in his voice and still all-of-a-tremble from the shock of the Nevsky-Grangeshield Memorandum of Understanding existing for anyone to read. Nicholas reached into his robe and pulled out a parchment scroll and handed it over to her.

On the other side of the room Lord Easton observed what was happening and it was subsequently only the work of a moment for him to fish out a small eyeglass and raise it to his eye to spy from across the room on the document Isabel was taking in her hands. With his other eye (the left one) he observed Nicholas observing Isabel, and realising from his past experience of observing young men in Isabel's company that Nicholas would not be doing anything except keeping his gaze fixed on Isabel he looked through the eye glass with his right eye. To forestall the detection of his spying by the practice of macchato by Nicholas he tilted his head and cupped the palm of his hand around the eyeglass, so it would appear as if he was doing no more than hold his head in his right hand. Thus it was that he was enabled to spy in complete freedom on the document in Isabel's hands. The eyeglass was so effective that it was as if he was holding the document in his own hands, and it was not long before he recognised what the document was. He took down his eyeglass and returned to his earlier position of simply sitting there as an observant but not intrusive chaperone.

'Did you see what it was?' Lady Easton asked him.

'Yes,' Lord Easton replied, 'it was the Nevsky-Grangeshield Memorandum of Understanding.'

'The what?'

'The Nevsky-Grangeshield Memorandum of Understanding which Captain Nevsky took away with him after we were all obliged to sign it,' Lord Easton told his beloved.

Lady Easton took some time to absorb this news. 'But what on earth is Mr Raspero doing with it?'

'Ah,' Lord Easton said thoughtfully, 'that is the question, is it not? I must think about this.'

Lord Easton contemplated the mystery that had just manifested. The logic of substance struggled against charmingly persuasive golden-haired appearances, but Lord Easton won through eventually. 'Ah,' he said, 'I think I have the solution to the mystery.'

'And what is that solution?' Lady Easton asked.

Lord Easton leaned towards his wife and spoke in a low voice. 'Mr Raspero is the only man in New Landern known to be capable of defeating Nevsky in a wandfight. Mr Raspero visited Isabel last Sunday and left, as you may recall, in a state of some anger. Captain Nevsky was killed two days later on Tuesday by a man of a certain appearance, our golden-haired Lord of the North. Now suppose that our golden-haired Lord of the North was really our very own Mr Raspero in a disguise, wearing a wig and well-dressed for once. The servant and flying carriage are merely details; the key point is that only Mr Raspero was capable of killing Nevsky. Now that would explain how Mr Raspero comes to have the Nevsky-Grangeshield Memorandum of Understanding in his possession at the present time. It would also explain why this Lord of the North has baffled every attempt to uncover his identity for the reason that he simply doesn't exist. He is an illusion created by Mr Raspero to act on Isabel's behalf in a matter of honour.'

Lady Easton looked at Nicholas sitting at the other end of the room, innocently oblivious to all this unmasking of Lords of the North by Isabel's chaperones. 'Goodness!' she gasped, holding her hand over a mouth opened in shock at finding herself sitting in the same room as a man who had not only killed the feared Nevsky, but slaughtered Nevsky's dogs while he was at it. 'But what do we do?'

'We keep our mouths shut and pretend we don't know anything,' Lord Easton told her sternly.

TWENTY-FOUR

The Conversation Between Miss Sophie Nicholson and Mr Nicholas Raspero over Dinner

6:20 PM, Sunday 17 July 1544 A.F.

Isabel was reading the Nevsky-Grangeshield Memorandum of Understanding for the first time; she had never actually read it before, although her signature was one of the ten signatures on the document. She had signed it without reading it when the nightmare was happening because signing this document had helped to bring that nightmare to an end. The document, which she was now reading for the first time, was not long but the detail was brutal. The document told how Isabel had openly offered herself to Nevsky, assuring him of marriage if he would only satisfy her desires. Nevsky had insisted on witnesses to the offer and the deed, and these had been provided. She had misled Nevsky into hopes of marriage, and in recognition of this fact she would pay Nevsky one million strada in compensation. Whether or not she had actually yielded her virginity was not defined, but what was made abundantly clear was that Nevsky had had her, virgin or not, and that was the key point — an event admitted to by Lady Isabel Grangeshield and others who had been witnesses.

Isabel came to the end of her reading and while she sat there feeling sick she felt Nicholas taking the document out of her hands. She looked up to see him hold up the document in a silent show-and-tell before walking over to a nearby fireplace. The fire, which had been brightly blazing when Nicholas arrived, was now slumbering, its flames low and jumping here and there over the shimmering heat of the blackened embers. He twisted the document in his hands slightly and threw it into the flames. It wasn't long before bright, cheerful flames danced along the sides of the parchment, which subsequently grew browner as it crumpled in towards itself. The flames rose like the tongue of a torch above the paper, which turned into a grey ash as they watched. The clocks all read six thirty-eight.

Nicholas returned to his chair and sat down, propping up his feet on the Footstool of Mangatha. Isabel looked at him, feeling ashamed and humiliated, her confidence gone now, anciently wrapped up once again in her grandmother's yellow dress to hide her beauty from the attentions of the world.

Nicholas looked at her. 'Lady Grangeshield,' he said, 'I know that was a pack of lies. I swear it on my honour. It was evil, pure evil.'

Isabel looked at him, her trusting brown eyes looking directly into his admiring grey eyes. As what he had said sank in she came back to herself. Nicholas had not believed any of what the Nevsky-Grangeshield Memorandum of Understanding had said; he had just sworn it on his honour. She looked down at her fan, unfolded it to scrutinise its Delphic markings, and for the first time since she had learned the news she rejoiced that Nevsky was dead. He was dead, dead, dead! She had not yet learned how Nevsky had died but she thirsted to know all the details of how his head had been removed from his neck, how all his blood must have gushed out of his body at his beheading. Nicholas had said that Nevsky had known the reason for his death before he died and she wanted to know about that too. For the first time since Nicholas had arrived, she was ready to hear what he had come to tell her.

Isabel was fully coming back to herself now. She straightened up in her chair, folded up her fan and said to Nicholas, 'Mr Raspero, did you say that you do not believe that document?'

Nicholas looked directly at her. 'I swear on my honour that I do not believe a word of it.'

Isabel nodded as if she had expected no less. 'Mr Raspero,' she said, 'you will tell me of the means by which you brought about the death of Captain Nevsky, and furthermore, you will explain to me all this business about the Lord of the North which has been in all the newspapers, and you will tell me this now!' She was back in charge and she was letting Nicholas know it.

'I had no choice but to kill Nevsky in a duel,' Nicholas told her. 'But I could not call him out in a public duel because I would have had to state the nature of my complaint before witnesses. However, if I only said that it concerned the honour of a lady, then he might choose the venue of our duel to make public what had happened and your reputation would be destroyed. Yet, I could not kill him with a bolt through the neck from around a corner. I am not a murderer. So I realised I had to summon him to a secret duel and there confront and fight him.'

Nicholas stopped then as the door was flung open in an abrupt manner and a figure stormed into the room, closely followed by a hapless Benson, who looked like debris in the wake of a storm, his arms flailing as if overwhelmed by these meteorological forces. His attempts to stop this invasion of the drawing room had clearly been ineffectual. The figure who had stormed into the room stopped as if to take stock of where everyone was, and then set forth for where Nicholas and Isabel were sitting. It was Sophie.

Benson followed behind as if dragged along in Sophie's wake by a vortex of forces, while other figures entered the room cautiously as if keeping their distance from this unfolding drama, their demeanour proclaiming themselves to be spectators and nothing more; they were only there by circumstances, they seemed to declare by the very shiftiness of their collective posture; this had nothing to do with them.

Isabel, who had been listening attentively to every word Nicholas had been saying, was not pleased by this invasion. She had, in fact, invited Sophie to be a friendly face after what she anticipated would be the ordeal of receiving Nicholas, but as it happened she had found in Nicholas's company that life had become interesting once again and now that Nicholas was about to tell her the absolutely fascinating account of how he had cut Nevsky's head from his shoulders, Sophie's was an unwanted, if invited, intrusion.

Nicholas politely rose to his feet to acknowledge Sophie's approach.

Sophie came up to them and burst out, 'Izzy, what on earth is going on? Why are we being kept waiting so long?'

'Well, really, Sophie, you are being very impatient,' Isabel said dismissively.

'Impatient? We've been waiting for hours. Surely you could at least have told us that you had such important business.' Sophie looked then at Nicholas, who was following their exchange without expression. 'What are you doing here, Mr Raspero?'

'I might ask the same question of you, Miss Nicholson. What are *you* doing here?' Nicholas asked with mock sternness.

Sophie raised her chin defiantly. 'I have come to dinner, Mr Raspero. Does that answer your question?'

'It'll have to do,' Nicholas said with a wary look as if he doubted her.

'Now it is your turn to answer the question, Mr Raspero,' Sophie told him. 'What are *you* doing here?'

'Like you, Miss Nicholson,' Nicholas said, 'I am a guest for dinner.'

'So you say, Mr Raspero,' Sophie said mischievously, doubting him in her turn.

'Time will tell on us both and the clock is ticking. Are you ready, Miss Nicholson?'

Sophie giggled and unfolded her fan flirtatiously.

'Benson,' Isabel said, 'set another place. Mr Raspero is staying for dinner.'

Sophie was trying to make sense of what was happening, even as Isabel was rising from her chair and meeting and greeting her guests. Mr Raspero had said he was staying for dinner before Isabel had instructed Benson to set him a place, which was very strange, surely: it was as if Mr Raspero was instructing Isabel that he would stay for dinner and Isabel's subsequent instructions to Benson had been as a result of his instructions (but who was Mr Raspero to Isabel?), and certainly the two of them, Isabel and Mr Raspero, had been conversing together all this time, regardless of the world at large. Something was going on, that was apparent to Sophie, who had been kept waiting for *hours* (it had been forty minutes or so) by these two so deep in conversation that they were oblivious to everything else going on around them. Furthermore, it had not escaped Sophie's attention that Mr Raspero had been using the Footstool of Mangatha — as a footstool!

Nor were these the only puzzles for Sophie. Why on earth was Isabel wearing that horrible yellow dress and with her hair so unattractive? Furthermore, Isabel was not wearing any jewellery at all. What was going on?

The mysteries multiplied for Sophie as they entered the dining room and she observed Benson directing another servant to set a place for Mr Raspero furthest away from where Isabel would be sitting at the other end of the table. Why was Mr Raspero being kept at a distance when he seemed to be in a position of such importance? And why had Isabel not introduced Mr Raspero to any of her other guests? It was an omission that the guests had all very obviously noticed, but Isabel simply appeared oblivious to everything, despite the peculiarity of such behaviour.

As they approached the dining table Mr Raspero spoke to Benson in such a familiar way as to make Sophie wonder further.

'Are you all right, Benson?' Nicholas asked. 'You're acting very normally today.'

'Yes, Mr Raspero, everything is perfectly all right,' said Benson, watching a footman bend over to light a candle.

'It's just that when you're not acting like a madman I worry about you. I think that something must be wrong. But everything's all right then?'

'Yes, Mr Raspero,' replied Benson, struggling not to laugh.

'That's good,' said Nicholas and laughed out loud. At that Benson could no longer restrain himself and burst out chuckling a wheezy, shaking laugh.

'Mr Raspero,' said Isabel, 'you will not tease my servants.'

Nicholas looked at her with a cheerful grin. 'Never again, Lady Grangeshield.'

The other guests all looked at each other as they took their seats, the same thought in their minds — Mr Raspero appeared to be too familiar with the servants of the household to be anything other than a privileged guest.

The dining table stretched from end-to-end like a shipping canal. At one end Isabel sat in the ornate wooden chair of the Mistress of Grangeshield House; at the other end was an equally ornate wooden chair reserved for the Master of Grangeshield House. When Isabel married her husband would sit there. Some way down the table Nicholas sat opposite Sophie, with Sophie's parents beside them; Isabel's other guests sat in the places of honour nearer her chair with the Eastons seated in between.

'But surely, Sophie, you will introduce us,' Lady Sabina said, finding herself seated across from Mr Raspero, a man to whom she had not yet been introduced, and who would be sitting there for the whole of dinner.

Sophie introduced her mother and father to Mr Raspero, taking the opportunity to scrutinise him closely, as if by such an inspection she could find the answers to her questions, but Mr Raspero seemed the same as ever and her scrutiny came to naught; or perhaps not naught, for her detailed inspection of Mr Raspero did not escape Isabel's attention. Isabel's suspicions of Sophie's motives in inspecting Nicholas so closely, once aroused, would only grow from that beginning to a definite end, which would ultimately have certain consequences as the subsequent drama of the evening would show. But for now, the guests, unaware of the firestorm which lay ahead, tucked in their napkins and lined up for a run at the steaming soup being ladled into their bowls.

Lady Sabina's curiosity was shining too brightly to be hidden for long, and so with apparent casualness she asked Nicholas, who was unfolding his napkin, 'So how long have you known Lady Grangeshield, Mr Raspero?'

'We were introduced back in early May,' said Nicholas.

'Early May!' gasped Sophie, looking up the table at Isabel, who was too far away to have heard this exchange.

'Yes, early May,' Nicholas confirmed. 'Why the great surprise?'

'Oh, no reason,' Sophie replied, not looking up from her soup bowl to meet Nicholas's gaze. Yet, as Nicholas bent down to his own soup bowl, she gave him a long look, purely in the disinterested way in which anyone might gaze at a man always surrounded by mystery. Isabel, too far away to hear what was being said, yet able to observe everything, noted the length of the look Sophie gave Nicholas and was not at all happy about it. It was the second long look she had given him in as many minutes and it seemed to Isabel that Sophie's behaviour verged on impropriety. Isabel's suspicions were now more than merely aroused; they were beginning to smoulder.

Sophie, happily unaware of the trouble already brewing for her, had decided that the best strategy to employ in order to resolve the always returning mystery of the enigmatic Mr Nicholas Raspero, was to engage him in innocent conversation, which imperceptibly would uncover the layers of mystification with which he was surrounded. Sophie wanted to find out why Isabel had, as Sophie had come to think, concealed her knowledge of Nicholas from The Gang by pretending not to know Nicholas a couple of weeks ago, when she had, in fact, all along known him since early May! Sophie was, in fact, being far too clever; if Sophie had directly asked Nicholas how he had come to meet Isabel, he would have told her quite openly that he had been introduced to her by Mr Timothy Boylent at the engagement party of Mr Carver and Lady Lachance, which would have taken Sophie part of the way to resolving this mystery but Sophie was being much too clever to adopt such a simple approach because she had decided, to her own satisfaction, that the mysteries she was faced with were too deep to be solved by a simple approach.

Sophie schemed silently to herself throughout the soup course, not saying a word but quickly looking up every now and then at Nicholas. She was deciding on the questions she would put to Nicholas over dinner in the course of a conversation that would be full of hidden enquiries which would, in time, peel off all these layers of mystery — a conversation resembling nothing less than a fishing expedition.

Isabel was now monitoring Sophie closely from afar, and she caught every one of these quick looks Sophie gave Nicholas. In the meantime, Nicholas chatted politely to the Sabinas about international trade, the latest tax proposal and the lawlessness that had been abroad recently in the capital. No-one knew what was going on, but one theory was that a powerful criminal had recently died, resulting in power struggles amongst his subordinates. Nicholas knew as little about this as anyone, or so he said at any rate. Isabel continued to keep an eye on Sophie, while Sophie continued to keep an eye on Nicholas.

Sophie was a pretty girl. She was not one of society's beauties, but her freckled face had a certain attractive cheerfulness about it, with her turned-up nose and delicate mouth and vivacious manner of talking. Her figure was slim and elegant, especially in the figure-hugging dress she was wearing tonight. Her light-brown hair was piled up high and draped with rubies and emeralds; diamonds sparkled in her ear-lobes; her pale blue eyes had an intelligent humour that could captivate the unwary male — one young man had fallen backward off his stool when Sophie had arisen too suddenly, while still talking to him, leading to jokes about "the Sophie manoeuvre". She had turned down three proposals of marriage to date.

This then was Isabel's scheming guest sitting across the table from Nicholas. Isabel was starting to feel trapped in her grandmother's absurd yellow dress. She could hardly believe this betrayal of her hospitality, and from Sophie of all people! Sophie was almost a sister to her; they had even shared the same cot on occasion as babies! And now look at her, look at this Sophie, such a so-called friend as this! Isabel began to feel a certain fury that such impropriety as this could be going on in her own house — her own house! She realised that Nicholas was innocent of any wrong-doing, because after all he was not looking at anybody, but as for Sophie, who she had formerly considered to be a friend, well ... ... Sophie was clearly guilty of such an appalling breach of impropriety as to make her an unwelcome guest in Grangeshield House, a very unwelcome guest indeed.

As the soup bowls were cleared away, Sophie began her campaign.

'It is interesting to meet you once again, Mr Raspero,' Sophie said as she folded her napkin, 'given that you have been the subject of so much talk lately.'

'I'm still the Talk of the Town, am I?' Nicholas said with a grin. 'Well, that's nice.'

At the sight of Sophie talking directly to Nicholas, Isabel started to brood under a darkening brow.

'But it is deserved, is it not, Mr Raspero, however pleased you must be by such fame?'

'I took down Nevsky, or the late Nevsky I should say,' Nicholas commented with a shrug, 'but that was a while ago now. Surely it's time to move on.'

The next course was being served up so Sophie bided her time, then resumed her campaign as they started to eat. She started with a stab in the dark. 'Yes, you were the Talk of the Town for having defeated the late Nevsky, but there is far more to you than merely the defeat of the late Nevsky in a duel, is there not, Mr Raspero?' Sophie was nearly sure that Nicholas tensed ever so slightly on hearing this.

'There most certainly is, Miss Nicholson,' Nicholas agreed. 'But modesty prevents me from proclaiming my merits.'

'You do not hesitate to proclaim your modesty though, Mr Raspero.'

Nicholas grinned to acknowledge the hit. 'I very modestly proclaim my modesty, Miss Nicholson.'

'It seems there is no end to your modesty, Mr Raspero.'

Nicholas laughed. 'My modesty ends where my conceit begins. How about you, Miss Nicholson?'

'My conceit cannot compare with yours, Mr Raspero, given all that you have been up to.'

'Surely conceit need not have a basis? It is conceit, after all.'

'Your conceit reflects what you are up to,' Sophie replied, 'which is the subject of such talk.'

'What talk is this, Miss Nicholson?' Nicholas asked.

'What would you guess as to what people are saying about you, Mr Raspero?'

'How would I go about guessing?' Nicholas asked. 'Would I not need to suspect something?'

Sophie wondered if he had used the word *suspect* in a slightly elliptical way. Did he suspect that she knew something, or did he only suspect that she suspected something?

'How do any of us go about guessing, Mr Raspero?' Sophie asked. 'We start with what we know, and then go on from there, do we not?'

'And what if we know nothing at all, Miss Nicholson?'

'But surely you know what you have been up to, Mr Raspero!'

'Of course I do, but nothing that I have been up to can be the subject of talk because I have really been up to very little of interest lately.'

'I see that your modesty has returned, Mr Raspero,' Sophie said with a smile.

Nicholas laughed again, gave Sophie an amused look, but said nothing in reply. Nicholas did not know what Sophie was about because what Sophie was about (namely, to uncover the reason why Isabel had concealed her acquaintance with Nicholas from The Gang) concerned a matter that existed nowhere but in Sophie's mind (given that Isabel had not been doing any such concealing). For his part, Nicholas suspected that Sophie must have heard something of what had happened to Jolly but he preferred to avoid discussing this story, if possible, just because it was all so long and complicated. It was inevitable in such circumstances that confusion could only grow and it was also inevitable that Sophie's attentions were in consequence all taken up with Nicholas to the exclusion of all else.

So this confusion grew at one end of the dinner table while its twin grew at the other. Isabel's brooding was growing and darkening into thunder clouds at the sight of Sophie quite outrageously talking to Nicholas in such a direct and continual manner. She simply wouldn't stop talking to Nicholas! And furthermore, Nicholas seemed to be laughing and enjoying the conversation which was surely indicative of its impropriety. She could not blame Nicholas for what was happening: men were so easily led astray. Sophie was entirely to blame for the pleasure Nicholas took from her company, and all this was happening in her own house — her own house!

'And what is your view of the identity of the Lord of the North?' Lady Sabina asked Nicholas, trying to get a more interesting conversation going than Sophie's obscure meanderings.

To Sophie's annoyance, much of the remaining dinner-time conversation was taken up with this topic. Nicholas, in particular, took it up very enthusiastically and both Lord and Lady Sabina had been following the story closely. Nicholas and her parents discussed the leading theories that had emerged concerning the identity of the Lord of the North, the latest being whether he was even from the North at all. The cryptic references of the Lord of the North's letter, such as *the hat by the road*, had already been the subject of innumerable commentaries, including the suggestion that this all had something to do with a secret society, with *the swinging gate* being some kind of ritual of initiation. The fact that he had signed the letter by saying that he signed the letter as the Lord of the North suggested he had another identity known to both Nevsky and his opponent, and why the Lord *of* the North and not the Lord *from* the North? Did the letters *f* and *m* which differentiated *from* and *or* indicate the author of the letter as having the initials F. M., or M. F.? Every now and then Nicholas laughed merrily at all these mysteries, and Lord and Lady Sabina joined him in his laughter, for they were enjoying this conversation. Sophie waited impatiently to resume her campaign to uncover what was going on between Isabel and Nicholas, her campaign having been side-tracked by this apparently irrelevant matter of the Lord of the North. She kept an eye on Nicholas to achieve her objective, while Isabel kept her eye on Sophie keeping an eye on Nicholas. Sophie's patience was rewarded as her chance came eventually.

'How long have you been in New Landern, Mr Raspero?' Sophie asked, taking aim at Nicholas once again.

'Since the second of May,' Nicholas replied.

'But surely you have done much more than merely defeat the late Nevsky since your arrival all that time ago,' Sophie asked.

'I am having dinner with you, Miss Nicholson,' Nicholas replied, 'which is much more interesting than a duel with the late Nevsky.'

'But we are not having a duel,' Sophie pointed out.

'No, Miss Nicholson, we are conversing over dinner,' Nicholas agreed.

'Yes, here in Grangeshield House. Do you have dinner here often, Mr Raspero?'

'This is the first time I have had dinner here.'

'You usually come for lunch, then, I take it.'

'I have never sat at this table before tonight, Miss Nicholson.'

'Do you normally eat elsewhere in Grangeshield House?'

Nicholas sighed. 'I have never had so much as a bread roll here before today, Miss Nicholson, anywhere in the house. Please let me know if any more comment is required to clarify this matter.'

'But surely you have taken tea with Isabel.'

Nicholas sighed again but at the same time he was nearly grinning. 'No, Miss Nicholson, I have not taken tea with Lady Grangeshield, nor consumed any kind of beverage here in Grangeshield House. I hope I haven't left anything out.'

'I am surprised that such a frequent visitor as yourself has not been offered any hospitality at all.'

'This is the second time I have been here, Miss Nicholson,' Nicholas told her. 'One of us must misunderstand the meaning of the word *frequent*, but my modesty, which has returned yet again, forbids me from saying who.'

This made Sophie pause for a moment; she found herself facing another mystery. How could Nicholas have achieved such familiarity in Grangeshield House as to use the Footstool of Mangatha and talk to Benson so teasingly and be head-to-head with Isabel in conversation, while her dinner guests were kept waiting, if he were only here for the second time? It didn't make sense. Her mother took advantage of her long pause to re-direct the conversation to the issue of whether Anglashia should support Yelyntrade or Gathnatun in their territorial dispute over the region of Trentland, and what with the conversation moving from one topic to another, Sophie found she was unable to continue the pursuit of her quarry for the remainder of dinner.

Sophie had done enough, more than enough, to bring Isabel's blood to the boil. Lightning was beginning to flash from the heavy, dark thunder storm clouds around Isabel's head.

Now that Isabel came to think of it, she began to attribute a new significance to past events which rendered them into a pattern of deception. Sophie, she remembered, had eagerly followed the departing Nicholas at Lady Starfeld's party and ambushed Miss Dahl into introducing her to him; Sophie had then failed to introduce Isabel to

Nicholas, even though the whole strategy of getting Nicholas to Lady Starfeld's party had been instigated by Isabel, a failure which Isabel had seen as accidental at the time but which she now saw had been all too clearly deliberate and premeditated, and Sophie was now carrying on with Nicholas right before Isabel's very eyes! In her own house!

Sophie arose from the dinner table ready to continue her crusading campaign during the next phase of the evening.

Isabel arose from the dinner table ready for war.

TWENTY-FIVE

....

The Great Quarrel Between Lady Isabel Grangeshield and Miss Sophie Nicholson

9:15 PM, Sunday 17 July 1544 A.F.

They all returned to the Red Drawing Room, Isabel leading the way with her fan lashing the air like the tail of a lioness. Had Sophie been more attentive to the mood of her hostess, she would have noticed these warning signs, but she flirtatiously placed her hand every now and then on Nicholas's arm as they walked along chatting of this and that in order to soften Nicholas up for her later interrogation of him; Isabel, observing this behaviour in the reflections of the hallway mirrors she passed, was made even angrier than before. When they reached the Red Drawing Room Isabel turned to survey her guests.

'Benson, please see to the needs of my guests,' Isabel said. 'Miss Nicholson, I will speak to you now, if you please.'

'Miss Nicholson?' asked Miss Nicholson in astonishment.

Isabel moved away to the other side of the room, then turned to face Sophie, who followed after some hesitation due to her perplexity as to what was going on. Benson escorted the other guests to various chairs that stood around near the fireplace where Nicholas had earlier burned the Nevsky-Grangeshield Memorandum of Understanding. Isabel had started to speak to Sophie but they were too far away for her words to be audible. What was obvious to the onlooker, however, was that Isabel's words were clearly not friendly.

'... this is absurd ... ' Sophie said loudly enough for the words to carry across to them.

'Nice painting,' Nicholas said to Lord Sabina, gesturing to the painting of a mountain landscape above the fireplace.

'Yes, isn't it,' he replied.

'You cannot deny it!' Isabel declared from afar.

'That figurine is also very pretty,' Nicholas commented further, pointing to a shepherdess on the mantelpiece.

'How dare you!' Sophie shouted.

'It is indeed,' Lord Sabina agreed, bending his head forward so as to study the flute-playing maiden in her voluptuous robe.

' ... your behaviour ... '

Messrs Tabatha and Fabian and Yago and Mesdames Tabatha and Fabian and Yago were sitting down, talking to each other in low voices, chuckling among themselves now and then. Lady Sabina stood next to Nicholas and her husband as if she were following their conversation and nothing else was happening, but her head was tilted to one side as she tried with all her might to hear what Isabel and Sophie were saying to each other.

'I would also draw your attention to this beautifully carved and decorated box,' Nicholas continued, pointing to a wooden box on the mantelpiece next to the shepherdess, featuring scenes of the life of a woodchopper in the forest.

'I can only thank you for doing so,' Lord Sabina said politely, 'for its beauty is quite extraordinary.'

'... never ... so insulted ... think you are ... ' were fragments of Sophie's furious sentences that came floating across to them.

'Shall we praise the presentation of this amphibious creature?' Nicholas asked, pointing to the next object along, an elegantly rendered frog in pure silver, its head pointing up and turned around almost as if in conversation.

'... in my house ... disregard ... of what is to be expected ... as you have disregarded...'

'I think we must,' Lord Sabina declared, examining the frog closely.

'How can we not praise such an exquisitely made object of art? Its beauty is quite extraordinary.'

'... saying such things ... guest in your house ... never been so treated ... unforgiveable ... '

'I believe this frog has been drawn from life,' Nicholas observed sagely, as if uttering a saying of the greatest import. 'Would you not agree?'

'... deny it all you wish ... obvious ... disgraceful ... '

'I think you might very well be correct in your estimation of the matter,' Lord Sabina replied, nodding with a sagacity fully the equal of anyone else's. 'This frog has without doubt been drawn from life.'

'... insulting ... came here ... only to be ... '

'Consider the legs,' Nicholas continued, as if he was onto a winner here with the frog. 'The due proportion of the limbs, the arrangements of the limbs and torso; surely we must concede that it is from life itself, that the artist has rendered a real frog in silver.'

'We must concede this,' Lord Sabina agreed.

Nicholas had more to say about the frog but Isabel and Sophie were storming across the room towards them and all those present ceased talking and looked at them expectantly. Messrs Tabatha and Fabian and Yago rose to their feet politely (and prudently).

'Mother, we are leaving,' Sophie declared, her face flushed, tapping her folded fan furiously on a knuckle.

Isabel said nothing but turned a cold eye on Lord and Lady Sabina.

'Why? Is anything the matter?' Lady Sabina asked solicitously, her eyebrows raised, looking as twitchy as a rabbit in a pit full of snakes.

'Izzy ... Lady Grangeshield has asked me to leave, but in any case I refuse to stay one minute longer in this household.'

'You are not welcome to!' Isabel snapped.

Sophie turned to Nicholas and looked directly at him. 'Do you know why Iz ... Lady Grangeshield has asked me to leave, Mr Raspero? It is because she says that I have been flirting outrageously with you!'

'Well, you're a wild one, aren't you?' Nicholas commented, looking her up and down, trying to make a joke of it.

'Tell me, Mr Raspero,' Sophie ploughed on, unaware at that moment that humour even existed, 'do you believe I was flirting outrageously with you?'

'Not so that I noticed,' Nicholas replied, not knowing whether to laugh or not, but deciding it was safer not to.

'There!' Sophie exclaimed in triumph, turning to Isabel. 'I was not flirting with Mr Raspero. He has himself confirmed it!'

'He only said he did not notice,' Isabel replied, seizing in a flash on Nicholas's form of words, 'but I most certainly noticed your brazen behaviour.'

'Brazen behaviour!' Sophie shouted. 'How dare you, you ... moron!'

'You will leave this house and you will leave now!' Isabel stated in a fury sheathed in ice.

'I will never set foot in this house again!' Sophie shouted. She whirled around and headed towards the door. Her parents stood where they were, as if frozen. Lady Sabina's mouth was hanging open slightly.

'Nice to have met you,' Nicholas said politely to Lord and Lady Sabina.

'It was likewise very pleasant to have met you, Mr Raspero,' Lord Sabina said as genially as he could manage. Much of his income was derived from trade with the Grangeshield Estate and this was not far from his presently troubled thoughts.

'A pleasure, Mr Raspero,' Lady Sabina said, much less genially, as if she would like to have seen Nicholas spitted and roasted on the spot.

'Oh, Mr Raspero,' Sophie said, tapping her fan on her thigh as she walked back towards the group, having clearly decided that she was not yet done, 'before I leave it may interest you to know that Lady Grangeshield is a liar.'

Lord Sabina felt an icy trickle go down his spine on hearing these words.

'I am sure that is not so,' Nicholas said to her in his most reasonable-tone-of-voice.

Isabel said nothing but her lips tightened into a thin, white line as she glared at Sophie.

'You have said that you and Lady Grangeshield have known each other since early May, yet it was only two weeks ago that Lady Grangeshield said she did not know you.'

Nicholas immediately leapt to Isabel's defence. 'She did not say so,' he declared with authority, hoping it was actually true, 'you merely assumed it.'

Sophie made the fatal mistake at that critical moment by openly pausing, while she all-too-obviously tried to remember what it was exactly that Isabel had, in fact, said.

'I said no such thing!' Isabel immediately proclaimed. She couldn't remember what she had actually said any more than Sophie could but the matter had already been settled in her favour. 'You are simply muddle-headed!'

'You pretended not to know Mr Raspero,' Sophie insisted. About this much at least she was certain. 'If you deny that, you are a liar.'

Lord Sabina's legs weakened so he had to lean slightly on the mantelpiece. No-one but Nicholas noticed.

'Why-are-you-not-lea-ving-Miss-Nich-ol-son?' Isabel asked, completely avoiding the valid point Sophie had raised. 'You-are-not-wel-come-here!'

Sophie took a deep breath, gave Isabel a scornful look, wrinkled her nose and upper lip with the greatest disdain she could muster, turned away and stormed off towards the door, swinging her fan as she went.

'Friends do quarrel, don't they?' Lord Sabina observed in his most friendly tone of voice.

At the door Sophie turned around and shouted, 'Deceiver!' before disappearing through the door.

'Benson will show you out,' Isabel stated coldly. As far as she was concerned, the father of her enemy was also her enemy. 'Goodbye to you both!' With that she turned her back on them and walked to a nearby chair and sat down, legs crossed, tapping her fan on her knee.

Lady Sabina gave Nicholas a dirty look, as if wanting to blame him for everything that had gone wrong, inclined her head to all those present and stalked off to the door. Lord Sabina followed, taking deep breaths as he shakily walked along after her.

Nicholas wandered over to a nearby window, opened it and looked outside, breathing deeply of the fresh evening air. He looked down from the windows into the moonlit garden below. Isabel stayed in her chair, opening and closing her fan, preoccupied with her thoughts. The Eastons sat nearby, silent and watchful as ever. Messrs Tabatha and Fabian and Yago and Mesdames Tabatha and Fabian and Yago looked at each other and said nothing. The scene had a certain striking quality to it — the man standing at the window looking out, the lady in the chair by the fireplace, the three gentlemen and three ladies to one side, the couple sitting on the other side — it was a tableau that would have made a pretty work of art to hang on the wall. None of those present, however, gave any consideration to any such point of view; they were caught up in their own thoughts.

Nicholas was looking down at the garden in the moonlight, struck by its beauty. It was such an astonishingly grand garden, he thought, but then, this was such an astonishingly grand house.

Isabel was too upset to pay attention to anything or anyone. What she saw as the betrayal of her hospitality by Sophie had churned up her stomach and left her prey to imaginary fears.

The Eastons were each separately thinking the same thing — that the sooner Nicholas was out of Grangeshield House the better. Lady Easton could not look at Nicholas without seeing a pile of dead bodies around him. Lord Easton was wondering if the man who killed Nevsky might thereby have a claim on Isabel's affections, especially given her jealousy tonight, and he was sceptical that Nicholas was a suitable match for Isabel.

Messrs Tabatha and Fabian and Yago and Mesdames Tabatha and Fabian and Yago were feeling increasingly uneasy as time went by and everyone in the room simply ignored each other. Isabel had begun the dinner with polite chit-chat but as time went on had increasingly appeared to not even know they were there, not appearing to hear what was said directly to her, until all conversation dried up and they had finished their meal in a complete and gloomy silence. Now there was another complete and gloomy silence, but it was a different kind of silence because it trembled in the aftermath of the blazing row between Isabel and Sophie like the silence that follows a loud roar of thunder. Messrs Tabatha and Fabian and Yago and Mesdames Tabatha and Fabian and Yago sat there not daring to say a word.

Tabatha broke ranks first. Declaring that it was time for him to leave, he stood up. Fabian and Yago followed suit, as if tied to Tabatha with invisible strings, which given the business deal they were involved in courtesy of the Grangeshield Estate, they were. Mesdames Tabatha and Fabian and Yago all followed their lead. Isabel looked up from her chair, pulled the cord for Benson, and accepted their farewells with a vague politeness, and then Messrs Tabatha and Fabian and Yago and Mesdames Tabatha and Fabian and Yago left. The Eastons walked with them to the door then returned to their seats.

Nicholas walked over to Isabel, pulled up a chair with his wand, pulled over the Footstool of Mangatha, and sat down and stretched out with his feet on the Footstool of Mangatha. (No other footstool would do for Nicholas nowadays.) 'Are you all right, Lady Grangeshield?' he asked.

'I am perfectly all right, thank you, Mr Raspero,' Isabel said determinedly.

'You look upset,' Nicholas pointed out.

'Do not presume to tell me how I look!' Isabel snapped at him.

'I'm starting to get the general idea, Lady Grangeshield. No-one can tell you anything. Is that right, or am I missing something?'

Isabel ignored his continuing impertinence. It was beneath her dignity to reply.

'We have to finish our conversation, Lady Grangeshield, but not now. I would suggest that we finish our conversation tomorrow. Do you agree?'

Silence from Isabel.

'Shall I return here tomorrow morning?'

Isabel opened and closed the latch of her fan as if wondering how the design could be improved.

'I will make my farewells, Lady Grangeshield,' Nicholas said, shifting his position preparatory to standing up.

'What do you mean, Mr Raspero?' Isabel asked.

'I mean I'll say goodbye and go.'

'But you are most certainly not leaving, Mr Raspero. You are staying here tonight.' Isabel pulled the cord for Benson.

Nicholas considered this, looking about him. It was certainly an amazing house, and it would be interesting to spend the night there. Such a chance might never come his way again. It was precisely because he so much wanted to stay the night that he dragged his feet.

'I would be honoured to spend the night in such a magnificent house as this, Lady Grangeshield, but unfortunately my uncle does not know I am here,' he said carefully in an oblique reference to the confidential nature of his visit, 'and I am sure he will wonder where I am if I don't return tonight.'

'But you will notify him by private messenger of your current plans,' Isabel explained to Nicholas, 'and this obstacle is thereby removed.' Isabel had made up her mind that Nicholas was staying the night and nothing would stop this happening.

Private messenger? Nicholas was not used to a world where there were such things as private messengers but he could grasp the concept. 'Well, I suppose,' he said vaguely feeling that he had run out of logical objections. 'But I really wouldn't want to put you to any trouble.'

Benson had turned up by now in response to Isabel's summons. 'Benson, Mr Raspero is staying the night. Prepare the Rowland Room for him and see to it that Mr Raspero is enabled to send a message to his uncle tonight.' Like a general making plan after plan to achieve an objective, Isabel was not going to rest until she had got what she wanted.

'Yes, my lady,' Benson said obediently and bowed to Nicholas. 'Will you please come with me, Mr Raspero?'

Nicholas stood up, accepting defeat. He followed Benson, expecting to be provided with writing materials in order to dash off his letter, but he was to learn just how naïve such a notion was. He was a guest of Grangeshield House and there were forms to be followed. He was preceded by a servant carrying a lamp and followed by a servant carrying a lamp and taken to a writing room with no fewer than three scroll-topped writing desks and an array of scrolls and writing implements. The entire room was lit up with lamps by the servants in attendance on him after which he was invited to make his selection from the scrolls and notepads and loose-leafed sheets of paper on offer, whether scented paper or coloured sheets of paper or watermarked paper or lightly illustrated sheets of paper; after which he could choose from trays set out with fountain pens, pencils, and a variety of other writing instruments all in their separate grooved compartments. Keeping his face carefully impassive and trying not to roll his eyes, Nicholas took a sheet of paper and a fountain pen and wrote a quick letter to his uncle. He then chose an envelope from a cabinet which seemed to contain every size and kind of envelope ever devised; addressed the letter and handed it over to an attentive servant.

Despite himself Nicholas had to reluctantly concede that there was a certain style in going about the tasks of life in this way; he felt like a barbarian perceiving the limits of functionality for the first time. The act of sending a letter had been turned into a celebration of civilisation; the idea that life was more than a material process was no longer only a philosophical point but a lived experience.

After saying goodnight to Isabel (but not to the Eastons, to whom he had not yet been introduced) Nicholas was escorted by Benson and two other servants to the Rowland Room. Nicholas refused to let them undress him, saying that he could manage such a feat on his own, and sent them on their way, and then it was that Nicholas found himself on his own in the Rowland Room of Grangeshield House late that evening of that topsy-turvy day.

The Rowland Room was about sixty-feet long and forty-feet wide; it had a large four-poster bed with golden bedclothes; the walls were lined with red and golden velvet; the ceilings were twenty-feet high with five chandeliers in a pentagonal arrangement hanging down over an expanse of armchairs, coffee tables, card tables and writing desks; there was even a piano. Paintings of various scenes of Rowland's life were hung here and there with crossed swords and masks and mirrors in between them and there was a large fireplace with carved stone figures of lions and deer on either side of the grate. There were bronze statues of figures of mythology placed here and there about the room, while the polished wooden floorboards were covered in a variety of carpets with clever geometric designs. It was altogether the most amazing room Nicholas had ever seen, in the most amazing house he had ever been in! This was living, he thought! This was something else!

He was still too keyed up to go to bed just yet so he wandered about, looking at all the details of the room, looking out through the windows at the garden below in the moonlight. It had been quite a day! Isabel's crazy letters over the past week had been only a prelude to the lunacy of today, topped as it had been by the bizarre episode of Isabel quarrelling with Sophie over Sophie's supposed flirting with Nicholas. He wondered if Sophie really had been flirting with him. He wouldn't have thought so himself, but Isabel certainly had, and women could usually tell these things.

He reflected that his life had recently experienced a great deal of turbulence, but now everything was nearly over. He undressed and went to bed and lay there in the dark taking account of his current situation before going to sleep.

He would finish his conversation with Isabel tomorrow and then it would be over and done with and he could put it behind him and move on, never giving it another moment's thought; or so he believed at the time.

TWENTY-SIX

The Deception of Mr Nicholas Raspero by Lady Isabel Grangeshield

10:30 AM, Monday 18 July 1544 A.F.

Nicholas was sitting in the Library with his feet on the table in front of him, absorbed in reading the Book of the World 1543. It had maps of different countries, and drawings of animals and statues, with comments on all the different peoples and customs of the world.

The Library was circular with bookcases lining the walls. Twelve large, curved windows were positioned above the bookcases, encircling the room. In the centre of the room was a large round table surrounded by armchairs and sofas. Twelve chandeliers hung down from the ceiling. Bronze statues, large bowl compasses and an armillary sphere were placed here and there to form a carefully structured geometric harmony. The Library was designed to remind the visitor of the meaning of civilisation.

Nicholas had slept well, enjoyed a large breakfast and was lazily reading an article about the people of Trentland. It had once been believed that the people of Trentland only took on a human form when observed by other people, but when left unobserved by others reverted to their natural non-human form which could only be guessed at from cave paintings; they only had to be observed by humans to once again appear to be of human form, but this belief, once a favourite topic of the deliberations of philosophers, had been discredited in more recent times although it could not, obviously, be entirely disproved. Modern day visitors to Trentland, at any rate, reported the people of Trentland as appearing to be normal in all respects, and it was these modern day reports that Nicholas was reading that day.

Isabel entered the Library, looking so impossibly beautiful that Nicholas momentarily froze where he was, looking across the room at her; the sight of her would have made a flying carriage fall out of the sky. She had, in fact, spent half-an-hour longer than usual on her appearance, after having ordered her grandmother's yellow dress to be burned. Isabel was followed by her chaperones the Eastons.

'I see you have managed to make yourself comfortable, Mr Raspero, as always,' Isabel said sharply.

Nicholas started to stand up, a bit late, as he was only now recovering from the appearance of Isabel.

'Oh, please don't bother to stand up, Mr Raspero.'

'I might try that if I had the courage,' Nicholas joked as he finished standing up, 'but maybe another time!'

'It does not take courage to behave without manners, Mr Raspero, it only takes stupidity.'

'You're not a morning person, are you?' Nicholas commented.

'I beg your pardon?'

Nicholas sighed. 'Nothing. I was just about to wish you a good morning, that's all. Good morning, Lady Grangeshield.'

'Good morning to you as well, Mr Raspero,' Isabel said frostily.

Nicholas looked meaningfully behind Isabel at the Eastons, but Isabel ignored the look and they remained unintroduced.

'You have enjoyed yourself this morning, I trust?'

'Yes, Lady Grangeshield, very much,' Nicholas said, turning towards the book as if to comment on it but then giving up on the gesture. Isabel, usually so astute in these matters, missed this danger signal. She was still too upset about the Carenthetian table.

'Do you know what this table is?' Isabel asked, pointing to the table on which Nicholas's feet had been perched shortly before. She had lost her inner battle not to discuss this issue.

'It's a table. I think that pretty much covers it,' Nicholas replied shortly. Isabel again missed the significance of the shortness of his reply along with his tone of voice; she was too focused on the Carenthetian table.

'It is a Carenthetian table. There are only ten of its kind remaining in the world today. It is priceless. Yet, you see fit to put your feet on it! Your feet! On the Carenthetian table!'

'Yes, well, there we are,' Nicholas replied. 'Is this where I get another lecture on courtesy from you? Given that you know nothing about this subject yourself?'

He said this so sharply that Isabel paused on the edge of her forthcoming tirade. Nicholas said nothing more but waited in a furious silence.

Isabel was now hard at work wondering what was wrong. As the silence continued and spread out horizontally around them Isabel unfolded her fan and held it spread out horizontally in front of her in order to look down on it as she said, 'I see I am at fault in some matter. If you could be so courteous as to inform me of the issue of contention, I would gladly take immediate steps to set the matter aright, Mr Raspero.'

Nicholas took a deep breath, then said, 'You quite deliberately refuse to introduce me to your guardians after all this time, while you do nothing but talk about your furniture!'

Isabel understood then and everything snapped into focus. 'You are quite right, Mr Raspero. You should most certainly have been introduced to my guardians by now.' Using her fan to make a sweeping gesture she said, 'Mr Raspero, this is Lord Bentley Easton and Lady Dacia Easton. Uncle Bentley, Aunt Dacia, please allow me to present Mr Nicholas Raspero.'

They all said how delighted they were, while Isabel folded up her fan. She turned back to Nicholas and waited in silence for him to speak, looking at him wide-eyed.

Nicholas took another deep breath. 'Lady Grangeshield, I would suggest that we finish our conversation from yesterday and then I must go.'

'Yes, I quite agree,' Isabel said. 'We must certainly finish our conversation and I can only thank you for your courtesy in waiting for me this morning.' She noted carefully that her best manners had little effect on Nicholas, who still seemed to be imbued with a spirit of dangerously defiant independence.

'I would suggest that we talk outside,' Nicholas said, 'as it is such a nice day, but of course we can talk indoors if you prefer.' Nicholas wanted to be outside with the free sky overhead, not cooped up inside with furniture that was not supposed to even be used!

'That is an excellent idea,' said Isabel, who was going to agree to everything Nicholas said until his mood changed. She turned towards the door. 'Let us go outside.'

They all trooped toward the East Door, Benson following discreetly behind. Isabel ordered Benson to bring shawls and blankets. She eyed the weather as she stepped outside as if it were an animal that might turn dangerous. She led Nicholas to the Grotto of Peace, while the Eastons discreetly sat down out of earshot but where they could keep the couple fully in view.

Isabel took some time appearing to settle into her chair, but in reality she was considering her options. She settled on the bare-faced lie.

'My guardians strictly forbade me to introduce them to you, Mr Raspero,' she told Nicholas.

Nicholas took this on board with some surprise. 'But why?' he asked eventually.

Isabel sighed. 'They are my chaperones, Mr Raspero, and I cannot oppose them in a matter of this kind. I hope you understand the limits to which I can affect their conduct when it comes to being my chaperones.'

'Ah, I see,' Nicholas said awkwardly. 'Right.'

'Why they should stipulate such a condition I am not entirely sure. Perhaps they feel that they are more effective chaperones in certain circumstances such as this if they have no direct acquaintance with you. But that is only a guess. I did not enquire too closely for that would be improper. I cannot, for obvious reasons, take too close an interest in the way in which my chaperones formulate such principles, as I am sure you understand.'

'Ah, yes, so you can't subvert their chaperoning in any way, I understand,' Nicholas said even more awkwardly than before.

'Precisely so, Mr Raspero. I cannot argue or question too closely in a matter of such importance as this.'

She spoke so sweetly and gently that Nicholas was starting to feel guilty for having been so abrupt earlier in the library.

'I see, Lady Grangeshield. Yes, it is all clear to me now.' Nicholas obviously felt that it was time to move on. Seeing this, Isabel turned up the heat.

'I felt myself to have been placed at an enormous disadvantage yesterday, and even more so this morning, in being obliged to conform to a requirement that placed you, my guest, in such a position as to have felt slighted by your reception. I am sure you must realise how I must feel about all this.'

Nicholas was now regretting having said anything about anything. 'This is now all very clear to me, Lady Grangeshield,' he said, giving Isabel a keen eagle-eyed look to show how clear it all was to him now. 'Yes, very clear.'

Isabel, however, was not letting him off so easily. She was going to make him sweat before she was done, so she turned the heat up even further. 'Naturally, as you must understand, when I realised the distress my thoughtless guardians had caused you by their incomprehensible policy, I immediately rebelled against their arbitrary and authoritarian decree and introduced you on the spot. I hoped in this way to make amends for the injustice that had been done to you.'

'Yes, well, there we are,' Nicholas said.

Isabel let the shawl slip from her shoulders as if the sunlight was warming her more than she had anticipated. Her low-cut dress with a sheathing of fine transparent gauze around her shoulders and arms was now encircled by the shawl tucked into her shapely elbows.

'You must think badly of me, Mr Raspero.'

'No, not at all,' Nicholas said fervently to the most beautiful girl he had ever seen in his life, 'I couldn't ever possibly think badly of you, Lady Grangeshield.'

'Then you understand that the strict policy of my guardians in this matter resulted in the way you have been treated, about which you have so rightly complained, and that I had nothing to do with it.' Isabel's warm mahogany brown eyes gazed into Nicholas's cool cloud-grey eyes.

'Absolutely,' Nicholas agreed without hesitation.

The Eastons continued to watch from afar, entirely and blissfully unaware of how they were being misrepresented. Isabel now turned her attention to seeing that things remained that way.

'I am now in a rather difficult position, Mr Raspero. You have quite naturally protested at the shabby way in which my guardians have treated you, and I have been obliged out of my natural sympathy with the justice of your cause to take sides with you over this issue. What my guardians will say to me over the way I have behaved I dare not think. But I cannot possibly prevent you from making everything much worse by confronting my guardians over their policy in this matter. It is after all your right, and I cannot stand in the way of you exercising your right.'

Nicholas was having difficulty in following all this, but it was clear to him that he should not make anything worse for Isabel than he already had. 'Naturally, Lady Grangeshield,' he said cautiously, not wanting to appear slow by not understanding everything that she had just said, 'as you are my hostess I would not dream of placing you in a difficult position.'

'But you are only being kind,' Isabel said.

'No, not at all, so you said you don't want me to confront your guardians about their policy in this matter,' Nicholas said even more cautiously than before, trying to work out what she meant, 'but what kind of confrontation do you mean exactly? I mean, I don't for a moment dispute their right to make such decisions as they see fit while fulfilling their duty as your chaperones.'

'But if you say anything at all to them about this matter it might indeed be seen in such a light as this,' Isabel said, 'but I cannot possibly prevent you from speaking to them about your complaint given the way in which they have treated you.'

'Ah, I see,' Nicholas said, understanding what she was getting at, 'well, in that case, I simply won't say a word to them about anything. We can forget the whole thing.'

'But if you sacrifice your own rights in this dispute, Mr Raspero, it will place me at a disadvantage as your hostess.'

'Oh, it really shouldn't be a dispute,' Nicholas said hastily, alarmed at being thought to be objecting to matters of chaperoning, 'I mean, they have a perfect right to make such a decision, of course, and I really have no complaints about anything. I mean, chaperones have a solemn responsibility, I mean, it can't be said seriously enough, what they do, no-one should object to their decisions, I really wouldn't myself. Good on them, I would say.'

'Do you really think so, Mr Raspero?'

'Absolutely,' Nicholas said firmly. 'It's exactly what I think.'

'Are you sure, Mr Raspero? You are quite sure that you will not say a single word to them about their refusal to allow me to introduce you to them?'

'Definitely not,' Nicholas said, racing like a horse to the finishing line, 'I most certainly will not say a single word to your guardians about this matter. It is closed, finished, over and done with.'

'That will help me greatly in my own dealings with them on this matter,' Isabel said with an air of relief. 'I will say to them merely that I could not allow you to remain at such a disadvantage as the one under which they had placed you. They cannot condemn me for courtesy. As you will say nothing to them about the matter, it can all be left behind without any further fuss.'

'So that's settled then,' Nicholas said hopefully.

'Yes, it is settled, Mr Raspero,' Isabel said, settling herself back in her chair and pulling her shawl back around her shoulders. 'Now I do believe we may continue our conversation.'

Nicholas cast his mind back to where he had been when they had been interrupted yesterday. 'Shall I begin with when I left Grangeshield House on Sunday,' he asked, 'and go on from there?'

'That is an excellent plan, Mr Raspero,' Isabel agreed, still all sweetness and light.

So Nicholas set forth to explain how he had arrived at the Thorburn Bridge without knowing where he had been going, and continued on from there. It was not long before Isabel was interrupting him, and it was not long before she was casting a critical eye over much of his strategic thinking and tactical execution. She did not actually say she could have done better herself, but the implication was there. Nicholas said nothing. He was descended from Daniel of Sacramento, one of the greatest military commanders of history, and he had been raised on detailed accounts of Daniel's military campaigns that were not in the history books, but he had also been raised never to speak of these matters, so he raised no defence against Isabel's attacks.

The use of Bailey, *a child*, was a matter of some headshaking for Isabel; Nicholas made no attempt to argue or defend himself but ploughed on regardless. He only held Isabel in check twice that day: the first time came when Isabel wanted to know what *Rasparos seakrit* might be and Nicholas told her very coldly that he got fed up with being asked questions like that. Isabel immediately dropped the subject.

When Nicholas came to the part of the story where he looked through the window and saw Nevsky and his party guests, he tried to skip over the scene of debauchery he had witnessed but Isabel was having none of it. She insisted on knowing everything, reminding a reluctant Nicholas that he had promised to tell her everything, and Nicholas obeyed her in some embarrassment. Isabel then, as Nicholas had known she would, thoroughly rebuked him for having witnessed such a scene. It was one thing to be a burglar, she said, but quite another to be a voyeur, and to be both at the same time was surely to be the lowest of the low, to belong to the dregs of humanity if such a creature could even be said to belong to humanity at all. She wanted to know if Nicholas was now properly ashamed of what he had done; Nicholas rolled his eyes in reply, exasperated by all this and simply shook his head in silence. Isabel also wanted to know if Nicholas had taken a *good look* at Lady Montlait in her undergarments; definitely not, Nicholas lied. Isabel did not look convinced and wondered at that point if her opinion of Nicholas could sink any lower than it had. *Could one sink any lower than the very bottom of the gutter?* she asked herself as if thinking out loud, and she then explained that she was asking this question because the very bottom of the gutter was surely the only place in the world where Nicholas could feel at home.

He felt incapable of defending himself against her attacks for a variety of reasons. One was the endlessly fascinating way her lips moved as she formed words. Another was the way she tapped her fan on her knuckles, an ordinary action in some respects but the way she did it seemed somehow astonishingly elegant. The way she looked at him, even when disapprovingly, her eyes, her hair, her sweetly formed face, her shapely body and the way she turned her head, were all further reasons for his helplessness in the face of her attacks. His emotions were somehow just out of reach, leaving him unable to be even mildly annoyed at anything she said. Nicholas kept his face as carefully impassive as he could while he looked at her, not knowing that Isabel had seen that exact impassive face on the more smitten of her many admirers so many times before as to know exactly the feelings which lay behind it.

Nicholas weathered this tirade and then proceeded with his story. When it came to the snakes Isabel fell silent and remained silent. She didn't want to hang around in a part of the story that had snakes in it. Snakes! Isabel pulled the shawl up around her head and wrapped it around her face so that only her eyes were peeking out of a narrow slit in the midst of the hiding place of her shawl. Isabel had a horror of snakes. She even passed by the mention of Nicholas's uses of Lady Montlait's dress and undergarment on the floor without any adverse judgement on Nicholas despite the delicious chance it offered to spit and roast Nicholas yet again.

The second time Nicholas held Isabel in check that day was when Isabel wanted to know what the wand combinations in Whittington's letter to his son had been. Nicholas gave her one very cold look and she asked no more about it.

When Nicholas reported Nevsky's words *like I already told you, Mr Raspero, I never refuse a challenge,* Isabel wanted to know when Nevsky had told Nicholas this and as it had been on the occasion of their first duel Nicholas then had to tell her the story of this first duel with Nevsky in all the detail she insisted upon. Then he returned to his duel of Final

Combat with Nevsky. Isabel's hands whitened in fury where she gripped her fan as Nicholas reported Nevsky's characterisation of her in the duelling arena towards the end.

After he had told her of Nevsky's last words, namely that he had refused Nicholas's challenge, whereupon Nicholas had immediately killed him, Isabel declared, 'So Nevsky died a coward.'

Nicholas had already considered the issue and his answer was prompt. 'No, he died an animal. Only a man or woman can be brave or cowardly.'

'An animal cannot speak or reason, Mr Raspero,' Isabel pointed out. 'Nevsky died a coward!' She almost spat the words out.

'It is a philosophical point,' Nicholas conceded. He then continued with how he had recruited Bailey to spread the false reports of Nevsky being killed by the man with golden hair, who would then be equated with the Lord of the North of the letter which Nicholas had placed in Nevsky's pocket. He then ended with the next day, when he had sent Isabel a letter and given Bailey the remaining part of his money. 'And so my tale is done,' Nicholas said with a slight air of relief. It would have been done much quicker with a less argumentative audience but Nicholas was not going to complain given that his audience could not have been more beautiful.

Isabel bowed her head, opened up her fan and contemplated the markings on it. She looked up to see Nicholas watching her and said, 'You have kept your promise to tell me everything, Mr Raspero. I see you are a man of your word.' Isabel was far too subtle to thank Nicholas directly.

It was over, Nicholas realised. He had done what he came to do. He felt as far from Isabel as he had ever done and to stay here any longer would be only to dwell on the distance he would always be from her. It was time to go.

'And now I am leaving, Lady Grangeshield,' Nicholas said, straightening up in his chair.

'Leaving, Mr Raspero?' Isabel asked. 'What do you mean?'

'I mean that I'm going on my way,' Nicholas said by way of reply.

Isabel didn't want to let go of him that easily. 'But surely you are not leaving now, Mr Raspero.'

Nicholas was already standing up. 'I would like to thank you for all your hospitality, Lady Grangeshield.'

Isabel remained seated in order to get Nicholas back into his chair. 'I quite understand that you will be leaving very shortly, Mr Raspero. But this is very abrupt of you.'

'I will see myself out, Lady Grangeshield,' Nicholas said. 'Goodbye.' He set off then and Isabel was obliged to stand up and follow him. Nicholas stopped by the Eastons to make his farewells. They had arisen courteously and before Isabel had a chance to say anything Nicholas was walking towards the driveway on his way to the Rose Garden door.

Isabel trotted quickly after him, trying to think of something to say. She remembered then that Benson believed that Mr Raspero had travelled on his first visit to Grangeshield House by the highly unusual expedient of walking.

'Please allow me to provide you with a carriage for your return journey,' Isabel offered.

'No, I want to walk, thanks.'

'But it is really no trouble,' Isabel insisted.

'Neither is walking.'

'But to refuse my offer of the use of my carriage would seem to be more trouble than simply to accept it.'

Nicholas thought about this, trying to come up with an answer to it. Eventually he just did the best he could. 'To change my mind about walking would be more trouble than the walking itself.' He thought it didn't sound too bad.

Isabel was infuriated by his stubbornness. 'You do understand, Mr Raspero, that it is very rude of you to refuse my offer of help. But I will say no more. It would be rude of me in my turn if I did.'

'So that's settled then,' Nicholas said.

Isabel immediately broke her pledge to say no more. 'It is quite all right that you have thrown my offer of the use of my carriage back in my face. I can assure you that I am not deeply offended by your brutal selfishness. I have offered to help, you have bluntly refused my assistance. You are of course quite within your rights to refuse, as I am quite within my rights to make this suggestion. Or perhaps you would argue that I should not have lifted a single finger on your behalf?'

Nicholas gave up then. 'All right, Lady Grangeshield. I would be happy to return home in your carriage. Perhaps you could have it made ready for me now.'

'But of course, Mr Raspero,' Isabel said, pleased to have won the battle.

The instructions having been given, Isabel waited with Nicholas, her guardians standing to one side.

She felt abruptly nervous. She didn't want Nicholas to go. She stole glances at him standing there, perfectly relaxed, his hand on the hilt of his wand, looking about him as if he, not she, was the ruler of this domain. She cast about for reasons to get him to stay but nothing came to mind, and time was running out. The carriage was already on its way to them. It was in the air before them, descending to the ground.

A feeling of panic gripped Isabel tightly. Nicholas was leaving and when would she see him again? She did not ask herself why this mattered to her. The carriage was already settling onto the ground in front of them.

'Mr Raspero,' she said abruptly, 'have you heard of the robbery at Fordham's the other day?'

'The robbery at Fordham's?' Nicholas queried, turning to her from his absorbing contemplation of the sweeping lines of the Balladur flying carriage. 'No, I haven't. I've had a lot on lately.' He gave her a conspirator's grin, which Isabel ignored.

The driver of the flying carriage came down to the ground and stood at attention, ready and waiting in the red and gold livery of the Grangeshield estate.

Isabel told Nicholas of how the twenty or so patrons of the Fordham's restaurant had found themselves taken prisoner by an armed band who had robbed them, even going so far as to strip the rings off their fingers. 'And of course it could have been even worse,' she concluded.

'They planned it all that way in advance,' Nicholas replied, understanding her implication, 'so they would only have so much of the law after them, not a whole stampeding country.' He held out his thumb and forefinger opened apart to measure out the *so much of the law* he meant.

'But what if I had been there, Mr Raspero?' Isabel said, turning to him. 'Would they have kept to their plan?'

Nicholas's blood turned cold as he considered how Isabel's beauty could make anyone lose their heads and forget even their own names. 'You were not there, Lady Grangeshield,' he said eventually, not able to think of anything else to say, but his attention was gripped by what Isabel was saying, exactly as she intended it to be.

'I have been invited to the Randell's party on Thursday,' Isabel said, 'but I am sure you will laugh at my apprehensions about the lawlessness abroad in this country as I contemplate attending this party. You must think I am very foolish to worry so, Mr Raspero.'

Nicholas was himself starting to feel apprehensive at the thought of a defenceless Isabel being at the mercy of a gang of armed robbers, and it mattered not at all that this apprehension was entirely irrational. 'It is never foolish to pay attention to your personal security, Lady Grangeshield. It is foolish not to.'

'I cannot possibly ask you to do more for me than you have already done, Mr Raspero.'

Nicholas looked at the Eastons, who were standing right next to them listening to all of this. 'I have done nothing for you, Lady Grangeshield,' he pointed out pointedly.

'I see you choose not to help me,' Isabel said as if resigned to an unspeakable fate in a lawless world.

'Help you how?' Nicholas queried.

'I could not help but wonder if you would agree to be my escort to the Randell's party on Thursday in order that my fears could be laid to rest. But I understand that I could not possibly ask you to do so much for me.'

'Well, I like parties,' Nicholas said, trying to carefully avoid saying how much he liked even more the idea of being Isabel's escort, 'so going to a party would suit me fine.'

The driver of the carriage remained waiting like a statue in the red and gold livery of the Grangeshield estate.

Isabel turned to Nicholas in surprise. 'Are you agreeing to be my escort to the Randell's party, Mr Raspero?'

'Definitely,' Nicholas said.

'I must first equip you with new clothes, Mr Raspero,' Isabel said.

'What's wrong with my clothes?' Nicholas asked, looking down at his robe.

Isabel let this question pass by unanswered. 'I will be much obliged to you if you could come here tomorrow morning at eleven o'clock,' Isabel said. 'I will send a carriage for you. A tailor will be here to take your measurements. We will have new clothes ready for you the following day, which you may wear to the party.'

'My other robe's in the wash,' Nicholas said, 'maybe that would do. It's better than this one.'

Isabel had seen his other robe and as far as she was concerned it could stay in the wash and never return to the daylight world of men and women ever again. 'I will supply you with new clothes, Mr Raspero. Surely you cannot object?'

Nicholas considered this. 'I need to wear these new clothes to go to the party?'

'So that is settled,' Isabel declared. 'You will come here at eleven o'clock tomorrow morning.'

Nicholas resigned himself to his fate. At least he would see Isabel again. 'Very well, Lady Grangeshield, it shall be as you say,' he said.

'But of course it will,' Isabel said, as if surprised that anything else could even be implied. 'I will see you tomorrow at eleven.'

Nicholas looked at the Eastons, said goodbye to them and they said goodbye back; said goodbye to Isabel, who merely gazed at him over the top of her fan in farewell, and went and ascended into the carriage. It soon took off and he found himself flying back home.

Isabel stood where she was and watched the flying carriage depart. She didn't move until it was out of sight. The Eastons exchanged glances but said nothing.

Nicholas stretched out and took in his new surroundings. The flying carriage had four sofas facing inwards, arranged like the sides of a square; they were upholstered in soft green leather and positioned around a large square oak table with the Grangeshield crest of lions embedded as solid gold filling in the tabletop. Inset lamps in the walls, drinks cabinets, bookcases all in rosewood and a bathroom all decorated in red and gold formed the picture of luxury; it was as much a flying home as a flying carriage. Nicholas leaned back and closed his eyes, awash in the feelings of softening pleasure evoked in him by all this luxury of a world which had swallowed him whole.

TWENTY-SEVEN

The Turn and Turnabout of Miss Angela Ashton

10:30 AM, Monday 18 July 1544 A.F.

Angela sat at her desk writing a letter to Nicholas. She chose her words carefully, yet with a feeling of freedom and abandon. She felt as if she were stepping out onto the floor to dance at a merry party.

She had broken off relations with Lord Foxley, and she was currently a free woman. This was what she wanted Nicholas to know. As she came to the end of the letter, she signed it merely "Angela". He would understand what this meant. Once she had suggested to him that they be on first name terms and he had refused, saying that she should not be on such familiar terms with him, while she was still on such familiar terms with Lord Foxley. Angela had not properly understood him at the time, but she had come to. She could not become Nicholas's mistress, while she was still Lord Foxley's.

Angela was starting to change and she could feel it. It was as if her life since her father had died was a level of permafrost that was beginning to thaw. Long forgotten memories were starting to re-surface, such as the time when she had been with her father in the garden burning rubbish on the fire; there had been a large crack as a branch sent up a shower of sparks and she had ducked behind her father's back, clutching onto his left arm, while peering around his side at the danger. She had felt happy to feel so warm, safe and protected, and she remembered now what happiness had been like. Her mind flew up with a whirring of joyful wings from that memory and, like a bird alighting on a branch, came to where she was now writing a letter to Nicholas.

She had always been well treated as a child, even if they had never had any money and her father had been away so much. She had been eager and curious and cheerful, laughing as she ran along the road on an errand. With her blue eyes and blonde hair and perfect doll's face she had been nicknamed *the little angel*. Jolly had once told her in one of his more expansive moods that he had chosen the name *Angela* from her childhood nickname.

Along with the good memories came the painful ones. A few days ago she had awoken crying — how strange was that? Yet, at the same time she felt that none of it mattered any more. She herself remained unaffected by what had been done to her. She could still be the little angel once again; everything since was merely an interlude, a temporary enslavement. The girl she had been could return.

She read the letter again that she had written to Nicholas and she found then to her surprise that her hands were shaking. She put the letter down and stood up and walked around the room to try to calm down. She brought herself to face the main point she was avoiding. It was no use pretending that Nicholas would be just another client, an interlude between her main business. She could not become his mistress just to ensure his continued protection. Once she had gone to him, she would never be able to leave him. She sensed this somehow, she could feel it in her stomach. She knew that he would be the last client.

She looked at the gifts spread around the floor, sent by all those who had been waiting for her to end things with Foxley. They varied in value but there was one in particular that caught her attention. She picked it up off the floor and inspected it for the twentieth time. It was a necklace, of gold plates studded with gemstones. It was worth a good twenty thousand strada, she was sure of it, and how much money did she currently have? Having sold Foxley's gifts and invested the money, she now had one hundred and forty three thousand strada. She also owned the apartment she lived in; the ownership papers had been sent to her the day after her meeting with Tagalong. She had enough money to live a life of modest gentility, but it would not bring her the luxury she craved. Would Nicholas ever have money? What kind of man turned his back on twenty million strada? If he had taken that money he could have had her, all of her, and she would have gone off with him without a backward glance. She felt angry at Nicholas then. Why should she choose him? What kind of life would a life of modest means be like for her, a woman accustomed to luxury? Her hands were still shaking and she was frightened.

She put the necklace on and immediately she became calm and still. She considered the necklace carefully. The man who had sent her this necklace meant business, and it was the kind of business that she understood. She looked again at the name of the sender: Lord Weatherby. She knew of him. He was very rich. He would do.

She knew now what she had to do and she did it without another moment's thought. She took the letter she had written to Nicholas, crumpled it up and threw it into the wastepaper basket. She wrote another letter, beginning "Dear Lord Weatherby", inviting him to attend her in her dressing room after tomorrow night's performance. After finishing and addressing the letter, she looked at all the remaining gifts lying around on the floor. She would have to return them to their senders. It was a wrench but this was business and she could not afford to lose her good name as a businesswoman.

She left the room to post the letter to Lord Weatherby, not looking back at the crumpled letter lying in the waste paper basket.

TWENTY-EIGHT

The Elliptical Dialogue Between Mr Nicholas Raspero and Lord Bentley Easton

11:30 AM, Tuesday 19 July 1544 A.F.

The tailor was a man with a large moustache forming a bracket around his mouth; he was dressed in fine clothes worn in an almost careless fashion, the seeming carelessness no doubt the fruit of his applied mastery of all things sartorial. He seemed deeply unimpressed by the mere physical existence of Nicholas, which he measured with his measuring tape as if Nicholas was all wrong, muttering what sounded like expressions of shock, horror and loathing under his breath, while every now and then saying numbers and terms such as "Capurdem 39" out loud which his assistant, a thin young man with shifty eyes, wrote down as carefully as if they were the pronouncements of an oracle. Nicholas stood there obediently raising his arms and adopting various positions as instructed, feeling that he was in some kind of play, although his audience was, in fact, waiting next door as he had disrobed in order to be measured by the tailor.

The measurements done, they went next door where Isabel was waiting, along with the Eastons, Benson and two or three eagerly attentive fashion-following servants who had sneaked into the room by somehow pretending that their presence was required.

Once the tailor had finished taking his measurements, there followed a lengthy and detailed discussion between Isabel and the tailor of the clothes Isabel was commissioning: the materials, the colours, the cut of the cloth, design and appearance, the buttons, sleeves, thread, and a variety of other aspects of said clothes which were referred to by obscure and incomprehensible names that Nicholas had never heard before; he understood then why people's eyes often glazed over when he was explaining to them some of the finer details of wandlore.

It soon became clear to Nicholas that his presence was superfluous. Nicholas was not one to surrender to circumstances so he made his way over to where Lord Easton was standing and asked abruptly: 'Will you show me around the garden?'

Lord Easton was taken aback by the peremptory delivery of this unexpected request, but his boundless courtesy was equal to any challenge. 'But of course, I would be delighted to show you around the garden,' he replied.

Taking his new duties seriously, Lord Easton provided the necessary commentary on features of the garden as they strolled with Nicholas as a politely attentive audience. After a while, at Nicholas's suggestion, they sat down.

There was a silence during which Nicholas's eyes shifted uneasily about the garden. After a while he said, very cautiously, 'I'm sure you must be wondering about all the time I have been spending here at Grangeshield House lately.'

'No, not at all,' Lord Easton said hastily, praying that Nicholas wouldn't suddenly confess that he was Nevsky's killer. Lord Easton didn't want to know, but now that he knew, he most certainly didn't want Nicholas to know that he knew. Lord Easton placed his hand on the bench out of sight in order to surreptitiously cross his fingers, for even though he was not a superstitious man he needed to do something to calm his nerves.

'But surely you must have wondered a little bit,' Nicholas commented suspiciously.

'It is indeed true, Mr Raspero, that I have not been so fortunate as to have been made acquainted with the reasons for your recent visits,' Lord Easton replied evasively, praying once again that Nicholas wouldn't suddenly take it into his head to confess the murderous truth and readying himself to divert Nicholas from any such confession.

'As these reasons are highly confidential, I cannot tell you why I have been coming here.'

Lord Easton was deeply (and privately) relieved. Not appearing to know anything seemed far safest. 'I most certainly will ask no questions, as these reasons are so confidential,' he said.

'I think that is best,' Nicholas said, and Lord Easton heartily (and privately) agreed. 'But I do wish you to know that everything is over and done with now and the matter which we cannot discuss, no longer exists.'

'Then as it no longer exists, we need not even refer to it,' Lord Easton commented.

They sat for a while in silence then Nicholas unexpectedly asked, 'Have you ever looked at the sunrise without thinking of yourself, Lord Easton?'

'I beg your pardon?'

'It's difficult to look at the world, even in one of its most splendid aspects, and even then not think of yourself. Wouldn't you agree?'

'We are all egoists,' Lord Easton said cautiously, 'if that's what you mean, Mr Raspero.'

'So you see my point?' Nicholas asked him.

'Not really,' Lord Easton confessed.

'Well, has Lady Grangeshield ever made up clothes for her escort to a party before?'

Lord Easton frowned, as if trying to remember. 'Not that I recall, Mr Raspero,' he said with the utmost seriousness, desperately trying not to laugh.

'Do you know what the definition of a gentleman is, Lord Easton?'

'I know of several,' Lord Easton said as cautiously as before.

'It is to be able to look at a sunrise without thinking of yourself.'

Lord Easton was struck by this. 'That is an interesting definition.'

'My grandfather taught it to me.'

'It goes to the heart of the matter.'

'Exactly. It does. But how can I look at this current situation without thinking of myself?'

'What do you mean?'

'Why is Lady Grangeshield having clothes made up for me? How can

I understand this if I do not think of myself? It's not happening without me being present, is it?'

'I think you can only understand this by referring to your presence,' Lord Easton replied, wondering how to tactfully tell Mr Raspero that his clothes were shabby, very shabby indeed. 'But surely this is not a sunrise, Mr Raspero.'

'It all comes to the same thing,' Nicholas observed cryptically and said nothing more.

For the first time Lord Easton found himself considering Nicholas as a young man in a large world, rather than as a mathematical function which had erased Nevsky from the scene. He understood then that Nicholas was trying to figure out things as he went along and Isabel's interest in him was one of several mysteries which he faced, but he also understood that he could not fully enter into a dialogue with Nicholas without revealing what he knew and that he would not do, but he had to say something.

'The confidential matter to which you referred which no longer exists, must be the source of Isabel's interest in you,' Lord Easton said carefully, 'and so it is that she wishes you to be her escort to this party and so it is that she wishes you to be properly attired. Isabel is clothing you in this manner, not to make you happy, but to make Isabel happy. There is really nothing more to the matter than this.'

Nicholas considered this for a while, his head tilted to one side. 'I see your point, Lord Easton, but I also see much more than this. However, it does come down to a question of knowledge.'

Cryptic as this closing comment was, Lord Easton understood it perfectly. He knew that Nicholas knew that he knew what Nevsky had done because Nicholas would have read the Nevsky-Grangeshield Memorandum of Understanding; yet Nicholas did not know that he knew that Nicholas had killed Nevsky and this was why Isabel was paying such attention to him. It did indeed come down to a question of knowledge. But Lord Easton had not been the chaperone of Isabel Grangeshield all this time for nothing and he knew what this was all about deep down. In the same instant that this came into focus he saw what he should do.

'Do you seek this knowledge to which you refer, Mr Raspero?' he asked.

'What do you mean?'

'You are really asking what Isabel's opinion of you is as a young man who is the recipient of the attentions of a beautiful woman, are you not?'

Nicholas blushed bright red. 'Um, well, ah, recipient, yes, recipient, well, I suppose … ' he trailed off into silence.

Lord Easton had his duty to perform and he performed it. 'Isabel most certainly has no interest in you as just another of her many admirers. I am sorry to shatter your illusions, if such they are, but you are utterly unfit to presume to receive her attentions in any way that your imagination might conceive in your wilder moments. Do not read more into these clothes than anything other than the clothes which are all they are. They are not symbolic of a deeper affection.'

'Well, of course not, I mean, I never —' Nicholas began to say.

Lord Easton cut him off. 'You are not a man to whom Isabel is directing her affections because, to put it bluntly, you are not in her social circle. These clothes are a gift Isabel is providing to you and it is a gift which is nothing more than a gift. They are, at the end of the day, only clothes.'

'Absolutely,' Nicholas agreed hastily, still blushing bright red. 'I mean, absolutely, of course, yes, it's just that … '

'Have I spoken too bluntly, Mr Raspero? While I do not know of the confidential matter, to which you referred, I do indeed know of other matters and it is of these that I have spoken.'

'No, not at all, Lord Easton, you have not spoken too bluntly,' Nicholas said as composedly as he could, feeling that he had been gutted like a fish being prepared to be baked in the oven, 'as I have to say, yes, I suppose I was wondering, now that you mention it, but that's cleared everything up, I mean, no, not at all, yes, they are only clothes and I have to say that everything is very clear to me now. Yes, very clear.' Nicholas nodded like a sage on a mountain who has grasped the meaning of the mountain.

Benson was making his way over to them then and they watched him approach, their conversation at an end. Isabel had sent him to bring Nicholas back to her and her tailor for further clothes-making activity and so they set off back to the house, each with their own thoughts.

Isabel gave them both a sharp look as they appeared as if wondering what mischief they had been up to but she made no comment other than to instruct Nicholas as to where he was to stand while she and the tailor conversed in their indecipherable language. There followed a second round of Nicholas playing the tailor's dummy while matters proceeded to a conclusion. The tailor shook his head emphatically on hearing that one set of clothes were to be delivered in two days' time. It was impossible! He even laughed, and his assistant also laughed after a moment of watching his master's laughter inattentively before belatedly realising it had to be seconded and amplified by his own laughter; Isabel then insisted as imperiously as only Isabel could insist; the tailor refused even more emphatically than before. His objections now, however, largely seemed to be concerned with the cost of meeting such a deadline and so by dint of driving his prices sky-high and complaining every step of the way he eventually agreed to Isabel's deadline, the artist and the merchant at peace in the tailor's soul; the enormously rich Isabel was as always indifferent to a mere matter of money, agreeing to an outrageously inflated price tag with a dismissive wave of her hand, and so the deal was done.

The tailor having departed, it was time for a very late lunch as it was by now two-thirty in the afternoon, after which they retired to the Red Drawing Room. Nicholas decided it would soon be time for him to leave which roused Isabel into a state of concern: *but surely Nicholas was staying for dinner?*

No, Nicholas was about to depart so he would not be staying for dinner as it happened, but Isabel was now joined by Lady Easton who commented that she had wished to improve her acquaintance with Nicholas before he left so surely he was not leaving just yet? Nicholas was put on the spot at the centre of their collective gaze, which impaled him like three radial spokes of an imaginary wheel, so he wound up saying that of course he would be happy to stay for dinner, and so it was that Lady Easton questioned him at length about his background, his family, his upbringing, his education and his future prospects. It was during this examination of Nicholas's life and character that Lady Easton ceased to fear him. Up until then, whenever she had looked at Nicholas she had seen him surrounded, so to speak, by a pile of dead bodies, but during this prolonged observation of his relentless ordinariness the pile of dead bodies shrank away into the ground and Lady Easton was no longer afraid of Nicholas Raspero.

She might as well have been vetting him as a possible suitor of Isabel, and Lord Easton kept an uneasy silence throughout, disapproving but not sure how to intervene. Isabel for her part paid close attention to everything that was being said, while appearing to ignore everything that was being said in favour of studying the design of her fan. Dinner came and went and then they were all back in the Red Drawing Room.

Nicholas was by now telling Lady Easton about Alexandre's travels before coming to Anglashia. 'He had fun,' Nicholas said. 'He would sign up as a guard in a blue uniform and cap.' Nicholas made gestures through the air with his hands to illustrate what this had looked like, a cheerful grin on his face. Isabel listened to this very suspiciously. She wondered if this had been entirely proper behaviour on Alexandre's part, inclining to the view that it had not been entirely proper behaviour on Alexandre's part. She was also irritated by Nicholas's evident amusement. Nicholas looked like he was enjoying himself much too much as he told the tale of his wayward grandfather.

'But surely I have not heard you correctly, Mr Raspero,' Isabel said eventually, in a voice loud enough to peremptorily disconnect even a pair of thoughts joined by Aristotle himself, 'are you saying that your grandfather performed menial tasks?' She glared at Nicholas as if to say that now was the time to deny this.

'Have you ever picked up a pair of gloves from the table, Lady Grangeshield?' Nicholas replied without hesitation, prepared for this fight. 'If so, then you have yourself performed a menial task, have you not?'

Isabel rotated her fan in her hands as if grinding a world beneath a millstone and said, 'I have never picked up a pair of gloves from a table for money, Mr Raspero.'

'That is only because money had rained down from the sky the night before,' Nicholas said promptly, 'but that is not my point. Work is done one way or the other, is it not? Or is it menial for you to even consider this matter?' He raised his eyebrows to show that he had finished forming his question and it was now time for Isabel to reply.

'But I am sure that I did not hear you correctly before,' Isabel said calmly, her fan half-opened as if she had paused in mid-thought with her mind caught by a passing distraction, 'when you said that your grandfather worked as a guard for the Meridian Line because such menial work would be an indication of a low character on his part. But perhaps your point is that your grandfather is a low character?'

Nicholas groaned out loud and leaned back in his chair as if overwhelmed by his weighty thoughts. 'You will never meet my grandfather, I am sure, Lady Grangeshield, but he is a fierce gentleman all too aware of his noble heritage as the second son of the twenty-fourth Baron of Raspero. You would be very ill advised to call him a low character.'

'But it is not I who call him a low character, it is you who do so,' Isabel immediately protested. 'You are the one who has told us these things. Or do you deny now what you have said previously?'

'Oh, for Heaven's sake,' Nicholas said, starting to become genuinely irritated, 'he was travelling the world on his own account taking work where he found it. What is your problem, anyway?' Nicholas was also aggrieved that he had been making conversation only to now be subjected to such scrutiny. It did not seem to him to be fair.

Reading his mood Isabel immediately backtracked. 'But you misunderstand me, Mr Raspero. My question was not concerning the impeccable heritage of your grandfather but your re-telling of his voyages. It was your representation that was under question, not your grandfather's conduct.'

Nicholas felt that his enemies were multiplying around him. 'Well, why I should answer any questions at all I don't know,' he said truculently, ready to start quarrelling if he was criticised just one more time. 'So what am I doing wrong? Making conversation? Is that it?'

Isabel faced a choice between soft-pedalling even more to defuse the situation, or going forward into conflict; it was a split-second choice and she made it on the spot. 'I would not say that you do everything wrong, Mr Raspero, but I would most certainly say that you have represented the conduct of your grandfather in such a way as to cast doubt as to the wiseness of his choices. But surely you will not blame me for your own failings?'

In effect Isabel had just slapped him and Nicholas straightened up in his chair as if about to take his feet off the footstool. 'Not at all, Lady Grangeshield, but I would most certainly blame you for your own failings,' Nicholas commented.

'Really?' Isabel smiled like an executioner being pointlessly insulted by a condemned prisoner even at the very last moment. 'And what are those failings?'

'Oh, being snobbish, critical, endlessly proud and self-satisfied,' Nicholas said vaguely, as if selecting haphazardly from an enormously long list.

Isabel's lips thinned. 'I hope you will excuse my surprise in being criticised in this fashion by a guest in this house. I have little experience in such matters. I am at a loss to know how such a dissatisfied guest as yourself can be made content once again.'

'By leaving this house,' Nicholas said sharply, taking his feet off the footstool and looking ready to stand up. 'I will be a happy man once I am out of here, trust me.'

'And why is that so, Mr Raspero? Is it because your happiness derives from saying goodbye to common courtesy?'

'Common courtesy?' Nicholas snapped. 'What do you know about it?'

Isabel sat straight-backed with her back as straight as straight could be as if geared up for battle. 'I know far more about courtesy than an ignorant man such as you could even dream of learning by eavesdropping at a banquet of buffoons, even if you were the guest of honour thereof.'

Isabel's insult was like being stabbed with a knife of multiple blades so Nicholas was temporarily distracted by wondering which insult to reply to first; then he just gave up on the whole business. 'I bid you farewell, Lady Grangeshield, as I am leaving now,' Nicholas said, suiting his actions to his words by rising to his feet.

'Oh, that is very fine!' Isabel snapped, rising to her own feet in response, her fan folded in her hands like a deadly blade ready to strike, 'you may come and go as you please on this day or any other!'

Lord Easton was cautiously pleased to see Nicholas about to leave, while wary of any intervening complications; he looked across at his beloved wife to see that she was gazing at the quarrelling couple with a fond smile; Lord Easton noted this fond smile with a certain puzzlement.

'Right,' Nicholas said with a certain caution, absolutely unable to see anything to disagree with in Isabel's comment but suspecting a trap, 'so I'm off then. Bye.'

'Mr Raspero!' Isabel nearly shouted, 'I forbid you to go! You will remain here in Grangeshield House. Is that clear?'

Nicholas looked at her for a moment in which his disbelief nearly cancelled out his temper. 'No, Lady Grangeshield,' he said with a pretense of calmness, 'it is not clear. How exactly is it that you can forbid me anything? Perhaps you might explain?'

'You are my guest, Mr Raspero,' Isabel said, breathing heavily as if running flat out in a foot race, 'and as such you are bound by the laws of hospitality to remain here until I say you can go.'

This was simply flat-out not true. Nicholas had enough sense not to be drawn into an utterly childish and pointless argument.

'I was your guest, Lady Grangeshield,' Nicholas said with a careful enunciation of each word, 'but I am leaving now. Goodbye.'

'Oh, it is no wonder that you have turned out to be a murderer, Mr Raspero!' Isabel shouted then in her fury.

There was an awkward silence. Nicholas carefully avoided looking at the Eastons; Lord Easton carefully avoided looking at Nicholas, but Lady Easton, for her part, gazed wide-eyed at Nicholas as if amused by all this awkwardness among friends. Isabel studied Nicholas almost apprehensively as if wondering if she had gone too far.

'Goodbye,' Nicholas stated as if this was the answer to a mathematical equation which he had just found at that very moment, and he turned on his heel and walked off toward the door. Isabel did not waste a single moment in hesitating — she ran straight after him.

'I have spoken hastily, Mr Raspero,' she said as she caught up with him. 'But surely you will not utterly condemn my momentary hastiness.'

Nicholas said nothing as he strode onward toward the door. From the expression on his face, his only thought was of how to leave that place without delay.

Isabel reached out and took hold of the sleeve of his robe. Where his whole body had responded to her touch earlier that day, now she felt only a stiff arm under her hand. She seized his arm and used the momentum of her running to swing around in front of Nicholas so as to stop him in his tracks. She then rolled her eyes back and sank carefully towards the floor, lying spread-eagled with her arms spread out as if she had fainted and was now lying unconscious.

Nicholas felt doubly challenged. Was he really supposed to believe that Isabel had fainted given that it was all so absurd? And was he really supposed to give up on his plan to leave Grangeshield House? For a wild moment Nicholas contemplated stepping around the prone body of Isabel on the ground and going on his way, but clearly that was impossible. He was as trapped as Isabel had intended into picking her up and carrying her back to her seat.

'Is everything all right?' Lady Easton asked in wild-eyed innocence.

'You tell me,' Nicholas replied shortly, still not in the best of moods.

As Nicholas set Isabel back in her chair she said plaintively, 'Mr Raspero, I don't feel well.'

'You're in perfect health,' Nicholas replied. 'Send for a doctor.' Despite his attempted bravado, there was no force in his words. The experience of holding the warm body of Isabel in his arms with her arms around his neck as he carried her along in a cloud of her piquant perfume had knocked all the fight out of him.

'But surely you will not leave me while I am feeling so unwell,' Isabel pleaded with him. 'Surely you will stay with me until I recover.'

Nicholas sighed in exasperation as he stood by Isabel lying in her chair, but it was an exasperation he did not really feel. He was struck all of a sudden by how little he knew of Isabel. Where were her parents? He was rich in family; perhaps she was poor where he was rich; what did he know of what was going on except that whenever he was near her the compass needles of his heart pointed directly at her?

'I am sure the Eastons must be wondering what you meant by what you just said, just as I am myself wondering about it. So feel unwell all you want because what else do you expect? Well?' Nicholas decided that to make his point clearer he would turn to look at the Eastons one after the other, with results he did not anticipate.

'We know that you killed Nevsky,' Lady Easton said.

'No, not at all,' Lord Easton burst out, giving his wife a sharp look. 'We only suspected it at one time, briefly but in passing, but of course naturally we no longer think anything of the sort.'

Nicholas ignored Lord Easton's feeble attempt to unsay what his wife had said. 'Does anyone else know?' he asked angrily.

'You will not use that tone of voice with me, young man,' Lady Easton said sharply.

Nicholas's mouth dropped open. It was exactly like being rebuked by his mother. 'May I enquire, Lady Easton, if anyone else knows about this?' Nicholas said carefully, still angry but on his best manners.

'That's better,' Lady Easton said approvingly. 'No-one else knows, Nicholas, except those of us in this room. And don't worry, we will be sure to keep it secret.'

Lord Easton, his eyes shifting as if his brain was making numerous calculations, set out to explain things further in order to smooth out all relevant concerns, 'We naturally suspected the truth on the basis of a simple logical inference given what information was to hand.' In this way Lord Easton folded layers of truth and prevarication like a chef folding layers of egg-whip with the back of a spoon.

'Please don't go, Mr Raspero,' Isabel pleaded.

Nicholas sighed so loudly that he almost groaned. He sat down and put his feet up on the Footstool of Mangatha once again. 'Very well, I will stay, Lady Grangeshield.'

Lady Easton had not yet finished with him. 'But I must ask you to promise me, Nicholas, you will not cut off any more heads in future.'

'I had good reason,' Nicholas said a little defensively.

'You had excellent reason, Nicholas,' Lady Easton told him consolingly. 'You were in a temper because of what that monster did to Isabel. But you must not make a habit of such behaviour. Once is enough. There must be limits on your future conduct with regard to such matters as these. Do you promise never to do such a thing again?'

'Never again, Lady Easton. I promise.'

'Excellent, Nicholas,' Lady Easton said approvingly, 'that is very well said.'

'Can I go back to being angry at Lady Grangeshield now?'

'But of course you can, Nicholas,' Lady Easton said with all the kindliness of a doting mother.

Nicholas looked back at Isabel and smiled reluctantly. Isabel gazed at him wide-eyed. The Eastons observed them both: Lord Easton with a sense that matters were taking their own course, Lady Easton with a friendly approval. Nicholas did not manage to leave Grangeshield House that evening; he did not manage to leave the following morning either because Isabel asked him to be her escort to a garden party that afternoon, and so it was that he found himself attending dinner at Grangeshield House in the evening of the following day with the Audocavars as his fellow guests.

TWENTY-NINE

The Match-Making Ambitions of the Audocavars for Lord Algernon Bomboodle

6:00 PM, Wednesday 20 July 1544 A.F.

Seeing that the death of Nevsky had brought Isabel back to life, the Eastons had resumed their matchmaking. After retiring to their writing room, which was campaign headquarters, on 13 July and carefully examining their database of eligible candidates they had chosen Lord Algernon Bomboodle as Isabel's next prospective suitor. Algernon was a mild, inoffensive soul who would not issue a duelling challenge if he ever found out the truth about Isabel which had been concealed from him. Isabel's damaged condition was now something the Eastons had to take into account for their match-making. They were essentially committing fraud by pretending Isabel was still an eligible bride and if this fraud was ever discovered they would be in a lot of trouble.

So it was that the Eastons had arranged for Algernon and his parents to come for dinner on 20 July, having no idea that Nicholas would happen to be at Grangeshield House on that evening. It was as if their plans seemed to be derailed from the start. After all, no prospective suitor could be expected to be happy about finding another man seated by the side of their prospective bride on arriving for dinner, even one as mild and inoffensive as Algernon.

Lady Petronel Audocavar was all smiles and effusive welcomes, obviously determined to overlook any and all anomalies, such as Nicholas's presence, in her eagerness to discuss her son's matrimonial qualities. Despite being short and plump she was like a sharp sword in a leather scabbard ready to cut down anyone in her way at a moment's notice. Lord Apolinar Audocavar was quieter and more reserved, with a trim, blond beard and vague, pale green eyes and an ever-ready, polite smile; he was much cleverer than he looked.

Algernon had pale blond hair, a long face and no chin. He seemed to be in awe of Nicholas Raspero the wandfighter, perhaps from having witnessed Nicholas break Hubert Hupppenstall's arm and then publicly mock Lady Starfeld to her face in front of all her guests; Nicholas was his usual cheerful and self-assured self; Isabel sat by not saying a word which slowed down everything from the very beginning. The very ground of the entire assembly seemed tilted by this convergence of factors resulting in the Eastons' matchmaking plans sliding helplessly on a journey to nowhere. Lord Easton realised within five minutes that the entire evening was going to be a disaster, but he had no idea even so just how much of a disaster it would prove to be, and so while he was apprehensive he wasn't nearly as apprehensive as he should have been.

Algernon had pride of place to the right of Isabel seated at the head of the table, but it was not long before Lady Audocavar noted how often Isabel was looking further down the table at Nicholas chatting away cheerfully to Lady Easton, and how distracted she was from any or all of Algernon's attempts to engage her in conversation. By the second course the only cheerful people in the dining room were Nicholas and Lady Easton and dinner seemed to drag on for everyone else until it was over and they returned to the Red Drawing Room.

Now that it was time for their after-dinner conversation it was seemingly inevitable that the subject of the Lord of the North should arise at this point just as it was seemingly inevitable that Algernon should have a theory about the Lord of the North, which Nicholas was immediately keen on hearing. It was Lady Audocavar who was instrumental in getting this ball rolling, however much she might have complained later about where the ball ended up. She started it as an attendant angel might have pointed out on a day of reckoning. Keen to have Algernon as the centre of attention and knowing that he was mad keen on this topic of conversation, she declared, 'Algernon has solved the mystery of the Lord of the North.'

All eyes turned to Algernon, just as Lady Audocavar had planned. She settled herself back in her chair with a satisfied air.

Nicholas was delighted to hear this. 'And what is this solution?' he asked Algernon eagerly. 'I am personally baffled by this mystery.'

'You may well be baffled by this mystery, Mr Raspero,' Lady Audocavar said patronisingly, 'but Algernon is not.' She looked meaningfully at Isabel as she brought Algernon's brilliance to the attention of the entire assembled company.

'I know who the Lord of the North is,' Isabel declared grandly. She looked meaningfully at Nicholas as she said this.

Lord Easton nearly had a heart-attack.

'Take your place in the queue, Lady Grangeshield,' Nicholas told her mock-sternly with a little smile. 'You may speak later.'

'You may well be baffled by this mystery, Mr Raspero, but I am not,' Isabel continued as grandly as before. 'It is the mark of a low person to be baffled.'

'Perhaps you have arrived at the same answer as Algernon,' Lady Audocavar suggested as if struck by how all this convergence was so obviously meant to be. Two young people whose minds moved as one! Why, their hearts would be beating as one next!

'All right Lord Bomboodle,' Nicholas said cheerfully, 'you're on stage. Go for it!'

It turned out that Algernon had signed up for the rapidly developing school of thought which argued that the fight between the Lord of the North and Nevsky had to do with a secret society of an esoteric nature. The use of the term *swinging gate* was considered to be evidence of this, the *gate* in question being that of a doorway to supernatural knowledge, and *swinging* meaning that something had been found out by the gate being opened through some kind of ritual. Nevsky had been found out by this knowledge obtained via this swinging gate and it was this that had brought on his head the wrath of the Lord of the North.

Lord Easton thought he had never heard anything so nutty. 'You might well be onto something there, Algernon,' he said approvingly. 'Good work, excellent work. That might very well be the solution to this mystery. I can remember back in '35 when —'

'And is this also your solution to this mystery, Isabel?' Lady Audocavar asked abruptly, heading off Lord Easton's reminiscences given that they threatened to change the subject entirely. Algernon seemed to be on a winner here and Lady Audocavar was not having the subject changed.

'Certainly not!' Isabel declared imperiously. 'It is utterly absurd and utterly beside the point!'

'All right Lady Grangeshield, you're on next,' Nicholas said as cheerfully as before. 'State your case. We are listening.'

Lord Easton's hands were sweating so profusely that he tried as unobtrusively as possible to dry them on his trouser-legs. He did not know it but he had gone as white as a sheet. He could not believe, he simply could not believe at all, how insane Nicholas and Isabel were being. It was simply beyond reason to see them dancing together at the edge of an abyss.

'I have said that I know who the Lord of the North is. Therefore, I have solved the mystery.' Isabel looked at Nicholas with a superior look as if to dare him to find any fault with this statement of her case.

'And?' Nicholas asked, looking directly at Isabel with raised eyebrows. 'Who is this Lord of the North?'

There was a silence. Everyone looked at Isabel, who for her part looked at Nicholas. Lord Easton learned a new definition of eternity.

'I choose not to say,' Isabel said eventually.

Lord Easton found himself remembering to breathe.

'Oh great!' Nicholas said very critically. 'You choose not to say! Well, that's sorted out the whole mystery, hasn't it?'

'But how is it that you know his identity?' Lord Audocavar asked Isabel.

Lord Easton had forgotten to breathe again.

'I will not,' Isabel said emphatically, flourishing her folded fan in the air like a debating pamphlet, 'be badgered by questions on this matter. I simply declare that I know who he is and that will have to do.'

'So that's settled,' Nicholas commented, leaning back in his chair as if accepting defeat. 'Well, it seems that you are never at a loss, Lady Grangeshield, unlike the rest of us. Congratulations!'

Lord Easton, remembering to breathe again, noted that Nicholas had managed to give the impression that he didn't believe a word Isabel was saying. Looking around him, Lord Easton saw to his relief that neither did anyone else. Everyone present thought that Isabel was simply pretending to know who the Lord of the North was.

'I beg your pardon, Mr Raspero?' Isabel asked with an edge to her voice.

'For what?' Nicholas asked casually, almost yawning.

'For your manners, Mr Raspero!' Isabel said fiercely.

'My manners?' Nicholas complained. 'What about yours?'

'Sarcasm, Mr Raspero, is not tolerated in this house,' Isabel snapped. 'When you said *Congratulations!* you were being sarcastic, were you not?'

'Well, what do you expect?' Nicholas fired back. 'If you say you know who this Lord of the North is, then say who he is. Otherwise you're just talking, aren't you?'

Lord Easton thought then that he could detect the terrible sub-text under all this. Nicholas and Isabel were each daring each other who could step closer to the abyss. The exposure of Nicholas would expose Isabel and they would both then die in different ways: Nicholas would sit down with Langston and Isabel would be a social outcast even if she avoided prison as an accessory. He looked across at Lady Easton only to see that she was watching all this with an interested and relaxed amusement. Praying that his beloved spouse had some insight into this drama that was beyond his, Lord Easton concentrated on remembering to breathe.

Isabel considered Nicholas's challenge with a glint in her eye. 'Let us employ deduction, Mr Raspero. This Lord of the North is known for having left a letter, is he not?'

'Indeed.'

'Given that is all that we know, who is to say who wrote this letter? It could have been a fool having fun, could it not?'

Despite his nerves nearly snapping Lord Easton noted this comment. He had already deduced that Nicholas had written this letter but this was confirmation that Nicholas had simply made it all up without giving any intentional significance to any of the contents.

'Nevsky went to the duel because of that letter, Lady Grangeshield,' Nicholas said as smoothly as a lawyer in court swatting away a dissenting opinion. 'So, it meant something to *him*.'

There were nods all around from the assembled company. Nicholas had landed a telling blow in this battle of wits.

'Nevsky may have gone to the duel because of another letter, one that was replaced by this one full of nonsense,' Isabel pointed out calmly, her fan held immobile in her hands, so intent was her concentration.

So, that was how it happened, Lord Easton noted with interest, for despite everything his logical mind was pleased to be finding out how things had gone: Nevsky had been summoned to the duel with one letter, which had then been replaced with another meaningless one. It was all starting to make sense.

'Highly conjectural, Lady Grangeshield,' Nicholas pronounced without hesitation. Once again there were nods all around. 'There is one letter, then there is another. But why not another one after that? As each letter must be explained by a following one you have embarked on an infinite regress of letters, have you not, Lady Grangeshield? Yet, the postal service is not infinite in extent, is it not? Therefore, as the postal service could not have conveyed an infinite sequence of letters, there could not have been such a sequence. Therefore, there was only one letter.'

There were not only nods all around, but there were respectful looks being directed towards Nicholas by those present. Such a dazzling display of logic and erudition could not but command respect.

'There were two letters, Mr Raspero,' Isabel declared emphatically, 'neither of which was conveyed by the postal service. Your argument has failed for its premises are faulty, the derivation of its conclusion laughable and the conclusion itself merely a joke.'

'I have enjoyed your fantastical observations, Lady Grangeshield, which I shall not designate as an argument because they entirely fail to form a coherent whole. But alas, now I am obliged in the interest of serving the truth to come to a brutish, yes, brutish, regretfully, for the charm of what might have been must give way to what was, brutish observation that the witnesses who saw Nevsky felled by the Lord of the North did not see letters being shuffled around like cards in a gambler's hand. The facts are clear: Nevsky fell, the Lord of the North departed. The testimony of the witnesses refutes your assertions, Lady Grangeshield.'

Yet, again there were nods all around. There was nothing to be said against what Nicholas had said.

'Witnesses? Do you say witnesses? I say drunks who were not even there,' Isabel said scornfully.

Despite his alarm that the truth was about to come out with a clattering crash, Lord Easton took note of this sudden puzzling statement. How could the witnesses be *drunks who were not even there*? What kind of sense did that make?

'To discredit the report of witnesses is a *common* ploy,' Nicholas observed, emphasising the adjective to annoy the elitist Isabel, 'a *common* ploy,' Nicholas continued with a little smile, 'which is the last refuge of those who have run out of all else to say. You cannot dismiss these witnesses in such a cavalier manner.'

Isabel glared at Nicholas. 'How dare you be so insolent to me in my own house?'

'Is the defence of the truth insolent in this house?' Nicholas riposted with raised eyebrows, still smiling. He was enjoying himself, especially given that he wasn't defending the truth at all.

'As I am your hostess and you are my guest in this house, Mr Raspero, you are obliged to behave appropriately. Are you really too low to see this for yourself, Mr Raspero?'

'As I am your guest and you are my hostess, Lady Grangeshield, you are obliged to behave appropriately. Are you really so far off the ground on your high horse that you can't see that far down, Lady Grangeshield?'

'How dare you speak to me in such a fashion!' Isabel said sharply, pointing her folded fan towards Nicholas's chest like a sword.

'In what fashion? That of a guest speaking his mind?'

'You are not to speak your mind in this house, Mr Raspero!' Isabel snapped furiously.

'Well, that's nice!' Nicholas said and laughed merrily. 'Perhaps I should thank you now for your kindness, Lady Grangeshield.'

Isabel was made even angrier by Nicholas's merry laughter. 'Shall I tell you why I do not speak of this Lord of the North, Mr Raspero? It is because he is too low to speak of. It is because he is nothing but a common murderer. It is because he is not a gentleman!'

At that instant, at the suddenly expressionless look on Nicholas's face, Isabel realised that she had blundered one step too far. Her temper evaporated on the instant in a moment's panic and she immediately set herself the task of working out how to backtrack from where she had gone.

Nicholas was trying to work out if Isabel had just said that he, Nicholas, was not a gentleman, given that he was in effect the Lord of the North; yet he could not be said to be the Lord of the North given that the Lord of the North was entirely fictional. To say that the Lord of the North was not a gentleman was not to say that Nicholas was not a gentleman, but surely, like the swipe of a bear's paw dealing a glancing blow, Nicholas could not be said to be entirely uninsulted when everything was taken into account.

Isabel knew exactly what thoughts were taking place behind Nicholas's stone-faced demeanour and swiftly set forth to redeem the situation. 'I have spoken too hastily to a gentleman such as yourself concerning the Lord of the North. Naturally, a gentleman of such noble character as yourself must wonder about the appropriateness of my comment about the character of another gentleman.'

Nicholas was barely listening. He was still trying to work everything out. *Had he been insulted or not? Had it been Isabel's intention to insult him? If so, did that count or not?* The thunderous expression on his face came from the thunder of his feelings that he might have been insulted but the thunder was muted as it was possible that he had not been. *Aristotle himself couldn't have figured this one out*, he thought.

Isabel noted Nicholas's expression and also his silence and continued to soothe his wounded feelings as best she could. 'Naturally, I withdraw the comment I have just made without hesitation and indeed I apologise for casting any aspersion on the noble character of the Lord of the North, who is no doubt a gentleman just as you, Mr Raspero, are without doubt a gentleman.'

Nicholas gave up on trying to figure this out but Isabel's attempt to reconcile with him had failed. He decided to simply leave. Anyway, what was he still doing in Grangeshield House when it came to it? It was time to go! 'I do not believe, Lady Grangeshield,' Nicholas said icily, 'that you have any idea at all of who this Lord of the North is. I do believe, however, that you wish to strike airs and pretend that you know who he is for some pathetic reason or other. That is because you lack all proportion, that you know no better, that you are, in short, ignorant not only of the subject under discussion but of how to conduct the discussion itself.'

Isabel noted the icy way in which Nicholas had spoken. Above all else Isabel additionally noted that Nicholas had straightened up in his chair and taken his feet off the footstool they had been resting on and she understood that he was about to leave. 'I do confess, Mr Raspero,' Isabel said placatingly, 'that I do not know who this Lord of the North is. I am sure that he is a gentleman, whoever he is. I have no doubt about this whatsoever. I merely made a jest which I have carried too far and I can only apologise and I unreservedly withdraw everything I have said.'

Lord Easton wondered when the ground under his feet would become a hole by which to swallow him up and end all this. Could anything be more obvious than this? Isabel had just said that the Lord of the North (who was Nicholas) was not a gentleman, and Nicholas was quite rightly offended, but who could not see that Isabel had offended Nicholas when she had offended the Lord of the North? As far as Lord Easton could see, their dance had ended with a plunge into the abyss. (Lord Easton's fears were groundless. No-one was ever to suspect Nicholas of being the Lord of the North, whether on this evening or any other.)

'I will leave now, Lady Grangeshield,' Nicholas declared, rising to his feet just as Isabel had feared he would. 'I will see myself out. Goodbye.'

With that he set forth for the door, ignoring everyone else present in his temper.

'Mr Raspero!' Isabel squeaked, shooting to her feet and running after him. 'Wait one moment, Mr Raspero. What I have just said was unpardonable. Oh, surely a gentleman of such a noble character as yourself can pardon the unpardonable.'

Nicholas made no reply but strode onwards towards the door. Isabel ran ahead of him, stepped in front of him to bring him to a stop, rested the palm of her hand on his chest and said pleadingly, 'Please forgive me, Mr Raspero.'

The sight of the proud and imperious Isabel being so humble and apologetic to a man dressed in rags, who should not even have been present when Algernon had come to dinner, made Lady Audocavar start to come back to life from the complete astonishment she had been in ever since this quarrel had begun.

'Please step out of the way, Lady Grangeshield,' Nicholas said, stepping to one side himself as he said this in an attempt to get past Isabel.

Lord Easton felt that he was dreaming. It was as if the strain of everything had proved too much for him and life itself had become dreamlike. He looked around him and saw that everyone was following this drama with rapt attention, as well they might. This was going to provide the fodder for the next week's gossip of New Landerners, he reflected, and where was this going to end?

Isabel stepped sideways to block him. 'Mr Raspero, I entirely withdraw what I have just said and I deeply and humbly apologise.'

Nicholas leaned closer to her and whispered so no-one else but Isabel could hear, 'Your behaviour is unacceptable, Lady Grangeshield, and so I am leaving.'

'Mr Raspero, how can I persuade you of my repentance?' Isabel whispered back. 'Please tell me and it shall be done as you have commanded.'

Nicholas's temper was fast ebbing away, given that Isabel had only said that the Lord of the North, who did not exist, was not a gentleman, and this was not only a logical statement to make, given that the Lord of the North did not exist, but also an empty one; further, Nicholas still couldn't work out if he had been insulted or not and what role Isabel's intention to insult him had played given that she had strictly technically not insulted him at all; furthermore, Isabel's hand was resting on his chest and her pleading brown eyes were all he could see before and around him, and further furthermore, Isabel's close presence always had the effect on Nicholas of making him fascinated with everything she was to the exclusion of all else that was.

Nicholas was weakening, and seeing this, Isabel rolled her eyes upwards as she carefully sank towards the floor and lay down sideways. It was the world's least convincing pretence of fainting and would not have fooled a small child but it had the effect Isabel sought, which for her was all that counted: Nicholas was obliged by upbringing and circumstances to pick her up and carry her back to her chair.

'But what on earth is going on?' Lady Audocavar asked, still nearly too astonished to be able to speak at all.

'Lady Grangeshield *appears* to have fainted,' Nicholas said, with the merest emphasis on the word *appears* as he settled Isabel back in her chair.

'Mr Raspero, I do not feel well,' Isabel said plaintively like a child.

Nicholas looked like a man in danger of forgetting his own name. The experience of carrying the warm body of Isabel in his arms had had its effect on him. 'Well … er … just … um … rest for a while,' Nicholas said as if trying to give medical advice.

'Surely you will not leave me alone while I am so unwell,' Isabel pleaded. 'Surely the age of chivalry is not dead, Mr Raspero.'

Nicholas sighed, trying and failing to be exasperated. 'Of course the age of chivalry is not dead, Lady Grangeshield. Naturally I will stay a while longer if you wish.'

Nicholas sat down and put his feet back up on the Footstool of Mangatha. Every now and then he looked across at Isabel who in her turn kept her gaze unwaveringly fixed on his face. The silence dragged on, becoming increasingly awkward for Lord Easton who could feel the restrained fury of Lady Audocavar. Lady Audocaver had come to dinner expecting to encounter preliminary developments for her son to become Isabel's suitor, only to be the unwilling audience for what looked like for all the world to be a lover's quarrel. Lord Easton looked over to his wife for support only to see that she was gazing at Nicholas and Isabel with a fond smile as if pleased to see the children having such fun. No-one was saying anything and the silence was now becoming an increasing burden for Lord Easton to bear.

Lord Easton had often observed that silence made people think. And while he was, as a general rule, all in favour of people thinking, and would even on occasion encourage it whole-heartedly, he was not in favour of it now. The answer to a riddle is all too obvious to those who know what that answer is and it was all too glaringly obvious to Lord Easton that Nicholas was known to be the only man in New Landern capable of killing Nevsky and only one man had killed Nevsky. It seemed to Lord Easton that to put these facts together in such a way that their identity became apparent was the work of only a moment's thinking and this was why Lord Easton was deeply opposed to such a moment being provided by circumstances. He forgot, of course, that it had taken him some time, even with the benefit of a very helpful clue, to have solved this riddle himself. Lord Easton set himself the task of driving away all this threatening silence.

'I am sure that heated discussion like this concerning this mysterious Lord of the North must be taking place all over our great metropolis at this very moment,' he said eventually, desperate to get the conversation away from the topic of Nevsky's slayer and taking this as his starting point.

'Not quite like *this*, I am sure,' Lady Audocavar said in a marked manner.

'No, not quite like this,' Lord Easton hastily agreed with an attempt at a light-hearted chuckle, 'but these differences do constitute variety, do they not? Variety, ah yes, speaking of variety I remember well back in the summer of '23 when I visited my old friend Burrayford —'

'A fascinating anecdote, I have no doubt,' Lady Audocavar interrupted with a deliberate rudeness, 'and one which I am sure would have diverted our attention away from the quarrel we have just witnessed. But can you match such entertainment, Bentley?'

Lord Easton was taken aback by how sharp Lady Audocavar's tone was. Seeing his difficulty Lady Easton stepped in.

'Nicholas and Isabel were having fun as young people so often do,' she remarked. 'I can remember when you were young, Petronel, and having fun.'

Lady Audocavar understood this veiled warning all too well as referring obliquely to an embarrassing episode of her youth which Lady Easton had witnessed but she was too angry about her disappointed hopes to completely change course. She had hoped that Algernon would become the suitor of Isabel because even had his suit failed, as it perhaps would have realistically speaking (although you never knew what might happen!), the glory of having once been Isabel's suitor might have improved his chances of making a match elsewhere. Not everyone got to be the suitor of Lady Isabel Grangeshield of Grangeshield House and such an accolade would be sure to have got him more noticed than he was, because frankly hardly anyone noticed him at all, but what had happened instead was that she had brought Algernon to Grangeshield House only to find herself in the midst of what looked very like a lover's quarrel between Isabel and another man of whom Algernon was all too visibly afraid. Her mother's fondness for her boy was the source of her outrage at these adverse circumstances which she blamed on the Eastons more than Isabel, who everyone knew was impossible.

'We all remember when we were young, Dacia,' Lady Audocavar said sharply, firing her own warning back, for she too could drag up embarrassing episodes from the past if needed, 'but how shall we remember this evening? Did anything else other than a quarrel happen here tonight?'

'The food wasn't bad,' Nicholas said to Lady Audocavar with a serious air. 'I mean, that beef stroganoff was just amazing, I thought. Very, very tasty.'

Isabel covered her sudden smile with an unfurled fan.

'And this young man,' Lady Audocavar commented, looking at Nicholas with an evident dislike, 'is addressed by Bentley as Mr Raspero but by you, Dacia as Nicholas. I find this a puzzle, as I find much else about this evening's, ah, entertainment shall we call it, to be a puzzle.'

'Nicholas and I are great friends,' Lady Easton decreed calmly.

'How nice for you,' Lady Audocavar said acidly, 'given that no-one else had ever heard of him until yesterday.'

'I must protest at such a characterisation of my public standing, Lady

Audocavar,' Nicholas said as seriously as before. 'I am very well known in Little Batton.'

'And where is Little Batton?' Lady Audocavar asked with a veiled viciousness.

'I could also ask rhetorical questions, Lady Audocavar,' Nicholas said as if he was too polite to ever actually do such a thing.

'My question was not rhetorical, I assure you,' Lady Audocavar said with a nasty smile.

'Oh, do you really not know?' Nicholas asked with an air of surprise. 'I am only too happy to tell you if you really want to know. After all, it would be discourteous of me not to, and we mustn't be discourteous, must we?'

'No, we must not!' Lady Audocavar snapped, goaded into a flash of temper by what she saw as a provocation. She thought it a bit rich that Nicholas should lecture her on courtesy after the way he had been carrying on with Isabel. 'We must not quarrel in public and make things uncomfortable for others, must we not? *That* is being discourteous!'

'What's your point, Lady Audocavar?' Nicholas asked a little impatiently. 'I mean, do you want to know where Little Batton is or do you not?'

'No, Mr Raspero,' Lady Audocavar told him with massive restraint, 'I do *not* want to know where Little Batton is.'

'Then it *was* a rhetorical question all the time,' Nicholas pointed out with the air of a vindicated philosopher. 'I thought so.'

'My question, Mr Raspero, of *Where is Little Batton?* had the meaning that I could not possibly imagine myself ever setting foot in such a place myself.'

'Just as well,' Nicholas observed cryptically.

Isabel giggled behind her fan, which Lord Easton thought was not at all helpful.

'Home is where the heart is,' Lord Easton said in his pleasantest manner.

'Home is also where a person is known,' Lady Audocavar pointed out, 'and while I do not doubt for a moment that Mr Raspero is very well known in his own home, he is all but a stranger here in New Landern.'

'Lord Zinia patted Mr Raspero on the shoulder, as you well know,' Lord

Audocavar said to his wife, by way of giving his own warning. 'We cannot say whether or not Mr Raspero is perhaps better known than we know.'

'Lord Zinia patted you on the shoulder, Mr Raspero?' Isabel asked in surprise. What with one thing and another she had not heard this before.

'*She* doesn't know,' Lady Audocavar told her husband with a gesture of her chin towards Isabel as if to imply that no-one knew anything about what was going on.

'I vaguely recall some such pat on my shoulder,' Nicholas said with a furrowed brow, as if only vaguely recalling this.

'And why did Lord Zinia pat you on the shoulder?' Isabel asked.

Everyone present looked at Nicholas. They all wanted to know the answer to this question.

'Oh, we chatted a while and then said bye,' Nicholas said evasively.

'That hardly answers my question,' Isabel said sternly. 'Why did Lord Zinia pat you on the shoulder?'

'It was a confidential matter which is none of your business,' Nicholas said, and given that he had given his word to Zinia not to speak of what had been said during their meeting he gave Isabel such a hard look that she widened her eyes and looked away from him with her eyebrows raised.

As much about Zinia was confidential the matter was dropped by all those present. Lord Easton seized his chance to tell an anecdote which started off about confidentiality and ended some time later with a skeptical observation concerning the fifteenth clause of a trade treaty between Anglashia and Pashtunvale. Lord Audocavar was then inspired to reminisce about his days as a diplomatic envoy to Tregebund, once so closely allied to Pashtunvale. Lady Audocavar said nothing and she said nothing in a very thin-lipped manner. Isabel gazed wide-eyed at Nicholas, who for his part listened politely to what was being said, every now and then looking across at Isabel. Lady Easton studied the markings on her fan with a far-away smile. Algernon darted sideways looks at Nicholas. Soon it was time for the guests to begin making preparations to leave (but not, Lady Audocavar noted, Mr Raspero!) and with polite thanks, best wishes and effusive proclamations the guests were on their way and the evening was over — or nearly over.

'I have to say, Isabel, and Mr Raspero,' Lord Easton said as fiercely as he could, 'that your conduct this evening was reckless in the extreme.'

'How so, Lord Easton?' Nicholas asked, sitting back down in his chair and putting his feet back up onto the Footstool of Mangatha.

'How so?' Lord Easton repeated incredulously. 'The way you and Isabel were talking about the Lord of the North in such a way as to draw attention to yourselves, that is how so. I couldn't believe my ears.'

'I have every intention of participating in every conversation about the Lord of the North which I can, Lord Easton. To not do so would be to draw attention to myself given the widespread interest in this topic.'

'You challenged Isabel to say who he was!'

'I responded to a comment which Lady Grangeshield made herself. To have done anything else would have seemed suspicious. After all, who would not have insisted on knowing who the Lord of the North was?'

This was all sophistry to Lord Easton. 'Your behaviour tonight was beyond anything, Isabel,' Lord Easton said. 'How on earth can you have been quite so insane as to carry on in such a fashion?'

Isabel said nothing but looked at Lord Easton like a guilty child.

Nicholas as always leaped to her defence. 'Lady Grangeshield was very clever,' he declared. 'By claiming to know who the Lord of the North was and then refusing to say, she gave the impression of having overplayed her hand with the result that she now truly appears to not know who the Lord of the North is. No doubt there are numerous people all around New Landern at this very moment who are dropping hints that they know far more about this matter than they are saying; Lady Grangeshield simply seems to have been found out in this matter. What could be less of a problem?'

Lord Easton looked deeply unimpressed by this spurious defence. 'And the letters? I did not know myself about the switch of these letters, which I learned thanks to what you call Isabel's *cleverness*. Tell me what the bright side of that blunder was!'

Nicholas looked taken aback by this. 'Well, you may have a point, Lord Easton,' he said and looked across at Isabel. 'Lady Grangeshield, it would be best if you said nothing more about the letters in question. Do you not agree?'

Isabel still said nothing, looking back at Nicholas wide-eyed.

Lady Easton stepped in at this moment. 'Perhaps you might tell us all about these letters yourself, Nicholas, given that there is so much of this story which Bentley and I do not know.'

So it was that Nicholas told Lord and Lady Easton the story of how he had summoned Nevsky to their duel, of the burglary of the Nevsky residence and of how drunks who were not even there had come to be witnesses to the duel between Nevsky and the Lord of the North.

Lord Easton privately thought that the entire plan had been the wildest and most hare-brained scheme he had ever heard of in his life. 'An interesting and imaginative approach to the whole business,' he said when Nicholas had finished telling his tale, 'which succeeded in the end completely.'

Nicholas understood what he wasn't saying. 'Yes, Lord Easton, so many things could have gone wrong. But isn't that true of life in general?'

'Well, yes,' Lord Easton admitted, feeling that he had been found out, 'but now that it is over and done with it would be best if you and Isabel knew no more about anything than everyone else. Do you not agree?'

'Yes, I do agree, Lord Easton,' Nicholas said, nodding emphatically to demonstrate his agreement and looking across at Isabel. 'Lady Grangeshield is also in complete agreement as well.'

Isabel tilted her chin up, unfolded her fan and fanned herself while looking up at the ceiling.

'That is just as well,' Lord Easton said a little dangerously, giving Isabel a hard look, 'because I am not here in Grangeshield House under compulsion.'

Isabel understood the implicit threat in what Uncle Bentley had just said. Uncle Bentley and Aunt Dacia were her closest family and after the death of her father they had been her guardians, her chaperones and even, in a sense, her friends, but if they chose to walk out and leave her alone there was nothing she could do to stop them and she would be obliged to replace them with comparative strangers in order to maintain her reputation as a chaperoned woman.

Later that night, after they had all retired to their respective bedrooms,

Isabel reflected more on what had happened than on Lord Easton's reprimand that it had happened at all. She distinctively recollected how Nicholas had talked with a degree of freedom that she found intolerable. He really had no place at all in Grangeshield House given his lack of manners. She really should tell him to leave without delay. He should get out! And that reminded her that Nicholas had nearly walked out and she had barely managed to prevent him leaving. She was not pleased to remember how Nicholas had seemed to think he could just leave Grangeshield House whenever he chose. He behaved as if he could simply leave whenever he pleased! Such behaviour bordered on insolence, if it was not actually insolence itself! Nicholas would leave Grangeshield House when she told him to leave and not one moment before!

She couldn't sleep for a while for thinking about Nicholas. It gave her a warm and protected feeling to think that Nicholas was under the same roof at that very moment. She was safe with him here. It seemed somehow appropriate that Nicholas was in Grangeshield House. *He belonged in Grangeshield House,* she thought. She had to make him stay but at the same time she also had to make him leave. At any rate, he most certainly could not leave until she told him to leave — that was beyond dispute!

Isabel dreamed that night that her father came into her room, stood at the foot of her bed and said, 'What is necessary remains to be done.' The dream was so real that Isabel awoke with a start to find that it had only been a dream and that her father was not really there. But the words he had spoken were still all about her in the air as she fell asleep again.

THIRTY

....

The New Clothes Given to Mr Nicholas Raspero by Lady Isabel Grangeshield

11:00 AM, Thursday 21 July 1544 A.F.

The tailor came out to Grangeshield House as a nervous man. Pale and breathing in tightly controlled gasps, he looked like a man whose time had come. His assistant followed behind carrying a large bundle in his arms, like an ant struggling along with an enormous blade of grass.

Benson led the tailor and his assistant and Nicholas and three servants of the household to the Rowland Room, where Nicholas was dressed in his new clothes under the attentive supervision of the tailor. His new robes were made of cotton interwoven with silk, pleated and tucked with swirling movements which brought out the indigo and green cross dyeing of the interlaced denim and cotton sections around the torso, while the russet velvet sleeves flared like cones displaying their cashmere lining. The closure of the attire upon Nicholas's person was like the proud unfolding of a lily in the clear light of a fresh new-born day and it was attentively followed by the tailor pacing around Nicholas in wide circles, looking him up-and-down from head-to-toe with an almost lustful candour, while visibly relaxing into being a man at peace with himself and the world. He looked at his assistant with a delighted smile; the assistant smiled back; the tailor chuckled and then laughed out loud, his head thrown back and his arms upraised in the air like the fore-limbs of a praying mantis. The tailor was a happy man.

Benson and the other servants watched these artisan antics with expressionless faces.

Nicholas might or might not have been holding back a smile.

'Is that not better?' the tailor asked Nicholas in a rhetorical fashion with a little smile and a twinkle in his eye; it seemed that for the tailor it was as if Nicholas had just been released from prison and his rhetorical question was his way of expressing his own personal happiness on seeing Nicholas so blessed by fortune.

'These clothes are excellent, thank you,' Nicholas replied, looking at himself in the mirror and trying to sound enthusiastic.

The tailor's good humour faded a little as he contemplated Nicholas standing in front of him. Nicholas had said the right thing but in the wrong way; the tailor could not but suspect Nicholas of heresy. The tailor shook himself like a man emerging from entrancement and gestured for Benson to lead the party back to the captain of these proceedings. They all accordingly trooped back to the Red Drawing Room, where Isabel and the Eastons and attentive servants were waiting.

Isabel's immediate and unqualified praise were all that the tailor needed to make him a happy man again. Isabel's insightful and appropriate comments so pleased the tailor that he stood like a cockerel puffed up in bright sunshine, his very being at one with the golden sun itself. While Isabel nodded in approval and voiced her appreciation of his artistic achievement, the Eastons also nodded in their turn to everything she said. The tailor walked here-and-there looking at Nicholas from all sides as if unable to leave just yet; Isabel waited patiently as if she understood his feelings completely; eventually the tailor and his assistant left, looking as if they had just saved a person's life and been well paid for it as well; everyone was happy and even Nicholas found that his new clothes were growing on him, as they were very, very smart and generally impressive.

'You will wait for us here, Mr Raspero,' Isabel ordered peremptorily, still in her captain's mode.

So it was that Nicholas waited for Isabel in the Red Drawing Room. It was peaceful and quiet in the midst of the enormity of all that

Grangeshield splendour; so enfolding was the stillness that the very paintings on the wall seemed to be watching Nicholas closely; the far-away sounds of Grangeshield House going about its daily business seemed to be felt as the faintest of tremors in the air rather than heard distinctly. Nicholas felt almost sleepy as the silence made his very thoughts slow and heavy.

In a spirit of calm contemplation Nicholas considered his circumstances as if from a distance. Here he was in Grangeshield House about to take Isabel onto his arm for the evening; he was about to be where he never thought he would be. It was in a sense the middle part of happiness as a food which created a new hunger. After tonight his dreams could only be of a larger happiness, and where could this end? Nicholas felt an impartial uneasiness at being in circumstances that could easily become a predicament; yet like a man on a boat being swept out to sea there was not a lot he could do about it.

Isabel's appearance interrupted these meditations. She entered the Red Drawing Room looking resplendent in the same red-and-blue gown she had been wearing when Nicholas had first seen her in Regana Palace. Nicholas rose to his feet and escorted her to the waiting flying carriage, her arm tucked through his, the Eastons following behind.

This flying carriage, a Compreadur, was even larger and more magnificent than the Balladur Nicholas had flown in before. The wooden fittings were again of rosewood, with a large oak table with the Grangeshield crest embedded in the table-top in solid gold filling.

Isabel was impassively (and happily) not smiling while Nicholas was his usual cheerful self. Lady Easton also seemed to be enjoying herself and so it was left to Lord Easton to bear all the apprehensions of this occasion which it seemed only he could see. Isabel of course had always been tempestuous but to be chaperoning Isabel and Nicholas together made him feel as if he was setting out in the company of a lioness and a lion who might or might not behave themselves. The flying carriage was well under way on its journey by now but still Lord Easton was taking calming breaths.

Isabel was staring directly at Nicholas, a slight look of amusement playing on her face. It was as if his mere presence was a source of pleasing puzzlement for her.

Nicholas felt that he had to say something. 'You look beautiful tonight, Lady Grangeshield,' he said with complete sincerity.

'Oh, I look beautiful tonight,' Isabel said in reply, mimicking his intonation mockingly. 'Not long ago, Mr Raspero, my escort for the evening read to me a poem he had composed on the subject of my beauty as we travelled together to our evening entertainment.'

'How did the poem go?' Nicholas asked.

Isabel couldn't remember a word of it. 'I suspect that the literary quality of the poem would be entirely lost on you, Mr Raspero, given that you cannot even properly write a letter. In any case, I merely draw attention to the deficiencies of your feeble attempts to play the role of the escort by contrast to others who are far more accomplished in these matters.'

'Well, thanks for that,' Nicholas said in a neutral tone, although he was trying not to grin. 'I'll bear all that in mind. Although, by the way, I have escorted ladies to dances before and none of them expected me to have written them a poem to honour the occasion.'

'I am sure that in the more backward parts of the world, such as where you are from, the very concept of the poem is entirely unknown. Grunting and pointing are no doubt the favoured methods of communication. Your lady companions were very likely impressed if your mouth wasn't hanging open.'

Nicholas grinned and shook his head in disbelief. 'You just never give up, do you, Lady Grangeshield? I will give you full credit for consistency, though. Nothing I ever do is ever right, is it?'

'Yes, you will complain, of course,' Isabel said dismissively. 'I expect no less from a man such as you. You will refuse any chance of self-improvement out of stubbornness, will you not? You will cling to your primitive condition because it is all that you have ever known.'

Nicholas laughed cheerfully. 'Naturally, Lady Grangeshield, out of courtesy I will let you have the last word.'

'Out of courtesy, Mr Raspero? I think not. I think it is rather that you have run out of things to say in your defence.'

Nicholas laughed again and looked out of the window. Isabel contemplated him and said nothing more, a slight smile on her face as if she were enjoying herself. Isabel let the silence continue up to a point precisely calibrated by her intuition before speaking again, 'So, Mr Raspero, tell me about these lady companions of yours.'

'What about them?'

'Well, did you say to them that *you look beautiful tonight*?' Isabel asked scornfully.

This was, in fact, Nicholas's usual compliment in these situations, as it happened, but he certainly wasn't going to say so now. 'None of them were as beautiful as you are, Lady Grangeshield, if that's what you mean.'

This was, in fact, so much exactly what Isabel had meant that she failed to notice that Nicholas had dodged her question. 'Once again your inept attempts to pay me a compliment fall far short of what is required,' she commented, looking away from Nicholas so that he could not see how pleased she was, 'but I do well understand that you are gallantly doing your best.'

'I am always a gallant escort,' Nicholas said immodestly, 'as you also no doubt, well understand.'

If he hoped to annoy Isabel he hoped in vain. 'Were these lady companions of yours all your sweethearts?' Isabel wanted to know.

'No!' Nicholas said emphatically, embarrassed at the turn their conversation was taking. 'Definitely not!'

'Was any one of them your sweetheart?' Isabel persisted in knowing with complete insensitivity.

'No, not at all,' Nicholas lied, looking out of the window.

Isabel's eyes narrowed in suspicion. 'You must be a man entirely lacking in romantic sentiment, Mr Raspero, to have never had a sweetheart.'

'And what about you, Lady Grangeshield?' Nicholas asked defensively. 'Have you ever had a sweetheart?'

'How dare you be so impertinent as to ask such a question?' Isabel snapped furiously.

'You're dodging my question, Lady Grangeshield,' Nicholas said, 'by getting onto your high horse, aren't you?'

As this was precisely what she was doing, Isabel opened her fan, turned her head away to look out of the window, and held her fan up and over her face. It was a gesture that expressed like no other the indignation of a lady subject to impertinence beyond measure. It was a gesture that was intended to make Nicholas feel guilty and ashamed, but he actually felt that he had fought Isabel to a draw for once.

They continued in silence while Isabel brooded behind her fan. As it happened, Isabel had never had a sweetheart. She always avoided discussing this issue because she knew that it was unusual. Perhaps it had been her early assumption of responsibility as Mistress of Grangeshield House, or the eager multitudes of admirers throwing themselves at her feet, too multitudinous for any one of them to be discernible, but for whatever reason Isabel had never had a sweetheart, and she did not like to be reminded of it. Isabel contemplated with a certain savagery about how to make Nicholas pay for the impertinence of his question.

The Grangeshield Carriage arrived at Randell House and descended to the landing area.

Nicholas descended to the ground first and waited for Isabel to descend, followed by the Eastons.

'Lady Grangeshield,' Nicholas said, offering her his left arm.

'What are you doing, Mr Raspero?' Isabel asked coolly, inspecting his proffered arm as if it were a work of art in a museum.

'I am offering you my arm as your escort tonight, Lady Grangeshield,' Nicholas explained.

'That is very amusing,' Isabel said, tapping his arm with her fan and marching off towards the entrance to Randell House. 'Now stop playing the fool and come along with me, Mr Raspero.'

They entered Randell House and were admitted by the doorkeeper to the party within. The announcer said, 'Lady Isabel Grangeshield and Mr Nicholas Raspero, Lord Bentley Easton and Lady Dacia Easton,' as they entered the Blue Salon. They attracted a certain amount of attention as they entered given that the gossip of today had all been about the goings-on at Grangeshield House the night before. The Audocavars had apparently arrived at Grangeshield House to find themselves in the midst of a full-blown lover's quarrel between Isabel and Nicholas. Crockery had been smashed, accusations had been thrown like spears and it had all ended with a weeping Isabel in Nicholas's arms begging for forgiveness, or so the wilder version of the story went. No-one knew what to believe, but some kind of fire must be behind all this smoke, and so Nicholas and Isabel were the subject of intense scrutiny by all those present.

Isabel made her way to Lord and Lady Randell, their host and hostess for the evening. She greeted them and remained chatting with them for a few minutes, while Nicholas waited patiently at her side. She did not introduce Nicholas or even look at him. When she had finished chatting to Lord and Lady Randell, she turned away as if Nicholas was not even there and walked off to the side where she greeted some more people. Nicholas followed, amused more than anything by her behaviour, not least because he had suddenly been granted an unexpected insight into Isabel's recent deception of him as they had talked in the garden. It was now apparent to him that Isabel's failure to introduce him to her guardians had had nothing to do with them at all. Nicholas realised that he had been expertly rolled and he could not help but be admiring of the way she had done it. He admired expertise in any of its many and varied forms.

He actually found it quite curious to stand there by Isabel's side as if he wasn't there as it was a new experience for him and he generally found new experiences interesting. He could not help but have a slight smile on his face as he followed Isabel around the room. Those he already knew he greeted politely, those he did not know he glanced at with a friendly amusement to show them that he recognised that he wasn't being introduced and it had its funny side. He saw Sophie and the friends she had been with at Lady Starfeld's party standing in a nearby room pretending not to be looking at Nicholas and Isabel, but Isabel herself might as well not have seen them, preoccupied as she was with meeting and greeting her fellow guests and ignoring Nicholas, who for his part was following everything, including Isabel's deliberate plan to treat him shabbily in public, with an amused alertness.

Lord Easton noted all this with alarm, feeling like a mortal who had wandered into Valhalla when things weren't looking so good.

The gong sounded, giving the signal to begin to prepare for the next dance.

'Lady Grangeshield?' Nicholas said.

Isabel completely ignored him.

Nicholas stepped up to Isabel's side and caught her lightly by the wrist, turning her around to face him.

'Lady Grangeshield,' said Nicholas, 'would you like to dance?'

Isabel stepped back, pulled her wrist out of his grasp and coolly replied, 'But I am not dancing at present, Mr Raspero.'

'Suit yourself,' said Nicholas and turned around and walked off.

Isabel turned back to her earlier conversation as if nothing at all had happened, but it was only a moment or two before she was admiring a detail of someone's dress, a closer inspection requiring Isabel to change her position; a change of position which gave her a view of where Nicholas had gone to after his departure.

Nicholas had gone directly to where Sophie was standing with The Gang.

'Good evening, Miss Nicholson.'

'Good evening, Mr Raspero.'

Nicholas exchanged greetings with the rest of The Gang while Sophie waited to pounce on him once he had finished. 'I see you have come here tonight with Lady Grangeshield,' she said to Nicholas.

'I see there is nothing which escapes your eagle eye, Miss Nicholson.'

'There is much which escapes my eagle eye, Mr Raspero, if it is sufficiently well *hidden*.'

Nicholas had to stop and think about this one for a moment. 'Not everything that is out of sight is hidden, Miss Nicholson.'

'But surely you are not *hiding* anything, Mr Raspero?'

'You're not flirting with me again, are you, Miss Nicholson?' Nicholas asked her with mock sternness, evoking a ripple of laughter from The Gang, who appreciated this shaft of wit.

'I was not aware that I had ever flirted with you, Mr Raspero,' Sophie said coolly.

'And why not?' asked Nicholas, with raised eyebrows.

Sophie paused for slightly too long while trying to think up a witty riposte, which provided an opening for Uliana to step briskly into the conversation.

'Is it true, Mr Raspero, that you were introduced to Isabel in early May?' asked Uliana.

'Yes.'

'But we have never seen you until very recently,' Penny blurted out.

'Well, the river of life has many tributaries which only meet up now and then,' Nicholas said casually. 'Or so I have been told, at any rate.'

The Gang all looked at him.

'How did you meet Lady Grangeshield?' Berg enquired.

'I was introduced to Lady Grangeshield by Mr Timothy Boylent at the engagement party of Mr Carver and Lady Lachance,' Nicholas told him.

'Are you acquainted with Mr Boylent?' Berg asked.

'I was introduced to Mr Boylent half an hour before.'

'And who introduced you?'

'You are being very inquisitive,' Nicholas told him, the tone of his voice distinctly frosty as he started to turn away from the group, 'so if you will all excuse me, I will move on.'

'No, no!' Penny cried out, slapping Berg on the upper arm reprovingly. 'You can't leave now!'

'Watch me!' Nicholas said, but they all relaxed on seeing that he was smiling as he said this.

'You dare not leave us now, Mr Raspero,' said Sophie. 'We have uncovered your secrets.'

'Should I be worried?' Nicholas asked quizzically.

Sophie only smiled in reply.

'All right, I'll bite. What secrets are these?'

'Those secrets which you have inherited from your baronial ancestors,' Sophie said meaningfully. It was an informed guess but Sophie had no idea how good a guess it was.

Nicholas looked unimpressed by this. 'Does this have to do with the baby from the windswept lake?' he asked with a smile, looking sideways across at Penny.

'Etienne da Silva is said to have not made public everything he knew,' Sophie said as meaningfully as before. She had gone to the library to research the Rasperos, even taking a look at the *World Compendium of Baronies,* and she was trying to stretch out what little she had managed to find out to give the impression it covered much more that she chose not to say. 'But surely what the eleventh Baron of Raspero knew was given in full to his descendants, was it not?'

'And what does that have to do with me?'

'But Mr Raspero, you are descended from the Barons of Raspero.'

'I am Anglashian, Miss Nicholson. The Barons of Raspero are Westrigonian.'

'But you are descended from them, Mr Raspero,' Sophie persisted.

'And you know secrets of wandlore which no-one else knows,' added Penny. 'You could beat Nevsky.'

'My grandfather and father did see to it that I was rigorously trained in the use of the wand. However, there are no great secrets in what I have received. Just a lot of hard work.'

'But of course,' said Penny, 'if there *were* such secrets, you would pretend there *weren't* any, wouldn't you?'

Nicholas laughed cheerfully. 'I suppose so,' he said. 'So there we are.'

'Those are very nice clothes you are wearing,' said Kora, who had been waiting all this time to ask about them during all this tedious talk about wandlore secrets.

'Yes,' Nicholas agreed.

'May I ask who the tailor was?' Berg enquired.

'What's a tailor?' Nicholas asked evasively, given that he didn't want to admit that he couldn't remember the man's name.

'I see you are *hiding* your knowledge of tailors from us, Mr Raspero,' Sophie said sweetly.

'You're back to hidden things already, are you, Miss Nicholson?' Nicholas asked.

'No, Mr Raspero, you are,' Sophie shot back instantly. This raised a chuckle from The Gang and Nicholas smiled as well in acknowledgement of the hit. The gong sounded for the next dance.

'I'll tell you what is hidden from me at the moment, Miss Nicholson, and that is my dance partner for the next dance. She could be hidden in plain sight for all I know,' Nicholas said meaningfully, looking directly at Sophie. 'But don't worry, Miss Nicholson, I won't ask you to dance given that Lady Grangeshield will bite your head off again.'

'Are you asking me to dance, Mr Raspero?' Sophie asked Nicholas, flapping her fan flirtatiously.

'You have found me out, Miss Nicholson. I was indeed.'

'I would be delighted,' Sophie said, holding out her hand, whereupon Nicholas promptly led her off to the dance floor.

The Gang watched them go and then fell into an animated discussion of all these mysteries. Berg spoke darkly of concealed affections; Penny wondered if Mr Raspero was hiding from deadly enemies with only Isabel knowing of his secret identity; Uliana sniffed at what she called nonsense, saying everything had a perfectly simple explanation if only this were known. They all agreed, however, that something was going on and they were determined to find out what it was.

Seeing Sophie going hand in hand with Nicholas to the dance floor Isabel was so taken aback that she dropped her fan. Mr Seward reacted faster than anyone, and got to the dropped fan first, picking it up and handing it back to Isabel with a slight bow, while his slower rivals looked on enviously. As Sophie and Nicholas went around the corner out of sight Isabel asked a companion where the nearest refreshments were, knowing full well that the nearest refreshments were lined up along the side of the dance room. Her group of male devotees obediently all trooped along with her as she went in search of these refreshments.

Isabel sipped a glass of punch while talking to Mr Seward, resolutely determined not to look at the dance, which was now in progress. Once, however, as she looked across, she noted Sophie shooting her a triumphant look as she whirled past with Nicholas. Isabel's stomach was clenched tight into knots. She did not blame Nicholas. Men were so helpless in these situations. Nicholas was being taken advantage of by Sophie.

The Gang had come into the dance room as well; Penny had seen Isabel drop her fan, and The Gang scented a drama.

The dance seemed to Isabel to simply drag on for ever but eventually it came to an end, as all things do, good or bad. Isabel paid no attention to Nicholas leading Sophie back to where The Gang were now standing; or rather, she appeared to pay no attention with her head turned away from them, her head casting a shadow on the wall by the side of a mirror in which they were all reflected.

'Well, that was fun,' Nicholas said to Sophie as they rejoined The Gang.

'Yes, indeed,' Sophie said, slightly flushed.

'You dance very well, Mr Raspero,' said Penny.

'And do you dance yourself, Miss Earlson?' Nicholas asked. 'If so, then my eagle eye is now on you.'

Flustered, Penny couldn't think of anything to say, especially as Sophie was now giving her a hard measuring look as if at a rival.

Nicholas by now had seen a variety of people he knew to talk to so he decided that it was time to move on. 'With any luck I'll see you again later,' he told them and was gone. The Gang veiled their gaze so as not to appear to watch Isabel, but it did not escape their attention that within a minute or so she was also departing the room in the direction taken by Nicholas.

'Now we have her!' Sophie said fiercely. 'Timmy can tell us about his introduction of Mr Raspero and Iz ... Lady Grangeshield will be exposed as a liar.'

'Timmy's here!' Penny said excitedly. 'I saw him earlier.'

'We will find him and bring him here,' Sophie decided, taking charge of the campaign. Sophie and Penny accordingly went off and soon found Timothy Boylent talking politely to some friends of his parents.

'Timmy!' they cried out and swooped on him. 'Come with us!' They each took an arm and with a 'Please forgive us!' to the Shermans they shepherded Timothy away. Not at all reluctant to be taken away from being grilled about all the various aspects of his life that the Shermans wanted to know about, Timothy allowed himself to be escorted away from that place.

'Am I being kidnapped?' Timothy asked.

'Yes, and the ransom demand will be to tell all that you know!' Sophie told him.

'That's not much!' Timothy joked. 'I'm glad I'll soon be free.'

'It is very ungallant of you, Timmy, to be glad of your freedom from our custody.'

'Ungallant is my middle name,' Timothy agreed. 'I was named after a knight of the Elliptical Table.'

By now they had reached The Gang, who all greeted him so joyfully that Timothy placed himself on full alert. It was obvious that they were after something. He didn't have to wait long to find out what.

'Timmy!' Uliana said briskly, taking hold of his attention, 'is it true that you introduced Mr Nicholas Raspero to Isabel at Sofiya's engagement party?'

Timothy wondered when people would stop asking him about this. First Isabel, now this lot. A wary look settled over his face, which did not escape the collective attention of The Gang.

'Yes,' he confirmed briefly.

'Are you acquainted with Mr Raspero?'

Timothy tried to recall how he had got away from Isabel; then it came back to him. 'Am I under interrogation, Uliana? If so, why? And what am I charged with?'

'You are indeed under interrogation, Timmy,' Uliana confirmed breezily. 'The charges have yet to be determined.'

Noting that the grip on his arms of his captors had slackened, Timothy decided to make a break for freedom. 'Oh no!' he burst out, raising a hand to his forehead as he suddenly appeared to remember something, which freed one arm, 'I forgot to speak to Ralph about, um, something.' He raised his other hand to place both hands on the top of his head, which freed his other arm. 'I've got to go. Bye!' With that, Timothy stepped back and with some deft footwork he was off and away.

The Gang watched their prey escaping from them in silence. The mystery had deepened — it was obvious Timothy was somehow involved in whatever was going on as his behaviour was highly suspicious.

'Is there no end to this mystery?' Penny cried out in delight.

'Well, we do know that Iz — Lady Grangeshield lied when she said she did not know Mr Raspero quite recently,' Sophie said furiously, her war against Isabel still in full swing.

'Technically she may not have lied,' Berg said, defending Isabel for two reasons: one was that Isabel was wealthy, the other that he admired subterfuge and was instinctively inclined to defend those capable of clever deceptions because they were his own sort. 'We cannot recall the exact words she used.'

'She asked *Who is Mr Raspero?* when she knew!' Sophie pointed out. The Gang had retrieved this item from their collective memories.

'That does not necessarily or factually mean that she did not know him,' Berg pointed out right back. 'It could have been intended as a rhetorical question.'

'She pretended not to know Mr Raspero,' Sophie said, 'and that is a lie.'

Berg was shaking his head in preparation for his reply but Uliana beat him to it. 'To pretend not to know something is not to lie about it,' she declared, 'unless you make such a statement outright. Looking back, she only implied such a lack of knowledge, she did not say so in so many words.'

'She only said she would look for him and find him without us,' Penny added, backing up Berg and Uliana. 'And then we all decided to look for him together.'

Kora was nodding to this. Sophie was on her own, but that did not daunt her for one moment. 'Mr Raspero seemed to be a familiar figure at Grangeshield House, judging by his familiarity with the servants. And do not forget that he was using the Footstool of Mangatha as a footstool! I saw it with my own eyes!'

And so The Gang wrangled while Nicholas moved here and there chatting to people. He was naturally sociable with a certain degree of ready wit, so he found a generally good reception. Isabel followed him about without appearing to, or so at least she believed.

Nicholas took note as the evening went on of the change his new clothes brought in the estimation of others. Where before people had been friendly, now they were friendly and respectful. His opinions now had more weight, his jokes were wittier and his mere presence was like a light unto others. He had become a larger and better person because of his new clothes. It was a lesson that Nicholas learned with surprise although once learned it of course seemed as if it had always been obvious. More than anything, though, Nicholas found that he was more of the world than he had been before, in that his clothes were wings by which he could now fly. He felt that he had become more than merely human thanks to his new clothes.

There came a time during the life of the party when the announcer at the door in the reception room called out, 'Lord Frederick Weatherby and Miss Angela Ashton.'

Nicholas turned to look at the latest arrivals. He was not the only one. The hubbub of noise quieted and there as a perfect hush as the assembled company turned their gaze as one on Miss Ashton.

She looked stunning in a white strapless evening gown, the gentle swell of her breasts needing only the merest hint of cleavage to accentuate their perfect restrained roundness. Her white-blonde hair was pulled up with careless-looking strands artfully falling down to the sides. Her bright blue eyes looked out over her audience as if she were on a stage and they were a distant audience, unable to approach her. Her companion, Lord Weatherby, a thin young man with untidy light brown hair and a cheerful moustache, looked about the room with a world-weary gaze as if unaware of the attention his companion of the evening was attracting; then people started to turn away from the spectacle and talk amongst themselves again.

'I thought Miss Ashton went around with what's-his-name, Lord ... Foxley,' Nicholas commented.

'She changes her paramours now and then,' Mr Fenton, who Nicholas was talking to at the time, replied.

'But what on earth is she doing here?' Mr Woods, another person present, exclaimed.

'She has been invited, I would assume,' Nicholas said.

Mr Woods looked as if this was not an assumption he would have made himself but he only said, 'Yes that must be it.'

Seeing Miss Dahl passing by with her long tennis-playing legs as the gong was sounding for the next dance, Nicholas intercepted her and a moment later was leading her onto the dance floor.

Isabel remembered then that Miss Dahl had been the acquaintance Nicholas had sought out at Lady Starfeld's party on his arrival. Isabel only vaguely knew Miss Dahl and she found herself wondering how well Nicholas knew her. She had certainly accepted his invitation to dance quickly enough. Isabel drifted towards the dance-floor, stopping to chat briefly to her fellow guests, moving by stages to a position from which she could observe what Nicholas was up to without appearing to be actually following him. The Gang drifted after Isabel in their turn. Timothy drifted in the opposite direction, keeping out of everyone's way.

After dancing with Miss Dahl, Nicholas took her over to where Mr Tarell was standing and chatted for a while before going off on his own. Angela deftly broke away from the ranks of the male admirers clustered around her and departed across the room on a trajectory intended to intercept Nicholas. Seeing Angela coming his way Nicholas stopped politely. Isabel watched all this from across the room.

'Good evening, Mr Raspero,' Angela said cheerfully, delighted to see Nicholas again.

'Good evening, Miss Ashton,' Nicholas said. 'No more Lord Foxley, I see.'

'We all change, Mr Raspero,' Angela replied pointedly, gazing at Nicholas's attire, 'even our clothes.'

'You are not the first to comment on my new clothes, but I suspect that I am the first to comment on your change of men.'

'And why do you say that?' Angela asked with one raised eyebrow.

'If you guess correctly I will confirm your guess,' Nicholas said playfully.

Nicholas was thinking to himself how odd it was that Angela's beauty and Isabel's beauty each reversed the other. Angela's slim shoulders seemed delicately sculpted compared to Isabel's sizeable presence; yet Isabel's superbly curvaceous shoulders made Angela's shoulders seem bony and skinny. Angela was slim and delicate where Isabel was large and bulky; yet Isabel's voluptuous figure made Angela by comparison seem like a stick figure. Where Angela was finely drawn, Isabel was overblown, but where Isabel was gently rounded, Angela was a pole with a mop of hair on top; Isabel's face was sweetly formed where Angela's face was drawn thin; yet Angela's face was so finely rendered as to make Isabel seem puffy.

'But how can I guess at what you suspect?' Angela laughed. She was enjoying this conversation and so was Nicholas.

'Are you confessing that you do not understand how my mind works or that you cannot catch a reflection with a shadow?'

'I never confess to anything, Mr Raspero,' Angela said flirtatiously, laughing again and opening her fan to hide more laughter behind it. 'And besides, I do not understand you.'

'A guess is a shadow because it is thrown by the light cast on an idea, a suspicion is a reflection because the mind works indirectly. Now you understand me, I trust.'

'You are too clever for me, Mr Raspero.'

'I confess in my own turn that I am living off the hard work done by another. I only repeat what I have heard another say. My cleverness is stolen.'

'Well, you are an honest thief then to tell me this.'

'Must I steal from you the knowledge of how Lord Weatherby has replaced Lord Foxley?'

Angela's good humour faded away. 'You are very inquisitive, Mr Raspero.'

'Only when I am curious.'

'I have told you that we all change, Mr Raspero, but you have not told me from where you got your new clothes.'

'From a tailor, Miss Ashton. From where else are new clothes obtained?'

'Which tailor was this?'

'I don't remember his name.'

'And did this tailor require money for his services?'

'Now you are inquisitive, Miss Ashton.'

'Only because I am curious, Mr Raspero.'

'Or evasive, Miss Ashton.'

'No, Mr Raspero, now it is you who are evasive.'

'I see I have lost a battle of wits while looking for a new dance partner,' Nicholas said meaningfully. 'I hope not to lose that battle also. Can you advise me where to find such a person?'

'In another place than this, Mr Raspero.'

'Will you be in that other place, Miss Ashton?'

Isabel's temper had been growing for some time. She was furious that Nicholas had ignored her all evening, spending his time talking with other guests and dancing with other women. She had already realised that she had made a mistake in asking Nicholas to be her escort this evening and had further decided to rectify that mistake by never making another one like it: after tonight Nicholas would be out of her life for good. She would have nothing to do with him ever again. Yet, the evening simply dragged on as if it would never end. She found herself nearly trembling at times from the strain of carrying on as if everything was as it should be. She had formulated the resolve not to approach Nicholas until it was time to go home, whereupon he would accompany her home and she would leave him outside her front door. Furthermore, she decided, and this cheered her up a lot, he would walk home given that he was so fond of walking!

It was only when she saw Nicholas talking to Angela for such a long time that Isabel's temper erupted into a solar flare, incinerating all earlier plans, decisions, observations, reflections, perceptions and comments into smoking ash. She had had enough and would take no more of this. Isabel charged over to them.

'Mr Raspero,' she snapped, 'I will talk with you immediately!'

She turned away and stormed off.

'As you see I must leave you now,' Nicholas said to Angela.

'Yes, you must do as you're told, of course,' Angela said a little maliciously. 'I understand your position.' Not having her own freedom she could not help but be a little malicious where she saw that someone else was not free either. Now she knew how Nicholas had got his new clothes.

Nicholas refused to take the bait but only grinned at Angela's comment before turning to go after Isabel.

She was waiting for him near the doors leading outside to the garden, tapping her fan furiously on a clenched fist. Nicholas stopped in front of her, his hand resting casually on the hilt of his wand.

'May I ask you, Mr Raspero, why you have decided to humiliate me this evening?'

'Shall we go outside, Lady Grangeshield? If we are to have a heated discussion, it might be better to conduct such a discussion in the cool evening air. Also, everyone here is looking at us, either openly or hiddenly. Clearly they expect you to make a scene.'

Isabel took a look around and realised Nicholas was right. They were the subject of the attended gaze of the assembled company, whose entire appearance as they talked and looked around was merely a disguise for the avid attention they were paying to Nicholas and Isabel.

Without saying a word, Isabel marched outside. Nicholas followed and they went to a place by the side in the garden, well away from the house. A nearby fountain was at play, the cool water talking to itself as it splashed down the sides of the sculpted figures of a centaur and a mermaid. Overhead the Milky Way stretched through the vault of the nighttime sky, the glowing silver dust of its path flanked by myriads of stars which glittered with varying degrees of brilliance. The sky seemed almost like a crumpled ceiling made of light and dark, the ice-white brilliance of the stars and the velvety blackness of space seeming to fold into each other as if the light came out of the dark to form a shaped surface that could almost be reached up and touched, so close to earth had the sky come that night.

'The stars look beautiful tonight,' Nicholas said appreciatively, looking up and around.

Isabel didn't give them even a glance. She had seen the stars before.

'Do you know what it means to be a gentleman, Mr Raspero?'

'Lady Grangeshield, when we arrived here you did not introduce me to any of the people you were speaking to. You ignored me as if I did not exist. You — '

'You are merely my escort for the evening, Mr Raspero. Do you really believe that you are entitled to anything more than the privilege of being here tonight?'

'Then when I asked you if you wanted to dance you said *But I am not dancing at present, Mr Raspero*, very snootily, and so — '

'Did you say *snootily*, Mr Raspero?'

'And so I decided, very understandably by the way, in case you don't realise it yourself and need to be told, very understandably, I decided to go and spend time talking to people who realised I was standing there and dancing with women who wanted to dance with me. And so that is what I have done. Do you have a problem with that?'

'Of course not, Mr Raspero. You may go off and dance with all the women you want. Why should I care less?'

'You're not angry because I didn't stay with you and I danced with other women?'

'No, I am not, Mr Raspero. It means precisely nothing to me.'

'Then what is it that you're so angry about then?' Nicholas asked, not knowing what to think now.

'You are here, Mr Raspero, as my escort for the evening. This means that your conduct reflects upon me. Do you understand that? Yes or no?'

'Yes, absolutely.'

'When you went to talk to that … woman, you showed the whole world that you are unfit to be my escort tonight, that you lack character, that you belong in the gutter, that you have no morals, that you have no place in civilised society.' Isabel threw each relative clause at Nicholas as a boxer throws a punch.

'That woman? Miss Ashton, you mean? Well, I know Mr Ansel Horado, the playwright and actor. He gives me free tickets to his plays and I go and watch their rehearsals sometimes. Miss Ashton is a member of his company so I know her to speak to. I just said hello, how's your latest play going, and so on. That's all.' Nicholas was somehow inspired to lie through his teeth with perfect composure, his inspiration perhaps coming from the stars overhead.

'Do you know what Miss Ashton is, Mr Raspero?'

'She's an actress.'

'She is a … whore, Mr Raspero. I fear I may have shocked you by speaking so plainly. Or perhaps you did not know this?'

'I know she is the mistress of wealthy men, but you are being —'

'There are no "buts", Mr Raspero. She is a whore. And by talking to her so openly, right in front of everyone in the way you did, you brought disgrace upon me. If I had known you were so degenerate, Mr Raspero, I would never have asked you to be my escort for the evening. How dare you behave like this! How dare you!'

'There is a flaw in your logic, Lady Grangeshield. You overlook the fact that Miss Ashton is a guest here tonight. If she is present here as a guest, then other guests may speak with her.'

'She was not invited. She has come as the … companion of Lord Weatherby, who was invited. She should not have been granted admittance to this gathering.'

'But she was. And I maintain that you can't blame me for talking to another guest. However,' Nicholas continued, to forestall Isabel's next attack, 'while you're about it, go and tell Lord Weatherby that he's a degenerate also. And —'

'Lord Weatherby has behaved disgracefully. It might well be the case that he is not invited to other gatherings of this sort in the future given the way he has flaunted his whore tonight in all our faces. He has shocked us all tonight. He will not be readily forgiven for this.'

'Very well,' Nicholas said, 'if you don't want me to talk with Miss Ashton any more tonight, fine, I won't. Happy now?'

Isabel found her temper abating greatly. While still furious with Nicholas, she realised that perhaps he simply hadn't known any better. She opened her fan and fanned herself with the cool night air. He was clearly unpolished, she reflected, or rather, while being highly polished in certain regards he was unpolished in others. He had at any rate promised not to talk to Miss Ashton *any more tonight*. That would do for now, though she noted that he had not promised not to talk at all to her ever again. He clearly had not yet learned his lesson, she reflected.

'I would not say I was happy, Mr Raspero,' Isabel said coolly. 'However, I have noted that you will no longer converse with Miss Ashton tonight. I shall regard that as sufficient reform on your part. I cannot excuse your misbehaviour tonight on the grounds of your utter and complete ignorance of what is expected of you if that is what you are hoping. The fact that you know nothing, the fact that you are completely and utterly ignorant of the most basic requirements of civility, of how to dress, your uneducated buffoonery, your imbecility, all your failings in short, do not excuse what you have done. You cannot say you did not know better because you should have known better. Your ignorance is no excuse. You are unfit to be my escort, Mr Raspero.'

'Yes, so you keep saying,' Nicholas said a little impatiently. 'But let me make something clear to you in my turn. I came here expecting to dance with you tonight but no more. I would refuse a request from you to dance with me. You may kick up all the fuss you like but I would say no. Why? Because that's your only hope of giving the appearance to all those present tonight that everything has been resolved between us, plus your only chance of getting level with Miss Nicholson. Yes, you'd like that, wouldn't you? Everyone would see us on the dance floor together and realise that everything was smoothed out and the gossip will fade away and everything will be as it was because they would no longer have anything to talk about. But I will not dance with you tonight, so dream on!'

Isabel considered this without saying anything in reply. She immediately reversed her earlier decision not to dance with Nicholas tonight. She would not be defied in such a manner. Nicholas was going to dance with her tonight whether he liked it or not!

The gong for a dance sounded in the distance and Nicholas said, 'That's the second last dance for tonight. I've been keeping count. I will be on my way if you'll excuse me. I just might have time to find someone to dance with me.'

Seeing how little time she had left, Isabel discarded the subtle approach. 'I only wish you had allowed me to finish what I was going to say earlier, Mr Raspero. I was going to say, *But I am not dancing at present, Mr Raspero. However, I would be delighted to have the next dance with you.* But before I could finish what I was about to say you simply charged off!'

'You were going to have the next dance with me?' Nicholas asked, pretending to believe her.

'But of course I was, Mr Raspero. I also expected us to dance together tonight. It would be absurd for us not to dance together, given that you are my escort for the evening.'

Seeing that his trick was working, Nicholas's heart began to beat faster at the prospect of feeling Isabel's hand in his. 'Well,' he said as if reluctant to change his mind on this issue, 'I suppose I only said I would refuse a request from you to dance with me. I suppose that's not the same as the request coming from me.'

Seeing things moving her way, and oblivious to the fact that she was for once being out-manouevred by Nicholas, Isabel seized on this concession. 'Precisely so, Mr Raspero. You have decided to refuse a request from me to dance with you. However, such a resolution does not preclude the presentation of a request from you to dance with me.'

'Could you give me a moment?' Nicholas asked, and looked away as if deep in thought. He then looked back at Isabel, held out his hand and said, 'Lady Grangeshield, would you do me the honour of dancing with me?'

'I would be delighted, Mr Raspero,' Isabel said as she placed her hand in his.

Nicholas felt the weight and warmth of her hand resting on his and for a moment couldn't move. Some kind of energy was dissolving his fingers without detracting from his razor-sharp perceptions of precisely how each separate finger felt together in his hand. They looked each other in the eye without moving for a moment, then Nicholas turned away and led Isabel back towards the house. Nicholas's heart was beating a lot faster than usual, and so was Isabel's, who was not fanning herself as they walked along for nothing. Nicholas was careful not to look at Angela, who was standing outside by the doors with two or three men in attendance, watching them as they passed by. Isabel looked over at Angela purely to give her a disdainful look as they passed by and Angela indifferently looked back at her.

As they entered the dance floor they found the dance that had been signaled earlier well under way. Nicholas led Isabel to the side, and as they came to a stop Isabel withdrew her hand from his and looked about the room without seeing anything, still fanning herself, unaware that she was blushing hotly.

The gong rang for the next dance and Nicholas held out his hand for

Isabel. She placed her hand in his, looking up into his eyes, which were no longer amused but serious as he led her out onto the dance-floor. Isabel found her heart beating faster and she fanned herself vigorously as the thought had occurred to her that she would not be able to fan herself while they were actually dancing so she might as well try to cool off as much as possible now. It was a sight that was not lost on those who looked their way, because even though it was a commonly seen affectation, it was not an affectation adopted before by Lady Isabel Grangeshield of Grangeshield House.

Isabel was not enormously fond of dancing as a rule because she was always concerned that she might look ridiculous, but she found that tonight was different. Although the dance floor was crowded, there seemed to be no-one else but Nicholas out there with her, and what she seemed to notice most were his observant grey eyes whenever their eyes met, which was often. The dance seemed to speed past and it seemed to Isabel that it was not long at all before Nicholas was leading her off the dance-floor, their dance together at an end.

'You were amazing,' Nicholas told her as he let go of her hand, 'leaping around the floor like a gazelle.' The fingers of his left hand jumped around in the air as if to illustrate how gazelles leapt about.

Isabel was not sure if this was really an effective compliment. Did she really want to be compared to a gazelle? 'Thank you, Mr Raspero,' she replied sweetly, gazing up at him with wide-open eyes, 'it is very kind of you to compare me with a gazelle.'

'Think nothing of it,' Nicholas said generously. 'Shall we go somewhere and sit down and talk for a while?'

'I would so much enjoy this very activity,' Isabel said with extreme seriousness, 'yet I must leave you now while I converse with other guests. Yet, surely I have put you out by this decision?'

'No, not at all,' Nicholas said breezily. 'Not put out at all.'

The gong rang for the next dance. 'I thought that we have already had the last dance,' Isabel said.

Nicholas looked around, a puzzled look on this face. 'So did I. I must have lost count.'

Isabel was too focused on the chance this gave her to make an anti-Raspero comment to pay the attention she should have to Nicholas's supposed mistake. 'Ah, I see you do not count very well, Mr Raspero. Yes, it is not an ability shared by everyone. It can, I believe, test the limit of a person's intelligence.' With the delighted malice of that parting comment Isabel turned away and departed without another word.

Far from appearing rebuked, however, Nicholas adjusted the sleeves of his robes with a very self-satisfied look on his face.

Just then Timothy turned up at his side and said, 'Could I have a word with you, Mr Raspero?'

'Of course you can,' Nicholas replied with a genial graciousness born of just having danced with Isabel Grangeshield. 'Follow me.'

As Timothy had a hunted look on his face and was carefully not looking across the room at certain people who were standing where he was not looking, Nicholas took him out of the dance room and then along a circuitous route through various rooms and corridors to a tucked-away out-of-sight corner of the party, sat down and gestured for Timothy to follow suit, and then asked cheerfully, 'What's up, soldier?'

THIRTY-ONE

The Public Quarrel of Mr Tread and Lord Weatherby

10:40 PM, Thursday 21 July 1544 A.F.

As soon as she was out of the dance room, Isabel went looking for someone to talk to, and as she had grown up with all these people all her life, it was merely a matter of walking in any direction. Almost by instinct, she manouevred herself to face the door of the room she had just left, where Nicholas would no doubt emerge from at some point.

As she engaged in chit-chat with someone or other whom she was talking to at the time, she kept her eye on the room she had just left. There was no sign of Nicholas, and she found himself wondering what he was up to now. She also found herself wondering if she had ever met anyone as infuriating as Nicholas. When he was in front of her, she wished him gone; when he was gone she could not stop wondering where he was and what he was doing. After some time she excused herself and returned to the dance room. Nicholas was nowhere to be seen. She went off in search of him, concealing the nature of her quest by an apparent desire to mingle with the guests and talk to them about the various topics of the day. There was still no sign of Nicholas anywhere. Where had he gone? How could he have simply disappeared like this? She continued looking but still with no success.

Isabel was by now holding panic at bay. Nicholas was nowhere to be seen and she had looked everywhere. Where had she not looked? What was he up to while he was out of her sight? He surely would not bring disgrace on her head by behaving improperly with one of the women he had been dancing with all night. His behaviour would reflect on her as she had brought him to this party. She spotted The Gang standing to one side and went up to them.

'Delightful party, is it not?' she said to them pleasantly.

'It is indeed, Isabel,' said Berg. 'You have aptly characterised the very nature of this happy gathering.'

Isabel cast all politeness aside, unable to make chit-chat while she worked her way to what she wanted to know, and asked, 'Have you seen Mr Raspero, by any chance?'

'He went off with Timmy Boylent, I believe,' Berg told her.

Timothy? Isabel's panic lessened. So Nicholas had not gone off somewhere with a woman. But what was going on? 'Did you see which direction they went in?' Isabel asked.

'They went in that direction, Lady Grangeshield,' Sophie said, pointing to her right at the door leading to the Violet Salon.

Isabel was so distracted that she nearly fell for it, but she caught the barely perceptible stiffening of Penny and Kora as they looked sideways at Sophie, and realised that of course Nicholas and Timothy had gone in precisely the opposite direction to that indicated by Sophie. 'Thank you, Miss Nicholson, you have been most helpful,' she told Sophie with a malicious impassivity and immediately set off in search of Nicholas and Timothy. Behind her Sophie's fan snapped shut loudly.

Isabel remembered that she had still not yet given Timothy a scolding for his behaviour in providing an introduction to her as a wandfighting prize, and she realised that now was the perfect time to give that very scolding. This time around, guessing that the two party guests were sitting down somewhere secluded to talk with each other, Isabel succeeded in tracking them down. They were in the Room of the Globe, sitting on the low-set window ledges, out of sight from anyone just looking in at the door, which was all she had done before. Isabel walked up to them. They both politely rose to their feet.

'Timmy,' Isabel said, pointing her fan like a sword at Timothy's chest in a distinctly hostile manner, 'it has come to my attention that you have been providing introductions to me as prizes for wandfighting. What do you have to say for yourself?'

'Um,' Timothy said, giving Nicholas a sideways look, 'well, um, yes, ah, well, what you have to realise, Isabel, is that Mr Raspero did the Three and that —'

'I have no interest in what Mr Raspero did in securing this prize from you, Timothy,' Isabel said severely. 'Am I to wonder from this time forth what someone has done to gain such a favour from you as an introduction to me? I simply had no idea that you did this kind of thing, Timothy. I am shocked, shocked and disappointed, very disappointed in you.'

'Isabel, do you have any idea how hard it is to do the Three? Any idea at all? It's not as if —'

'How can you be sure that a man whose only recommendation is that he can do the Three is a gentleman?'

Timothy cast Nicholas another sideways look to see how the best wandfighter in New Landern was taking this. The best wandfighter in New Landern was gazing at Isabel with a fascinated smile.

'Well, um, Mr Raspero is certainly a gentleman, Izzy,' Timothy said, 'and that was clear before he did the Three so —'

'The man who introduced you to Mr Raspero was not a gentleman, Timothy. Are you aware of this?'

Timothy looked uncertainly at Nicholas. Nicholas looked across at him and nodded. 'I later discovered that Mr Longman is most certainly not a gentleman, Mr Boylent. I demanded satisfaction from him for an offence and he declined my challenge. He is a liar, a rat, a cheat, a man without honour.'

'Well, I never met the man until ten minutes before you came along,' Timothy told Nicholas.

'Fair enough,' Nicholas said.

It was not *fair enough* for Isabel. 'That does not excuse your shocking lapse of judgement,' Isabel told Timothy sternly. 'You should be ashamed of yourself, Timothy Boylent, deeply ashamed of handing out introductions to me to thuggish wandfighters who you merely happen to come across in the more debauched corners of a party.' With that Isabel turned and left.

'Isn't she amazing?' Nicholas said to Timothy admiringly as he gazed after the shapely figure of the departing Isabel.

'Ah, yes,' Timothy said as if agreeing. He was, in fact, agreeing, but perhaps not in the way that Nicholas would have assumed. Timothy had already had his Isabel experience. When they had both been fourteen, Timothy had fallen madly in love with Isabel. He had declared his feelings to her one day and Isabel, with a glint in her eye, had decreed that he must prove himself worthy of her. He had been required to write an essay of not less than ten pages on the duties of a husband to a wife, with reference to all historical sources available; Isabel had read through his essay and marked it, giving him an "F" for "Fail" because she thought he had failed to properly examine the issue. He had been obliged to write her love letters once a week, which she had returned with his grammatical errors underlined in red ink. She had criticized his clothing, the way he stood, the way he walked, the way he talked, his opinions on any subject of the day, and his hair style. It was not long before Timothy had decided that all the happiness in the world was not worth this kind of treatment, and he began to retreat from the ground of his earlier declaration of his feelings for his beloved, browbeaten all the way by a furious and contemptuous Isabel who made observations such as that his eternal love hadn't lasted long, had it?

'Let's sit down,' Nicholas said, but hardly had they sat down when Nicholas observed Isabel on her way back to them and they stood up again.

Isabel had been peacefully on her way when it occurred to her that she did not know what Nicholas and Timothy were talking about sitting so out of the way in the corner. She therefore decided to return to find out what they were talking about; it was not that she had any real interest, but just to be sure that these rascals were not up to mischief, she returned to interrogate them.

'Timmy, what are you two talking about?' she asked imperiously.

'Isabel, this is a private conversation, and it is none of your business what we are talking about. Goodbye. The door is behind you.' Timothy spoke with a certain cold authority, secure in the citadel of courtesy from whose ramparts he addressed the enemy.

Isabel, her head bowed down as she inspected her fan which she was slowly unfolding while listening to Timothy's defiant declaration, took her time in fully unfolding her fan, and then looked up at Nicholas and asked, 'Mr Raspero, what are you two talking about?'

Timothy was not surprised to see Nicholas immediately surrender without a fight. 'Well, Mr Boylent is concerned because The Gang are after him because he introduced me to you and they believe that you are deliberately concealing an acquaintance with me that precedes a time when they believe you were saying that you did not know me. You know all of this anyway. You are welcome to sit in on our conversation if you wish.'

Isabel said nothing, examining the markings of her fan as if they contained a secret message that she was only then just deciphering.

'I'll get you a chair,' Nicholas said, and waved his wand to set down a chair behind Isabel. 'Let's sit,' he said and sat down himself, followed by Isabel and, more reluctantly, by Timothy. 'So, as I was saying, The Gang believe that Lady Grangeshield deceived them into believing that she did not know me earlier this month when she did, in fact, know me. However, she did not know me in actual fact because she did not remember our introduction in the Dacian —'

'I remember our introduction perfectly well,' Isabel interrupted him.

'As she did not remember our introduction in the Dacian Room of Regana Palace,' Nicholas resumed, 'she was not deceiving The Gang concerning this matter.'

'I-re-mem-ber-our-in-tro-duc-tion-ver-y-well!' Isabel insisted, tapping out each syllable of each word on Nicholas's knee with her fan.

'So this matter can be cleared up very readily,' Nicholas continued, ignoring Isabel's repeated interruptions, 'by simply telling The Gang how things stand.'

'Mr Raspero,' Isabel said firmly, 'you have many faults, but you are not forgettable. I remember you very well.'

'You didn't even look at me,' Nicholas pointed out. 'There was nothing for you to forget because you didn't even see me.'

'I remember our introduction very well,' Isabel insisted yet again, not giving way a single inch on this matter, 'and I will not go along with such a falsehood as you propose. Let the glorious Truth stand forth. Its light will dazzle those who hide in the dark!'

'I keep on forgetting that no-one can tell you anything,' Nicholas told Isabel, 'but never for very long because you're always so quick to remind me, aren't you?'

'I keep on forgetting how insolent you are, Mr Raspero,' Isabel replied, 'but never for very long because you are always so quick to take refuge in your insolence in order to dissemble and evade the issue.'

Nicholas turned to Timothy. 'Mr Boylent, what do you think? Is it not very likely that Lady Grangeshield did not remember me at the time The Gang believe she was pretending not to know me?'

Timothy nodded even as Isabel continued to protest, saying that it was very clear that Isabel could not possibly remember the introduction, and in any case Isabel had even asked him if he had made this introduction; Isabel said it had been a rhetorical question; Timothy asked scornfully if Isabel even knew what the word *rhetorical* meant; Isabel asked in her turn if Timothy could even spell the word "retorikle" without help. She had once underlined with red ink this mis-spelled word in one of Timothy's love letters. Timothy reddened but seemed determined to fight on.

Nicholas rose to his feet and they broke off their bickering and looked around. The Gang had entered the room and were standing before them, spread out in a determined manner which showed that they meant business.

'May we join you?' Berg asked pleasantly, as if their grim and determined postures did not make it clear that this was merely a rhetorical question as they had already taken their places between them and the door.

'Of course you may,' Nicholas said equally pleasantly. 'What could delight us more?' It was a rhetorical question, as obviously nothing could have delighted Nicholas more than to have The Gang join him and his companions.

'I see that you have *hidden* yourself away, Mr Raspero,' Sophie observed.

'Only to talk in private, Miss Nicholson.'

'May I ask what you are talking about, Mr Raspero?'

'Memories and misunderstandings,' Nicholas replied cheerfully.

'And are these misunderstandings *hidden*, Mr Raspero?'

'They wouldn't trip us up if they were hidden, Miss Nicholson.'

'Ah, it is the memories to which you refer which are *hidden*, I take it.'

'Nothing is being *hidden* from you, Miss Nicholson. Trust me.'

'Should I trust you directly, Mr Raspero, or in a *hidden* way?' Sophie asked sweetly.

'You should only place your trust in providence, Miss Nicholson,' Nicholas said, as amused as ever. 'Spooky, isn't it?'

'Providence works in *hidden* ways, does it not, Mr Raspero?' Sophie asked.

'Who's to say, Miss Nicholson? Providence is inscrutable, after all.'

'Are you inscrutable, Mr Raspero?'

'You tell me, Miss Nicholson.'

'Shall I tell you directly, Mr Raspero, or in a *hidden* way?'

'Stop flirting with me at once, Miss Nicholson!' Nicholas said with a broad grin. 'Remember what happened last time!'

'I see you are not *hiding* your amusement,' Sophie observed, 'but you are surely *hiding* something else, I think, Mr Raspero.'

'You manage to hide your intelligence very successfully, Miss Nicholson,' Isabel said, unfolding her fan as a declaration of war, 'indeed, so successfully you appear to have none at all.'

'Oh, is that what I am hiding, Lady Grangeshield?' Sophie asked, unfolding her own fan right back. 'Now I know. But tell me, Lady Grangeshield, what is it that you are hiding?'

'How dare you presume to question me!' Isabel snapped.

'How dare you deceive me as you have!' Sophie snapped right back.

Isabel closed her fan and started to say, 'I believe you have —'

'Shush!' Nicholas said loudly, holding his left hand out high in the air, his right hand on his wand as always, 'shush!' He tilted his head, listening. 'Why has everything gone so quiet?'

While everyone was still catching up with him, Nicholas said, 'Excuse me,' and used his wand to flip himself through the air over the heads of The Gang, landing so smoothly on his feet that he was already walking towards the door as a continuation of his motion through the air. Timothy promptly followed suit, but landed more awkwardly, so he staggered slightly as he went after Nicholas.

'A difference of ability, I think,' Berg observed.

'And how would you do?' Uliana asked.

'That would be yet another difference of ability,' Berg laughed.

Isabel shot to her feet and trotted after Nicholas, crying out, 'Wait, Mr Raspero, wait!'

Isabel got to the door to find Nicholas and Timothy already at the far end of the corridor, turning left down a flight of stairs. There was indeed a silence that was a fearful absence of noise throughout the entire house, at least to Isabel's ears, given that she was now remembering she had mentioned attacks by armed gangs when asking Nicholas to be her escort tonight. Terror struck at Isabel's heart at the thought of being defenceless at the hands of an armed gang; she threw all decorum and dignity to one side and ran at top speed after Nicholas. She reached the top of the flight of stairs and started rushing down them. She could see people standing around looking downwards; to her right she saw Nicholas and Timothy standing by a balcony railing, looking down into the Main Hallway below. Isabel rushed up behind Nicholas, grabbed onto his left arm and hid behind his back while she peered around his shoulder, wide-eyed and fearful, at the drama unfolding in the Main Hallway below.

The sight upon which Isabel gazed was a spectacle dramatic enough to gladden the hearts of all theatre-goers. It was clear at first sight that some kind of confrontation was taking place. On the one side stood Mr Tread, resplendent in his red coat with its silver and gold buttons, his side-whiskers neatly trimmed, his hair rising into the air in carefully folded waves, his knee-length black leather boots so highly polished that they reflected everything around him like a cunning mirror designed by an eternal mind. On the other side stood Lord Weatherby, clearly much the worse for wear; his moustache was if anything even more cheerful than before, his hair more rumpled and sticking out at the sides, his clothes seeming somehow to be in a state of disarray because even though technically everything was buttoned down and tucked in he gave the impression that a good tug upon his person would bring everything undone.

Lord Weatherby and Mr Tread were facing each other like two cockerels in a farm-yard, surrounded by concerned friends, well-wishers, merchants of conciliation, and drama-hungry spectators.

'I was not aware that you are a guardian of propriety,' Lord Weatherby was saying loudly, 'nor of your qualifications to claim such a role.'

'I am not alone in my complaint,' Mr Tread said equally loudly, looking about him for support. There were nods from some of the men, and the fluttering of fans from many of the ladies, to back Mr Tread up in his stand against Lord Weatherby. 'Your behaviour tonight has been one of reckless misconduct, Lord Weatherby. You have brought your whore here into our very midst without regard to propriety or decency.'

'I am sure you keep your whore in a private room where no-one can see her because she's so ugly!' Lord Weatherby roared, looking about him with a fierce grin. He evoked a modest wave of appreciative laughter at his wit.

Isabel looked about for Angela and was not pleased to see that Angela had already noted Nicholas's presence and was looking in Nicholas's direction.

'You are unaware of the requirements of civil society which govern the conduct of a gentleman,' Mr Tread said as if addressing a political gathering rather than a degenerate opponent. 'Your private life is your own affair but to bring your whore here tonight is an unacceptable breach of decorum. Your behaviour is that of a degenerate.'

'Ho hum! Ho hum!' Lord Weatherby yawned loudly, his face flushed and sweaty, 'your private life is no doubt too boring to discuss, so you must discuss mine! You are nothing but envious, Mr Tread, and that is the cause of your true complaint!'

Some nods, and one or two fluttering fans, backed up Lord Weatherby's contention, but the majority of heads and fans were on Mr Tread's side and stayed motionless. Seeing this, Mr Tread was encouraged to continue. 'But perhaps this lack of discretion is a family failing on your part, Lord Weatherby. After all, your great-grandfather, Lord Cross, was none too discreet about his withdrawal from the Battle of Staynes, was he not?'

'I demand satisfaction!' Lord Weatherby roared in a fury. 'How dare you insult my great-grandfather! Answer my challenge!'

'I accept your challenge,' Mr Tread replied. 'What form of satisfaction do you require?'

'First Combat.'

'When and where?'

'Here and now.'

'Very well, let us go,' Mr Tread said, and the two combatants turned away from each other, and set forth for the garden, with the party guests following them.

Isabel let go of Nicholas's arm and stepped back. She stayed by his side as they took their places in the flow of party guests leaving the house to watch the duel. Outside in the cool night air people took their places in the garden while Lord Weatherby and Mr Tread squared off against each other, and began their duel.

The duel proceeded for a while, both men equally handicapped by drink. Then Mr Tread, by a flurry of moves, managed to bring Lord Weatherby down to a rousing round of applause from his supporters.

The two men squared off for the second round and resumed battle. Angela set forth from where she was standing and came towards Nicholas. She looked like a swan in a yard full of chickens as she made her way through the party-goers, her white dress gleaming in the moonlight with its cunningly woven fabric. Angela stood before Nicholas with her fan folded in her hands and said, 'Mr Raspero, would you be so kind as to take me home?'

'No, Miss Ashton, that is out of the question. I came here with Lady Grangeshield and I will leave with Lady Grangeshield.'

'You must do what you think is right, of course.'

'And what about you, Miss Ashton? Do you always do what you think is right?'

Angela paused, looking at Nicholas. She either had too many answers to choose from or none at all; it was as if she couldn't even be certain about being uncertain. 'I will answer that question when we next meet, Mr Raspero,' Angela replied serenely and turned away.

The next man she approached took up her offer immediately and with obvious enthusiasm and they left the party together. Nicholas continued to watch the duel while feeling a vast impatience with everything, just everything. Isabel looked across at him, feeling nervous for no good reason that she could think of except for the faraway look on Nicholas's face. She knew that he was thinking about the departed Angela.

Isabel was struck by how grand Nicholas looked as he stood there. He stood so still he looked like a statue, like a statue of a nobleman, grave and distinguished. Isabel didn't like to see Nicholas as a statue thinking of Angela, so she interlinked her right arm with his left arm and said, 'I wonder if you could explain to me what is happening, Mr Raspero. I do not have an extensive familiarity with this kind of thing.'

'They're idiots and this is pointless,' Nicholas said abruptly. 'I think that pretty much covers it.'

Isabel could feel from the stiffness in his arm that Nicholas was in a mood. 'I must say that we are in agreement that this is unnecessary, Mr Raspero. There are surely more reasonable and civilised ways of settling disagreements of this sort. Even if Mr Tread did insult Lord Weatherby's ancestor.'

Isabel could feel the tension in Nicholas's arm lessening. The sound of her voice was having an effect on him. The Gang was following this exchange while not giving them a single look. Timothy was too absorbed in following the duel blow by technical blow to be aware of anything else. 'Yes,' Nicholas agreed, 'but given the sheer ineptitude of both combatants, it is no more uncivilised than children playing at soldiers.'

'There are of course many reasons for there to be duels,' Isabel continued, still being polite and on her best behaviour, at least until Nicholas stopped being in such a mood. 'If one of those reasons is so that children can play at being soldiers, then I can only agree that this is not necessarily uncivilised but rather a diversion from more serious matters.' She could feel that his arm was completely relaxed now; there was no longer any tension in his body.

It dawned on Nicholas then that he had the dazzling Lady Isabel Grangeshield on his arm. She was actually holding his arm! The last thought of Angela disappeared from his mind and he looked across at Isabel. 'Precisely so, if I may borrow a phrase from you, Lady Grangeshield.'

Isabel could see from his look that she had him back. She let go of his arm, stepped away, unfolded her fan like a swordsman drawing his sword as she turned to face him and said coolly, 'I would rather you paid attention to principles of conduct than turns of phrase, Mr Raspero. Please feel free to borrow all the phrases you wish to from me. But what of the principles of conduct which you so evidently fail to observe? Why do you not borrow them as well?'

The Gang had given up all pretence of watching the duel and was now watching them openly. Nicholas and Isabel were so focused on each other they paid The Gang no attention. Timothy carried on watching the duel, oblivious to anything else.

'What do you mean?' Nicholas asked with a certain resignation; he was wondering what he had done now, given that he could see that Isabel was gearing up to scold him for something or other.

'I thought that we were in agreement that you were not to speak to Miss Ashton again tonight. Did you not promise me this? Have you not now broken your promise? Or perhaps I am mistaken?'

Nicholas felt trapped. The logic of her attack was irrefutable. He realised he somehow had to confuse the issue. 'Are we not bound by a wider promise that as guests at this party we are to observe those rules of courtesy that govern our conduct? So there are promises within promises, Lady Grangeshield. The wider promise of our circumstances simply over-rode the particular binding nature of my promise not to speak to Miss Ashton again.' Nicholas thought that this didn't sound too bad.

'I see,' Isabel said, folding her fan and closing the latch as if locking Nicholas into a cell. 'You will dissemble, you will evade the issue and in the end no doubt you will tell me that I am the one who is in error.'

Nicholas sighed. 'All right, Lady Grangeshield, I broke my promise not to speak to Miss Ashton again. I will confess that I am in error.'

'And what am I to make of your conduct, Mr Raspero?' Isabel said furiously, unfolding her fan again. 'Clearly I cannot trust you to keep to whatever promises you make, yet I am glad to have uncovered this now.

I would never have asked you to be my escort tonight had I known your true nature, which has now been revealed to me.'

'Well, things happened as they happened,' Nicholas said a little helplessly.

'Oh, did they so?' Isabel said scornfully. 'Is that an argument, Mr Raspero, or the cackle of a goose?'

'It is neither, Lady Grangeshield. It is merely a statement.'

'Mr Raspero, I must insist that you apologise to me for your conduct.'

'No, I will not!' Nicholas snapped, tired of being brow-beaten by Isabel day in and day out. 'You can think what you like, Lady Grangeshield. No doubt your behaviour is always perfect and you can tell us lesser mortals how you manage it.'

Isabel realised that she had pushed this as far as she could. She started to backtrack. 'No doubt you regret now having made that promise to me in the first place.'

This was an unexpected and skillful change of direction from Isabel that floored Nicholas then and there. 'Not at all, Lady Grangeshield,' he said eventually, remembering that it was making that promise that had led the way to him dancing with Isabel.

'Perhaps you believe that I am not entitled to extract such a promise from you in the second place,' Isabel continued.

'Not at all, Lady Grangeshield,' Nicholas said again, finding himself thrown back on the floor again. 'Naturally I am here as your escort this evening so you are perfectly entitled to make such a demand.'

Isabel felt that it was time to wrap this all up. She knew exactly when to stop: she could judge it to within a hair's breadth. 'Well, I am relieved to hear that this at least is perfectly clear to you, Mr Raspero. There is no need to say any more about this. You admit yourself that you are in error, and this at least is to your credit.'

'So that's settled then,' Nicholas said hopefully.

Isabel turned away from him and folded her fan like a general accepting the surrender of the enemy. 'Yes, Mr Raspero, the matter is settled.'

The Gang all turned away from their contemplation of this exchange back to a contemplation of the much less interesting duel. Mysteries remained, but one thing at least was perfectly clear to them all.

THIRTY-TWO

A Decision is Made by Mr Nicholas Raspero
Concerning Lady Isabel Grangeshield

12:20 AM, Friday 22 July 1544 A.F.

The Grangeshield Estate flying carriage was high in the air on its return journey to Grangeshield House while Nicholas and Lady Easton chatted pleasantly and a brooding Isabel tapped her fan lightly on her knuckles. At some point Isabel asked, 'Did you enjoy yourself this evening, Mr Raspero?'

'I enjoyed every moment,' Nicholas told her. 'What about you, Lady Grangeshield? Did you enjoy yourself this evening?'

'I would not say I enjoyed every moment, Mr Raspero,' Isabel said meaningfully. 'So we differ there. But then, we are so different in so many ways, are we not?'

'You can say that again,' Nicholas agreed with a grin.

Isabel looked away, unfolding her fan and folding it up again. She felt a desire to crush Nicholas, to inflict such pain on him that he would whimper and beg for mercy. Above all else, she wanted to wipe that stupid grin off his face.

She had spent much of that evening in an agony. The conduct of her escort would reflect on her, and there he was dancing with all those other women. What if he had behaved improperly in their company? She would be blamed for having brought him. Nicholas was a jumped-up nobody who had only been present tonight as her escort. Yet, he had complained that she had not introduced him to her fellow guests, as if he was something more than a jumped-up nobody! Who did he think he was?

'But surely you are not being entirely truthful,' Isabel told Nicholas, 'when you say that you enjoyed every moment.'

'Do you have a particular moment in mind?' Nicholas asked warily.

'I do believe that you complained about not being introduced to my fellow guests. You cannot have enjoyed those moments if you later complained about them.'

Nicholas shrugged. 'That's all right,' he said casually. 'I have no complaints now, if that's what you mean.'

'How kind you are being, Mr Raspero, until of course you lose your temper again.'

'You could make a saint lose his temper, Lady Grangeshield.'

'Are you saying that *I* am to blame for *your* loss of temper, Mr Raspero? Am I to take responsibility for your failings?'

'Absolutely!' Nicholas said with a perfectly straight face that might as well have been the most crooked of grins. Seeing his merry mood made Isabel angrier.

'Do you know why I did not introduce you to anyone tonight, Mr Raspero?' The way she said this was like a knife-fighter taking out his knife in a studied fashion in full view of his unlucky opponent.

'Because you're a snob?'

'You are being rude, Mr Raspero.'

'I learned it from you,' Nicholas said promptly. 'All right, I'm going to hear this anyway whether I like it or not, aren't I? Why did you not introduce me to anyone tonight?'

'Because you are a *nobody*,' Isabel said with a very deliberate emphasis on her very deliberate description of Nicholas Raspero as a *nobody*. 'That is why.'

Nicholas tried to keep a straight face but it was impossible. His cheek muscles simply convulsed of their own accord and he burst out laughing. To Isabel's enormous annoyance, the laughter was genuine. 'Well, there we are,' Nicholas said as his laughter subsided into chuckles. 'Now I know! At least you're not blaming your guardians this time, are you?'

This made Isabel pause like a swordfighter encountering an unexpectedly skillful move from an under-estimated opponent. She looked at Nicholas, who was grinning cheerfully at her.

'*Blaming your guardians?*' Lord Easton asked Isabel. 'What does he mean by that, Isabel?'

'I have absolutely no idea,' Isabel said defiantly. 'But I must insist that we talk no more about this subject given that Mr Raspero is clearly out to make trouble. We must not give him the satisfaction of responding to his provocations.'

'But what are we blamed for?' Lady Easton asked, half-laughing over the latest antics of the children.

'This subject is closed!' Isabel declared imperiously.

'May I ask what you meant by your comment?' Lord Easton asked Nicholas.

'Ask Lady Grangeshield,' Nicholas told him and looked away.

Lord Easton rarely put his foot down, but when he did Isabel obeyed him. 'Isabel, you will explain to me what this is about and you will do this now!'

'Mr Raspero believes that I did not introduce you to him on your instructions,' Isabel said carefully, trying to imply that this was not her fault but Mr Raspero's.

'Are you saying that you lied to Mr Raspero about us?' Lord Easton said very coldly.

'She did not lie, Lord Easton!' Nicholas said, immediately springing to Isabel's defence with his very own bare-faced lie. 'She only implied it. I was the one to make this attribution.'

'Precisely so!' Isabel declared with relief. If anyone was lying now it was Nicholas. She was in the clear. 'I cannot be blamed for Mr Raspero's muddle-headedness.'

Lord Easton found his prey escaping from under him. 'I cannot say that to have implied such a thing was a matter which leaves you entirely blameless, Isabel.' The word *blame* had resurfaced and it was now being stuck on Isabel.

'The demands of courtesy often require implication, do they not?' Isabel said coolly.

Lord Easton was set back on his heels by this. As Isabel well knew, he prided himself on his courtesy and his logic, and this was not a statement he could brush aside. 'Well, yes,' he admitted, trying to see what next to say, 'but that does not entirely —'

'It is time for us to disembark!' Isabel declared. The carriage had settled down to the ground some time ago but no-one but Nicholas had noticed at the time. Isabel had just noticed it now, and she grasped at this chance to put time and distance between her and this argument. By the time the argument resumed, if it ever did, everything would have cooled off and she could simply blame Nicholas for entirely misunderstanding what she had been saying.

They disembarked from the carriage, first Nicholas, as he was the escort, then Isabel, then Isabel's guardians.

'You will come inside, Mr Raspero,' Isabel said when they arrived at the front doors of Grangeshield House. She said it as if giving an order to a servant. Lady Isabel Grangeshield of Grangeshield House had returned to Grangeshield House.

Nicholas put up with her bossiness as if he hadn't noticed it. 'Thank you, Lady Grangeshield.'

On the way in Lady Easton murmured to Lord Easton, 'We will say no more of this subject, Bentley. I will explain everything to you later.'

Lord Easton considered this for a moment then agreed. 'Very well.' He had not been sure how to continue the debate in any case.

They entered the drawing room. 'I will have a glass of red wine, Benson,' Isabel told Benson. 'And what will you two have?' she asked her guardians.

They wanted red wine as well.

Nicholas was not asked if he wanted anything to drink.

'Let us sit down,' Isabel said to her guardians.

They all sat down, Nicholas slouching back in his chair with his feet thrust out on the Footstool of Mangatha.

'And what will you be doing with yourself this week, Mr Raspero?' Isabel asked Nicholas.

'Oh, this and that,' Nicholas said. 'Thanks for asking.'

'It is obviously something very personal and very private,' Isabel said maliciously. 'I perfectly understand if you do not wish to say what you will be up to.'

Nicholas couldn't help smiling reluctantly at that comment. 'Oh, I'll wander along to the Emperor Theatre and watch a rehearsal or two. The Kerrick Company is going to be performing *The Kingdom of Happiness* next month. Visit some friends, go to Kenina Park, that kind of thing.'

'We already have tickets for *The Kingdom of Happiness*,' Lady Easton confided to Nicholas. 'I am greatly looking forward to attending the performance. Such a wonderful play. I have seen it five times.'

Benson brought red wine for Isabel and her two guardians. Nicholas watched them being served with an amused expression on his face.

'Oh, goodness me!' Isabel exclaimed. 'I have forgotten to ask you if you wanted something to drink, Mr Raspero.'

'I don't want anything to drink as it happens,' Nicholas said, looking such a picture of laziness as he sat there stretched out with his hands on the armrests of his chair that it was clear that he preferred to avoid even the effort of lifting a glass. 'But thank you for asking.'

'Are you quite sure, Mr Raspero?'

'Yes, I am quite sure, Lady Grangeshield.'

'But are you quite, quite sure, Mr Raspero?'

'Yes, Lady Grangeshield, I am quite, quite sure.' Nicholas couldn't help grinning.

'Very well,' Isabel said doubtfully, as if uncertain that Nicholas was really able to make such a decision unaided. 'But you will, of course, let me know if you change your mind, won't you, Mr Raspero?'

'Of course I will,' Nicholas said with perfect seriousness. 'Definitely!'

'So you are attending the rehearsals of the Kerrick Company,' Isabel said without a pause, as if this followed on from what they had just been saying. 'You will no doubt pursue your acquaintance with Miss Ashton.'

'Miss Ashton this, Miss Ashton that. Do you ever talk about anything else other than Miss Ashton?'

'I see you prefer to hide from my question. Very well, grovel before Miss

Ashton all you like. At least you are too ashamed of what you are doing to confess to it. That shame is the only virtue you possess, Mr Raspero.'

'I talk to Miss Ashton for thirty seconds and —'

'It was much longer than that, Mr Raspero.'

Nicholas sighed. 'I am not pursuing Miss Ashton. In any case, I don't have any money.'

'Yes, without money you cannot buy a whore. Miss Ashton, I believe, is an expensive whore.'

'I know she is the mistress of wealthy men, one after the other, but that's not exactly being a whore. You are being a little bit unfair. She receives gifts, I think.'

'She exchanges the use of her body for these gifts. In what way is that not being a whore, Mr Raspero?'

Nicholas sighed again. 'I take your point, Lady Grangeshield. I have never said I didn't.'

'But you will also take the opportunity to converse with Miss Ashton again, will you not, Mr Raspero?'

Nicholas said nothing but looked for a while at Isabel. She merely gazed back impassively.

'Do you want me not to?' Nicholas said at last.

'I could not care less what you do, Mr Raspero. You are conceited to suppose that I do.'

'It's time for me to go,' Nicholas declared. 'It's getting late.'

'You will stay here tonight, Mr Raspero,' Isabel declared right back. 'I will have a room made up for you.' She then and there pointed her wand and pulled a cord for Benson to come.

'I don't think that's such a good idea,' Nicholas replied. 'But thanks anyway.'

'Why, are you planning on visiting someone tonight, Mr Raspero? Is that why you must leave now?'

'No!' Nicholas said emphatically. 'I am not visiting anyone. I am going home and straight to bed.'

'But you can go straight to bed here in Grangeshield House. Unless of course you find this accommodation to be beneath you?'

'You are very bossy and critical, Lady Grangeshield.'

'How dare you call me bossy and critical!'

'I took a deep breath first,' Nicholas told her as if alarmed, but with a smile.

Isabel did not smile in return, as if completely unaware of the disarming humour he had just displayed. 'I see that you choose to be rude simply because of the enormous courtesy I have shown you in offering you a room for the night. But you will, of course, stay here tonight no matter what you say to me. Courtesy will always triumph over discourtesy.'

'Why are you so insistent on this point, Lady Grangeshield?'

'Why are you so insistent on leaving, Mr Raspero?'

'Not for any particular reason,' Nicholas said, a little weakly, suddenly and inadvertently giving ground in this battle. 'I mean, I had no other plans but to return home tonight so —'

'But your plans have changed, Mr Raspero, and that is all there is to it.' Benson had already materialised in response to Isabel's earlier signal. 'Benson,' Isabel ordered, 'Mr Raspero is staying the night. Prepare the Rowland Room for him immediately.'

'Very good, your ladyship,' Benson replied obediently and disappeared out the door.

'So, that is settled,' Isabel declared, not looking at Nicholas. 'We shall all retire shortly, Mr Raspero, so you need not complain about being kept up.'

Nicholas sighed and leaned back in his chair, defeated. 'Very well, Lady Grangeshield, I will stay the night.'

'But of course you will, Mr Raspero. The matter has already been settled.'

'So I see,' Nicholas said with resignation. He was not too displeased at the thought of staying another night in the Rowland Room. It was an amazing room and Grangeshield House was an amazing house. He would leave in the morning and that finally would be it. He would very likely never see Isabel again, or perhaps he might see her in passing at a party or out walking in the park. She might or might not even speak to him, but for now he would enjoy her company. She was looking down at her fan and he took the opportunity to study her. Her dark brown hair shone with a reflected light from the lamps; her neck and bare shoulders gleamed like alabaster. She looked like a painting as she sat there, Nicholas thought, a masterpiece that would entrance all who gazed upon it.

Isabel looked up at Nicholas to see him watching her. He continued to gaze at her, now looking into her eyes, which Isabel found infuriating. Usually when she caught a man watching her, he would look away guiltily, having been caught out. But they, of course, had been civilised men, Isabel reflected, whereas Nicholas was nothing of the sort.

'If you ever have a painting made of you,' Nicholas said thoughtfully, 'it should portray you exactly as you look now.'

'I have had several paintings made of me, Mr Raspero,' Isabel told him abruptly to put him in his place, given that she had started sitting for portraits from the age of seven onwards, 'and I think I will not seek your advice on the matter of any future ones!'

'Yes, well, there we are,' Nicholas said.

'Mr Raspero, what is your great interest in Miss Ashton?' Isabel asked him with a gentle tone to her voice, as if she understood that he was ultimately not to blame. Nicholas could trustingly confide in her, she seemed to suggest by the gentleness of the tone to her voice. The watching Eastons kept their usual silent counsel.

'Lady Grangeshield, are you concerned on my behalf or on behalf of Miss Ashton? I mean —'

'I am not concerned about either of you, Mr Raspero. She lives in the gutter and you seem determined to join her there. What you do with each other is no concern of mine.'

'We're not doing anything with each other,' Nicholas insisted. 'We're not even on first name terms.'

'It is only a matter of time, I am sure. Well, you will do what you must.'

Nicholas sighed. 'I find Miss Ashton a puzzle, to tell the truth.'

'And why is that?'

'Well, Miss Ashton is actually very refined and elegant. She is even a very nice person, by the way. Yet, I am not unaware, as you said earlier, that she is the mistress of one wealthy man after another. She —'

'She is a *whore*, Mr Raspero,' Isabel interrupted savagely. '*That* is what I said.'

'Have you listened to a word I've said? That's exactly my point. She is elegant, nice, refined but … she is a person of low morals, it has to be said. So that's the puzzle.'

'She is a person of low morals, so she cannot be elegant or nice or refined, Mr Raspero. Do you have any understanding of the meanings of these words?'

'However you characterise it,' Nicholas said, 'the fact remains that she is … striking. That's the puzzle for me, the way she is and what she does.'

'She is an actress, Mr Raspero,' Isabel said dismissively. 'She plays a role, that is all. She is a monkey who imitates what she sees. I cannot blame you for failing to realise this because you are a dimwit who lacks judgement.'

'No,' Nicholas shook his head, ignoring Isabel's provocation, 'Miss Angela Ashton is a nice person and she is herself. She plays roles on stage, but off-stage she behaves as she is. And that is the puzzle for me. I can't make sense of it.'

'You are easily deceived, Mr Raspero,' Isabel said scornfully. 'Perhaps the family you come from has failed to raise you properly. I begin to believe that it is not your fault that you are so low. You come from a family of foreign adventurers, bandits in the forest, and no doubt others who are so low even you dare not speak of them. It is because of this that Miss Ashton deceives you so easily.'

'Why does Miss Ashton drive you into such a fury?'

'You vastly over-estimate the significance which I attach to a passing whore. My concern is that you appear to be unaware of the judgements which you should be making concerning Miss Ashton.'

'Since when have you been so concerned about me?' Nicholas asked quizzically, raising his eyebrows.

'Mr Raspero,' Isabel replied, leaning back in her chair and opening up her fan, 'you vastly over-estimate the significance which I attach to a passing wandfighter. You will be on your way tomorrow and the manner in which you conduct your life thereafter will be entirely a matter of your judgement. I merely seek to instruct you while you are here. That is all.'

'Yes, you're all heart,' Nicholas replied, trying not to grin. 'Well, I think we have completely dealt with this issue as thoroughly as it needs to be dealt with. Do you not agree?'

Isabel thought about this, tapping her fan on a knuckle. She actually felt that the matter had not been dealt with as thoroughly as it required. For a start, she had not led Nicholas to the point to which she wished to lead him, namely that he was never to speak to Miss Ashton again. This was for his own good, and she realised that he would not agree to such a decision until he could be led by her of his own accord to see this for himself. *You can lead a horse to water,* Isabel thought, *but you cannot make it drink.*

She could feel Nicholas looking at her as she thought things over. Let him look, she decided, while she considered how to reply to his question; he is at least occupied. What should she reply to him?

She had not at all liked the way Nicholas had stood while he spoke to Miss Ashton. There had seemed to be a certain friendliness there. There had been something she could not put her finger on exactly but which she had nonetheless felt strongly. Nicholas liked Miss Ashton, and he liked her a lot. That had been obvious to her. Naturally, Nicholas was a man, and so he could not be entirely blamed for his stupidity in being perhaps slightly attracted to a whore. That was why whores existed, after all. Men were supposed to find them attractive. What had really troubled Isabel, however, was the way in which Miss Ashton had looked at Nicholas. She had laughed, had flirted with her fan, had even given Nicholas appraising looks while Nicholas was not looking at her. Miss Ashton, in short, had not seemed to be entirely as indifferent to Nicholas as a whore in the pay of another man should have been. Miss Ashton knew that Nicholas did not have money, yet she had looked at him with appraising looks. What kind of whore was that?

Isabel knew that Nicholas was still looking at her. He had been looking at her continuously ever since she had fallen into these thoughts she was having. She knew that he was smitten with her beauty, and the longer he looked, the more smitten he would be. Fine, let him look longer then. She had to think this matter through. He would not interrupt her thoughts while he had the chance to look fully at her without distraction. Besides, looking at her would keep his thoughts away from Miss Ashton. She still had not come to a decision. What was it that Nicholas had just said? Ah yes, that they could agree that they had thoroughly discussed this issue. Well, that was absurd. They most certainly had not. When Nicholas understood that he should never speak to Miss Ashton ever again, then and only then, could it be said that they had thoroughly discussed this issue, and not a moment before.

Isabel reflected then on how much Nicholas had done for her. He had restored her honour. He had gone past snakes for her. Snakes! He had braved enormous dangers, and he had done it because he was in love with her. Yes, Isabel reflected, Nicholas was no longer merely smitten, he was in love with her. She said to herself with a hot exultant fierceness that Nicholas was in love with her, she owned him body and soul, he belonged to her entirely, he was hers to do with as she pleased, anything at all; whatever she wanted from him, he would give. She owned him. He belonged to her. She could wrap him around her finger, take him in her hand and crush him to a mashed lump of dripping blood and shattered bone if she chose!

Surely therefore, she reflected, she was duty bound to save him from Miss Ashton, that scheming whore who would give a man appraising looks even when he had no money. Isabel saw then the logical conclusion to which all this led. She could not allow Nicholas to go his own way until he had come to understand that he must never speak to Miss Ashton again. Only then could she let him go and not a moment before. She was duty bound to save him from Miss Ashton, given all that he had done for her. It followed then that they had not finished thoroughly discussing this issue. But what answer should she give Nicholas now?

She would think of a way to keep Nicholas here in Grangeshield House until he had come to his senses as far as Miss Ashton was concerned. She looked up at Nicholas then. He was looking at her, and she looked into his eyes without speaking for a moment; she was struck then by how handsome he was. His face was actually quite striking, the face of a nobleman, she thought, grave and distinguished.

'I believe it is time for us to retire for the night, Mr Raspero. Do you not agree?'

Nicholas leaned back in his chair with an amused look. 'Yes, Lady Grangeshield,' he said, 'I do agree.'

Isabel folded up her fan and stood up. 'Good night, Mr Raspero.'

'Good night, Lady Grangeshield,' Nicholas said in reply, standing up as well.

The Eastons said good night and went off with Isabel, while Benson took Nicholas to the Rowland Room.

Nicholas undressed for bed slowly, looking about him, enjoying his surroundings. This was an amazing room to sleep in, he thought. Well, it would be his last night here. As Isabel had said, he would be on his way tomorrow and his association with Isabel would be at an end.

Or so he believed at the time.

7:30 AM, Friday 22 July 1544 A.F.

The first thing Isabel thought of the next morning when she awoke was how to keep Nicholas in Grangeshield House. She had thought the matter over last night until she had fallen asleep, but nothing had come to her. She rolled over and looked at the clock. It had just gone seven-thirty. Isabel wondered why had she awoken so early. Then she remembered that Benson had told her that Nicholas was an early riser. He would already be up and about by now.

She wondered again if she should offer Nicholas a position. Logical though the idea was, her intuition had warned her against it last night, and her intuition warned her against it now. Besides, if he was her employee she would not feel quite so free to insult him, and she did not want to give up just yet on the pleasure she derived from insulting him.

The answer she sought to this question still evaded her as she entered the library some time later. Nicholas was sitting reading what looked like the same book as before, his feet up on the Carenthetian table. Isabel let the Carenthetian table go; she had expected no less.

'Oh, please don't bother to get up, Mr Raspero,' she said, as Nicholas started to climb to his feet.

'Don't tempt me!' Nicholas joked. 'Good morning, Lady Grangeshield.'

'Good morning, Mr Raspero. You are still reading, I see?'

'Yes,' Nicholas replied. 'I was just passing time to say goodbye to you before I left.'

'That is very courteous of you,' Isabel replied.

Nicholas gave her a surprised and wary look. He had come to realise that when Isabel was being nice to him she was up to something. 'I am always courteous, as you know,' he said, just to annoy her.

'Indeed,' Isabel agreed, barely listening. 'Shall we sit down?' She promptly went to a chair and settled herself down, giving Nicholas no choice but to sit down as well. He put his feet back on the Carenthetian table, noting that there was no reaction to this from Isabel. She was definitely up to something. 'What are your plans for today, Mr Raspero?'

Nicholas shrugged. 'This and that, but nothing dramatic. Why do you ask?'

'I had hoped to go to Kenina Park today,' Isabel said, 'but I have no-one to escort me.'

Now Nicholas knew why she was being so nice to him. 'I would of course only be too delighted to escort you myself.'

Isabel's eyebrows rose in surprise as if she had not anticipated this response. 'That is very kind of you, Mr Raspero. I can only thank you for being so considerate.'

'However, I do have to go home at some point to let my aunt and uncle know that I'm still alive,' Nicholas commented. 'What if I meet you at Kenina Park? I really should at least show my face around the door at home, my uncle and aunt, go and see Ben in his office, I mean, yes, then catch up with you later.'

'Very well,' Isabel agreed promptly. 'That sounds very sensible. I will meet you at Kenina Park at three o'clock.'

'Excellent,' Nicholas said, rising to his feet. 'I had better borrow a carriage from you then. The Balladur one would be fine.'

'So it is all settled,' Isabel said, rising to her feet and leading the way.

As they were outside waiting for the flying carriage to arrive, Nicholas said suddenly, 'Wait a moment!' It had come back to his mind that he had seen nothing of his own clothes when getting up this morning, and he had forgotten to ask Benson about them earlier. 'Where are my clothes?' He looked around and caught sight of Benson standing nearby. 'Benson, where are my clothes?'

'Your clothes, sir?' Benson asked nervously, looking to Isabel for help.

'Yes, my clothes,' Nicholas said impatiently. 'The ones I came here in.'

'I had your clothes burned, Mr Raspero,' Isabel said calmly.

'You what? You burned my clothes?' Nicholas asked in genuine astonishment. He couldn't believe it.

'They were not clothes, Mr Raspero. They were rags.'

'This is a blasted outrage!' Nicholas protested.

'Mr Raspero, I do not tolerate the use of that kind of language in my house.'

'No, you just burn other people's clothes instead. You burned my clothes? Are you mad? Are you out of your mind? It is a tiny mind, is it not, Lady Grangeshield? One step and you're in the abyss, utterly demented and raving and burning other people's clothes!'

'Mr Raspero, I shall overlook your intemperate abuse on the grounds of your emotional immaturity.'

'Oh, will you? How very kind of you. Thoughtful, even. That makes everything all right, doesn't it?'

'You are making such an enormous fuss over nothing, Mr Raspero.'

'I'm leaving now. You'll have to excuse me for leaving before any more of my belongings get destroyed.'

'You have so few belongings in your abject poverty, Mr Raspero, that this can hardly be a concern for you.'

'You just don't give up, do you?'

'Really, Mr Raspero, you are behaving like a spoiled child. I have provided you with far superior clothes, have I not?'

'That,' Nicholas said with slow heaviness, 'is not the point.'

'I believe it is precisely the point, Mr Raspero. You no longer have need of your rags, do you? So they were burned. You are really making an enormous fuss over nothing at all.'

'Well, now I know,' Nicholas replied sarcastically, still shaken by disbelief. He could not help but feel an absolute certainty that he should not be treated like this, that it was outrageous that Isabel had burned his clothes. Yet, he could see quite clearly that there was not the slightest uncertainty about Isabel's feelings of rightness about what she had done.

'I do not expect thanks from you, Mr Raspero,' Isabel said sharply. 'Your ingratitude is no more than I did expect, so there is no surprise there!'

Nicholas decided not to say another word. He merely gave Isabel one look of disbelief and marched off towards the carriage. Isabel watched him go, concealing what might have been a smile behind her fan.

Nicholas returned home, then went to visit Ben.

'Another night at Grangeshield House?' Ben asked.

Nicholas threw himself into Ben's chair for clients. 'That is such an amazing house!' he said in admiration.

'Nice clothes,' Ben said.

'Lady Grangeshield had them made for me. Then she burned my own clothes! Behind my back! Can you believe that?'

'They were looking pretty ragged,' Ben commented.

'Fine, I knew I could look to you for sympathy,' Nicholas said. 'But tell me, people can't behave like that, can they? I mean, burn other people's clothes?'

Ben laid down his fountain pen, leaned back in his chair and steepled his fingers before him. 'That is a more complicated question than it might at first appear to be.'

'Blasted lawyers!' Nicholas told him. 'You just talk like that to pump up your fees.'

'Women can be difficult to understand,' Ben said cautiously.

'You don't say!' Nicholas said sarcastically. 'Do people really pay you for these insights of yours?'

Ben hesitated and then commented, 'You seem to be spending a lot of time with Lady Grangeshield lately.'

'What's that supposed to mean?' Nicholas replied a little sharply.

'Nothing,' Ben said, picking up his fountain pen again absently.

'No, go on, say what you have to say,' Nicholas insisted.

Ben paused and sighed, fiddling with his fountain pen. 'There's a lot of talk about the two of you. Even in the law courts. That's all.'

'What kind of talk?'

'Gossip.'

'What kind of gossip?'

'The gossip kind of gossip.'

'There's nothing going on to merit gossip,' Nicholas said, feeling nervous for no good reason.

'That's not what the gossip says.'

'What does the gossip say?'

'That you spend your nights at Grangeshield House,' Ben said, examining the tip of his fountain pen as carefully as a jeweller squinting through an eye-glass.

It was a blow that made Nicholas feel momentarily stunned. He felt that he should have seen this coming. People believed what they wanted to believe and in general they would grasp any excuse, no matter how slim, to believe something scandalous of someone else. It excited them, the mongrels.

He should not have stayed even a single night at Grangeshield House. His weakness in being unable to refuse her had endangered Isabel. She could not afford to even have the mildest of gossip about her, let alone this kind of salacious talk.

He had failed to protect Isabel. He stood up and left Ben's office without another word. He went out onto the streets and walked along blindly, not looking where he was going as his thoughts were very much elsewhere.

He found himself forced now by circumstances to examine what he intended to do anyway about the time he was spending with Isabel. He had known for some time that he was in love with her, but he had avoided the topic even in his own mind. But did she return his feelings? That was the question. He was not the first man in history to contemplate this question, and he would not be the last, but like every man who had ever been in his situation he felt utterly isolated by having an answer to the question implacably and mercilessly demanded of him.

He had briefly during their dance together the night before thought that maybe she did return his feelings, but he had no very good reason to believe it now. It was true that there had often at last night's party been jocular comments about what a lucky man he was to be Isabel's escort, not to mention hints and innuendo. Looking back on it, he realised now that he had not realised at the time that it was a matter of general knowledge that he had spent a few nights at Grangeshield House, but he should have done, of course. Little Batton had been no different; gossip was the same everywhere.

Did she return his feelings? It had to be said that she was continuously critical of him day in and day out, but who understood women anyway? Yet maybe that didn't mean what it looked like it meant; or maybe it did. It was very difficult to be sure one way or another and his own scrambled emotions were of absolutely no help to him in thinking about it; in fact, they were worse than useless; in fact, they made it impossible for him to think at all.

He found himself at the Thorburn Bridge, where he had killed Nevsky. There were picnickers nearby so he kept on walking. The Thorburn Bridge was back in business as a popular spot for visitors now it had become infamous as the scene of Nevsky's death at the hands of the mysterious Lord from the North, about whom epic poems were already being written. The mysterious Lord from the North was already growing into a figure of legend whose identity would be endlessly speculated over, perhaps for centuries to come. Three paintings of his titanic duel with Nevsky had already been commissioned, which explained the easels standing about the place. Nicholas would have found it funny if it wasn't that he was in no mood to laugh about anything.

Nicholas directed his steps to the Montague Monument, and there at least there was no-one about. He sat down out of the way where he had sat down with Bailey and tried to think what to do.

He started by using logic. Either he would continue to see Isabel or he would not. If he stopped seeing her, then the gossip could be hosed down somehow. Perhaps Isabel could say that Nicholas had been fixing the security systems of Grangeshield House or something.

If he continued to see Isabel, then it could only be on changed terms. He could not avoid seeing what those terms would have to be. He would have to declare himself to be a suitor for her hand in marriage. If she received him as a suitor that would end the gossip, or at least the gossiping kind of gossip. Then he would court her, propose, she would accept or refuse his proposal, and that would be that.

Logic was doing a grand job at clearing this matter up, Nicholas thought. Things were becoming clearer. He would have to declare his feelings for Isabel. She would agree to receive his suit or tell him to get lost. Most likely, she would tell him to get lost. But at least everything could then settle down and the drama would be over.

Nicholas stood up. He had a plan of action, and now he only had to implement it, and then his troubles would be over. Or so he believed in his innocence, entirely failing to realise that his duel with Nevsky would seem like a walk in the park compared to the hurricane with the name of Isabel that would break out over his head once he, Mr Nicholas Raspero of Nowhere, declared his intention to become a suitor for the hand in marriage of Lady Isabel Grangeshield of Grangeshield House.

THIRTY-THREE

The Declaration of his Feelings by Mr Nicholas Raspero to Lady Isabel Grangeshield

2:30 PM, Friday 22 July 1544 A.F.

Nicholas wasn't sure what time of day it was as the sky was clouded over so he went straight to Kenina Park, where people were standing about like figures in a painting. Isabel was nowhere to be seen, as it was still only two-thirty by the public clock, so Nicholas chatted to people he knew who were passing by. It was a sunny day and everyone seemed to be very relaxed, which was just as well for Nicholas, who was starting to feel nervous. It was dawning on him what he had let himself in for, and the palms of his hands were sweating and he took very deep breaths. Now that he considered his decision again, it seemed to him like the craziest idea anyone had ever had in the whole of history. He asked himself if he had gone insane. How would he himself know? Watching the Grangeshield carriage settle to the ground was like hearing the bell ring to signal the start of a bare-handed fight with a lion.

Isabel seemed very gracious and kindly to him as she stepped out of the carriage to find him waiting for her. The Eastons followed and greeted Nicholas with such affability that Nicholas wondered all of a sudden if his decision to become Isabel's suitor was really quite so crazy. What if the Eastons were thinking the same thing?

They took a turn or two about the park, stopping to chat with people here and there. Berg and Uliana from The Gang came along, and they stopped to chat with them.

'You like those clothes so much you are still wearing them, I see, Mr Raspero,' Berg commented. He still wanted to know the name of the tailor.

'Lady Grangeshield burned my own clothes,' Nicholas told him. 'Can you believe that?'

'Oh, really, Mr Raspero, stop being such a child,' Isabel snapped impatiently. 'Am I never to hear the end of this?'

Berg had been ostentatiously considering Nicholas's question, tapping his forefinger on his lips while Isabel was speaking. 'Can I believe that, did you ask, Mr Raspero? Indeed I can, with the greatest of ease. You can only be congratulated, Isabel, for slaying such a dragon. The whole of New Landern can only thank you for what you have done.' Berg gave Isabel a very ostentatious bow after saying this.

Isabel forgave him on the spot for being such a coward when Nevsky had been tormenting her. 'I am glad that you understand the necessity of this action which I was obliged to take, Berg. There are others who do not, and it seems that nothing I can say is of any use in aiding their limited and dim-witted comprehension.'

'What do you think, Miss Newman?' Nicholas asked her. She was his last hope now. No-one at all seemed to be taking his side in this issue.

Uliana backed Berg up without hesitation. 'Even the flames which consumed your clothes, Mr Raspero, must have trembled at the task set before them. Flames are said to dance but not, I think, these ones.'

Nicholas groaned out loud. 'Very well, Lady Grangeshield, I will accept defeat. I will say no more on this matter. Clearly it seems that you did the right thing.' Clearly it seemed that Nicholas himself did not really believe what he was saying, given the expression on his face.

Isabel took his words at face value, hiding her smile behind her fan. 'There is hope for a man, Mr Raspero, who can accept how very wrong he has been. The recantation of your error can only redound to your credit. If you were now to thank me for the deed I have done on your behalf, your rehabilitation would be complete.'

'Dream on!' Nicholas told her defiantly. 'I am not thanking you for burning my clothes. I'm only giving up complaining about it and nothing more.'

'I am disappointed in you, Mr Raspero. You have managed to come this far and no further.' Isabel was still hiding the same smile behind her fan.

'Yes, well, there we are,' Nicholas said.

They said farewell to Berg and Uliana. Uliana was hiding her own smile behind her own fan while Berg was wishing that he had a fan to hide his smile behind. They walked on. Isabel was in an excellent mood over her recent victory, openly smiling now as she gave Nicholas triumphant looks now and then. She even began to blatantly flirt with him, tapping him with her fan while making some comment, or leaning on his arm to whisper something into his ear. Isabel could feel how the pressure of her hand on his arm and her hot breath in his ear sent shudders through Nicholas's body and so she teasingly fanned him with her fan as if to cool him off. In other circumstances, Nicholas would have delighted in the attentions which Isabel was paying him, but not now. Nicholas's nervousness, never entirely absent, was returning to him, creeping in under his ineffectual attempts to ward it off. The Eastons followed on behind.

'What are your plans for the rest of the day, Mr Raspero?' Isabel asked him. It was getting on to four o'clock. Isabel was trying to work out a way to get Nicholas back into Grangeshield House.

Nicholas had been turning over in his mind a variety of schemes which would provide a way to get Isabel to invite him back to Grangeshield House. He realised it was there that he would have to declare his suit, for several reasons. One was that Isabel would be on her home ground, where she could receive such a declaration feeling herself to be at her strongest; that was only chivalrous on his part. Another was that they could be alone with the Eastons at a distance. Another reason was that it deferred the declaration itself into the future, which is where Nicholas wanted it to remain for as long as possible.

'We are about to go our own separate ways, Lady Grangeshield,' Nicholas said. 'Is this not so?'

'That is a strange thing to say, Mr Raspero,' Isabel said, 'on such a lovely day as this.'

Nicholas nodded, barely listening. 'But it does seem, that for a time we have walked the same way together. Would you not agree?'

'We have walked hand in hand together along the great journey of life for a time, have we not, Mr Raspero?' Isabel said, still in a flirtatious mood. The Gang had all agreed that Brecky had come up with a great line when he had said to Isabel that *I want to travel hand in hand with you along the great journey of life,* Penny had even declared that she would not have been able to refuse the proposal of a man who could express such a wonderful sentiment.

'Ah, yes, exactly,' Nicholas said, thinking to himself that this was exactly the kind of poetic thing he would need to say to Isabel when he declared his feelings for her. 'But I thought that surely it would be very abrupt if I were to suddenly leave you right now without another word. So perhaps I should come back with you to Grangeshield House to talk a little bit more so that when we go our own separate ways, the transition will be more gradual and thus less disruptive.'

'I can only praise your consideration,' Isabel said appreciatively. 'Indeed it would be abrupt to make our farewells at this very moment, given that we must surely make our farewells with the courtesy and care fitted for such occasions. You speak to the point, Mr Raspero, and I can find nothing to add to what you have already said.'

'And in Grangeshield House,' Nicholas added. 'You are at home there. That place suits you. I would like to leave you there when I say goodbye.'

Isabel was not paying any particular attention to what Nicholas was saying. The main thing was that he was coming back to Grangeshield House *right now,* and that was what mattered. She would have him sitting in her carriage, and once at Grangeshield House he would not find it easy to get away.

'That too,' Isabel agreed absently. 'Very well, we shall return to Grangeshield House at once, shall we not?'

'Excellent,' Nicholas said approvingly.

The Eastons did not look surprised to find that Nicholas was coming back with them to Grangeshield House. They climbed up into the Grangeshield carriage and left Kenina Park.

Nicholas was not feeling talkative due to his nerves, which simply would not go away so he said nothing. The Eastons maintained their usual silent vigil. Isabel was reflecting that there were several matters which required her immediate attention on their return to Grangeshield House. Nicholas would just have to wait to make his farewells. Then it would be dinner time, and Nicholas would have to stay for dinner. After dinner they would all be talking for a while, as the Eastons could hardly be shunted off to one side; after which it would be late enough so that Nicholas would have to wait until the following day before he left.

Such was the plan Isabel formulated in the carriage on the way home, and so it was that things turned out as she had planned. She sat him at her right-hand side, in pride of place as her guest at the table; she had said this was "to keep an eye on you so you mind your manners for once" but she had said this gently, almost flirtatiously, and Nicholas had said nothing in return. He had come to understand for the first time why the nervous system was called the nervous system.

The guests sitting up and down the table stole covert glances at him. Nicholas somehow got through the dinner by going through all the necessary motions and taking part in table talk that he was later never to remember; then it was the after-dinner conversation in the Red Drawing Room and the guests all sat around talking politely of this and that; then all the guests left until Nicholas alone remained.

The Eastons were sitting nearby and Nicholas realised that the time to make his declaration had passed by, or more accurately it had never materialised at all. It was with a sense of relief that he realised he would not have to declare his feelings to Isabel until tomorrow. Tomorrow would be Declaration Day. He could postpone it that much further. He felt like a condemned man given a brief reprieve.

'Lady Grangeshield,' he said, 'I would like to talk to you tomorrow morning, if possible.'

The Eastons exchanged meaningful looks.

'But of course, Mr Raspero,' Isabel said, 'most certainly.' She believed that Nicholas had come to see for himself that he could not say farewell to her this late in the evening, and so he was arranging to make his farewells to her the next day. She pulled the cord for Benson on the spot. 'I will instruct Benson to make the Rowland Room ready for you.' She had already given him this very instruction on her return from Kenina Park, and had even visited the room herself to check that the flowers were fresh and everything was as it should be, while Benson looked on impassively.

Soon after that Nicholas went to his room to prepare for Declaration Day.

10:20 AM, Saturday 23 July 1544 A.F.

It was now the morning after his decision, the morning of Declaration Day itself, and Nicholas was sitting in the library with his feet on the Carenthetian table and the Book of the World 1543 in his hands. It was opened but he could not bring himself to even look at it.

His hands would not stop sweating and he was having second thoughts about everything. He felt an emotion something akin to terror at the thought of declaring his feelings to Isabel. It was not that she might refuse to receive his suit. It was not even that she might agree to receive his suit; or perhaps it was. He could not help feeling intimidated by her impossible beauty, her very womanliness, by the desire her impossible beauty brought forth from him. He both wanted and feared intimacy with her. He desperately wanted to have her and he was desperately afraid of having her. It was all very strange and he uttered an age-old groan. The very sinews of that groan were as ancient as the days when the first caveman grunted to himself, 'She looks all right!' Even that first caveman, Nicholas thought, must have felt nervous when he declared his feelings.

It was now Declaration Day and the more he thought about telling Isabel that he loved her the more his head parted company from his neck and started floating up towards the ceiling. There was something about the prospect of telling Isabel that he loved her that smoothly scooped out the insides of his stomach. It was a feeling exactly linked to his feeling of being smitten that overpowered him whenever he looked at her. Nicholas had never heard of the Guardians of the Hidden Flame, who believed that the only true love was that which was never declared, but he was well on track to become their latest recruit.

He felt now on Declaration Day that he was about to trespass into a sacred realm by taking this step of declaring his feelings and it was the very wrong-doing of the trespass itself which made him feel half-dead with nerves. If he was punished in consequence, fine, all well and good, he had no concerns about that, he would even welcome it as he probably deserved no less. He had no concerns about the consequences which might be visited on his head as it was the actual trespass itself that terrified him. He had tried to talk himself out of his fears a thousand times, yet his fears followed him around like his own shadow and refused to go away. There was nothing else to do but just go through with it in the state he was in, feeling as if he had sprouted two heads and the world was upside-down.

For the thousandth time he felt the temptation to let it go for today, to leave it until later when perhaps the times were more propitious, but he knew that this was cowardice masquerading as strategy. This was Declaration Day. And then the moment he had been dreading all morning arrived: Lady Isabel Grangeshield, looking impossibly beautiful and dangerously regal, entered the library.

The Eastons followed behind her. They recognised the look of concealed terror on Nicholas's face immediately. They had seen it many times before.

'Good morning, Lady Grangeshield,' Nicholas said, putting the book down and standing up.

'Please don't bother to get up, Mr Raspero,' Isabel said a little stiffly, looking at the Carenthetian table where Nicholas's feet had been. Usually so astute in matters of the heart, she was too preoccupied with trying to think of a way to sabotage the farewell which she believed Nicholas was about to make to recognise the look on his face. Her annoyance with Nicholas's use of the Carenthetian table further blinded her.

Nicholas was too nervous to try to make his usual variant on a theme of a joke. 'Let's go outside into the garden,' he suggested. 'It is such a beautiful day.'

Isabel considered this suggestion then inclined her head. 'Very well, Mr Raspero, if that is your wish.'

Something of Nicholas's nervousness might have communicated itself to her but she was still behaving stiffly in any case as they left the house and wandered through the garden. Nicholas directed them to the Grotto of Peace.

'Let us sit down here, Lady Grangeshield,' Nicholas advised.

'Did *you* just tell *me* to sit down?' Isabel exclaimed indignantly.

'Oh, get off your high horse. I have something important to tell you,' Nicholas said as he sat down himself, thankful that his legs no longer had to support him.

Isabel gave him a look but sat down without further comment.

'Although you look good on a high horse, I must admit,' Nicholas said, suddenly reflecting on what he had just said and realising that it might not have sounded very romantic. 'In fact, you look excellent on a high horse. Very, um, majestic and everything. Being on a high horse suits you perfectly.' Realising that he was babbling, Nicholas forced himself to stop talking.

The Eastons were already seated at a distance, watching the show.

After a long silence, that stretched on for quite a while from Isabel's point of view, but raced past in a couple of panicked heartbeats from Nicholas's point of view, Isabel asked, 'And what is this important communication of yours?'

'I'm just getting to that,' Nicholas said. 'One moment, if you please.'

Nicholas was desperately trying to find some poetic sentiments with which to clothe an eloquent expression of his undying love, but absolutely nothing was coming to mind. His mind was a complete blank. He summoned all his courage, straightened his back, turned and looked at Isabel. She was sitting looking away from him. She saw him turn to look at her and turned in her turn to face him. Her forest brown eyes were looking directly into his sky grey eyes and he realised that this was the moment. It was now or never. Taking a deep breath he said, 'Isabel, I've fallen in love with you.'

Her eyes widened and her lips parted slightly as what he had just said sank in; then she turned away from him and looked into the distance.

'Isabel,' Nicholas said again. Isabel visibly stiffened on hearing this second use of her first name but did not look at him. 'If we continue to see each other, it's only a matter of time before I make you a proposal of marriage.'

Isabel fiercely said nothing.

'Isabel, if I came to you as a suitor would you receive my suit?' Nicholas asked.

The palms of his hands were sweating profusely. He was only too well aware of how badly he had handled this. He had dived in where he should have circled around. He had spoken plainly where he should have teasingly (and delightfully) meandered in spirals of obscure phrases never exactly equidistant from an undefined yet perfectly obvious point; he had in short blundered from the beginning where he should have gracefully danced. He had once heard someone discussing how all this worked, and he wished now he had paid more attention, but it was too late for that now.

Yet on the plus side he had done it! He had declared his feelings. He couldn't help feeling proud of himself, a pride that leaned cheerfully against an overwhelming sense of relief, each supporting the other like two drunks whose legs were too enfeebled to perform locomotory functions. He had messed it up as badly as it could be messed up, but at least he had done it!

After a while Isabel said slowly, 'You are very clever, Mr Raspero. Very clever indeed.'

'Well, thanks,' Nicholas said awkwardly, despite having a very strong feeling that Isabel was not being complimentary.

'I did not know until this moment that you were a fortune hunter, Mr Raspero. Rather I have been deceived by your dissembling into believing you quite otherwise. But that is what the fortune hunter does, is it not? Deceive by dissembling.'

Nicholas knew then that a storm was coming. He inwardly braced himself. 'Are you saying that my attentions are unwelcome, Isabel?'

'How dare you call me by my first name!' Isabel shouted at him. 'You are guilty of the grossest impertinence! How dare you!'

The Eastons, too discreetly far away due to their unending courtesy to hear anything of what was being said, even Isabel's shouting, nonetheless realised that things were not going well for Nicholas. They resigned themselves to the outcome they now saw coming.

'We've been spending a lot of time together lately, Isabel,' Nicholas said. His mental paralysis had vanished now that it was clear that he would be lucky to get out of this alive. 'I have now declared my feelings for you. It is time for you to decide whether to receive my suit or not.'

'Ah, it is the time we have spent together that has emboldened you in this fashion. Yes, I realise now my error. It is always a grave mistake to show too much familiarity to one's social inferiors. It gives them ideas above their station.'

'Well, there is that,' Nicholas cautiously agreed, looking for an exit from this situation within whose folds he was now unavoidably enwrapped.

'I took you in as a beggar off the street,' Isabel continued as if Nicholas had not spoken. 'I clothed you, I fed you, I gave you a roof over your head, and I introduced you to a level of high society far above what you can have even dreamed of achieving. I was so gracious as to allow you to stay here in Grangeshield House. And what is my thanks for my kindness? How am I repaid? What do I find but an insolence such that no words can describe it, an impertinence, an insolence, an insolence shocking beyond all measure? How dare you presume to say what you have said! How dare you! Such presumption! Such grotesque and unprecedented insolence and presumption beyond anything I could imagine! From you, a dog off the streets, a jumped-up nobody, a grotesque and insolent nothing of a man!'

'From the general tenor of your remarks —' Nicholas began to say but Isabel ploughed on regardless.

'Your uncouthness, your use of foul language, your general low-born state, your unworthiness, all this I have striven to overlook and forgive, but your presumption today has gone too far. This cannot be overlooked! How dare you! It is one thing to lack all manners, it is quite another to lack all proportion. From the very day I met you I have been appalled, simply appalled, at your lack of manners, your rudeness, your blatant disregard of all propriety. But I have overlooked all your faults on the grounds that you simply know no better, you are incapable of the finer feelings that characterise the gentleman, but to what end? You have come here, a vagrant from nowhere, a common murderer from a family of bandits, a family of a foreign adventurer, a family that lives in the gutter where you were raised to murder people, a family that raised you as a common murderer, a bloodthirsty wandfighting murderer. This is simply indescribable, this is beyond anything, to be told to sit in my own garden by the offspring of a foreigner, whose family would not even be given employment here to sweep the leaves, a low-born family of no worth.' Two red spots were burning on Isabel's cheeks, her eyes were narrowed and her face was like a rigid mask.

Nicholas was suddenly seized by a desperate desire to laugh but every fibre of his being warned him to fight against this desire as if it were his mortal enemy. Luckily Isabel started speaking again and listening to her helped distract him from his laughter, which started to die away of its own accord.

'You are no gentleman, Mr Raspero. You have no place here, you are a common thug of no repute, no name, no fortune, a man driven by greed, a lustful, lustful insolent man who does not know his place, who presumes to rise higher than he merits or deserves. A man who lacks all proportion, a man who has no honour, a man whose lack of honour has created a void into which all the lusts and unclean behaviours of the lowest of men have rushed to take up their place in the filthy cavern of your mind. You have no honour, you are not a gentleman, and you presume far beyond what can be tolerated by a person of gentle birth such as myself.'

'So you're saying no, then, I take it,' Nicholas said calmly.

Seeing that Nicholas had not even been made the least angry by her insults, into which she had poured every ounce of fury she possessed, Isabel's fury reached a white-hot incandescent level of utterly indiscriminate incineration.

'Get out! Get out of my house! Get out now!'

Nicholas nodded and stood up perfectly calmly. It was over and he accepted everything without complaint or regrets. He looked down at

Isabel as he straightened his robes automatically and spoke to her with a certain cold authority, 'Lady Grangeshield, from this time forth we do not know each other. Goodbye.'

He stood up then and walked away. Isabel had said nothing as he left and as if in a dream he realised that he had had the last word for once. He kept on walking without looking back, walking down the driveway. He was vaguely aware of Benson trotting up behind him and then slowing down to keep pace with the departing guest of Lady Grangeshield.

He stopped to allow Benson to open the door. 'Goodbye, Benson,' he said.

'Until you come again, sir,' Benson said with unfeigned friendliness.

'Dream on,' Nicholas replied, and walked off through the door.

Benson closed the door gently with a smile on his face. *A lover's quarrel,* he thought.

THIRTY-FOUR

The Reflections and Contemplations of Lady Isabel Grangeshield

11:15 AM, Saturday 23 July 1544 A.F.

Isabel sat where Nicholas had left her for a while. She could not remember when she had last felt so upset. Her stomach was tangled into knots, she was breathing heavily, she wanted to break something, and she was even trembling from head to toe.

How dare he even think of such a thing! She had done nothing to encourage such ideas! She had been nothing but polite, courteous, helpful in the matter of providing him with clothes, helpful with introductions to people of high society. He had been so eager to be introduced to her fellow guests at the party she had taken him to that she should have realised then that he was a fortune-hunter, precisely the kind of fortune-hunter she had been warned against so many times. She had overlooked his slovenly behaviour and his use of the Footstool of Mangatha, not to mention his feet on the Carenthetian table. She had gone out of her way to make him welcome in Grangeshield House, and he had had the sheer presumption, the audacity, the brazen shamelessness, to tell her that he loved her. She had done absolutely nothing to give him the least reason to suspect that any such approach from him would be even remotely welcome, yet he had simply gone ahead anyway.

She realised then that while she had been absolutely blameless in her conduct, while she had given him no reason whatsoever to consider her responsive to his advances, yet it was not entirely outside of the very remotest possibility that she might well have spent the slightest bit too much time with him lately. Yes, now she reflected on the matter, a desperate beggar such as Mr Raspero might well have seized on the merest illusion to grasp at when it came to clawing his way out of the gutter. In whatever hovel he lived in, it might well be the case that even a letter from her might look like money to him.

It was best, she thought, if she never saw that man Raspero again. Luckily he had himself declared the matter to be so. What had he said? *From this time forth we do not know each other,* yes, very well, let it be so. She was very glad that he had said it so plainly that he could not pretend that he had any right whatsoever to even speak with her again. He might well attempt to sidle into her good graces again, he might try to contact her in one way or another. Well, she would simply ignore him.

So everything was clear: they would not see each other again, *from this time forth we do not know each other,* and so everything was clear. He had said that, she would hold him to it. If he ever even tried to speak to her again she would remind him that they did not know each other. He had said it himself, luckily.

Fine. Isabel felt herself calming down. The peace of resolving the matter dissolved her nervous tension. She had made the mistake of spending too much time with a man who was nothing but a wandfighter, a common murderer, an uncultured brute of a man who put his feet on the table and failed in general to speak to her respectfully. He had sawn off another man's head, for Heaven's sake. What kind of behaviour was that? She had most certainly not expected anything quite so brutal. She had merely expected him to dispose of Nevsky in a civilised way. A gentleman would have disposed of Nevsky in a civilised way, by poisoning him or something like that, yet this wild man of the woods, this savage, had sawn off Nevsky's head with his own disc. But luckily he had now said that *from this time forth we do not know each other* and so she was fully entitled to take him at his word, to shun him like the plague, because as he himself had said *from this time forth we do not know each other* and so that was that!

She wondered why she had put up with his insolence all this time. Now that she thought about it, he had spoken to her with far greater freedom than she should have allowed. *Oh, get off your high horse,* he had said. What kind of way was that for a beggar to talk to Lady Isabel Grangeshield of Grangeshield House?

She would never speak to him again, she decided. If she saw him from a distance she would ignore him, and if he ever had the presumption to approach her again, she would remind him that they did not know each other. She rose to her feet, feeling that everything had been resolved.

Her resolution to never see Nicholas again lasted all that day and she was in fine fettle. She was too busy with affairs concerning her estate, replying to invitations to social engagements and generally tidying up loose ends, to give any more thought as to what had happened that morning. She padded happily about Grangeshield House dealing with domestic matters. She wrote a letter to Lady Tranell, who was to have been her hostess that evening, explaining that she was unable to come because Something (she hinted that it might have been the End of the World) had happened, thus rendering her presence impossible. Lady Tranell wrote back to say she quite understood — so that was that.

It was after dinner that evening, as she sat in the Red Drawing Room, that her resolution began to waver. Should she really never see Nicholas again? She took herself in hand and renewed her resolution, impatient with herself for even granting such doubts a moment's consideration. She would never again see that presumptuous man. The matter was not even up for discussion. There was nothing to reconsider about her decision.

Yet it was not long before the doubts returned. It was perhaps a bit extreme to never see Nicholas at all. Perhaps she could see him now and then, provided he behaved himself. She had allowed him far too many liberties. He would say things like *Oh, get off your high horse,* and why on earth had she not been firmer in restraining such talk? It seemed to her then as if she had not been herself at all lately. Somehow she had tolerated a degree of impertinence from Nicholas that she would not have tolerated from anyone else, but that was not exactly so. Somehow it had seemed perfectly natural for Nicholas to speak his mind so freely. It had not seemed like impertinence because he was so obviously smitten with her. For whatever reason, she had never really minded him speaking his mind the way he had. She had even liked it in a way.

He just said what he thought and in a way she had enjoyed feeling relaxed and comfortable with him because he was simply himself. However, he had most certainly gone too far this morning. Clearly, however, if he kept to his place, it could not be completely out of the question for him to visit her again, perhaps even escort her to a dance or two. And if, on occasion, he spoke to her freely, well, maybe she would overlook it. It was really as if she had not been herself at all during the time she had spent with Nicholas. She had not objected to his behaviour because she somehow had not been herself, had perhaps been distracted by irrelevant considerations such as his hair not being brushed properly or his grey eyes being amused at something she had said when he should have been apologetic.

Yet he had declared his feelings to her that morning, and clearly that was unacceptable. It was preposterous for him to have even entertained such a thought! She had never given him any indication at all that such attentions from him would be welcome. What on earth had he been thinking? In any case, he was certainly not the first man to declare such feelings for her.

She had lost count of her suitors; they had declared their undying love for her, written her poems, compared her to the most extravagant landscapes, extolled her qualities in the most operatic of manners and thrown themselves at her feet in a variety of calculated fashions. She could not remember exactly what any of them had actually said on these occasions, yet the general idea had been clear enough; or rather, the general idea had been as clear as a generality ever is; or to say this again, they had all been interchangeable each with the other. She remembered hardly anything of any of them.

On the other hand, she could remember every word Nicholas had said. She could remember how crisp the raked gravel of the driveway had looked in its sharp hard lines of frozen motion, how floatily green the short-cut grass had been stretching out in its opulent leisure along the ground, how deeply red the carnations all around the Grotto of Peace had looked in their flower-beds, when he had said, *Isabel, I've fallen in love with you.* Really, he could not even make such a declaration with any decorum. How brutal of him, how common, to make such a declaration in such a way as to stamp the scene on her memory with such crystal-clear clarity. He simply lacked finer feelings. And then to declare that he would propose to her, that was simply too much. It was outrageous! Who on earth did he think he was?

She realised then that she had been wrong to doubt her resolution. It was simply out of the question for her to ever again even look upon that adventurer, that fortune-hunter, that common vagrant from nowhere. She would avoid him completely. *If we continue to see each other, it's only a matter of time before I make you a proposal of marriage.* Really, to speak so plainly that every word he had spoken was stamped on her memory was not the mark of a gentleman. She vividly remembered watching a public flying carriage pass by as he had said this, she remembered how blue the sky had been, how white and fluffy the clouds, how the flying carriage had had red panelling that flashed in the sunlight, the heads of the passengers looking out through the windows at the world below. She would not have remembered all this so vividly if he had been cultured enough to speak less plainly. He simply lacked education, breeding and culture.

No other suitor she had ever received had ever spoken to her in such a way that she could remember anything at all of what they had said, and that was just as it should be. They at least had been cultured, they had been gentlemen. They had passed through her life without being so difficult, so badly behaved, as to burden her with any memory of them.

On the other hand, she reflected, it might not necessarily be out of the question to see Nicholas now and then. *Isabel, if I came to you as a suitor would you receive my suit?* A red-breasted robin had perched on a nearby shrub when he had said this, she remembered how cheerful it had been, it was almost laughing at her as it ruffled its feathers, ducked its head as if nodding, turned its head one way and the other to look at her with first one eye then the other. He would have to be kept at arm's length, she realised. If she saw him again, which could of course only happen very rarely; if at all, which, of course it could not because she would never see him again, but *if* she did see him again, even if once, even if only now and then, he would have to be kept at arm's length.

Naturally, he would be desperate to regain her favour; *from this time forth we do not know each other,* well, he had over-reacted to a few very unintended and barely offensive comments she had made in circumstances which were entirely understandable and meant little. For him to say *from this time forth we do not know each other* was simply an exaggeration on his part, he most certainly had not meant it. He had only said *from this time forth we do not know each other* because he may have misunderstood her comments at the time, which she had perhaps expressed a little carelessly. It was true that he had seemed to speak with a certain decisiveness but nonetheless he would not have meant what he said when he said *from this time forth we do not know each other* because he could not really intend that to be the case.

She felt a chill clutch at her all the same. She knew he had not really meant it, but then he had seemed to be quite decisive when he spoke. Of course he had not meant it, he had not really meant it at all, he had over-reacted and no doubt he was already regretting his intemperate over-reaction. Isabel realised, however, that it was a matter of some urgency to smooth out any misunderstandings that may have occurred, especially if the idea that *from this time forth we do not know each other* was to be removed from the scene immediately without delay.

She should probably write to him before too long had passed, she decided. After all, he had not really meant that *from this time forth we do not know each other* but even so she should write to him just to clear things up. Of course she should wait a while before she sent him such a letter, but that would not stop her writing it now. Yes, she might as well compose the letter now, after all she had nothing else to do. She could leave the date out and put it in later. She found her hands were shaking, even though she knew full well he had not really meant that *from this time forth we do not know each other.* He had only said it due to an absurd misunderstanding of a few perhaps careless comments she had made only in passing. He could not possibly have meant that *from this time forth we do not know each other* simply because it was really unacceptable for him to take such a decision.

So she wrote him a letter that night. She was up until late, because clearly she had to make it clear that his advances were unwelcome, but at the same time she wished to make it clear that she forgave him his indiscretion, he would visit her again soon and that everything was just water under the bridge.

Having written him the letter, she decided that she might as well date it now and have it sent off immediately by private courier. He would receive it tomorrow morning. Which meant that his reply would come the morning after.

Except that no reply came the morning after. She wondered if her letter had somehow been mislaid. Surely he would have replied had he received the letter. Yet, it was possible that he had not received the letter. She realised then that she would have no peace of mind until his reply had come. So she wrote him another letter. This time she expressed her apology in unambiguous terms, in case her earlier letter had not been clear enough. Still no reply. A sense of panic was starting to grip her. She wrote a third letter, and this time she wrote phrases like *please forgive me* at one point; *I fully apologise for what I have said* at yet another; *please accept my apology*, and to make sure that there could be no mistake, she re-phrased these phrases and even cast all epistolary eloquence out of the door in order to make plain that her apology was genuine, heartfelt, unambiguous and that she couldn't be more sorry for what she had said. And then she cast all caution to the wind and wrote *I have decided on due reflection that I will receive you as a suitor for my hand in marriage*, thinking to herself that once she had safely got him back in Grangeshield House she could always turn down his proposal in the end. And this time she sent her letter by her own personal messenger whose very clear instructions were that he was not to return to Grangeshield House until he carried a reply to her letter from Mr Raspero. If that reply never came, then neither would he.

The messenger brought back a reply addressed to her in Nicholas's handwriting. It was a thin letter, but then she had expected no less. She opened it to find a blank piece of paper; she turned it over to find that the other side was blank as well; she turned it around, as if the piece of paper might have had more than two sides to it, but still the page was blank. This was his reply and she understood it so perfectly that she felt a sudden pang of loss like a knife thrust in her stomach, and then her panic overwhelmed her and she wept as if her heart was breaking in two.

11:45 PM, Tuesday 26 July 1544 A.F.

Isabel lay awake that night, unable to sleep. She rolled over in her enormous bed, diving under her bedcovers and pulling them over her head. She curled up into a ball and lay there.

That blank page! The letter Nicholas had sent her affected her more than she could say. It was as if she was forced to face the question of what she would write on that page.

She had to get Nicholas back into Grangeshield House. She simply had to! There were no whys or buts or maybes. Nicholas had to be in Grangeshield House right now. Right now! The thought that he might never again be present in Grangeshield House was too terrible for her to contemplate; she turned away from it without acknowledging its importunate existence; she ran from the sting of that bee.

Isabel had never in her whole life ever stopped for a single moment's reflection; why should she? Let others reflect, if they cared to! Such an activity was not for her; it even seemed undignified in some unspecified way. Yet, now she was reluctantly, grudgingly, being grabbed by the scruff of the neck and forced to face facts. She was infuriated by the implacable necessity of the question she faced, but there was no avoiding it, no matter how much of a ball she curled herself into. She wanted Nicholas back in Grangeshield House; why? She had gone into the library earlier that day and felt a sudden stab of loss not to see Nicholas sitting there with his feet on the Carenthetian table, looking up at her with a smile. She had known then at that moment how much she missed him.

Perhaps she should have accepted one of her various suitors, she thought, even Brecky, who had later voted for Miss Ashton, and perhaps would have voted for Miss Ashton anyway even if Isabel had been his betrothed at the time, but so what? What did any of it matter? Wasn't life easier that way, if nothing mattered and you just went through the motions?

For no reason at all her father Amyas came to mind then, grim-faced but with his kindly moments. She had been fourteen years old, and dreamily looking out of the window, and he had stopped while passing by and asked her what she was thinking about and she had replied, with a directness and honesty that had surprised them both, that she was thinking about whom she would marry. He had looked at her and said, 'Marry a man who will fight the good fight, and he will do.'

She had thought later in life, looking back, that her father's advice was not very specific and certainly not at all helpful. What had he meant by what he had said? Had he even thought about it at all? Was it merely an idle comment which he had made in passing, or was it the cryptic product of a lifetime's thinking? Her father himself had known full well, none better, that the man she married would take his place as Master of Grangeshield House. And she now found herself wondering: what would her father think of Nicholas? He was certainly a man who fought the good fight in the sense that he had killed the monster Nevsky, but this only placed him in a general category, and a general category that was not even clear. What had her father meant? That she could marry any member of this category, all else being equal? That she only had to identify a general characteristic of this sort carried along as if like a banner on a pole in the hand of any man who came along, and he would do?

Isabel was all too well aware of the responsibilities which she bore to the Grangeshield legacy. She had to marry a man worthy of being Master of Grangeshield House. Her personal feelings were secondary. Yet, her personal feelings were all she knew, so what was primary was unknown, and so what was she to do? Those who saw Isabel as selfish, spoiled, willful, brattish, uncaring, arrogant and snobby, certainly saw Isabel as she was, up to a point, but those who thought she was nothing more, knew nothing more themselves. In some secret recess of her private self, Isabel felt her Grangeshield legacy keenly, carried it about in her innermost heart, and above all else, she knew that the next Master of Grangeshield House had to be worthy of this role. She could not just marry anybody, nor would she.

None of this was getting her anywhere, so Isabel rolled herself up tighter in a ball buried in the middle of her enormous four-poster bed. She had to get Nicholas back into Grangeshield House, but she could not run forever from the question of why she had to do so. The whole large expanse of Grangeshield House around her felt like an enormously large, enormously blank page. That blank page! She rolled herself around into a ball, rolling smaller and tighter and more curled up than before. That blank page! It was beyond impertinence, it was beyond even rudeness, it was beyond anything. Surely he was not so angry as that! And why was she still thinking about Nicholas Raspero, long after she should be sound asleep? Nicholas's blank letter was a wall that Isabel had run into. That blank letter had expressed his feelings about her treatment of him with such eloquence that even Isabel was at a loss for words for once. It said everything and it said everything perfectly.

She had written in her third letter that she would accept him as a suitor, but had she really meant it? No, probably not. Then why did she feel so strongly that she had to get him back into Grangeshield House? What did it matter where Nicholas was?

So it was that reluctantly, dragged by the scruff of her neck by the hand of logic, Isabel had to face the question she had been avoiding all this time: had she fallen in love with Nicholas Raspero?

She knew immediately that the answer was no, she had not, because it could not possibly be so, but she obliged herself to go through the issue systematically, just to be sure. She had admired his self-assurance from the beginning, but that was not because of being in love with him; she admired self-assurance in general, but she certainly didn't fall in love with anyone who was self-assured. He had a way of looking her directly in the eyes with a sort of amused curiosity, but that did not mean anything either; if anything he annoyed her at such times, not always, but sometimes. She had seen from the beginning that he was smitten with her, but then so were many others; he was just another man who rolled over when she told him to roll over. It was true that he was handsome but one could not judge a man by his looks. He had refused her one million strada despite being poor, which did show integrity, but really, a hairy holy man living in a cave would have done the same. She liked being with him, she enjoyed his company, he did amuse her at times even if she was careful not to show it, but none of these things made her heart beat faster; although her heart had indeed beat faster when she had gone to dance with him, but no doubt that was merely happenstance, because there was nothing about Nicholas that she could think of, apart from his good looks, the looks of a grave and distinguished nobleman, that set him apart.

Was there anything at all about Nicholas Raspero that recommended him as a suitor for her hand in marriage? Not one thing, as far as she could see. Not one thing! Yet why then was she so desperate to get him back into Grangeshield House?

Isabel rolled over yet again in her bed, still curled up under her bedcoverings in the midst of the sea of her bed. She forced herself to be logical once again: perhaps she should simply accept that Nicholas would not return to Grangeshield House. She would simply never see him again. Her emotions kicked and protested and threw a tantrum but Isabel forced the thought across her mind, pushing it like a wagon whose horse had bolted. She would never see Nicholas again. That was all. After all, why should she?

Yet she simply had to have him sitting in front of her in order to reject him. He would not reply to her letters; fine, what did he know? She needed to have him right in front of her in order to tell him that he was too inferior to be her suitor all over again; that was all that could be said, that simply could not be doubted, no logic or truth or reason was needed to prove this, you only had to look and there it was! She had not sufficiently berated him for his insolence. He had not even been angry at her insults; yet now he would not even reply to her letters; so perhaps he had been angry; yet he had not seemed so; so what was to be done? His insolence in presuming to be her suitor could not be overlooked; yet perhaps she would forgive him, but she had to have him in front of her to do this; because of course she could not forgive him, even if she did, which she didn't, but she would not in any case forgive him, yet above all else she had to have him back in Grangeshield House in order to tell him that she would never, *never*, accept him as her suitor! What was the good of him being elsewhere when he should be here in Grangeshield House?

Perhaps she would not berate him for his insolence; she would be kind and understanding, given her vastly superior social rank, and that he had no money, and that she was very rich and that her understanding of his nothingness would sting him like acid and make him suffer! He had to suffer for his insolence! How dare he presume to ask to be a suitor for her hand in marriage? How dare he!

The more she thought about it, the less she could identify a single characteristic of Nicholas that was singular or outstanding. He had no money, no title, no distinguished background. At least no distinguished Anglashian background, no matter how elevated the social status his bandit ancestors in Westrigonia might have been held in the eyes of their peers as they robbed merchant caravans or whatever they had done all that time ago. His other relatives were all schoolteachers and lawyers. Isabel was a snob to the core, and she could not overlook Nicholas's social inferiority.

The logic of Isabel's thoughts led unavoidably to the conclusion that she simply should decide never to see Nicholas again. Yet, at the very thought her stomach turned to empty ice and she rolled over in her bed, still curled up in her ball under the bedcoverings. Never see Nicholas again? No! She would not simply never see Nicholas again. That was out of the question. It was absolutely and completely and utterly out of the question! She had to see him again just in order to tell him that he was utterly unworthy of being a suitor for the hand of Lady Isabel Grangeshield of Grangeshield House. She hadn't made her rejection of him plain enough, he probably didn't understand what she had said, even though he refused to reply to her letters, but that was no doubt just laziness as no doubt the effort of putting pen to paper was beyond him. She remembered that her initial decision had been to never see Nicholas again, to cut him out of her life mercilessly, but then she had gone back on that decision; now she tried to decide why she had reversed that decision all over again, and should she reverse that reversed decision? And still she could not sleep! It was the middle of the night, and she should be asleep, and still she could not sleep! Surely she would sleep if this could all become clear to her.

She remembered then, it came back to her like a cool refreshing glass of water to a thirsty woman that initially she had only wanted to save Nicholas from Miss Ashton. That was it! She remembered now! That was why she was so keen to get Nicholas back to Grangeshield House! She had to keep Nicholas away from Miss Ashton. She remembered the mood he had been in when Miss Ashton had left the Randell's party with another man during Weatherby's duel. She had felt everything through his arm which she had been holding at the time. He had been bound by etiquette to refuse Miss Ashton's request that he take her home, but Isabel knew that without that restriction he would have taken Miss Ashton home, and why had Miss Ashton asked him to take her home in the first place? She liked Nicholas, Isabel could tell, and Nicholas liked her, and so maybe she should leave the two of them to roll around in the gutter together where they belonged, far below the notice of grandees such as Isabel. No! She could not abandon Nicholas to Miss Ashton. She would be very bad for him. She would destroy his moral character; not that he had any moral character, but she would destroy it anyway. This was the man who presumed he could court her! A man to whom Miss Ashton gave appraising looks! Let the two of them roll around together in the gutter! Isabel would accept her very next proposal, her very next proposal, from whomever that proposal might come from, given that it was from a man who was in her own social rank, and she would no longer find herself beset by questions such as these! Why should she not? Why not? Did not everybody? She would go through the motions of life, and so be it!

Furiously, Isabel tried to look for a single quality of Nicholas's that presented him to his advantage as a suitor for her hand in marriage. No money, no title, no family background, and few — very few — personal qualities that recommended his character to a prospective bride; his use, or misuse of her furniture; yes, he could cut off people's heads like nobody's business, but was that really an attribute she should look for in a husband? Her father hadn't said to her to marry a man who could cut off people's heads. Nicholas had acted on her behalf in a matter of honour, but what had driven him to storm off and kill Nevsky? Certainly not the plight of Isabel herself, who Nicholas did not even know. It was the plight of any woman in her situation, it had been the abstract idea of what Nevsky had done that had driven Nicholas; although admittedly he had been smitten with her, but so what, what had he known of her? What had he been smitten with? How deep could those feelings be for a girl he had seen in the distance at a party? He had not killed Nevsky for her, he had killed Nevsky for an idea, whether that idea had been Isabel in her red and blue gown or some grand scheme of things. Was there anything about Nicholas, was there just one single thing, just one point in his favour that she could identify? No, there was not. Yet, why could she not then stop thinking about him? Maybe there was one thing in his favour that she was overlooking, something to recommend his suit, but what could it be?

He was the best wandfighter in New Landern but she had never been that impressed with wandfighters, though she knew that some women threw themselves at wandfighters, perhaps out of a perversity she did not herself share. Miss Ashton, for example, might be such a woman. Yes, no doubt she would be perverse to the core, shuddering with longing for violent men who would satisfy her debauched desires.

She remembered again that night when Nicholas had escorted her out and she had seen him talking to Miss Ashton. Now that she came to think of it, she had felt furiously jealous at the very sight, though at the time she had not recognised her own jealousy for what it was. *Perhaps I was in love with him already by then*, she thought dreamily, beginning to fall asleep at last. Except she was not in love with Nicholas, so why was she asking herself such questions? She was not in love with Nicholas now, so she was not then, so she had not been jealous at all. She had been furious to see how Miss Ashton had flirted with Nicholas, and that fury must have been jealousy; so she had been in love with him then. Otherwise why would she have been so jealous? Her thoughts were becoming tangled because now she was wondering if Nicholas was talking to Miss Ashton these days, perhaps at the rehearsals of *The Kingdom of Happiness* which would soon be showing at the Emperor Theatre, and suddenly an idea jumped up into her mind like a cat jumping up into her lap. With the arrival of that idea she found herself wide-awake again, but this time with a reason to be wide-awake.

She had to see Nicholas in person but she could not go to him like a supplicant asking for him to receive her. He might see her, or he might not; he might talk to her politely, or he might not, but she knew in her stomach that such an approach would not work in any case. Furthermore, it was very important that she need not speak a word if she chose not to speak, whereas if she went to see him she would be obliged to speak from the beginning. The blank page he had sent her had told her everything she needed to know in order to make these judgements. Somehow she had to have him sitting next to her without her having gone to see him and without needing to speak. She knew instinctively that if that happened she could win him back. He refused to see her, she could not go directly to him, but there was a third way and she had just now seen what it was.

Isabel uncurled herself from the ball she had made of her body while she had wrestled with this issue. She worked her way back up her enormous bed until she lay with her head on her pillow and her bedclothes drawn up to her chin, breathing the nighttime air again. She now saw, with a feeling of delirious freedom, that she had no need now to resolve this issue. She had to have Nicholas sitting in front of her, she had to have Nicholas sitting in Grangeshield House, and she had to have Nicholas back in her life again, in order to make everything quite clear to him and to her. Yes, she thought, to him as well as her. Nicholas probably hadn't understood her properly when she had last spoken to him, with regard to her rejection of his suit, or rather, with her rejection of his desire to be a suitor for her hand in marriage. She had to get him back into Grangeshield House! She *had* to get him back into Grangeshield House! She had no doubt that if she could get him back into her presence under her own conditions, Nicholas would be hers again. He would do whatever she said. He would come back to Grangeshield House if she told him to, and he would stay in the Rowland Room again, and then ... and then what? *Well,* she thought, *one step at a time.* She would take one step at a time. The next step would be to get Nicholas back to Grangeshield House, and she had seen what that next step would be.

Oh, yes indeed, she knew what to do next! She saw what trap to set for Nicholas. The idea had just jumped into her mind; she knew now what to do. She would set this trap for Nicholas, he would be caught by it, he would come tumbling down to land at her feet, and there he would be, and she would say nothing and he would be there at her feet, and she would have him back, and then he would be back here in Grangeshield House, where he belonged, and naturally he would not stay at her feet here in Grangeshield House, she would allow him to walk about, but he would be here, here in Grangeshield House.

Isabel fell fast asleep then at last, knowing then that Nicholas would be back at Grangeshield House, where he belonged. With the plan she had formulated, it was all as good as done. She plunged into sleep like a diver swooping from a great height into deep waters, happy now that Nicholas would soon be back in her life, and that he would be back in Grangeshield House where he belonged.

Yet she knew deep down she had avoided answering the real question that had kept her awake all this time, but as she dived happily into sleep, happy, beyond happiness that Nicholas would return into her life because she had seen how to do it, she knew also that answering that question could wait. She had time, and she would find her answers, but most of all, Nicholas would be back in Grangeshield House, *where he belonged* ...

THIRTY-FIVE

The Letters of Lady Isabel Grangeshield to Mr Nicholas Raspero

11:15 AM, Saturday 23 July 1544 A.F.

Nicholas felt fine as he walked down the street away from Grangeshield House. Walking suited his mood right then, walking was being independent, not riding in someone else's carriage; walking also helped him breathe properly, because his chest felt so tight that he couldn't seem to get deep breaths of air into his lungs.

He felt fine about everything, especially about having everything resolved so clearly with regard to Isabel. He would never see her again, except perhaps in passing. He would be distant and polite, he would nod and say as few words as possible and try to keep at a distance from her. It was just as well that all this had been so cleanly and clearly resolved so that now he could move on. He had not done what he had done for Isabel, and he had done it for the sake of justice, so that was the main thing. He quite sincerely wished Isabel well for her future, but he had his own future to consider and it was time to move on.

He really felt fine about everything, but he also felt a little bit light headed and so he stopped by a tree to lean on it for a moment. For some reason the tree turned sideways, which puzzled him as the palms of his hands scraped over the rough bark which he also didn't understand and he found himself lying on the ground, looking up into the sky around the crown of the tree. The sky overhead was a deep blue with sketchy white streaks of cloud like a white lacery finery over the deep blue of the heavens above. Nicholas decided to lie there for a moment just for fun, because what was the rush anyway?

The tree stretched high into the heavens above like a tent pole, with the blue of the sky the tent itself in some strange way; the tree seemed supernaturally enormous to Nicholas, its brown length in the blue air bulging like a perspective onto a planetary landscape. It came to Nicholas then that he could stretch out where he was and lie there for a while and explore this strangely inviting vista by falling into the blue and that was all there was to it!

A passing flying carriage swooped down towards the well-dressed gentleman lying on the ground. Nicholas heard voices coming towards him, but they seemed to be far away, even though as he turned his head he could see two women towering over him, one of them older, perhaps sixty or so, and vigorously fierce looking, the other younger, perhaps thirty or so, and much more gentle looking.

'Are you all right, Mr Raspero?' he heard the older one ask.

He looked at her. She looked vaguely familiar, but he was sure he had never been introduced to her. 'Introductions are by third party,' he said, by way of telling them to go away.

'Oh, stop talking nonsense,' the older woman said. 'Lord Zinia patted you on the shoulder, did he not, and that will serve as your introduction. I am Lady Saranna Presley, and this is my daughter-in-law, Lady Emilia Tatton.'

'Oh, you were at Lady Starfeld's party,' Nicholas said, remembering now where he had seen her before. 'Well, to answer your question, yes, I'm perfectly all right. So you can go on your way now, I'm fine.'

'You are not fine, Mr Raspero,' Lady Presley said sternly. 'We live very near here. You will return home with us and have a rest to regain your strength.'

'Women,' Nicholas said bitterly, 'no one can tell you anything, isn't that right?'

'Oh, I see, your fainting fit is over a woman. How very brave of you, Mr Raspero! How lucky we women are to have such bravery to lean on ourselves! Otherwise we would be the ones who fainted!'

'You are mistaken in your diagnosis, Lady Presley,' Nicholas said. 'I just have a slight touch of the flu, that's all.'

'Yes, I can tell from your coughing and sneezing,' Lady Presley said sarcastically. 'Now, on your feet and come with us, young man, and stop being so foolish!'

Nicholas realised from her tone of voice that she was going to nag him until he did what she wanted. Reluctantly, because he was actually feeling very comfortable where he was, he struggled up into a sitting position and then managed to stand up. 'I'm feeling perfectly all right now,' he said, leaning against the tree, 'but thank you for your kind help anyway.'

Lady Presley came and grabbed his arm, gesturing to Emilia with her head to take the other, and Nicholas found himself being marched towards their flying carriage. He decided not to protest any more, although he did, in fact, feel much less light headed than before. The two women sat him between them in their flying carriage and they were airborne again. Nicholas closed his eyes, more to avoid being drawn into conversation than for any other reason, and it wasn't long before he felt the flying carriage descending to the ground. He opened his eyes to see a mansion before him, with the flying carriage settling into its landing spot.

Nicholas insisted that he could walk unaided, and in fact, he did feel a lot better, even practically back to normal. They took him inside and settled him down into the drawing room. Lady Presley brought him a glass of brandy and insisted that he swallow it all, despite his protests that he wasn't much of a drinker.

'This is medicine, Mr Raspero, and you are my patient. Drink up!'

The brandy burned his throat and made him splutter, but it did seem to do him some good. He was told by Lady Presley that he was much less pale, the colour had come back into his cheeks, and this was confirmed by Emilia with a nod. The ladies sat down in nearby chairs and opened their fans and hid their faces behind their fans, with their eyes peeking over the tops of their fans as they studied him.

Nicholas looked around him. His attention was caught by a huge wall-hanging opposite him on the far wall, perhaps five-feet wide and twenty-feet long. It was made of some white material, perhaps a fine wool, with black markings all over it that Nicholas realised, on a closer inspection, was a drawing of mountains with writing in various places. Lady Presley turned her head to follow his gaze and said, 'Those are the Mountains of Weiden, Mr Raspero.'

'I've heard of them from somewhere,' Nicholas commented. 'I mean, they ring a bell.'

'They rang a funeral bell for my father,' Lady Presley said, 'that tapestry was his work, by his very own hand, he spent twenty years mapping those mountains, but they killed him in the end.'

'So what was the big deal about the Mountains of Weiden for your father?' Nicholas asked.

Lady Presley sighed. 'My father had a lifelong obsession with the Doctrine of Duplication. Are you familiar with this theory?'

'Not really,' Nicholas shook his head.

'Well, according to the Doctrine of Duplication, apparently our own society is a duplication of a society that existed before The Fall, and this is maintained either to prevent another Fall, or as an experiment of some kind, or in order to carry out some kind of programme towards a specific goal, depending on which school of thought you are listening to. According to the believers in this doctrine, such as my father, it is possible to prove this by gaining access to records of the past. Now the Mountains of Weiden, my father believed, contained such records. But they are very dangerous territory and in the end they killed him, those mountains.'

'Oh, the stories you hear about those mountains are horrible,' Emilia asserted, managing to overcome her shyness enough to speak at last. 'There are monsters there, creatures that have heads like hawks but bodies like bears, creatures that have intelligence but are evil predators.'

'My father believed these stories were inventions designed to keep people from going there to see what was going on for themselves,' Lady Presley added.

'I would never go there myself, whether those stories are inventions or not,' Emilia insisted.

The wall-hanging was having an odd effect on Nicholas. It seemed almost three dimensional, almost illusory, a numinous portrayal of a magical place that seemed to call to him to go there. 'Couldn't you just fly over it in a flying carriage and have a look down from above?' Nicholas asked. 'I mean, these bird-headed bears can't fly if they don't have wings, so wouldn't you be safe enough doing that?'

'That is precisely how my father drew up his maps,' Lady Presley said, 'but the time came when he was determined to land on the ground and explore more thoroughly. The carriage returned to the place where he had been left at a pre-arranged time, but he never returned, nor any of the fifteen members of his party. None of them were ever seen again.'

'Bad luck,' Nicholas said sympathetically, 'I mean, that must have been hard on you.'

'Oh, he waited until his son and heir was of age to have gotten married and produced his own son and heir, he provided a good dowry for my own marriage, so his affairs were settled and he was ready for the last adventure of his life. I am actually quite proud of him, to tell the truth. There comes a time in life, Mr Raspero, when it is best to choose how you will die rather than pretend that it will never happen.'

'That sounds a bit gloomy to me, Lady Presley,' Nicholas protested.

'It is horribly gloomy and very morbid,' Emilia complained.

'You are both young,' Lady Presley responded, shrugging off their objections, 'you will understand when you are older.'

Nicholas laughed merrily. 'I've heard that all my life and I still don't understand anything about anything!'

Emilia giggled and Lady Presley brightened up as well, as if laughter was not heard often enough in their house. 'You must have patience, Mr Raspero,' Lady Presley said reprovingly but with a smile.

And so it was that Nicholas learned of the Mountains of Weiden. He stayed chatting with the ladies until lunch, and then accepted their invitation to stay for lunch, and then stayed chatting with them until mid-afternoon, and then accepted their offer of a loan of a flying carriage to take him home. He lay awake that night thinking about the Mountains of Weiden, which had already seized his imagination. He gave no further thought to Isabel; the thought of going to the Mountains of Weiden was now all he could think of and the more he thought about it, the more he decided to do it.

He asked Ben if he would like to come with him.

'Haven't we already had this conversation as children?' Ben said impatiently. He was in a bad mood. Nicholas wasn't the only one whose love-life was going badly. 'We were going to travel around the world in a flying carriage, I believe. It was a fascinating conversation to have then. It has no interest for me now.'

The idea of going to the Mountains of Weiden had now seized hold of Nicholas's imagination. He went to the library and spent all day there looking at the accounts that had been compiled from travellers who had been there themselves, or who claimed at any rate, truthfully or untruthfully, to have been there themselves. After the library had closed he went off to get himself his usual free meal from a street vendor, and then wandered around New Landern.

To be free, to be a bird in the blue sky, to be high in the mountains on constant alert against the danger of imminent death, seemed to Nicholas to be the only place in the world to be right then. The philosophical implications of finding out that the society he lived in was some kind of stage-managed affair were of little interest to him; *so what* would have pretty much summed up his entire response to such a discovery. It was the idea of going into the wilderness away from everything that was the attraction for him.

Nicholas was not the world's most reflective person, so it did not occur to him that his sudden compulsive desire to go into the wilderness might have had something to do with the crushing rejection of his romantic advances by the beautiful girl he had fallen in love with. As far as he was concerned he felt fine about everything with regard to Isabel and he had already moved on and put everything behind him. So it was that the arrival of Isabel's letter, which he did not receive until he had returned late the next evening, left him indifferent. Her carefully constructed letter irritated him to the point where the bird-headed bears of the Mountains of Weiden, no matter how evil and predatory they were, seemed excellent company by comparison to Isabel.

"*Grangeshield House,*
New Landern.

24 July 1544

"*Dear Mr Raspero,*
I trust that this letter finds you well and in good health, as surely it must
(I refuse to allow things to be otherwise, I positively refuse to allow this!
— and so there we are, if I might borrow a phrase from you! — all is well
with you, I am sure).

My dear Mr Raspero, I hope and pray that you will excuse me
if I express a certain puzzlement as to the somewhat abrupt nature
of your departure from Grangeshield House. It has retrospectively
occurred to me that perhaps some of my comments may have been so
freely spoken as to be liable to misinterpretation, and yet you left so
abruptly that I had no opportunity to clarify any ambiguous points
which may have given rise to some kind of misunderstanding; had you
remained a moment longer to discuss any point, which may have been
unclear to you at the time, I am sure that all misunderstandings and
misinterpretations of my perhaps slightly too freely spoken comments
might have been rendered much more intelligible than they perhaps
were."

Nicholas stopped here to roll his eyes and groan out loud. He
remembered only too clearly how Isabel had shouted, *Get out! Get out of*
my house! Get out now! and he was not at all impressed to be told that this
was an ambiguous statement he had somehow misinterpreted. Isabel's
complete disregard for the truth, or perhaps more accurately her regard
for the truth being defined entirely by how much it would allow her to
have things her own way, had somehow largely lost its charm for Nicholas
as he sat there reading this letter.

My dear Mr Raspero, it is a matter of some concern to me that
this misunderstanding should not persist one moment longer and that

it really must be cleared up without any delay. You have been such a welcome guest at Grangeshield House that it is with a good deal of surprise that I now must contemplate a determination on your part to no longer visit me, and I am sure that this determination on your part has arisen from a misinterpretation of certain statements I may have inadvertently made during our last meeting.

I do confess, my dear Mr Raspero, that I may well have spoken a good deal more freely than was perhaps called for or intended, and some of my comments might even perhaps have seemingly verged on the slightly intemperate, which if so was certainly not intended on my part. I believe that the simplest course of action is this: I withdraw completely and entirely, without any qualification, all of the remarks I made on the occasion of our last meeting, and I withdraw all these remarks without hesitation or reservation. Let what was said be unsaid; or, if this is not possible, at least let what was said be understood to be revoked.

Naturally, this leaves the declaration of your feelings to be without a response on my part, which I cannot countenance for a moment, as it is highly discourteous for a man of your outstanding quality to be treated in such a way. I therefore suggest that you return to Grangeshield House in order that I might make a response to the declaration of your feelings which is fitting and appropriate, which is much clearer and less uncertain than the perhaps slightly ambiguous character of some of the remarks which I may have made perhaps a little too carelessly.

My dear Mr Raspero, do not let us be parted on such terms as this, please do not allow such an absurdity as a slight misunderstanding between such good friends as us to be an occasion for us not to continue to remain on such good terms as formerly. I would be greatly pleased if you could come and visit me Tuesday 26 July at three o'clock in the afternoon so that we can resolve this misunderstanding. Our acquaintance may be short of duration, but it is long indeed in thought and feeling, is it not, my dear Mr Raspero — we are already old friends, you and I, we are already much too close to each other to have such a distance between us. How absurd is this? — to be close yet far, to be next to each other yet be in different places. This is absurd, surely you must agree, this terrible misunderstanding must be cleared up without delay.

I await your arrival eagerly, nothing could possibly please me more than to see you return to Grangeshield House, surely you will not leave me to be so unhappy as I am now, to sit here without the prospect of having you in Grangeshield House again; yes, my dear Mr Raspero, I would go so far as to declare that I am unhappy that you are not here now, and that I must write a letter to you instead of being able to speak to you directly. Yet, I look forward to speaking to you directly once again, when you come and visit me here in Grangeshield House.

I remain your most affectionate friend,

Sending you this letter with the warmest affection,

Lady Isabel Grangeshield.

Nicholas considered this letter for a while, then crumpled it in his hands and threw it into the waste paper basket. He leaned over his desk, pulling out his notebook and studying once again a map of the Mountains of Weiden.

10:30 AM, Monday 25 July 1544 A.F.

Isabel's letter had had some effect on Nicholas because he was reminded that he had unfinished business to attend to remaining from his clash with Nevsky. Whittington's letter to his son would have to be forwarded somehow and Nicholas would have to do this in such a way as to avoid being asked awkward questions. It would be simplest, no doubt, to simply post it without comment, but it was something which Nicholas should deal with before leaving Anglashia for the Mountains of Weiden, just in case he never came back.

Another remaining issue was Jolly's sole surviving notebook, divided into two parts headlined Friends and Enemies. Nicholas looked through this notebook again, noting as he had before that Lord Zinia headed the Enemies' section; it was this backhanded endorsement of Lord Zinia which prompted Nicholas into deciding to take the notebook to Zinia.

He wrote Zinia a letter asking to visit him, using the address Jolly had written down in his notebook, and sent off the letter that morning.

He then turned his attention to studying techniques of surviving in the wilderness. He studied diagrams that showed how to bend tree branches together to form a shelter for the night, and how to stay downwind of places where there were indications of dangerous and predatory animals. He looked through books that showed how to identify edible plants and fruits, and other books that showed how to do many interesting things such as the correct way to skin snakes before cooking them over an open fire.

His plans to go to the Mountains of Weiden were proceeding apace. Ben was not the least impressed with these plans. 'I see that your promise to be a completely normal person hasn't lasted long,' he would say disparagingly whenever Nicholas mentioned his great adventure. 'You do understand, of course, or perhaps you don't, that this is not the kind of thing that a normal person does. I do note that it won't result in innocent relatives getting murdered in their beds late at night, but apart from that, I can see no merit in your scheme whatsoever.'

Nicholas ignored these criticisms. He had never felt so fired up about anything before in his life. He was going to go right the way through the Mountains of Weiden from one end to the other, and then turn around and make the return journey all the way back. That would be something! Ben could scoff all he liked, but Nicholas was going to do it!

Isabel's second letter came in the midst of all this. Nicholas opened it a little impatiently, as reading it was interfering with learning the top twenty most useful knots to use when tying up ropes in the wilderness.

Grangeshield House,
New Landern

25 July 1544

My dear Mr Raspero,
I can only believe that my earlier letter must have gone astray, and

so I write once again. I have written, as you cannot know, having not received my earlier letter, of my concern that the remarks I made at our last meeting may well have been misinterpreted; or if not misinterpreted, at least taken the wrong way, given that I most certainly did not intend that such a distance should have grown between us, such a distance, such a distance that surely we cannot allow it to remain, this distance that must be removed immediately. I know you did not receive my earlier letter. How do I know this? Because you are a man of such infinite courtesy, such infinite courtesy that you would certainly have replied had you received this letter.

Nicholas rolled his eyes and groaned aloud. Fine, when it suited Isabel for him to be a man of infinite courtesy that was what he was, only until the precise opposite was what she wanted to be so and then the opposite it was!

As you cannot have received my earlier letter, I must briefly reprise it. I entirely withdraw everything I said on the occasion of our last meeting, and furthermore, I even apologise to you for certain remarks that I do not deny were intemperate. Yes, I spoke rashly. I have nothing but admiration for your wholly admirable family, your very distinguished Westrigonian baronial heritage, a heritage of which I am sure that you are justly proud, your wholly admirable grandfather who settled here in Anglashia, your wonderful relatives who comprise your family whom I can only praise.

Mr Raspero, there has been a terrible misunderstanding. Please Mr Raspero, do not be so angry with me as perhaps you are. I do not deny that I spoke foolishly, rashly, intemperately, that I said very stupid things that I did not mean at all and which I now completely withdraw without reservation or hesitation or qualification. My dear Mr Raspero, I deeply apologise for everything I said. I am truly sorry. I did not mean anything I said. I was very foolish. Surely you are not so angry with me as to ignore my letters! Surely not so!

Please come to visit me at 3 PM Tuesday so that we may immediately and without delay resolve a foolish misunderstanding. It was only that you caught me by surprise when you spoke as you did, I expected you to be saying farewell, I was perhaps a little taken aback, yet I do not make excuses for my behaviour, which was inexcusable, I do not pretend otherwise, I say only that I did not expect such a declaration at such a time. Yet, this is my own failing, not yours, it is just that formerly I had always known when such a declaration would be forthcoming, but on this one occasion I did not see this coming. It was so soon — yet we have known each other for so long, have we not — surely such matters as these are not measured in days and hours. I have no excuse, I do not know, I only know that I am sorry now for what I said.

Mr Raspero, please come to see me at 3 PM tomorrow afternoon. I must see you in person to resolve this matter. It is a terrible misunderstanding. Naturally I meant nothing that I may have said. I withdraw everything I said.

Your very own affectionate Isabel Grangeshield.

Nicholas crumpled up the letter and threw it into the waste paper basket, and returned to studying his knots.

3:00 PM, Wednesday 27 July 1544 A.F.

Nicholas waited patiently while Lord Zinia filled his pipe with tobacco. They were sitting in Zinia's study in Aranrhod House.

Lord Zinia obviously had an interest in foreign exotica. The walls of his study had a variety of strange masks from around the world hanging in between paintings of the ruins of long-plundered cities of old. Peculiar objects made of bronze or tin that could be anything from weaponry to bodily ornaments sat on tables and shelves here and there. A stuffed tiger's head with a wide-open snarling mouth and black opal eyes was mounted on a wall-plaque to one side, giving Nicholas the odd feeling that the study was moving and changing shape.

Zinia lit his pipe, puffing clouds of aromatic smoke in the air, and leaned back in his chair behind his desk and said, 'It is very kind of you to pay me this visit, Mr Raspero. I can only say how appreciative I am of your consideration.'

The insincerity of this kind of talk often made Nicholas impatient but he swallowed his scepticism and said, 'Not at all, Lord Zinia, it is your kindness in receiving me that I appreciate. You are the one being considerate, not me.'

'Far from it,' Zinia disagreed, the stem of his pipe poised in the air before his lips, 'very far from it indeed, in coming to see me today you have demonstrated an exemplary courtesy which I can only applaud.' Zinia puffed on his pipe, while contemplating Nicholas as if to say that he could do this all day.

'When we last spoke I left out one or two details about my evening out with Jolly,' Nicholas said, ending these polite exchanges as abruptly as a man slapping dust off the palms of his hands.

'Did you? What details are these?'

'Jolly had a number of notebooks in his safe detailing personal matters concerning leading individuals of New Landern. These notebooks could be used for blackmail, burglary, and all kinds of mischief.'

'Who were these leading individuals?'

'I forget their names. In any case, I burned all those notebooks except one, so it doesn't matter now who they were. Their foolishness need not survive in such records any more; Mr Taggart Longman witnessed the destruction of these notebooks if you require further testimony.'

'You spared one notebook from the flames, did you say?'

Nicholas took the notebook out of his pocket, stood up, walked over and laid it on the desk in front of Zinia, then returned to his chair. Zinia contemplated the notebook without moving for a moment, then laid his pipe down carefully to one side and picked up the notebook and started looking through it.

There was silence in the room while Zinia turned the pages of the notebook and Nicholas tried not to look at the tiger's head, which was still playing optical tricks on him.

'May I keep this for a while?' Lord Zinia asked, having come to an end of the notebook.

'Keep it, it's yours,' Nicholas said with a brisk wave of his left hand, feeling that he had mishandled the gift-giving; he should have made more of a ceremony out of it. Still, it was done now. 'I came here to give it to you.'

'I can only thank you for your kindness,' Zinia said, but this time he sounded as if he meant it.

'That's all right.' Nicholas straightened up in his chair as if preparing to leave any moment now. 'I would've given that notebook to whoever was Jolly's main enemy; it happens to be you, that's all.'

'An excellent line of reasoning,' Zinia said approvingly. 'You have a good head on your shoulders, Mr Raspero.'

'I have been called one of the leading minds of our age,' Nicholas said casually.

'Indeed?' Zinia's eyebrows rose. 'And who was your admirer on this occasion?'

'Lady Starfeld, in her party invitation,' Nicholas said, and after a moment's silence laughed merrily.

Zinia laughed as well. 'I have also been praised by Lady Starfeld in her party invitations over the years,' he commented. 'You are certainly a talented young man, Mr Raspero, in any case. May I ask what your plans are at this time in your life?'

'I'm going through the Mountains of Weiden,' Nicholas said.

'Why is that?'

Nicholas shrugged. 'Because it's there to be done. Why not?'

'I would counsel you against such a plan of action, Mr Raspero. You would be highly unlikely to survive such a journey.'

'We'll see,' Nicholas said, feeling that he was surrounded by critics day in and day out.

Lord Zinia re-lit his pipe, taking his time about it, then said casually, 'I thought you had made such good friends with Isabel Grangeshield.'

Nicholas took a deep breath to steady his nerves. 'We've quarrelled and we're not on speaking terms.'

Zinia didn't seem surprised. 'What did you quarrel about?'

Nicholas sighed. 'I suggested that I should be a suitor for her hand in marriage and she, well, never mind the details but that's all over now.'

Zinia nodded understandingly. 'Do you know what Isabel looks for in a husband?'

'Do you?'

'Isabel Grangeshield will only marry a man who is worthy of being Master of Grangeshield House. Remember that.'

'Well, she doesn't want me anyway.'

'I would not be too quick to turn away at the sight of the first obstacle,' Zinia told him in a tone of rebuke. 'A man who is worthy of being Master of Grangeshield House will not turn away at the first sign of trouble.'

'Everyone is always so good at giving advice,' Nicholas said a little impatiently. 'Well, aren't they? It makes you wonder why their own lives are in such a mess. Doesn't it?'

Zinia didn't smile but looked very seriously at Nicholas. 'My life is not a mess, Mr Raspero, and I am giving you good advice. Forget about this madness of Weiden and set your sights on becoming Master of Grangeshield House.'

'I will, of course, give your very wise and welcome advice a lot of careful deliberation,' Nicholas said as sincerely as he could despite not meaning a word of it; he then stood up and said, 'I'm off, Lord Zinia. Thank you for your kind hospitality.'

Zinia accompanied him on his way out, his pipe in hand, waving away his butler. He stood puffing on his pipe on the top step outside his front door, looking after the departing figure of Nicholas with the bright eyes of a fox.

10:30 PM, Wednesday 27 July 1544 A.F.

Nicholas had wandered around New Landern all afternoon after his meeting with Lord Zinia, feeling at a loss; his own certainty about going to the Mountains of Weiden was being undermined by external considerations. He felt like a believer whose faith was being challenged by logical thoughts. Isabel's letters and Zinia's advice were suggesting to him that it was time to think again, but the activities of thinking and upholding the faith were pointing in two different directions. It was in this mood, feeling like a man stranded between two warring gods, that Nicholas eventually returned home to find that a third letter from Isabel had arrived for him.

Isabel's third letter was in the hands of a messenger dressed in the red and gold livery of the Grangeshield Estate sitting waiting in the Clark household. He had been waiting there since eleven-thirty that morning. Although, he had not had too hard a time of it as he had been well taken care of by Mrs Clark, who admired his red and gold livery.

He arose as Nicholas entered to present him with the letter with which he had been entrusted. Nicholas took it with a brief nod.

'Mr Raspero,' the messenger asked, 'may I take your reply back with me?'

'Not today,' Nicholas said, in a manner even more brief than the nod which he had already given.

"May I ask when, sir?' the messenger asked.

'What's it to you?' Nicholas asked in a tone that suggested the messenger was being impertinent, which, as far as Nicholas was concerned, he was.

'Lady Grangeshield has instructed me that I may not return to Grangeshield House until I have your reply in my hand,' the messenger said in reply. 'Sir,' he added hastily, realising he had forgotten to say this.

'What? Never?' Nicholas asked in surprise.

'Yes, sir,' the messenger said in some embarrassment, aware that everyone was staring at him, including the Clark children in hiding on the stairs.

Nicholas sighed. 'Why am I not surprised?' he asked rhetorically, although, in fact, he had been surprised. 'What's your name?' Nicholas had seen the man about before on an earlier visit to Grangeshield House.

'Stanwick, sir.'

'All right, wait here. I'll see what I can do.'

'That is very kind of you, sir,' said the messenger.

Nicholas went back to his own room, still clutching Isabel's latest letter in his hand. He took several deep breaths, feeling overwhelmed by events; what should he do now? All of a sudden he knew just what to do as a sharp-edged impatience seized hold of him. She wanted a reply from him? Very well, he would reply to her. So be it — he would give her a reply that said everything. He took a blank piece of paper, folded it up and stuffed it into an envelope. He addressed it to "Lady Isabel Grangeshield, Grangeshield House" and sealed the envelope with red molten wax. He left his room and handed the envelope to Stanwick, and so it was done.

Nicholas returned to his own room where he sat down and opened Isabel's letter.

Grangeshield House,
New Landern

27 July 1544

Dear Mr Raspero,
Where are you, my dear Mr Raspero? I call for you but there is no reply. Where are you? I write you letters that you do not answer —— surely you are not still angry with me. Are you well? I worry that you have fallen ill, that you cannot reply to me because of some happening that has befallen you, and that surely you would reply if you had received the letters that I have written.

Mr Raspero, I deeply apologise for everything that I said. I did not mean a word of it at the time. I fully apologise for what I have said; please accept my apology. I can only ask you to please forgive me. Surely you have received my earlier letters and you know this already. My dear Mr Raspero, I miss you all the time — I simply must see you, even if it is only to learn that you will no longer see me. Will you not at least grant me this one simple request? I spoke very badly, I did not mean anything I said, I was taken by surprise, I have no excuse, if only I had foreseen that you would speak so I would have been so much more temperate, I would have told you much more truly how I felt about what you said.

Mr Raspero, I have decided on due reflection that I will receive you as a suitor for my hand in marriage. Yes, I will. But perhaps you no longer wish to court me? But you will let me know if this is so, will you not, Mr Raspero? Surely you will at least grant me this one simple request, you will at least tell me in person that you no longer wish to court me so at least I know.

Mr Raspero, who knows whether I might marry you after all? Surely a suitor must surmount all such obstacles in his path if he is driven by true love. If it was true love that drove you to speak as you did to me, you will surely come to see me and speak to me in person because you will at least understand that I regret everything that I said to you when we last met. If you love me, or at least if you did love me but no longer do so, then surely you will come and see me whichever it is because you are not false, your heart is true, Mr Raspero, I am very sorry for what I have done, I know that I acted very badly, please forgive me.

Do you still love me, Mr Raspero? Perhaps not, very well, I understand, I have driven you away. But surely you loved me once, you would not have spoken falsely, you said that you loved me and so it was true, you are an honourable man, you would not have spoken falsely; so then, as you once loved me, then reply to my letter, let me at least know that you still live.

I remain your loving Isabel.

Nicholas folded up this letter and carefully stowed it away in an inside pocket of his robes. He hesitated then, sitting at his desk, his head bowed. He couldn't decide on a thing right then. Isabel's letter had reached him; suddenly his heart was beating faster; Isabel almost sounded as if she would marry him given the least effort on his part, but what did she really mean? Women, Nicholas decided, were erratic: first it was one thing, then it was the opposite. Isabel had not wanted the least thing to do with him before; now she simply couldn't live without him. Well, which was it?

Nicholas, unaware of the masterstroke he had just played in sending Isabel a blank letter, was assailed by a sudden doubt. Perhaps he had just blundered in what he had just done. But it was too late now to undo his action.

Nicholas buried his head in his hands and thought the matter through, rising above his emotions in order to be logical. Soon he saw that given their role on this particular stage, and given that they were very likely on his side if appearances could be trusted, he should write a letter to the Eastons.

71 Norell Street,
Dejaville,
New Landern

28 July 1544

Dear Lord and Lady Easton,
It is clear to me that Isabel's wellbeing is of great concern to you and so I therefore write to you with regard to recent developments and future possibilities. What is to be done? Isabel has said that she will receive me as her suitor, but I am away very shortly and so everything is divided into two.

As no doubt you know I recently suggested to Isabel that I should be her suitor and she said definitely not. And so there we are. But now I have received three letters from Isabel even though I am making plans to depart Anglashia briefly and so my thoughts return to making a clear statement on these issues now before I leave.

My point is this: Isabel has decided to receive me as a suitor, very well, I will be a suitor for her hand in marriage, all well and good, but not now. I mean, what does she expect? The world doesn't simply stop spinning on its axis because Isabel has a brainwave. I have decided to go to the Mountains of Weiden and traverse that mountain range from beginning to end from Weiden to Ardal and back again. And after I have done that I will return to Anglashia and I will be a suitor for Isabel's hand in marriage. This is what I have to say and this is why I am writing this letter to you. It is all clear enough as it stands but there are nonetheless complications, as so often in life.

I foresee numerous instances of varying permutations. You may well say, well, what if Isabel has moved on and does not even remember me by the time I return from Weiden? I say that is all well and good, and I will say no more. So it is done. Clearly love is impossible. I would much prefer not to be in this situation; obviously it would be best if Isabel moved on, I will also move on, so I am sure we can all agree that there is nothing more to be said. But perhaps she will receive me still, well, we shall see.

Nicholas paused, his pen raised in the air. He was really writing this letter for Isabel, on the off-chance that the Eastons might give her the letter to read, which he thought they should do, everything considered, even if he couldn't count on it, but what did he have to say to Isabel?

I completely accept the apology for her comments which Isabel has made in her letters. This is no longer an issue for me. I was naturally offended at the time, and I resolved in consequence that our association was ended, but her apology has removed the offence and as I am still in love with her I am naturally still keen to be her suitor in the future. But does Isabel want to be married? Is she ready to be married yet? Perhaps not. So all well and good and there is nothing to say. She just wants everything her own way all the time which means that she is not yet ready to be married.

Nicholas paused then, realising that he was sounding perhaps a bit too critical. On the other hand, it was true that Isabel wanted to have things her way all the time. *Being in love with Isabel was an impossible situation to be in*, Nicholas thought.

Clearly love is impossible. But there are complications even beyond what a normal lover might expect. I declared my feelings for Isabel at a time which you might well consider to have been much sooner than necessary. Believe me, I would have much preferred to have waited until later, much later, the longer the better. Why then did I not wait? Well, it came to my attention that there was a good deal of gossip throughout New Landern concerning my overnight stays at Grangeshield House and I reflected that Isabel's reputation could not have a question mark raised against it because of my behaviour. I should not have spent so much time at Grangeshield House, I realise that now; well, what is done is done. Anyway, my point is that I declared my feelings to Isabel when I did because of my concern to protect her reputation from any damage done by this kind of gossip, the gossip kind of gossip as it was put to me, and so that is how things were.

Nicholas wondered what else to say. Surely Isabel would read this letter. What did he have to say to her?

I understand that Isabel will only marry a man who is worthy of being Master of Grangeshield House, because that is her legacy, and in the end that is what counts despite every impression she likes to give about being self-centred. Isabel is self-centred in many other respects, but not in this regard: with regard to her Grangeshield legacy she is entirely without thought of self. It is not enough that I love Isabel and that she loves me, if she does: there is the other side of this particular coin. I understand this completely. I have to say in all honesty that I have no idea whether or not I am worthy of this role. If I am to court Isabel this issue will no doubt become clearer.

I thank you for all the kindness you have shown me. Being Isabel's chaperones can't be the easiest job in the world but you nonetheless are unfailingly kind and courteous. However things turn out, it was an honour to have known you both.

All my best wishes and best regards,
Yours sincerely,
Nicholas Raspero.

He tried to go to sleep but he was too wide awake. He cast his mind back to where he was with his progress along the Mountains of Weiden but for some reason the Mountains of Weiden no longer held quite the same fascination for him as they had done. Isabel's letter had distracted him. Surely she hadn't actually meant to tell him that she might marry him; it was a trick, she had written it without thinking, or while thinking the opposite; she would be saying the opposite the very next day if he went to see her. Yet, his heart beat faster simply from the memory of having read those words; so he lit the lamp again and read her letter again; he half-wanted to crumple up her letter and throw it into the waste paper basket but he couldn't so he carefully stowed it away and turned off the lamp and lay there until eventually he fell asleep in the darkness.

THIRTY-SIX

....

A Letter from Mr Nicholas Raspero is Received by Lord and Lady Easton

10:30 AM, Friday 29 July 1544 A.F.

Isabel sat at the breakfast table, too gloomy and sick with apprehension to move. She had barely managed to eat or drink anything and now the rest of the day stretched before her like a long road which she had to walk along whether she liked it or not. She couldn't face going to the library, where Nicholas would not be sitting. She couldn't face going anywhere right then.

'We haven't seen anything of Mr Raspero lately, my lady,' Benson commented from where he was standing to one side. 'His lordship and her ladyship received a letter from him today. Perhaps they might know something of what he's up to these days.'

Isabel considered this news, her head tilted to one side. All of a sudden, there was sunlight in the room as if a hand had reached across and wrenched away an obscuring curtain. A letter from Nicholas! A ray of sunlight was actually falling directly onto her breakfast plate, making the white china glint as if blinking its eyes. The world was suddenly interesting again.

'I will go and sit in the Whitfield Room,' Isabel declared.

'Very good, my lady,' Benson said.

So it was that Isabel was in the Whitfield Room when Lord and Lady Easton entered some time later. They greeted her with a pleased surprise, but it wasn't long before they realised why she just happened to be in their writing room that morning. It all became clear to them when Ravenone brought to them their letters, including a letter from a "Mr Nicholas Raspero". Someone had obviously tipped Isabel off that Nicholas had written to them.

Isabel watched Lord Easton closely while he read Nicholas's letter, which Lord Easton found exasperating. It was like trying to eat a meal, while being watched by a hungry beggar. But then Lord Easton read something so startling that he forgot all about his discomfort. 'What?' he exclaimed. 'Nicholas is going to the Mountains of Weiden!' He looked across at Lady Easton to see if she had heard this.

'A young man who is disappointed in love might well wish to go into the wilderness,' Lady Easton commented.

'Well, there's that,' Lord Easton acknowledged. He looked across at Isabel and said sternly, 'I don't know what you said to that young man, Isabel, but perhaps it's best if I don't. You can be very intemperate at times, young lady.'

Being rebuked by Lord Easton entirely lacked any terrors, for there was nothing whatsoever scary about that gentle and educated man. Nonetheless, Isabel was so desperate to get her hands on Nicholas's letter she lowered her eyes and unfolded her fan as if in a state of contrition.

Feeling that his rebuke had sunk home, Lord Easton returned to reading Nicholas's letter. He read it with a certain interest and then said, 'Well, Isabel, you once commented that Nicholas could not write a proper letter but I must say that I disagree. He lacks polish but he has passion and his own point of view. In fact, he is very like you, Isabel. You do realise how similar the two of you are, do you not?'

These comments represented Lord Easton's unsophisticated and slightly naive attempts to play the match-maker. Like Lady Easton, he was now keen to see Isabel and Nicholas married, but unlike Lady Easton he failed to recognise the necessity of the oblique reference in such circumstances. Logic had to take second place to association where match-making was concerned. It was no use pointing directly to what was plain to see given that this was already known; like the indirect progress of a dance in which every direction was optional, match-making had to at the necessary times go sideways.

Isabel, her eyes fixed on Nicholas's letter, was closing her fan in a stealthy fashion as a preliminary movement to seizing hold of that letter, but Lord Easton was already taking the letter over to Lady Easton and giving it to her, and now it was Lady Easton's turn to read the letter while Isabel was obliged to wait until Lady Easton was done. Isabel's fan stayed closed, however, for nothing now would open in her hands except that letter. Lady Easton enjoyed every moment of reading Nicholas's letter with Isabel as her audience. She understood that such events only happened once — she would never again read such a letter in such circumstances and she lapped up every milky mouthful of drama.

Lady Easton folded up the letter and took it across to Isabel, holding it out and saying, 'You may of course read Nicholas's letter yourself if you wish, Isabel.'

Isabel took the letter without a word, opened it and bent her head to the task of reading the letter which Nicholas had sent to the Eastons; he had not sent this letter to her — oh no! She had only received a blank page as a letter from the man who had said that he loved her! While the Eastons had actually received a proper letter, as in a page with actual writing on it. Nicholas would never properly appreciate the unwitting brilliance with which he had handled these matters, given that this brilliance had been unwitting, but Isabel, despite the bruises to her feelings resulting from being thrown around in this fashion, had to grudgingly and reluctantly acknowledge the exceptional skill which Nicholas was displaying on this occasion. From Isabel's point of view, Nicholas was laying down the law that she had to stop mistreating him or else he would not come back, and given that she could not mistreat a man she would marry, he was in effect making his courtship a foregone conclusion. It was very clever, very clever indeed, Isabel had to concede, and it was in this frame of mind that she read Nicholas's letter. She read this letter attentively, her alert mind fully alive to every implication and innuendo of every comment. As Lord Easton had observed earlier, Nicholas might lack polish but he certainly had something to say.

Most telling of all, as far as Isabel was concerned, was Nicholas's observation that she would only marry a man worthy of being Master of

Grangeshield House. Not even the Eastons, judging from the suitors they had selected to date, had ever realised this key point. She could never, for example, have married Percival Breckenridge. It was not just the stories about his hedonistic lifestyle, although they were legion. An eye which could have seen the future would have discerned the hidden rivers of dissolution which were already hollowing out his handsome features, leading to the day when his face would collapse into the semblance of a wrinkled prune. It was also that Lord Breckenridge was far too wealthy in his own right to place the Grangeshield Estate at the centre of his affairs; he might or might not have even chosen to reside in Grangeshield House, having a castle or two of his own. Throughout his courtship, as conventional as it was and entirely lacking in one original thought or feeling, it had never crossed Breckenridge's mind to even mention the importance of the role of the Master of Grangeshield House.

As only a man worthy of being Master of Grangeshield House would be capable of such an insight, Isabel had to concede that she was like a swordfighter driven onto the back foot by the most brilliant swordplay. The thought that Nicholas could see into her very soul with such keen insight made Isabel pause for a wide-eyed moment. It was no longer a matter of Nicholas being so handsome as to make her heart beat faster; he had character as well, character that was like the weight of gold held in the hand, weighty and valuable, made by the sun itself.

She came to an end of the letter and folded it up thoughtfully.

Lord Easton was a methodical man who was already wondering where to file Nicholas's letter, so it was almost absently that he walked over to Isabel with his hand outstretched saying, 'You may return the letter to me now, Isabel, thank you.'

Isabel looked up at him wide-eyed and without a moment's hesitation rolled the letter into a tube and slipped it into the cleavage of her dress, after which she opened up her fan and hid behind it so that only her eyes still showed as she gazed up at Lord Easton as if there was nothing more to be said about the letter which was now in her complete and entirely enclosed possession.

Lord Easton groaned. 'Of course, you may hold on to the letter for a while longer if you wish,' he said in resignation, defeated by these womanly wiles.

Nicholas's letter did not remain in the warmth of its hiding place for long. Isabel was soon re-reading it. Furthermore, Isabel appeared to have decided that the Eastons, as the designated recipients of Nicholas's letter, were also the designated recipients of her views on life in general and Nicholas in particular.

Isabel conceded that she may have spoken a little intemperately to Nicholas on the occasion of their last meeting. Isabel quoted approvingly from Nicholas's letter: *clearly love is impossible.* She emphasised that Nicholas still loved her by reading aloud what Nicholas himself had written. Isabel reminisced about the last time she had seen Nicholas and acknowledged that it was possible, or at least not entirely unlikely, that she had spoken ever so slightly in a more forthright manner than she would have done otherwise, but as Nicholas himself had said, *clearly love is impossible.* Isabel said that she could not help but wonder if she had perhaps spoken to Nicholas in perhaps slightly too blunt a fashion, but she pointed out that Nicholas had written himself in his letter that he still loved Isabel: he had said so directly in so many words, which Isabel read out aloud. For example, Nicholas had written that *as I am still in love with her I am naturally still keen to be her suitor in the future* which Isabel pointed out meant that Nicholas still loved her and intended to be her suitor in the future. But then *clearly love is impossible,* Isabel continued, quoting directly from the letter with an upraised forefinger, but furthermore, Isabel went on then and there to say without even a pause for breath, Nicholas had written that *I love Isabel and she loves me* which, Isabel inferred, clearly showed a certain constancy in Nicholas's feelings.

Lady Easton listened attentively to all this, or at least appeared to listen attentively, with a sympathetic and understanding air, nodding and making the occasional response such as, 'Yes, that is quite so,' or 'Of course, that must be the way things are,' or 'That is very true, Isabel.'

Lord Easton hung onto the remnants of his everyday mind, exasperated by this never-ending repetition of the same points over and over again, nodding politely in response to Isabel's repeated statements.

All that day Isabel read and re-read Nicholas's letter, commenting on it and quoting from it in turn.

It seemed to be Nicholas's fate that year to write letters that would be intensely studied by a dedicated readership.

THIRTY-SEVEN

The Courtship of Lady Isabel Grangeshield by Mr Nicholas Raspero

1:50 PM, Sunday 7 August 1544 A.F.

Nicholas was puzzled by circumstances as he neared the Emperor Theatre. People nodded to him as he strolled along Shakespeare Street but that made perfect sense. What did not make sense was that the Emperor Theatre was nearly empty of wands, or so his particular brand of macchato was telling him. Yet, where was the audience for the show he was about to attend given the Sold Out signs for the afternoon matinee?

Someone was obviously watching out for him, because as he mounted the steps of the Emperor Theatre (whose doors were closed) the doors opened and Mr Harold Maynard himself appeared to say, 'Welcome, Mr Raspero.'

Mr Maynard, the manager of the Emperor Theatre, had travelled to Dejaville in person to present Nicholas with his free box seat ticket several days ago and Nicholas had accepted on the spot, having been only too pleased to be given the chance to see another play, and so it was that Nicholas was here as promised, but where was everybody else? Nicholas was suspicious of everything, given that he was entering a nearly empty theatre which was supposed to be full in a city in which he had a fair number of enemies who wished him harm. So he said, 'So where is everybody?'

Mr Maynard said in reply, 'Please enter, Mr Raspero. The show will begin shortly.'

Nicholas couldn't help but notice that Maynard had completely avoided his question, but given that he had been raised from birth to never reveal his inheritance, he wasn't in a position to argue the issue. After all, he wasn't supposed to know that the theatre he was entering was practically empty. So, readying himself for battle, he said, 'It had better not begin before I'm sitting down, Mr Maynard.' It was an oblique and pointless warning intended to rattle an opponent precisely by being pointless.

Maynard laughed briefly before replying, 'But of course not, Mr Raspero. But please come with me.'

Nicholas knew countless stratagems for battle, a thousand wandfighting responses that were not so much memorised as instinctive, and with his hand on the hilt of his wand as he entered the theatre, he readied himself for what the moment might bring.

Tracking every wand in the macchato space around him as he entered, he followed Maynard through the lobby and along a corridor and up the stairs. There were only three wands ahead of them in the space of the theatre they were entering, all the other wands about them being on the peripheries. Maynard took Nicholas to the entrance of one of the boxes, then stepped aside, and with a deferential bow gestured for Nicholas to enter.

Ready for anything, Nicholas stepped past the curtain.

As soon as he saw the backs of the heads of the Eastons and Isabel seated at the front row of the box Nicholas started to relax a little. He wasn't faced with three assassins set on killing him where he stood. He went down the aisle slowly, aware by macchato of Maynard entering the box behind him.

The Eastons, turning their heads and then standing up as he approached, were all relieved smiles as they greeted him. Nicholas returned their greetings courteously, still a little keyed up given that Isabel had remained sitting immobile.

'Your seat is here, Mr Raspero,' Maynard said, gesturing to the empty seat next to Isabel's as he spoke.

'Yes, I understand the seating arrangements,' Nicholas said in a tone of rebuke, although he had only realised just then where he was supposed to sit. He was still catching up with everything that was going on. The Eastons sat down, and slowly, as if with an eye to the aesthetics of calm deliberateness Nicholas sat down next to Isabel.

Maynard withdrew after casting the necessary beady eye on Nicholas sitting next to Isabel to confirm that he had earned his bonus as Isabel had made it clear to him that it was this outcome which she sought and which alone would bring him his bonus. There was an equation in Maynard's mathematical mind at that moment which meant that Nicholas seated next to Isabel equaled five thousand strada and so he verified before departing that Nicholas was indeed sitting next to Isabel as commissioned.

The theatre all around was completely empty. Nicholas was still catching up with everything even now and it was dawning on Nicholas then that Isabel had bought out all the seats in the theatre in order to get him to sit next to her. He could not help but be impressed by such a dramatic gesture. Coming on top of her letters, his young heart overthrew its restraints on the spot and he was happy once again to be sitting next to the beautiful girl he had fallen in love with. Everything was once again possible.

Nicholas looked across at Isabel. Given that he was sitting right next to her, she could hardly have been unaware of his gaze, but she looked straight ahead as if absorbed in her thoughts.

'Isabel, it's good to see you again,' said Nicholas.

Isabel appeared to have not heard him for all the response she made; in fact, she couldn't speak because she was paralysed with nerves. As Nicholas sat next to her she could feel his physical presence like waves of heat from a fire radiating outwards.

Nicholas looked away. There was a silence. Nicholas looked back at her. 'I received all your letters. But as it happens I'm leaving Anglashia for a while. We'll talk about everything later,' Nicholas told her.

Again silence from Isabel.

Nicholas leaned forward, looked down over the side of the box into the empty seats of the stalls below, then looked up and around for his vision to encompass the thoroughly empty theatre, and then leaned back in his seat with a sigh of exasperated submission. He looked across at Isabel again. 'I'll give you full marks for the dramatic gesture, Isabel. This is something else. You're quite a girl,' Nicholas said admiringly.

'I beg your pardon?' Isabel said, turning to look directly at him for the first time. Her large brown eyes looked straight into his observant grey eyes.

'I said you're quite a girl.'

'Quite ... a ... girl,' Isabel repeated slowly, as if baffled by this particular sequence of words.

'It's a compliment,' Nicholas explained.

'Ah, I see, it's a compliment,' Isabel exclaimed with exaggerated comprehension. 'That's what it is!'

'Isabel,' Nicholas said firmly, 'we are not going to quarrel. I have only just arrived.'

'Do you still hope to marry me?'

'Yes, definitely,' Nicholas replied without hesitation.

'Well, Nicholas, in that case, you must do better than simply grunt like a cave man while courting me. Or perhaps you think that I am asking too much?'

Nicholas thought about this and then said, 'You look beautiful. How about that as a compliment?'

'Trite, tedious and over-done,' Isabel said immediately, pronouncing her judgement in such a tone of voice as to make it clear that her verdict was definitive.

'But you do look beautiful,' Nicholas insisted. 'Beautiful, dazzling, gorgeous and stunning.'

'To say that I am a list of adjectives is hardly a compliment, Nicholas,' Isabel declared. 'Adjectives have their place, but you would be very unwise to place too much reliance on them in your quest for a worthy compliment.'

A trumpet had sounded and the stage curtains had started to open while Isabel was saying this, so Nicholas gave Isabel a look intended to show her that he was more amused than alarmed by her demands, and then turned to face the stage and watch the play.

The play was about a witch who had two daughters, one of them honest and good and beautiful, the other ugly and lazy and wicked. The hero was in love with the good daughter but he had been apprenticed into the Guild of Thieves and so could not pursue his courtship. One day the hero stole a talking dog, who told him that the only way to win the good daughter's heart was by stealing the witch's purse which always magically refilled with gold when emptied and then bringing the magical purse back to the talking dog. The hero did this, only to be turned into a dog himself, while the original talking dog regained his human form as an exiled prince and left to return to his homeland.

Angela was playing the good daughter, Gertrude, but what she was doing on stage, contrary to all rehearsals, was looking directly at Nicholas whenever she was not speaking, and sometimes when she was. Whenever this happened, Isabel turned in her seat to gaze closely at Nicholas as well while looking back and forth between Nicholas and Angela. Nicholas carried on watching the play with the air of an interested spectator as if nothing at all out of the ordinary was happening. This of course was all an act because he felt like a man in a world made of differing parts moving in a complicated fashion whose harmony was episodic.

As the curtain came down for the intermission, Nicholas and the Eastons clapped (but, pointedly, not Isabel). The isolated sound of their applause seemed tiny in the large space of that empty theatre; Lord Easton found it oddly embarrassing.

They made their way downstairs, the only figures moving along the corridors and down the stairs. They were like characters in a play themselves, requiring only an audience to make their progress in the empty theatre a scene all in itself. They wound up at the bar for their intermission drink. There it was that Isabel broke her silence.

'I did not applaud,' she declared as if decreeing that this question must have been preoccupying them all this long while, 'because I am entirely baffled as to how it is that Miss Ashton should have been as cast as Gertrude.'

Seeing a quarrel on the way, as was always the case whenever Angela's name surfaced in conversation with Isabel, Nicholas said diplomatically, 'Ah, yes, casting people in plays, a tricky business I am sure.'

'No, Nicholas,' Isabel corrected him, 'there is nothing tricky about the unsuitability of Miss Ashton to play Gertrude. She is only fit to play Felicity, the daughter of unhappiness.'

'Perhaps this is yet another dimension of make-believe,' Nicholas said, still determined to be diplomatic.

'Ah yes,' Lord Easton said with interest, 'that is something to consider, Isabel. It is an interesting logical point.'

'It is nothing at all to consider,' Isabel declared grandly, far above such things as logic. 'It is too much make-believe to believe Miss Ashton to be Gertrude. She is far too notorious a whore for anything good to be believed of her.'

'So how have the rehearsals gone?' Lord Easton asked Nicholas, trying to change the subject given Isabel's choice of words.

'I haven't been to any of them, as it happens,' Nicholas replied, with a glance at Isabel, 'what with one thing and another.'

'You have been spared much, Nicholas,' Isabel said, resting her hand on his arm, 'as to see Miss Ashton as Gertrude, even in rehearsals, is to suffer greatly. She cannot be believed as Gertrude. She can only play Felicity.' Isabel wasn't having the subject changed.

'Well,' said Lord Easton, blinded by logic, 'Gertrude must be played by a beautiful woman, while Felicity must be played by a not-so-good looking woman, so from that point of view Miss Ashton is clearly a good choice to play Gertrude, as she is a beautiful woman.'

Nicholas tried not to groan. This was like waving a red flag in front of a bull.

There was a silence all around as no-one said anything for a lengthy moment or two. Nicholas knew that Isabel was mainly complaining about how Angela had kept looking at Nicholas from the stage; Lady Easton understood this as well; Lord Easton, however, seemed to be taking Isabel's complaint purely at face value.

'But this is precisely my point!' Isabel said. 'Miss Ashton is not at all beautiful. Is that not so, Nicholas?'

'No, that is not so,' Nicholas said firmly. He was not going to be browbeaten by Isabel into uttering falsehoods. 'Miss Ashton is a beautiful woman, as it happens. However, she is not as beautiful as you, Isabel, if that is your real concern.'

'The Club of Appreciation certainly thought Miss Ashton was beautiful,' Lady Easton commented, throwing her weight behind Nicholas's point of view.

'What's the Club of Appreciation?' Nicholas asked curiously.

'Those geese!' Isabel said with contempt. 'I see. We are now to trim our judgement accordingly. To think that this should be our decision! This is what has become of us today!'

Lord Easton commented on the subjective nature of aesthetic judgements; Isabel spoke loftily by way of reply of the objective nature of moral ones; Lord Easton discussed the inter-dependency of the subjective and the objective; Isabel waved all this philosophising away by pronouncing her verdict on Miss Ashton as the truth plain and simple; Lord Easton, with a touch of acid in his tone, questioned how we could know what the truth was given all the complexities of life; Isabel explained to Lord Easton, with a touch of condescension in her tone, that she simply looked and there it was, the truth plain and simple, such as in this case the utter gutter-ridden lowness of Miss Ashton, the whore of Weatherby and Foxley; Lord Easton explained to Isabel how unpersuasive her argumentation was, and all the while Nicholas and Lady Easton stood to one side listening to all this talk with cheerful expressions.

The bell rang for the end of the intermission.

'Shall we return to our box, Isabel?' Nicholas asked.

Isabel took his arm as if acknowledging that the intermission was over but with a set expression to her face that suggested she was not done with anything just yet.

The play continued. The hero, who was now a talking dog himself, went to the witch's house for help in returning to his human form. The witch agreed to return him to his human form if he performed seven tasks for her. Each task was supposed to kill him but somehow he managed to complete each task helped by the good daughter until he came to the seventh task, which was to marry the evil daughter. With a heavy heart he agreed but thanks to a technicality his marriage was annulled as soon as he returned to human form. The witch and her wicked daughter died in a battle at the hands of the exiled prince who had returned with his father's magicians. The prince, it turned out, was the brother of the good daughter who was not really the daughter of the witch at all but an exiled princess. The hero thus married the princess and became king, and they all lived happily ever after.

The Eastons and Nicholas applauded while the cast bowed. Isabel studied the design of her fan in a deliberately rude manner. The curtain fell again and the applause, such as it was, ended. It had been the second play Nicholas had ever attended and there had been a curious contrast between these performances given that the second performance had hardly had an audience. *Was a play without an audience a play?* Nicholas wondered. It seemed to be a philosophical point that was not easy to address from scratch, so he gave up on the question. Besides, he realised that he needed to keep his wits about him, given the nature of Isabel's silence as they walked along to the Grangeshield Estate flying carriage. He could tell that she was up to something.

In fact, Isabel was fully focused on seeing to it that Nicholas got into the carriage and came back to Grangeshield House with her.

'Thank you for everything, Isabel,' Nicholas said politely as they reached the carriage and he disengaged his arm from hers. 'I am glad to see that you look well and I am sure that we will meet again soon.'

Isabel looked at him in astonishment. 'But whatever do you mean, Nicholas? Surely you are going to escort me back to Grangeshield House?'

'Well,' Nicholas prevaricated, playing for time, 'I did have other plans for today, as it happens, so perhaps I can visit you another time.'

'But surely you cannot mean to leave me here all alone,' Isabel protested. 'I cannot believe such a thing of you, Nicholas, I simply cannot. I refuse to believe it.'

Nicholas sighed. To tell the truth, it had been a half-hearted attempt on his part to leave in any case. He was already falling under Isabel's spell again. 'Of course I would be honoured to escort you back to Grangeshield House,' he said in defeat, and so it was that Nicholas found himself once again in the other-worldly luxury of the Grangeshield House flying carriage. He chatted to the Eastons as they flew along; Isabel had fallen silent and was contemplating her fan as if listening to their conversation but, in fact, she was preoccupied with getting Nicholas into Grangeshield House at the end of their journey.

Nicholas did, in fact, make another attempt to get away. As they left the flying carriage and stood by the side he said, 'Well, I will say goodbye for now, but now that we are on speaking terms again I'm sure that we will meet again soon.'

'But what on earth do you mean, Nicholas?' Isabel asked in surprise. 'Surely you will come inside now that you are here?'

'Well, my experience in the past has been that it's easier to go in that direction,' Nicholas said, waving his forefinger in a forward direction as if through the front doors, 'than to come back in the other direction,' he continued, reversing his forefinger through the air.

Isabel's mouth fell open in astonishment. She was a picture of puzzlement. 'But what on earth do you mean, Nicholas?'

'Well, I just want to make it clear that if I decide to leave and go on my way you will raise no objections to my decision,' Nicholas explained, though Isabel was staring so closely at him that he couldn't help grinning.

'But *of course* I will raise no objections, Nicholas,' Isabel said as if she had the greatest of difficulty in understanding anything of such obscure matters. It seemed that from her point of view Nicholas was in a world of his own.

Nicholas sighed in defeat. 'Very well, Isabel, I would be delighted to come inside for a while.'

Isabel made a point of not seizing Nicholas's arm too hard as he escorted her inside. She did not want to tip Nicholas off that, as far as she was concerned in her over-heated brain, Nicholas Raspero was taking a one-way trip through those front doors.

8:50 PM, Sunday 7 August 1544 A.F.

Time had passed since Nicholas had entered Grangeshield House once again. They had all chatted in the Red Drawing Room, then had dinner, then returned to the Red Drawing Room once again, where Nicholas observed Isabel instructing Benson to make the Rowland Room ready for Nicholas, as Nicholas would be staying the night. Seeing that this decision had been taken on his behalf without any kind of consultation whatsoever, Nicholas readied himself to discuss the matter of his courtship of Isabel. As the door closed behind the departing Benson he said, 'Isabel, as I mentioned earlier, I received your letters. You have decided to accept me as your suitor, but as it happens I'm leaving Anglashia for a while, so we will have to wait a few months, maybe three months, maybe six months or so, before I can court you on my return.'

'But what on earth do you mean, Nicholas?' Isabel asked him.

'Exactly what I say.'

'But how on earth can you court me if you are not here to do so?'

'I will court you later, after my return.'

'But what kind of courtship is that? Do you not want to marry me, Nicholas? Is that it? But why do you not say so from the beginning?'

'I certainly don't want to marry you if you just want to have your way all the time, which means that you're not ready to be married.'

'First you say you want to marry me then you say you don't! What have I done to deserve being treated in this way?'

Nicholas sighed. 'I am going abroad for a few months, Isabel. This is what I am trying to tell you. I am going to the Mountains of Weiden. Then I will return and if you still want to receive me as a suitor, my courtship of you can begin then.'

'I will come with you to the Mountains of Weiden, Nicholas,' Isabel said tearfully.

'You don't get it, do you, Isabel?'

'No, I don't get it,' Isabel wailed. 'You said you loved me and wanted to be a suitor for my hand in marriage and now you're going off to the mountains!'

'Now wait a moment, Isabel,' Nicholas said firmly, determined not to suddenly find himself in changed circumstances in which he would be in the wrong, 'you rejected my declaration of my feelings in no uncertain terms and so I made other plans.'

'I understand, Nicholas,' Isabel said, breathing heavily as if labouring under a heavy load, 'you have decided to go to the Mountains of Weiden and so I will come with you. You can begin your courtship during our travels together.'

Nicholas groaned out loud. 'I have news for you, Isabel. The world does not revolve around you. Yes, I know,' Nicholas continued, holding up his hand to prevent Isabel from interrupting even though Isabel was sitting perfectly still, listening wide-eyed to what Nicholas was saying, 'I know that you must consider this an impertinence on the part of the world, but that's just too bad, Isabel, that's just how it is. The world will just have to struggle along in the face of your disapproval.'

'No, Nicholas,' Isabel replied sorrowfully, 'you are the one who thinks the world revolves around you. That is why I am obliged to follow you to the Mountains of Weiden so that you can court me.'

'Isabel, you can't come with me to the Mountains of Weiden,' Nicholas said decisively. 'It is out of the question. I will have enough to do just watching out for myself let alone for you as well.'

'I will bring three flying carriages with camping gear, food supplies, servants and all necessities,' Isabel continued, as if thinking aloud, 'and that will be all. You cannot accuse me of not being able to rough it if that is the source of your objection.'

Nicholas decided to switch the battle to another front. 'This situation is in part of your own making, Isabel. After all, when I declared my feelings, you told me to get lost! So, I have gone off and made other plans in consequence. Do you refuse to accept responsibility for the consequences of your actions, is that it?'

'But of course I accept responsibility for what I have done,' Isabel said calmly, although, in fact, she had no intention of accepting responsibility for anything. 'I do not deny for a moment that I have not yet received the declaration of your feelings with the proper consideration it deserves.

However, surely you must understand that I am expected to behave with a certain modesty on such occasions.'

'A certain modesty?' Nicholas said, repeating her phrase with a certain emphatic irony. He was remembering how Isabel had shouted at him to get out of Grangeshield House after insulting his family and his ancestry.

Isabel could see that he was remembering this and that she had lost a little ground. 'Yes, Nicholas, a certain modesty,' she insisted, and then added. 'It was only that I was taken by surprise on that occasion.'

Nicholas was reminded that he had himself felt he had not handled the business of declaring his feelings as well as he could have. 'Yes, well, I don't dispute that I didn't declare my feelings with sufficient finesse,' he acknowledged, 'so there is that side of things.'

Nicholas didn't know it, but he had just made a fatal blunder. He was trying to be fair to everybody, while Isabel understood that the higher requirements of justice meant that she could ignore such technicalities as actually being fair to anybody so foolish as to stand in her way. 'Finesse, Nicholas?' she queried, opening her fan with a twirl like an ice skater jumping through the air, 'finesse, did you say? You were like a bull charging through a meadow at an innocent rambler passing by. I was greatly taken aback by your forcefulness.'

'Yes, quite,' Nicholas agreed with a nod of his head, a little embarrassed, 'as I have already said, I do not dispute that I spoke with a certain lack of polish, it has to be said.'

'A *lack of polish*, Nicholas?' Isabel commented, not ceasing for a moment to press home her advantage. She had Nicholas on the back foot now. 'A *lack of polish* is a description that hardly begins to do justice to the situation which I found myself in through no fault of my own.'

'Yes, yes, as I have already said I acknowledge all this,' Nicholas said a little impatiently, feeling that Isabel was harping on and on about a matter which he had already conceded as not in his favour, 'so that's settled. But that is not —

'What is settled, Nicholas,' Isabel interrupted, 'is that your hasty and intemperate behaviour forced us both into a situation in which no possible outcome existed that could be favourable to either of us.'

Nicholas woke up then to the danger of the position he had been driven into. Isabel's treatment of him was now all his own fault. Whatever the truth of the matter, he could no longer say anything in his own defence as it had been his own error that had set Isabel's temper in motion and now she was in the clear. 'Now, wait a moment, Isabel,' Nicholas protested, not giving in without a fight, 'you shouted at me to get out of Grangeshield House, so don't make out now that you're the injured party.'

'Yes, Nicholas, I was very upset,' Isabel agreed, not looking up from the fan spread out in her hands. 'The abrupt manner in which you spoke to me so shocked me that I was really not myself. But surely you will not avoid accepting responsibility for the consequences of your own actions?'

'So in the end I'm to blame for everything you said,' Nicholas said with a certain resignation. 'Why am I not surprised?'

'No, Nicholas,' Isabel said with the air of an innocent victim, 'I am to blame for everything you said.'

Nicholas laughed out loud despite himself and shook his head. 'I have to give you full credit for a skillful argument, Isabel, but that is neither here nor there. I mean it always turns out —'

'Oh, I see,' Isabel interrupted with an edge of anger to her voice, 'I have spoken the truth without fear or favour and that means no doubt that I have twisted everything about with my skillful argumentation. But had you declared your feelings in a proper fashion, with the required tact and sensitivity, with all due consideration for my own feelings, then I certainly would have agreed to receive you as my suitor then and there. But you did not, and now this is all my skillful argument, you say, but I will follow you to the Mountains of Weiden even though it is all no doubt my own fault that you are going in the first place!' Isabel sat straight-backed in her indignation, glaring fiercely at Nicholas, who for his part leaned back in his chair with an air of defeat.

As it happened, Nicholas was not too disappointed to have lost the argument. His desire to go to the Mountains of Weiden had greatly lessened since he had received Isabel's third letter; in fact, he had actually all but changed his mind about going; truth to tell, he had only really told Isabel that he was going to the Mountains of Weiden as a matter of form.

So it was not too great a loss for Nicholas to hold his hands up in the air, palms facing outwards, and say, 'All right, Isabel, you win. I will stay in New Landern for now and be a suitor for your hand in marriage.'

Nicholas lowered his hands and contemplated Isabel for a moment or two. Then he said, 'So all that remains for us to decide is how I should go about courting you. For example, how often should I come out here to visit you?'

'But what on earth do you mean, Nicholas?' Isabel asked with a perplexed look.

'Should I come out here to Grangeshield House every day, every other day, once a week, in order to see you?'

'But you will be staying here in Grangeshield House,' Isabel pointed out.

'I don't think so,' Nicholas said with a shake of his head. 'So ... how often should I come out here to visit you?'

'But why on earth do you refuse to stay here?' Isabel asked as if completely bewildered by Nicholas's inexplicable behaviour.

'Isabel, you may or may not know,' Nicholas said with a glance at the Eastons, 'but there has already been a lot of gossip about the two of us and so that is why it is not a good idea for me to stay here.'

'But you are surely not serious, Nicholas,' Isabel said, appearing to be still completely bewildered by all this. 'This cannot be your reason for not staying here. What is your real objection?'

Nicholas turned to Lady Easton. 'What do you think, Lady Easton?' He was reasonably sure that she would take his side in this dispute, but as it turned out he was mistaken.

'But of course you should stay here in Grangeshield House, while you court Isabel,' Lady Easton said without hesitation. 'This is a respectable household, Nicholas. Why should you not stay here? Naturally Bentley and I will continue to chaperone Isabel, so there need be no concern about her reputation.'

Nicholas turned to Lord Easton. 'What do you think, Lord Easton?' Lord Easton was his last hope.

'It would seem most appropriate that you stay here while courting

Isabel,' Lord Easton said promptly. 'After all, if you marry Isabel you will be living here anyway. It would seem to be the best course of action.'

Nicholas sighed at his latest defeat. 'I hope I get to win an argument now and then. All right, fine, I'll stay here then.'

Isabel leaned back in her chair with an air of satisfaction on hearing this, opening up her fan as if only now was she able to relax and enjoy herself. The rotation of the planet itself would now bring her the result she wanted. All she needed to do now was to wait.

10:50 AM, Monday 8 August 1544 A.F.

Nicholas was a man at peace with himself and the world on that sunny morning in early August. There seemed to be a certain inevitability about everything today, even such things as the cheerful sunshine pouring in through the windows of the library. Things were as they were because they could not be different. The ever-restless animal of life was momentarily at rest.

He watched Isabel enter the Library in a sea-green dress, low-cut to emphasise her cleavage; she seemed to him then as resplendent as the day itself. Isabel was, in fact, seized by nerves. For the first time in her life she had some understanding of how nervous her suitors had been as their moment of destiny had approached, that moment from which their doom would unfold one way or the other, to the right or to the left. She knew she would accept Nicholas's proposal, which meant that she hoped that he would not propose today, but she wanted him to propose today so that it would all be done, but she did not want him to propose today because she knew that she would say yes, and she wanted this all to be over while at the same time she did not. She was struck by how gravely good-looking Nicholas was as he rose to his feet and came to her and took her hand in his; her knees felt weak so she was glad to be guided to a chair where she could sit down; yet sitting down so close to Nicholas who was already sitting down by her side made her feel even more nervous than before, and so it went for Isabel on that sunny morning in August.

Nicholas suggested that Isabel show him around Grangeshield House;

Isabel agreed absently, hardly listening. It was the Eastons who had to supply the necessary commentary as they strolled around; Isabel clutched onto Nicholas's arm, peaceable and silent.

So peaceable was Isabel that Nicholas pointed to the empty chair of the Master of Grangeshield House in the Gold Dining Room and said, 'If I am to marry Isabel I will sit in that chair, will I not? In which case, I should try it out now.' Upon which Nicholas boldly walked up to the chair of the Master of Grangeshield House which had been unoccupied for the past seven years, and sat down. He looked down the table imagining what it would be like to sit in that chair for the rest of his life; then he looked across at Isabel and said, 'So how do I look?'

'You look splendid, Nicholas,' Isabel said slowly, unable to take her eyes off him sitting in the Master's chair. 'Benson, from now on you are to set Nicholas his place at the table exactly where he is sitting now.'

'Yes, my lady,' Benson said obediently.

Nicholas stood up and the party resumed its tour of Grangeshield House, and at the end of the tour they came to the end of all things, and the way by which they came had not changed over the centuries — this at least was still the same as in the beginning. At the side of the Great Hall was a carved wooden panel that, in fact, consisted of two wooden panels, so cleverly carved that they seemed from a distance to be all one panel, but as they came closer the illusion shivered and snapped into two and it became apparent that there were two panels, one set further back from the first, with the gap of a doorway between them, and through this doorway they went, preceded by three servants carrying lamps and followed by three servants carrying lamps.

They were at the head of a staircase cut out of the bedrock itself; the servants preceding them lit lamps hanging on the stone walls as they went down so that a pathway of light unfolded ahead of them down the dark cold stone stairs. The stairs turned to the right; then to the right again, and then ended at the entrance to a large chamber. Nicholas had long ago guessed that they were on their way to a crypt.

Isabel told Nicholas to stand still by a pressure of her arm through his; he looked across at her and saw on her face her interest in this place. The servants ahead of them were lighting lantern after lantern on the walls at the sides as they made their way along until they reached the far end of the crypt and stood there at attention.

The crypt was about one hundred feet wide by about one hundred and sixty or so feet long. Stone sarcophagi were placed about on the stone-flagged floor, and on ledges at the sides and stacked on raised platforms; some of child-sized lengths, and from the sight of them all around it was made plain that there was nothing but death in this place of death. From the pressure of Isabel's arm through his he understood that it was time to move; as they set forth through the crypt it seemed to Nicholas at first that they walked in a spiral fashion, then in a zig-zag fashion through all the Grangeshield dead, and then in no discernible form at all as if the designer of the crypt had understood that death, whatever the precise nature of its systematic progress, did not proceed in a right to left fashion; yet it was clear that Isabel was guiding him through the chronological sequence of Masters and Mistresses of Grangeshield House as made plain by the carved lettering on the stone sarcophagi. The ceiling seemed to be low, although it was, in fact, above head height for a tall man, but still with a sense of being so low that the visitors needed to bow their heads.

'So this is the Grangeshield crypt,' Nicholas said, trying to keep his voice sounding casual.

Isabel looked at him without reply, as if aware that this was not his real point. They had come to a halt in their wanderings through the stone sarcophagi. The crypt was all around them.

'So if I marry you we'll be buried here, is that it?' Nicholas asked, still trying to keep his voice sounding casual, although to tell the truth he felt a little light-headed. 'So where will the two of us be interred?'

'Why, here, of course,' Isabel said very gently as if to avoid drawing attention to Nicholas's inability to observe the next term of a simple sequence, pointing slightly ahead of them to her right.

Nicholas walked to where she had pointed and leaned his hands on the cold stone of the platform on which his sarcophagus would rest. All of a sudden he felt the gloom of the crypt fall over him like a fallen cloak. 'So

do you come here often?' he asked, more to make conversation than out
of any real interest.

'Only on Ancestors Day,' Isabel replied. 'That's when we light candles
for our ancestors.' A thought struck her. 'Just think, Nicky,' she said
cheerfully with a big, happy smile, 'when we're dead and lying here for all
eternity our descendants will light candles for us!'

Nicholas nodded, or tried to nod, which perhaps he hadn't, as he
felt dizzy and nauseous to the point that it affected his understanding
of what motor actions he had recently performed or not performed or
even attempted to perform, if he had done or not. He leaned on a nearby
sarcophagus for a moment, a tiny fountain of saliva shooting up under his
tongue, intending to comment on how little air there was but before he
could do this everything turned around for him. He couldn't understand
how this had happened, but the ceiling above him was now sideways
and still moving and what was down had become up. He could feel cool,
smooth stone slipping across the palms of his hands and then he was
lying on the floor looking up. He heard Isabel call his name.

It occurred to Nicholas that he would be happy just to lie there for a
while but oh no that was much too simple an idea as everyone was fussing
around him, clearly intent on not leaving him alone; Isabel was kneeling
over him, her eyes wide and worried; the Eastons formed a second array
of concerned attendants, with the other servants also gathered around in
yet a third array, and so Nicholas allowed himself to be brought to a sitting
position and then helped to his feet and then walked along with his arm
around Isabel back up the stairs and into the Great Hall and outside into
the sunshine where they sat down on a stone bench. Nicholas breathed
deeply of the clean air, feeling as he sat in the golden sunshine that the
world was returning to him; or he was returning to the world.

The Eastons asked Nicholas if he was feeling all right.

'Stop fussing, I'm fine,' Nicholas snapped, irritated by their unnecessary
attentions.

Isabel waved the Eastons away and took hold of Nicholas's left
arm protectively, gazing closely at her suitor as if awaiting his next
pronouncement.

Nicholas felt that he had to explain himself, even if he didn't properly understand himself what had happened, but he could, of course, guess. Like anyone else, Nicholas knew in an abstract sense that he would die one day, but to see the actual place where he would be buried was something else entirely.

'It's strange, isn't it, to see where you'll be buried.'

'Strange, Nicholas?' Isabel replied cautiously. She obviously had no idea what he was talking about. 'Yes, it is. That is a very astute observation on your part.'

'I mean, it's kind of spooky, don't you think? That's what I really mean to say, that it's spooky.'

Isabel considered this, her eyes shifting uneasily about the garden, still obviously unable to understand the point Nicholas was making. 'It is indeed spooky, Nicholas. Very spooky indeed.'

'Maybe not for you, of course,' Nicholas conceded, 'if you've grown up with the idea and everything.'

'Even so, Nicholas, it is spooky for me anyway as well. Very spooky indeed. We are of one mind on this issue.'

'Let's walk about the garden and look at green and growing things,' Nicholas suggested.

'Yes, Nicholas, that is exactly what I was about to suggest,' Isabel agreed. 'Isn't it curious how we are always in such close agreement about everything?'

They stood up and walked off through the garden, the Eastons following, but with Lady Easton holding her husband back to give the courting couple space.

'Well, I'm in love with you,' Nicholas said, 'so what hope is there for me?'

This didn't make complete sense to Isabel, so she took the part of it that she did understand. 'Are you really in love with me, Nicky?' she asked.

'Trust me, I should be locked up,' Nicholas agreed.

Isabel considered this comment for a moment. 'Oh, Nicky, you are being so witty!' She gazed up at him in a transport of admiration, clutching onto his arm in another transport of delight. 'I do believe that wit is important in a man. I could never marry a man without the ability to express his sense of humour in a delicate, refined yet energetic manner. I must say that you are courting me with enormous success given that you have shown such wit on this occasion.'

Nicholas understood more than what she was saying. Isabel had taken Nicholas into her scorpion soul, and now he could do no wrong in her eyes. Whatever he said and did would be regarded as the perfect expression of the perfect courtship; he understood that Isabel had already decided to accept his proposal of marriage, and he knew beyond this that there was no way on earth he was not going to marry her now.

They sat down again on a bench, while Nicholas thought things through. What freedom did he have to choose anything other than Isabel? Did he want anything other than Isabel? No! There was, for this reason, no why in what he did when he chose her because there was no choice.

Yet, just to be logical he thought things through. What if he just ran for it? He could do, in the sense of being able to do what was logically possible, and then what?

He was twenty-two years old and marrying Isabel would in certain respects settle the rest of his life beyond contention or change. He would be Sir Nicholas Grangeshield, a wealthy and powerful man with a respected position in society, and the beautiful Isabel would be his wife. She would be in his arms all his life, and that was happiness.

What he would lose by gaining this good fortune he would never know because it could never now happen. He felt the limits of his life then, and he felt that by making the choice of marrying Isabel he was accepting a form of life within which he could find freedom and happiness. His life could have taken many different forms, but by accepting this one form of life and precluding all others, he was spreading forth his arms and growing wings, that what he had no choice but to do was where all his choice lay. Strangely, there was freedom where there was no choice, and while none of this made any sense to him, he felt that it was the complete truth.

'Isabel, sweetheart,' he said, 'I'm not sure what to do about something.'

'What is it, Nicky?' Isabel asked, sounding concerned.

'I want to propose to you but I don't have an engagement ring.' Nicholas paused. He intention was to say that he would have to go home to talk to his parents and grandfather about getting hold of an engagement ring with which to propose, but Isabel immediately took over.

'Nicky, you silly billy, I have lots of rings. You will inspect them and make your choice of an engagement ring after lunch.'

'So that's all right, is it?' Nicholas asked, because beyond his knowledge of wandlore and obscure aspects of Westrigonian history he often felt unsure about basic aspects of his own society. 'I mean, I can use one of your rings to propose with?'

'Well, of course,' Isabel said with an evident surprise that he should even need to ask such a question. 'After all, I'm going to get it straight back anyway, aren't I?' After a pause she added, as if she had been too obvious, 'Whether I say yes or no.'

'Well, if you're sure,' Nicholas said uncertainly, not sure if this was something like when she had burned his clothes, having decided to her own satisfaction that she could, but then, he reflected, perhaps conventions were adaptable in circumstances like this. After all, so what if he proposed to her with her own ring? He was going to take her family name after all, he was going to be buried in her family crypt; perhaps this was another development that was all part of the whole process and in those terms made perfect sense. 'I mean, it's normal and everything, I mean, to propose to you with your own ring?'

Isabel's mouth fell open in astonishment as she gazed at him. 'But of course it's perfectly normal, Nicky. Why on earth should it not be?'

'I'm not perfectly conversant with all the varieties of social distinctions with regard to every exact application of this particular rule,' Nicholas said, feeling he was babbling but still not really sure if Isabel, the immensely skilled and subtle Isabel, was just having things her own way as usual.

'But I am!' Isabel exclaimed, laying her hand on his arm reassuringly and patting his arm to help him believe what she was saying. 'I am perfectly conversant with everything, my darling Nicky, absolutely everything, and it is perfectly, perfectly all right to propose to me with a ring which has come from my own jewellery box. You are being a silly-billy and I insist that you stop at once.'

Her insistence was a far cry from the days when she would spit and roast him on the spot for saying the wrong thing, but Nicholas felt anyway that he was going to propose to Isabel with one of her own rings in any case no matter how mild her insistence. 'So what happens exactly, I take a look at your jewellery box and pick out a ring, is that it? And when should we do that?'

'Directly after lunch,' Isabel declared.

'Which can't be far away,' Nicholas commented. 'What time is it now?'

Isabel fished out her watch and inspected the time. 'Goodness me, Nicky, it is already ten-past-one! How the time flies when I am with you! I believe it is the happiness I gain from your very presence. Time itself goes faster! Is that not curious?'

'So it's lunch time then,' Nicholas observed, standing up and offering Isabel his arm. 'So let's go.'

1:30 PM, Monday 8 August 1544 A.F.

Nicholas sat in the Master's Chair; Isabel sat in the Mistress's Chair; between Isabel and Nicholas stretched the long dining table of the Gold Dining Room; at Isabel's right hand sat Lady Easton, and at Nicholas's right hand sat Lord Easton. No-one was saying anything. The servants stepped forward to serve the courses; Isabel and Nicholas glanced at each other now and then; Lord and Lady Easton seemed each amused by their memories of long-ago times, and so the lunch went.

After lunch Isabel gave Benson some instructions, and so it was that some time later Benson approached Nicholas in confidence. Nicholas was waiting alone in the Red Drawing Room.

'If I may offer some advice, Mr Raspero,' Benson said deferentially, 'I would advise you to choose the amethyst ring.'

'The what?' Nicholas said.

'The amethyst ring, sir.'

'What are you talking about?'

'It has not escaped my attention, sir, that you are to select an engagement ring this very afternoon. It is my humble duty to serve you in the matter of giving you my advice on this auspicious occasion.'

Nicholas gazed suspiciously at Benson, who for his part stood there with a deferentially downcast appearance; Nicholas frowned as if uncertain what to say next.

'What's an amethyst?' he asked eventually.

'It is a purple gemstone,' Benson replied, as if this was only the beginning of his knowledge of amethysts, although truth to tell he had never heard of them until that day. 'The ring is an amethyst in the shape of a square, enclosed in a fine gold netting with two gold lions on either side of the ring.'

'What's your point about this amethyst ring, Benson?'

'That's the ring for you to choose, sir,' Benson said.

'And you know this how?' Nicholas asked.

'I have been forty years in service in this household,' Benson answered with dignity, dodging the question quite nimbly for a man his age.

Nicholas guessed by an instinctive appraisal of what was going on that Benson was, in fact, relaying Isabel's own advice; so he nodded dismissively and said, 'Well, so now I know.'

Benson bowed and departed, only to return some time later to escort Nicholas to the anteroom to the Master Bedroom of Grangeshield House. This anteroom was a chamber in its own right, with ornately carved wooden panelling of trees and animals of the forest such as deer and squirrels lining the walls. Isabel and the Eastons were there waiting for Nicholas with an open chest waiting on the table. Nicholas approached the chest and looked inside. There were rings and necklaces and various ornaments in a glittering pile like a pirate's treasure hoard. Nicholas stirred the pile around until he saw what he was looking for: a gold ring with a large square-cut purple gemstone inset in a gold netting with two lions holding the gemstone in place with their paws. He picked up the ring, examined it carefully as if making complicated calculations, although, in fact, he was only pretending to, and then declared, 'This is the ring I choose.'

The Eastons looked at each other meaningfully, while Isabel looked wide-eyed at Nicholas holding the ring in the air; it was like passing a test in a fairy tale, Nicholas thought.

'Why did you choose this ring?' Lord Easton asked.

'I just like purple, and look at those gold lions!' Nicholas said, hoping he wouldn't be questioned any more about it.

Isabel stepped in. 'Nicky just knew, didn't you?' she said admiringly.

'It just came to me,' Nicholas agreed, 'just like that!' He clicked his fingers.

'When things are meant to be, everything simply falls into place,' Lady Easton commented with a sage air.

'What is this ring anyway?' Nicholas asked.

'It was the engagement ring of the Lady Marigold, the first Mistress of Grangeshield House,' Lady Easton told him.

Nicholas took the amethyst ring and carefully stowed it away in an inside pocket. As everyone was looking at him without saying anything, he realised that he was supposed to take charge. 'Perhaps we should put away all this jewellery,' he suggested.

The jewellery was put away. There was another silence, while everyone again looked at Nicholas.

'Isabel,' Nicholas said, 'let's go out into the garden. I have something important to say to you.'

3:20 PM, Monday 8 August 1544 A.F.

Lady Isabel Grangeshield of Grangeshield House sat in the Grotto of Peace in her magnificent garden on that beautiful sunny August day. Nicholas sat in the neighbouring chair, gathering his thoughts together. For the first time ever on such occasions Isabel felt nervous; she noted that Nicholas seemed perfectly relaxed, which made her feel even more nervous; the silence was making Isabel feel almost floaty.

Nicholas cleared his throat and sat up straight and turned to face her. Isabel darted him sideways glances but was too paralysed by nerves to turn to face him herself. Nicholas launched himself into what he had to say. 'Isabel, you're impossible, but I love you anyway. I don't even know why I love you because there's something about you that makes my brain stop working. You're special in some way that I don't understand and probably never will understand. You burn my clothes and do nothing but give me a hard time, but I would trust you with my honour and my life just because you are never anything less than yourself. Even when you give me a hard time I can't take it seriously because you look too beautiful for me to believe you mean anything by it. There's no hope for me because I am already completely in love with you and I will only fall more deeply in love with you as the years go by. I want to marry you, even if that means I've gone completely crazy. You're selfish, autocratic and opinionated but you are beautiful and good and true at the same time. I want us to walk hand in hand together along the great journey of life.'

Nicholas stood up, took out the engagement ring from his pocket, lowered himself onto his right knee and held the ring out before him and said, 'Isabel, will you marry me?'

Isabel gave no thought to an evaluation of Nicholas's proposal, although it seemed to her that it surely didn't sound entirely right, because she had already decided to marry Nicholas anyway. Mind you, she thought some of what he said had sounded very romantic, but she wasn't sure if it was really a proper proposal on the whole, given that he had sounded critical during parts of it; however, he had at least got onto his knee and offered the ring and asked her to marry her, so that, she thought, would do as the proposal of marriage, whatever he had been babbling about before then.

'Yes, Nicholas,' she said, 'I will marry you.'

Nicholas stood up and pulled her to her feet and put the ring onto her finger. It fitted perfectly, which was no surprise as she had made sure two years ago that it would fit perfectly. Nicholas then pulled her to him and kissed her, and that was a surprise, Isabel thought as she stood there eyes closed in Nicholas's arms, feeling his lips on her lips; this was indeed a surprise, Isabel thought, as Nicholas continued to kiss her, and as the sensation of being kissed spread throughout her whole body, she fell against Nicholas and opened her arms to close around him and floated for the moment in the joy of wanting this moment to last forever.

THIRTY-EIGHT

The Second Employment of Bailey by Mr Nicholas Raspero

The news that Mr Nicholas Raspero was engaged to be married to Lady Isabel Grangeshield started spreading through New Landern as soon as Isabel placed an announcement in the *New Landern Recorder*. Naturally, all those men who had hoped, even if utterly hopelessly, to marry Isabel themselves one day, were disappointed and expressed their strong disapproval of the forthcoming match; they said that Raspero was the fortune hunter of the century. They continued to lament their loss even when it was pointed out to them that someone has to marry the most beautiful girl in the world. Given that someone has to marry the most beautiful girl in the world it followed that everyone else would miss out and that was just how the world was and how the world had always been and how the world would always be. Their complaint remained unaddressed, however, as their complaint was beyond reason. Only time could heal their wound. The disappointed admirers of Isabel Grangeshield were hunched over their bitterness like beggars in the rain.

Nicholas was not without his own admirers. Sophie especially took hold of Nicholas's arm to tell him that if his engagement fell through, he had *other* options. She leaned close into him, an emerald fastened to the front of her strapless dress gleaming brightly as if to attract attention to her modestly sized but enormously interesting cleavage. Nicholas felt himself swaying for a moment, as if losing his balance, but recovered himself sufficiently to say that a man in love had no options.

The pat on the shoulder that Lord Zinia had given Nicholas was enough for the grandees of New Landern. The next Master of Grangeshield House would be one of them, and the love and beauty of marriage was not relevant compared to knowing that the wealth and power of the Grangeshield Estate would be in the hands of a man they could trust. Rumours that Nicholas had slain a dragon in the depths of the New Landern demi-monde had long ago percolated into the higher echelons of New Landern society, although no-one seemed to know exactly what had happened. The romantics of New Landern seized on how Isabel had bought out all the seats of the Emperor Theatre in order to see Nicholas again after their quarrel as proof that love really did exist after all, no matter what the cynics might say, but the cynics, of course, were not so easily refuted, saying in their turn that it was only yet more evidence of Isabel's high-handedness and nothing more. For a brief time Nicholas was nearly as talked about as the golden-haired Lord of the North who had slain Nevsky, but then the fuss started to die down and before long it became an accepted feature of the New Landern landscape that Grangeshield House was about to have a new Master. It soon enough became yesterday's news.

One man who still dwelt on this news long after everyone else had moved on, even Isabel's disappointed admirers, lived in the depths of Angramain Ville, itself in the depths of the demi-monde. His name was Alpin Balustrade and he was an Advocate. He sat in his darkened room, the curtains drawn to keep out the light and brooded over this latest development.

He had been the one to have spotted Nevsky's talent, he had been the one to have thought up the Grangeshield Venture and he had been the one to have brought Nevsky to Jolly. He had introduced Nevsky to Jolly and the two of them had taken to each other like a long-lost father and son who each saw their fulfillment in the other. Jolly had told Nevsky that a man of his talents could be of some use to him. Nevsky had said that a man of his talents expected to be paid, and paid well. Jolly had told Nevsky that he could make him a millionaire in less than a year. Nevsky had said that now Jolly was talking. Jolly had then laid out the Grangeshield Venture which Nevsky had agreed to on the spot.

Somehow Jolly had known everything that needed to be known to set up the scheme of things whereby Nevsky could get to work. Jolly had somehow known that Lady Isabel Grangeshield would be attending a party at the house of Lord Nieves, he had known how to gain access to the house, how to breach the security systems, which servants could be bribed and the routine of the household necessary for Nevsky and his dogs to do their business without hindrance or interruption. The information provided by Jolly to Nevsky had made this possible and so everything had been arranged, including the division of the spoils. Had Nevsky succeeded in becoming Master of Grangeshield House, that would have been one outcome, but the million strada that was the other more probable outcome was to be divided by five hundred thousand going to Jolly, four hundred thousand to Nevsky, fifty thousand to Balustrade and ten thousand each to Nevsky's dogs. Nevksy had kicked up a fuss at only getting forty per cent after doing all the work, a fuss which Jolly had observed with a fatherly smile and then soothed by outlining the next venture after the Grangeshield one, a venture which would net Nevsky a bride who would be Nevsky's introduction to the world of politics where Nevsky would go far beyond even Jolly himself. Nevsky had allowed himself to be soothed and even joked about how he would see Jolly right when the time came that he was that far beyond Jolly, and Jolly had smiled with a smile that did not reach his eyes and said that Nevksy was his long-lost son that he had found at last which was why Nevsky's progress through the world of politics was a progress that he, Jolly, would personally supervise. Balustrade had watched all this with fascination, feeling himself to be one of a triumvirate of monsters.

Jolly's plans to enter politics were not idle or recent. Jolly had penetrated the authorities and grown more powerful than even Zinia knew and the time was approaching when what Zinia knew would not be enough to control Jolly. Zinia would wake up one day to find Jolly standing over him.

Nevsky was a new piece on Jolly's chessboard that would eventually be sacrificed when the time was right, but for now Jolly was all smiles with his new protégé.

But then the world itself had turned crooked. Like a stick pushed into the water that changed its straightness into a puzzling non-alignment of its length between ends, the unexpected had intervened from one ordinary day to the next. A comet should have heralded the death of a king but there was no warning of what came next, nor of what followed. Jolly had gone and gotten himself killed in bizarre circumstances, having tripped over a previously unseen newcomer called Nicholas Raspero, and then Nevsky had gone and gotten himself killed in bizarre circumstances, sprawled full-length on the rough ground of his final duel, headless, with an obscure letter over where his heart should have been, and Balustrade reflected uneasily that if it were true that trouble comes in threes, then he would be third. Greed and fear pulled Balustrade in opposite directions.

After Jolly had died he and Nevsky had agreed to proceed with the Grangeshield Venture. This time, Nevsky had taken nine hundred thousand, Balustrade fifty thousand, and Nevsky's dogs ten thousand each. The Grangeshield Venture had worked like a well-designed clock. The Walherich Venture had followed like another smoothly turning piece of machinery, another legacy of Jolly's unique insight into the world of the grandees of New Landern, and Nevsky had gotten engaged as planned. Weakened though they were without Jolly's backing, they had prospects nonetheless, but then Nevsky had been killed by this Lord of the North who no-one knew anything about. First this unknown Raspero; then this unknown Lord of the North, and if he, Balustrade, was endangered, from what yet different but of course equally unknown source would the next deadly blow be dealt? These were Balustrade's thoughts.

But Balustrade's thoughts were not only of danger. The Grangeshield Venture was far from over when it had been done. That had been only the beginning. The plan had been to wait a while and then return for more money. Nevsky would turn up now and then and throw a scare into Lady Isabel Grangeshield. She would become weakened, fearful, beaten down, and then the demand would be made for another million strada. After all, she still had fourteen million strada, so what was merely one more taken away compared to her position in society? And then another million after that, and another. She would be bled of her lifeblood and she would not resist. The reasons that she had her money would be the same reasons that saw her money taken away. Would she put up a last stand at some point? Probably. But she would turn to the authorities to do this and Jolly would have a direct report on when she had done this and to whom she had spoken because Jolly was a man with influence who was watching closely what was going on. At this point she would be kidnapped and thrown into a brothel known only to a privileged few with her tongue cut out so she could not talk; there were those of Jolly's following among the authorities who would be among her first eager clients in this case. Jolly had devised a number of scenarios one drunken evening while Nevsky had laughed and Balustrade had laughed and the Burke Tavern around them had shuddered from basement to attic with all the thrust of its business underway.

Jolly had been killed; Nevsky had been killed, and now he, Balustrade, the last living, had to decide what to do with what he knew. The pieces on the board had shifted again. Lady Isabel Grangeshield was marrying Nicholas Raspero and this might well be an opportunity that if missed would never occur again. There was a limit now as to how much Lady Isabel Grangeshield could be bled for. After she married Raspero she could no longer be blackmailed directly, which meant, given that this was Raspero, she could not be blackmailed at all. Raspero had a reputation for direct action. But before she married Raspero ... ... well, now, that was the question, was it not? Surely Lady Isabel Grangeshield would not want Mr Nicholas Raspero to know that Nevsky had enjoyed her very personal favours previously to her marital happiness to come? Surely, Lady Isabel Grangeshield would be very keen, very keen indeed, for Raspero not to know the condition of the woman he was marrying? Surely one million strada, given that she had fourteen more, would be a small price for Lady Isabel Grangeshield to pay to keep Raspero from knowing what he should not know? Lady Isabel Grangeshield would surely not want Raspero to know about her past.

There was one million strada there for the taking. It was there waiting for him to take it, as if it were sitting on a table ready to be shovelled into his pocket. All he had to do was to demand it and it would be his. All that stood in his way were his doubts; yet they were several.

Balustrade was puzzled. As Nevsky's lawyer he had demanded possession of Nevsky's documents. He knew all too well that he might be found guilty to being an accessory to rape and extortion; he would not sit down with Langston but the jail sentence would be so heavy that a man of his age (sixty-eight) would not outlive it. The authorities had insisted on inspecting all documents first. Yet, when they had opened Nevsky's safe, after five hours of intense work by the experts, the scrolls in Nevsky's safe had all been blank, while all the money had been there. That was a puzzle, and Balustrade had no idea what to make of it. So where were the original documents? Who had them and how had they gone missing in the first place? It was a puzzle and a doubt thereby.

Another doubt was the death of Jolly. Another doubt was the death of Nevsky. All these doubts had their separate causes, as far as Balustrade knew, but they all pointed to the same end — the black blankness of death where the lack of space was curved to the lack of time in the unthinkingness of the lack of soul which yet might be endured perceivingly. The fear of death was Balustrade's major doubt. Yet, there was one million strada waiting for him. He only had to claim it and it was his.

One million strada! A sum of money like that seemed to encompass a whole world. It was a world that could be held in the hand and from which any kind of satisfaction could be brought forth, and all he had to do was demand it and it would be his.

It was at that moment of excitement in his contemplations that everything converged of its own accord into a single point of perspective and he knew exactly what to do. Yes, he would blackmail Lady Isabel Grangeshield for one million strada for one last time and he would do it now.

10:20 AM, Friday 16 September 1544 A.F.

Nicholas could see that Isabel was upset when she arrived at the library but he said nothing, knowing that it would not be long before Isabel spoke out about whatever was troubling her, and indeed it was not too long before Isabel spoke out.

'I am perplexed by the existence of insolence in the world, Nicholas,' Isabel declared, unfolding and folding and unfolding her fan in quick succession. 'It is a mystery, is it not?'

'Why, what's happened?' Nicholas asked.

Isabel folded her fan closed and tapped it impatiently on her knuckles to signify her displeasure. 'Insolence must be bred in swampland conditions of humidity by slithering creatures of the dark,' Isabel observed with the air of a zoologist discussing the place of a species in its ecosystem. 'It must be fed with the pale slug of envy; it must be emboldened by such hatred as to overcome its natural cowardice and then, Nicholas, it will rear up from the swamp with its sharp fangs bared, ready to strike at any of those whose only fault is to walk upright with a vertebrate spine. This is where we stand today, Nicholas, where to be upstanding and noble and virtuous is to invite the hatred of those creatures whose natural baseness is all the life they have ever known. In their darkness they hate and fear the light because the light shows them their own condition. They seek to extinguish the light so they may know nothing of their own state of corruption.'

'Absolutely!' Nicholas agreed lazily, stretched out with his feet resting on the Carenthetian table. 'That is very well put, Isabel. But just out of curiosity, do you have a particular example of insolence in mind at the moment?'

Isabel considered this question for a moment or two; or more accurately, she considered the time at which the question had been put in order to decide whether it should be answered now or later. She considered the matter a moment or two longer; the silence stretched on while Nicholas waited patiently.

'An insolent creature named Balustrade has written to me demanding an audience with me,' Isabel complained indignantly. 'I most certainly refuse to see him. I shall not even trouble to reply to his letter. This matter is beneath my dignity, Nicholas. I shall simply ignore it entirely.'

It took Nicholas a moment or two to place the name. 'Balustrade? He was Nevsky's lawyer, wasn't he? Did he say what he wanted to see you about?' Nicholas was struck by Balustrade's timing: the engagement party of Nicholas and Isabel, held at the Regana Palace of such vivid memory, had just taken place the night before.

'But he will not be seeing me, Nicholas. Have you not listened to a word I've said?'

Nicholas knew Isabel well enough to see that underneath all her bluster she was frightened so he said diplomatically, 'Isabel, I have listened carefully to every single word that you have said. However, someone will have to see him. Perhaps Lord Easton can see him on your behalf.'

Isabel's point of view was that no-one at all should see Balustrade; Nicholas fended off her insistence that he should agree with her on this point. The Eastons then arrived and entered the conversation; like Nicholas, they believed that someone would have to see Balustrade, and so Isabel was over-ruled. Isabel took this development graciously enough as she was by now feeling much safer and therefore much braver.

By an instinct whose prompting he obeyed without question Nicholas decided that he would be present but hidden during the meeting and so he selected the Room of the Concealed Turning as the venue for this meeting.

The Room of the Concealed Turning was an L-shaped room on the ground floor of the north-east corner-tower of Grangeshield House, the long side of the L facing out onto the garden. A fresco running along the walls above head-height showed a flying cherubic figure in blue and white robes in a succession of stages in its flight, and in the corner where it turned through a right angle to fly along the neighbouring wall there was drawn a leafy tree whose plentiful foliage concealed the flying figure so that only a foot could be seen of the figure going behind the tree and only a hand could be seen on the other side of the figure emerging from the tree, and thus it was that the room had been named the Room of the

Concealed Turning as the turning of the figure in its flight was concealed behind the tree.

The incoming Master of Grangeshield House, however, was not a master of wandlore for nothing, and so it was that Nicholas had realised that the name of the Room of the Concealed Turning was intended to both reveal and conceal what it was that was being concealed. The name of the room revealed what was being concealed by letting the observer know that the room had something that was concealed, and so by looking for what was concealed the observer decided that what was being concealed was the turning of the cherubic figure in mid-flight; yet this very attribution was an act of misdirection that itself concealed what was really concealed, which was namely a hidden alcove by the side of the room. This hidden alcove was behind the façade of an apparently solid carved wooden seated figure that was embedded in the wall; the façade was hinged and opened outwards, revealing a bench where a person could sit; the façade could then be closed upon this person, who would then be able to see and hear everything that happened in the room, while remaining perfectly concealed. Not even Benson had known this particular secret of Grangeshield House. Nicholas, who had devious ancestors of his own, thoroughly approved of the devious mind behind this scheme.

Isabel no longer objected to Balustrade's visit, now that Nicholas would be present; Lady Easton also volunteered to be present, and so they were all in agreement, whereupon Lord Easton wrote to Balustrade inviting him to come to Grangeshield House, and so things were in motion.

3:10 PM, Monday 19 September 1544 A.F.

'Please allow me to congratulate you on your forthcoming marriage, Lady Grangeshield,' Balustrade said with an attempt at a smile that made his face look more like a death's head grin than anything; although perhaps it also looked like a pumpkin with a crooked ragged wedge cut out of the middle; or like a roundish weathered stone that had been chipped and cracked by the weather.

Isabel said nothing, wide-eyed and pale, too frightened to speak, looking away from Balustrade across the room. Her nerves had suddenly attacked her at the last few minutes as Balustrade had arrived, leaving her paralysed; she stared at the carved wooden figure by the side of the room, as if appealing to its mute wooden face. Lord Easton reflected in exasperation that Isabel's behaviour was not exactly helping their deception to remain undetected, but luckily Balustrade could not see the direction of Isabel's gaze, as her gaze was directed behind him, and furthermore, Balustrade was too busy sniffing out the money trail he sought to follow to pay attention to anything that did not smell of his personal gain.

'That is very kind of you, Advocate Balustrade,' Lord Easton said with not even an attempt at his usual urbanity. He made no effort to hide his dislike of Balustrade. 'Please allow me to thank you on Lady Grangeshield's behalf.'

'That's quite a catch you've got yourself,' Balustrade continued with his grotesque grin, 'Nicholas Raspero, no less! With a husband like that, no-one's going to give you grief, are they? Best wandfighter in New Landern. Even Nevsky ran from him.' Balustrade grinned even wider than before to display even more rotted or missing teeth. 'Nevsky! Now there's a name to bring back memories, Lady Grangeshield, hey?'

'May I ask what all this is about, Advocate Balustrade?' Lord Easton asked coldly.

'Ah, you're a man after my own heart, Lord Easton,' Balustrade said, still with a fixed stare on Isabel, 'straight to business, enough chit-chat, off we go, heads down, get things done without delay.' He unexpectedly banged his fist on the table, which made Isabel jump uncontrollably; Balustrade sneered with satisfaction at the sight, as he had only banged his fist to see if Isabel would jump, and jump she had. He was gaining a creeping ascendancy over the meeting, his cold and clammy presence like a wet smell in the air.

'Shall we then proceed without delay?' Lord Easton suggested, but his voice had lost some of its force. Balustrade's death's head grin was draining Lord Easton's vitality in some unknown way that made him feel apprehensive; or was it his apprehension that was weakening him while he watched Balustrade's scuttling approach towards some unknown destination? Everything was difficult to tell in these circumstances. It was as if seeing and hearing had become blurred by the warping presence of Balustrade's malevolence.

Balustrade swung his gaze with a stealthy deliberation away from Isabel to point like a sword at Lord Easton and then said, 'Patience, Lord Easton. We shall all move along together on this occasion. I say only, for now, Nevsky, Raspero, Lady Grangeshield, marriage.'

Lord Easton had the good sense to say nothing in reply. Instead he gazed straight back at Balustrade thinking how glad he was that Nevsky was dead and buried. He well remembered his dealings with Balustrade when Nevsky had been in the room, threatening to break down doors and storm upstairs to where Isabel was hiding, even leering at Dacia, bullying and threatening. Balustrade had been right about one thing — Nevsky was a name to bring back memories. By an association of ideas it occurred to Lord Easton that Nicholas was nearby and he found that to be an encouraging thought.

Balustrade sensed strength returning to the silent Lord Easton and decided to pick up the pace. 'Lady Grangeshield,' he said abruptly, turning back equally abruptly to face Isabel again, 'there is a matter of missing money to be accounted for, a debt not paid. You are surely a person who pays her debts, aren't you?'

'What debt is this, Advocate Balustrade?' Lord Easton asked with a sense of coming now to what this was all about.

'Ah,' Balustrade responded, raising a finger to point up towards the ceiling, 'I wondered if you might play the innocent and pretend not to know.' He said the phrase *play the innocent* while staring at Isabel with a malicious sneer that made the word *innocent* itself seem far from innocent.

Once again Lord Easton had the good sense not to say anything. He continued to find strength in the thought that Nicholas was nearby listening to all this.

Balustrade sensed himself losing momentum again and resumed speaking. 'You promised my client Captain Abner Nevsky the payment of one million strada for ... ... services rendered, hey, hey-hey-hey, yes, but the money never arrived and the time has now come for payment of this money. On behalf of the numerous dependents and associates and creditors of the late Nevsky I am authorised to collect the said money to which I have repeatedly referred, namely the one million strada owing. This is the debt of which I speak: the one million strada promised to Captain Nevsky but never delivered.'

'That money was paid in full,' Lord Easton stated flatly. 'There is no debt.'

'That money was not paid at all,' Balustrade stated equally flatly. 'There is a debt and surely Lady Grangeshield pays her debts.'

'We are not paying this illusory debt,' Lord Easton declared. 'This is nothing more than extortion. If this is why you have come, Advocate Balustrade, you may as well leave now.'

Balustrade looked as if he had no intention of ever leaving. 'You will pay this debt if you wish to avoid the consequences which will follow from not paying this debt,' Balustrade declared in his turn, leaning back in his chair in a relaxed manner, 'and may I say now, Lord Easton, that I am pained to be accused of extortion. This is a harsh way to treat a man who seeks only what is rightfully his. If you refuse to pay the money owed I will be obliged to take my complaint further, to a higher authority, shall we say.'

'There are financial documents which prove the payment of one million strada was made to Captain Nevsky,' Lord Easton said coolly.

'But do you want to prove a point which is not in your favour?' Balustrade said meaningfully, turning now to face Lord Easton directly.

'You acknowledge that the payment was made,' Lord Easton said, completely missing the point, 'by admitting that I can prove that the payment was made.'

'I say to you that the money was not paid. It is still owed. I say again that I will take my complaint to a higher authority if you do not pay this debt and I ask you again if you really wish to prove to this higher authority that the payment was made.'

Now at last Lord Easton asked the question he should have asked earlier. 'What higher authority is this?'

'Mr Nicholas Raspero,' Balustrade said.

This was so unexpected that Lord Easton could only repeat the answer, 'Mr Nicholas Raspero.'

'The fiancé of Lady Grangeshield,' Balustrade explained as if defining a philosophical term. 'Mr Raspero would not be pleased to learn that Lady Grangeshield played the whore with Nevsky. Mr Raspero might re-consider his engagement to Lady Grangeshield. Mr Raspero might feel that he had been deceived. Mr Raspero might issue you a challenge, Lord Easton, and surely nothing less than Final Combat would suffice to provide satisfaction for such an offence as this.'

As all this started to come into focus for Lord Easton he started to feel in control of events for the first time. Balustrade was in a world of his own and Lord Easton looked forward to telling him so. But just as he was about to send Balustrade flying with a few carefully chosen words he felt a sharp pain in the shin of his left leg as Lady Easton kicked him under the table and he gasped involuntarily, his fingers twitching as if about to drive through the table-top to provide a healing massage to his injured leg. Balustrade, believing Lord Easton's pained reaction to be the result of what he had just said, allowed himself a satisfied smile.

'Nicholas must never know,' Lady Easton declared loudly, looking across at Isabel. 'But surely, Advocate Balustrade, you will not carry out your threat to reveal Isabel's past to her fiancé given what the consequences would be.'

Lord Easton, rubbing his aching shin as best as he could with the calf muscles of his right leg beneath the all-concealing table-top, prudently let his wife take over.

'I have no choice in this matter, Lady Easton,' Balustrade insisted. 'I will have justice done, as is my right.'

'But surely Isabel has suffered enough, Advocate Balustrade,' Lady Easton continued, as if appealing to Balustrade's finer feelings. 'Why should you threaten her happiness in this manner?'

'I threaten nothing and nobody,' Balustrade said, shaking his head as if to emphasise the truth of this statement. 'I am only asking for what is rightfully mine.'

'I see,' Lady Easton said with an air of resignation. 'But surely we are within our own rights, Advocate Balustrade, to ask for some time to think this matter over. This is reasonable, do you not agree? Or will you dispute this?'

Balustrade was delighted to see how everything was running his way. He had been sure by his own calculations on the balance of probabilities that the outcome would be the one he sought but it was always nice to see things work out as planned. 'But I most certainly do not dispute this inalienable right of yours to have time to think things over, Lady Easton. You have three days. Then you will agree to pay me the one million strada owed or face the consequences that will follow.'

'Very well, Advocate Balustrade, we shall have an answer for you in three days,' Lady Easton said in a tone that by itself said that everything that needed to be said had been said and the meeting was therefore concluded. Satisfied with what he had achieved, Balustrade left the room.

Nicholas emerged from his hiding place and went directly to Isabel. She was white-faced and breathing heavily, her mouth half-open, her eyes slightly unfocused. Nicholas gently took her hands and raised her to her feet and, ignoring her chaperones sitting nearby, took Isabel into his arms and kissed her. Isabel looked at him.

'You were amazing,' Nicholas told her. 'I was wondering, is that my Isabel or is that a lioness?'

Isabel was coming back to herself. Her eyes focused on Nicholas. 'Oh, Nicky, what are we going to do?'

'What has to be done, of course,' Nicholas said as if he knew exactly what he was talking about. 'You just sit back and take it easy. I will sort this out, don't worry.'

'Will you kill him, Nicky?'

'Of course.'

Lord Easton stirred and raised a hand as if about to say something but then apparently thought better of it and lowered his hand again.

'Benson,' Nicholas said sternly, mindful that Benson was bound to have overheard this exchange, 'you don't know anything about anything.'

'I do not require you to tell me my duty, Mr Raspero,' Benson said sharply, stung by this directive. 'I have been forty years in the service of this House, and I have never known anything about anything in all that time, nor will I ever know anything about anything at any time in the future.'

'That's good. Now listen carefully, Benson. I want you to clean that chair,' Nicholas ordered, pointing to the chair where Balustrade had been sitting, 'And that part of the table in front of that chair, and all along here,' Nicholas continued, pointing with his finger along the floor where Balustrade had walked. 'And then all along to where our visitor entered,' Nicholas continued further, waving his finger in the air in the vague general direction of the remaining parts of the house, 'until you have cleaned this house of the filth of all the places where our visitor has been. Is that clear?'

'Yes, Mr Raspero,' Benson said immediately. 'That is perfectly clear.'

Nicholas turned back to Isabel and the Eastons and said, 'Let us go to the Red Drawing Room.' He offered his arm to Isabel and they all set off.

Isabel was coming back to herself. Like someone rescued from drowning she was breathing properly again and taking stock of her surroundings. Nicholas's house-cleaning directives had also had its effect on her, reminding her that she was Lady Isabel Grangeshield of Grangeshield House.

'Right,' Nicholas said after they had all sat down and he had his feet stretched out on the Footstool of Mangatha, 'there's no need for any of you to trouble yourselves about this matter further. I'll deal with it.'

'Remember, Nicholas, you promised not to cut off any more heads,' Lady Easton reminded him.

'I will have to break that promise, Lady Easton,' Nicholas replied without the least air of regret.

'And why must you?' Lady Easton asked pleasantly.

'Well, fine, if I had poison then I would make him drink it, but I don't have poison, do I?'

'I can get you poison,' Lady Easton said calmly.

Lord Easton would have spoken but he was speechless.

'Can you? Excellent. When?' Nicholas sounded impressed.

'Perhaps by tomorrow, but certainly by the day after at the latest.'

'That is an offer which Nicholas most certainly will not take up,' Lord Easton said, managing to find his voice, 'given that you should not have made such an offer in the first place, Dacia.'

'It had better be guaranteed to work,' Nicholas said to Lady Easton as if Lord Easton had not said anything at all. 'I don't want him to wake up in the morgue with a tale to tell of the consequences of blackmail. If Balustrade survives he'll go to ground and be impossible to find. He might even go to the authorities with all the problems that will involve. At least cutting his head off has the merit of being guaranteed.'

'It also has the demerit of being uncivilised,' Lady Easton said sternly. 'Surely we should consider the sensibilities of our fellow New Landerners. It is one thing for Langston to cut off heads; that is only proper and to be expected. It is quite another thing for headless corpses to appear elsewhere in the city. It is not expected and is therefore unsettling and shows a lack of proper consideration for others.'

'Not to mention that he was Nevsky's lawyer,' Nicholas said as if thinking out loud, 'and a headless Balustrade might well be related to a headless Nevsky in a way that might get people thinking. Very well, poison it is.'

'Dacia!' Lord Easton protested. 'You understand that this makes you an accomplice.'

'Yes, Bentley, I do understand that this makes me an accomplice,' Lady Easton agreed. 'An accomplice I shall be! I look forward to it.'

'I'll need Balustrade's address,' Nicholas said, still thinking things through. 'I'll scout things out today.'

'You will do no such thing, Nicholas,' Isabel told him firmly. 'You are now a man with responsibilities. You simply cannot run around killing people anymore.'

'Who will do it if I don't?' Nicholas asked.

'I am sure that assassins can be procured if required,' Isabel said with an airy wave of her fan as if nothing could be simpler. 'I will provide the necessary fee.'

Nicholas saw an argument coming his way and tried not to groan out loud. 'Very well, Isabel. I'll leave all this for you to sort out. If you haven't done so by tomorrow night I'll have to take care of things myself. Or perhaps I am being unreasonable?'

'You are most certainly being unreasonable, Nicholas,' Isabel said heatedly. She had fully recovered now from the scare Balustrade had thrown into her. 'You are not to place yourself in danger. Is that clear? You are a man with responsibilities now. You cannot —'

'This *is* my responsibility!' Nicholas said loudly, cutting her off.

Isabel noted the sharpness of Nicholas's tone and subsided a little, but from the restless movements of her fan the battle was far from over.

'There is, of course, an alternative course of action,' Lord Easton said in his most reasonable tone of voice. 'Nicholas can simply be present when Balustrade returns to inform him that the money will not be paid.'

'What if it then occurs to Balustrade that the one man in New Landern capable of killing Nevsky is the fiancé of Lady Grangeshield who knows what he did to her?' Nicholas objected without bothering whether his tone of voice was reasonable or not. 'Balustrade might cease to believe in the Lord of the North. He might go to ground and become impossible to find. He might even arrange to have a letter delivered to the authorities in the event of his death which would expose me, thus making him immune from any action I might take. He might then blackmail me as well as Isabel. No, Balustrade has to be dealt with now.'

'It is more likely that Balustrade will retreat and give up on his blackmail,' Lord Easton insisted.

'And then out of sheer spite talk to all his pals in the demi-monde about how I'm the Lord of the North after having given up on his blackmail?' Nicholas asked. 'How long will it be before that news spreads? How long before I'm taken in for questioning? Even if I escape conviction due to lack of evidence I'll be a marked man. Not only that, if Balustrade talks about Isabel, which again he will out of spite because he didn't get what he wanted, her reputation will be ruined. He only keeps his mouth shut now in order to blackmail her; if the chance of blackmailing Isabel is taken away from him what is there to keep him from talking? No, Lord Easton. To delay striking our blow is much too dangerous. This has to be dealt with now.'

'He will be like a monster who simply grows another head when one is cut off and return with another threat on another day, more dangerous than before,' Lady Easton agreed. 'He must be dealt with now, while he can be disposed of decisively.'

'In any case, justice must be done,' Nicholas said in a tone of voice that made clear there could be no arguing against this statement of principle.

9:20 AM, Tuesday 20 September 1544 A.F.

Nicholas had visited Ben earlier but had decided against subtly finding out what he needed to know about Balustrade by indirect questions for two reasons: one was that Ben was too sharp to fool easily, and the second was that Balustrade would shortly be dead and Ben would undoubtedly remember that Nicholas had uncharacteristically been asking about him. So Nicholas left Ben and walked off through the streets of New Landern; at the sight of three street urchins loitering near a street corner, without doubt up to no good, the thought of Bailey came back to Nicholas's mind.

Nicholas called over a street urchin. All three came running over.

'Where's Bailey these days?' Nicholas asked.

'Dunno, Mr Raspero,' one of them said. 'We don't see nothing of him these days.'

'He got hisself a good job,' urchin number two added. 'He's too good for us now, is Bailey.'

'If you see Bailey, tell him to meet me at the same place he last saw me this evening at seven o'clock. Bailey will give five strada to whichever of you finds him first if you deliver this message in time. Got that?'

'Yes, Mr Raspero,' they chorused, and they were off chasing that five strada like racehorses galloping down the final stretch.

7:00 PM, Tuesday 20 September 1544 A.F.

Bailey was a mixture of emotions as he waited for Nicholas at the Montague Monument. His heart was bowed down like a stooped old man. The smooth hopes of material gain were juxtaposed with sharp fears of undefined pain. He had withdrawn himself from the world and wrapped himself in the folds of the money he had acquired, but a messenger had arrived to turn him out of doors. He felt like a tortoise being dragged out of its shell for unknown reasons.

Nicholas looked every inch the wealthy young gentleman as he strolled towards Bailey. The resplendence of his attire was an almost visible aura surrounding him, but Bailey, as observant as ever, noted that he still kept his hand resting as casually as ever on his wand with the usual air of alertness. His clothes had broken through his skin and taken root but he still walked as freely as before. In short, Bailey thought, he hadn't changed at all.

'How are you, Bailey?' Nicholas asked in a friendly manner.

'I am well, thank you, sir,' Bailey said in a state of half-terror.

'Good, good, excellent,' Nicholas said affably, his observant grey eyes taking in not only every detail of Bailey but also of his surroundings. 'I have another job for you, Bailey, if you are interested. The conditions are the same as last time. Discretion, you will do as I tell you, and for payment you will receive whatever chance throws your way. Do you accept this employment given these conditions?'

Bailey hesitated, giving Nicholas a quick nervous look while he thought about what to say.

Bailey was more frightened of Nicholas than he had been of Nevsky because he had understood Nevsky. It was easy to understand what Nevsky had been about. Bailey was not frightened of Nicholas because he had killed Nevsky; that alone just made him Nevsky on a larger scale. He was frightened of Nicholas because nothing about what had happened made any sense to him. He knew that Nicholas had not killed Nevsky without reason, but he also knew, or at least strongly suspected, that he would not understand the reason even if it was told to him. He was also sure that Nicholas had given him ten thousand strada that Nicholas did not have himself at the time, which made no sense at all. Nicholas was beyond reason, just like a god should be, and it was that more than anything that made Bailey afraid of him.

This was why Bailey's hero worship of Nicholas was now tempered by fear. Nicholas was still something of a god to him, but he understood now that the gods were to be feared not because of what they could do but because of what they were. An angry god could radiate through the heart and brain like a toothache made visible. His earlier vision of Nicholas was of a regal presence, a quiet wandfighter who Nevsky ran from, and that was all. Nicholas had been like a statue to place an offering before. He had never thought that his offering would be taken, or if so, what the result would be. Yet, that statue had come to life, taken his offering of hero-worship and placed him in service.

Bailey knew, none better, that he had profited from the arrangement. He had received the fortune of ten thousand strada. His careful spending had meant that he still had nine thousand and five hundred and thirty seven strada left, but by calculation Bailey had come to realise that it was only a matter of time before the money ran out. He had only just turned thirteen and the fortune which he had thought beyond limits was, in fact, exceeded by the years of his life, which would continue long after the money had gone. Bailey was older and wiser than the boy who had delivered Nevsky the letter.

But a boy talking to a god has limited choices. There was little else Bailey could say except what he did say, 'Yes, Mr Raspero.'

Nicholas nodded as if he had expected nothing else, which, in fact, he had not. 'You will deliver a letter for me, and then you will place yourself at my service for what follows. Just like before. Is that clear?'

'Yes, Mr Raspero.'

10:00 AM, Wednesday 21 September 1544 A.F.

Nicholas and Bailey were walking along Defender Street near the Law Courts. Nicholas was giving the apprehensive boy instructions as they walked along.

'Bailey, you will take this case to the Law Courts and ask for Advocate Alpin Balustrade. As before, you will insist that only you can deliver this case to Advocate Balustrade. If you are asked by Advocate Balustrade who has sent this case, you will say that it was a tall gentleman in a green cloak wearing a hat. You could not see his face and you know nothing about him. You have been paid one hundred strada to deliver this case.'

'One hundred strada, sir?' Bailey said hopefully.

'This is all pretence, Bailey,' Nicholas reminded him. 'You are pretending to have been paid one hundred strada to deliver this case to Advocate Balustrade. Now Balustrade might well ask you about this gentleman in the green cloak and hat in which case you will say that he had a silver clasp at his throat holding the cloak together and this clasp was in the form of a design showing a rabbit and a stag facing each other over an apple. Is that all clear so far?'

'What's a stag, sir?'

Nicholas stopped, took out a card from his pocket and showed it to Bailey, 'A stag is an animal such as this with antlers on its head. This is the design which you will tell Balustrade that this unknown gentleman was displaying. You see the rabbit, the stag, and the apple. Do you understand everything so far?'

'Yes, sir.'

Nicholas handed over the case to Bailey. The case was about a couple of hand spans in length and a hand span in width, thin, made of highly polished and delicately carved rosewood; it was a beautiful and expensive thing and merely to hold it in his hand made Bailey feel that he was the bearer of a treasure. It was in this slightly awe-struck manner that he entered the Law Courts and asked to see Advocate Balustrade. As he entered Balustrade's office, his treasure in hand, he presented just the picture that Nicholas would have liked to see: a messenger bearing a valuable gift.

Balustrade was seated at his desk, a fat man with a bald round head like a pumpkin, a bulbous nose bulging like an over-ripe fig above moist, red, rubbery lips. There was something grotesque about Balustrade that made Bailey's skin crawl but he approached the desk holding the case out in front of him saying as formally as he could manage, 'I have been asked to deliver this to you, Advocate Balustrade.'

Bailey laid his delivery on the desk-top before the Advocate and then retreated a few steps and stood there patiently. Balustrade looked down at the expensive case lying before him and then asked, 'Who are you, boy?'

'I'm Terry, sir,' Bailey replied, just as Nicholas had instructed him.

'What is this that you have delivered to me, Terry?' Balustrade asked, still not reaching for the case, his pudgy hands resting before him like bloated spiders waiting to move.

'I dunno, sir,' Bailey said truthfully, 'it was what was given me by a gennelman what to give to you this very day.'

'A gentleman? Who was this gentleman?'

'I dunno, sir,' Bailey continued, much less truthfully, 'he was dressed in a green cloak and a hat, I never saw him before.'

'You have never seen him before?' Balustrade queried. 'You are sure of this?'

Bailey started to feel under pressure. Why couldn't Balustrade just take the case and be done with it? But then again, Bailey reasoned, it was kind of funny to be sent a case from someone unknown. 'Well, no, sir,' Bailey said hesitantly, 'that is, I saw, well, nothing really.' Bailey was reluctant to get into the further details of Nicholas's instructions, but he was realising now that Nicholas had foreseen that Balustrade would question him.

'What did you see?' Balustrade asked sharply.

'This gent, he had a, a silver, a silver,' Bailey was floundering, trying to remember the word *clasp* but it had gone clean from his memory as it had been such an unfamiliar word, 'at his throat, it was a rabbit and a funny animal with things on its head, I dunno, something like that, sir.' Bailey was starting to fall apart but as it happened his faltering performance was far more believable than a more polished performance would have been. His very incoherence seemed to be articulate of the deeper truth that all this had really happened.

Balustrade sat more upright on hearing this, if a bag of sand could ever be said to be upright, stood up and waddled over to the side of his office where a number of leather bound books were lined up on shelves fastened to the wall. He took down a large book, waddled back to his desk, flipped through the pages and then beckoned Bailey over, tapping at an image on the page and saying, 'Was this the shield you saw, Terry?'

Bailey reluctantly came across, not wanting to be near Balustrade, and looked at the image; it was the same image that Nicholas had shown him on his card. 'Yes, sir.'

'Are you sure about this, boy?' Balustrade asked emphatically.

'Yes, sir. But I never saw this gennelman before.' Bailey moved away from Balustrade to stand once again where he had been before.

'I am sure you have not,' Balustrade said eagerly, almost jovially. This shield was of a powerful and wealthy dukedom. Now it was that he sat down and reached for the case. He opened the latch and levered the lid open and there, in its green velvet lined interior, there lay a letter addressed to "Advocate Alpin Balustrade".

Nicholas had started to compose this letter in the company of Isabel and the Eastons only to find that the task was very soon taken out of his hands; he tried to regain control over the venture by battling against Isabel's conception of a letter — a letter had to be lengthy and literary, according to her — Nicholas managed to get around this obstacle by suggesting that Balustrade didn't deserve a proper letter, and the mere functionality of the message was itself an appropriate expression of disdain. This was an argument which made Isabel pause, but Lord Easton used this pause to try to take charge himself of writing the letter, holding forth to the others on a variety of espionage-related concerns about which he himself apparently had an expertise of some description, or at least a pretended expertise, such as for example the art of invisible writing and how a pipe stem could be used to smuggle a roll of parchment. Nicholas was very polite in replying that this matter was not really that complicated as he was only writing a letter to arrange an appointment with an adversary; which brought Isabel back into the argument. In the end the final version of the letter had been written by Isabel herself with her very own superbly trained calligraphic hand.

Balustrade lifted up the letter in his pudgy hands and cut it open, observing the quality of the paper, the elegant flowing letters of a quality fountain pen wielded by an expertly proficient hand. It was just what would be expected of a letter from a noble person in a wealthy dukedom.

Tuesday 20 September 1544

Dear Advocate Balustrade,
Your name has come to our august attention concerning that claim to
confidentiality in which it seems that you stand so high in the estimation
of your peers. We refer of course not to the demands of conscience
but of law, and in the matter of law you stand well-appraised by all
accounts. Thus it is that we seek your services in a matter of the highest
confidentiality whose remuneration shall be proportionate to this
aforesaid secrecy. Let it be understood that your reputation, acquired so
deservedly over the years, is the cause of this, your possible commission
from our hands. Once again we say that it is to law not conscience that
we look to on this singular occasion.

We send to you tonight an emissary who is empowered to negotiate
on our behalf the terms and conditions and remunerations of this our
proffered employment, although not yet the nature of the task to be
performed itself, this remaining undisclosed for the time being; this
emissary may visit you at seven o'clock this evening at a place of your
choosing but not, as you will understand, in a public place where his
identity may be discerned by others. Please be so kind as to send a reply
by way of the messenger who has delivered this letter nominating the
venue of this meeting.
We must remain anonymous for the present,
Yours sincerely,
Anonymous.

Balustrade's thoughts on reading this letter were trotting along like
obedient sheep following the exact paths that Nicholas had intended.
The letter contrasted conscience versus the law, hinting that this
matter was illegal, or at least immoral; the only estimation of his peers
which Balustrade enjoyed was that of a crooked lawyer, as Balustrade
himself knew as well as anyone; the secrecy of this business was to be
proportionate to the fee Balustrade could command, which given the
nature of the supposed client involved should prove to be a substantial

amount, and the initial meeting being concerned only with contractual matters while the business itself would remain undisclosed for the time being was a tantalising suggestion of just how much money Balustrade might make from this whole mysterious business given how highly secretive the client was being.

The only potential flaw in his plan that Nicholas could see was that Balustrade might connect this unexpected client with his visit to Grangeshield House and suspect a trap. He had therefore made sure that it would be Balustrade who would nominate the place of their venue in order to make Balustrade feel more in control of events and thus more secure; furthermore, Balustrade would choose to meet this emissary in the place where his security was most assured, and that would be where he would keep his most guarded secrets, such as his documents concerning his dealings with the Grangeshield Estate.

Balustrade looked up from his letter to see Bailey waiting patiently before him. He took up his fountain pen and wrote a reply to "Your Unknown Eminence", attempting in this way to rattle his prospective client by having guessed his title and also to impress his prospective client by showing his cleverness in having guessed his title. He invited his unknown client to visit him at his home that evening at seven o'clock and wrote down his address, gave the letter to Bailey and sat back in his chair with a fat feeling of satisfaction.

7:00 PM, Wednesday 21 September 1544 A.F.

A figure in a green cloak with a hat pulled low over his face walked leisurely along Voltaire Avenue in Angramain Ville. He walked up the steps to number 17 and knocked briskly. The door was opened by a burly man with a scowling expression and he stepped inside; following the gesture of the burly man he walked up the stairs. The stairs ended at a hallway and at the end of the hallway was an open door where the welcoming figure of Balustrade stood in a pool of yellow light. Balustrade stepped aside and the man in the cloak entered the room; Balustrade waved for the burly man to leave and closed the door.

'Please be seated,' Balustrade said in his most effusive manner, but now he noted, as he had not properly noted before, that the "face" of the man in the cloak was really a flesh coloured mask as worn in a masquerade ball, and furthermore, that the silver clasp at the throat of the visitor fastening his cloak together was not in the shape of the insignia he had been told about, and it was then, much too late to do him any good, that Balustrade felt himself to be in danger.

Balustrade was not a fighter, so he did not wear the magnetised bracelets around his wrists and ankles, but he heard, or perhaps sensed, the movement of magnetised bracelets through the air; he was grabbed by them on the instant; it all happened so fast that he had no time to cry out before another bracelet with a mouthguard seized him and gagged him, and then he was lying abruptly on the floor, his eyes shifting about the room like a trapped animal as he was bound to the leg of a heavy chest of drawers so he couldn't roll about. He was able to see, across the room at an angle, the horizontal figure of the man in the cloak and hat walking improbably out of the room as if moving vertically.

It was time for recriminations and Balustrade indulged in them: he should have suspected that something was wrong; he should never have agreed to this meeting; he should have had his visitor stopped and searched and disarmed; he should have … It was then that it occurred to Balustrade that his captor had entered his private office without breaking step, despite the heavy wand security he had bought at great cost, and at the thought that he was about to be robbed Balustrade felt a righteous indignation and a resolve to have revenge on this man who was doing him such injury.

Nicholas was in a room with polished floorboards, paintings of men and women in various erotic poses, a large fireplace and a large leather-topped desk with a carved wooden chair behind it. There was an unusually heavy wand protection around the fireplace, which on closer inspection looked as if it had not been used for many years; Nicholas located the hidden lever, which was hidden in plain sight as a poker seemingly hanging on a fire bracket; pulling on this poker caused the fireplace to swing outwards to reveal a safe stored behind it. Nicholas had this safe open in seconds: it was filled with money and files and notebooks. Nicholas took all these over to the desk and sorted through them. There was nothing on Isabel in any of the files so he turned his attention to the rest of the room. On one side of the room was an enormous filing cabinet locked with heavy wand security; Nicholas opened it and found the Grangeshield file under "G"; he took out the Nevsky file from the "N" drawer; he tucked these files into his cloak and then turned his attention back to the contents of Balustrade's safe. In addition to the money in banknotes and coins there were some valuable artefacts made of gold; there were also a variety of financial documents of a similar nature to the financial documents he had found in Jolly's safe, which added up to a total of one hundred and seventy thousand strada. Nicholas took the blue velvet cushion from the chair and unbuttoned it in order to pull out the filling and use the blue velvet upholstering as a bag into which he stuffed Balustrade's money and valuables. He then locked the safe, replaced the fireplace, threw the cushion stuffing into the bin, and left the office after checking that everything was in order. He returned to the living room where Balustrade still lay bound on the floor, although he had managed to struggle up into a half-sitting position.

'Balustrade, your life is forfeit because you are blackmailing Lady Isabel Grangeshield for one million strada,' Nicholas declared; he then ungagged Balustrade, because a condemned man should always be given a last chance to speak in his defence.

'I understand that I have the honour of speaking with the famous Lord of the North,' Balustrade said in his most fawning manner. His mind, leaping madly about like a frightened frog, had leapt to this conclusion as soon as he had heard his death sentence pronounced because after all Nevsky had earlier been killed; his logic might have been cross-eyed but his conclusion was not far off being true.

'It does not matter who I am,' the masked figure told him. 'It only matters what you have tried to do. An innocent lady was greatly wronged and for this you sought to blackmail her.'

'I understand the error of my ways, my lord,' Balustrade said with all the sincerity he could muster. 'I truly and deeply apologise and I withdraw my claim, which I freely acknowledge to have been unjust.'

'You are going into the afterlife, Balustrade,' Nicholas said as matter-of-factly as a ticket inspector on a public flying carriage stating their destination, 'so make peace with this life before you leave it.'

'But surely you will show me mercy,' Balustrade protested, still not really believing that the Lord of the North meant to kill him, 'I am unarmed, I am repentant, I have changed my ways because I have seen that I was greatly in error. You will show me mercy, will you not?'

'Not a chance,' said Nicholas, withdrawing a bottle from a pocket inside his cloak. 'It is really out of the question.'

'But I withdraw my claim, which I acknowledge was false,' Balustrade argued, his eye on the bottle in Nicholas's hand. 'I humbly apologise to Lady Grangeshield for my offensive conduct and solemnly pledge to trouble her no more.'

'But you will tell the tale of what Nevsky did to her and of how the Lord of the North avenged her honour, will you not?' Nicholas commented. 'Out of sheer spite you will do what damage you can, will you not?'

'That is most certainly not true,' Balustrade denied most insistently. 'I will say nothing to anybody of the past. This I pledge to you on my deepest honour.'

'You have no honour, Balustrade. Of the various dark forces which rule your life, spite is prominent, is it not? You will say whatever you can now in order to escape this fate but when you are no longer under this compulsion, and you are free to choose what you want to do then you will choose to do what is spiteful and vicious because you are yourself spiteful and vicious.'

'You gravely misjudge me, my lord,' Balustrade insisted fearfully, his bulging eyes never for a moment leaving the bottle in Nicholas's hand. 'I am a meek and mild man. I am innocent of wrongdoing, except on this one occasion on which I have fallen into error and for which I truly repent.'

Nicolas knelt down by Balustrade and suddenly seized Balustrade's neck in his hands, pressing down on a pressure point to paralyse

Balustrade while he forced the mouth of the bottle into Balustrade's mouth and tipped the bottle up. He shifted his grip on Balustrade's neck to massage his throat so Balustrade was involuntarily forced to swallow the bitter liquid contents of the bottle; then Nicholas stood up and stepped back to look down on Balustrade.

'If there is an antidote, my Lord of the North, I beseech you to have pity and mercy on my soul even at this very last moment,' Balustrade pleaded.

Nicholas said nothing further while he waited for Balustrade to die; death was not long in coming. Balustrade gasped and shuddered, his flabby body rippling like quicksand in an earthquake; then with a convulsive heave of his body in its bonds he died. Balustrade lay there like a dog who had been put down.

Nicholas untied him and took back his bonds and pocketed them and turned on his heel and left the room.

Nicholas walked down the stairs in his cloak and hat, feeling like a character in a play. Isabel had provided him with the cloak and hat and mask, and now she was waiting for him in Grangeshield House, suffering the torment of a thousand throbbing nerves at the thought of Nicholas in danger. He had identified six wands in the downstairs area of Balustrade's house but he could leave easily enough as the hallway was clear to the front door. Yet, there was unusually heavy wand protection below him to the right of the entrance hallway; he hesitated and then, realising that he could not leave this job half-finished, he opened the door to his right, lit a lantern standing on the top step of a flight of stairs going down into the darkness and stepped onto the top step, pulling the door closed behind him. He walked down the stairs, the light of the lantern showing stone steps going down, his wand in his hand held at combat readiness. There was a wooden door at the bottom of the stairs, locked with the heavy wand protection which had attracted his attention in the first place; there were no wands on the other side of the door; Nicholas opened the door and looked through, his lantern held high to see into the room beyond.

He saw a young girl, perhaps ten or eleven, sitting on a bed in a dirty, faded frock that was too small for her. She sat with her legs tightly drawn up to her body, her arms locked around her legs. She stared blankly at

Nicholas as he entered. The doll's beauty that had brought this fate on her head was faded but still evident.

She made no attempt to resist as he picked her up; she seemed to be aware of what was going on but only as a far-away matter that did not concern her. Nicholas carried her in his arms up the cellar room steps; she was so thin and starved that she was as light and brittle as a bag of bones. Nicholas stepped back into the entrance hallway, closed the door behind him, opened up the front door without triggering the alarm, and set off down the street, still carrying the unresponsive girl cradled in his left arm throughout.

Nicholas made his way to the nearby Langtree Park where he had told Bailey to wait for him. He detected a wand out of sight behind a tree in the darkest area of the park so made his way over there. Bailey stepped out into plain view as he approached, privately awed that Nicholas had so easily spotted him in the dark; he was reminded that Nicholas had abilities beyond the ordinary; even Nevsky had feared him.

'There is no need to mention my name, Bailey,' Nicholas said by way of greeting as he set the girl he was carrying down on the ground.

'Ah, yes, Mr, ah, yes, sir.'

'Do you know how much money is in this bag, Bailey?'

'No, sir.'

'One hundred and seventy thousand strada.'

'How much, sir?'

'There's a catch, though.'

'A catch, sir?'

'It's a different kind of money.'

'A different kind of money, sir?'

'It is in the form of financial documents. You will need an education to know how to cash in this money.'

'An education, sir?'

'You can make a start in the public library. Now, the completion of your services to me tonight will be to take this girl away with you and take care of her. She is your responsibility now. You will take care of her. Is that understood?'

'Who is she, sir?'

'Balustrade had her locked up in the cellar. You're probably not old enough to understand why.'

Whatever the customary limits of knowledge of someone his age, Bailey did, in fact, understand why but he said nothing about it. 'Why am I taking care of her, sir?'

'Because you want this money, don't you? You want this one hundred and seventy thousand strada, don't you? Yes or no?' Nicholas spoke very sharply.

'Yes, sir.'

'Yes, sir, what? Yes, sir, I want the money so I'll do as I'm told? Well?'

'Yes, sir, I want the money so I'll do as I'm told.'

'Then I am telling you that she is your responsibility now. You will take care of her until she is married or can make her own way in the world. If you fail to perform this duty I will consider that you have wrongfully acquired this money and I will take it back from you. Now take her and go. Remember, Bailey, discretion always.' With that Nicholas handed the bag over to Bailey and turned and walked away.

It struck Nicholas with the force of a revelation that he was going home. A man returning home from a war is conscious of his destination in the very soles of his feet and this was how Nicholas felt at that moment: Grangeshield House was now his home. He had sealed his fate as the next Master of Grangeshield House with love and blood and the demands of justice and it was done. He had pledged nothing less than his soul to this life and there was no turning back now.

THIRTY-NINE

....

The Visit of Bombasto the Elephant to New Landern

8:20 PM, Wednesday 21 September 1544 A.F.

Bailey watched the departing figure of Nicholas with an almost superstitious dread. He had an unimaginable fortune in his hand that resolved all the material problems of life then and there and yet he did not know what to believe. Would this all be snatched away from him even now? Was this all a cruel trick? Yet Nicholas walked away without alteration; the magical bag in his hand, which might or might not contain the essence of a material world, was real enough in this moment and this moment was lasting longer than a moment, it was stretching out in time like a lazy cat yawning with its legs extended and its claws extracted, and still the bag was in his hand and Nicholas had gone around the corner.

Bailey turned to his newfound companion. She was sitting hunched up where she had been set down, looking at him with a curiously blank gaze as if looking at him through a glass wall. Bailey only saw her at that moment as a problem he had to deal with.

'Come on, let's go,' he said, speaking politely as he still had no idea who she was. She made no response. 'Come on, let's go,' Bailey repeated a little more loudly, but still she made no response. Bailey leaned down over her and pulled on her arm but she did not resist him nor did she move.

A sense of his predicament came into focus then for Bailey. He had a strong feeling that the bag in his hand had once belonged to Balustrade and an even stronger feeling that Balustrade was now dead; after all, he had been here with Nicholas before. In fact, to be completely honest, he had pretty much guessed from the beginning that Balustrade was always going to wind up dead after what had happened to Nevsky — and he was pretty sure now that Balustrade had, in fact, wound up dead. In the midst of this situation was a girl who was a complete unknown and who was his responsibility. All Bailey knew right then was that he wanted to get out of there, but he couldn't leave this girl behind given what Nicholas had said. He had to go and she had to go with him, but she seemed all but dead to the world.

Bailey groaned out loud but bowed to his task. He took hold of the girl around her shoulders and knees, and picked her up in his arms. Bailey was not a strong boy but she was light in his arms and he was energised by his magic bag. He carried her along, silently cursing her unresponsive weight, every now and then pausing to quench the fire flaring through the muscles of his arms but almost immediately driven onward by the knowledge of his magic bag which contained a fortune greater than the years of his life. He made his way through the streets of New Landern attracting no attention from those passing by until by force of will and all the strength he possessed he managed to get home where he could lay his burden down on the floor of his room and rest with his arms afire.

Bailey rested for a couple of minutes but he was still as driven as before: he got to his feet, lit a lantern and took out some bread, salami and tomatoes, and cut himself a sandwich. The sight of food brought the focus of sentience to the girl's eyes so Bailey placed these foodstuffs in front of her. Even Bailey, accustomed to hunger as he had been during his short life, was taken aback by the way the girl flung herself like a starving animal on the food placed before her. She ate as fast as she could, always with one eye on Bailey as if afraid that he would stop her; Bailey let her be and turned his attention to the bag he had carried so determinedly all this time.

He pulled open the drawstring holding the neck closed and upended the bag onto the floor and started sorting through its contents. The banknotes and coins he understood but the remainder of the contents of the bag he did not understand at all. Yet, Nicholas had said that these paper scrolls were a different kind of money. Bailey could see that there were strada amounts listed here and there but he had no idea how these documents could be used as money.

The girl had by now finished eating and was sitting on the floor staring at Bailey.

'What's your name?' Bailey asked her. She made no response. It was as if he had not spoken at all.

'I'm Bailey,' Bailey said, pointing to himself; 'who are you?' he continued, pointing at her.

She looked back at him blankly.

'I'll call you "Tamara", then,' Bailey decided. 'All right?' He was prompted to choose this name by thinking of a famous actress.

The girl might as well not have understood that she had just been named, and over the days that followed she seemed as blank as always, although, in fact, sentience and a sense of the world was beginning to return to her. Tamara was encountering the world as if for the first time. Behind her lay a dark room, which contained hunger and fear and the repeated visits of a crocodile man who hurt her; her mind had glazed over and frozen and become a snowball. Now she was thawing out and seeing the world as if she had never seen it before, but at the same time other memories stirred within the newly-named Tamara of times and places and faces that she must have once known. A field with red and white flowers, a rocking chair, the smiling face of a woman, a cemetery with an open grave, a hand holding hers; change, pain, hunger, the dark room. Now she was becoming aware of a world of sunlight, fresh air, food, lots of food, all she wanted to eat, and Bailey studying his newly-acquired documents.

Bailey would have abandoned Tamara at the first chance he had if it hadn't been for Nicholas's stern warning. Tamara was a mute who had nothing to do with him. Bailey knew of nothing but taking care of himself; the world had taught him nothing else. He told others that she was his cousin and a mute; he bought her clothes and provided her with food and ignored her. Bailey's disinterest could not have been more perfectly suited to Tamara's recovery, or more accurately, rebirth. She spent a lot of time studying Bailey. She felt that it was Bailey who had taken her out of her dark cave into the wider world outside; the man with the funny mask-face had been merely a means of transportation from one place to another. Bailey was her rescuer and to him she gave her undivided attention. Her world had changed in a moment from dark to light and the change had pivoted entirely around the figure of Bailey. Bailey's disregard of her gave her all the time she needed to finish being born again. After a while she remembered how to speak again but chose not to.

Bailey in the meantime took hold of those financial documents Nicholas had given him like a monkey taking hold of the bars of its cage. Freedom lay in the space beyond the lattice-work of these letters and numbers; or so Bailey believed at the time. He had gone to the library and become a member in order to borrow books on finance to gain an understanding of these documents. He aimed to get hold of the money they represented and so now spent all his time reading his finance books. Bailey was a bright and highly-motivated boy and he was starting to make progress. Understanding was expanding within his mind like the light of the sun coming over the horizon. One of the great financial analysts of history was being born.

2:40 PM, Wednesday 5 October 1544 A.F.

Nicholas, Isabel and the Eastons were on their way to visit the Starfelds. Isabel was still in battle-mode, judging by the way in which she was holding her fan, but they were on their way to attend peace negotiations and soon the battle would be over.

The trouble had started when Lady Starfeld had invited Isabel but not Nicholas to her next party, the October Party. Isabel had immediately geared up for battle. Too subtle to directly confront Lady Starfeld over a decision that would become fixed only when openly defended, Isabel wrote a friendly, chatty letter to Lady Starfeld. She wrote about about her wedding plans, the arrangements whereby not everyone would be seated but some guests would have to stand like cattle throughout the ceremony and the uncertainty over the final guest list for the wedding reception. Isabel did not mention Lady Starfeld's party invitation.

Lady Starfeld wrote an equally friendly, chatty letter back saying how happy she was to learn that everything was going so well for Isabel but that she was not sure if she might not be out of Anglashia at the time of Isabel's wedding, as it happened, so she might have to write to congratulate Isabel on her coming happiness some time before she left, but all that remained to be decided.

Lady Starfeld had upped the stakes. The stage now was set for a lengthy bout of hostilities between the two. It would start with Isabel's non-attendance at Lady Starfeld's party (which could never be forgiven) and continue with Lady Starfeld's non-attendance at Isabel's wedding (which also could never be forgiven) into a future as indefinite as it was grey and bleak. This kind of quarrel could be expected to last a lifetime.

It was at this stage of hostilities that Nicholas and Isabel had been invited to a royal reception and they had been congratulated on their engagement.

'What would you like as a wedding gift?' the king asked Isabel.

'I would like an elephant, sire,' Isabel said firmly. She would not dream of insulting a king by asking for anything less than a kingly gift and she was only getting married once.

The king laughed uncertainly. 'We shall see, Isabel,' he replied.

In the end the loan of an elephant from Tregebund was arranged.

The news that an elephant was coming to New Landern spread swiftly through the metropolis. It was this that gave Isabel the decisive advantage in her battle of wills with Lady Starfeld because the news of the elephant changed everything. Lady Starfeld could not miss such an event which had never happened in anyone's living memory and which people would be talking about for years, but there would be only two ways to see the elephant: one was by means of being invited by Isabel as a fellow grandee of New Landern; the other was to attend as a paying member of the public. Lady Starfeld would rather have died than be so humiliated as to attend as a paying member of the public, so clearly she had no choice but to make peace with Isabel if she was to see the elephant in a manner befitting her station and rank. So she wrote to Isabel asking Isabel if she could be so kind as to confirm that she and Nicholas were attending her party as invited, and Isabel, rather than giving an answer then, wrote back to Lady Starfeld asking if she and Nicholas could visit Lady Starfeld in the near future. Isabel wanted to accept Lady Starfeld's surrender in person.

So it was that Nicholas, Isabel and their chaperones were on their way to Starfeld Manor with Isabel's fan firmly closed throughout their voyage, while her mind was focused on the outcomes she had already decided upon. Nicholas said nothing, resigned to whatever would happen and nearly half-a-husband already in terms of having accepted that he was enwrapped in his fiancé's schemes in any case. The Eastons were, as ever, along for the ride, Lady Easton enjoying herself more than Lord Easton who was on edge with anticipation of trouble given that Isabel might still lose her temper.

The Starfelds and various others present greeted their visitors with effusive welcomes; Isabel was all wide-eyed pleasantries, while Nicholas, perhaps remembering when he had last seen Lady Starfeld and rebuked her in public, had a half-smile on show that might have been the politeness of being welcomed with such polite kindness; while Lady Starfeld, perhaps also remembering the exact same occasion when she had last seen Nicholas, had a much more strained smile on show.

They were shown into the May Living Room and ushered to their chairs. Isabel, took her seat opposite Lady Starfeld like a minister of the opposition sitting down for peace talks. She looked up to see that Nicholas was still standing to one side.

'Lord Starfeld,' Nicholas said, 'do you have a billiards table?'

Lord Starfeld, taken aback by this peremptory question while everyone was staring at him, said eventually, 'Why, yes, Mr Raspero, I do.'

'Shall we play a game of billiards?' Nicholas asked. He then added, 'Plus, of course, anyone else present who would like to play as well.'

Lord Starfeld, realising then what Nicholas was about, agreed to this suggestion very promptly, 'But of course, Mr Raspero. That is an excellent suggestion.'

Nicholas looked across at Isabel. 'Behave yourself, Isabel, while I am away!'

'Run along, Nicholas,' Isabel replied, unfolding her fan dismissively. 'I understand how important it is to hit a ball with a stick in such a venue as a billiards room. Off you go!'

Lord Starfeld led the way, followed by Nicholas and Lord Beavis Engelbert and Mr Irving Tatton and the young and honourable Master Boyce Burkhard.

It soon became evident that Nicholas had no idea of how to play billiards. He had, in fact, only played the game once, and could hardly make a proper bridge of his hand in order to strike the ball with his cue; however, as Nicholas was the first to acknowledge this fact and propose his replacement, it soon enough happened that Lord Starfeld, partnered by the fifteen year-old Burkhard, wound up playing Engelbert and Tatton. So the game of billiards commenced.

Lord Starfeld had appointed himself without consultation as the scorekeeper, sliding along markers with an important air; the triangle of balls had been cracked and scattered fiercely and the game was on; the cue ball was struck hard, while billiard balls slammed into their pockets or careened wildly around the table slamming into other balls. Nicholas observed all the players with a perhaps slightly amused expression on his face. They were quivering fiercely like small terrier dogs with their teeth sunk into an innocent leg.

About halfway through the game Nicholas said, 'I would like you to know, Lord Starfeld, that I have decided to let bygones be bygones.'

'Excuse me?' Lord Starfeld replied, dragged out of the depths of his calculations about the billiards game.

'As you must have yourself realised,' Nicholas continued, 'I was aware of the game you played and thus it was that I expressed my displeasure but that is all past now. It is notable, is it not, that when we are upset we reach for the harshest punishment but after a week or so it no longer matters? Well, I do not dispute that I lost my temper on that particular occasion, and nor can you dispute that you were at fault, but so be it, it is done and we can all move on now. It matters little though I was angry then.'

'You were angry then?' Lord Starfeld queried.

The game had stopped as everyone's attention turned to Nicholas.

'Do you not realise that I had unmasked your game?' Nicholas challenged Lord Starfeld. 'Why did you invite me to your party? It was all a trap, was it not? You invited me to be provoked into fighting a duel with that Happenstance fellow, whatever his name was, in order to provide a spectacle for your guests. You cannot blame me for being so angry at the time although, as I say, it is all water under the bridge by now.'

Lord Starfeld was observing at least five different paths of thought unfolding before him but luckily he was an intelligent man and the confusion was narrowed rather than expanded at this point. He disregarded all extraneous detail in order to focus on what could be said simply. 'There appears to be a misunderstanding, Mr Raspero. We invited you to our party out of circumstances not of our choosing. But I am sorry to hear that you have suffered the experience of being angry and believing us to blame.' Lord Starfeld stopped there, as if he had accused Nicholas of too much already.

'What circumstances?' Nicholas asked with a puzzled air.

Lord Starfeld sighed, as if he was being asked to tell a truth he would have preferred to avoid. 'Marcella and I were the victims of the Sheltrades strategy. Numerous of our party guests congratulated us on having invited you as our guest; if you had not turned up it would have been seen as a failing on our part, and so it was that we sought to have you as our guest. This was the beginning and the end of our invitation.'

The image unbidden of Penny and her friends giggling when he had asked why he had been invited to Lady Starfeld's party came to Nicholas's mind then and from an entirely new perspective he made an entirely new understanding of what had happened. 'Ah,' Nicholas said, nodding, feeling thoroughly guilty of misbehaviour, 'right, well, there most certainly has been a misunderstanding then. Yes, indeed, it is clear that I have misjudged you. Well, hopefully, Isabel and Lady Starfeld have made peace by now.'

There was a silence while everyone looked at Nicholas.

'Continue with your game,' Nicholas advised them with movements of his hands as if to illustrate the pathways of convection currents, 'whose shot is it next?'

The others needed no more encouragement than that to dive back into their fiercely-fought game. The game resumed and such was the competitiveness of the players it seemed as if all had been forgotten, but Nicholas, watching them play, was aware that of all the games in play at that moment, this one was the only one which had clear numbers assigned to its outcome.

The Engelbert-Tatton alliance prevailed by a narrow margin much to the chagrin of Lord Starfeld and his young sorcerer's apprentice Burkhard. They were already gearing up for the next game when Nicholas commented that he would be returning to the May Living Room but he could remember the way and he could go on his own if necessary. The others reluctantly postponed their further reckoning like battle-ready cats sheathing their claws and smoothing their fur but tensions remained.

So it was that they all returned to the May Living Room. Nicholas observed on his arrival that everything seemed peaceful enough; Isabel's fan lay idly open in her lap. Soon after they had all sat down and been served tea Isabel turned to Nicholas and said with an air of surprise, 'Nicky, guess what? Lady Starfeld believes she mislaid your party invitation.'

Nicholas considered this news with a serious air. 'Did you check behind the writing desk?' he asked Lady Starfeld. 'Sometimes a piece of paper can fall between the desk and the wall and become lost in that way. You can never be sure what you might find if you pull your desk away from the wall and have a look at the space in between.'

Lady Starfeld gazed wide-eyed at Nicholas as if she wasn't sure if this was a joke at which she should laugh or not.

'Just a thought,' Nicholas added as if to place his advice in the proper context; he turned to Isabel and said, 'Well, that's all settled then.' He said this as if it was half a question.

'Yes, Nicky,' Isabel said in reply, 'it is all settled. We shall be attending Lady Starfeld's party next week.'

'Excellent! I find I enjoy having been at your party more and more as time goes on,' Nicholas told Lady Starfeld. 'It's a memory that improves with age, like the finest of wines.'

Again Lady Starfeld said nothing, so Lord Starfeld said on her behalf,

'We also have our own very fond memories of your attendance at our last party and very much look forward to seeing you again at our next party.'

There was a general and widespread approval of this friendly and welcoming sentiment, and the muscles of Lady Starfeld's face moved into the semblance of a smile.

11 AM, Sunday 30 October 1544 A.F.

Nicholas and Isabel exchanged vows and rings and were married two days before Isabel's birthday. They stopped to see Bombasto on their way back to Grangeshield House, where the wedding reception would be held.

Bombasto the Tregebund elephant had arrived the week before to a rapturous reception. Cheering crowds had lined the streets through which he had paraded. Bombasto was happy to be fed apples and to drink from buckets of water as he made his way along the route prepared for him. Every now and again he raised his trunk high into the air and trumpeted; the crowd went wild.

Nicholas and Isabel went into the giant marquee that was Bombasto's home during his visit to Anglashia. They each held out an apple in their hands and Bombasto ambled over and deftly snatched the apples from their hands with his trunk and munched them on the spot, while flapping his large ears amiably.

Isabel looked into the elephant's wise eyes. The elephant's dark friendly warm kind eyes looked back into her eyes and for a disquieting moment displaced in time Isabel felt that the elephant was inspecting her whole life from cradle to grave and she was relieved to see that the elephant still looked friendly even after having seen everything there was to know about her.

While they were leaving the marquee Nicholas spotted Bailey in the crowd to one side. Remembering that Isabel had once said that she wanted to meet Bailey, Nicholas beckoned the boy over. He came over cautiously, Tamara clutching his hand as always.

'Hello, Bailey,' Nicholas said cheerfully. 'How are you?'

'I am well, thank you, Mr Raspero,' Bailey said.

'I am addressed now as Sir Nicholas, Bailey,' Nicholas corrected him, 'and this is Lady Isabel.'

The enormously well-dressed figures of Nicholas and Isabel loomed over Bailey like friendly lions over an apprehensive rabbit.

'What are you doing these days, Bailey?' Isabel asked him.

'I am studying finance, Lady Isabel,' Bailey said in reply.

'That is good,' Isabel said approvingly. 'We cannot reply on whatever chance may throw our way all the time, can we, Bailey?'

'No, Lady Isabel,' Bailey said obediently.

'Who is your friend, Bailey?' Nicholas asked.

'Tamara, Sir Nicholas.'

'Are you taking good care of Tamara, Bailey?'

'Yes, Sir Nicholas.'

Isabel unfastened a diamond brooch from her lapel, and leaned over and fasted the brooch to the lapel of Tamara's dress. 'Today is my wedding day, Tamara,' Isabel told the girl, 'and so I have received many gifts. This is for you.'

'Thank you, Lady Isabel,' Tamara said distinctly, drawing a look from Bailey, who had not known until then that she could speak.

Nicholas and Isabel went on their way back to Grangeshield House for the wedding reception which would be followed by their wedding night.

1:00 PM, Sunday 18 December 1544 A.F.

Bailey and Tamara descended from the public flying carriage on their arrival in Second Brissle, the garden city of the West. They found their new accommodation and then walked around the town taking a look at everything.

They soon realised why Second Brissle was called the garden city. There were walled gardens, open gardens, parks, playground parks and more walled gardens. Second Brissle was a town for wealthy people who understood that the cultivation of gardens was a characteristic of civilisation along with other characteristics such as writing systems and trade routes.

Bailey had decided to leave New Landern and settle in Second Brissle now that he was making such good progress with his finance studies. While packing for the journey Bailey had come across the broken toy which he had kept all this time. Acting almost on instinct, Bailey threw away the broken toy into the bin. Almost at once, as if a curse had been lifted from him, Bailey started feeling cheerful. The sunlight coming in through the window was smiling and the world itself seemed friendly.

Something had changed for Bailey. He had never before had anyone to take care of, and being with Tamara was like waking up from a long sleep. He was no longer alone in the world.

Being no longer alone in the world changed everything about the world, starting with its geometrical structure; the world had changed from being a circle to being an ellipse, with Bailey at one centre of the ellipse and Tamara at the other. So it was that Bailey had decided to leave New Landern and move with Tamara to Second Brissle. The inner change had brought about the outer change.

Bailey and Tamara stopped for tea in their new hometown, arranged for purchases to be delivered to their lodgings, and continued on to visit yet another garden as hand in hand they set forth along the great journey of their lives together.

FORTY

....

Ancestors Day at Grangeshield House

11:00 AM, Wednesday 9 April 1553 A.F.

The sun was a bright and cheerful yellow disc in a sky that was a clear and cloudless azure blue from horizon to horizon. The garden at Grangeshield House was the setting for a number of separate scenes being conducted within the same space. To one side Nicholas was teaching his eldest son Alexander some tricks with the wand Alexander had been given on his seventh birthday a few months before. Alexander was happy and proud and serious all at the same time. Lord Templeton, Sophie's husband, looked on with a smile.

Acacia, the six-year-old daughter of Nicholas and Isabel, and Amyas the five-year-old son of Nicholas and Isabel, were screaming with laughter as they ran and played tag around the statues and hedges and benches of the garden, watched over by their gossiping nannies.

Camryn, the three-year-old daughter of Nicholas and Isabel, was building a sandcastle, with a very serious air, in a sandpit that Isabel herself had once played in long ago, a watchful nanny standing by.

Maximilian, the youngest son, at the grand old age of one year and a half, was sound asleep in his pram; in his peaceful repose, he could have been the lord and emperor of the visible world.

Isabel and Sophie were huddled together in a sisterly fashion on the Seat of Passing Contemplation. Isabel was talking into Sophie's ear in such a low voice that only Sophie could hear what she was saying. Isabel was talking to Sophie as frankly as one married woman to another about the repeated satisfaction she received from the continuously passionate company of her husband Nicholas. The recitation of the pleasures Isabel received from Nicholas's ardent attentions inflicted sharp pain on Sophie's soul as if Isabel's words were razor-edged lashes. Isabel might well have been unaware that by telling so many of the intimate details of her happy marriage she was inflicting enormous pain on a childless woman who had the sheer brazen audacity to be in love with her very own Nicholas. Isabel might have been further unaware that Sophie's jealousy was agonisingly amplified by the fact that Nicholas never looked at anyone but Isabel. Sophie herself certainly believed that her love for Nicholas was a secret that she had guarded so closely that no-one else knew — no-one at all.

Far away from this happy gathering in the castle of Anona, Angela sat with her elderly husband the Lord of Anona and waited for him to die. This was what her life had been reduced to, some would have said, but not Angela herself, who was not unhappy. She lived out her days as the extremely wealthy Lady Anona and her very endurance outlasted the scandal of her life before her marriage. There came a time when it seemed beside the point to be anything but courteous to this white-haired old lady, who had lived the life of a nun for fifty years ever since her widowhood. Seemingly indifferent to the end, Lady Anona passed from life to death during her sleep without a change of expression.

Ben had been able to court and marry Miss Eileen Radcliff. The Radcliff parents had dropped their opposition to Ben seeing their daughter on learning that his cousin was about to become the next Master of Grangeshield House. The couple had been blessed with two daughters and a son and the future Chancellor of Anglashia was a successful and happy man.

On this fine April day the newly married couple Bailey and Tamara strolled by the river in Second Brissle with their fine clothes and white gloves, happy and rich and in love. The world was at their feet and they had everything to look forward to in a world from which darkness had been banished. With the coming of children they became a happy family of five people. Along with Bailey's growing fame as a writer of commentaries on finance came an occasional public role which Bailey enjoyed, with only one exception: whenever his path happened to cross that of the Master of the Grangeshield Estate, Bailey was seized with vertigo, as if made aware by a direct vision that the path he walked through life was flanked with chasms. For his part, Sir Nicholas was friendly enough and always had an encouraging comment to make.

Bailey lived long enough to hear of the death of Sir Nicholas Grangeshield, and then it was that, robbed of his fear of the man he had known as Nicholas Raspero, Bailey felt betrayed for a second time. Once he had thought Nevsky invincible, or at least to have presented the similitude of invincibility; then he had thought Nicholas Raspero to be a god, or at least to have presented the similitude of divinity; now as he walked along the street behind Nicholas's funeral procession, Bailey bowed his head as he made his farewells to a man whose mortality was in the end as much of a mystery as divinity.

Tagalong sat in Jolly's chair on that April morning, far removed from the sunshine outside. In the end Tagalong had taken over from Jolly, precisely in part because he had never attempted to until no-one else was standing. The other successors of Jolly had in the end killed themselves one after the other in their attempt to get hold of the all-important nineteen million strada. Two entirely illusory factors had protected Tagalong like a magic shield making him impervious from harm: one was the pretended knowledge he was assumed to have concerning the magical nature of the financial documents in which all this money had been locked away; the second was the belief of everyone involved that Tagalong was not a rival to succeed Jolly. This had, bizarrely, led all four of Jolly's successors, one by one, to make Tagalong their partner in their duplicitous schemes to seize sole control of Jolly's empire; Tagalong had, one by one, betrayed each of them to their deaths with an utter unscrupulousness that in the end made him Jolly's worthy successor. Now he dealt with Lord Zinia as Jolly had done before him, but he was a much more modest man than Jolly had been. He could have seen himself as the unexpected king but he chose not to see himself as a king at all. In any case, there was always the fourteenth Master of Grangeshield House on the scene to remind him of his less than royal attributes. Sir Nicholas impaled him with a glare if their paths ever crossed, if Sir Nicholas even deigned to notice him at all, and Tagalong knew his place well enough to say nothing. Tagalong would have been surprised in the afterlife had he known that Nicholas came to visit his grave sometime after his funeral, but Nicholas was an old man by then with his own memories of when he had been young all those years ago and he had rescued Tagalong from his attackers who had apparently intended to do him harm, and to the elderly Nicholas Tagalong had seemed like the spring that launched the wind-up toy of the world into action, and to be curious about the past and to pay his respects to the dead seemed to be like one and the same thing.

Isabel remained Isabel while all else changed: staunchly loyal to Nicholas, deeply disdainful of all those below her social status, fiercely protective of her children and her heritage and steadily conscious unto death of the distinction between the high and the low as exemplified in her own person; that was Isabel right down to the very end.

Nicholas achieved mastery of his role as Master of Grangeshield House. Being a good judge of character, he made sure to appoint the most competent people to the appropriate positions of the Grangeshield Estate, and given his social standing, his impeccable public reputation and the air with which he played the role of Master of Grangeshield House as if he had been born to it, it followed that all his business dealings flourished and the Grangeshield Estate greatly prospered. Nicholas realised late on in life that he had achieved the standing of being one of the great Masters of Grangeshield House despite never having understood anything of business, but it was in passing on his Raspero legacy that he felt fulfilled. He had explained to Isabel from the beginning that it was important to him that the Raspero heritage was continued along with the Grangeshield heritage, and she had accepted this. The wandlore mastery that Nicholas had himself inherited was inherited in turn by his children, and that wandlore mastery, which went back to Daniel himself, lived on.

11:30 PM, 23 June 1875 A.F.

The waxing moon was a silvery hand span above the horizon, about to descend below the horizon as if to follow the departed golden sun; the stars glittered fiercely in clear patches between the fast-moving clouds; an owl hooted mournfully overhead as the trees swayed in the brisk wind. There was a sense in the air of forces at work in the sky above and in the earth below and in the middle realm between.

It was Ancestors Day at Grangeshield House and Matthias Raspero had come to pay his respects to Nicholas and Isabel. He was only fifteen years old but by then already the thirty-seventh Baron of Raspero, on the run with a price of five million strada on his head. His enemies were everywhere yet he had taken the risk to come here tonight to pay his respects to his ancestors.

He lit two candles at the door of the crypt and made his way with the slow steps of respectful observance between the stone sarcophagi; there were candles scattered like stars throughout the crypt, including several on the sarcophagi towards which Matthias was directing his steps: the sarcophagi of Sir Nicholas and Lady Isabel Grangeshield. Beyond them on paths vaguely like the veins of a leaf were the other sarcophagi of their children and grandchildren and later descendants winding their way along the floor of the crypt, but Matthias stopped and tilted his candles to drip wax on the sarcophagi of Nicholas and Isabel before fixing his candles to stand upright in the cooling congealed wax coatings on the rough stone.

Matthias placed his warm hands, alive with his sense of the hard cold stone underneath his skin-stretched senses, to rest above Nicholas and Isabel, and bowed his head in respect. Nicholas and Isabel were his very favourite ancestors. He had gazed frequently in fascination at their paintings in the Castle of Raspero as a boy. They had seemed to his boyish eyes like magical beings from another time and space, two of his Anglashian ancestors embedded within his Westrigonian ancestors who had lived in a time and place that now only existed in stories.

The paintings of Sir Nicholas and Lady Isabel Grangeshield hung side by side in the Great Hall of the Castle of Raspero to the right of the fireplace and there Matthias had gazed at them with a hungry gaze, greedy to drink them in both on the spot. He knew of their story, as he knew of the stories of all his ancestors: he knew how Nicholas had walked all the way to Grangeshield House when he had first visited Isabel because he was too poor to pay for a flying carriage; how Isabel had once bought out all the seats of an entire theatre in order to get Nicholas to sit next to her; how Nicholas had saved Isabel's honour from a villain by pretending to be a Lord from the North. Nicholas had looked back at Matthias with a calm and amused gaze, as if he sat at the centre of things watching everything pass by; Isabel had looked at Matthias with her wide-eyed appraisal of all things whose propriety pleased her, as if ready to bestow her approval on the young boy in the Great Hall if he only stood a little straighter and looked a little more dignified. Centuries had passed but his knowledge of what they had done made their images alive in his mind in his own day. He belonged to them because they had come before him and stood over him like two constellations of stars, encompassing him with the sheer range of their joined being; what they had done had made him and from that weaving there was no escape.

Now they lay in dust under his hands; their magnificent bodies that were once warm flesh had long ago become piles of dust below the arching expanse of their skeletons. What had once been an ironic smile was now the grin of a skeletal head; where there had been the heat of passion there was only the cold of the grave, which is the cold that makes cold to be cold; all quarrels had become stillness. Matthias shivered without thought in the presence of death; he took in a deep breath as if reminding himself that he was alive. He felt death like a fallen cloak all around him then; he felt the crypt close around him like a prison and he wanted to flee; yet he stayed where he was in defiance of his fear. The moment passed and he felt calm again; it had all been a passing illusion, he thought.

The obvious thought came to him then: *what we are now, so shall you be*. The thought was even expressed with the exultant hiss of a ghost, but Matthias was not the least bit impressed. He was, after all, fifteen years old, and death was only a dot in the distance. He was here because he was alive from head to toe with all the forces loose in the wide world above and below and within this crypt, and his heart was beating steadily. Yet, he was aware that he had not answered the ghost so he thought: *what I am will continue for a while*. It did not seem to be the world's best answer to the challenge of a ghost but it would have to do as it was all he could think of right now. It was perhaps no more than an exchange of insults, Matthias thought, but at least he had insulted the ghost right back. That was something!

Matthias opened his eyes and straightened up; even the candle-light seemed dazzling, forming passing geometrical patterns on the backs of his eyeballs, but he had been taught well enough to ignore their pretended advice, so he turned away and walked out of the crypt.

He made his way up the stairs and into the Great Hall of Grangeshield House and into the garden outside. The moon had disappeared; the sky overhead had largely cleared of clouds leaving a myriad points of light gleaming from horizon to horizon in all their variegated clusters. The world seemed wider than possibility itself. Matthias breathed in deeply of the cool night air and set off through the dark night under the brightly glittering stars overhead.

Life had passed on.

www.ingramcontent.com/pod-product-compliance
Lightning Source LLC
Chambersburg PA
CBHW020242030726
47499CB00001B/32